KEROSENE AND CANDLES

KEROSENE

AND

CANDLES

JOHN KINGSTON McMAHON

Matador
9 Priory Business Park,
Wistow Road, Kibworth Beauchamp,
Leicestershire. LE8 0RX
Tel: 0116 279 2299
Email: books@troubador.co.uk
Web: www.troubador.co.uk/matador
Twitter: @matadorbooks

ISBN 978 1789018 486

British Library Cataloguing in Publication Data.
A catalogue record for this book is available from the British Library.

Printed and bound in the UK by TJ International, Padstow, Cornwall
Typeset in 12pt Adobe Jenson Pro by Troubador Publishing Ltd, Leicester, UK

Matador is an imprint of Troubador Publishing Ltd

This story is dedicated to the boys who became men in the bloodied trenches of Gallipoli, and upon their return, fought to tame the barren lands of rural Australia.

I wish to express my thanks and acknowledge the assistance of Melissa Ferguson along with Angela Lardner of Melbourne in the development of this book.

I must also express my thanks and gratitude to my wife, Elizabeth, for her unwavering patience and assistance in compiling this work.

Contents

Introduction

1960

The old box telephone hanging on the hallway wall was ringing, its jangling bells were now magnified in the almost empty house. Hannah was sitting at the kitchen table, and the sound had startled her. She was daydreaming, as her fingers had slid across the dents and scars worn into the tabletop by her family over countless years.

Her mind had wandered back to a different time when they had first arrived here with almost nothing. She thought about the happy days, and the laughter that they had shared together. But, she also remembered their struggles through the lean times, and now she was wondering where the years had gone. The tea in her cup had gone cold as she waited for Charlie, her son-in-law, to arrive. It was mid-morning, and he had promised that he would be here early to pick her up to take her to her new life in Sydney.

She shuffled to the telephone and answered it. There was the click as the connection was made, and the voice at the other end of the crackly line asked, 'Hannah, is that you?' Mary, the telephonist, always asked that when she rang, and Hannah didn't know why as Mary knew that she was now living by herself.

'Hello Mary, it's Hannah speaking, is there some news?' Mary knew everybody's business, as she spent up to ten hours a day connecting people's calls that came through her exchange.

She usually listened in on everyone's conversations on what was known as a party line, and the town gossip usually emanated from her.

'Hannah, I have just received a call from your Charlie! He's broken down in his truck around Lithgow somewhere, and he asked me to tell you that he's waiting for someone to tow him to the garage. He doesn't think that he will get to your house now before it gets dark.'

Hannah swore, 'Damn! I knew that I should have caught the train.' She muttered it more to herself than to Mary.

'I'm sorry Mary, I'm not going crook at you! But I told Molly that I was happy to catch the train to Sydney and she wouldn't hear of it. I would have been there by now!'

'Charlie had sounded upset, and was apologetic. He said that once he got the truck to the garage it shouldn't take too long to fix it. I suppose that it will be tomorrow now before you get to leave?'

They spoke for a little longer, as they had known each other for many years, and their children used to attend the same school in Blackmore. She put the receiver back onto its cradle and made her way back to the kitchen. Hannah needed another cup of tea, and she raked the embers in the old black stove back to life.

She had always liked the sound of the crackling fire as it somehow comforted her, and now she expected that she would be staying for another night. As the tea brewed in its pot under an old tea cosy, Hannah wandered along the hallway and looked into each room again. The floorboards creaked, and the sound only intensified her loneliness. She had done this a dozen times already, and the few items of furniture left in the rooms would be staying in the house when it was sold. Her suitcases that she was taking with her to Sydney were now standing on the steps of her front verandah. She had lived a frugal life and her possessions reflected that.

A few blowflies buzzed irritatingly against the windowpane in her bedroom; and she remembered the sounds of her children playing and giggling in these rooms, what seemed like only yesterday.

She poured her tea, and carried the cup to the front verandah, and sat down on the old cedar miner's couch whose flouncing was now faded and worn. She and Tom would sit on it almost every evening in the summer months after the children had gone to bed. Tom would fill his pipe, and they would just watch the sky as the blue of the day melded into the velvet of the evening.

It was a simple pleasure, and they never tired of watching the changing hues of the heavens as the stars came out.

Later on, as the children grew older, they would also look at the heavens as they searched for the Southern Cross and the Saucepan hidden within the Milky Way.

Tom had built the old house over forty years earlier. It was shortly after he had arrived back from the war, and he had levelled out their allotment with nothing more than a pick and a shovel, along with a few sticks of dynamite. He and his horses had pulled the rocks from the hard ground where they had lain from time immemorial.

The house sat high on the brow of the hill. It afforded views right across the valley, and down to the stream that meandered through it. The stream could turn into a raging river when the rains fell heavily in the mountains behind their allotment, but for the most part it just flowed gently between the towering gums. As she drank her tea, Hannah stared across to the smoky, distant hills and the dry, yellowing paddocks that sloped down to the valley below.

The house was flooded with memories, both happy and sad and she really didn't want to leave, but she was old now and there was no one left. They were three miles from the nearest town, and a mile from their closest neighbour.

She didn't feel old, but she knew that her daughter Molly was right when she had said, 'Mum, what if you have a fall, or get bitten by a snake? It's too isolated to be out there by yourself. I know that it's your home, and that you love being there. It was all right when Dad was alive, but there is only me and Jack left now, and I can't move back...' She left the sentence unfinished as it upset her when she thought about her younger brother.

The thought of her only surviving son Jack was also painful to Hannah. She hadn't heard from him for almost a year. The last letter that she had received was postmarked from Goulburn gaol. In it, he said that he was being transferred from Bathurst where he had been since he was sentenced to the gaol at Goulburn. But Goulburn was too far for her to go and visit, so she had written to him every month, but he had never replied.

She squinted against the glare, as she scanned the road that ran through the valley and led to the farm. It was a back road, and it had always been referred to as *the ration track* from the days when the bullock trains had brought the supplies out to them. The surface was corrugated and potholed and baked hard by the endless summer sun, and she remembered that it had always been like that.

Dust from any vehicle moving along it could be seen for miles from her vantage point. She didn't expect to see Charlie coming, but she looked anyway.

The sunlight glinting on the water in the dam below the house caught her attention and held her gaze. The dam was in a natural fold of the hill, and it had never run dry since they had moved onto their parcel of land in 1920. To one side stood the old ironbark tree. It was old even before they had built the house, its trunk twisted and knotted and its bark as tough as leather.

Hannah put down her cup, and she slowly made her way along the rutted path that led down to the dam. She had walked along this path a thousand times before to sit in the shade of the old gum that her Tom had often referred to as the kiddies' tree.

When the children were young, and the relentless summer sun had parched the earth hard and dry, they would sit under its gnarled branches in the shade that they afforded, while the children splashed around in the cool, black water of the dam.

As she stared into its dark waters, she remembered the Christmas day in 1936 when they were all together. She had cooked the roast, and her kitchen was like a furnace. It was the first Christmas lunch that they had celebrated together since before the Depression, and their neighbours and friends had all been there. When the meal was over, they had all made their way down to the dam. They had bought each of the boys a pearl-handled pocket knife as a Christmas present, and they had spent almost an hour carving their names into the tree trunk along with the date. Jimmy, was born in 1920 followed by Billy a year later. Her eldest daughter Peggy was 11, and her two brothers had adored her. She had been crippled by polio at the age of 5, and she had struggled to walk for years with the iron callipers that had been fitted to support both of her weak legs. But the callipers didn't stop her, and the boys would piggyback her down to the dam, and then take turns to carry her back up the hill to the house.

When the boys had finished carving their names into the tree trunk, Jimmy held his sister's hand and guided it as she struggled to carve the letters. When she was finished, she squealed with delight, and Billy took his knife and gouged her name deeper into the trunk to match theirs. Hannah remembered, how Peggy had died shortly after that Christmas, and they had buried her near the base of the tree.

Tom had built a roughly sawn bench for them to sit on, and after the two boys had gone to the second war, he would regularly sit on it at the end of the day.

He would fill his pipe and stare off into the distance as his mind had wandered to a different place. He had once told Hannah that he felt close to his children when he was down at the dam. Only Peggy was buried there, as his two boys had never come back from France after World War Two, but every afternoon before he left there he would place his hand over their carved names, and in his mind he would say goodbye to them before climbing the hill to go back to the house.

She looked to the side of the tree, and at the two small, weather-beaten crosses lying side by side. Tom was now buried next to his daughter, and that was his wish.

She smiled, as she remembered what Tom had said as they sat out on the verandah one evening. 'I want to be buried down there Hani.' He had always called her Hani, 'under the kiddies' tree when I die.' She thought of how they had both laughed when she had said, 'You will have to dig the hole before you go, because I couldn't bury a potato down there, what with the ground being so hard.' But after the accident, she did bury him there next to their daughter, and next to the memory of his two sons. Her eyes welled, as she placed her hands over the names of her children. The bark had swollen around them, but the gouges were still plainly visible almost twenty-four years after they had been cut.

Part 1

Sydney 1907 – 1919

1.

Sydney 1907

Claire Townsend and her husband Davin were childless, and it had always been a burden to them. They were desperate to have a child, and had all but given up hope of ever having one.

Five years after migrating from Ireland to Sydney, Claire had received a letter from the Mother Superior at Saint Joseph's Convent in Cork. Its contents explained the circumstances of Claire's sister's incarceration into an asylum, and her subsequent death. Mother Superior had asked if it would be possible for Claire to adopt her niece Hannah, who was now eleven years old.

Claire reread the letter, and her heart skipped a beat. She mused over how wonderful it would be to have a child live with them.

Davin worked at the Darling Harbour railway yards as a carriage maintainer, and Claire had waited anxiously for him to return home. When he did, she showed him the letter and asked,

'Do you think that we could have her here with us Davin? It would be lovely to have a youngster around!' Davin read the letter. He was the practical one and said, 'I don't mind if the child comes to stay darlin'. It would be a blessing to have a child who we could give some comfort and a home to, but we don't have any room.'

Claire had been thinking about where Hannah could sleep, and she had suggested to Davin that she should look for a larger house.

They lived in a small two-roomed, single-storied terraced house in the suburb of Pyrmont. Most of the other workers who worked at the railway yards also lived there, as the state housing authority owned most of the workers' houses in the area.

They were barely habitable, as they all had dirt floors along with poor sanitation. Two houses shared a single tap in the backyard, and water had to be carried inside.

Pyrmont was an overcrowded, inner city suburb where the streets were narrow and cobblestoned. Grubby children, whose heads were shaved to keep the lice at bay, played amongst the filth and the rubbish. Tin pan toilets serviced some of the houses, while others made do with a pit in the ground, and the stench of raw sewage always permeated the air. It was a poor, working-class area, as were most of the inner Sydney suburbs.

It was also home to desperate women, who tried to get a few pennies from their husbands each payday before they had gambled, or drunk their wages away. When no money was forthcoming to feed their children, and out of desperation, some offered themselves to any randy male who would pay for their services.

Others still, tried to show an air of respectability by painting the door stoop with white paint and hanging a piece of lace in the front room window. This would be the one room that was kept clean in case the priest or district nurse should call. Also, it was usually the only one that had a wooden floor.

Many of the residents made no pretence of respectability, while many questioned why they had left the slums of Ireland, and other parts of Europe to come to a place where their lot was no better than what they had left behind. Some residents, who were desperate to better themselves, had small signs hanging in a front window. They advertised that washing and ironing would be done for a shilling a basket load. Others offered to do clothing alterations and sewing.

The area was a slum. Rotting weatherboards on the housing authority's dwellings, and rusty tin roofs all added to the air of despair that pervaded the suburb.

Claire had obtained work with the Pelaco Shirt Company. She was paid to sew buttons on women's blouses and men's shirts that would be sold in the town's emporiums. Once a week, she would walk the mile to the clothing factory. There, she would pick up the fifty garments that required buttons and she would load them into her old pram.

She then returned those that were finished, and received her wages of five shillings.

Most of what they earned was spent on paying the rent, with a little left over for food and tobacco, along with the occasional bottle of beer, but generally they struggled from week to week.

✳✳✳

Eighteen weeks later, Claire received a letter from the immigration department confirming that Hannah had arrived in Sydney and was being housed at the quarantine centre at North Head. Whilst Hannah was only quarantined for six weeks, for Claire, it seemed like an eternity.

On the morning of Hannah's release, Claire had left home when it was still dark. The nervous excitement that had been building within her for the past few weeks had woken her early, and she had a long journey to get to the quarantine station. She double-checked her appearance before leaving home, as she was desperate to make a good impression on her niece.

The gates opened at the quarantine centre, and Hannah tentatively walked through them and took in her new surroundings. She smiled nervously at her aunt, and as recognition dawned, she ran and gave her a hug.

'Let me look at you child, my goodness how you have grown, you were only a bairn when I last saw you. I've been worried sick since you left, but you're here now, safe and sound, thanks be to God!'

⁕⁕⁕

Some weeks earlier, Claire had gone to the tenants' office where the rent was paid each week. They held a list of houses to rent to anyone who had a job. She had seen the notice on the wall of the office advertising a two-bedroom house with an outside kitchen. The advertisement advised that the property was available for rent in the suburb of Redfern. Redfern was not far from Darling Harbour, and she applied to the clerk to have it.

'Sir, can you tell me how much be the rent on that home in Redfern?' The clerk opened a wooden filing cabinet and checked, but before he told her the amount he asked, 'Are you married missus?'

'I am at that, for a whole six years!' was her response. The clerk stared at her and then asked, 'And is yer husband working madam? I canna let ye have the place unless ye husband is in full-time employment, what is his trade and where does he work?'

'He is a blacksmith sir, and he works at the rail yards at the Darling Harbour.'

'The cottage is fifteen shillings a week, cana yer afford that amount missus?'

Claire was taken aback at hearing how much the rent was, she hadn't thought that it would cost as much as that. That was a whole five shillings a week more than what they were paying now, and she tentatively agreed that she could manage it, and almost in an act of defiance she said to the clerk, 'I would like to see it first though, if that would be all right?'

'See it! It's just a wee cottage. You either want it, or not, which is it to be?' Claire dug her heels in and retorted, 'I'll not be paying fifteen shillings a week without taking a peek at it. Why it might not be fit to house a goat in, and I have my niece to live with us now, so I wish to see the house, sir.'

The clerk could see that nothing would be achieved by refusing her request. He took a small strip of paper from his desk, dipped his nib into the inkpot and scratched down the address. He went to the rack holding an assortment of keys and handed one to Claire.

'If you catch the number 9 tram down George Street it will drop you in front of the house. Now I need you to bring me back the key today sometime, so make sure that you do madam, and make sure that you lock the door behind you when you leave. I don't want no squatters in there!'

⁎⁎⁎

Claire stood outside the house after alighting from the tram. The street held a mixture of businesses including a Chinese laundry. A short distance away was a general store, with the name of the proprietor, George Gretch, painted in large white letters across the front window. Below his name was a list of goods, such as honey and treacle, that could be purchased cheaply if the buyer brought their own jar. Another sign stated that candles could be bought singly for one halfpenny each. Boxes of fruit, along with square, four-gallon tins of kerosene, lined the area directly in front of the window.

A long wooden horse trough and a steel hitching post stood on the road outside of the shop. The road itself was paved in square wooden blocks buried lengthways into the ground. Spent cigarette butts lay in the gutters with assorted rubbish, and sheets of discarded newspapers collected against front fences and lamp posts.

Many of the houses were run-down. Some had dried gum tree branches holding up the remains of paling fences. Others had the weatherboards falling from them, exposing the inner canvas walls.

There was a general sense of decay surrounding the whole area. Smoke-stained glass adorned the gas street lamps attached to cast iron lamp posts. Most of the houses were single-storied terraces with rusty-stained roofs, as was the one that would become Claire's new home.

A short, buxom woman wearing a worn, floral-patterned dress, and faded pink slippers was standing in the doorway of her house. She yelled out at Claire, 'Are you lost love?'

Claire looked towards the woman, and replied, 'No, I'm just looking for number 6.'

'It's right there in front of you dearie, are you gunna move in?'

'I might be, but I wanted to see it first.'

'It's a good house that one; it's got two bedrooms and a parlour. And it's got wooden floors! Not many houses around here with proper floors. Most of the older ones still got dirt ones. The people living there,' and she nodded at the house next to hers, 'was evicted! He was a no-good drunk, and he used to belt her, and his kids, when he was drunk. Mrs Fisher was her name, dearie me she had the patience of a saint that one, putting up with the way that he treated her and the kids. I think that she's living down by the Parramatta River in a tent now, such a shame!'

The woman smiled and said to Claire, 'Anyway luvvy, me name's Doris. Doris Fields, I live in number 8, so I'll be your neighbour if you move in. Now, where're me manners? I'll go and put the kettle on, and I'll make us a nice cup of tea. So, go and have a look inside luvvy and then come over, the tea will be brewed by then.' She wiped her hands down the front of her dress before holding out her hand to shake Claire's.

Claire introduced herself. 'My name is Claire Townsend, and please don't bother with the tea, I don't want to trouble you.'

'Don't you be silly luvvy, it's no trouble. We can have a nice cuppa and a natter, so I'll see you shortly!'

Claire unlocked the door, and went inside. The house comprised of two small, dark bedrooms, divided by a narrow hallway that split the house from the front door to the back. There was an even smaller parlour room that had a fireplace against the back wall. The front door opened directly onto the footpath. At the back of the house was a short dirt path that led to the kitchen, which was covered by several sheets of corrugated iron.

The kitchen was small. The walls were lined with horizontal wooden planks all showing the remnants of faded green paint. Against the back wall stood a cast-iron stove.

There was also a small table, with several rickety chairs against it. Two small, open cupboards hung from the walls above a handpump that would provide water.

Behind the kitchen was a small plot of ground that was mainly dirt. A few shrivelled weeds struggled to grow within the confines of the hard-packed earth. It was barely big enough to plant anything, let alone some vegetables. The brick outhouse stood against the back fence. The remnants of a dead pumpkin vine lay across the flat roof, and a struggling choko vine clung tenaciously to the toilet wall. Behind it was a small laneway, where the night soil man would come with his cart to change the toilet pans once a week.

As Claire stood in the small yard, she could just hear the distant sound of a steam engine whistle along with the crashing together of railway wagons, before they were lost amongst the cacophony of street sounds. She was thinking that although the house was slightly bigger than where they were now it would still be a squeeze. Also, it would cost another five shillings a week more than what they were now paying. Davin couldn't work any more hours than what he was already doing, so she would have to get some more work sewing or ironing to make up the shortfall. She thought that the rooms could do with painting, but there was no mould on the ceiling, so at least the house was dry. Claire locked the door behind her and made her way next door

Doris greeted her and asked, 'How did you go luvvy, do you think that you will take it? It would be nice to have some new neighbours!'

Claire was still thinking about the extra money that she would have to find, but replied, 'We have to find a bigger house, cause my young niece be arriving soon from Ireland, and she will be staying with us. But the rent is dearer, and I'm not sure if we will be able to afford it.'

'Come in luvvy, and sit down. How do you like your tea?' Doris had placed two chipped china cups down on the worn tabletop. 'Excuse the cups dearie, I've been meaning to get some new ones, but the money has been a bit tight since me old man died. They want two shillings for a new cup down at Gretch's store can you imagine that? Two whole shillings for a wee cup and saucer!' Then she changed the subject and said, 'You could see China Sam down at the laundry, and he might give you a few pennies to do some ironing.'

Claire had taken an immediate liking to Doris and her down-to-earth nature. 'Don't you be a worrying about a few chips. What's important is that they hold the tea.' She smiled at Doris as she said it and Doris relaxed.

'Are you married luvvy, and have you got any kiddies?'

'Yes, I'm married, but we don't have any children. But, I am looking forward to having my niece to take care of.'

Doris poured the tea and asked, 'What sort of employment does your husband have luvvy?'

'His trade is blacksmithing, but he works on repairing carriages down at the Darling Harbour goods yards. Do you have any children Doris?'

'I have two boys, Jack is me eldest, he's 12, and Tom is me baby and he's 10. They are both good boys, and I don't know how I would have coped after Barry died if it wasn't for the boys. Barry was me husband!' Doris's voice trailed off to a whisper as she mentioned her husband's name. Claire wasn't sure how to respond but asked, 'When did your husband die?'

Doris replied in a matter-of-fact way, 'It's almost three months since the accident. He worked down at the rail yards. He was a shunter, and there was a terrible accident down there. A train ran away with no brakes. Barry was coupling some carriages together when the runaway train crashed into them, and he was between them.' She stopped talking, as she wiped away a tear with a scrunched-up hanky that she had taken from up her sleeve.

'I'm sorry Doris. I heard about that accident as my Davin was working that day. He came home and told me about it. It sounded dreadful.'

Doris wiped her eyes, 'No, it's all right luvvy, it's just one of those things that happen. It was hard for the boys at first, but they have coped well. I miss him a lot, and I still expect him to walk through the door some nights.'

She dabbed her eyes again and said, 'But at least we still have a roof over our heads. This house is owned by the railways department. After the accident, Barry's boss, who was at the funeral, came over and seen me after the service. He said that because Barry was killed at work the railways would let us live in the house for as long as we liked. Then he told me that we didn't have to pay no rent ever again! They even sent us a fancy letter with a cheque for five pounds! The letter said that we would be regarded as protected tenants until I died, or moved away. They even pay us ten bob a week as well. It's not much, but we manage. At least we don't have to find the rent out of it, and me boys help out a bit!'

'Jack, he's me eldest, he gets a bit of work at Mr Johnston's fuel yard bagging up coal. Mr Johnston is a good man, and he pays Jack a shilling for every bag that he fills. Some weeks my boy brings home all of ten shillings, and he gives it all to his mum, but I always give him back a bob for himself!

'Tom has been cleaning windows for some of the shopkeepers. He doesn't earn as much as his brother, but every shilling helps. My Barry always said that we should be grateful for small mercies and I am. Look at poor Mrs Fisher, the lady who used to live in your house. She's now living in a tent down by the river!'

They finished their teas, and Claire needed to get back to the housing office to return the key and make the arrangements to swap houses. As she left Doris said, 'It was nice to meet you luvvy. I hope that I see you again soon.'

¥¥

Bailey Street, Redfern, where they now lived, was a half-mile long. It was two streets behind Redfern station where the railway workshops were situated. Chimneystacks from the factories, and the railway workshops towered above the workers' grimy, smoke-stained cottages. The billowing smokestacks dotted the skyline, and belched soot-laden grime across the roofs and streets. Each morning, the factory whistles and hooting alarms shrilled out the start to a new working day for hundreds of sullen-faced men. Some wore stained overalls along with battered hats as they trudged along the streets to fill in another day that was the same as the one before.

Most of the houses had minimal space behind them. The children all played amongst the grime and rubbish-filled streets. Some mothers were trying to bring their daughters up in a refined manner, in an area where poverty and struggle was a part of everyday life. Dirty urchin boys would poke fun and tease the girls who were clean-faced and wore starched dresses, along with lace-up boots.

Most of the children went to the only school in the area. It was a combined school that was known as the Jubilee Ragged School, and the sisters of the poor ran it. The nuns survived on charity, and all the pupils shared the few schoolbooks that were available.

Many of the children only went to the school for the free lunch, as most would have had little or no breakfast. The pannikin of soup, and the slab of bread that they received there, was the biggest meal that they would have all day. They learnt the basics of reading, writing and arithmetic and little else. There were around twenty children at the school when Claire enrolled Hannah.

Young Tom Fields knocked on the door, and Hannah opened it. He was expecting to see Mrs Townsend, and he was momentarily tongue-tied before saying to Hannah, 'Me mum sent these scones for ya,' as he clumsily thrust the plate towards her. Hannah smiled a wispy smile and said haughtily, 'Bring them in, Aunt Claire is out the back.' She turned without taking the plate. Tom followed her through to the kitchen, and he placed the plate on the table and repeated to Claire, 'Me mum sent these scones for ya!' Claire smiled and said, 'How nice Tom, now you make sure that you thank your mother for me, and would you like one?'

'Yes please, missus.'

'Hannah take down a plate, and get the butter and a jug of milk from the icebox please, now you just sit there young man and help yourself.'

'Thanks missus.' Hannah sat opposite him, and stared while he devoured a couple of his mother's scones. He said to her, 'I seen you at school the other day, you're in sister Mary's class, ain't ya?'

'Yes, she's a dragon.'

Tom sniggered, 'Too right she is.'

'Hannah, that's no way to talk about the nuns, I'm sure that they do their best, and why is she a dragon?' asked Claire, with a hint of a smile.

'I 'ad her for awhile, and she was always going crook and calling us dunces,' replied Tom before Hannah could speak.

'Well, I've got sister Judith now, and she is nice, and she said that she was going to take us on a picnic one day.'

Tom changed the subject and said, 'I'll hafta walk to school tomorra, cause I've got a puncture on me bike, so I'll wait for you in the morning if ya like Hani?'

***

That was the first time that he had called her Hani, and Tom never fixed the puncture the next day, or the day after, or even the week after. They walked to school together for the next two years, until he left.

2.

Davin and Claire

The chill of winter had arrived, and Jack was still working at the fuel merchant's loading bags of coal. But now, he was able to load the dray unassisted with the full chaff bags. Mr Johnston increasingly relied on young Jack, and he would get him to make the deliveries by himself more often than not.

The people who couldn't afford to buy bags of coal would go down to the rail yards where coal was plentiful. It would lie on the tracks after falling from the coal tenders of the steam engines.

Several steam engine drivers worked out of the Redfern depot and lived nearby. When they were shunting around the yard, they would bang the engine harder than was necessary to couple up to the carriages and other vehicles. This ensured that lumps of coal would spill from the engine tender, so that there was always a bit on the ground for anyone who needed it. Each night, people would sneak through the holes in the fence armed with a milk pail, or a tin bucket, and they would scurry along the track picking up the loose coal. The railway authorities frowned upon it, but nobody ever stopped them doing it.

Claire had hung a sign in the front window shortly after they had moved in. She advertised that she could do clothing alterations, along with dressmaking and ironing, and Claire taught Hannah how to sew.

Davin had dug over their small garden plot, and he had filled it with horse manure gathered from the street. He grew a few potatoes, along with carrots and a few cabbages, and at other times he would swap some of the vegetables for a few eggs from the neighbours who had chickens.

He had been looking for another job, as blacksmithing was his trade. He had looked after the horses back on the farm in Ireland, re-shoeing them, and doing general ironmongery work. But, try as he may the railways would not transfer him to their boiler-making section where they had a large casting forge.

Claire snuggled up to him as they sat on the couch one evening. She had sensed his restlessness and asked, 'What's troublin' you my love, are ye not happy here?' He wrapped his arm across her shoulder, and thought for a moment before answering her.

'It's not that I'm unhappy living here, but I miss the horses and the open fields. I would do anything to work at a forge again, making shoes for the horses and welding a bit of iron, but the foreman said that they could use a boiler-maker, but not a blacksmith. The man's a fool, cause anyone knows that if you can shoe a horse you can work a forge. If we had some money I'd be tempted to start me own business, I know that I could make a go of it!'

They sat in silence for a few moments and then he said; 'It's orright darlin', I'm just feeling a bit down. We come out here to make a new life, and I can't even support you and the child without you both havin' to sew buttons just to pay the rent.'

Claire gave him a squeeze and said, 'Don't you be talkin' nonsense now. We don't mind sewing buttons. Look at us here in this nice house with friendly neighbours. Isn't this far better than where we were? If we can save a few pounds you can still start up a forge.' She gave him a cheeky smile and said, 'Now I know what you need, so take me to bed!' He smiled and replied, 'You be a right hussy Claire Townsend.' And he playfully smacked her bottom as she brushed past him.

***

Many families were striving to have some form of domestic comfort, and they wished to be seen as moral people.

However, if there was any hint of a scandal it would spread throughout the neighbourhood like a wildfire.

Doris was making a pot of tea, and she could hardly contain herself with self-righteous indignation. She asked Claire, 'Did you hear about Mrs Crawley luvvy?' Claire shook her head and Doris said,

'The coppers were around at her house last night, and apparently there was a big fight between her and her old man. He drinks a bit you know! Anyway, she was seen down at the docks a few times and apparently, she's been selling her wares,' Doris raised her eyebrows knowingly before going on, 'if you know what I mean luvvy.

'She goes and meets the ships, as they come into Circular Quay in the afternoons when her old man is still at work. Apparently, she had the use of a room at the Royal Hotel and the coppers caught her at it, and they have charged her with prostitution. So, the coppers came around to her house last night with a warrant for her to go to the courthouse, and her old man was at home. When he heard about what she was doing, he punched her right in the gob, and when the coppers tried to stop him he belted a couple of them too, and so he was locked up.'

Claire responded with, 'That's awful, the poor woman.'

Doris snorted, 'Poor woman nuthin', she's been carrying on like a two-bob tart, and she got what she deserved.'

Claire, a little more compassionate replied, 'She mightn't have had any money if her old man drinks it all, does she have any children?'

'She has six, and with her shenanigans they might all belong to different blokes, I'm sorry luvvy, but it don't matter how poor she is, it's immoral to do what she was doing, and there is no excuse for it, and her being a Catholic too!'

'What do you think will happen to her now Doris?'

'I dunno, but I won't be surprised if her old man just clears off. He might get locked up though, because I think that he has been in trouble with the coppers before, what with his drinking. It depends if the beak is in a good mood or not I suppose.'

The door opened, and Hannah came in followed closely by Tom. 'Aunt Claire, may I go with Tom down to the wharf please?'

'Where are you going Tom?'

'We might go down to the Parramatta River at Glebe, and I can teach Hani how to fish.'

The river was almost a mile away, and Tom would ride his bike with his fishing tackle in a rucksack on his back whenever the opportunity arose. He took Hannah fishing almost every weekend, and as Tom fished she mostly just sat on the wharf and prattled on about nothing. He was always calling her a chatterbox, but he still wanted her to be with him.

3.

The Forge

It was 1909, and Davin was still working for the railways, but he still dreamed of going back to his trade of blacksmithing.

Burt Davis worked at his forge on the outskirts of Erskineville, and he had been there for more than ten years. Erskineville was several miles from Redfern and it was still more rural than suburban.

Most of Burt's business came from shoeing horses, of which there were still more than automobiles. He had a small store on one side of the forge, and he sold a myriad of small items that he made there.

He also made steel rims for wooden cartwheels. As he fitted the last of a set of four, the heavy cart broke free of the pulley rope that was holding the back axle off the ground. He was working alone, and as the rope broke free, the cart came crashing to the floor. The steel tyre flew off the wooden wheel and hit Burt in the head. The blood flowed freely from the great gash on his forehead, and Burt was dead before his body had hit the ground.

It didn't take long for the news to spread about the accident that had killed the local blacksmith. Mr Davis had no next of kin, and the speculation was that the forge would remain closed. Doris was in the kitchen telling Claire about the accident.

'The poor chap going just like that, it just goes to show that you never know when your time on this earth is up!'

She blessed herself as she remarked, 'At least it was quick, and he didn't suffer by all reports, but you know what luvvy? I thought that this could be a golden opportunity for your Davin.'

'What do you mean Doris?'

'Well, as Mr Davis had no kin, your Davin might be able to take over the forge from whoever owns the building. He should go over and see how much the rent is before someone else snaps it up.'

Claire thought for a moment, and could see the logic in what Doris had said. 'That's a good idea Doris, because I know that he misses his forge, and if he could get the equipment for the right price I'm sure that it wouldn't take him long before he started to make some money. I'll talk to him as soon as he gets home.'

✻✻✻

Claire waited anxiously for Davin to arrive home, and she had spent the day thinking of the possibilities of Davin working at his own business. She had no idea of how much it cost to shoe a horse, and she speculated about what they would they do if Davin couldn't make a wage from the forge. The doubts were creeping into her mind, and she even thought of not telling him about the opportunity, but dismissed the thought instantly.

Davin arrived home tired and dirty, and Claire, anxious to talk to him, said, 'Darlin' go and wash up, I need to speak to you before I get your supper.' He gave her a quizzical look, but said nothing and made his way outside to the washhouse.

He had a quick wash, changed his shirt, and then went inside to hear what his wife was so anxious to tell him. Claire recounted the circumstances of the death of Mr Davis.

'Darlin', I think that you should go around there as soon as you can and talk to the owner of the forge. Mr Davis only rented the shed according to Doris.' Davin was quiet for a few moments, digesting what his wife had told him and then he asked, 'How could we afford for me to leave my job? I would love to work a forge again, but not if it means that we can't pay the rent here.

'What would we do if I couldn't make a go of it?' He was excited about the prospect, but the thought of failure was holding him back until Claire said, 'I have something for you.' She took down a canister from the mantelpiece, and handed it to him.

He looked at her, and then took off the lid. His eyes opened with surprise and he asked, 'What's this?'

'It's my little stash darlin'. I have been putting a few pennies away every week ever since we moved here. I knew that it would come in handy one day and that day is now.' He looked at the coins in the tin and asked, 'How much is there?'

'Six pounds and three shillings, and that should be enough to get you started, so I don't want to hear any argument. I want you to go and see the owner of the forge first thing in the morning. If you can get the business, then use that money to secure the place!' Davin was overwhelmed with the thought that maybe he could finally work for himself.

He was up at first light, and rode his bike along the rutted road to Erskineville. He had wrapped the tin that held the coins in an oilcloth before securing it in his haversack that was slung across his back. Doubt crept into his mind, and he was trying to contain his pent-up excitement. What if the owner wouldn't rent him the forge? What if he couldn't afford the asking price? And, if after all that he did manage to secure the forge, could he run a business?

He was well aware that he had limited schooling. While he could count, read and write, which was more than some others could, the reality was that he had never run a real business. Back on the farm in Ireland he was just the farm blacksmith. He didn't have to worry about doing the books and looking after the pennies. All that he had to do was shoe the horses and forge a few drawbars and iron brackets for the farm wagons.

His mind was churning over with these thoughts as he pedalled past the houses and shops. Soon he was pedalling through open farmland.

He had no idea where the forge was situated, but he would ask someone when he got to the town.

A few factories were under construction nearby, and there was also a small church, a general store, haberdashery and a butcher's shop along with a smattering of houses. He rode past the forge, and as it was boarded up he rode back towards the butcher's shop, which was the only place where there was any sign of life. He leaned his bike against the verandah post and went inside. The butcher was hammering at the bones of a cow's carcass with a meat cleaver.

He stopped and looked at Davin. 'Yes sir, what would you like?' He put down the cleaver and wiped his hands on his striped apron.

'Good morning, could you help me with some information on who owns the forge building at the end of town, I would like to rent it if I could?' The butcher looked a little surprised, as it was less than a week since Mr Davis had been buried.

'Old Mrs Darcy owns the site; she owns most of what you see around here including my shop. I don't know what her plans for the building are Mr...' and his voice trailed off.

'Townsend, Davin Townsend,' He held his hand out for the butcher to shake.

'I'm Jack Burrell, and this is my establishment. I run it, just me and me son.'

'Could you tell me where I might find Mrs Darcy?'

'You a blacksmith are yar?'

'I useta be, back home! Can you point me in the direction of Mrs Darcy's?'

'If you follow the road past the forge it goes down to the bay. You will see a big red brick place near the beach. You can't miss it; it's the only house down there. Do you want to open the forge again? Old Davis had a good business down there, you will be set if she lets you have it.'

'Thanks fer your help Mr Burrell.'

'Call me Jack, and call back and let me know how you got on, orright?'

'I'll do that.'

He pedalled down the road, his heart pumping faster with the anticipation of meeting Mrs Darcy. It was now fully light, and he could see the sunlight glinting off the water as the seagulls squabbled and squawked amongst themselves at the water's edge. The smell of rotting seaweed filled the air as he arrived at the front of the house. He hoped that he wasn't arriving too early, but the thought had no sooner crossed his mind than he saw the woman scattering seed to the chooks milling around her. He gave the bell on his handlebars a tinkle, and the old lady looked across at him.

Mrs Darcy was wrinkled and small, but her eyes were bright and she appeared sprightly. Davin guessed that she would have been at least seventy. As he approached her he raised his hat and said, 'Good morning to you ma'am, would you be Mrs Darcy?'

'I would, and who might you be young man?'

'Me name is Townsend ma'am, Davin Townsend, and I was wantin' to see if I could rent the blacksmith's forge offa you.'

She looked him up and down before speaking, and then said, 'I don't know what I'm going to do with the forge, I hadn't given it much thought. The poor man is hardly mouldin' in the ground, and I haven't even been back to the place since he died.

'If I did let you have it, it wouldn't be cheap you know. It was a good little business, and Mr Davis worked six days a week. I'll have to think about it for a bit. Now tell me about yourself young man. Are you married, and do you have any children?'

Davin was twirling his hat between his hands, and he was starting to relax as he spoke, 'Yes ma'am, I'm married, and the missus and me look after our niece, and we don't have no children of our own. But Hannah, that's our niece, is as loving as any child and she be part of our family now for around six months!' Mrs Darcy was watching him as he spoke, and then asked him, 'Are you a blacksmith, and are you working now?'

'Yes ma'am, I work down at the Darlin' Harbour rail yards, and I been there about five years, give or take. I haven't been at a forge for some time ma'am, but that's all I useta do!'

'I done me apprenticeship back home on the farm, and I been looking fer a long time for a chance to get back to hammerin' some iron again ma'am.'

'You do know that Mr Davis had a shop at the forge, and if I let you have it, I would expect the store to stay open. A lot of people bought their ironwork there, and this little town is growing. He had a bit of stock on the shelves, and I suppose that it's all mine now too, not that it's any good to me. If I let you have the forge you would have to buy the stock as well, do you understand that, young man?'

Davin was beginning to worry. The way that Mrs Darcy was talking she would want more money than what he had. However, he asked her the questions that he needed to know. 'Ma'am, could you tell me how much it would cost me to take over the forge and the stock? To be honest with you, I don't have a lot of money, but I'm a hard worker, and I'm sure that I could run the business if you gave me the opportunity.

'I don't want to waste any more of your time ma'am, so if you could just tell me how much it is, and if you want more than I have then I'll be off and I'll wish you a good day.' Mrs Darcy put down the pellet bucket, and the chooks went back to scratching around.

'Now don't you be getting impatient with me young man, I need to think, and I need a nice cup of tea! Bring those eggs with you.'

She pointed to the basket sitting on the ground. 'We will go inside, and I'll make us a cuppa.'

He followed her, and taking off his hat at the back door he scraped his boots on the doormat that led into a spacious kitchen. He looked around as he had never seen an inside kitchen, let alone been in one. The workers' houses always had an outside one and they were nothing like this.

On one wall stood a large dresser, which held an assortment of blue and white plates. Shelves and cupboards lined the other walls, and two large kerosene lamps hung from the ceiling with a pulley system to lower them down. Davin guessed that this kitchen was as big as his whole house and he thought of how Clair would love to see it.

Mrs Darcy poked and prodded the fire in the large stove to life, before moving the kettle to the flames. She took down two china cups and saucers from the dresser, and then brought out a jug of milk from the icebox and placed it near to the cups. Davin was watching her and felt the need to say,

'Excuse me ma'am, but I don't mean to impose on yer good nature, so please don't go to no trouble with tea, just fer me.'

'It's no trouble young man, and if I didn't want your company I wouldn't have invited you in, so you just sit there while I pour.'

'Thank you, ma'am.'

She poured the tea through a tea strainer, and asked Davin if he would like milk with it, 'No thank ya ma'am, I just has it black.'

'Well young man, I've been thinking! And I believe that I will charge you a pound a week for the forge. That's what I was getting from Mr Davis. Now before I let you have it I would need a month's rent, and I'm not sure how much stock would be in the store, but at least twenty pounds I would think. So that would be twenty-four pounds in total, and for that, you get all of Mr Davis tools to keep and anything else that is inside.'

Davin was crestfallen, and it must have shown on his face. He put the cup down and stood up, 'I'm sorry to have troubled you ma'am, but I can't afford that. I could make a go of a pound a week, but I couldn't pay twenty pounds for the stock. I'm sorry to have bothered you ma'am.' Mrs Darcy looked up at him and said, 'Sit down young man, and tell me how much money you have.'

'I have six pounds, and three shillings ma'am, and that would be every penny I own!'

'Now, let me think for a minute. You are a blacksmith, and the town needs a blacksmith, and I think that you could make a go of it, so I'll tell you what we can do.

'Now, you pay me five pounds, and I will take four of that for the months' rent, and I will take one pound as a deposit for the stock. So, what if you pay me five pounds a month for nineteen months, and that way you can pay for the stock as you go, now how's that?' Davin didn't have to think too long, and he replied,

'That's very generous of you ma'am, and I'd be pleased ter sign an agreement with you.'

'Well, that's settled then, I'll go and get a strip of paper, and we can draw up the details now, and then I'll get the key for you.'

Davin was twirling his hat frantically, and then he thought about the money. Mrs Darcy had gone off to get the paper, and he took the money tin from his haversack. He carefully counted out the five pounds.

Mrs Darcy came in carrying a small writing slope, which she placed down on the table and opened it up. She unscrewed the inkbottle, dipped the nib, and then started to write out the contract. When it was finished, she blotted the document carefully and then handed it to Davin to read. He read it slowly, but his mind was in a spin, and when he finished reading it he said, 'I would be happy to sign that ma'am.'

The document was signed, and Mrs Darcy pushed a large key across the table to Davin.

'That's yours now young man, now you had better get up to your forge and start working.' She gave him a smile and said, 'I'll give you a few days, and then I will come and see how you are getting along. Now be off with you, and tell that wife of yours that you are now working for yourself.' He put out his hand to shake hers, 'I cannot thank you enough for your generosity ma'am, and I'll look forward to seeing you at the forge. Good day to you ma'am.'

She brushed away his thanks and said, 'Now get along with you!'

He straddled his bike, and pedalled back to his new forge. The excitement was building within him as he spent an hour checking out the tools and the stock. Everything was as it was before the death of Mr Davis. The reality of having his own forge and a business gave him so much to think about, but first, he would go home and share his news with Claire.

***

Over the next three years, Davin worked to settle his debts with Mrs Darcy, and he had expanded the forge to now include a small foundry.

4.

The Apprentice

The government railways were expanding across Sydney. They were also building an underground loop system that would allow trains to travel around the city.

Davin had successfully applied for a contract to supply the brackets for the cast-iron lamp posts for the new stations. He had employed the services of a young labourer to help him with the increased workload, but they were still so busy that Davin decided that he should hire an apprentice.

Claire was busy cutting up a rabbit to make a stew for dinner, and Davin was sat at the kitchen table having a beer.

'I was thinking of asking young Tom if he would like to be me apprentice. I sure could use some more help, and Tom, he be a good lad. I was thinking that seeing as him and Hannah are such good mates, I thought that I should teach him a trade. What do you think darlin'?'

Claire smiled, 'Could it be that you believe that we might have him for a son one day? And you want to make sure that he could support our Hannah. Would that be the reason that you want to take him under your wing?'

'Can't hide nuthin' from you Claire Townsend, but I got eyes in me head. I might be a bit slow, but I seen the way he looks at her, not that I disapprove, or nuthin' like that.

'You have brought her up proper, and she's a right young lady now, but I seen how the other young urchins look at her too. She won't be left on the shelf that one won't, and I think that she could do a lot worse than young Tom.'

'For goodness' sake Davin, the child is barely sixteen! And here you are marrying her off already. I know that she likes Tom, and she likes Jack also, but they are like her big brothers, so we should just let things develop naturally. What will be, will be, and there's no need for you to be a matchmaker, but by all means offer Tom a job, but he mightn't want to be a blacksmith.'

'Well, I might as well go and ask him as there's no time like the present, and I need an answer.'

Tom and Hannah were sat on the front door stoop playing jacks. Tom was winning, and Hannah was squealing along with calling him a cheat as she grabbed for the knucklebones as Davin came out the door.

'Can I have a word with ya boy?'

Before Tom could answer Davin asked, 'Would ya like to learn a trade boy? I need an apprentice, and if you be interested, I could give yer a start. Wada ya think lad?'

'I would like that Mr Townsend, and I'd be happy ta learn a trade.' Hannah jumped up, and gave Tom a kiss on the cheek before they went back to their game.

5.

The Coal Yard

Jack had grown tall and muscular, and had almost taken over the complete running of the fuel yard. The years of lumping coal had taken its toll on Athol Johnston. His lungs were full of coal dust, and his coughing had gotten progressively worse. He smoked a pipe, and when a coughing fit had finished, he would immediately light it up and drag more smoke into his weakened lungs.

When Jack arrived at the yard one morning, Mr Johnston called him over to the tin shelter that served as the office and said, 'Son, I think me days are numbered. As ya know, I don't have no family, and that's probably a good thing. I know that ya aren't, but you are the nearest I got to kin, and you 'ave been me right hand man for a long while now. I trust yer son, so I want ya to take over the running of the yard for me.' He stared at Jack through bloodshot, watery eyes, but not really expecting an answer. He was wheezing, and trying to suppress a cough, but he continued talking.

'You've bin running the place almost by yerself these past two years and you're a good boy, and a good worker, so I'll increase ya wages to ten bob a day if ya can run the place by yerself, wada ya say lad?'

Jack was shocked, not only because of the offer of a pay rise, but he hadn't actually taken a lot of notice of Mr Johnston's deteriorating health until just now.

He had never taken much notice of his coughing and constant wheezing because he had always done it, ever since he had known him. But now, listening to the wheezing, he had just come to understand how sick his boss actually was.

'Thanks, Mr Johnston, I can run the place for you, and do the deliveries, and I don't mind looking after the horses.'

'You're a good boy Jack. I might plan a trip back home now that I've got this settled.'

'Where's home, Mr Johnston?'

'I grew up in Bathurst on the other side of the mountains boy. It's a lot warmer there than it is here in Sydney, and I got me a sister still living there. I haven't seen 'er fer some time, and if I don't go now I might not make it. We was always close when we was kids. I writ her a letter recently and she's expectin' me to go.' He handed Jack a bunch of keys and proceeded to show him which was which.

'There's the front gate one, and the smaller one is fer the safe, and inside the safe is the cash box and the little key is fer that. Now, there is about fifty quid in the safe, and ya use that money to buy the coke and coal from the mine company, and the feed for the horses. The mining company only take cash; you gotta work out how much ter order when the salesman comes around. You buy more in the winta, and ya buy more coal than coke. Only the blacksmiths buy coke, and when yer sells the stuff you take the money to the bank. Take out yer wages first, but always leave fifty quid in the safe for yer supplies.

'Now, I'm gunna see old Jones at the bank, and tell him that you're in charge of the accounts from today. Just remember always keep fifty quid in the safe!'

He started coughing again as he went out the front gate.

6.

Young Love

Tom started his apprenticeship, and he learned quickly. Davin's forge generated most of its income from shoeing horses, and Tom started making horseshoes from his first day. He was taught how to stoke the forge with the big bellows, and turn the coals white-hot. Then he hammered the glowing steel until his arms ached.

The city was expanding, and there was a growing need for cast metal objects from lamp posts and brackets to metal casings for the town's gas lamps. Tom worked twelve hours a day, six days a week. On Sunday they went to Mass, and sometimes they had a picnic in the park, or they went fishing down at the pier.

Davin had purchased a horse from a customer, and he would ride it to and from the forge. There was no room at home to stable a horse, but there were public stables at the back of Redfern Park that was only a ten-minute walk from his home.

Hannah had left school, having turned 16. Claire had taught her to be a seamstress as her small business had become busier. There was now a constant stream of ladies wanting a hem altered, or a new blouse made.

Davin was now also earning a regular income from the forge and he had spoken with Claire.

'We be doing orright for money now, and I'm going to get a lot busier what with the railway contract, so there be no need for you and the child,' he still referred to Hannah as the child, 'to keep working as you do. I can easily support you both now, so you don't have to keep sewing buttons darlin'.'

'Don't be silly, we enjoy our sewing, don't we Hannah? And it's nice when the ladies come as we get to gossip and catch up on all of the news, but I might stop working for the mill and sewing their buttons. They still only pay me five shillings for all of the garments that we do, and after all these years they have never increased what they pay me. I've seen the prices that they charge, and a shirt might cost five shillings more now than what it was last year.'

She threaded a needle, and then said, 'If I don't have to sew buttons for them, then we will have a lot more time for ourselves. I could make a few more blouses, and maybe a dress or two and even a bonnet and sell them myself. Hannah can help me, yes, that's what we shall do. I'll take the last basket back to the mill, and when they pay me, I'll tell them that I won't be doing any, anymore.'

✳✳✳

Doris had come around to see Claire. 'It's my Tom's birthday next Saturday. I thought that we might put on a bit of a do for him, nothing special because he hates a fuss. But I thought that I would make an apple cake, that's his favorite. I'll stick a few candles on it, so I want you all to come around for tea. I was wondering if you could get Davin to close the forge a bit earlier luvvy. That way, he can have time to have a bath and change his clothes, and then you could all come around, and we will have a bit of a party.'

Claire responded with, 'I'll have a word with Davin, it shouldn't be a problem.'

Hannah said, 'I know how to get him home early, he promised that he was going to teach me how to ride a horse, so I will nag him to take me horse riding on Saturday afternoon.'

She nagged at him to the point that he gave in and said, 'Orright, orright, I'll teach you how to ride a horse on Saturday arvo.'

When Tom arrived home, Hannah was waiting for him and said, 'Go and have your bath, your mother was heating the water an hour ago, so as soon as you are clean we can go to the stables and get a horse for me to ride.'

'No, we can go now, and I'll have me bath tonight.'

'Oh no you won't Tommy Fields, I'm not sitting in a saddle with you like that, you smell, so go and have your bath!'

'You sound like me mother Hani, and I won't get no peace until I've had it, will I?'

'And make sure that you put on a fresh shirt, now get along, and hurry up.' He did as he was instructed, and then they walked to the stables.

'Do you want to double up on my horse and I'll sit behind you, or do you want to start off by yourself?'

'No, we will double up Tommy, just like when you used to dink me on your bike.' With that, he held the halter as she climbed into the saddle and then he swung himself up behind her.

'Take hold of the reins like this, and loosen them off when you want to go forward, and pull back on them when you want to stop. If you want him to turn to the left then just pull on the left strap and the same for the right. Have ya got that?'

The lesson continued until he was happy that she could control the horse. Up to then, he had been loosely holding the reins as he had an arm around each side of her. She had also been holding them, and now he let them go completely and said, 'He's all yours now Hani, I'll just hang onto you.' He folded his arms around her waist and rested his chin on her shoulder. He felt her stiffen, and then she relaxed. His face was close to her hair, and he could smell the lavender soap on her skin, and now he didn't understand what had suddenly changed. He wanted to hold her, and he was enjoying holding her.

The horse was just plodding along, and Tom had no real need to hang onto her so tight, but he didn't want to let her go. His arms were just below her breasts, and he felt them resting there. She turned her head and said, 'Where should we go?'

'I don't care, you have the reins, so go wherever you like.' She did not attempt to release herself from his grip, and she turned the horse and headed for the river.

As the horse ambled along the unsealed road Tom was quiet and lost in his thoughts. For seven years he had tolerated her. He and Jack had played with her. They had put up with her temper tantrums as well as being berated by her when she wanted to play a game that they didn't want to play. She was like an annoying little sister, who wasn't their sister, and there was no doubt that she regarded them as her protectors and big brothers.

She had even taught them both how to play hopscotch, much to the derision of the other boys in the street.

'Look at the Fields playing a sissy's game as they had tried to outscore her on the squares. She would muscle in on them, and demand to play marbles with the other boys.

Then there was the day that she had accused little Billy Morris of cheating. Hannah had ended up wrestling him to the ground until Tom had grabbed her around the waist and dragged her off the hapless boy. Now here he was with his arms around her waist, and not understanding why he was feeling the way that he did, and he was enjoying it.

They reached the river, and Tom reluctantly let her go as he slid backwards off the horse. He took the reins from her, and then took her hand as she climbed down. He held it for longer than was necessary, and then the moment was gone.

'So, do you think that you could ride him by yerself Hani?'

'Not yet Tommy, I think that I will need a few more lessons before I could trust myself to be able to handle him.' Tom tied the reins to a bollard on the bank, and was about to sit down when Hannah exclaimed, 'Oh I forgot, we have to get home now!'

'What for? We only just got 'ere. I got to teach you some more about horse riding and how to check his feet.'

'I'm not checking his feet that's your job. I just want to be able to ride a horse so that we can go on picnics out in the bush together, but we have to get back home.'

33

'Why?'

'It's a surprise, so you will just have to wait, now come on we have to go now!'

They made their way back home slowly, Tom hanging on to her tighter than he needed to, but she didn't complain. Hannah led him through the front door and into the parlour.

'Happy Birthday son.' Tom looked sheepish and muttered, 'What's all this, it's just me birthday?' He looked at Hannah and smiled, 'So that's why we had to go for a ride, just so you could spring this ambush on me?'

Doris handed him a small parcel wrapped up in brown paper and tied loosely with string. She gave him a peck on the cheek, and said, 'Go on, open it.' He cut the string with a pair of scissors and tore at the paper. Inside was a long, silver-handled pocketknife. For a moment, he just looked at it, and then he recognised it, 'This was Dad's!'

'Yes son, it was your father's, and he was going to give it to you last year,' her voice trailed away, and her eyes welled up. 'Anyway he wanted you to have it as it had belonged to his father, your grandfather. He would be so proud of you son, seeing you working as hard as you do. Now that's enough of this, I baked your favorite cake, so now you have to blow out the candles.'

'Ma, I'm too old to be blowing out candles.'

'I know son, but it was Hannah's idea, so go crook at her.' He looked across at her, smiled and shook his head. The cake was eaten, and Tom, anxious to be outside, asked Hannah, 'Do ya wanna go for a walk?'

✳✳✳

It was almost dark, and the lamplighter was walking along the road lighting the gas street lamps. As they walked along, he nervously touched her hand, expecting her to flinch and move it away. When she didn't, and with his heart beating hard in his chest he clasped her soft hand with his rough and calloused one. He was still expecting her to withdraw it, but she didn't.

She said nothing, as her heart beat rapidly with nervous excitement, and she bowed her head not wanting him to see her face lest her feelings showed. He was nervous, and expecting rejection, but hoping that she wouldn't, and neither sure of what to do or say. They strolled towards the park, where the gas lamps showered a soft glow on the overhanging trees.

Hannah's mind was spinning with emotional turmoil, and Tom's was grappling with insecurities and not knowing if he was overstepping his boundaries. In the end, he just stopped walking. Hannah looked up at him in surprise as he said, 'Damn it Hani, you be doing me head in!' With that, he drew her to him, and clumsily wrapped his arms around her. She stiffened at first, but in an instant, she relaxed as their eyes locked together and then their lips met. A couple of children ran by and giggled as they embraced. The kiss lingered, and then they sat on a park bench, the shadows hiding the emotions on their faces. As they sat, she snuggled into him as he wrapped his arm around her shoulder.

Old Mary Hardy, the flower seller, sat at the entrance to the park. She sat on a stool under a gas lamp in the same spot every evening selling ribbons and flowers. Tom took a small posy from the bucket sat at her feet, and peeled off a length of blue ribbon from the coat hanger hanging from a nail in the tree trunk.

'That will be one shilling young man!' Tom handed her the flowers first and then the ribbon. 'You can put that on yer bonnet Hani.' She wrapped the ribbon around her hand that held her posy, and took hold of Tom's with her other one as they walked home in silence.

7.

The Inheritance

It was April 1912, and the newspaper boys were standing on their corners extolling the latest local and overseas news.

'The Titanic has sunk, 1200 souls lost! Read all about it! Get your paper here!' Two months earlier, the same boys had been spruiking the news about the same ship being almost ready for its maiden voyage. The newspapers had then proclaimed that she was *unsinkable*. People were now grabbing papers from the young sellers quicker than the boys could fold them over. They paid their three pence, and then stopped to read the news that had already spread to every corner of the globe.

Australia still relied totally on mail and goods being brought to the country by ship, and most shipping news was big news. Every ship that berthed bought a new wave of mainly British migrants to its shore, each one hoping to make a better life for themselves in the harsh and vast brown land that they would now call home.

Sydney was expanding in every direction, and some of its residents were becoming more affluent, as others sunk deeper into debt and despair.

The state and federal governments were funding major infrastructure programmes across the cities and towns with money that was borrowed from the Bank of England. There were more jobs than people to fill them. Men would work 12 and 14-hour days at the docks, and at the rail yards.

Labourers lay the crushed rock on the roads, and others dug trenches to lay cast-iron water and sewage pipes. At the end of their working day, most would invariably head for the pub.

Urchin children would hang around outside of the pubs and wait for their fathers. Women were not allowed inside hotel bars. Some would send their children into the pub to extract a few shillings from their fathers before they became too drunk and spent their rent money on booze and gambling. Fights and squabbles between drunken husbands and desperate wives were common.

✱✱✱

Jack had settled into running the fuel yard alone. It had been more than a year since Mr Johnson had left him in charge, and not a letter nor a message of any sort had reached him to explain how long he would be away. He did the banking, along with the ordering of stock, and he paid for the horses' feed bills upon receipt of the invoice. He was loading the dray with his daily deliveries when the postman stopped at the gate. Usually, the postman would just drop the mail in the box and give a blow of his whistle, but today he got off his bike and leaned it against the wall.

'Mornin' Jack, and how's things with yerself?'

'G'day Bert, can't complain. I got a few deliveries on taday, have ya got some bills fer me?'

'No Jack, just one letter, it looks official though, it's from a solicitor, and I hafta get a signature from you if you don't mind?'

Jack dropped the coal sack that he had just filled onto the dray. He was curious now, as solicitors' letters were usually letters of demand.

'Dunno what it could be Bert, is it addressed to Mr Johnson?'

'Nup, it's your name on the front, so you had better sign me book and I'll be off.' He took the envelope, and gave his signature and then stared at the front of it. In one corner was the name, Horace Taylor Solicitor, with the return address. He slid the blade of his pocketknife under the flap and sliced through it.

Dear Sir,

We represent the estate of the late Athol George Johnson. We wish to advise you that Mr. Johnson passed away recently. He left no kin other than an elderly sister, and we further wish to advise you that Mr Johnson has left his entire estate to yourself. The estate comprises the fuel yard and the dwelling at 112 Brickworks Road Redfern, and includes all the chattels there upon it. There are no caveats, or encumbrances on the said property.

Further to wit, Mr. Johnson held a Bank of New South Wales savings account with the sum of fourteen hundred and sixty-one pounds, seven shillings and sixpence therein. This money also forms part of Mr. Johnson's estate, and the entire amount is also bequeathed to you.

Would you be kind enough to make an appointment at your earliest convenience to attend this office so that the formalities of this will may be settled?

Your humble servant
Horace Taylor, Solicitor
443 Saint James Square
Sydney.

Jack reread the letter, but the details of the contents had not yet sunk in. His boss and mentor Mr Johnson was dead, and Jack was shocked to learn of it. He thought back to the last time that he had seen him. He remembered the wheezing and the raspy, wracking cough. *I wonder when he died*, he thought. He put the letter down on the old desk and sat down. He was dumfounded, as he slowly contemplated the change in his circumstances. He had never given any thought to what he would do if he had money to spend and became a property owner.

Jack sat at his desk for some time, as he tried to make sense of how the contents of the letter would change his life.

8.

The Present

Tom's feelings towards Hannah had changed since he had taught her how to ride a horse. No longer was she like a pesky little sister, and she was in his thoughts more each day. As he beat the red-hot metal into shape he was thinking of her, and he wasn't quite sure why.

At the end of each day, and after he had had his dinner, he would go and see her. Some nights they would just sit on the doorstep and talk about nothing, and on other nights they would walk to the park and sit under a gas lamp. Occasionally, on a Saturday night they would go and see a pantomime in a music hall, or go to a circus. Sunday mornings they would all go off to Mass, and afterwards the two of them would go to the stables to pick up the horses and go for long rides along the river. Hannah would pack a picnic hamper, and they would find a secluded spot to have their lunch.

Tom had been shoeing a horse, and the customer had mentioned that he had a couple of ponies to sell. A price was negotiated for one of them, and he had bought it for Hannah for her birthday.

It was her birthday on Saturday, and Tom had not come home from work any earlier than he did on weekdays. Claire, Doris and several of Hannah's friends had come around to celebrate with her.

The blossoming relationship between Hannah and Tom had not gone unnoticed by Claire and Doris.

Claire could see that her niece was continually looking towards the front door in the hope that Tom would appear, and she saw the disappointment on her face when he didn't. It was dark by the time that Tom came home, and Hannah was sitting on the front step when he finally arrived. She tried to ignore him, but he bent down and gave her a kiss on the top of her head.

'Happy Birthday Hani! I didn't forget ya, but I hadta finish doin' a couple of shoes. Anyway, I got ya a present.'

'Where is it?' she asked coolly.

'You will hafta wait till tomorrow before ya can 'ave it.' He was smiling as he said it, but Hannah kept on pestering him.

'Where is it Tommy, tell me I can't wait until tomorrow, please.'

'Nah, you will just hafta wait until we been to Mass in the morning and then ya can 'ave it.'

She cajoled and nagged him, and when that didn't work she pouted and said, 'I'm not talking to you Tommy Fields you're just mean. I'm going inside as I have to set the table for dinner!'

Still pouting, she gathered up her skirt, did a pirouette and closed the door behind her. He stared after her, and then laughed loud enough for her to hear it before he went home.

***

Sunday morning, they all went to Saint Bridget's Catholic church to attend the Mass, and afterwards he said, 'Hani, I'll come and get ya after breakfast, and we can go and get yer present.'

'I'm not talking to you Tommy Fields, I don't know if I shall ever speak to you again, anyway where are we going to get it, why can't you just bring it around after breakfast? Why do I have to go anywhere to get it?'

He turned around, and put his hands on her waist and tickled her, making her jump. She almost knocked off her bonnet that was now sporting a blue ribbon.

'Yes, you will, you just wait and see.'

It was mid-morning by the time that Tom took Hannah to the public stables in Redfern Park.

'G'day Harry!' Harry was the general hand and lived in a small room at the back of the stables.

'Mornin' Tom, is this the missus?' Harry was looking at Hannah, and she blushed.

'Nar, but sometimes she's just like me mother the way she nags me.'

'Tommy, that's not nice you've upset me now, I think that I shall go home.'

'Harry, you had better go and get her before I put me other foot in me mouth.' He smiled as he said it. Harry disappeared, and returned shortly after leading a roan-coloured pony that was already saddled. Before Hannah could say a word, Tom said, 'Happy birthday Hani, she's all yours!'

Hannah put her hands to her mouth, 'Mine, is she mine! Really? Tommy, you're not foolin' again are you?' Harry led the pony through the gate and handed the reins to Hannah.

'There yer go miss, she's been rid and she be a gentle ride.'

At first, she didn't take the reins from Harry, but turned to Tom and threw her arms around his neck, 'Oh Tommy, she's beautiful!'

Then she kissed him fiercely. Tom put his arms around her and squeezed her, 'Have ya forgiven me now?'

'Oh Tommy, I wasn't really cranky with you, how could I be? Cause I love you Tommy Fields.' She lowered her face, embarrassed by her forwardness.

Harry turned his head, as it wasn't the done thing to intrude into a young couple's intimate moments.

Tom lifted her face, with a finger under her chin and bent down to return the kiss.

'I love ya too Hani.' Hannah pushed her face into his chest, and they embraced without speaking.

Harry gave a short cough, just to remind them that he was still there, and they both looked at him sheepishly as Hannah took the reins of her new pony. The horse stood slightly taller than her, and she stroked its neck and said, 'Now what shall I call you? I know! I shall call you Florence! Come on Tommy, we have to show her to everyone, now give me a hand to get up.'

'I don't think that you can ride her dressed like that, let's go home so you can change yer duds and we can go for a ride.'

She was wearing a long skirt, and she knew that it wouldn't be ladylike to throw her leg across the saddle while dressed as she was, and conceded that she should change back into her jodhpurs.

9.

Past History

Doris was making a pot of tea when Claire came in to the kitchen.

'I need to talk to you Doris about our two lovebirds.'

'What's up dearie, do you think that they are too young to be getting so serious?'

'I don't know Doris, but she asked me the other night about, you know, the differences between boys and girls. We have never spoken about, well, you know, what goes on between a married couple and I'm not too sure what to say!'

Doris poured the tea, and placed the cup in front of Claire.

'I never much thought about it dearie, what with having two boys, but do you think that it's that serious? I know that my Tom is smitten with Hannah, but they have grown up together, and I saw them more like a brother and sister up until recently. Mind you, I would be happy if they did marry someday, and if it helps, I could have a word with her. I'm far from being an expert on the subject, but my Barry, well, he could get as randy as a ram in a paddock full of ewes at times, and neither of us knew anything about sex. It's not something that people talk about, is it? Mind you dearie, once my Barry worked out what he was supposed to do after we were married there was no stopping him, not that I wanted him to stop when he was in the mood.'

She said it with a hint of a smile, as her mind went back to the nights when Barry was still around.

'I just want to prepare her, even if they aren't all that serious. My mam told me nothing, and I had no idea of what to expect on my wedding night, and it was a shock as I suppose it is with a lot of girls.'

'Stop your worrying luvvy, if it gets to that point then I'm sure that they will work it out just like the rest of us did.' Claire didn't look convinced but said, 'I suppose that you're right Doris, but I want to do what's right for her. She's growing up so fast, and the other night she asked me why her mam had gone the way that she did.'

'Have a piece of cake dearie, I just baked it'. She didn't wait for an answer, but cut a slice and pushed the plate across the table to Claire.

'You have never told me what happened back home, other than her mother was put into the asylum. I gather that her pa died before that, and I'd be interested in knowing how come she was sent out here. I don't want to poke me nose into her affairs, but she has said a few things over the years, and I'm just curious that's all!'

'Tell me to mind me own business dearie, if you want, but I love her almost as much as I'm sure that you and Davin do. Goodness me, she is the closest thing to a daughter that I will ever have, and I love it when she just pops around and makes herself at home.'

'It's a long story Doris, and it's one of the reasons that we immigrated out here, but I'll tell you if you want to know, it's no secret, but I need another cuppa first!'

⁂

Claire stirred her tea before saying, 'There was so much going on around the farm back then, and I don't know where to start.

'Hannah's parents were tenant farmers, as we all were. Our lives revolved around the seasons. Eight families were living on the one farm.

Our farm was in a really remote area of West Cork, and we had to grow and make everything that we needed to get us through the whole year.

'We planted the praties, that's what we call potatoes; on Saint Patrick's Day and harvested them in the autumn. We would bury them in pits in the ground, and we covered the mounds with straw to protect them from the snow and the ice through the winter. If we didn't do that the crops would rot because the winters were so bitterly cold, and praties were our staple diet.

'We would take a few chickens, and occasionally a spare goat if we had one, to the monthly market in town.

'Life was always a struggle for all of us, that was until Hannah's father got mixed up with Francis Duffy.' Claire took a sip from her cup and then continued.

'Francis was a bit of a rogue, and he had been fined once for making the poteen. When he had been caught again they had locked him up in Cork prison for a month.'

Doris asked, 'What's poteen dearie?'

'It's homemade grog. It's a very strong drink, and it's illegal to make because the authorities don't get any taxes from the people who make it. It's made from the skins of the praties, mixed with a smidgen of barley.

'Anyway, Francis had met up with Sam Declan, that was Hannah's father, at the local tavern after the Saturday market and that's where the trouble began. They had been talking about their struggles as tenant farmers and never having enough money. Francis suggested that an enterprising man might make a pot of money if he didn't mind bending the rules a little. Sam made the mistake of asking Francis about his plan, and that's when Hannah's father had started making the grog.

'The family started to prosper, that was until the rumours from gossipin' tongues started about where the family's new-found wealth was coming from. The authorities and the excise men had offered rewards to anyone who reported any illegal distilleries, and it was only a matter of time before Hannah's father and Francis Duffy were caught and brought in front of the local magistrate.'

'What happened then?' asked Doris.

'Her father received a stern warning from the visiting magistrate, and a penalty of ten pounds as he had not come under notice before. Francis was sent back to prison for two months.'

Doris interjected, 'Ten pounds! Goodness me, such a lot of money, did he have that amount of money?'

'No, but we all scraped together what we had, and it was enough to pay the fine. If he hadn't paid it, they would have sent him to the debtor's prison. My sister had begged her husband not to make any more illegal grog, and for a while he had stopped brewing it. But we had gotten used to the few extra pounds that he was making, and he was such a generous man that he would slip us a pound or two after he had sold his batch.

'We all missed the money when he had no liquor to sell, so I suppose we were all guilty for what eventually happened.'

Doris asked, 'So he stopped makin' it after that, did he?'

'Sadly, no.' Claire took another sip from her cup. 'A month after Francis was released from prison they had decided to try their luck again, but this time they were determined to find a secure location in which to set up the still. They had to keep it a secret, because the less that knew what they were doing, the less likely the chance was of them getting caught again. A chap called Willy Hayes had grown up with Hannah's father and Paddy Townsend. He was Davin's father; he was the oldest of them. They were a tight group. Paddy was the farm blacksmith. His skills were utilised in the making of the equipment that was required for the distillery.

'We all lived in little stone houses that were scattered around the farm. Tenant farmers in Ireland had to make their own cottages. None of us had any real money, so we had to use what material was available. There were plenty of stones, so we all used them to build with. The land was very hilly, and behind Hannah's house the ground rose up to the woodlands. The higher up it went, the stonier it became until it reached the summit. It was such a beautiful place, but there was always something eerie about it. It afforded views right across to the next county of Kerry on a clear day.

'At the very top of the hill were the remnants of an old building. Someone had said that it was an ancient church, but nobody really knew.

There was also a circle of stones, and an old twisted hawthorn tree. I had been up there when I was a child, and it was really mysterious. I was glad to get away from there, and I never went back up the mountain.

'In Ireland, the thorny hawthorn trees grow everywhere. Legend has it that they are the home of the fairies and the leprechauns. Whenever you see a hawthorn tree growing next to a circle of stones, it was regarded as a sacred place, and woe betide anyone who disturbed the site.'

Doris was smiling, and Claire said, 'I know that it sounds far-fetched, but don't laugh Doris. Legend had it that bad luck would befall anyone who interfered with a stone circle, or who cut down a hawthorn tree. You have to understand, Doris, that Ireland is a very ancient land. We all grew up with stories of leprechauns, banshees and strange happenings. Anyway, at the very top of the mountain was what was know as a fairy fort. There were seven large stones in a circle and about twenty feet away was a large solitary rock. It was flat, and balanced precariously on two smaller stones. Beneath the large flat rock was a small opening that a man could just squeeze under if he lay on his belly.

'These rock formations were not all that common, and the small opening, no more than two feet above the ground, was seen as the entrance to the dark underworld of the fairies and the little people.' Doris's tea had gone cold, as she listened to the story that her friend was telling.

'Once through the opening, it dropped down into a small cave where a man could just stand up. I never saw it of course, but Davin said that it was dark and damp and that the place had a strange eeriness about it. They thought that it would be an ideal place to set up the still. Davin had helped them carry up the equipment, and when he had told me about the place it gave me goosebumps. I said that I had been up there when I was a child and that the place scared me. He agreed that it was a really spooky place, and that he wasn't going to go back again either. He believed in the inhabitants of the underworld, and strange things had happened to people who had crossed their paths. Paddy was the most superstitious of the group, and he told us that he was uncomfortable working in there.

'Paddy tried to convince Sam that they should find somewhere else to set up the still. He said that they were playing with fire if they were to mess with a spiritual place. I could tell that Paddy was worried, and he said that it was a place where one should tread lightly, so as not to disturb the inhabitants of the underworld. Sam dismissed the legend as just folklore that had been passed down through the generations.

'Nothing that Sam could say would stop Paddy feeling nervous, and he told us that he had known about the legend that had surrounded that area since he was a child. I got the shivers when Paddy told us the story. We were all huddled around the fire in our house one evening, and the only light was from a solitary candle that was stuck in a stone on the wall and from the turf fire. It was always breezy inside, and the shadows danced around the room like demons, and I wanted to hide because I was so scared.

'Sam was determined that this was where he would site his still, and be damned with the legends. He then set about making the entrance larger so that they could get their equipment in. At the same time, dozens of other small distilleries had sprung up in the hills around West Cork. His previous customers had gone elsewhere looking for a drop, and now Sam was anxious to start making some money again.

'There was bad blood between Sam and our landlord's gamekeeper. Sam had almost been caught poaching in the forest behind their tenement several years earlier, and the gamekeeper suspected Sam, but he couldn't prove it.

'He had called up the Constabulary, and they had questioned Sam, but he was not about to admit that he had been out poaching on the landlord's property, so Sam had escaped being charged.

'It had not taken long for the rumours to spread about Sam making the grog again. The gamekeeper's name was Ted Mulligan. He was known as a sleveen.'

'What's that, dearie?'

'It's what we call someone who is sly; you would probably call him a shifty person. Apparently, he had spent a week watching them from his hiding spot in the forest until he was sure that they were operating a still. Anyway, Mulligan reported the location to the constabulary so that he could claim the reward. The excise men lay in wait in the forest as Sam and Paddy made their way to the hideout. When they were inside the cave, the police rode up to the entrance and challenged them to come out.

'As you can imagine Doris, Sam was shocked that his hiding place had been discovered so soon after setting it up, and the Sergeant told him that it was the gamekeeper who had reported him. Paddy then cursed him and said that he would sort him out at a later date.

'Paddy and Francis were both sentenced to two months in jail and Sam to one month. Willy Hayes was not caught, as he had gone into town for more supplies when the raid had taken place. The jailing of Sam had devastated my sister, but Davin and I helped her with looking after her plot. Mary had continued looking after Hannah and their smallholding, and she tried to carry on as normal, but she was a frail person and relied completely on Sam.'

Doris interrupted, 'Keep talking luvvy. I'll just make us another pot of tea.'

'We were all counting down the days until Sam would come home. His cousin Tom Barry, who also worked on the farm, went to get him from the prison after he was released.

'Mary and Hannah both cried when they saw the condition of him. I did too. We were shocked by his appearance. His hair was matted, and he was so thin that he looked like a skeleton. It looked as though his skin was the only thing that held his bones together. Mary bathed Sam and set about nursing him back to health.'

Doris was enthralled with the story, and asked, 'Did he get better?'

'A few weeks later he had almost recovered, and was just about back to his old self. He promised Mary that he would now devote all of his energies to improving his plot and his livestock, and forget all about making the easy money from the illicit grog.

'Mary was so relieved, and I think that in hindsight she may have wished that he had been kept in prison.'

'Why, what happened then?' asked Doris.

'Sam was still worried about the roof of their house. The pine shingles had split, and he didn't know if the roof would hold out until the spring.

When it rained, they had to resort to placing bowls and pots on the floor to catch the leaks. So, Sam set about looking for a larch tree, which he knew would make long-lasting shingles. When Paddy and Francis had both recovered after being released, they set about looking for a tree to fell.

'It was full winter when Paddy and Willy Hayes searched the woodlands looking for a larch tree. The only one that they could find was on the landlord's property, and he wouldn't take kindly to anyone stealing his trees.

'Nobody had seen Mulligan for some time. The general consensus was that he would be keeping well away from Sam Declan and his friends. He had been told that Sam and the others were aware that he was the one responsible for getting their still shut down and for them being sent to prison. He knew that they would be waiting for the moment when that score would be settled.

'In the end, they decided that they would just fell the landlord's larch tree, but heavy snow had fallen shortly after Christmas, and that had put their plans on hold. It was early in February before the ground was solid enough to take the log jinker into the forest. It was just Sam, Tom and Paddy who set out for the woods early that morning, as Willy Hayes had gone into town to pick up the farm supplies.

'They had chopped the tree down, and had dragged it about a half a mile when Mulligan appeared from the forest with his shotgun tucked under his arm. We later guessed that he must have been watching them as they chopped down the tree.'

'Oh, my goodness,' exclaimed Doris. 'What happened then?' The tea had been brewing, and she stood to pour it.

'Sam had been waiting for this moment when he could confront Mulligan, and now was his opportunity. He had said that he would knock his block off when he saw him, and Sam was a man of his word.

'Hostile words were exchanged, and Mulligan demanded that they unchain the tree, as it was the landlord's property. Sam said that they were taking it, and there was nothing that Mulligan could do about it. But Mulligan had other ideas, and he levelled his gun at Sam.' Doris had both of her hands covering her mouth, her eyes wide with the thought of what she was about to hear.

Claire continued, 'No one thought that he would shoot, and I'm sure that Sam didn't either. He had had enough of Mulligan, and he grabbed hold of the barrel of the gun that was only a couple of feet from his chest. We think that his intention was to just push it sideways, but the gun went off, and Sam took the full force of the blast in his shoulder.

Doris quickly blessed herself and exclaimed, 'Oh my Lord!'

'Mulligan was equally shocked I think, before claiming that it was self-defence. The others weren't listening though; they were kneeling on the ground with Sam, and they could see that his wounds were fatal. Tom held Sam, as the light of life in his eyes faded, and Sam breathed his last.

'Oh, the poor man, what happen then? Did they catch Mulligan?'

'Mulligan ran off. Tom and Paddy were in shock, but picked up Sam's body and put it across the tree trunk. They dragged the log behind them, and soon they were at the house. Mary came out to meet them. I came over just as Mary saw Sam. She froze for a few moments before she broke down. Tom held her as he told her of the circumstances of Sam's death. She went and looked at her husband before composing herself, and she said that they needed to get him inside. We spoke to Hannah, who couldn't quite comprehend what had happened to her father.

'Paddy rode into town, and informed the authorities of Sam's death. He didn't trust Mulligan to give a correct version of what had taken place. Several hours later the constabulary arrived, and they said that they had spoken to Mulligan, and that he had claimed that the gun had gone off accidently. They had taken Mulligan's word because Sam and the others had stolen the tree. The undertaker came, but Mary had already decided that she would bury Sam on the land down by the river.

'The local doctor had arrived, and he wrote out the death certificate. Then the undertaker took Sam's body back to his establishment to make it ready for the funeral. Two days later he returned to the farm with the coffin. A hole had been dug down near the river. The Glen had always been Sam's favourite place with its moss-covered trees and the tinkling sounds of the flowing water.'

Doris said, 'Sounds like a lovely place dearie, better than being dropped into a hole in a church cemetery like my Barry was.' Doris blessed herself with the mention of her departed husband's name.

'After we buried him, there was talk of revenge, but then was not the time. We were all in shock, I think.

'The funeral was a simple service, and we all went back to the house to hold a wake and toast his life.

'That's what we do when someone we love dies. We tell stories, and play music and dance and drink because that's what is expected.'

'Oh, that sounds lovely dearie, I think that I would like a wake when I go, mind you they could probably hold it for me in the undertaker's broom cupboard for all the people who would come to it for me.' She smiled as she said it, and Claire responded with, 'I'll come and dance at your funeral Doris, we all will, but you're not planning on going just yet are you?' she laughingly asked. Doris was still smiling as she asked, 'So what happened then?'

'Well, when Willy Hayes had returned from town and learned of Sam's death, he was inconsolable and vowed revenge. He was going berserk, and even Davin had trouble controlling him. Willy had drunk heavily for two days after the shooting, until finally passing out inside the cattle stalls. When he had recovered from his binge, he was sullen and moody and nobody could talk to him as he stared at Sam's graveside. Paddy tried to pacify Willy by saying that he knew a man who could take care of Mulligan for a fee.

'That's what happens in Ireland Doris; there were always feuds, vendettas and killings! But no words would satisfy Willy; his only focus was on avenging his friend. He was still drinking as he saddled up his horse. We watched as he tightened the girth strap and looked around at the place that was his home; it was as though he knew that he wouldn't be coming back. He checked the magazine on his rifle before climbing into the saddle. We tried talking to him, but his mind was made up.

'He galloped across the fields like a man possessed as he made his way to Mulligan's place. Willy did not say a word as he looked at the person that he held responsible for killing his friend and he pulled the trigger.

He would probably have gotten away with what he did except that Jimmy Whichard, a farm worker, had been standing in the stables when Willy had ridden up to Mulligan's house. He had watched the drama unfold, and he had to report the murder to the authorities. It was at Willy's trial when we learned what had happened after he had left our farm.

'After the shooting, Willy made his way back home, but he didn't stop. He continued through the forest, and up to the ridge and the stone circle where they had made their last still. He walked to the flat rock that had hidden their cave where the still had been. He sat on the rock, and I'm sure that Paddy's words would have came back to haunt him.

'*We shouldn't mess with the stones; it's bad luck to mess with the little people.*'

'Willy was still sat on the ridge when the constables arrived. They handcuffed him, and charged him with murder before they took him to Cork prison. After a short trial, he was found guilty of murder.

'The judge entered the courtroom, and he placed a square of black fabric upon his head. It was the sign that he was about to impose the death sentence.

'We were all in the public gallery when the sentence was handed down. Willy was manacled in the dock, and he took one final look up at us, and he gave us a nod of his head and a weak smile.'

Claire stopped talking for a moment, as the memories that she had spoken to Doris about were still raw.

'A few months after Sam had died, Paddy got kicked by a horse, and he died a few weeks later. Davin could have taken over his father's forge, but too much had happened, and he didn't see any future on the farm. It was shortly after that when Davin had suggested that we should immigrate to Australia. We didn't do it just then, but after all that had happened; there was nothing to keep us there.'

***

'Later, Davin made the arrangements for us to immigrate here. It was so hard leaving my sister and everyone that we had known behind. But our passage was booked before they hanged poor Willy, and if we had cancelled our passage we would not have been allowed to apply again.

'It was also an Irish tradition to hold a wake for family members who were immigrating. Most farm workers were illiterate, so there would be no communication between them ever again due to the tyranny of distance. Every friend and family member would drink a toast to those leaving in the same fashion as if the family member had died. The thinking was that they might as well have been dead once they had left! We had been here for almost two years before the execution took place.

'A friend of Davin's had posted us a copy of the Cork newspaper in which they reported the hanging. About fifty people had stood outside the jail on the morning of his death. A few police were on duty in case of trouble, but there was none. When they placed the noose around Willy's neck, a black flag was raised up on the prison tower flagpole.

'Within a minute of the flag rising, the lever controlling the trap door was pushed forward, and Willy fell the eight feet to his death and was left to slowly strangle.

'His body was left to hang there for an hour before a doctor examined it. When this happened the black flag was lowered, and those watching on the outside knew that the prisoner had met his maker. They took his body to a corner of the prison cemetery reserved for those executed inside the prison walls, and there it would stay.'

'Oh, Mercy be,' exclaimed Doris, and she crossed herself again and asked, 'When was that?'

'That was around 1902.'

She mused for a moment, and then said out loud. 'I can't believe that it is over ten years since that happened. I can remember it as though it were yesterday.'

Doris asked, 'So tell me dearie, what happened to Hannah's mother?'

'After the death of Sam and with me gone, Mary had trouble managing their plot. According to the nuns, she withdrew into herself and eventually lost all reason. Hannah was about seven years old, and she spent most of her time looking after her mother. She got some help from a few of the other farm workers, but they had their own troubles. The rent had not been paid for almost six months, and they had been threatened with eviction. Everything that they had owned was sold off bit by bit, and then there was nothing left to sell. Within two and a half years of Sam's death, Mary was placed into a sanatorium in Skibbereen, that's a little farming town about twenty miles from where we lived on the farm. Hannah was sent to live with the nuns in Cork after that. That's when they wrote to us asking if we could take her!

'We were married four years earlier; Davin was ambitious and dreamed of having his own forge somewhere in the city. After the killings, he was more determined than ever for us to start a new life. He had seen the immigration posters plastered along the walls of the docks in Cork. They suggested that a better life was waiting for anyone who would make the long journey to Australia or America. There was also a long list of trades that were required, and blacksmithing was one of them. So, after making many inquiries, it was decided that we would immigrate to Australia.'

Claire said, 'I was so shocked when I received the letter from the convent informing me of my sister's condition.

'We had always been close, and I miss her terribly, but of course the silver lining on the clouds of despair is that we got to give Hannah a home. Well Doris, that's the story. It's not a very happy one, but at least Hannah settled in really well, and we have no regrets about moving over here at all!'

They sat in silence for a few moments. Doris was thinking of the story that she had just heard, and Claire was feeling melancholy after narrating it.

10.

The Drums of War

In times of uncertainty, the community would look to the church for reassurance and guidance. The newspapers had recently featured stories that inferred that the assassination of the Archduke of Austria, Franz Ferdinand, and his wife could lead to conflict within Europe. Most people had chosen to ignore the warnings, partly as Europe was so far away, and furthermore, because most had never heard of Franz Ferdinand.

However, the headlines on the following edition of the weekly newspaper had caught everyone's attention: *Germany Declares War on France*. The article was ominous, as it predicted that a war in Europe was now inevitable.

On the following Sunday morning, Saint Bridget's was packed with people each dressed in their Sunday best. The men had hung their hats on the racks in the vestry, and there was an air of anticipation amongst the congregation as they shuffled into the pews. They waited for the service to begin, and for Father Damien to give them an update on what may happen if there was a war.

The vesper bell rang, and all those present rose as the priest and the altar boys made their way along the aisle to the altar. Father Damien stood in the pulpit and glanced around at his congregation. He didn't speak at first, and a few people coughed and fidgeted, as they prepared themselves for what they were about to hear.

'My friends,' he stated solemnly, 'I stand here today with a heavy heart. I believe that shortly we will be at war. Unconfirmed reports coming through to the newspaper offices from England, tell us that Germany has invaded Belgium in the last few days. The reports also say that if this is the case, then England will surely become involved. I want to prepare you all, because if that happens then our young men here will be called upon to stand up for their king and country. Let us pray that common sense will prevail throughout the corridors of power, and that the dark forces of evil will not take us to war.' He then led the congregation in prayer.

After Mass, people gathered outside in small groups. Jack, Davin, Tom and a few others stood together. They rolled cigarettes, and shuffled their feet until Davin spoke. 'Gunna be interestin' if what the father says is gunna happen.' Jack replied, 'Dunno how any of us could be involved, by the time we got over there it would be over, what do ya think?' He hadn't directed the question to any one of the group, but Tom said, 'I reckon that I'd go if they wanted me, could be a bit of fun, and I'm not a bad shot!'

'Yeah me too, dunno who would run the business though!' Jack thought out loud.

The conversation waned, as they all became immersed in their thoughts about what they would do if war became a reality.

∗∗∗

It was a week later, and the headlines read, *Rising Tensions in Europe* and *First Shots Fired*. Then, a few days later the news came via the Overland Telegraph Service directly to every newspaper throughout the country. The headlines declared in bold print, *Britain Declares War on Germany*. The *Sydney Herald* newspaper proclaimed that Prime Minister Joseph Cook had pledged full support to Britain. He had offered 20,000 soldiers with a promise to increase that number to 50,000 as soon as they were trained up.

Davin and Tom were both working at the forge, when they heard the newspaper boy spruiking out the news. *Australian Troops to Fight in Europe.* It was the news that they had all been expecting, but it was still a shock to know that Australian involvement in the war was now a reality.

Davin gave the boy his three pence and took the paper. He stood on the road as he read the news and devoured every word. Then he went back to the forge, and he handed the paper to Tom.

After reading the articles he asked Davin, 'Would you be able to manage if I enlisted, boss?' Davin was pumping the bellows, and the coals were glowing red.

'I'd hav'ta manage, but I won't say that I wouldn't miss you lad, but if you decide to go, then I don't envy you telling Hannah. She's gunna be upset. I know that she loves you, and I reckon you feel the same about her. Am I right boy?' It was the first time that Davin had mentioned the growing relationship between the two of them, and Tom didn't have to think before he answered.

'Yep, she means the world to me boss, and I s'pose that I will probably ask her to marry me one day. But now that the stoush is on, I dunno what to do. Maybe I'll just wait awhile and see what happens. I would feel bad about leaving you boss cause you have been good to me.'

Davin put down the red-hot poker that he was hammering into shape and picked up the paper again. He turned the pages and grunted. 'It says 'ere that the government expects the war to be over by Christmas, crikey that's only three months away! Hardly seems worth the trouble of training any troops if that's the case. By the time they get over there it will be all over if that report can be believed.'

Tom kept hammering the steel all day, but his mind was elsewhere. If he signed up to enlist and the conflict was over before he got to wherever the war was on, then at the very least he would get to see something of the world before coming home. But, he was struggling with what he would say to Hannah. She was as gentle as a kitten, however when something upset her she could get as mad as a hornet, and Tom had no desire to upset her.

He thought that if he asked her to marry him, she might not be so upset, but then he thought, *What if I got meself shot, or even killed? That wouldn't be fair to her.* As he rode home, he had resolved nothing in his mind. He decided that he would go and see her as soon as he'd had his bath.

Hannah was in the kitchen with Doris when he came in. 'Hello, ma,' and he gave her a peck on the cheek.

'Don't I get one too?' He put his hands on Hannah's shoulders and kissed the top of her head. She responded with, 'I hope that your hands are clean, Tommy Fields!' And he laughed.

'Did you hear the news about the war?'

Doris retorted, 'Of course we did, that's what everyone was talking about today. They are already sticking up enlistment posters all over the place. I read one when I was down at the Chinese laundry earlier. I saw Mrs Preston there, and she said that her Jerome had already signed up.

'Old Jack Turner, the street sweeper, was talking to Mavis Jennings outside the butcher's shop. He said that he was thinking of enlisting too. Silly old coot, he must be seventy if he's a day. God help us all if he started swinging a rifle around like he swings that broom of his!'

Hannah smiled, but she was dreading Tom telling her that he was going to enlist. The thought had no sooner crossed her mind than he said, 'Well I might as well tell ya both now, I think that I will give it a go too.' He was looking at his mother, and afraid to look directly at Hannah. 'The paper said that it would be all over by Christmas, so I shouldn't be gone fer long!' He then tried to make light of the situation, 'In any case they mightn't have me; they reckon that you hav'ta pass a medical examination of some sort before you can get in.'

Doris was looking at her son. She knew that there was nothing that she could say that would make him change his mind.

'If that's what you want to do son, then it's not up to Hannah or me to stand in your way, but think carefully before you make up your mind. What will you do if it's not over in a few months? Once you sign up you won't be allowed to change your mind, I'm just saying, don't be in a hurry to sign up, just give it a few weeks and see what develops. Will you do that for your mother?'

'Well I wasn't gunna go down there tomorrow; besides, I have to finish doing about fifty sets of horseshoes for the police barracks. I spoke with Davin, and I won't leave him in the lurch. I'm just sayin' that I wouldn't mind signing up, but there's no hurry!'

Hannah was quiet; disturbed on one hand that the love of her life was even thinking of going off to join the army, but relieved on the other. He appeared not to have made up his mind completely, and she wondered if she would be able to talk him out of enlisting.

Tom could feel the tension in the room and said, 'Hani, do you want to go to the music hall tonight? They are having a singalong, and I thought that we might go and kick up our heels a bit, wada ya say?'

'I don't know Tommy, I'm a bit down tonight, and I wouldn't be much fun, what with all this talk of the war. It's all right for you. To you it's just a big adventure, but if you go off to Europe, your mother and I will be worried sick every day that you are gone. How will we know if you're safe? It takes weeks for a letter to arrive from the other side of the world, I'm sorry Tommy, but I feel sick to my stomach just thinking about it.'

Doris moved over to Hannah and gave her a hug, 'There, there dearie, don't you go upsetting yourself, now go and pretty yourself up, and go and have some fun. Let tomorrow take care of itself. Now son, you go and have your bath, and dinner will be ready by the time that you're clean. Hannah has cooked us a lovely rabbit pie, so let me get the veggies started.'

✳✳✳

Six large gas lamps hung from chains at the front of Aggie's Music Hall in Chinatown. A young woman sat in a bright red painted box selling entry tickets at sixpence each. The advertising signs, along with gaudily coloured banners hanging from the walls, promised a night of laughter, fun and magic.

The music hall stage was adorned with long red velvet curtains and glittering gaslight chandeliers hung from the ceiling. Waiters, wearing black waistcoats and bowler hats over pinstriped shirts, attended to the tables scattered below the stage. These characters would occasionally group together, and then burst into song while wearing fake moustaches and slicked-down hair.

The gaslights were dimmed, and a musical melodrama began. The audience was encouraged to hiss and boo the villain, who was played by Aggie, and cheer and clap when the heroine got the upper hand. The night ended with the waiters and Aggie linking arms and singing a medley of melancholy songs that seemed to reflect Hannah's sombre mood.

After the show, Hannah and Tom walked home slowly. The streets were almost deserted, save for an occasional drunk leaning on a lamp post.

All along George Street, shop fronts and light poles had recruitment posters on display. The posters enticed men from 16 to 40 to enroll. Some were blunt and screamed, *Don't be a coward, do your bit for king and country, enroll now, and don't shirk your duty.*

Others were subtler, and suggested that by enrolling it would be a good way of seeing Europe and the mother country of England. They gave the impression that it would be akin to taking a holiday rather than going to war.

Tom was struggling with what to say to Hannah. For a few short hours, they had forgotten about the impending war, and they had laughed, hissed and booed as they stomped their feet on the wooden floorboards along with the others. But now, they were alone. They were holding hands, but each was thinking of the other, as they grappled with their own fears of the future.

Tom stopped at the corner of their street. A late tram trundled by as he took Hannah into his arms and said, 'I truly do luv you girl, but I need to go and do my bit. Don't you ask me why cause I can't tell you, all I know is that I gotta go. I don't want to upset you and Ma, but if I don't go and the others do, then I couldn't see me self as a man, and I would never be any good to you! I wanna marry you girl, but how could I marry you if I saw me self as a coward? I'm sorry Hani, but maybe you don't wanna marry me, but if you do how would you look at me when the others came home, and I didn't go?

'I couldn't stand it if others looked at you, and them knowing that yer husband didn't go, and I buried me head in the sand like an ostrich!

Hani, I would poke me own eye out before I done anything to hurt you, but I have to go an enroll, and before I do I just want you to understand the way that I feel!'

Hannah looked into his face, but his eyes were hidden in the shadows, and she couldn't see them. 'Oh Tommy, I love you so much. Go and fight your silly war, and I will be waiting for you when you come home. You will come home won't you Tommy?' Her words trailed away as she held his face between her hands.

Tom looked down at her and whispered, 'Will you marry me Hani, will you?'

'Yes, Tommy, I will marry you when the war is over, and you have come back to me.' As they kissed, a shudder of fear ran through her.

11.

New Friendships

Desmond Carney had emigrated with his father from County Wicklow in Ireland three years earlier. He was the son of a cabinetmaker, and now worked for his father in the family business.

Des was eighteen and had befriended Jack and Tom shortly after he had arrived in Sydney. He was quiet and somewhat shy, but he possessed a sense of humor and a ready smile.

The three of them would regularly fish together, but all that changed after Tom had started spending most of his time with Hannah. At first, Des almost resented her presence, but then one day Hannah had introduced her friend Brigid to him, and he was smitten. Des was much too shy to talk to her, other than to say, 'hello.'

Brigid was tall, lanky, and wore a face full of freckles, and her ginger hair was plaited in pigtails. Brigid was the middle one of ten children. She was a tomboy who had a tendency to be loud and brash. Her mother had long ago given up on trying to get her to act in a ladylike manner. In moments of frustration she would say, 'You should have been a boy; how many times have I told you that little girls don't play in the creek and catch tadpoles?' But her mother's cajoling fell on deaf ears, and hardly a day passed by when her clean dress wouldn't be splattered with mud and dirt.

Brigid was relaxed around boys, and she took the lead in forming a bond with Des; and over a few months he began to feel comfortable around her. They were fishing, and sat with their legs dangling off the pier when Des had asked her what she was going to do when she started working.

'I want to be a doctor, or a nurse if I can't become a doctor,' she said matter-of-factly. Des retorted, 'Girls can't be doctors, who ever heard of such a thing? I never heard of any lady doctors anywhere.

'My old man always sez that outside work is fer blokes, and so is doctorin'. What would you do if you had to saw off a bloke's leg that was hanging offa him?'

Brigid ignored the sarcasm and asked, 'Why can't girls be doctors? Just because no girl has become one yet, is no reason why a girl shouldn't learn how to patch up people and make them better when they are sick. Don't you think that I could be a doctor?' She was now on the defensive and ready to argue her case with him, and if necessary wrestle him to the ground just to make her point.

Des didn't want to upset the only girl that he was friends with and said, 'I didn't say that, but how would you become a doctor? They hav'ta go to a special doctor's school, and I bet they wouldn't let you in. Have you been to the hospital to ask 'em?'

'Why would I go to the hospital?' asked Brigid.

'Well that's where all the doctors work, and if you don't go to the hospital how would you know what you gotta do to become a doctor? If I was gunna be a doctor that's where I'd go first, or why don't cha just ask the district nurse? She's always riding around on that bike of 'ers, she'd know.'

Up to that moment, Brigid had never given much thought to being a doctor because Des was right. Girls didn't become doctors because being a doctor was a man's job. But, she was curious about all living and dead things, and it had just dawned upon her that maybe she should go the hospital and ask someone, like Des had suggested.

'All right, I will go down to the hospital tomorrow and ask someone, and I'll tell you what they said!'

Brigid made her way to the Barracks Hospital the next day. The hospital had been built one hundred years earlier to service the needs of the Sydney Garrison and those who were seen as being the 'upper classes' of Colonial Sydney. She saw a nurse dressed in her uniform. Her hair was tucked up tightly under her wedge-shaped veil, and Brigid politely asked her, 'E'scuse me ma'am, but might I ask you a question?'

The nurse looked at Brigid and replied, 'Yes, what is it child, are you here to see someone?'

'No ma'am, it's just that I would like to know what I would have to do to become a doctor.'

The nurse wore a bemused smile. 'A doctor! Goodness me young lady, why on earth would you want to be a doctor?'

'I just wanted to know if a girl could become a doctor, or not ma'am. It's something that I'm interested in. I'm not squeamish with blood or guts ma'am. My mates think that I'm strange because I like looking inside dead animals and lizards and things, so I think that I would make a good doctor!'

The nurse asked, 'How old are you child?'

'I'm almost seventeen ma'am.'

'Do you work now; do you have a position with anyone?'

'No ma'am, I still live at home with all my brothers, and I help my mother.'

'How many brothers do you have child?'

'There's ten of us all together, and I'm the only girl, and I thought that I would like to be a doctor, so that's why I came here ma'am.'

'Can you read and write child?'

'Yes ma'am, I did seven years of schooling and left when I turned fourteen.'

'What's your name child?'

'My name is Brigid Blake ma'am, and if I can't become a doctor, then I shall become a nurse. I will study as much as I can, so that I will know how to save people and help them. That's what I want do ma'am.'

'So, you would like to become a nurse, would you? Well young lady, you would have to start off as a nurse's aide. That means that you would have to do all of the unsavoury jobs that a nurse or doctor tells you to do. That means cleaning out bedpans and washing bloodied bandages and bedclothes along with working strange hours. Is that what you want to do young lady? Because, before you could become a nurse you would have to do all of those things and more, for at least three months while you are being trained. You wouldn't be paid during your training period, although we would provide you with accommodation and meals. Once your initial training period was over, you would have to train for a further year, and then you would get examined to see if you could become a junior nurse.

'Being a nurse is a vocation child, it's a particular job where strength and compassion are needed, do you have those qualities, Brigid?'

Brigid was quiet for a moment and said, 'Yes ma'am, I could do those things.'

'Very well child, how about we see if you will make a nurse or not? I will put you on probation for three months, and if you work out, we will give you a full-time job with pay. Now my name is Sister Emmitt, and I am the matron in charge of the nurses. Now, you go home and think about this, and if you decide that this is something that you want to do then come back here at 7 am on Monday. Now be off with you as I have work to do. Goodbye, and I may see you next week.'

12.

Decisions

Over the following weeks, and all across the remote areas of the country, recruitment marches had been organised. At first, just a few men gathered in their towns, and then a small group started on the long walk to Sydney. Wives, girlfriends and young children joined with them for a mile or two, until the marchers were out of sight. Some were on horseback, but most were on foot, and they travelled up to eight miles a day. Soon, there were volunteer recruitment committees in almost every town across the state, and they would help set up the camps. Food and water was provided to the marches, and local nurses attended to blistered feet.

As they marched into a new town the soldier with the megaphone would call out, 'C'mon lads, there's no time to waste, your king and country need your help. Join up here lads. Get six bob a day and all the tucker that you can eat, c'mon lads the war's this way.' This drew more volunteers, and the ranks swelled to such an extent that each night they would have to be put up on the town's parks and ovals.

As the volunteers passed through each town people stood on the footpaths and clapped, and when a group of young men were seen to hesitate the megaphone would boom out, 'Don't be a shirker, are you gunna let your mates do the fighting for you?' By the time that the march had reached Sydney, they were as many as five hundred strong.

This took the authorities by surprise, and they had to hastily organise camps in the parks and the botanical gardens. Some of those who had come from the furthest corners of the state had been walking for almost a month. The volunteers were directed to the registration tables, and to the army doctors who questioned the recruits.

'How old are you boy?'

'Fifteen sir.'

'Go home and milk the cows for your mother son, and come back next year!' While others were at the opposite end of the spectrum, and may have been full of fight, but were clearly on the wrong side of fifty. There were no niceties, and the doctor, or his assistants, would send them packing.

'You're too old for this war granddad, if we get desperate we will send for you!' The selection process went on well into the night, and those that had passed were now in the army.

⁕⁕⁕

The morning after Tom had proposed to her, Hannah should have been happy, but her mind was instead in turmoil. She had slept a restless sleep, and had risen early. By the time that Claire and Davin were up she had the kettle boiling, and the porridge was simmering at the back of the stove. 'My goodness child, you're up early this morning.' Claire still called her niece 'child' even though Hannah was almost 19. 'You're not ill are you dear?'

'No, Aunt Claire, I'm well, and I should be happy because Tommy proposed to me last night.' Claire had taken over stirring the porridge, and stopped what she was doing.

'Why child that is wonderful, and what did you say?'

'I said yes, of course Aunt Claire, but he's going to enlist, and he promised that we would be married as soon as the war was over. Aunt Claire, I'm so scared that he won't come home. I love him so much, and I couldn't bear it if something happened to him while he was away!'

'Now, now, don't go getting yourself upset! The papers are saying that it's only going to be a short war, why he mightn't even get to Europe! Has he signed up yet?'

'No Aunt Claire, but he told me last night that he was going to as soon as Uncle Davin can get someone to help him at the forge.' Claire asked, 'And what about Jack, is he going to sign up too? Those brothers are very close, and I can't see Jack not going if his brother goes.

'My heart goes out to Doris, because as you well know both of those boys are her life. She told me that she was dreading them both leaving home, and that was ages ago before we even knew that there was going to be a war.

'I suspect that Jack will also go, although I haven't spoken to him recently.'

¥¥¥

Jack had been distracted at work throughout the day. Earlier, Tommy had told him that he was going to marry Hannah after the war. He had said that he was going to enlist on Monday now that Davin had found someone to replace him at the forge. He had been thinking about the war for weeks.

At first, he didn't take much notice of the advertising, or the recruitment marches that were going past his door on an almost daily basis. Jack was largely indifferent about whether he would sign up or not. But now that Tommy had confided his plans to him, Jack was reassessing his options. He had made up his mind that if his brother signed up, then he would too. Jack surprised his mother coming home early as he did.

'Hello son, you're early! I haven't even started the dinner yet; didn't you go to the pub?'

'No Ma, I wanted to see Tommy before he went out with Hannah, I assume that he's gunna see her again tonight. Anyway, I thought that I would enlist with him. I thought that as he would need someone to look after him when he was overseas then, it might as well be me!'

Doris stopped shelling the peas. The blood had drained from her face. 'Oh Jack, what can I say, you are a grown man with your own business, but you and your brother will always be my little boys. I knew when your brother told me that he was going that you would follow him. You have always looked after him, and I'm proud of you son, but are you sure that this is something that you really want to do? Tommy won't expect you to go with him; he has always been more boisterous than you were.

'You two are my everything since your father had his accident, but if you have to go, I will pray for both of you every day until you come home.'

'Oh Ma, nothing will happen to us, I won't let the Germans or the Turks use us as target practice I promise.'

He gave his mother a peck on the cheek before saying, 'I'll go an 'ave me bath before me brother gets 'ome.'

'The water in the copper should be hot as I put it on an hour ago, but when you empty it you had better fill it up again so that it will be hot for your brother when he gets home!'

Tom and Jack were sat at the kitchen table and Doris put their meals in front of them.

'Ma, where's yours?'

'I can't eat tonight. I'm worried sick about both of you. Now don't say that I'm being silly, because that's what mothers do, we worry about our children. I'm going next door to talk to Claire; she'll understand how I'm feeling. Just tell me when you're leaving.'

'Probably next week Ma,' replied Tom. 'We are gunna go down to the recruitment office on Monday, aren't we Jack? So, we don't know if we go straight inta training, or what. Billy Nugent signed up last week and nobody's seen 'im since, so he probably went in then and there.'

Jack was filling his mouth, but managed to say, 'Ma, I was wondering if you could get someone to look after the yard for me. I been meaning to find someone to do the deliveries, and I was thinking that if you did the ordering and took the money, then we would only need someone to cart the coal, and look after the horses until I got back.' He was looking at his mother to see her reaction to his proposal.

'I dunno son, I could open and close the place I suppose, but I couldn't fill the bags let alone put them on the cart. Did you have anyone in mind? It might not be that easy, because everyone that could lift a coal bag will be signing up like you two?'

'No Ma, I don't want ya to do any of the hard work, but if you can't look after the business, then I will just close the place down until I come back, whenever that might be. I thought that it might give you something to do, and get you out of the house for a while, but only if you wanted to. I don't want to twist your arm or nuthin' like that!'

'Look son, if I could get someone to do the hard stuff, then yes I could do your banking and ordering because people will still need fuel to cook with, war or no war. All right son, I'll put an advertisement in the newspaper next week and see if I can get someone to work. How much will I pay them?'

'Give 'em a quid a week Ma, and that's to do all the deliveries as well as bagging up the coal and to look after the horses. You will have to pay Harry at the stables two quid every week to take care of them.

'Before you give anyone the job, make sure you get them to lift a couple of bags of coal onta the dray. No good giving them a job if they can't pick up a bag of coal!'

Doris was feeling slightly better than what she was before dinner. At least she now had a purpose. If she couldn't look after her boys, then at least she could take care of her son's business.

'Are you two going out tonight?'

Jack was the first to reply and said, 'Yeah Ma, I am. Now that I've made up me mind, I thought that I would go and see me mate Des, and tell 'im that I'm goin.'

13.

Lovers

Des was sitting on the front step when Jack turned up.

'What are ya doing out this way?'

'I come to see ya, to tell you that I'm gunna sign up on Monday, Tommy, too. So, I dunno if I'll get ter see you again after tonight.'

'I been thinkin' of signing up meself, but I'm still doin' me apprenticeship with the old man. Don't think he'd be too happy if I told him that I was pissin' off ter join the army.'

'Well do you wanna go or not?'

'Gunna be a bit quiet around 'ere if yer all gone. I was reading some of them posters sayin' that you get to go to London and Paris when you ain't fightin. Be nice ta see them places. Yeah, I wouldn't mind goin'. Tell ya what Jack, the old man's inside getting pissed, so I'll just go and ask 'im. Come in, he's out the back, but be ready to duck if he's holdin' a beer bottle cause he gets a bit narky when he's been drinkin.'

'Hello boy, ya gunna have a drink with yer ol' man? Who's dat standing with ya?'

'It's Jack, Dar, Jack Fields, me mate from the fuel yard! Dar, I was thinking of signing up. Jack and Tommy are goin' on Monday. Do yer reckon that you could do without me fer a while; I could finish me apprenticeship when the war's over Dar, wot do yer think?'

'Yer might get yerself shot, why dontcha just stay ere and finish yer apprenticeship.

'The business is gunna be yours one day, let somebody else do the fightin' son, it's not our fight. Back 'ome, we been fightin' the Brits for years, why do yer think we come out 'ere in the first place? Not ter fight for the bloody Brits jus' cause one of their royal family got 'emself killed. It's not our fight boy, so stay outa it. Now come and 'ave a drink with yer ol' man.'

'I don't wanna drink Dar, I just wanna join the army to have some fun. I don't care what the fight is about, it's just that I wanna be with me mates and see the world. The war might be over before we get there, so I might only be gone fer a few months. I wanna do this Dar. I'm eighteen now, and I can join up anyway, but I need your signature on the enrolment papers. I would like to go with yer support Dar.'

'Well, if yer gunna take that tone with me then ya can just bugger orf, go on, bugger orf now! Get out yer ungrateful bastard, now clear off an' leave me alone!'

'Come on Jack, I can't talk to 'im when he's like this.'

Jack replied, 'You can come and sleep at my joint, grab yer stuff and let's get goin'.'

'Yeah right oh, I'll come back and see 'im tomorrow, but bugger it Jack, I made me mind up, I'll be coming with ya ter sign up on Monday!'

✻✻✻

Tom went next door, just as they were finishing dinner. 'I thought that we might go for a walk tonight Hani, unless yer wanna do somethin' else.'

Davin knew that tonight was the night that Tom was going to tell Hannah that he was signing up on Monday. Tom had told him a few days ago, but made him promise that he wouldn't say anything to Hannah until he had spoken to her first.

Davin had employed the services of a young man who was eager to learn the blacksmithing business. At fourteen, he was too young to join up, and Davin had been teaching him for the last few days.

Tom knew that his replacement would work out given time, and now he was happy to leave.

He had been putting off telling Hannah. But now, as it was Friday night, this would be their last weekend together for some time. Hannah looked across the table at Tom, and she could tell by his face that he was intending to tell her tonight.

'No, I'm happy just to go for a walk. Just let me wash the dishes first, and then we can go.' Claire had also guessed and said, 'No, leave the dishes dear I'll do them. You go and get your shawl, and I will see you in the morning.'

Hannah put her arm through his, and they walked side by side. Tom didn't speak as he was just enjoying her closeness, but his mind was in turmoil and he was looking for the right moment to tell her.

They walked along Pitt Street, occasionally stopping to look into a shop window that was illuminated by a gas lamp.

'You're going to sign up, aren't you? Tell me when?' There was a note of resignation in her voice.

'We are all going down to the recruitment office on Monday mornin.'

'Who else is going beside you and Jack?'

'Des is coming with us, he had a bit of a stoush with his old man and he's camping at our place till then.'

***

They walked in silence, both having a thousand things to say to each other, but neither knowing how.

At the park, they sat on a bench that was bathed in the soft glow of a path lamp. He had his arm around her shoulder and she turned her head towards him. There were tears in her eyes as he gently kissed her. He tried to be jovial and said, 'Ma wanted to tell you that she had a new catalogue from the David Jones Emporium. It had pitchers of weddin' dresses in it direct from Paris, and she's gunna bring it around to show you.'

'Oh Tommy, I couldn't afford a dress from Paris. I couldn't even afford one from the David Jones Emporium. Besides that, Aunt Claire still has her wedding dress, and she is going to alter it to fit me. My grandmother wore it, and Aunt Claire was married in it in Ireland, and I'm happy to wear it for my wedding.'

'Well my girl, you make sure that it's ready to wear when I get back, cause I'm gunna marry you as soon as we can arrange it after the war. So, don't you forget that? I'm not good with words Hani, but you gotta understand that you mean the world to me and I love ya.

'Yer do know that don't cha? But sometimes, saying I love yer don't seem to be enough. I can't explain what yer do to me. I just wanna hold you and touch you, and touch you all over. I'm sorry to be blunt Hani, but I get all these strange feelings, and I can't stop thinking about you.

'I dream about laying' on a feather mattress with you like we was married. Do you know what I'm saying Hani? I can't explain it no plainer!'

Hannah blushed in the soft light before saying, 'I get those feelings too, and sometimes I feel like I'm going to bust my girdle and then I have to think of something else. Goodness me, I'm talking' like a hussy now. See, that's what you do to me Tommy Fields!'

She snuggled in closer to him as the night drew in around them. Later, they wandered home in silence and kissed at her front door.

'Tommy, I think that we should go on a picnic tomorrow. Let's take the horses way out into the country, and find a place where there is nobody else. I will pack a basket in the morning, so pick me up early. I know that we have Sunday together, but by the time that we have been to Mass half the day will have gone. So tomorrow we can be by ourselves all day. Goodnight Tommy.' She kissed him again, and the taste of her kiss lingered on his lips.

¥¥

They were up early. Both of them had slept badly before they walked to the stables and found their horses. They trotted down the road to Erskineville, and they followed the contour of the river for almost an hour.

They stopped at the top of a grassy knoll, and the area was completely deserted other than for the squawking of a myriad of seabirds.

A faint breeze blew in from across the bay, and Hannah said, 'This is beautiful Tommy, let's have our picnic here.' Tom took the saddles from the horses and laid them on the ground facing towards the bay. Hannah spread the picnic blanket in front of them, and they tied the horses to a saltbush tree. 'Let's go for a walk Tommy.'

Not waiting for him, she half walked and half ran down the grassy slope to the beach stopping to gather up some shells. 'Look Tommy aren't they pretty? I shall make a shell necklace, look these are the ones that I want!' She held one up to show him. Tommy stood and looked at the love of his life, and he thought that she was just like a child. She skipped from the shells that she had searched through to a fresh pile washed ashore with the last high tide.

'C'mon Hani, show me what you have in that picnic basket, I'm hungry!' Hannah had picked up a piece of driftwood, and was scratching the end of it into the wet sand.

'Just a minute Tommy, I have to finish doing this.'

'What are you doing girl?' He walked across the beach to where she was.

She had scratched a large heart in the sand, and inside the heart were the initials H.D. loves T. F. He had just enough time to see what she had drawn before the water rose and filled the indentations. Smiling, he put his hands around her waist before he lifted her off the ground, saying, 'I luv yer too Hani, more than I can ever tell you, and I will think of you every single day that I'm away.' He then kissed her, but she didn't close her eyes, and looked at him intently. 'Oh Tommy, I'm so scared that I'm going to lose you. I don't know what I shall do while you are away. You will come back to me, won't you?'

'Just try and keep me away. I will swim back if I have to, just you watch me, now what have we got to eat? C'mon I'll race you back up the hill.'

'Tommy, I can't run in this dress now look at my hem it's all wet. You will just have to wait for me to get there!'

***

She laid their small feast onto the blanket, and they ate in silence.

They were completely alone, as Tom lay down with his shoulders resting against the saddle. Hannah was staring out over the bay. She was sat with her knees tucked up under her chin.

In the distance, a steam packet ship could be seen billowing plumes of black smoke behind it as it made its way across the bay. He lay there looking at her as she gazed across the water. 'A penny for your thoughts.'

At first, she didn't respond, but after a few moments she said,

'Touch me Tommy.' He moved his hand and placed it on hers, but she pulled it away and lay down beside him. She looked at him shyly, and said, 'No Tommy! I need you to touch me, touch me all over! I want you Tommy Fields, and if we can't be married until the war is over then I want to pretend that we are married now. Don't think of me as a hussy please Tommy, but think of me as your wife. I love you desperately, and I need a memory of you that is only ours.'

She snuggled into him as he placed his arm under her neck. She took his other hand and placed it upon her breast, but then she sat upright and removed the bolero jacket that she was wearing.

She then loosened the laces and buttons of her camisole before lying down again. He gently placed his hand over her breast, but she guided it inside her vest. As his fingers touched her nipples, they became hard, but then he removed his hand. She looked quizzically at him, but his manhood had swelled within the confines of his trousers, and he had to loosen them. He smiled sheepishly at her and muttered, 'I hav'ta loosen me duds Hani.'

He quickly stood, and dropped them to below his knees. He lay facing her, and as his fingers tentatively touched her nipples, she kissed him passionately before pushing his head down to her chest. Her cheeks were flushed as his warm breath washed over her breasts, and his tongue explored her.

He was lying close to her, and she could feel the hardness of him pressing against her leg, and this excited her more. As they kissed, she took his hand and guided it down under the waistband of her bloomers. His hand lightly crossed her belly, and his fingers felt her silky hair as soft as down.

Tommy was breathing hard now, and he could barely contain his desire. Hannah's face was flushed, and she let out a small gasp as his finger pressed into her, and their senses mingled with unbridled pleasure. She moaned again, and he stopped for a moment and asked,

'Are you orright Hani, I'm not hurting ya am I?'

'No, you're not hurting me.' She buried her face into his chest, and quietly moaned.

'I want you Tommy, I need you now!' Their passion was now so inflamed with lust that modesty was thrown to the wind. She let go of him, and he removed his hand as she sat up and quickly removed her bloomers before lying back down. He sat up, and removed his boots along with his trousers and the long johns that were around his ankles.

She gave a grunt, and a gasp of pain as he entered her and pushed into her narrow, unbroken passage. But, as the pain diminished she gently rocked her pelvis to the rhythm of his thrusting. The ecstasy was building within them both, and Hannah was blushing more from heated desire than from a lack of modesty. He gave a final thrust as his passion exploded inside of her. He lay over her, panting and breathing hard, before kissing her and saying, 'I love you Hani.'

Now that their passion had abated she felt embarrassed. She dare not look at him in case he now despised her. They rearranged themselves in silence.

Hannah was now feeling bashful, and worried about what he might think of her, but her fears were unfounded. He sat behind her, a leg on either side of her hips. He placed his arms around her and buried his face into her neck and said, 'Do ya still love me Hani? You don't think of me as a disappointment now, do you?'

She put her arms around his and squeezed them tightly. She turned her face sideways to his and whispered, 'Oh Tommy, I love you more than ever, and you could never be a disappointment to me.'

⁂

By the time that they had returned the horses to the stables it was dark, and they kissed again at her front door. 'I'll see you in the mornin' Hani, are you gunna go to the early Mass?' The first Mass was at seven, with two other services after that. 'I think that we should go to the nine o'clock service as I can lie in for another hour because you have utterly exhausted me Tommy Fields. Now I need to go and boil the water, so that I can have a bath.' She kissed him again before gently pushing him away.

The next morning, they all walked to the church. Small groups of people were going to their own places of worship. The churches were now the unofficial places where the population could get an update on the war.

The second service was almost full as they found places to sit. There was an air of expectation within the church. Children fidgeted, while the adults whispered among themselves. The vesper bell rang, and a hush descended throughout the church. Three altar boys walked in single file followed by the priest, as they made their way past the pulpit to the altar.

When it was time for the sermon, the priest climbed into his pulpit. He appeared troubled, and he rested both of his hands on the railing.

'Brethren, yesterday we received news over the inland telegraph wire that our first troops have landed in Egypt. The authorities in London had decided that because it is winter in the northern hemisphere, the combined Australian and the New Zealand troops should do their training in Egypt. The climate there is of a similar temperament to our own. They are now under the authority of the British army, and will be utilised when and where the British authorities want them sent. So, we should all be proud of those boys who have already volunteered their services! Our own Prime Minister has stated that many more will be required before peace will be won in Europe.

'I see many young men here in this church today, and I implore you to go and do your duty, sign up now I say! Do not shirk from your duty and let others do the fighting for you. When you come home, you will be able to hold your head high, unlike those cowards who don't see any need for our involvement in this war. If you shirk from your duty, you will be regarded as a coward and a bludger, and you will have to hide in the shadows of our society.

'Unlike those of you who will think of others, and who will go to the recruitment offices tomorrow, and offer themselves to the service of their king and country.'

The priest was looking around the room, and focusing his gaze on anyone who was of the age to join up. Some fidgeted uncomfortably, and others like Tom and Jack sat back and wondered what tomorrow would bring.

***

Doris had arranged for everyone to be at her place for the Sunday lunch and she had proclaimed, 'This might be the last proper meal that my boys will get for a while! I got a large leg of mutton from Mr Birrel at the butcher's shop. When I told him that it was for my boys because they were signing up on Monday, he gave it to me for free! Can you imagine that? Such a kind man and him with his only son already gone. He said that his Jimmy had left Sydney a month ago. He might be one of those that the priest mentioned was already over in Egypt.'

The table was set up in the backyard, and Doris had covered it with a cotton sheet. Jack had bought a few bottles of beer, and they were cooling in the galvanised bathtub with a chunk of ice taken from the icebox. Doris had wanted the meal to be like a regular Sunday dinner, where her boys would laugh and joke and eat like there was no tomorrow. But, although Claire, Davin and Hannah were there, the lunch was a sombre affair, and when a conversation did start it invariably ended up talking about the war.

Hannah picked at her food, even though she was coaxed by Doris to eat more, 'C'mon dearie you have to eat more than that, goodness me you will fade away to a shadow soon.'

'I'm sorry Doris, but I'm just not hungry. Maybe I'll feel like something by dinnertime.'

Jack broke into the conversation and said; 'Now Ma, leave Hannah alone! We know that you are all upset, but it's not as though we won't see you before we finish our training.

'I dunno how long the trainin' lasts, but I'm sure that we will be home when it's finished and before they ship us out. Anyway Ma, the war might be over before we even get there. The papers are still sayin' that with the British and the French along with us, and the New Zealand blokes all fightin', that the Turks and Germans might surrender before Christmas. If that happens we mightn't even get to London or Paris. So, stop worryin' Ma. I'll look after yer baby for ya; I won't let nuthin' happen to him.'

'I know that you will son, but I can't help worrying about you both, that's what a mother is for, to cook and clean and worry about her children.'

Des got up and thanked Doris for his lunch and said, 'I need ta go and see the old man and see if he's calmed down yet. I don't want to leave without saying goodbye. I think that I will stay at home tonight, even if he is still annoyed with me. So, wish me luck, and I'll see you all in the mornin'!'

After Des had left, the conversation around the table waned. Doris stacked the dishes, and Hannah busied herself with scraping the mutton fat from the roast into a jug. She then placed it in the icebox, where it would be left to harden to be spread on bread later on. Davin took a bottle from the bathtub and removed the top. He topped up the boys' tin mugs that they were drinking from and filled a china teacup with beer for himself. He took a sip, and they all laughed at the sight of a man drinking beer from a teacup. He smiled before saying, 'I'm gunna miss you boys, and I'm already missing you at the forge Tom.'

'How's the new bloke going, he seemed keen the other day when I was there.'

'Yeah, he'll be orright when he gets the hang of things, and when he gets to the stage where I can leave him by himself. You were me right hand man Tom. Don't get me wrong son; I think that you are doin' the right thing in signing up. I been wonderin' if I shouldn't be signing up meself, but if I do there won't be any money comin' in, and I got me government contracts that I have to fill. I couldn't bear the thought of Claire and Hannah having to go back to sewing just to make ends meet.'

They could see the dilemma that Davin was facing. Tom said, 'Ah, yer too old anyway Davin. They wouldn't have ya', and besides that, I seen how ya shoot when we been out rabbitin'. You couldn't hit the side of a house with a shotgun, and once they seen how ya shoot they would tell you to go home anyway.' They all laughed including Davin, and he knew that Tom was right.

***

It appeared as though the whole street was up early on Monday morning. Old Jack Turner swept the streets, and he was a regular sight as he pushed his cart with its oversized wheels around the streets. He would sweep the gutters, and clean up the horse manure with the brooms and shovels that were fitted to the side of his cart. He was always one of the first out on the street each morning, and one of the last at night, but this morning he was waiting outside of Doris's house. He was patiently packing his pipe with tobacco when Doris opened her front door.

'Hello Jack, what are you doing here, are you waiting for someone?'

'Mornin' Mrs Fields, its just that I 'eard that yer boys was leavin' ter sign up terday, and I wan'ed to say good luck to 'em before they went. Yer should be proud of them lads of yours, why it seems just like yesterday when they was just young whippers. They used ter push me barra down the road fer me. I wishes that I could join em Mrs Fields, but I'm neerin' seventy now, and I ain't as sprightly as I was once. So ifa ya don't mind me intrusion Mrs Fields, I would like ter give yer boys me best wishes.'

Doris had stoked the fire before dawn, as she was determined to give her boys the biggest breakfast that she could cook them. 'That's very kind of you Jack. The boys are up and just havin a bit of a wash so come in and have a cuppa with us, c'mon, come inside, the kettle's boiling.'

'Why thank ya, Mrs Fields, but I'll not be intrudin' on ya hospitality, but if yer could just tell the boys that I'm out 'ere and just wanna wish em well, I'd much appreciate it, thank ya Mrs Fields.'

'All right Jack, have it your way, I'll just go and get them.'

Jack said goodbye. He gripped each of their hands with a strength that belied his age. He congratulated them, and offered a wish for a speedy and safe return. Without another word, he took hold of the handles of his cart and started his morning rounds.

Hannah had slept badly. Claire and Davin had risen early so that they could say goodbye to the boys one last time.

Des arrived just as Doris was laying out the breakfast plates. She was frying the eggs and said, 'Come on son sit down, I've made enough for you as well, I didn't expect that you would have eaten at your father's, by the way did you make your peace with him?'

'Yes, Mrs Fields, he was a bit grumpy when I come home last night, but we sat down and had a coupla beers. He got all soppy and told me that I could finish me apprenticeship after the war. He said that he was gonna miss me bein' around the place.

'I think that he's going to be a bit lonely, what with everything and me gone. He's been missing Mum since she died, and he never made any real friends since we been out 'ere. I told him that I'd write ter him from wherever we was.'

Doris had thrown a few slabs of bread into the frying pan, and now they were crispy with fat. She lay the eggs down on the three plates and said, 'I'll make us all a nice cuppa tea; now eat up before it gets cold. I'll go and see him occasionally for you Des, so don't worry. I suppose that we will all have to get used to things being a bit different from here on in.'

She dabbed her eyes with the corner of her apron. The other two had their backs to her, but Jack noticed and he got up and said, 'C'mon Ma, yer promised not ta cry.' He put his arms around her and kissed the side of her cheek. 'Why Ma, you will be so busy looking after the fuel yard soon, that you won't even miss us in a coupla weeks!'

'I will miss you both every single day that you are gone, you too Des, and I will light a candle for the three of you every Saturday night when I go to the church for the Novena.'

The breakfast was finished in silence, save for the clattering of the cutlery on the plates. They were taking nothing with them other than the clothes that they were wearing. Jack looked around the kitchen for a final time. He knew that once they had signed the papers, there was a good chance that they would not be back until the war was over. Doris went to the front door with them and said, 'I was going to walk with you for a bit, but I would rather we said goodbye here. Go and see Hannah, and tell Claire that I will be over later on, so go on give your mother a hug.'

The tears welled in her eyes, and she dabbed them again before tightly hugging each of them. Her voice wavered as she spoke her last words to them. 'I'll pray to the Blessed Mary every day to take care of you, so God bless you all, now go!' She turned without a backward glance and went back inside her now empty house. She closed the door behind her, and leant against it as the tears streamed down her cheeks.

✳✳✳

Davin was standing in his doorway as the boys left home. He greeted them with a simple, 'G'day, so today is the big day, eh?' Tom was the first to reply and muttered, 'Sure ain't looking forward to this.'

He took a deep breath, and went inside followed by the others. Claire and Hannah were sat at the table.

They could see that Hannah had been crying as her red eyes told the story. The atmosphere was strained, and Jack was the first to speak, 'We just wanted to say goodbye, and thanks for everything.'

Hannah started to cry again, and Tom went to her as she stood up and buried her face into his chest. He put his arms around her and said, 'Don't cry, or you will make me cry, and these blokes will never let me forget it. C'mon, let me wipe your tears away, it's only for a little while and you never know we might be lucky enough to be back by Christmas.'

Tom was the last to go. He gently kissed Hannah, and then pushed her away from him as he turned and hurried out the door.

14.

Recruitment

They walked in silence, each deep within their own thoughts. When they reached the end of Redfern Street, Jack would usually turn right and go the fuel yard, but today they kept on walking straight ahead. The recruitment centre was on York Street in the city, and when they arrived, they were surprised to see a lengthy queue that had already stretched back a couple of hundred yards from the entrance.

A few men stared at the new arrivals, and Jack asked no one in particular, 'Is this where we sign up?' One of them replied, 'Sure is,' but it was another hour before the queue moved forward, and by that time the line extended for almost the entire city block. Those inside were in various stages of undress, as men in white dustcoats poked and prodded at them. It was finally their turn, and the sergeant behind the desk asked, 'What's your name, son?'

'Jack Fields, and this is me brother and me mate,' pointing towards Tom and Des.

'We will get to them in a minute, now how old are you?'

'I'm twenty.'

'Sergeant! From here on in you will call all of your superiors Sir, or Sergeant, or Corporal do you understand that?'

'Yeah, righto, I got that.' He winked at his brother.

'Listen to me lad, this is the army, and when you are told to do something by a superior officer you do it immediately, and you say, "Yes Sir", or "Yes Sergeant", so have I made myself clear?'

'Yeah, I understand ya, but I'm not in the army yet, so I don't see why I should call you Sergeant, or Sir.'

'What are you, a smart alec? You had better change your attitude quick smart around here son, or you will be making smart remarks while you are doing a hundred push-ups, now do you have a trade?'

Jack decided that he should stop fooling around as it had suddenly dawned on him that a sergeant could make his lot very uncomfortable and he replied, 'No Sir, I don't have a trade, but I own me own fuel yard.'

'Right, I'll just put you down as a labourer, and you call me Sergeant, not Sir. Now go and stand over with those other fellows and strip down to your underwear.' He was pointing to where he wanted Jack to go. The process was the same with Tom and Des, and they too waited their turn to be examined by the army doctor.

It was mid-morning by the time that they were kitted out with their uniform. Their civilian clothes were wrapped up in brown paper, and their names scrawled on each bundle before it was thrown on top of all the others in the corner. There were around several hundred new recruits in total, and when they were dressed the sergeant spoke to them through a tin megaphone.

'Right you lot; you are now in the army! Shortly, you will take the oath of allegiance to the King, after which you will be taken to the training ground at Liverpool. At this stage, your training will take about eight weeks, and depending on circumstances you may get a few days' leave before being shipped overseas. You will be informed of this when the time gets closer, now get into single file and go through that green door behind you. There will be trucks outside, and these will take you to the camp, now off you go, and good luck!' There were a few muttered grumblings, but for the most part, they sat in the trucks in silence. They were each coming to terms with the fact that the army now owned them, and it was too late to change their minds.

The convoy took over an hour before it reached the camp at Liverpool on the far reaches of Sydney. They were greeted with the sight of several hundred tents on what used to be the Liverpool horseracing track. As soon as the trucks had stopped another sergeant bellowed, 'You men assemble over here!' He was pointing as to where he wanted them.

'You are all assigned to the third battalion, and your training will start tomorrow, now when you hear the bugle call at daybreak that is known as the "Reveille".

'When you hear that bugle, you don't roll over and get some more sleep, you get out of your bunk and get dressed, and then you make your bed! You have five minutes to do that before you run to the parade ground.' They were then instructed on the various bugle calls from 'Boots and Saddles' to 'Taps', which meant that all tent lights were to be extinguished. Equipment was still in short supply, and the new recruits were handed broomsticks to practise drill with instead of rifles.

Their first full day started with the bugler waking up the camp. They staggered out of bed, and still half asleep they quickly splashed their faces with the cold water that was in the tin bowls on the shelf outside their tents, and then they shuffled their way to the parade ground as the sun was casting its first rays over a distant horizon.

✲✲✲

Over the following days and weeks, the training intensified, but now they had been issued with rifles and bayonets.

Target practice was carried out every day, and straw-filled sacks, roughly shaped as a man, were slung from beams. Each man was required to run and stab at the dummy with his bayonet. Then, there was another ten-mile march with full kit. Day in and out the routine was the same. Exercise, eat, and close combat practice along with marching.

They had been at the training camp for almost eight weeks without a day off, and the rumours abounded that shortly they would all get a few days' leave before being sent to Egypt.

The newspapers had been reporting that the first group of Australian and New Zealand Army troops had been engaged in battle with the Turkish forces on the Gallipoli Peninsula and they had suffered many casualties. They also speculated that if the casualties kept mounting then many more reinforcements would be urgently needed.

On the Sunday at the start of the eighth week, they were all on parade when the camp commander addressed them. 'Your training is almost complete. You will no doubt have read or heard about the fight at Gaba Tepe, which our people are calling Anzac Cove due to the involvement of our troops along with the New Zealand fellows. This division, along with several others, will be leaving shortly for overseas duty. The details are still being worked out, but we expect that you will be shipped out within a week. Our ships are presently in Sydney Cove loading coal and supplies. When they are fuelled and ready, I expect to get our orders to board.

'Now leave passes and rail warrants will be granted to each of you next Friday. The pass expires at 10 pm on Sunday night. Anyone who has not returned by then will be regarded as a deserter, and may be subjected to being shot if found guilty of desertion by a military tribunal. I would advise that you all make sure that your personal affairs are in place for your families and loved ones. But, let me caution you that if our orders come through sooner, you may not get an opportunity to have weekend leave. That's all men. Take over Sergeant!'

The sergeant bellowed, 'If anyone has a letter that they want posted give it to the corporal, and he will ensure that it will be sent out with tonight's mail. Today will be regarded as a rest day. Nobody will be allowed off the base, but feel free to relax. Play a game of cricket, or cards, but no money must exchange hands. Enjoy your free day today men, because I cannot say when you will get another one. That's all men.'

They stood around, not too sure of what to do as they digested the news that they were about to go to war.

15.

The Dilemma

Life was getting back to a form of normality for the families whose sons had enlisted up to two months earlier. Nobody knew when they would get the opportunity to see them again, as none had received any information on how long the training would last.

Hannah had immersed herself in dressmaking for the ladies who had the money to indulge themselves. She had not been feeling well both physically and mentally for some time now, but had said nothing to Claire or Doris. Emotionally she was missing Tom, and she was still feeling insecure after she had given herself to him. She didn't take much notice when her menstrual cycle hadn't come as it had always been irregular, but now it was over two months since her last one. Hannah was now having bouts of feeling sick, mainly in the mornings, but sometimes at any time. She had also lost her appetite.

Hannah had made up her mind that she would tell Claire about how she was feeling, as she thought that she should visit the district nurse. She remembered the last time that she had gone to see her, and how she had been given a bottle of castor oil to consume. The nurse had told her that she would need to digest the entire contents over the following week. She smiled as she thought of how the cure had ended up being worse that the illness. Just the thought of taking castor oil was making her feel better already. Claire was making a stew from the chicken that Davin had dispatched the day before, when Hannah came into the kitchen and sat down at the table.

'Why child you look terrible, what is it?'

'I don't know Aunt Claire; I haven't been feeling well for some time now. I thought that I should go and see the district nurse if that's all right. Do you think that I could have a shilling to pay her?'

'Oh goodness me child, of course you should see the nurse, we are not paupers, so if she wants a shilling to see you then she shall have a shilling. We will go down to the clinic first thing in the morning. Now I have made a nice chicken stew, but I will drain off some of the broth, and see if you can keep some of that down.'

Nurse Nugent was middle-aged and single. She had devoted most of her working life to looking after the ills and ailments of everyone who lived in her district. Her days were filled with dispensing pills and advice in almost equal quantities. She greeted Hannah and Claire as old friends, as she did with everyone who visited her room. The front room of her modest house was where the consulting was done when a patient came to see her, although mostly she would ride her pushbike to the homes of her patients.

Claire was the first to speak and said, 'My niece has been feeling a bit off color and is off her food, it's probably just a tummy bug, but we thought that we should seek your advice nurse!'

'How old are you girl?'

'Nineteen miss.'

'Now tell me, do you have any pain, or are you just feeling sick?'

'I have been feeling sick, and I don't feel like eating.'

Claire broke into the conversation, 'Which is unusual, as the child has always had a good appetite.'

'How long have you been feeling like this, and when do you feel sick?'

'Maybe for a few weeks now, and I usually feel sick in the mornings, but sometimes it can be at any time.'

'Lie down on the daybed girl, and we will have a look at your tummy.' Hannah did as instructed, and the nurse gently pressed down on her stomach and asked her some more questions. Then, as she sat up again the nurse asked, 'How long is it since you have had your last menstrual cycle?'

'More than two months now.'

Claire interrupted, 'Why child you never told me!' She expressed it as though it was something that she should have been told about.

'I'm sorry Aunt Claire, but I didn't think that it was important.'

The nurse then asked, 'Are you still a virgin, girl?'

The question shocked Hannah as she was not expecting it, and she hesitated before answering. The hesitation was enough to provoke suspicion in both Claire and the nurse.

'Well are you girl? It's a simple enough question.' Hannah had gone bright red, and her face told them the truth. She lowered her head and murmured softly, 'No.'

Claire was shocked with what she had just heard and asked, 'When, who… was it Tommy?' She stamped her foot before saying, 'Oh Hannah, how could you?' But, before Claire could say anymore the nurse said, 'It's not for me to judge you girl, but I believe that you are pregnant. I can assume that you are not married, and that is an issue that you and your aunt will have to deal with. My involvement will be in keeping both you and the baby healthy. Now give me your address, and I will call and check up on you when I do my weekly rounds. I advise that you get plenty of rest and don't exert yourself. Now, today's consultation will cost you a shilling!' Claire paid the money, and with apprehension Hannah walked outside.

Claire was absolutely horrified with the knowledge that her niece was pregnant. At first, she said nothing, and when she did speak it was short and abrupt. 'We will need to have a long talk when we get home my girl!' As they passed Saint Bridget's Church, Claire said, 'We need to go and say some prayers to the blessed Virgin and ask for forgiveness and guidance, and if the priest is there you will need to get him to hear your confession! Goodness me child, I hope that you understand how much trouble you have caused us. Now go and ask the good Lord for forgiveness, and I will light a penny candle.'

When they arrived home, Doris was standing at her front door and said, 'That was good timing I'm just making a cuppa.' Claire replied curtly, 'I'm sorry Doris, but I have just received a big shock, and my head is all over the place. I don't think that I can talk right now.'

'Oh luvvy, what is it, has something happened to Davin, can I help?'

Claire composed herself for a moment and said testily, 'Oh well, you will find out sooner or later so let's go inside, Hannah has something to tell you.' Doris wore a concerned look on her face as she led the way inside. The kettle was singing, and she removed it from the hotplate and poured the boiling water over the tealeaves.

'Sit down. Take your coats off, and tell me what the problem is.'

For a few moments, they all sat in silence as each one waited for someone to say something first, then Hannah decided that she should speak.

'Doris, we have just been to see the district nurse.' But before Hannah could go on Doris interrupted, 'Is everything all right, what is it luvvy, you're not sick or anything bad are you?'

'Doris, I'm pregnant,' she said it with a hint of defiance in her voice as she looked directly at her, 'and Tommy is the father!'

Doris was pouring the tea, and for a moment the tea missed the cup altogether, and splashed into the saucer before she could put the pot down.

'Goodness me luvvy is that all?' She gave a nervous cackle before going on. 'I thought that you were going to say that you had pleurisy, or something as bad as that. So, I'm going to be a grandmother. Oh luvvy, we will get through this together, so who else knows?' Doris came around the table and hugged Hannah as she cried.

Claire was taken aback by Doris's reaction to the news. At the very least, she thought that Doris would have taken the moralistic viewpoint that sex before marriage was not allowed. Not only was it morally wrong, but it was against the rules of the church. Then as she thought about it, she conceded that Doris had always been a little unconventional with her thinking.

Claire was mortified, and her mind was in turmoil, even more so now that she had seen Doris's reaction and she said, 'But Doris, you know what the church thinks about unmarried mothers, and what will the neighbours think? We won't be able to walk down the street without people talking about us. No, it's too shameful, I will have to send her off to the nuns when she starts to show.'

The conversation went around Hannah, but didn't include her, as she sat at the table and quietly wept. Doris asked, 'Does Tommy know?' Then she answered herself, 'No, of course he doesn't know, how could he? But he will do the right thing by you anyway luvvy.' She then asked, 'Does Davin know?' Again, she answered herself, 'Of course he doesn't know. How will he take the news Claire?'

'I really don't know Doris, I really don't know.'

Doris was thinking out aloud, 'Now let's not worry about what the fuddy duddy's think, how far gone are you luvvy?'

Hannah had come back into the conversation and said, 'About eight or nine weeks. I don't think that it could be any longer than that. Tommy left nine weeks ago next Monday.'

As she spoke, she remembered the last glorious day that she had shared with Tommy, and the thought brought back her tears.

Claire was tapping the tabletop as she thought about their dilemma. I don't know what we should do really, as I haven't even spoken to Davin yet.

'I have no idea of what his reaction will be.' She looked at her niece and said, 'I suspect that he will not be happy with you, and he may want you to leave the house. I don't know if that will be his reaction or not, but you will need to be prepared for it. You have no idea of how disappointed I am with you child.'

Doris snorted, 'He wouldn't throw her out onto the street, surely not! Well if he does luvvy you can sleep in Tommy's room.'

Hannah started to cry again, and she said, 'I'm sorry that I have caused everybody so much trouble, but I love Tommy so much, and I'm glad that I'm having his baby.' She buried her head into her arms that were across the table as she sobbed uncontrollably.

16.

Deployment

The news had spread across the camp that they were to be deployed at anytime. Now that their training was over, they were all looking forward to going home, even if it was only for a couple of days.

On the Tuesday morning at roll call they were all informed that they would be paid, as they had received no money since signing on. A private was paid six shillings a day. The army had a policy that one shilling a day would be held by the military until the soldier was discharged, or in the event of his death the money would go to his next of kin in the form of a pension. They had all been given a form to fill in, and they could nominate a certain amount to be paid to a relative or spouse. Tom had decided that half of his pay would be paid to Hannah.

There was an air of expectation amongst them, when they were informed that the captain was going to address them after breakfast.

'Stand at ease men. Just over an hour ago, I received a dispatch from army headquarters informing me that our ships are loaded and fuelled and are ready for boarding. As such, the proposed leave for this weekend has been cancelled. We will be boarding tomorrow, and will be sailing on the afternoon tide from Garden Island dockyard.' There were a few audible groans from within the ranks along with men fidgeting uncomfortably. The captain continued, 'I do understand that some of you will be disappointed with this news.

'I regret that you will not be able to spend time with your families before we ship out, but the news from the front is not too good. Our lads already overseas will need all the reinforcements that the army can provide. What I can tell you though, is that each of your families is being sent a telegram informing them of your imminent departure. So, you may get a chance to see them before we embark. Tomorrow, a special troop train will take us to Central Station. It will depart at 7 am from Liverpool and on arrival at Central Station, you will march along George Street to Circular Quay. From there, ferries will take us to the Garden Island dockyards where we will rendezvous with our steamers. Once on board, you will be informed of our destination, and not before.'

***

The telegram boy from the General Post Office knocked on Doris's door, and then on Claire's. The telegrams were short and identical and read:

> *Please be advised that your relative will be embarking on overseas duty tomorrow the 9th day of November 1914. Please be further advised that the troops will be arriving at Central Station at approximately 10.30 am. They will then proceed down George Street, Sydney, where they will be ferried to their embarkation point. Families are asked to line George Street from 10 am if they wish to see their relative.*
> *Department of Army.*

Even though they were all expecting the news, they were still shocked when the telegram arrived. Doris was filled with mixed emotions, as she was proud to say to her neighbours and acquaintances that both of her boys had signed up to *do their duty*. But on the other hand, the reality of possibly never seeing her sons again played heavily on her mind.

Hannah was devastated. She read the telegram and burst into tears. She was desperate to see him, not just to shake off the insecurities that she was feeling, but to once again tell him that she loved him. Would he still love her after she had given herself to him? What if he now despised her and thought of her as nothing more than a woman with loose morals? She was also grappling with how, or whether, she would even tell him that she was pregnant.

She thought back to several nights ago when Claire had spoken to Davin about her condition and his response.

He had come home tired and dirty, and after he had bathed, Claire had said to him, 'Sit down Davin we need to talk.'

He sat at the table as Claire informed him of Hannah's condition. At first, he didn't respond at all. He just stared at a knot in the tabletop before he rolled himself a smoke. He had mulled over what he was about to say, and then he spoke softly, 'Hannah, I won't say that I'm not shocked and somewhat disappointed, but as you know I'm not much of a God person, and I haven't had a mind to bother him with me problems lately, so I don't care much of what the priest and others think. Now, I have come to look at Tom and Jack as part of this family, and Tom is as close to a son that I'm ever likely to get, and you, well, you are like me own daughter, and a more lovin' a child I couldn't expect ta have!

'Now, I don't wanna start moralisin' because these things happen and we are livin' in different times, but people are gunna start talkin', and I haffta think of your Aunt Claire and her feelin's. And what about Doris, does she know?' he asked, looking at Claire.

Claire told him of their conversation, and how she had suggested that it might be a good idea for Hannah to go and live with Doris's sister in the mountains during her confinement. Davin thought about this and then asked, 'What other options are there?'

Claire responded with, 'She would have to go and live in a convent with the nuns, and they would take the child and find it a home. That's what they do, and Hannah would have to stay with them for some months to pay for her keep.'

Davin drew back on his smoke, and thought about this option before speaking, 'And when Tom comes home we tell 'im that we didn't wanna keep his bairn, and so we got rid of it, is that what yer telling me woman?' His voice rose slightly.

Claire knew that Davin was getting annoyed, and she was feeling confused, as she had been brought up with the belief that sex before marriage was not only morally wrong, but was also a sin. Her feelings were in conflict as Doris, her friend and neighbour, along with her husband, were now prepared to ignore the things that she believed in. On the other hand, she loved her niece, but could not condone what she had done.

Claire went and sat next to him. She held his hand and spoke quietly as she looked at him. 'No darlin', if times were different and Hannah had brought shame to us by foolin' around with every Tom, Dick or Harry then I would be the first to turn her from our door. But, how could we?

'She be like our own child, and her bairn will be part of this family. I care naught about what gossipin' tongues say, and I know that Doris feels the same way.'

The tension that was building fell away, and Davin looked at the two women before saying, 'Well that's settled, if anyone asks then we will say that they got married just before Tom left, and if they don't believe it then we shouldn't care as to what they think.' He smiled as he said, 'It will be nice to have a bairn around the place before Tom gets back.'

Hannah jumped from her chair, and came around the table. She threw her arms around Davin's neck before kissing him on the cheek and saying, 'Thank you Uncle,' as her tears ran down his face.

Part 2

1914 – 1919

17.

Departure

Most of the troops were wide awake before reveille. There was a mix of excitement along with trepidation amongst them. After a hurried breakfast, each man collected his kitbag and a rifle along with their tin hat and leather bandolier.

The trucks that they had arrived in took them back to the station where two trains were waiting to transport them to Sydney. Black smoke rose from the engine's funnels, and steam hissed from brake cylinders and safety valves as the men jammed into the wooden carriages. Porters loaded kitbags, rifles and equipment into the baggage wagons, and eventually, a thousand men were being transported to the docks. Upon arrival at Central Station, they assembled with more troops who had arrived from other camps. Orders were being shouted, and there was a general sense of organised pandemonium. They all grouped into several columns, and the mile-long march along George Street to Circular Quay commenced. By the time that they had reached the Sydney Haymarket, the column of men was two thousand strong, and it became more of a gaggle than a march.

The word had spread, after so many families had received their telegrams. Thousands of people had lined the street since early morning, in the hope that they would get a glimpse of their son or husband once more before they departed.

The crowds clapped at the passing parade, and young boys sat in the gutter and played with home-made wooden rifles.

Claire, Doris and Hannah had made up their minds to catch the tram down to the ferry terminal at Circular Quay. They hoped that if they could get a glimpse of their boys, they might get to spend a moment together as the troops milled around and waited for their ferry.

The hours rolled by, and the crowds were thinner where they stood, and then someone shouted, 'Here they come!' They all turned their heads as one. For the soldiers, it was more of a quick stroll than a formal military parade. From the crowds, there would be a shout, followed by a wave, and sometimes someone broke ranks to scoop a loved one up in his arms for a final embrace. The sea of soldiers kept rolling by until finally Hannah yelled, 'There they are!' before she ran out onto the road calling, 'Tommy Fields, Tommy over here.' She waved her gloved hand madly hoping to catch his attention.

Jack saw her first, and nudged his brother at the same time pointing, 'Look who's over there!' Tom let out a whoop, as they locked eyes before he pushed past a couple of soldiers. He dropped his kitbag before wrapping his arms around her. Doris and Claire were standing next to them, as Jack followed his brother and gave his mother a bear hug.

Tom held her tightly as the seconds ticked away. He gave her a kiss before asking, 'Do ya still love me Hani?' The tears were running down her face and she didn't want to let him go, but those words chased her fears away. With her arms wrapped around his neck she shouted, 'I still love you Tommy Fields, and I will always love you! Write to me whenever you can, and I shall write to you every week!'

The Sergeant's bellow caught their attention, 'Private Fields, both of you Fields boys get back into formation, now!'

Jack gave Hannah a quick embrace and whispered, 'I'll look after him and bring him back to ya Hannah, that's a promise.'

Both boys gave their mother and Claire a final embrace and fell into line with the others. The parade had started to thin out, and the three women just stood on the footpath all lost within the turmoil of their own thoughts and fears.

⁂

The passing parade of young men kept rolling by until they were jammed shoulder to shoulder at the quay.

The ferries kept up a constant relay transporting the troops to the Garden Island Dockyard until finally, several thousand troops were boarded onto five ships.

Below decks had been modified to house several hundred men who would sleep in hammocks slung back to back. The rest were housed on the various decks, but the facilities were primitive with less than a dozen toilets and six washbasins to service an entire ship.

It was late afternoon by the time the tugboats guided the convoy of ships into the harbour. The soldiers lined the railings to take in the sights of Sydney Harbour as the ship steamed up the channel and out through the heads. Once they were in the open water, most had gone below decks again to climb into their hammocks as the rolling swell took its toll on queasy stomachs.

18.

Brigid

After her conversation with Sister Emmitt, Brigid had gone home and told her mother of the job offer.

'A nurse, why would you want to be a nurse? For goodness' sake girl do you have any idea of what nurses do?' Before Brigid could reply her mother continued. 'All that you will be doing is emptying bedpans and washing people, along with working all night. No, I don't think that's a good idea, why don't you see if you can get a position in the kitchen down at Kelly's Hotel? You know how to cook and clean, and I think that you would be much better suited to a job in a kitchen. At least you will be getting paid for your work at the hotel. I cannot believe that they expect a trainee nurse to work for three months without pay. I think that if you really want to get a job, then you should at least get one that pays you something!'

Brigid was not happy with her mother's response, but she had already made up her mind. She couldn't explain it, but something within her told her that nursing was what she needed to do.

'Mummy, Sister Emmitt at the Barracks hospital was very nice. She said that if I turn up on Monday morning, she would make me a nurse's assistant. She would give me a uniform to wear and all, so I think that I will go and see if I can do the job. If I can't, then I will try something else, but blood doesn't bother me, and nor would emptying bedpans.

'Please, Mummy, it's something that I would like to do, and if I can become a nurse, I might be able to help the soldiers if they get wounded.'

Her mother knew that there was no use in arguing with her daughter, and so she relented like she usually did with any of her children. 'Very well, if that's what you want to do then go ahead and give it a go, but if you don't like it then just tell the sister and leave!'

*⁂

Brigid started working as an unpaid nurse's assistant, doing all the unsavoury jobs that went with the position, while the senior nurses were already discussing the possibility that shortly they may be working on the hospital ships which were being painted white and fitted out on the harbour.

19.

The Voyage

The convoy was heading south, down along the east coast before sailing across the Great Australian Bight and out into the Indian Ocean.

By the time that the ships had reached the west coast, those on board had gained their sea legs. They had settled into the routine of life on board, which included exercising and target practice from the stern of the ship. They were also taught how to read and send semaphore signals, but for the most part, the men just lounged around and dreamed of being somewhere else. A few kept diaries, and some read books.

Des was leaning against the railing when he heard the shout, 'Des, Desmond Carney, is that yerself?' Des looked towards the caller. At first, he didn't recognise the face, but as recognition dawned he gave a holler and yelled, 'Doughy, Lenny Doherty, I can't believe it, where did you spring from?'

Des had made his way across to his friend and pumped his hand vigorously.

'Beejeebers man, it's good to see ya, what would yer be doin' here? The last time I seen yer was back 'ome, God, how long ago was dat?'

'Yeah, I been over 'ere a bit over a year now. The old folks are gone, and as yer know Des things wasn't too good back home.

'So, I put me name up fer a cheap passage, and I landed here. But I had a dozen jobs since, and I've had a hard time settlin' in. I was thinkin' of goin' to America an seeing if I could get a job there. Then this thing starts up, and I sez to the missus, at least I'm gunna get paid if I sign up and here I am!'

'Did ya say that yer married Doughy, who is she, do I know her?'

'It's Sarah, Sarah McKee, you remember 'er, she sat in front of you at school, and you were always pulling her pigtails.'

'Well I'll be dammed, little Sarah marryin' you. So, have ya got any young'uns, how long have you bin together? C'mon Doughy, tell me what's been 'appenin' back 'ome?'

Doughy rolled a smoke as Jack and Tom joined them. Des did the introductions, and Des continued asking his friend questions.

'So, where you been living since ya been 'ere, Doughy?'

'We got a little two-room joint over in Surrey hills. It isn't much, but it only costs ten bob a week. We got kicked out of the other place we 'ad in Redfern cause we couldn't pay the rent. It was hard trying to get a job with half decent money. When I first got 'ere I got meself a job diggin' holes fer the water pipes. Bugger me mate, I 'ad blisters on me blisters after swingin' that pick all day. I worked for three solid weeks, and the boss bastard only paid me for one. He give me a quid for three bloody weeks of slavin' me guts out. Said it wos normal practice to hold back two weeks' pay, which he reckons is what he pays me at Christmas when we don't work. I told the bastard that I would 'ave me money now as I mightn't be 'ere for Christmas, and he sez nup, it was company policy to hold me money and If I didn't like it, then too bad!'

They were all listening intently to the story, and Jack asked, 'So what did ya do?'

'I belted 'im in the gob, and tipped the bastard upside down ter see how much money he 'ad in his pockets. He 'ad a couple of quid, and I took it. Then bugger me, a bloody copper was walking by and saw the bloke on the ground. He woke 'im up, and the bloke said to the copper that I had robbed 'im, and that he 'ad never seen me before. So, the copper tried ter handcuff me, but I give him a shove and took off. I never told the boss where I lived, so they never found me.

They all laughed at the story as Doughy said, 'Geeze it's nice to see a familiar face, and I'll be happy when my Sarah starts getting me pay packet from the army. Now tell me about yerselves.'

***

The days were getting warmer as the ships went north. The sleeping quarters were getting too uncomfortable to sleep in, and many men had taken to sleeping on deck. Letters had been written to loved ones, but they would not be posted until the convoy had reached Colombo. There, they would replenish the coalbunkers and take on fresh supplies. Jack had already written to his mother, and Tom found a quiet corner and penned a letter.

December 1914.

Dearest Hannah,

By the time that you receive this letter, we will possibly be at our destination. Rumour has it, that it will be Egypt. We cannot be sure, as the brass hasn't officially told us. We were of the opinion when we first sailed that we were to sail directly to England, but all that has been told to us is that our destination will be in the Middle East somewhere.

We expect to reach Colombo sometime tomorrow, and we are hoping that we can get off this ship to stretch our legs for a short period while they replenish the coalbunkers. We have been told that all of our mail will be censored, so even if I know where we are going, I cannot tell you, but wherever we are you will always be in my thoughts. I can tell you that it is very crowded on board, and the brass has us doing all kinds of things. We exercise every morning, and they have taught us how to read semaphore signals, which is how they communicate between the ships in the convoy. They have also taught us how to tie things with various knots; although for the life of me I don't know what use that knowledge will be to me when I am back home.

There is a small shop on board where we can buy our tobacco, beer, or lemonade. The beer is only available after midday, but we can buy cold lemonade at any time during the day. They charge us four pence for a pint of beer and tuppence for a glass of lemonade. They also make fresh bread on board, but we are expected to provide our own jam to have with it. I purchased a tin of plum jam from the comfort store. That's what it's called, and they charged me sixpence for the tin.

The food has been generally good, and thankfully there is plenty of tucker to be had. We had a sports day arranged last week, and different teams of men competed in a tug-of-war contest along with having wheelbarrow races.

We didn't actually use a wheelbarrow, but the object of the game was that one fellow would stand on his hands and have his body horizontal to the deck and the other chap would hold his ankles. The teams would line up until the starter's gun went off, and the poor chap would have to pedal with his hands whilst having his mate hold his legs and running forward.

Some chaps were having sly bets on who would win, but they frown on betting, and anyone caught has to spend several hours down in the coalbunkers shovelling the stuff into the furnace as punishment.

Did you receive a letter from the army yet? I signed over a portion of my weekly pay to you, and you should have received notification on where you should go to collect the money. I was told that you would need to go into the York Street army office once a week to collect it. I want you to use it as you wish as it is of no use to me here. We are paid six bob a day, and some wag suggested that we were six bob a day tourists.

I wish that we had been married before I left, because if something were to happen to me and we were married, then you would have been entitled to a widow's pension. However, because we are not married you would not be entitled to anything should something go wrong. So, Hani, I hope that you will save some of the money for a rainy day. However, buy yourself a pretty bonnet, or some such thing, and think of me when you wear it. This letter will be posted from Colombo tomorrow, and I have no forwarding address at this time, but if you have a mind to write to me then send it c/o the third battalion, and I'm sure that it will eventually reach me. I will see you in my dreams Hani, and I shall write again once we reach our new camp.

Forever yours

Tommy.

20.

Patricia and Mary

Mary Bridges was barely 16 when she became pregnant. Uneducated, and with no prospects, her mother had tolerated her condition because she felt partly responsible for it.

Patricia Bridges had never married, but she had made a meagre living by whoring. She was now on the wrong side of forty, and her features that had once made her attractive to men were now fading.

Lines on her face, bags under her eyes and her breasts that had once stood proudly erect were now sagging. Where once she could be selective in whom she took to her bed, her conquests now were more likely to be middle-aged married men and drunks. She had always enjoyed sex, but now it was just a means to an end.

She and her daughter lived in a single room, of a four-roomed house with a shared kitchen and a pit toilet out the back. When Mary was young, she was left to her own devices as her mother had entertained her male friends in front of her.

As Mary got older, Patricia had slung a cotton sheet around her bed in a futile attempt at gaining some privacy. It was also to protect her daughter from seeing her naked and humping her clients, but the sheet didn't stop the sounds of her copulation. It also didn't stop the sound of the occasional slap that she received from a client because he was too drunk to get his manhood hard and functional. But the client was never too drunk to belt her because of his inadequate condition.

Times had been lean for Patricia over the past few weeks, and she had only managed to bed one client for which he had begrudgingly paid her a pound. She now had an infection *down there*, which made having sex painful.

Mary had long been used to being in the room, as her mother satisfied the basic needs of another man. She had lost her virginity to a randy lad three years older than her when she was just 14. And as painful as the initial experience was to her, she had come to enjoy it. By the time that she had turned 15, she was letting any good-looking young stud give her a quick poke.

Harry Lauder worked down on the docks at Garden Island, and he was in his mid-twenties. Tall and slim, with a flat belly, he had no trouble finding plenty of women who would give themselves to him for a fee. He had been using Patricia's services for a year, even though she was older than the women that he usually got to service his needs. In his words, 'She was a good root considering her age!' But now he had his eye on Mary.

He was lying naked on the bed, and having a smoke when he first suggested to Patricia that he could go again.

'Pat, how old is Mary?' Pat retorted, 'You get yer eyes offa her yer randy bastard. If ya want a root then ya can shag me!'

Harry kept coming around once a week on payday. As he was shagging Patricia, he would suggest to her that she should share him with her daughter. 'I'll give ya 30 bob if ya let me shag her!'

But Patricia still refused, until finally the infection was so painful that sex was out of the question altogether. She knew that if she didn't come up with the rent money soon, then they would be evicted.

'I'll hafta talk to 'er first, and if she agrees then it's two quid, orright?'

'Two quid! I could 'ave me pick of any of the girls that hang around the Cross for that amount of money.'

'Sure, ya can, and ya better go and find one, because two quid is the price for me daughter, so pay up or bugger orf!'

The deal was done, and for a couple of months Harry laid with Mary every payday, and he paid Patricia two pounds for the privilege. That was until Mary had told him that she was pregnant, and then Harry disappeared.

Patricia was annoyed because of her daughter's condition, and she was now anxious about her own future. The home nurse had suggested to her that she might have a case of the 'pox'.

'What's the pox?' Patricia asked, and the nurse explained that it was a disease called syphilis, which caused ugly legions to grow on mouths and noses along with the genital areas.

The nurse suggested that she should get herself to the Barracks hospital where they may give her a potion to ease the pain. But now that her daughter was pregnant, her immediate problem was how they could they earn enough money to pay the rent and buy food.

'Mary, yer mother is sick, and me shagging days is over fer a while. You won't be any help in paying for ya keep soon, so we will hafta see if we can farm your bub out after ya 'ave it. I know a woman who runs a baby farm, and she reckons that ya can get ten quid for a healthy bub. If we sell it to 'er, she will give us a coupla quid up front. She sells 'em to well-ter-do people, so either that, or ya will hafta get rid of it now, so ya can get back to earnin' us some money.'

It was a lot for Mary to take in, but she knew enough to know that getting rid of it was messy and painful, and might even kill her. She had remembered how Mavis Broome was after she had let the old hag from Smith Street get rid of her unwanted child. She had bled for several days before the infection had taken hold, and it was finally the infection that had killed her. So, after thinking about what her mother had told her, she had decided that having the baby and selling it later was her best option. In the meantime, she would let the local boys give her a quick shag, but this time she would charge them a couple of bob, and that would help pay the rent.

21.

Hannah

Hannah was now twelve weeks pregnant, and she had been having pains in her belly for days. Claire had called the nurse, and when she had finally arrived she took Hannah's temperature.

'I've been bleeding a little, nurse.'

'When did this start?' she asked as she took hold of Hannah's wrist and monitored her pulse.

'About two days ago, and then it stopped, but I don't feel well. Something is not right, I know that something is wrong, what's the matter with me nurse?'

The nurse turned to Claire and asked, 'Has she been eating normally?' Claire replied, 'Not really, she only takes small amounts of food, and considering her condition she should be eating a lot more than she is. Oh, and for the past few days she has been bringing it all back and has hardly kept a thing down.'

The nurse had her hand on Hannah's stomach, and was pressing down and trying to find the source of the pain. She then touched her breasts and asked, 'Do they feel sore or tender?' and Hannah replied, 'No.'

At that moment, Hannah gave a groan, followed by a scream. She rolled over onto her side clutching at her stomach.

The nurse yelled at Claire and said, 'Get some linen, or towels quickly now.'

Hannah was now sat up with her legs dangling over the side of the bed. Doris had entered the room just before the miscarriage, and watched with apprehension as the drama unfolded.

Claire brought in a few towels, and stood in stunned silence as Hannah gasped for breath just as the bloodied fetus mixed with mucus and bodily fluids flowed from her.

Hannah had fallen backwards on the bed, and was now curled up and clutching her stomach. She was deathly pale, and her breathing was shallow. The nurse rechecked her pulse, before lifting her stained nightgown. The bleeding had almost stopped but she needed to clean Hannah, and she asked Doris to bring a bowl of warm water and a sponge.

Claire washed Hannah down, and removed the soiled nightdress. The nurse wrapped up the tissue in a bloodied towel and said, 'We need to bury this.' Claire had started to clean the floor, but Doris knelt down and said, 'Here luvvy, let me do that, you sit with our girl.'

Davin was in the kitchen when Claire said to him, 'Hannah has lost the bairn, and we need to bury it.' He said nothing, but rose and went to the wall where his shovel was hanging. He dug a small hole to one side of the lemon tree that he had planted four years earlier. The nurse handed the small bundle of rags to Davin, and he took it gingerly before placing it in the hole and covering it up.

The four of them stood in silence looking at the small pile of fresh dirt. The nurse, who had seen this same scenario many times, took the lead and said out loud, 'Dear lord, we offer this little one for you to take to your bosom. For whatever reason, it was not in your plans for this little one to live, and so we ask that you will spare the life of its mother. Thank you, Lord.'

Doris wiped away a tear, and Claire was openly crying as Davin put his arm around her shoulders. The nurse went back to her patient and checked her blood pressure and to see if the bleeding had stopped. She put her hand on Hannah's forehead before whispering to her, 'Get some sleep now child, you will be feeling better soon please God.' She turned and walked over to the others.

'The bleeding has stopped, and she should sleep for some time now. I have given her some laudanum, but I have to warn you though, that if she starts to bleed heavily, she will probably die. I will call in and see the doctor and inform him of what has happened. If the girl gets worse during the night, you will need to get the doctor or me here quickly, but the best thing for her now is to rest and sleep.'

22.

Noreen Emmitt

Matron Emmitt had taken Brigid under her wing. She was impressed with Brigid's attitude, and she had suggested that as Brigid would be on call she should move into the nurses' quarters.

Matron Noreen Emmitt was now in her late fifties. She had spent most of her life in and around hospitals, as her father had been a doctor. Even as a child, she could be found wandering around the wards and generally finding her way into areas where children shouldn't be. Once she had finished her schooling, it had seemed to be appropriate for her to start working as a nurse's aide.

She had married a young medical student, but the marriage, and her prospects of becoming a mother, had been cut short prematurely. Her husband of six months had been killed after a bolting horse had hit him as he had left the hospital one evening.

She had never had the inclination of finding another husband. There had been a few opportunities for her to do so as she was still young, and her features were on the attractive side of plain. After her husband's death, she had thrown herself into studying midwifery, and not satisfied with that she had started reading all of her father's medical books. She had devoured medical knowledge from hospital journals and experience. Years earlier, Noreen had applied for the position of senior matron at the Barracks Hospital.

The hospital board members had questioned her extensively, and after the interview they had agreed unanimously that she would make an admiral Senior Matron.

Her work had generally fulfilled her, but as the years had passed she held regrets that she had never had any children. As her parents were long dead, there was nobody that she was close to.

That was until Brigid had come along, and Brigid was bright and eager to learn. Whatever tasks were asked of her, she attended to them without complaint. Noreen Emmitt had seen herself in young Brigid, and was pleased with what she saw.

Brigid had been studying, and had already sat her first exam. There had been talk about the hospital ships that were being fitted out down at the Garden Island Dockyards. The rumours were that nurses would be required to work on them once the modifications had taken place.

Brigid had thought about the possibility of working on a hospital ship, and she knew that it was something that had appealed to her. But she knew that only the most experienced nurses would be allowed to go, if in fact they were required at all.

23.

Egypt

When the convoy arrived at Colombo, the soldiers had been given twelve hours' shore leave. Mountains of coal had been deposited on the wharfs, and more was arriving in high-sided wooden wagons pulled by bullocks. The coolie labourers loaded the large wooden bins with sacks of coal before it was hoisted from the wharf by a crane, which deposited it into the bowels of the ship. A hundred or more labourers were filling each bin, and as the coalbunkers were replenished, the ropes were cast off and the convoy was under steam again.

The days were now sweltering, and it was common knowledge that their destination was Egypt. The menu had also changed after they had left Colombo, as crates of bananas, coconuts and exotic fruits had been added to the menu, much to the delight of the men.

It had taken them eight weeks of sailing to reach Egypt, and the convoy arrived into the port city of Alexandria. They were all heartily sick of the cramped quarters on board, and they were excited at the thought of leaving the ship for good.

A sergeant was bellowing through a megaphone, 'Our ships will be unloaded here, and we will all be transported by train to our camp. I'm told that the journey will take about seven hours and you must not get involved with any of the locals. They will try and sell you souvenirs, and they are very persistent. Now, don't start any fights as this is their country, and their ways are different to ours.

'When we arrive at our camp, there will be plenty of time to take in the sights and buy trinkets to send back home. That's all men, at ease.'

They all fell silent, and looked around at the new surroundings. Dirt roads crowded with more camels and donkeys than horses. Brown buildings that appeared to be made from solid earth, and the whole male population appeared to be wearing long white robes and sandals on their feet.

The train station looked more familiar. It was similar to British stations with iron pillars and cast-iron fretwork, except for the Islamic writing on the station signs. Food sellers were sitting cross-legged on the ground, selling their fare from cast-iron pots sat above charcoal burners.

The station filled with several thousand soldiers, and as each train arrived they were quickly loaded. They sat in the corridors, and some even climbed into the overhead luggage racks as the train rattled and creaked its way across the sand dunes and the otherwise barren landscape. It was nightfall when they finally reached the camp that would end up being their home for the next two months.

The following morning the camp Commander addressed them all. 'Stand easy men! We are now officially under the command of the British military, and our orders will come directly from them. You will be deployed to wherever you are needed. I can't say when or where that will be, but you have been sent here for several reasons.

'One is, that the British generals believe that you require more training to prepare you for what is already facing those who came before you. Two, you were to be sent directly to London, but as it is the middle of winter there at the moment, it was decided that it would be a pointless exercise to do your training while having to cope with a harsh northern hemisphere climate.

'So, while you are here, you will have a certain amount of freedom, but don't abuse it. Your training will be carried out between sunrise and midday, and unless you are restricted to barracks, or on guard duty, you will be allowed to have free time between 3 pm and 9 pm each day.

'Lights go out in the barracks by 10 pm. You may take tours of the pyramids, or the tombs, or anywhere else that you choose, but everyone must be back in barracks by 9.30 pm. Anyone caught returning later than that will be confined to barracks for as long as is necessary.

'Two divisions, including the Light Horse, will remain here indefinitely as they will be required to fight the Turks who are already in the Sinai area. The rest of you will be deployed to wherever you are required. That's all men.'

The camp was set up in view of the ancient pyramids, and the soldiers found the heat and the flies to be torturous. They soon came to realise why reveille was at 4 am instead of the usual 5 am.

Their days were taken up with target practice, attacking straw-filled dummies with bayonets and digging trenches. As the early afternoon heat became unbearable, the troops relaxed in whatever shady area they could find. The first mail had arrived from home, but few soldiers had received a letter, as most families had been waiting until they had heard from their loved one, which would tell them as to where they could write.

Jack had found a shady spot to relax in, and as he didn't feel like sleeping he decided to write to his mother.

He knew that she would be waiting for the postman to arrive every day. He had meant to write to her while on the ship, but the decks were so crowded and space was at a premium that letter-writing was almost impossible.

February 1915.

Hello Mother,

Well, here we are in Egypt at a place called Mena. We have been here for some weeks, and I cannot describe how hot it is, but other than the heat and the flies the place is not too bad. We get up at 4 am, and at that time the air is most pleasant. We are camped in what is called the Pyramid Valley, and it gives us views of these giant structures. We still do training, target practice and whatnot, although they have had us digging trenches.

It seems as though most of our daily lives revolve around digging trenches and filling sandbags. If we are not digging holes, we go on long marches across the desert. The sand is so soft that by the time we have completed our march our boots are almost full of it. There is certainly no shortage of sand around here. We start off with a barren piece of ground outside of our camp, and several hundred of us start digging, and we have to make the trenches big enough for a man to stand in, and when we have finished it, we have to fill it in again. We have been given the nickname 'Diggers' as we have all become quite adept at digging holes.

Tommy is well, and he wrote to Hannah, and one would hope that she had received his letter by now. He misses her, and is extremely worried that she will find someone else whilst we are away. We took a tour of the ancient pyramids last week as well as seeing a giant stone edifice that looks like a lion. It is called the Sphinx, and is said to be more than two thousand years old.

We also took a tour of the museum that housed some objects that were said to be thousands of years old. It was a very interesting place. We also climbed to the top of one of the pyramids. The view was wonderful, and we could clearly see our camp and how big it was. The place is like a large village, and from the top we could see how well it is set out with what looked like roads and paths between the tents.

We also visited one of the Digs, which is where they are digging through the ancient tombs looking for treasure. We all took a camel ride, and it was a most unusual experience. Des came with us along with a mate of his from Ireland, so if you happen to see Desmond's old man could you pass on to him that he is well.

They feed us very well, Mother, but the camp cook cannot hold a candle to your cooking, and I much look forward to sitting in your kitchen once again.

The heat has taken a huge toll on the poor horses that sailed with us, although now that they have had time to settle down after their long voyage they should be all right. At night, we are allowed to visit the bars and the bazaar.

The natives have named many of the bars and eating-places with Australian names, like the 'Wattle bar' or the 'Kangaroo café'. I suppose that it is their way of trying to make us feel at home. We are all expected to be back at camp by 9.30, but the rules are pretty slack. Nobody has a mind to enforce them, and many of the chaps don't get back to camp until late.

They have set up a couple of picture theatres and run a film every night. The Red Cross has also set up a hall to hold cabarets and pantomimes.

How are you managing at the fuel yard? And did you manage to find someone to do the deliveries? Well Mother, it is all very boring here really, and none of us actually knows how long we will be required to stay here, but I shall write again, maybe from this location and maybe not. Being 'diggers,' we are the last to be told anything.

We are glad to be off that blessed ship and back on dry land.

A few chaps got very ill on the voyage, and one poor devil died from pneumonia. All the chaps stood on the deck, and the chaplain spoke over him. They wrapped his poor body in the Australian flag and dropped it over the side. It was a sobering experience and something that I shall remember for a long time. Well Mother, we hope that you are well and would you give my regards to all next door? Do not worry about Tommy, as he is well although he is feeling a little homesick.

Pray for us please Mother.
With love from your son,
Jack

He finished the letter, and found the others as they were making plans for a night in the town. Des suggested that they should visit one of the many brothels that were in the area that was known as the French Quarter.

Tommy was the first to speak and said, 'I don't think that I will bother with the brothel. A couple of chaps have got the clap, and there is some talk that they might be sent home. Besides, you heard what the captain said. He said that anyone who was sent home with the clap wouldn't get paid. Anyway, I'm engaged, and I don't feel like shagging some Arab Shelia that's been rooting half the regiment. What if I got the clap and they sent me home now? What would I tell Hani? No, you chaps go ahead, and I'll go to that bar that we went to last week. I liked that place with the musicians, and the views over the water.'

Des was less troubled about catching anything, as his carnal desires had swayed his thinking and all that he was interested in doing was soothing the fire within his loins.

'You can say what you like mate, but I'm gunna find me a dark-eyed beauty,' he made a voluptuous curve with his hands, smiled and winked at the others, 'who will shag me silly. What about you Doughy? Are ya up for it?'

Doughy replied, 'Yeah, why not it might be the last one I get. I heard the Sergeant talking to the Captain before, and the Captain said that he was waiting for the orders to be confirmed. Now that could mean anything, but we been 'ere for over a month now, and they aren't gunna leave us at this holiday camp forever! So, lead the way to sexual paradise my man!' He gave them a wry smile.

Several mornings later, the call to parade bugle sounded unexpectedly. Everyone stopped what they were doing, and they all had the same thought. Two thousand men assembled on the parade ground, anticipating the announcement that they would be heading to the front.

They shuffled nervously until the camp commander and his aide stood in front of the assembled group. The commander spoke to the troops through a tin megaphone.

'Stand easy men, this won't take long. An hour ago, I received a dispatch from army H.Q. Our lads in Turkey are having a tough time over there, and I have been informed that there have been numerous casualties as the enemy is proving more resilient than what was anticipated. The third battalion will ship out at first light tomorrow. The Light Horse Brigade will remain here for the time being, but be on standby to head for the Sinai over the coming days. The rest of you will be the reinforcements for the first and second divisions already fighting on the Gallipoli peninsula.

'Tonight will be your last night of freedom, so make the most of it. From tomorrow, you will start putting all of your training into practice, and it will be some considerable time before leave will be granted again. At 6 pm tonight, the chaplain will conduct a non-denominational service here on the parade ground. If you have a need to make peace with your maker, then this will be the time for doing so! I am not going to dress this up.

'Tomorrow you will sail for Turkey, and some of you, unfortunately, will not return. If you have not already done so, may I suggest that you write to your loved ones and put your affairs in order? Letters will be dispatched tomorrow for home. By the time that they reach Australia you will already be on the front lines. You will not let them know your destination, but you may tell them anything else.

'We will be catching the train back to Alexandria at 4 am, and we will be sailing to Turkey on the evening tide tomorrow. Turkey is over six hundred miles from Alexandria, and it will take us about three days' sailing to get there. So, you will all be required to be back on base by 8 pm tonight. Make the most of your freedom, but be warned that any man who is not back at base by the designated time will be regarded as a deserter and will be liable to be shot! That's all men, dismissed!'

They looked at each other, and Tom was the first to speak, 'I've changed me mind, I don't think that I'll go inta town tonight, I'll stay here and write Hannah a long letter, that's the least that I can do.' The others decided that they should still go into town, and were more determined than ever that they would kick up their heels for possibly one last time.

⁂

The journey from the camp to the ship took over twelve hours, and by nightfall, they were all pleased to be back on board. Unlike their voyage to Egypt, the mood among the men was quiet and sombre. The realisation that within thirty-six hours they would be at the front fighting, and possibly dying, was something that they had yet to come to grips with.

After sailing for almost three days, the convoy had quietly glided to anchor about two miles off the coast of Gallipoli. The troops had been woken at 3 am with the instructions that no lights were to be shown on deck. They were given an extra-large breakfast, and kits were checked for the umpteenth time. At 4 am the landing barges were lowered, and as each barge was loaded they motored to the beach. As their eyes became accustomed to the dark, they could just make out the dark outline of the hills that they would soon be climbing. They reached the shore unscathed and unnoticed, unlike those in the first divisions that had arrived months earlier in a baptism of fire. They could all hear the sporadic boom of cannons, and see the fleeting glow of light as another shell momentarily lit up the dark sky in the distance.

As they gathered in small groups, the word was spread amongst them that they would stay on the beach until first light. The day dawned bleak and threatened more rain. All were wet and cold, as they squelched their way up and along the goat tracks that had cost their comrades dearly just a few months earlier.

They carried boxes of ammunition and other supplies with them, along with drinking water and machine guns. A curse could be heard as another soldier tripped over and fell into the waterlogged ground.

It was raining when they reached the camp that was less than half a mile from the front. The sound of sporadic gunfire could now be heard along with the distant explosions from the heavy artillery. They looked at each other, none speaking but all thinking the same thoughts. Orders were being barked, and whistles were blown as the new recruits stood around on the muddy ground unsure of what to do. A Sergeant yelled at them to get into formation.

'Righto lads, ahead of you are three rows of trenches each about a mile long. The first trench is the rest one. The second is the standby one, and the front one is where all the action is. You will all do four-day stints on the front line. Then you will return to the rear trench where you will have several days to rest. After that, you will go back to the standby trench. There, you will be about a hundred yards from the frontline. That will enable you to be brought forward quickly should the need arise. The lads already here now need to be relieved and rested. They have been fighting for some time, so I need a couple of hundred of you to make your way down that trench.' He was pointing to the entrance. 'You will be given orders when you get there. I want 100 or so to go to the standby trench, and the rest of you go to the rest area. Now keep your heads down, and I can assure you that you will be a welcome sight to those already there.'

A makeshift wooden ladder was propped up against the sandbagged wall, and one by one they climbed down. The entrance to the trenches was wet and slippery, and was barely three feet wide, and in some areas held almost a foot of water at the bottom. The smell was rank and overpowering, as overflowing toilet buckets had mixed with the muddy water that sloshed over the duckboards. They squeezed their way along the narrow passage, and past weary soldiers. Many of them were caked in mud, but still able to muster a grin to their replacements. As they moved forward, others moved back towards the rest area. It took them more than an hour to get to their final positions in the front-line trench, and someone called out, 'Welcome to hell boys.'

***

Tunnel entrances were propped up by sandbags, and diverged at right angles to the trenches. To one side was the communication trench.

This trench was to be kept open and free of soldiers at all times, as runners would use these to deliver orders from command headquarters. Soldiers were standing almost shoulder to shoulder, and all were standing in sodden boots, and wet, mud caked clothes.

A few already had their kitbags slung across their backs waiting for their turn to go back to the rest area, and hopefully to get a chance to dry out.

The captain addressed his new troops. 'You are a welcome sight men, and the next few days will no doubt be a shock to you. You will find somewhere to stow your gear inside the tunnels. You will need to keep your rations with you, as there is no camp kitchen on the front line, so I'm afraid that it will be bully beef and biscuits for the next few days.'

'You will sleep whenever you can get a few moments, and at best you may get four or five hours. However, take note, if you are rostered to do guard duty and you go to sleep at your post, you will be shot. Sentry duty is of vital importance, and each man will do a four-hour stint. All of our lives depend on sentries staying awake!

'The Turks send out patrols some nights, and try and infiltrate our lines, so make no mistake, if you allow yourself to fall asleep while on sentry duty, you will be court martialled and then shot. I hope that I have made myself clear!

'As this is your first time at the front line, I will give you all a rundown of what we do. Between here and the enemy is a distance of approximately one half-mile. We have rolls of barbed wire strung across what is called 'No-Man's-Land.' The purpose of this wire is to prevent the enemy from sneaking over to our lines at night, and surprising us. This is regarded as our first line of defence. The enemy has also laid out rolls of wire to protect their front lines.

'Some of you will be required to crawl out there during the hours of darkness, and repair or replace that wire that has been damaged. It is dangerous, but it is essential to protect the integrity of our lines. This job not only requires courage, but also must be done in complete silence. If you make any noise the enemy will hear you, and you will become sitting ducks, and they will target their guns at you, and there is no shelter.

'Volunteers will also be required to act as stretcher-bearers to bring back the wounded. We do not put ourselves at risk, or waste time trying to retrieve those that have been killed. We also have specialist teams whose job it is to infiltrate the enemy lines and disable the enemy machine-gun posts. Others of you will fill sandbags and reposition them on the walls. This is extremely dangerous as the enemy has snipers watching over our lines of defence, and if you raise your head there is a good chance that you will be killed.

'So, do your duty men, not only for those that you left behind, but also for your country. The empire is watching us, and we as a nation are untested in the theatre of war. So, it is every man's duty to stand up and protect this country of ours and make our families proud.'

They heard the whistle a second before there was a yell from within the trench. 'Duck,' and a few seconds later the earth shook as the trench mortar shell exploded a few feet from where they stood. Clods of dirt and mud rained down on those nearby. A second and third explosion followed shortly after. Everyone was crouched down, and the newcomers were the last to lift their heads.

Tom looked at his brother and his mates. They were all pale as the realisation came to them that the games were now over, and that this was war.

Shortly after the mortar attack, a volley of shots rang out with the bullets whistling like a swarm of hornets above their heads before burrowing into the sandbags with muffled thuds. Some soldiers were standing on the firing step, and returned fire through gaps in the sandbags placed at the top edge of the trenches.

Tom looked around and muttered out loud, 'So this is the front, God what a mess!' He was looking at the ground. A few wooden planks had been laid down and were now sitting an inch below the water and mud that filled the trench.

An older soldier standing next to Tom, stared at him before speaking in a hushed voice, 'That was a mild one; they do that sometimes, the bastards. They go for hours with nuthin', and then they let loose, sometimes for an hour, and sometimes for a few minutes, you never know. You just wait until they let fly with the big cannons. The first time that they did it I near shit meself!'

'Have ya got a fag mate, me baccy's all wet?' Tom looked at the man, his eyes were dull and weary, and something said that his mind was in another place.

'Sure mate, help yer self.' He handed the soldier his tobacco pouch. He took hold of it and removed some weed, and then rolled a generous cigarette.

'Have you got a light? Me matches are all wet too.' Tom struck the match and cupped his hands around the flame, and the soldier bent his head to reach it. He drew in deeply, and held the smoke in his lungs before expelling it with a gush.

'Thanks.'

'You been 'ere long?'

'Too long, we was the first here, not many of us left now. Dunno why I'm not dead like the others!' It was just a simple statement, and Tom didn't know what to say although he asked, 'How bad has it been?'

'Pretty bad, there was a few thousand, or more of us up on the hill when we first got here, but we lost at least the same amount when we landed. But I reckon there's only a handful of us left now, maybe two hundred, dunno really.

'These trenches go fer miles. The last time we went over the top they just picked us off like flies. Shit, there were so many blokes climbing over dead bodies just to get out.

'Most of 'em is still up there in no-man's-land.' He nodded his head towards the top of the trench.

'With so much blood and guts all over the place, it was what ya would expect to see in an abattoir. What fucking madness this bloody war is. We kill them, and they kill us. Then we have a truce, and we all stop fightin' so we can clear up the bodies, just to make room for more when we start fightin' again. Them bloody generals still wanted more, and we give 'em our all. There was hardly anyone left, so now they brung you lot up to be more cannon fodder. It's like a lucky dip at the fair, some live, some don't, and some become vegetables. I'd rather be dead than lose me mind!'

He drew back on his cigarette before continuing, and as he held the fag to his mouth, Tom could see that his hand was trembling. He had been bottling up his emotions, and now there was someone fresh to talk to, and to tell about the things that he had seen.

'I'll give ya a bit of advice, fer what it's worth. When you hafta go over the top don't stand up, lie as flat as ya can. Use the bodies up there as a shield. Some of them stink like hell, and sometimes you have ta step on 'em as ya run fer yer life. You can't help it, there's so many of them. They get peppered with bullets, but better they go inta a dead man than a live one, huh? And, if yer the first over the top crawl over it, don't stand up and make a target of yerself. The brass will be screaming at yer to move yer arse, but ignore them, and concentrate on makin a small target of yerself. If ya get a chance join the tunnel gangs."

Both Jack and Tom asked, 'What's the tunnel gangs?'

'Both sides dig tunnels under no-man's-land, and when they think they are under the enemy troops they blow them up, and they try and do the same to us, but you got a better chance of livin' if yer under the ground than above it. Does that make sense?'

'Yeah, I s'pose it does.'

Jack asked, 'So what's yer name?' He answered, 'Fred Schuman from Batemans Bay, that's down the coast, south of Sydney. Christ, I wish I was back there now, just sitting in me dinghy with a line in the drink catching a few fish.'

He was slow to offer his hand, but readily shook them one by one as they were offered. 'Christ, here comes another one,' and he instinctively ducked as the whistling projectile approached, and then exploded twenty yards from their trench. Nobody moved as they all listened intently to see if any more would follow.

'One fell right on the edge of the trench yesterday just up there.'

He pointed in the direction that he was speaking about. Tom asked, 'Was anyone hurt?' Fred replied with a voice that was louder than necessary, 'Hurt! Nobody was fucken hurt,' and his eyes blazed angrily as he remembered the moment, 'But that round killed a dozen of our blokes in one go. We think that it was a dozen, but who knows, there was body bits everywhere, there's probably still pieces of them lying up there now. It isn't easy picking up all the bits of a bloke and stickin' them in bags. That's what ya 'ave ta do when they tell ya ter do it. All that I know is that nobody has even identified who they were just yet. S'pose they will work it out when they have a roll call.'

Doughy had been quiet up to now, then asked, 'Why do they 'ave a roll call?'

Fred gave him a hard stare and said, 'The corporal comes by every now and then with his list and starts to call out names. If yer don't answer that means that yer dead, and he scratches yer name offa his list. I expect that he will come by today as the brass always wants ter know how many copped it during the last shebang.'

Fred had an air of resignation about him. He expected to end up the same as the others that he had come here with, and as he was so battle-weary he didn't seem to care when his time would come.

The sky had turned dark, and soon the rain was pelting down bringing with it more despair. The lookouts could barely see fifty feet into no-man's-land, and only those that were sheltered in the tunnel entrances and the dugouts were spared another soaking. The gunfire had stopped, as even the enemy could see no point in wasting ammunition by firing into the barren gloom.

24.

Letters From Abroad

Hannah had slowly recovered, but was still emotionally raw after her miscarriage. Doris had called in almost every day. The stress of now living alone was only made bearable by the fact that she could make herself feel useful by fussing over Hannah, and swapping gossip with Claire when she wasn't at the fuel yard.

Doris couldn't really start her day until after the postman had passed by. Charlie Stead would carry his sack of mail up one side of the street before crossing over to deliver the mail to the houses on the other side. He knew the houses where the sons were at war because like Doris, others were also waiting with anticipation for the sound of his whistle.

'Mornin' Mrs Fields, I imagine that this is what you've been waitin' for.' He handed Doris the letter with the postmark of Egypt stamped on the front.

'Hello Charlie, I can't tell you how glad I am to get this. This is the first one I got, and at least I will know how they are. Hopefully, I will have an address where I can write back to them.'

'Lota people happy today Mrs Fields. The ship came in yesterday with all the mail, and there musta been over a hundred sacks filled with letters from the boys. Well, I'll be on me way, still gotta lotta letters to deliver before I'm done.' With that, he doffed his cap and continued on his rounds. Doris carefully opened the letter from her son.

She would read it a dozen times before going next door to read it to Hannah and Claire. Doris looked at the envelope, and she noticed that it had been written more than six weeks earlier, and as happy as she was to have the letter it troubled her to wonder where they were now. It also worried her when she reread the last line that said, 'Pray for us Mother.'

She had been praying for her boys almost every night, along with lighting a penny candle at Saint Bridget's every Sunday when she went to Mass. She placed the letter back into its envelope and went next door. Claire had told her long ago to stop knocking, and to go inside, but she still gave a discreet knock before entering.

Hannah greeted her, and Doris couldn't contain herself, and said, 'I got a letter from me boys just now and they are in Egypt, or they were.'

Claire moved the kettle to the hotplate, and prepared the teapot and cups.

'How are they?' But before Doris could answer Hannah said, 'I got a letter from Tommy too, but his was from some place called Colombo. I hope that they haven't been split up.' She said it with a look of consternation.

They sat at the kitchen table, and Claire poured the tea. 'Read it out to us Doris.' They exchanged the letters and speculated as to where in the world the boys might be at that moment.

Doris turned the conversation to Hannah, 'How are you doing dearie? You know everything happens for a reason and what happened could be a blessing in disguise.' Hannah smiled, and said, 'You may be right Doris, but I have another dilemma now, and I'm not too sure how I should handle it.'

Claire looked at her charge and said, 'What's bothering you now child?'

Hannah replied, 'I had already written to Tommy before, you know, what happened!' she said sheepishly. 'I was going to tell him about the baby, but I didn't. I was scared of his reaction, but now I don't know if I should say anything about it at all. If I don't, will that be deceiving him? Should I say anything to him? I just don't know what to do!'

Claire reached over, and put her hand over Hannah's and said, 'My mother once told me, that what the heart doesn't know can't hurt you. Telling Tommy about your pregnancy and the bairn will achieve nothing. It will probably give him something else to worry about. What do you think, Doris?'

Doris was pouring another cup of tea, and said, 'I think that your aunt is right. It was a blessing in disguise that the child didn't live, and it was probably never meant to be. What happened, happened. I will never tell him what transpired, and neither should you. But, if it bothers you in the years to come when you are an old married woman, you can tell him then and not before! That's my opinion.'

Hannah stood up and gave both Doris and Claire a hug, followed by a thank you. 'That makes me feel a lot better, so I shall write to Tommy tonight. I've made them both some woollen mittens. Father Dixon said that it was very cold in Europe, and it would help if we all made them something warm.'

Doris added, 'I made them a dark fruitcake, but I have to get a tin from Gretch's store before I can send it. I know that they said that they were getting fed well, but they both love my fruitcake. So, I'm going to bake them one every month until they get home.'

Doris asked Claire, 'How is Davin? I haven't seen him for a while.'

'He is so busy, and he misses having Tom around. Young Billy, who he took on to replace him, is very slow, and Davin is loath to leave him at the forge by himself. Davin said that he is as slow as a wet week when he is hammering the metal, and that he has to watch him all of the time. He still has the police contract to shoe all of their horses, plus he has a big contract to forge the railway barrier gates for all of the new stations on the new city circle line.

'Old Ben Taylor is helping out a bit, but he mainly does the horses even though he must be seventy. But beggars can't be choosers, and good labour is hard to find these days. It seems that every young man has just disappeared since this blessed war has started. I shouldn't complain, but I worry about Davin. He is gone before sunrise, and he doesn't get home until late every night. If the forge weren't so far away, I would go around and cook him his dinner there. Some nights he has even slept there. Like he said, if he works to 10 pm it takes him an hour to ride home, and by the time he gets here and has his bath its almost midnight, and then he leaves again at five. No Doris, I won't be the only one happy to see an end to this war!'

'By the way, how are you managing at the fuel yard? Is that fellow still there, what's his name?'

'Harry, Harry Lupine, well there's a strange chap! I did what Jack told me to do. I asked him to pick up a bag of coal, and he couldn't get it off the ground, so then he went and tipped half of it out before he picked the bag up and loaded it onto the dray.

'Then he picked up the coal and filled up the bag again. I said, you can't do that; you haven't got time to do that every time that you do a delivery, and he said, why not? So, I told him that I couldn't use him, and he got all huffy, so I offered him a job filling up the bags. I offered him two bob a bag, and he said that he wanted five bob. I said that he could have five bob a bag as long as he could load them onto the dray and deliver them. But because he couldn't lift them, I would only give him two bob as I told him that I would have to pay someone else to do the deliveries.'

Hannah and Claire were listening intently, and they both asked, 'So what did he say?'

'First, he said yes, and then he said no. He wanted more money, and I told him to bugger off. Oh, excuse me French. I couldn't put up with this nonsense, and then he said he wouldn't work for a woman boss anyway.'

'So, what are you doin' now, how are you getting the fuel delivered?'

Doris chuckled, 'Jack would be so proud of his mum.'

'Why, what have you done?' Claire asked, a bemused look on her face.

'I got two young urchins that just live down the road. Big strappin' lads, but too young to go to the war. You know Mrs. Desmond?' They both nodded. 'Well they are her two boys, and her old man went off to the war too. She has just had another baby, and I suppose she could use a bit more money.

'So, I offered her two lads two bob each to fill the bags, and another five bob between them to deliver them. You ought to see them work. They both fill a bag each at the same time, and then they both get on each end and heave the bags onto the dray. Jack told me to pay whoever I got a quid a day including doing the delivery. Now I got these two young fellas sharing fifteen bob a day between them, and I get the deliveries done as well!

'The first day that they worked, I paid them a quid. I told them to make sure that they gave it to their mother. Well, Mrs Desmond came around to the yard with both of her lads in tow. She thought that they had pinched the money, and she didn't believe them when they told her that they got it for working at the fuel yard.

'When I told her that they worked hard for the money, and I could give them a couple of days' work each week she started crying. She couldn't thank me enough, because she hadn't got any money from the army because her old man hadn't signed any of his pay over to her.

'What a miserable sod he would be, what's he think they are gunna live off? Anyway, we had a cuppa and she said that she would make her lads do whatever work I had for them. So, I can write to Jack, and tell him not to worry about his yard.'

Hannah stood up and said, 'I think that I shall go and write to Tommy, and then I might get my pony and go for a ride.'

Doris smiled and said, 'That's nice dearie, I'm so glad to see you getting back to your old self. If you get your letter written today, I will post it tomorrow when I send the boys my cake.'

Davin had jammed a small desk into a corner of the parlour. She moved a few buttons, took some writing paper from the drawer and penned her letter.

March 1915.

Dearest Tommy,

It was so wonderful to receive your letter. Your mother has also this very day received one from your brother, and she was so happy to hear of your adventures.

It was so very generous of you to provide me with your army pay, and each week I go to the army office in the city, and they give me a pound note. I will not be frivolous with it, and have resolved to save most, if not all of it as it will come in very handy when you get back and we are married.

Life is so very strange here in the city at the moment. Only old men and young boys are seen on the streets these days, with no sign of the many young men that were always around. It breaks my heart, and the thought fills me with dread as I see more and more ladies on the streets wearing their black mourning dresses. The newspapers are saying that things have gone terribly wrong for the boys over there. I think that they were referring to the first batch of troops that had apparently landed at the wrong place and that, that mistake had cost them dearly, but no matter, the story is terrible, and we hope and pray that the story was an exaggeration.

I cannot imagine the hardships that you are all going through, and I pray to God every night to protect you, and bring you and Jack back home safely. Your mother is well, but constantly worries about you both, but the fuel yard is keeping her busy.

I am taking my pony for a long ride after I finish your letter.

I have been back to our private place, you know the one that I mean, several times since you have gone. I sit and watch the steamers cross the bay, and it takes me back to that wonderful day that you and I shared just before you left.

I miss you so much Tommy, and everywhere I go there are reminders of you. Since I have been coming back here to Erskineville, I have come to realise that I enjoy the solitude that being in the country affords. I know that it is not really the country, as more development has taken place since you were last here, but the space around me, together with the quiet solitude, seems to bring peace to my burdened heart.

When we are married Tommy, do you think that we could move to the real country? Somewhere where we can hear the birds sing, and the splashing of water in a stream. You could set up a little forge within a small town, and I'm sure that we would be so very happy.

I don't know as to why I have taken an aversion to the city. Maybe it's because of the constant noise and grime of the place, but since you have gone the city holds no joy for me. Stay safe and well my love, and come home to me soon.

Forever yours
Hannah.

25.

Empathy

The war had been raging for almost eight months before the advertisements calling for volunteer nurses and orderlies to work on hospital ships appeared. They were to join a medical team that would be required to work at various locations overseas. The ships were converted merchant marine vessels. They had been refurbished at the Garden Island dockyards as floating hospitals, and they were almost ready to sail.

Brigid was still a nurse's aide, and was some months off sitting her final exam that would qualify her as a junior nurse. Her mentor, Matron Emmitt, had given her books to study that were far in advance of what a first-year nurse was required to know. Noreen Emmitt saw in Brigid what she had been like at that age, when she had pestered her doctor father to let her read his medical journals.

She was aware that with the right training, young Brigid might even achieve her dream of one day becoming a doctor. She was so keen to learn, and she devoured the information on every page in the medical journals given to her. Nor was she squeamish when it came to cleaning up the blood and bodily fluids of the hospital patients. As much as she had a soft spot for Brigid, she insisted that all her jobs were carried out correctly. Noreen showed her no favouritism over the other nurse's aides, although she would regularly give her a quiet word of encouragement when they were alone.

Noreen now had a purpose, and she would gently guide her young charge through the early steps of her chosen career.

Brigid had seen the advertisement calling for volunteer nurses and orderlies to work on the hospital ships. She knew that she was not even a junior nurse, and also knew that the chances of her getting a job on a hospital ship were slim. However, from the time that she had first heard the rumour she had thought that it was something that she would like to do.

Brigid knocked softly on matron's door. Noreen looked up, and was surprised to see who it was, 'Why Brigid, you are not required for another hour, whatever is the problem?'

'Matron, I am sorry to bother you, but I would like to work on a hospital ship. I was wondering if there are any opportunities for someone like me to help out on board?'

'Oh child, I'm afraid that they only want fully qualified nurses on those ships. I believe that there are only limited quarters for staff as they have been modified to hold up to nine hundred patients. Anyway, I don't think that they will be nice places to work. If only half the stories that we read in the newspapers are true about the casualties, it may be somewhere you can't hide from the real horrors of war. It is very admirable, and brave of you to offer up your services Brigid. But even if I were going, I wouldn't be able to convince the powers that be to allow you to go, not only because you are not yet qualified, but because of your age.'

Brigid had expected that response, but was still slightly disappointed, and Noreen in an effort to give her some encouragement said, 'If the war drags on as the papers say that it now will, then there may be an opportunity for you to work on a hospital ship next year after you have done your exams. If I see an opportunity for you, rest assured that I shall inform you, now you had better go and get your uniform on.'

'Yes matron, thank you matron.'

As she made her way downstairs, she couldn't help but notice the woman pleading with a nurse at the front entrance for some help. Supporting the woman was a young girl about Brigid's age, and she was saying, 'Ya gotta help me mam miss, she is very sick and might be gunna die, please help us!'

The nurse was trying to explain that only doctors could admit patients. 'I'm sorry, but have you seen a doctor, and do you have a referral?'

'We can't just let people turn up here for treatment unless they are very ill, now if you haven't got a letter from a doctor, then there is nothing that I can do for you. I suggest that you go and see your local nursing sister, or go to the dispensary, now please leave!'

'We can't afford to see a doctor, they charge ya four bob, and we ain't got no money. We been to the dispensary, and they give us some stuff, but it done no good. Me mummy is really sick, look at the sores on 'er face an' she got em down below too, please ya gotta do somethin' fer 'er, please miss!'

Brigid was now standing behind the nurse and had overheard the girl's plea. One look at the girl's mother showed her that the woman was not well. Brigid had only worked on the wards, and she had no idea of the hospital policy that wouldn't allow them to treat sick patients who hadn't been referred by a doctor. Most of their patients were soldiers, or patients that could afford to pay their way.

The woman was sat on the front step at the front door, too tired and ill to plead further with the nurse. Her daughter was crying and holding her mother with her arms wrapped around her as the nurse closed the door.

Brigid was frowning and said, 'Surely we can't just leave her there!' The nurse looked at Brigid and recognising her said, 'I don't make the policies, but imagine if we just let every Tom, Dick, or Harry just come in and demand medical attention. Goodness me girl, we have enough patients as it is. Can you imagine how busy we would be if we had to treat everybody? No, she just needs to see the district nurse, and she could make her up a potion of something. If you want to keep working here young lady, you will have to learn that we cannot treat everybody that just turns up. That's just the way that it is, now haven't you got work to do?'

'Yes nurse.'

Brigid, headstrong and impulsive, went straight back upstairs and knocked on matron's door.

'Come in.' Noreen looked quizzically at her as she entered.

'Yes, child, what is it this time?'

Brigid blurted out, 'Matron, I'm sorry to bother you again, but there is a sick lady on the front steps. She looks terrible, and she has her daughter with her. And the nurse said that she couldn't come in, isn't there something that you can do for her? I thought that we helped people when they were sick, how can we ignore a sick old lady out the front? She might be dying, what happens if she dies on the steps?'

'Stop child, stop! Now take a deep breath, calm down and start at the beginning.'

Brigid relayed the story again, and Noreen said, 'The nurse was right; doctors have to refer patients to us. We only have a limited number of beds, and sometimes we can treat the occasional pauper patient for a minor ailment, but that's all. I'm sorry child, it's a harsh policy, and it goes against everything that we stand for. But, it is the hospital's medical board that makes the policies, and I have to take my instructions from them as well.'

The tears were starting to well in Brigid's eyes, but she was determined to make a final stand and said, 'If that's the policy, then the policy is wrong. We are a hospital, and hospitals are supposed to be a place where sick people can come to get better. It's wrong that only some people can get help, and all the rest can't!' She had said her piece, and now she broke down and started crying.

Noreen was taken aback with the outburst, but admired the conviction with which Brigid had spoken. Noreen knew that she was right of course. Hospitals should be a place of refuge, because if sick people could not be admitted unless they could pay, then many people would suffer and die needlessly.

She rose and said, 'I'll go down and see if we can help. If she is not too sick, I'll see if we can get the dispensary to make her up a potion, but I cannot promise anything. We will have to see what ailment she has first, so come with me child as you may have to help with her.'

143

Brigid was now feeling sheepish after her outburst and replied, 'Thank you matron, and I'm sorry for how I spoke to you.'

Noreen replied, 'That's all right child, I admire that you can feel empathy for a stranger, and that you can speak up for them. Now, let's go and see if there is anything that we can do for your sick patient.'

Mary Bridges was still holding her mother when Matron opened the front door. Noreen looked at the bedraggled pair and said, 'Can you stand? Here, let me help you!'

They half carried her to a small examination room. Looking at Brigid, Noreen said, 'Help her out of that shift, and let's have a look at her.'

Patricia wore no underwear, and they were all shocked at seeing the red and inflamed pustules that spread from between her legs and onto her lower abdomen. After taking one look at the patient, Noreen instructed Brigid to go to the nurse's station, and bring the duty nurse, and find the doctor. The nurse arrived, and Noreen gave instructions for her to run a salt bath. Patricia screamed as the warm water covered her.

Doctor Benjamin Conrad had been doing his rounds when Brigid found him. 'Excuse me Sir, matron asked if you could attend a patient downstairs with some urgency?' He frowned, and referred to his pocket watch, as he liked to keep a tight schedule when doing his rounds.

'Tell matron that I shall attend shortly.' He turned away as if to dismiss the messenger.

Doctor Conrad took one look at Patricia, and declared loudly, 'Matron, this woman has syphilis! You took me away from my patients to attend a whore with syphilis? Who referred her here, where is the referral letter?'

Benjamin Conrad was a man who relished his position of power at the hospital, and he expected everyone, including the senior matron, to bow to his authority. Noreen had worked at the Barracks Hospital for far longer than any of the doctors including this pompous one. Noreen knew that she was the one who had the final say on patient care.

'Doctor, this woman attended the hospital with her daughter of her own volition, and I made the choice to admit her. She is my responsibility, and all that you are required to do is give me advice on how to treat her.'

The doctor's face turned bright red. He was not used to being spoken to in this manner, and certainly not by a woman. Blustering, he said, 'How dare you speak to me in this manner matron, and in front of the staff, I will not have it, I say, I will not. Now put this woman's clothes back on her and discharge her immediately. Send her to the dispensary, and tell them to give her some metallic mercury ointment. Now, do as I say!'

Under normal circumstances, Noreen would have followed the doctor's advice and done as she was told, but she didn't like Doctor Conrad. Now that she could see the condition of her patient, there would be no likelihood that she would comply with the doctor's orders and discharge her.

'I'm sorry doctor, but this patient is ill, and I will not put her out on the street in her condition. My job is to care for the sick, and this woman is sick. I don't care how she got sick, or what her profession is. I am not here to judge her, and nor should you. However, I will look after this patient because it is my job to do so. You may report me to the medical committee, and I will report you for failing your commitment to the Hippocratic oath. Now, instead of standing there blustering, just tell me how I may treat this patient!'

Noreen glared at Doctor Conrad, and was ready to give him some more of her vitriol at the first sign that he wanted to stand his ground. But, he had had enough of a tongue-lashing, and begrudgingly gave in to her wishes.

'Give the woman full body massages with metallic mercury paste, several times a day until the legions go down.' In a concession to Noreen, he asked Patricia, 'Where do you have pain?'

'All over me doc, me bones is aching, and so is me muscles! Can't ya give me something to stop it hurtin' doc?'

He didn't answer her directly, but turned to Noreen and said, 'Get the dispensary to make up some licorice powder, and mix it with a mild dose of laudanum. Keep her on that for several days, and give her metallic mercury massages three times a day for the next two weeks. Now I have wasted enough time with this patient matron; so she is under your care from here on. I don't expect to be interrupted during my rounds again, is that understood?'

Noreen was about to start on him again, but thought better of it, and she replied, 'Yes doctor.'

Kathleen Thomson was the duty nurse, and matron gave instructions to her. 'Nurse, please see that the dispensary mixes up the potions for this patient, and I will have young Brigid administer the metallic mercury to this patient during her shift each day. Please make a note for the night shift nurse, that the mercury paste is to be administered every eight hours until further notice.

'Brigid, nurse will show you how to rub the lotion into your patient. You must wear rubber gloves when using the mercury, and you must not handle it without wearing an operating gown over your uniform, and that must be changed after each massage session. You must also wear a facial mask when you come into contact with this patient. Is that understood?'

'Yes matron, and thank you for your help. I will look after this patient to the best of my ability.'

'I know that you will child, now I have other duties to attend to.' She looked at nurse Thomson and said, 'Please start the programme as soon as the potions are made up. Thank you, nurse.'

Noreen was about to leave, when she saw Mary sitting in the corner and went over to speak to her. 'You can go home now young lady.

'We will look after your mother, and we will do our best to make her well again. You can come and visit her at 2 pm and again at 7 pm, now go home.'

Mary looked down and she started to cry, but she said nothing. Matron asked, 'Whatever is the matter child? Your mother will get all the treatment that she needs here, and you have no need to worry. Now go on, say goodbye to your mother and go on home.'

Mary sobbed, 'I don't have nowhere ta go. We wos evicted from our room cause we couldn't pay the rent. I tried to earn some money when mummy got sick and couldn't work no more. I got a bun in the oven miss, and I can't earn no money until I get rid of it, or 'ave it.'

Noreen was taken aback with Mary's story. The nurse and Brigid had also heard, but went about attending to Patricia.

'Are you telling me that you are pregnant child, and that you have nowhere to live?'

'Yes ma'am.'

'How old are you girl?'

'I just turned 16 a few months ago ma'am.'

'Have you no family that you can stay with?'

'No ma'am, it's just me and mummy.'

She hesitated a minute, and Noreen asked, 'What is it child, what is it that you are not telling me?'

Mary looked at Noreen in a defiant manner, before saying; 'The landlord said that I could stay in the room for another week if I gave 'im a shag, but he's awful with his yeller teef and fat belly, and he smells, and I couldn't shag 'im cause I'd be sick.'

Noreen had dealt with a variety of people, and had heard all manner of stories during her long nursing career, but she had never dealt with a situation like this, and was now feeling slightly perplexed.

'How far are you gone with your pregnancy?'

'About fifteen or sixteen weeks I think, ma'am. Mummy wanted me ta get rid of it, but I didn't want to cause I knew a girl who got rid of one, and she died. Mummy said that I could sell it when it wos born. She knew somebody that bought babies, and she said we might even get ten quid for it if some rich people wanted a bub.'

Noreen was shocked at the simple honesty of the girl. But, now that she knew of the problem she was left with no alternative, but to do something about it.

'Have you and your mother eaten anything today child?'

'No ma'am, mummy was too sick ta eat, but I sure could use a morsel.'

'Nurse, could you please go to the kitchen, and ask the cook to bring some broth and bread now, please?

'Now, let's get some food into you girl, and then you can have a bath, and we will find something clean for you to wear while I think of what we can do.'

'Thank ya ma'am, but some food would be good, and now that you are looking after mummy I don't wanna be no further bother, so I will just eat and be on me way.'

'Don't talk nonsense girl, I might know of a place where you can stay. I will have to make some enquiries; so, you just sit there and eat something, and nurse Brigid will take you to the bathroom. Brigid, make sure that this girl gets some clean clothes and has a bath. Now I really have work to do.' Noreen went back to her office and penned a note to the hospital chaplain.

'*Father, I have a situation involving a young woman who is homeless and pregnant, and I seek some advice. Could you call in and see me at your earliest convenience when you next do your rounds.*'

She gave the note to an orderly, and asked him to immediately take it to the presbytery.

26.

In the Trenches

The smell of death from the decaying flesh of men and animals permeated throughout the trenches. Small tunnels burrowed into the walls, and sandbags were positioned at their entrances. Frogs and moss clung to the damp walls of the dugouts, while telephone cables criss-crossed the trench walls forcing the soldiers to bend down to avoid becoming entangled in them. Drowned field mice floated in the putrid water in the deep sump holes designed to hold the excess water at the bottom of the trenches.

Candles burning in jam tins were placed between the sandbags, and kerosene lamps were hung on nails on the cross-beams that held up the roof of the officers' quarters. The senior officers tried to preserve some form of normality and civility amongst the carnage and the mud. Some officers ordered that their shirts should still be washed, and they insisted on using scarce drinking water to keep themselves and their clothes clean, which created animosity among the troops.

The troops themselves were only interested in keeping dry and surviving. Not a day would pass without more troops being carried along the trenches because they could no longer stand. The water in the trenches ensured that the soldiers' boots were always wet, and many men fell prey to what was called trench foot where their feet would start to rot inside of their boots.

The boys had been at the front line for three days, and had only been subjected to the occasional volley of sniper shots, and a few shells fired at them from the Turkish cannons.

Each evening they were all issued with a tot of rum, but as the nights became colder even the rum couldn't warm them, and as the night drew down the rats came out.

A corporal moved along the trench doling out a dram of rum to each man. As he came across Jack and the others, he stopped and looked at Jack in the fading light. Jack stared back, and recognition finally dawned and he yelled, 'Brownie, Billy Brown how the devil are ya?' He grabbed his friend's hand and pumped it vigorously. 'Fancy runnin' into you way out 'ere. Geez, and I see that you already got a promotion!' Jack nodded at the stripe on his friend's uniform as he wore a grin across his face.

Corporal Bill Brown was tall, gangly and sported a mass of red curly hair. Jack and he had become friends when they had attended school together. They had occasionally crossed paths around Redfern, but the last time that they had seen each other was shortly after Jack had been left the fuel yard by Mr Johnson. Jack had been having a quiet drink at Thomson's pub, and mulling over his good fortune when Brownie had wandered in. Now, here he was doling out rum to the troops.

'Brownie, you know me brother?' Tom shook his hand. 'And these are me mates,' pointing at Fred, Des and Doughy.

Brownie shook each of their hands in turn and said, 'I must go and finish spilling this rum, but I'll be back and we can have a catch-up Jack. Now the officers, even lowly ones like me, are not supposed to socialise with the troops, but stuff the rules, if the captain don't like it then he can send me home.' They all smiled as Brownie said, 'Cheerio chaps, and if I don't see you later tonight, I'll see yer all tomorrow.' Then he disappeared along the trench.

Doughy was dozing in the darkness of a tunnel, when he felt something chewing on his legs. He slapped at the creature that then jumped onto Des. Doughy was beating his legs, and managed to wake the others. Someone called out, 'What are yer doing Doughy, fer Christ's sake can't ya keep still?'

'It was a bloody great rat, shit the thing was as big as a cat, and it was chewin' me boot.'

Des called back, 'Stop exaggerating, you was dreamin' now go back ta sleep an' shut up.'

Doughy had to have the final word and retorted, 'I hope the bloody thing sits on yer head, and when it does I'll tell ya you was dreaming.'

From along the tunnel, someone called, 'Shut up you blokes, some of us are tryin' to sleep.' After a few more grumbles, and the rearranging of their kitbags, they all settled back down.

The sounds of gunfire woke them, and the captain was blowing his whistle and yelling, 'Get up there on the rim, and fix your bayonets!' There was no time for stretching, or wiping sleep from their eyes as they all found a position behind the sandbags. The whistling of bullets overhead and the thuds of shots as they hit the protective wall of sandbags brought terror to their hearts. As Tom stood on an empty ammunition box to take up his position, he heard the clang a split second before his tin helmet was ripped from his head. He stumbled backwards before falling into the bottom of the wet trench. Jack had thought the worst as he dropped down to help his brother, but was relieved when Tom asked, 'Bloody hell, what was that?'

He gingerly felt his head, and much to his relief he found no wound. His helmet was sitting upside down in the water. He retrieved if, and looked at the hole that had appeared on the edge of its rim. The hole was as big as his finger, and if it had hit another inch to the right, he knew that he would have been dead.

The others were returning gunfire between gaps in the sandbags, and as Jack helped his brother to his feet, Tom tried to make light of his near miss. 'Well, I guess I'll hav'ta keep me tin hat now as a souvenir, just to show everybody what lousy shots the Turks are.'

Jack smiled, but the realisation of how close death lurked to all of them now struck him. He gave a shudder at the thought of having to tell his mother that his brother had been killed.

The shooting stopped as quickly as it had started. It was their first serious confrontation since they had arrived, and they were all immersed in their own thoughts.

Ammunition boxes were passed along the trench, so that magazines and bandoliers could be refilled. Des was the first to speak and then asked no one in particular, 'Geez is it always like that?'

'Like what?' someone asked. 'The shooting, it just started, no warning, nothin' and all them bullets whistlin' past like angry hornets. Is it like that every time?' Fred Schuman was rolling a smoke, and he answered the question. 'That was only a small skirmish; wait until they start with the big guns. All them poor bastards lying out there,' and he nodded his head in the direction of no-man's-land, 'were getting blown to bits. Christ knows how many bodies are out there now. We been killin' our share of the Turks, and they are in the same boat as us. Wait until you get fence duty, an' then you will see how bad it's been!'

'What's fence duty?' Jack asked.

'Out there,' Fred replied, and he pointed, 'in no-man's-land are miles of barbed wire, just rolls and rolls of it. We put it out, and they put it out.

'It's so you can't sneak over there in the middle of the night, or in the fog. They get some mighty thick fogs hereabouts, and you can't see two feet in front of you. If the wire weren't there, we could sneak over and get the bastards in their trenches, mind you, they could do the same to us. But it is also a trap; cause if you make it to the wire, you then hav'ta get under it to get through. The barbs get caught on your clothes, and you can't get out and then you just become a sittin' duck for them to shoot you. They also leave gaps in some places. If ya see a hole in the wire don't run towards it.'

'Why not?'

'Cause that is where they have the snipers positioned. They aim at the gaps in the wire, and they can shoot everybody who goes through it. So, both sides got the wire up, and the brass sends us out every now and then to repair it.' Then we all start usin' the big guns, and it all gets blown up again. My advice to you, is don't volunteer fer fence duty!'

They all fell silent, as they digested what Fred had told them.

Tom asked, 'Why have they just left all those blokes out in no-man's-land? Don't seem right, just to leave em there.'

Fred drew back on his smoke, and thought about the question. 'Dunno, really, I suppose there are just too many to bury, but our brass take their orders from the English Generals. We are just the colonials. They seem to think that if enough of us got over the top, then it don't matter how many get shot because some of us might make it to the Turks' side. It's all about guts and glory, for those pricks. They got no idea how hard it is for us ta go over the top when we all know that we are probably gunna die.' Fred was speaking louder now, as the emotion took hold.

'You wanna know what it was like, and why there were so many killed in the first few minutes the last time we went over the bags?' Fred didn't wait for an answer, but continued. 'They told us to make our way to the assembly trench. It must 'ave been half a mile long at least, maybe longer. We all stood there jammed together like beans in a tin, and we all stayed there for almost two hours, not knowing when the order would come.

'We weren't stupid; we knew that once you got up the ladder, you would hav'ta run like hell, cause we knew that the Turks were waitin' fer us. I seen grown men prayin', and I seen the look on their faces and in their eyes, and they knew that they weren't gunna see their home, or their families again. And I seen men, well boys really, writing notes in their pocket books to their family.

'We are not supposed to keep a diary, or record nuthin' as ya know, but some of the boys kept 'em anyway. We all knew that we was rooted. If you refused ter go over the top, the captain would threaten to shoot ya, and when ya did go up them ladders yer knew that your chances of livin' were slim. And all the while, them fat bastard generals were hidin' in the dugouts, with their clean shirts on, an sippin' brandy, while thousands of blokes was dyin'!'

His voice trailed away.

Fred stopped for a moment; he knew that he had said too much, and he was aware that he could be court martialled for criticising senior officers. But, he had seen too much, and he was tired; and he no longer cared what the brass thought, as he never expected to ever leave there.

'So, to answer your question, when the order finally came, some officer blew his whistle and that went down the line, and then there was whistles blowing everywhere, and we all started to climb the ladders. I was down the line a bit, and I was watchin' them all go over the top. Some didn't even get off the ladder. Bullets hittin' em, and some were fallin' back inta the trenches already dead. Shit, there was so much fuckin' noise. There was blokes yellin', whistles blowin', mortar shells explodin' all round, and on top of that them Turks had them machine guns chattering and spittin' out death. Jesus, I just kept runnin', and they just kept fallin' all round me. I could hear the bullets whizzing all over the place, and I tripped over some poor bastard. I could see that his face was all gone. I lay there for hours, and fired off a few shots, but there was no one ter shoot at. When it all stopped, I crawled back along with a few others that had survived.

'There was one poor bastard I came across, and his hand was blown off. It was just a bloody stump left on his arm. He was lying there, and moanin' when I got to him. I tried ter drag him back, but there was too many bodies. I couldn't pull him over the others, so I hadta leave him.

'Sometimes, if they are close to the trenches, we can drag em back. Then they bury them over behind the rest area. Jesus, I felt so bad about leavin' that poor devil that I decided to volunteer to be a stretcher-bearer.

'We go out in pairs after each skirmish. We take a stretcher with us, and try and bring some of them back; cause if we don't go out, the poor sods will die slowly, and alone. I got to the stage now where I don't care about dyin', cause when I do I will be with me mates, and cause I don't care, that makes me a good stretcher-bearer!'

Nobody had moved as Fred spoke. The honesty of his story had left them to ponder their own mortality.

Several hours later, the dispatch came along the communication trench, and was handed to the captain. It read,

A NAVAL BARRAGE WILL COMMENCE AT FIRST LIGHT ON THE MORNING OF 2ND SEPTEMBER '15.

HAVE TROOPS READY FOR ASSAULT ON TURKISH LINES IMMEDIATELY ON CESSATION OF SHELLING. SIGNED GENERAL COMMAND.

An officers' briefing was held, and the belief was that the barrage by the ships in the harbour would be a surprise to the Turks. After which, all available troops would cross no-man's-land, and engage the enemy in hand-to-hand combat.

The word went down the line like wildfire that a big operation was about to begin. The troops were not told of the details, but were to be prepared for battle in a little over twenty-four hours' time.

'Well, this is it, I suppose that we have to face the Turks at some point,' said Jack.

Tom was silent. He was still thinking of the battle story that Fred had told them. He wondered if after tomorrow, he would also be lying out in the mud in no-man's-land. It wasn't that he was afraid of dying, but his dreams of marrying Hannah were burning strongly within him. He knew that he would feel no pain. But, those that loved him would cry, and all that they would have left of him would be his photograph that would sit on a dusty mantelpiece.

The thought saddened him, and he knew that he should write a letter to both his mother and to Hannah.

***

Des had been quiet all day, and Doughy had noticed. 'What's on yer mind? Are ya worried about tomorrow? Cause if yer are, there is nothin' that we can do except fight, an if we get it, then so be it!'

Des thought about what his friend had said, and he partly agreed with him, but he was thinking of his father.

He was an only child, and his mother had died shortly after they had arrived in Australia. He could only imagine the pain that his death would cause him. What would he think, and what would he do, when the telegram from the army arrived, and told him that his son was dead?

His father, who didn't want him to go to war, but in the end, had given him his blessing. Des remembered, how he had almost begged his father to sign the consent form that the army required a parent to sign if the son was under twenty-one. He mused that he was glad that he didn't have a woman in his life, but then he thought of Brigid. It had never crossed his mind that one day he might love her. He smiled as he remembered how headstrong she was. It crossed his mind that if he were to marry, then she would be the sort of girl that he would choose.

Tom rested his back against the trench wall, and used the bottom of an ammunition box as his desk. He had no ink and would write his letter in pencil. He had kept a folded sheet of plain paper in his top pocket so that he could write to Hannah when the need arose. He pondered on what to say and how to express his true feelings when this might be the last letter that he would ever write.

September 1915.
Somewhere in Turkey

My Dearest Hani,

I have recently received your most welcome letter, and as I opened it, the smell of your lavender powder wafted to my nostrils. I closed my eyes, and for a moment you were standing near to me, and I was home again.

We have been here now on the front line for several days, and already the weather has changed. Hardly a day passes without rain, and yesterday it was torrential, so much so that the trench that we are in was almost knee deep in water. Everything is soaking wet, including our kit and blankets.

I must say, Hani, that it is a most miserable place where we are. What with the cold wind blowing incessantly, I long for the warm weather of home. What we are also missing is some good tucker. We have no facilities to cook any food, not that we have any food to cook.

I will tell you of what our diet consists of here in the front-line trench. For breakfast, we have a Billy of tea together with a hard biscuit, so hard that one needs to dunk them in our tea for several minutes to soften them up. For lunch, we have another Billy of black tea, and for dinner, we have a bully beef stew concoction that comes in a tin, and if we are fortunate, we may share a half loaf of bread that has been cooked behind the trench area and brought up to us.

Many of the chaps are sick, due to the unhygienic conditions and poor sanitation, and I suppose our poor diet doesn't help. I would love an apple or two, or even some fresh vegetables would be nice. The place is full of rats, and I must say that I have never seen such big ones. Some would have to be the size of rabbits, and they show no fear of us and they really are huge. I do not exaggerate Hani. I do not wish to elaborate on what they eat, but it turns one's stomach if we dwell on it.

We have no idea of how long we will be stationed here, but I fear that the winter will not be pleasant. If you have some spare time, we could use some woollen mittens or gloves and possibly scarves. The wind whistling through our trenches is a lazy one as it goes right through us. It doesn't help that our clothes have always been damp since we have arrived.

It pleased me to read that you had revisited our secret place and I would have no objection to us moving to the country when this blessed war is over. Did you have a location in mind, or should we just go to wherever the wind blows us? I think that I should like to own a small farm and have some animals.

The noise here is horrific when the guns go off, and oh, how I would love to have a bath and change into some clean, dry clothes, not that we have any. We have been told that if we do stretcher duty, that is, taking the wounded down to the temporary field hospital, which is on the beach, then we could have a quick, if cold, dip in the water.

I spoke with a couple of chaps who have been doing stretcher duty, and I believe it to be a most arduous task. The track to the beach is barely a goat track, and so steep and treacherous that two chaps have to carry the stretchers sideways so as not to tip the poor sick chap off it, as they make their way down to the sea. But I should like to volunteer to do it at least once, soon, just so that I could wash the mud and grime away.

Could you say hello to Mother for Jack and I? I must go now, as I have to find the chaplain to give him this letter.

Hani, please know that I love you dearly, and if I should not come back to you, please do not spend your life grieving over me, for we shared our love for a brief time, and I could ask for no more.

Forever yours,

Tommy.

The chaplain made his way along the mud-filled trenches. He held a bundle of letters and a small missal. He stopped, and collected letters as he spoke with those who needed encouragement, and he gave them a blessing. A few soldiers had asked for him to hear their confession, but all that he could offer was to say, 'If you ask God to forgive you for your past indiscretions then he will.' Along with, 'We are all God's children, and some of you will sit with him in his kingdom shortly, and that will be his will. So, make your peace with him tonight, and pray for his forgiveness for your past misdeeds.'

He then moved along the trench.

They looked at each other after he had left, and Fred was the first to speak, 'Well, he was a barrel of laughs, I wonder if he's cheering all the boys up that way?' That brought a few smiles, but Des was thinking out loud when he said, 'I wonder if he knows something about tomorrow that we don't. The brass wouldn't send 'im down here to cheer us up like that, unless they thought that it was gunna be bad.'

As the darkness enveloped them, most settled down in their damp dugouts to a restless night. A match would flare in the darkness as another lit a smoke, too nervous to sleep. At 5 am the junior officers made their way through the trenches and woke those sleeping.

'No lights anywhere chaps, and that means no smoking either, and keep your voices down, we don't want the Turks hearing us. In approximately one hour's time, our ships in the harbour will unleash a barrage on the Turkish lines. When it stops, we will be over the top.

'Also, ensure that your water bottles are full and carry a hard biscuit or two, because we don't know how long this skirmish will last. Good luck lads!'

The air was still and cold, as an officer passed through the trenches and offered each man a tot of rum to warm their frozen bodies. They stood with wet feet and damp clothes, and now as they bunched together in the darkness, each was alone with their thoughts.

Some were pleased that the big guns from the ships would soften up the enemy, but most couldn't help feeling that this might be their last morning on earth. The four of them stood close together, and Tom whispered to his brother, 'Are ya scared?'

'I'd be a liar if I said no, but we will do our best and if our time is up then so be it. If ya lose me tell Mother that I was thinking of her, and if I get it then you can have me fuel yard and me bank account. Make sure Ma has enough ta live on though, and the rest is yours!'

'Don't talk like that! Your not gunna die, cause ya promised Mum that you would look after me. I don't mind sayin' that I'm shit-scared! I'm gunna run as fast as me legs will go, but I dunno what I'll do if I hafta kill a Turk with me bayonet.'

'Well ya stabbed enough straw dummies during yer trainin', so if ya get close enough to a Turk then think of him as a straw dummy! Hopefully, the big guns will blow 'em to smithereens before we get to their trenches!'

Doughy was standing beside Tom, and had heard the conversation, and he nudged Des, 'I writ a letter to me Sarah yesterday, but I didn't give it to the chaplain to post. Dunno why, but I didn't. Now listen mate, I got a bad feelin' in me guts, and I want yer to do me a favour if I don't make it today.' Des was staring at his friend, but couldn't see his face, and he whispered, 'Don't talk like that!'

But Doughy continued, 'Shut up, and listen to me will ya? I been sending most of me pay to Sarah, but I got a few quid stashed in me kit. Now, if I don't make it back I want ya to go and see Sarah for me, I left the address with the letter and me money. Now I didn't tell yer this, but she only came out 'ere 'cause I wanted to. I know that she would like ta go back 'ome. And because we are married, she will get the wider's pension if I cop it. Tell her to use the money I got to get a one-way passage back 'ome. Will ya do that fer me?'

'Listen you stupid bastard, yer not gunna die today, or any other day soon, so stop talkin' like that. But if it makes yer feel better, and somethin' does happen to ya, I will go and see your Sarah and do what yer asked, but I'm tellin' ya, nothin' is gunna happen to you, now get that into yer stupid Irish head!'

They spotted Corporal Brown making his way along the trench. He stood over six feet tall and towered over most of the others. He gave them all a nod and whispered; 'If we hafta do this, then I thought that I should be with you blokes when we go over the bags. You know that I was the best runner at school Jack, so when we are up there,' and he nodded to the top of the trench, 'folla me, and run like hell, you got that?' And they all nodded.

They were stamping their feet, and banging their hands together to try and get some circulation through their frozen bodies. When they spoke, their warm breath swirled in small clouds of wispy mist in the cold air. To the east, the darkness was beginning to fade. As they looked towards the lightening sky, they heard the first boom from the ship's cannon somewhere down in the harbour.

A shell arced across the sky, spewing up a mountain of dirt and rocks to produce another crater in the earth.

The first was quickly followed by a second, and then a third until the booms and explosions became one. The shells were exploding in all directions, and dirt and mud rained down on those sheltering within the trenches. Explosion after explosion rearranged the landscape, and as the shelling stopped the silence was eerie. But the silence only lasted moments, before the whistles blew, and the shouts rang out.

'Over the top lads, quickly, get up those ladders and over the bags.'

Two thousand men scrambled out of the trenches to cross the decimated fields. At first, only a few shots rang out from the Turkish lines, but then their machine guns started chattering. Soldiers were falling, but many had already made it across the churned-up fields, and were in mortal combat with their enemies. The Turkish mortar shells were exploding, and exacting a high toll on the remaining soldiers that were still running towards them.

The four of them had initially stuck close to each other, but had become separated as they had ducked and weaved their way towards the enemy lines. They could not keep up with Brownie who had surged ahead of them.

Doughy and the others had all spread out before falling to the ground to seek shelter in the muddy craters. The Maxim guns were spitting out tongues of flame until their barrels glowed red, while the spent bullets kicked up spurts of dirt across the ridges. Mingled among the explosions, would be the occasional cry of pain as another soldier fell. But most of those hit by the flying shrapnel and bullets were already mortally wounded, or dead before they silently fell to the ground.

Tom was lying face down in the mud, having tripped over a body and landed in a crater. He looked around, and was horrified to see parts of decaying corpses all around him. He couldn't see Jack, or the others, but there were frequent flashes of gunfire all around him. He crawled to the rim of the crater, and peered over the edge. He was only twenty feet from the enemy lines, and he could see the gaps in the enemy trenches where the roof had been blown away.

He looked in horror at the mutilated remains of what were once Turkish soldiers. The heavy shrapnel had torn limbs, and heads, and legs from those that had been sheltering below the roof of their trenches, and it was now a scene from hell.

As Tom lay in the crater, enemy mortar shells were exploding all around him. With each explosion coming nearer to him, so did the revulsion. Decaying bodies and body parts that had been lying in no-man's-land for weeks were now black and swollen, and were being pulverised further. As the smell of cannon smoke mixed with burnt and rotting flesh filled his nostrils, he had to fight the urge to vomit.

He sank lower into the crater as the mortar shells came closer, but then a round exploded thirty feet from where he lay. Tom heard the explosion, an instant before the darkness enveloped him.

A hundred yards away, Jack and Des had almost made it to the enemy trenches, but the withering machine-gun fire had forced them to take cover in a muddy culvert. Ten thousand bullets a minute were whistling death to anyone still standing. Corporal Billy Brown had led the futile charge from the trench, and he ran like a man possessed. With his rifle at waist height, and with the bayonet pointing forward and glinting in the gloom of smoke and drizzle he was looking for someone to engage with. But, a Turkish sniper held a bead on him, and the bullets slammed into his chest in quick succession.

Jack watched in horror, as his mate danced a slow, grotesque dance of death as the bullets tore the life from him. With his legs still in forward motion, they buckled beneath him.

Jack lay in the culvert. The others were with him, but at that moment he was alone with his thoughts. He was thinking of his hometown friend, and how he had just seen him killed, and he was having trouble coming to terms with what he had just witnessed. Billy was now lying somewhere above the ditch that they were in. Des was calling out to him, 'Jack, Jack are yer orr right. Jack, can ya hear me?'

Jack could hear him, but his mind was in another place, 'Yeah, I'm orright, but they got Brownie. Them bastards got him, geez, I can't forget the look on his face, the poor bastard!'

'Jack, have ya seen Tom? He ain't 'ere.' The question turned Jack's thoughts away from Billy, and he was trying to think of where he had last seen him.

'No, I dunno where he is, we got separated.' He was hoping that Tom was still alive and not lying dead like Brownie, but at that moment, there was nothing that any of them could do as another salvo came from the Turkish lines.

At least fifty men were sheltering in the culvert, and as the explosions drew nearer to them, Fred crawled across to where Jack lay half buried in mud. They were protected from the gunfire by the lip of the culvert, but the shellfire was so intense that if any of them lifted their heads it would guarantee their instant death.

'How yer doin' mate?'

'Been better, would rather be lying on the beach at Bondi drinkin' beer.' He gave a wry grin.

'Geez, I can't stop thinkin' about poor Brownie. Bloody hell mate, I feel bad about him. We can't just leave him there like the others to get blown ter smithereens. When all the damn shootin's over I want to come back and get him. Will yer help me, Fred?'

Fred hesitated for a moment, before saying, 'Sure mate, we will come and get 'im after all this bloody racket stops. That is, if we are still around, and we don't end up the same as him. But the first thing that we hafta do is try and find yer brother!'

He didn't elaborate, but both of them were thinking the same thing, hoping that Tom was alive, but sure that he wasn't.

They lay in the cold mud as the Turkish artillery kept pounding their position. The noise was incessant, and as the mortar shells grew closer, flying clods of dirt were hitting the group. Some were being slowly buried as the dirt and mud rained down. They were all terrified, and expected to be killed at any moment. There was no chance of returning fire such was the intensity of the bombardment. Fred was looking back over his shoulder as the explosions got closer, and he yelled at Jack and those nearest to him, 'We need to get outer 'ere.' Jack was already thinking of making a run, but his legs were frozen. He knew that he would need to get his circulation back before he would be able to stand, let alone run.

The shell landed on the rim of the culvert where they all lay huddled. First came the flash followed by the explosion. Three soldiers were instantly blown to bits. The shards of steel from the fragmentation bombs mutilated their bodies and stripped their clothes from them, and they now lay lifeless and limbless like animals in a slaughter yard.

Jack looked across the crater, and viewed the carnage. He was not a religious man and usually only went to Mass under sufferance from his mother, but he buried his face in the mud and whispered, 'I don't want to die like this God!'

Then everything fell silent. They lay in the mud, among the mutilated bodies, and the decimated remains of those that had died there weeks earlier.

The stench was overwhelming. Fred was the first to speak, 'Time for us ter bugger off outta 'ere.' As they extracted themselves from the putrid mud they heard the moaning.

Clive Patterson had arrived in Turkey at the same time as Jack and the others. He was a quiet boy, who had mainly kept to himself on the trip over. He had told them that he had wanted to be a newspaper reporter. He explained to them that he had just started working as a telegram boy at the *Telegraph* newspaper in Sydney two months before the call-up had begun.

He had been secretly keeping a diary, and he had told those that were bunked near him that he would be able to give a first-hand account of the war when he returned home. He had hoped that if he wrote a good enough article, then the editor might promote him to being a cub reporter. While the others had whiled away the hours on the ship playing cards and quoits, Clive had been scribbling in his notebook.

Fred crawled over to Clive, and took a look at him. His foot was covered in blood, and even though he still wore his boot, they could see that his foot was shattered. Jack could see that it would be impossible for him to walk, let alone run back to their trenches, and he asked him, 'Are ya hit anywhere else mate?'

Clive was barely conscious, but managed to shake his head. They were all crouched down trying to decide on how they could get back to their own lines without being killed, but now, they also needed to figure out how they could take Clive with them.

The guns and mortars remained silent, and they all hoped that they would stay quiet long enough for them to get back to safety. Jack spoke first, 'Listen Fred, we hafta get outer 'ere, and I'm used ter lumpin' coal sacks, so I need ya to cover me arse. I'll carry Clive on me back fer as far as I can, and you watch out fer anyone behind us, orright?'

'Orright, I'll go over the top first, and if no one shoots at me, you come up!'

Jack looked at the side of the culvert, which was now more of a crater. He saw how difficult it was going to be for the others to climb out because of the angle of the hole and the mud. He spoke to Clive.

'Listen, mate, I'm gunna carry you on me back. But, we won't be able ta climb out with you on me back, so me and Fred are gunna drag ya up the side of the crater.

'When we get to the top, you're gunna slide onta me back, and put ya arms around me neck and hang on.

'I know that yer foot's buggered, but yer gunna hafta get on me back even though it's gunna hurt like blazers, orright?'

Clive, pale and in shock, could barely speak, but he managed to give a nod of his head. The last of the group had disappeared from view having negotiated the rim of the crater, and now there were only the three of them left.

They rolled Clive onto his back, and with Fred on one side and Jack on the other they put a hand each under each of his armpits and slowly dragged him along. As his broken foot dragged along the ground Clive gave out moans of despair. When they finally reached the top and there was still no gunfire, Jack squatted down, but then stopped. He was thinking about Brownie, and he wanted to make sure that when they came back, they would have some idea where to look for him.

'Whatsa matter, what are yer waitin' for?' Fred asked.

Jack replied, 'I hafta find Brownie before we leave here, cause we will never find him in this mess after we go!'

Fred thought for a moment before saying, 'I was on yer left, and behind ya, and he was on yer right.'

He stopped talking, as he thought about where he had seen Brownie go down and then he said, 'Listen! We only managed to get here when the shootin' started, so he has ter be only a couple of hundred feet behind us, over that way,' he said, pointing. Sporadic gunfire could still be heard in the distance and Fred spoke again, 'I'm gunna go back over there,' pointing again, 'you stay 'ere with the young fella, and I'll go an' find him.'

Before Jack could say anything, Fred had gone. Crouching low, Fred stopped and examined a body, and then another. For what seemed like an eternity Jack watched his friend stumble from corpse to corpse. Then as Fred stopped again, he turned and gave a wave pointing downwards with his hand. Fred looked at Brownie. His chest had been ripped open, and his uniform was shredded and torn by the hail of bullets that had snuffed the life from his young body. His dead, staring eyes were still portraying the shock of the first bullet that had struck him. His rifle, with the bayonet still attached, lay a few feet away, along with his tin helmet that had fallen off as his body had hit the ground. Fred didn't dwell on thinking about him, but picked up Brownie's rifle and forced the bayonet into the soft ground before picking up his helmet and sitting it on the butt.

The marker stood out starkly amongst the carnage, but providing another barrage of shellfire didn't occur they would be able to come straight back and get him.

Fred helped Clive onto Jack's back. He then crouched down and faced the enemy trenches looking for any sign of a sniper as Jack gave a grunt, and stood up with Clive barely able to keep his arms around Jack's neck. As Jack stumbled forward, Fred whispered, 'I'll stay 'ere until ya get 'im back to the trench, now bugger off.'

Jack carried his load through the mutilated bodies, but couldn't help but tread upon some such was the carnage. Several soldiers had sprung from the trenches as they watched Jack carrying his wounded mate and took his load. As they lowered Clive into the safety of the trench, Jack yelled at a stretcher-bearer who was nearby. 'Help me mate, I hafta go back'. The stretcher-bearer appeared overwhelmed by the destruction all around and said, 'What are you doin'? Get in the trench man, you can't help any of them still out there.'

Jack could see the despair in his haunted eyes and growled, 'Give me the bloody stretcher,' and not waiting for a response took it without resistance. He ran across the field of dead men to where Fred was still crouching. They laid the stretcher alongside Brownie, and they rolled him onto it. Both men lifted the stretcher. Their back muscles tensed, expecting a sniper's bullet to strike them at any moment. For what seemed like an eternity they gingerly stepped over the shattered remains of men who they had both shared their trench with less than an hour earlier.

Corporal Billy Brown was carried to the field behind the reserve trenches and buried along with several hundred others in a mass grave. Small crosses, made with wood from ammunition boxes, marked their final resting places.

※※※

Tom opened his eyes, and for a moment wondered where he was, but as the fog in his mind cleared, he realised that he must have been knocked out. He had no idea how long he had been asleep. He was afraid to move in case he had another injury, but as the minutes ticked by, he felt no pain other than for the thumping in his head. He had trouble moving as large clods of dirt had fallen on him, and he lay half buried in the mud. He struggled to free himself, and then he stopped and listened. He could see movement, as others that had been buried also struggled to free themselves from the mud. He slowly lifted his head above the crater rim.

Giant mounds of dirt surrounded him, and he felt as though he was lying among large rabbit burrows. He crawled between the mounds until he could finally see the direction that he needed to crawl. All around him lay the blackened and pulverised remains of men and farm animals. His mind was screaming, and the sights that confronted him made him think that he had passed through the gates of hell. He wanted to stand up and run toward the safety of the trenches, but he knew that if he did, he would surely make a target of himself to a sniper.

He crawled across the field of death, and rolled over the sandbags to drop down into the trench below.

He looked around and saw a few familiar faces, but their eyes were dull and weary, and their faces wore the haunted looks of despair. The crowded trench that he had left several hours earlier was now eerily quiet. The soldiers who had made it back safely were all reflecting on their fallen mates. They pondered on how they had survived and the others didn't. Tom stumbled back to his dugout hoping upon hope to find his brother there. He was thinking the worst when he heard Jack shout.

'Tommy, Tommy you little bastard, I figured that you was dead. Geez, I was so worried about ya.' Jack was smiling, and grabbed his brother's hand and shook it vigorously.

'I'm so glad to see ya brother.' But then his tone took on a serious note, 'Look at ya, you look worse than we do, did ya get buried or somethin'?'

Tom relayed his story. Fred had managed to obtain a bucket of water and having cleaned himself in it offered it to Tom. The mud came off, but the horror and the images remained.

Stretcher-bearers were now carrying back the wounded and the maimed from across the now quiet battlefield. Some were missing legs, and others held onto the stumps of what were once hands. Others wore bloodied wounds across chests and faces. Moaning and the occasional scream could be heard as the field medics injected the wounded with morphine to help deaden their pain. Sometimes, they would deliberately inject a lethal dose into a dying man as an act of mercy. The alternative was to prolong the life and the pain of a fatally injured man's suffering.

They were all resting after sharing their tobacco. The men were mostly quiet when a corporal arrived with his note board. He was doing a roll call, as the brass had wanted to know how many casualties there had been from the last skirmish. He was aware that their losses had been heavy because the front-line trench was no longer crowded as it had been. However, the paperwork still had to be done, and he called out, 'Right men, when I call out your name yell out, "Here sir". If I call out a name, and you know that he is back, but was wounded tell me, so that I can check the hospital records.'

He called out the names on his list in alphabetical order. Sometimes there would be a response, but at other times there was only an uncomfortable silence, as a dozen names would be called before he received another, '*Here sir*' that was then followed by further silence.

27.

Reunion

Hannah had not read a newspaper for over a week. She really didn't like to read them at all. The news was always about battles that had been fought and lost, or about heroic actions that had resulted in numerous deaths.

Claire was sewing in the parlour when Hannah came in. 'I think that I shall go into the city today, Aunt Claire, I just want to do something different. Do you think that we could go to the emporium? I'm sorry Aunt Claire, I had assumed that you would come with me, will you?'

'Yes child, we could go and see what they have. We haven't been there for quite a while, and they might have some new material. I might even buy us a Devonshire tea. Give me a moment to change my dress, and while I'm doing that you might ask Doris if we can pick up anything for her while we are out.'

Doris was boiling her bed sheets. Thursday was always washday for her, and by the time that she had lit the fire under the copper and boiled the water to wash her clothes, the day was half gone.

'Hello luvvy, what brings you here?'

'Hello Doris, we are going into the city, and Aunt Claire wants to know if there is anything that we can pick up for you.'

'Where are you going luvvy?'

'I'm going to the army place to pick up Tommy's pay, and then we are going to the emporium.

'We thought that we might look for some material, something warm so that we can make some scarves for the boys.'

Doris smiled and said, 'I sent them a fruitcake last week, so I could use another tin if they are not too dear. Mr Lukin at the general store sells round ones for two bob. That's what I paid last week, so if they are any cheaper at the emporium then you can get me a couple otherwise I don't need anything else thanks luvvy. Tell Claire to come around for a cuppa when you get back.'

'I will Doris, goodbye.'

They caught the tram down George Street, and walked the two blocks to the army office and signed for Tom's pay. Claire whispered to Hannah, 'Have you noticed how many ladies are dressed in black? I'm sure that there weren't that many the last time that we came into the city!'

Hannah had noticed, but wasn't going to say anything, but now that Claire had mentioned it there was no point in ignoring it.

'Aunt Claire, not a day goes by without me worrying about Tommy and Jack. Sometimes I think that I shall go mad with worry. I think about Doris, and how she would cope if either, or God forbid, both of them got killed over there. I know that I should not think about the "what ifs", you have told me that so many times, but when I see all of these ladies wearing black it bothers me. I can't help wondering how bad it must be over there.'

Claire could see how her niece was getting upset and said, 'Let's go and have a look at the material. Jack wrote that it was dreadfully cold over there, so we will make something nice and warm for them to wear.'

As they approached the emporium lift, Hannah heard a familiar voice calling her, 'Hannah, wait, Hannah!' They both turned, and Hannah smiled as she recognised Brigid. They embraced, and Hannah said, 'Why Brigid, I haven't seen you for ages, where have you been?'

'I haven't seen you because I'm working at the Barracks Hospital. I got a job there as a nurse's assistant almost a year ago, and I live in the nurses' house next door to the hospital.'

Hannah asked, 'What are you doing here?'

'It's my day off, and I have to buy some white stockings. So, I thought that as I have been working so hard I would do some window-shopping before I went home to see Mother. I haven't seen her for a month, and I know that she misses me to help with the boys. But, I love my job even though the hours are long, and I don't get paid very much.'

Claire interrupted with, 'Hello Brigid, we are just going upstairs to have a Devonshire tea, would you like to join us?'

'Thank you, Mrs Townsend, yes, that'd be nice.' They made their way to the tearooms on the third floor. After placing their order, Brigid asked, 'How are the boys going Hannah? I haven't heard any news at all other than what we read in the papers, and some of those stories are dreadful!'

'We have received a few letters from them, but what with them always moving from place to place, it sometimes takes months before we get a reply. The last one that we received said that they were somewhere in Turkey, and that it was freezing. That's why we came here today. We want to buy some warm material to make them some scarves!'

Brigid wore a frown. 'They are in Turkey?' she asked, as though it was a complete surprise. 'Isn't that the place where all those poor chaps were killed, because some general got the landing place mixed up?'

Hannah replied, 'Yes, but I think that they were referring to the first lot that went over there. I read that article too, but I couldn't read it all because it upset me too much. But our boys went in the second, or third battalions, I can't remember, but from their letters I don't imagine that it was as bad as what the papers told us about the first landing. I hope not anyway.' Brigid looked uncomfortable before saying, 'May I ask you something?'

'Of course, you can, what is it?'

'Has there been any word from Des, are they still all together? I hadn't heard anything from him since before he left with Tom and Jack. Mind you, I didn't ask him to write to me, and it would be a little forward of me to write to him, don't you think? After all, it's not like we were engaged, or anything like that.'

'Why Brigid Blake, are you in love with him?' Hannah teasingly asked.

Brigid blushed, and she lowered her eyes before saying, 'No, I'm not in love with him, but I like him. I liked being around him, and I suppose that in some ways I miss him.'

The waitress arrived, and placed the teacups and napkins in front of them. Brigid waited until she had finished before continuing. 'I have thought about him often since he left, and I was just wondering how he was, that's all.'

Claire had been listening as she poured the tea and said, 'Why don't you just write to him. We have the army address where you can send the letters to, and we can give it to you.

'I'm sure that he would love to hear from you; I don't imagine that he gets much mail at all. I don't know if his father has written to him, and even if he did, I don't know of anyone else who would send him a letter.

'There was a notice in the church foyer recently. The lady's auxiliary brigade suggested that people should write to our soldiers like a pen pal. So, as you know Des, you could just send him a letter and tell him what you are doing. You could talk about the things that you used to do. I'm sure that he will write back to you, now have a scone!'

Hannah asked, 'Tell me about working at the hospital, is it interesting, and how long will it be before you are a proper nurse?'

'I have to be a nurse's aide for twelve months before I can become a junior nurse. So, I hope to sit for my exams shortly. But Matron is very kind, and she helps me a lot. She knows that I am really interested in hospital work, and she has been giving me lots of books to read on medicine and other stuff. You know that it was Des that I have to thank for me getting this job!'

Hannah asked, 'Why, what did he do?'

Brigid told them about the conversation that she had had with Des about women doctors.

'So, it was his suggestion that led me to the hospital to ask about what I should do to become a doctor. So here I am, almost a proper nurse. I was hoping to work on a hospital ship, but Matron said that they were only looking for experienced nurses to work on them, and besides that, she said that I was too young.'

'So, tell us, what do you do, do you actually look after the patients, or is it just cleaning and stuff like that?'

'At first, it was just cleaning bedpans and bathing people, but over the last couple of months, I have been given a couple of patients to look after. Do you want to hear about this lady that I have been nursing?'

'Yes, do tell,' said Hannah as she layered jam and cream onto another scone.

'Well, this lady and her daughter turned up at the hospital one day, and the woman was very sick. She had these dreadful sores all over her. Matron had a big row with the head doctor because he didn't want the hospital to look after her. Anyway, matron won the argument. Then she told me that I was in charge of looking after the sick lady, but I have to put this cream all over her body every day. The stuff smells dreadful, and I have to wear gloves when I'm touching her.'

'So, did she get better?' asked Claire.

'Oh no, I think that she is getting worse, in fact,' Brigid looked around before lowering her voice, 'I think that she might die, because yesterday when I was rubbing on the metallic mercury, that's what it is called, her teeth and her hair started to fall out, and her skin has gone all yellow. She looks worse now than when she came to the hospital.'

Brigid finished her tea before saying; 'I must go now, as I need to see mother and my brothers before I have to be back at the hospital. Thank you for the tea, Mrs Townsend.'

'You're welcome Brigid, and do write to your Des, I'm sure that he would love to hear from you. After you have seen your mother, call in and see Mrs Fields before you go back to the hospital. Ask her for the army address for where to send the letters.'

'I will Mrs Townsend. Goodbye Hannah, and I will try to see you next month when I have my next day off.'

'She is such a lovely girl Hannah, I do hope that she writes to Des, I think that they would be so suited to each other, don't you?'

'Yes, I do Aunt, but on the other hand, I think of how she would feel if she starts writing to him and then something happens to him. I don't know if it is the right time to try and start a relationship, considering how bleak the future looks.'

Claire looked at her niece, and tried to read her face. She had to ask her, 'Is that how you are feeling about Tommy?'

'I don't know Aunt Claire, I still love him I really do, but our lives are on hold, not just ours, but all of us who are feeling insecure about what tomorrow holds. What would I do if Tommy were killed? I hate myself for thinking about it, but I can't help it. The papers keep saying that thousands and thousands have been killed, and nobody knows how long the war will last.'

Claire could see that her niece was becoming upset again, and she changed the subject, but not before saying, 'I know what you are trying to say child, but even if the war was over, none of us has a crystal ball to know where our future lies. Look at poor Doris, and how her husband went to work one day and never returned.

'You cannot spend your days worrying about what might happen. The only advice that I can give to you child is to stay positive, and always look to the future. There will always be black storm clouds gathering on the horizon as we travel through life. But, it is up to each of us to learn how to skirt around them. Even if life throws you into the middle of those storm clouds, then you must learn how to come through them. I hope that helps you darling, and now lets's go and look at some material.'

They wandered through the emporium, and looked at the material and the latest furnishings. Hannah said, 'I thought that I should start collecting things for my glory box Aunt Claire, so I think that I should start making curtains and towels and things. Oh, and I might make us a quilt.'

Claire smiled at her niece and replied, 'By all means make yourself a quilt for your bed, but the first thing that you will have in your trousseau will be my wedding dress. Now, as a present I will get Mr Carney to make you a big chest to hold your dowry. Now don't argue with me, that's what I'm going to do! We can go over to his workshop in the morning, and he can show us some of his designs.'

'Oh, Aunt Claire, how very kind of you, but I'm sure that it will be much too expensive for us to buy. Why don't I just store my things at Doris's? I can stack them all on Tommy's bed, I'm sure that she wouldn't mind.

'Now, I don't want to hear another word about it young lady. You can busy yourself with getting all of your linen and towels and things together, but you will have a box to store it all in. Now I think that we have spent enough today, so let's go home.'

28.

Mary

Father Peter Aldridge read the note from Noreen, and decided that he would see her after he had conducted a special funeral service in the city.

The Bishop had suggested that a memorial service should be held for all of the soldiers that would not be returning from the war. He wanted the families of the fallen soldiers to have some form of closure, and he had arranged for a public funeral service to be held where all denominations would be welcome.

The newspapers had been giving updates on every battle that had played out in Europe. With each new publication, the casualty list grew longer. He was mindful that last Saturday's edition had screamed to the populace:

25,000 LIVES LOST in EUROPEAN WAR.

Buried within the article was a paragraph that mentioned that out of the thousands of casualties over half of them were from Australia and New Zealand. The paper had also made the point that a significant portion of those casualties was from New South Wales.

The Bishop had been informed that political dignitaries and government officials would also be in attendance. So, what was originally going to be a small service for grieving families would now become a major church function at Saint Mary's Cathedral.

The Cathedral had filled up quickly, and the choir had sung sombre tunes while many cried discreetly.

When the service was concluded, the church officials and the politicians had mingled as they had a pleasant afternoon tea on the church grounds. While the bereaved families went back to their lonely lives.

It was late in the afternoon by the time that the Vicar arrived at the hospital. A nurse greeted him, 'Good afternoon Vicar, whom do you wish to see?'

The vicar was a regular visitor at the hospital, and he usually arrived when it was time to perform the last rites on a dying patient.

'I would like to see Matron Emmitt, if you don't mind nurse. I believe that she is expecting me.'

'Please wait here Vicar, and I will go and find her for you.'

Shortly after the nurse returned and said, 'Matron will see you now Vicar, if you care to go to her office.' He made his way upstairs and greeted Noreen as an old friend.

'Good afternoon Noreen. I'm sorry that I couldn't get here any sooner, but I had a service to conduct for the families of the fallen. Now, what seems to be the problem?'

'Peter, I have a young woman downstairs whose mother has been admitted as a patient. She is barely 16, and she tells me that she is about three months pregnant. She has no family, other than her mother. Her mother is a prostitute, and she has a very severe case of syphilis. I do have concerns that she may not survive, but my immediate problem is the welfare of the girl! She has no money, and as things stand now, I don't believe that she would be capable of looking after a child on her own. I would appreciate some advice from you on what would be the best course of action for me to take.'

'She has no other family you say?'

'That's correct Peter, but if I let her go then I would hold grave fears not only for her, but for the unborn child as well.'

The vicar was silent for a moment before saying, 'I think that the best course that we could take with the child is if we send her to the nuns. I know Mother Superior at the Mary Magdalene convent in Surrey Hills. They have a commercial laundry, and they take in young women with loose morals along with pregnant ones. They can give her shelter, and she can work in the laundry and pay for her keep. They do the laundry for the army barracks, and for a few city hotels. I think that they do the laundry for the prison as well. They will look after her, and when she has her child they can find it a good Christian home. Would you like me to organise her transfer Noreen?'

Noreen thought for a moment before asking, 'Will the child be allowed any freedom; will she be allowed to visit her mother?

'I can see that she is very close to her, and if her mother does survive then I would expect that she would be an in-patient for a considerable time. I could only agree to her living with the nuns as long as she was free to come and go, after all, she isn't a prisoner!'

'Noreen, I have known Sister Margaret for many years. And while I concede that she believes in strong discipline, and is tough on her charges, she is also fair. No, I think that your patient's daughter would be well cared for there. Three months after she has the child, she will be able to leave without the worry of looking after a baby. And hopefully, by that time she may have gained some morals!'

'Very well Peter, I will go and have a word with Mary, that's the child's name. Do you want to take her tonight, or do you want to talk with mother superior first?'

Peter looked at his pocket watch before replying, 'Look it's getting rather late, so if you don't mind allowing the girl to stay here again tonight, I will have a word with mother superior first thing in the morning. That will give her time to organise the girl's transfer. Now I must rush Noreen, and I will be back to pick the girl up sometime tomorrow.'

'Thank you, Peter, now let me see you out.' After seeing him to the door, Noreen went directly to the ward, as Brigid was just finishing off massaging the ointment into Patricia.

'How is the patient, nurse?"

'She is not responding well today Matron.'

'What is the problem?'

Brigid moved to one side of the room and spoke quietly, 'Matron, she has not eaten anything in the past twenty-four hours, and today I found several more teeth on the sheets. As you can see, she has now lost most of her hair and she is delirious most of the time. The sores are spreading, as you can see from her face. Matron, is there nothing else that we can do for her?'

Noreen wore a frown, she was unfamiliar with treating patients with syphilis, and the few that she had dealt with had either ended up in the asylum, or had improved enough to be discharged.

'How many times a day are you delivering the metallic mercury to the patient nurse?'

'Twice matron, I do it at the start of my shift, and at the completion of my shift. The night nurse does it once, that was the instruction from the doctor, but she is still not getting any better.'

'Very well nurse, I shall have a word with Doctor Conrad, and see if we should change her dosage.' Noreen then turned her attention to Mary. 'How are you, young lady?'

'I'm orright ma'am, but I'm worried about me mummy. Is she gunna die ma'am? She hasn't spoken to me for a coupla days now, and why is her teef and 'er hair all fallin' out?'

'We are doing the best that we can for your mother, but I do have some good news for you.' Mary looked quizzically at Noreen.

'I have spoken with the vicar, and he has arranged some accommodation for you with the nuns. You will get all of your meals, but you will have to work to pay for your keep. The nuns will take care of your baby when it is time for you to have it, so you should be very grateful to Father Aldridge. He has arranged this for you, so make sure that you thank him when he comes for you tomorrow young lady.'

Mary wasn't sure of what to make of this information. She didn't want to leave her mother, and had very little to do with nuns, so she had no idea of what to expect.

'Can ya tell me where ya gunna send me please matron, and will I still get ta see me mummy?'

'Now stop worrying child, the convent is just down the road in Surrey Hills, why it shouldn't take you more than a half hour to walk from there to here. Father Aldridge has assured me that you will be able to come back here whenever you choose. Now you can sleep here again tonight, and you will be taken to the convent tomorrow. Now, in the meantime, you can just stay here with your mother.'

29.

Evacuation

After the last skirmish, all of those that had been on the front line were now rotated back to the rest trenches. The reserve troops then moved up to the front line.

It was autumn, and the cold was forgotten for a short period as they all took a long overdue bath in the makeshift bathhouse. Ragged uniforms were washed, and wet clothes were replaced with dry ones. The rest area was where the camp kitchens were set up, and the soldiers had their first hot meal in days.

Each day would bring on a dozen different operations, and each operation brought with it its own dangers, but the fighting was becoming more sporadic. The last month of autumn brought with it cold rain and misery for those still languishing in the trenches. It was three weeks before Christmas. As they huddled together during the long quiet hours, many of the troops were thinking of home along with blue skies and sunny days. Tom and the others had been in Turkey for over three months, and other than trench rotation they had not been granted any leave. Many others had to be carried down to the field hospital, as they

181

could no longer walk as their feet rotted inside their constantly wet boots.

After the last violent skirmish, the boys had become more sombre, and they were all suffering from battle-fatigue. They had received mail from home, along with woollen mittens and scarves. The fruitcake that Doris had sent was consumed in less than a day. Newspapers from home were read and reread and dog-eared books were shared amongst themselves. Their world revolved around their muddy trenches. The only news that they received about the war came from two-month-old newspapers. Doris had folded them up and placed them under cakes and chocolates that had been packed into tins. Dysentery was rife throughout the trenches, and as the weather deteriorated so did the morale of the troops.

Tom had wanted to write to Hannah, but after the last skirmish writing paper was no longer available. When they weren't on sentry duty they huddled inside their dugouts playing cards and smoking.

Corporal John Bradley had been sent from the reserves to replace Brownie. Friendly and unassuming, he had no interest in enforcing discipline unless there was a senior officer in his vicinity. He had joined up for what he thought would be an adventure and a cheap way to see the world. He had grown up in the small country town of Blayney in NSW, where he had worked on his father's farm. The lure of adventure, rather than any sense of loyalty to the King, was what had led him to the nearest recruitment office in Bathurst. But, fifteen months after signing up and more than six months in Turkey had him longing for the peace and tranquility of the green hills of his home.

The command headquarters was set in an area called Quinn's Post, which was behind the trench rows. The British officers in charge tried to maintain a sense of decorum that was out of place within this hostile environment. A small officers' mess had been set up, and the batman to the captain was required to set his table and lay out cutlery before each meal. Scarce drinking water was also used on washing officers' shirts. This caused enormous resentment among the lower ranks that for the most part were desperate for clean drinking water. It was from this environment that Corporal John Bradley had arrived into the front-line trenches.

He came to Egypt with Fred Schuman. They were of the same age and demeanor, and they had struck up an instant friendship. On arrival in Turkey they had been separated, and had not seen each other for more than six months. The Corporal was doing his first rounds and a roll call when Fred spotted him.

'Well look what the cat dragged in,' was Fred's response. Corporal Bradley glared at the speaker about to challenge this insolence, but as recognition dawned on him he smiled and clasped Fred's hand.

'So, you're still alive I see,' was the Corporal's response to Fred.

'Don't ask me how, cause I dunno why, what with all the nonsense that's been goin' on around here,' Fred stated resignedly.

'What happened to you, where did you get to? The last time that we saw each other was in Egypt. We been here fer over six months, and I can tell ya mate I've had enough. I dunno what we are fightin' about, or why all those poor bastards have bin blown ter bits out there.' He nodded his head towards no-man's-land.

'Hell, I know that we are not supposed to question what's goin' on, but Christ the papers are sayin' that there has been over twenty-five thousand people killed so far. And that information was from a two-month-old paper that one of me mates had jammed into a cake tin.

'How much longer is this goin' on for?' Fred didn't expect his friend to answer, but he was weary, and it was good to see an old face that could understand his frustration.

John looked at his friend, and then lowered his voice before saying, 'Keep this to yourself, but I overhead the brass talking earlier. I didn't hear the whole conversation, but the captain stated that HQ had mentioned that we might be pulling out soon, and goin' back to Egypt. Somethin' about a secret operation!

'I dunno anymore, but something is going on! The captain had sent a dispatch to London, or somewhere. He mentioned about the high number of casualties, so I don't know if the two things are connected, but something's up. Keep it under your hat, because I might have the bull by the horns, but we might get lucky, and be able to get out of this rat hole soon.'

***

It was the morning of the nineteenth of December 1915. The British Generals had finally conceded that the war on the Gallipoli peninsula was at a stalemate, and that nothing further could be gained by staying. Over thirty thousand Australian and New Zealand troops were to be evacuated as quietly and quickly as possible from the peninsular. The troop ships were stationed in the harbour, and the orders were sent along the lines that thirty men at a time would make their way down the cliffs to the temporary pier on the beachfront. Orders were given quietly by junior officers, and passed by word of mouth from trench to trench.

'We are evacuating this morning men. Only guns and ammunition boxes are to be taken, now move quickly and quietly. We don't want the enemy to know that we are pulling out!'

Shock, surprise, and finally elation overtook the ravaged troops as they walked and slid down the rocky hillside for the final time to gather on the beach.

The casualty clearing station where the wounded were first taken was now empty. The wounded were already on board the hospital ships that were now steaming towards the small island of Lemnos, which was a few miles off the Turkish coast where a hospital had been set up.

The landing barges relayed the troops from the shore to the waiting ships. Up to three thousand men were crammed together on each vessel, but there were few complaints as the men were informed that they were returning to Egypt.

Forty hours after leaving the shores of Gallipoli, they were all back at the camp in sight of the pyramids. New uniforms and supplies were given out after the troops had been deloused and showered. They had all been issued with a five-day leave pass, but most were on the base on Christmas morning.

After having the biggest breakfast that they had had in many months they all fell into line for muster. The mail had been waiting for them in Egypt, and along with the mail came what were known as comfort billies. Women's groups from across Australia had raised money by holding raffles, and eliciting donations from businesses. The money was used to purchase goods that would be sent to the troops fighting overseas. People were also encouraged to buy a billycan, and fill it with little luxuries along with writing a letter to the recipient. The billies would be dropped off at women's auxiliary organisations, where they would be sent to the men of different battalions. Each billy contained something different. Some held a pouch of tobacco, a cake of soap, or dried fruit. Whatever the contents were, the soldiers gratefully received them.

After breakfast, a non-denominational Christmas service was held. War-hardened and battle-weary men knelt with bowed heads, and prayed to a God who many had thought had abandoned them.

Afterwards, most lounged around in the warm sunshine. Some wrote letters, some played cricket, and some lay and grappled with their own personal demons. Tom was still coming to grips with the images that had been burned into his mind, but overriding those thoughts was his need to write to Hannah.

Christmas 1915.
Somewhere in Egypt.

To my Darling Hannah,

I am so sorry that I haven't written to you sooner, but we have been having a difficult time over the past couple of months. We have had no writing paper, and none of the chaps had any ink or pencil, but the reality was that the weather has been so foul, and hardly a day passed without us being involved in some skirmish or other. But nevertheless, I am pleased to say, that I am writing this to you on Christmas Day from our camp in Egypt.

Yes, Hani, we are finally somewhere safe, dry and warm. We are still together, Jack, Des and I, and I am sure that they will be writing home shortly as well. We have only just arrived here; in fact, we have been here for less than two days. It was a great surprise to all of us when they told us that we were leaving Turkey.

We have been lucky, as we only had to endure that hellhole for a little over three months. Some poor devils have been there since the beginning, and it was so demoralising being constantly damp, and standing in sodden boots for weeks at a time. I have seen some men having to be carried down to the hospital tent because they were no longer able to stand because of the trench rot in their feet.

I don't know if we were beaten in Turkey, but I believe that we can all hold our heads high for I can assure you darling, we gave our all when the need arose.

I can't help wondering if we have achieved anything with this entire killing. War is so depressing. The only things enjoying this madness are the rats. Giant nasty things that show no fear of us. They crawl over us as we sleep, and it is most unpleasant.

It was only a short while ago that a mate of mine and myself had to carry one of our chaps back to the trenches after a skirmish that we had been in had almost blown his foot off. Poor fellow, but he is out of it now, and should be in a hospital in England somewhere.

Anyway, Hani, I shall tell you as to how we spent our Christmas Day over here. Firstly, we all had a huge breakfast. The best breakfast in fact that we have had in many months. Then, they handed out the mail, along with the parcels from home. It was amusing to watch grown men acting like excited children as they opened their parcels. Not everyone received a package, or even a letter, as many of the chaps don't have family back home.

But they were not forgotten. The captain had informed us that complete strangers from across Australia had donated the comfort billies that were handed out to us.

Jack and I were lucky, as not only did we each receive a comfort billy, but we also received the parcels that you and mother had kindly sent us, so we have nothing to complain about. Between Jack and I, we have received two fruit puddings, soap, and dried fruit, not forgetting what you have sent along with the fruitcakes and tobacco that mother had sent.

The camp cooks outdid themselves with our Christmas lunch, and I must confess that I made a total pig of myself, as there was so much food on offer. I filled my plate, and then went back for seconds. Lunch consisted of Plum Duff, Turkey and Ham along with minced fruit pudding. Most of the lads are now sleeping off lunch, or just lounging around and playing cards. But we have all had a most wonderful day, but we can't help remembering all of those that we left behind in Turkey. I am so tired of this war, and how I long to be strolling through the park with you by my side. I cannot say how long we will be stationed here in Egypt, or in fact where they are likely to send us in the future, but I would be happy if I never heard another cannon fire again.

Would you give my regards to your family, and say hello to mother for me?

Until next we write,

Yours forever,

Tommy.

30.

The Convent

Patricia's condition had deteriorated overnight. Mary had slept on a blanket by the side of her mother's bed, but as her mother had moaned in pain, she had lain beside her and comforted her. By morning she still had not woken, and as the night shift nurse prepared to hand over the patient to Brigid, Mary heard her say, 'She's all yours now, but if you ask me I don't think that she will see the day out. I may be wrong, but if she dies it will probably be a blessing. Well, I'll be off now, I need some sleep, so it's bed for me!'

Mary asked, 'What she mean, won't see the day out, she ain't gunna die is she? Tell me she ain't gunna die, please miss!'

Brigid was taken aback with the night nurse's insensitivity. She took hold of Mary's hand before replying. 'Mary, your mummy is very sick, but I'm not a doctor, so I can't say if she will get better or not. But, we will do our very best to keep your mother comfortable.' Trying to change the conversation Brigid said, 'Matron says that she has found somewhere for you to stay, so that's good, isn't it?'

'I don't wanna leave me mummy while she is so sick. Can't I just stay here wif her? What if she wakes up and I'm not 'ere? I hafta stay 'ere miss, I just hafta.'

'I'm sorry Mary, I'm just a nurse's aide and I don't have any say in anything around here. If it were up to me then I would let you stay.

'But, if you go and get settled into your new place, then after you have your tea tonight you can then come back and spend some time with your mother, after all, it's not as though you are going to jail. You will be allowed to go out after you have done your work, so stop worrying, everything will be all right.' Mary didn't look convinced, even though what Brigid said made sense.

Father Aldridge had arrived before the doctor had done his rounds. He came straight to the ward where Mary and her mother were. He took a cursory look at Mary before saying, 'Have you got your things girl?' He didn't wait for her to answer.

'I don't wanna leave me mummy, I need ta be 'ere when she wakes up cause she won't know where I've gone, I hafta stay 'ere Father.'

'Don't talk nonsense girl, you can't stay here, and that's the end of it, so kiss your mother goodbye. You can come back and see her after you have settled in at the convent, now come on. I have other duties waiting as well as this, and I have a carriage outside, so it will only take a few minutes to get there.'

'But I hafta say goodbye to the nurse, she wanted to see me before I left. She said that she would be 'ere.'

'Look girl, stop wasting my time, you can see the nurse when you come back to visit your mother.' Father Aldridge was starting to show his annoyance, and his voice had raised an octave. 'Say goodbye to your mother now, and go!'

Mary started to cry, as she bent down to give her mother a final hug. Patricia was still asleep, and heard nothing as her daughter's tears ran across her face. 'Goodbye mummy, I will come back as soon as I am able, I will try an' come back tonight, but if not, I'll be back in the mornin'.'

Brigid made an appearance, just as Mary and the Vicar were walking towards the front door. 'Goodbye Mary, good luck in your new home, I'm sure that you will enjoy being there.' The tears were still streaming down

Mary's face as she said, 'Will ya tell me mummy where I've gone? Please nurse, an' will ya tell her I will be back tonight, or in the mornin'? And thanks fer looking after me and mummy.'

'I'll be sure to tell her that you are being well looked after Mary. Goodbye for now, but I'll see you every month when you come to have your check-up, now take care of yourself and that baby that you're carrying.'

Mary climbed into the vicar's carriage, and Brigid watched as it disappeared down the road.

Shortly after, it turned through a walled gateway before stopping at the front of a large imposing stone building. Above the portico and carved in stone stood the words 'Mary Magdalene Convent.'

'Come on child, don't dilly-dally.' He spoke irritably, as he pulled the cord on the side of the front door, and somewhere deep inside the building a bell rang. The door opened, and the vicar smiled before saying, 'Good morning sister. This is the child that I spoke to mother superior about recently, could I leave her in your capable hands?'

He gave a weak smile before saying, 'I'm actually running dreadfully late for another appointment. Please give my apologies to mother superior, and tell her that I shall be in touch shortly. Thank you, sister.' He turned around quickly, and without a goodbye to Mary, or the nun he climbed into his carriage and left.

'Don't you have any luggage with you girl?'

'No miss, me clothes that I'm wearin' is all I got.'

'Oh, very well then, follow me. We will give you your uniform after you have seen mother superior, now step lively girl.'

Mary walked along the corridor. She looked in awe at the wooden panels covering the walls and the mosaic-tiled floor. She thought that it was the grandest place that she had ever seen. They stopped outside a black painted door, and the nun knocked before entering. Mother Superior was sat behind a large desk. Hanging on the wall behind her was a framed print of the sacred heart, and on the opposite wall was a bookcase with the contents all neatly stacked.

Sister May Lukin looked up as the door opened. She gave a weak smile before asking, 'Isn't Father Aldridge with you Sister?'

'No Mother Superior, he asked me to convey his apology to you, but said that he was running late for another appointment. Here is the girl, and she has no luggage.' Mother Superior looked at Mary before saying, 'You should be very grateful for this accommodation that we are going to provide you with, what did you say that your name was?'

'Mary, Mary Bridges ma'am.'

'Don't call me ma'am. My name is Sister May, and I am the Mother Superior, and that is what you will call me, now do you understand?'

'Yes sister.'

'Now, I will tell you what we do here. We do the laundry for a number of establishments in the city. We wash, iron and fold. We do this five days a week, and on Saturday we scrub and polish floors, and the Sabbath is our rest day.

'Now, we give shelter to girls like you who seem to think that having loose morals is entirely acceptable, which it is not. But you will get plenty of time to pray for God's forgiveness for your whorish ways. Now tell me girl, what religion are you?'

'I don't have no religion Sister, me mummy said that goin' ta church was a waste of a good Sunday mornin'.'

Mother Superior stared at Mary, and her indignation was clearly showing, 'So, not only are you a whore, but you're a heathen as well! Well let me tell you girl, it's the good Lord that has brought you here to us, and you will thank him. You will go to morning mass at 6 am, and you will read the epistle when you have a spare moment. You can read, can't you girl?'

Mary, looking sheepish said, 'No I can't,' and then hung her head in embarrassment. Sister May sighed in exasperation, and rang the small brass bell sat on her desk. The door opened, and a nun entered the room.

'Sister Joseph, this is Mary Bridges. Please show her where she will sleep in the dormitory, then take her to the storeroom and find her a uniform. When she is dressed, she can start working immediately.'

'Please sister, me mummy is really sick, and I need to go and see her at the hospital. Can ya tell me when I can go?'

Mother Superior looked at Mary and said, 'What don't you understand girl, this is where you will be staying until you have had the baby, and you will stay here for a further twelve weeks after the child is born. You cannot leave here before that. This is not a hotel where you can come and go as you please!

'We give you accommodation, and two meals a day along with religious instruction. You repay our kindness with working in our laundry from Monday to Friday. On Sunday, your day will be taken up with prayers and meditation. If your mother wants to see you, then she will be allowed to see you for one hour, once a month!'

Mary was digesting this information and wailed at the nun. 'But I hafta see me mummy. She don't know where I am, and she is sick, I hafta go and see her sister, I hafta! Even the father said that I could go an see me mummy after I got settled in 'ere!'

'Stop talking back at me girl, I have told you what the rules are, and you will abide by them. Now go with sister Joseph, and I don't want to hear another word from you. Sister Joseph, please do as I have asked, now go.' She waved her hand disdainfully to dismiss them both.

Mary was fitted out in the workhouse uniform, and she was taken to the laundry, which was divided into three sections. The place was a hive of activity with girls of various ages all working at their stations. Sister Joseph asked Mary, 'Do you know how to use a flat iron girl?' Mary replied, 'Of course I can, I'm not stupid ya know.'

'Do not answer me in that tone of voice young lady, or you will regret it, is that understood?

'I don't wanna be 'ere, I wanna go back to the hospital! You can't keep me 'ere, now let me go!' She stamped her foot to make the point. Sister Joseph took hold of Mary, and placing both of her hands upon her shoulders she shook her vigorously. 'Now you just calm down, or I will have to punish you!'

Mary was using the bottom of her clenched fists to beat Sister Joseph on her chest. She was becoming hysterical, and stamping her feet. The other girls had stopped working and were watching Mary. Sister Joseph brought her hand back, and slapped Mary hard across her face. Her hand went to her face, and she rubbed the welt, but Sister Joseph had not finished. She turned her around, and pushing her in the back said, 'You are going to learn some manners while you are here girl, now move.'

The nun pushed Mary along the passageway, and when she reached the staircase, she opened the small broom cupboard built beneath it. Then she pushed Mary inside, slamming the door behind her before locking it.

'You can stay there until you calm down, and while you are in there you can think about your future. But no matter what you do or say, you will be staying here until you have had the baby.'

The broom cupboard was dark. The only light showing came from the cracks between the doorframe and the door. Mary was kicking the door and screaming, 'Let me out, let me out!' But her pleas went unanswered, and eventually her screams turned into harrowing sobs until finally, exhausted, she fell asleep.

※

Brigid checked Patricia, after Mary had left. She was going to give her another rub with the metallic mercury, but something about her breathing made her stop. She checked her pulse, but it was so faint that she thought that she had died. Patricia's face was deathly pale, and the skin around her temples was now yellow. She looked like an old woman.

Her teeth, along with her hair, had all fallen out, and her kidneys had almost failed.

The toxic mercury coursing through her body was now eating into all of her vital organs, and there would be no recovery. Brigid rang the ward bell to attract the attention of a nurse.

'What's the problem nurse?' asked ward sister, Margaret Bennett.

'I'm worried about my patient. I can't find a pulse, and I'm not even sure that she is breathing!'

'Let's have a look at her.' Sister Bennett held Patricia's wrist as she tried to find a pulse. She bent over the bed, and placed her stethoscope upon Patricia's chest, and moving it around she finally heard a tiny heartbeat. She stood erect, and looked at Brigid before saying, 'This patient is dying nurse, has she any next of kin?'

'She has a daughter. She has been staying here with her mother, and she has only just left with the priest. I don't know where he was taking her, but she was very close to her mother. She didn't want to go, but the priest was insistent.'

Just then, a final expulsion of breath left Patricia's mouth, and she breathed no more. Sister Bennett used her stethoscope, and when she was satisfied that Patricia had breathed her last she said, 'This patient is dead nurse; please go downstairs to the mortuary. Ask the attendant to bring his trolley and remove her.'

Brigid hesitated for a moment, and Sister Bennett asked, 'Yes what is it nurse, what's bothering you?'

'Sister, I was wondering if I could find out where they took my patient's daughter. The priest was going to take her to a convent somewhere. I wonder if I could go and tell Mary, that's her daughter, about her mother. She was very close to her, and when I last saw her she really didn't want to leave her mother's side. I know that she will be devastated, but someone should tell her.'

Sister looked at Brigid and said, 'That's very compassionate of you nurse; we should be able to find out where she was taken to. When I do I will let you know, but are you sure that you want to do this? Telling the child that her mother has died will not be easy. People react in different ways to that sort of news.'

'I felt so badly for Mary, sister. They were so poor, and they only had each other. I got to know her a little bit while she was here, so it would make me feel better if I could give her a shoulder to cry on.'

Brigid had obtained the details of where Mary had been sent, and when her shift was finished, she walked to the convent. After knocking on the door, she was greeted by a nun.

'Yes, what is it? What is your business here, do you not know what time it is?' she asked brusquely.

'I'm sorry sister, but I am a nurse at the Barracks Hospital, and I have only just finished my shift. I wonder if I could talk to a girl that was brought here today? Her name is Mary Bridges?'

'No, certainly not, we don't allow visitors here unannounced, and certainly not at this time! The girl that you are referring to is having trouble settling in. I wouldn't think that it would be a good idea for her to see anyone from the outside at this moment.'

'Please sister, it is important that I see her. I have some distressing news for her, her mother died shortly after she had left the hospital this morning. I wanted to tell her, seeing as how close she was to her mother. I thought that I could give her some comfort seeing as she has nobody else.'

The nun looked at Brigid, but was unmoved by her story. 'I'm really sorry, but I don't think that it would be helpful at this time to give her that news. Like I said, she has had a little trouble settling in, and giving her this news would not make the situation any better. If it helps, I will pass on the information to mother superior, and she can decide when would be the best time to tell the girl about her mother. That's the best that I can do, so goodnight young lady.' The nun then closed the door.

31.

Leaving Egypt

Christmas had come and gone, and the New Year had arrived without fanfare. None of the soldiers had any idea of how long they would be staying in Egypt.

The days dragged on with no variance to their daily routine, and boredom was a part of their everyday life. Some days the wind would blow, bringing waves of sand with it from the desert. It would fill their tents, and they would be forced to spend several hours cleaning machinery and equipment. They eagerly waited for the mail to arrive, and when it did, they could read about the war that was now raging throughout Europe, albeit being old news. The soldiers filled in their spare time with frequenting the bazaars, bars, and brothels. On other occasions, they went sightseeing and lounged around enjoying the sunshine of a Mediterranean winter.

¥¥

It was the end of March when their new orders came through. The horrors of the war in Turkey were fading, but not forgotten. As the peaceful weeks in Egypt had turned into months, many were secretly hoping that the war would end before they were sent elsewhere.

The call to muster was blown by the bugler, and they all gathered on the parade ground before the camp Captain addressed them.

'Tomorrow we will be embarking for France, so get your affairs in order. Write to your loved ones, as it will probably be the last opportunity that you will get for some time. We will ship out at 6 am tomorrow! A church service will be held at 5 pm this evening, so those that have a mind to should attend. That's all men! Dismissed.'

Two weeks steaming brought them to Southampton, and they were then informed that they would be staying in England until further notice. Their new camp was set up on the Salisbury Plains, in Central England, and about sixty miles from London. They filled in their days doing route marches, and repairing roads around the local villages.

The locals had complained to the authorities that the military traffic was making their roads impassible, and for the next two months, they drove converted army trucks, and laid gravel and repaired roads. But at the end of each day, when the work was done, most would spend their leisure time at the local pubs and taverns.

It was mid-June, and spring was turning into summer as their laid-back, balmy days in England were coming to an end. They had received their orders, and they would be sent to France within the week.

32.

Tragedy

Brigid left the convent grounds, and walked back to the hospital. She was troubled by the thought of how Mary would cope after hearing the news about her mother.

Mary had sobbed herself to sleep, but woke when Sister Joseph opened the cupboard door. 'You may come out as long as you are going to behave yourself, but if you give me any more trouble I will put you back inside, and I will leave you there all night, is that understood?'

Mary replied sullenly, 'Yes sister.'

'Good, now you can get back to the laundry and start earning your keep.'

Mary stewed with resentment, along with having bouts of guilt about leaving her mother. Mother Superior had decided against telling Mary about the death of her mother, and Mary soon fell into the drudgery of convent life.

The bell could be heard as it rang throughout the convent at 6 am each day. The girls, including those that had recently given birth, slept on iron-ended beds in a large dormitory. As the bell rang they would all rise and dress in their uniforms. Those that had babies would go to the nursery, where they would change their nappies, and be given ten minutes to feed the child.

Sister Marta was in charge of the nursery, and her instructions were that the babies were not to be breastfed, but instead were to be fed a formula of watered-down cow's milk, and when the baby was given up for adoption, the new mother could continue with the same formula. With the limited time given to feed the child, and the poor nutritional value of the watery milk, the babies were invariably hungry and wailed incessantly. The new mothers were not to show any affection to their babies. Kisses and hugs were forbidden, and any mother that flouted those rules was swiftly given a tongue-lashing.

It was also Sister Marta's job to find prospective parents for the newborns. Some babies would be adopted out within a few days while others would stay for several months. The convent nursery was managed as a baby farm, where prospective parents could pick and choose the child of their choice.

The babies had to be fed, changed and returned to their cribs before it was time to attend mass at 6.30am. An hour later, they would all file into the dining room to start their day with a bowl of cold porridge, a slice of bread and a glass of water. They were allowed half an hour for breakfast before spending the next ten hours in the laundry.

The nursing mothers would be given thirty minutes at midday to again attend to the needs of their child, and after feeding and changing them, they would be returned to the nursery.

The routine was the same from Monday to Friday. On Saturdays, the floors were swept and polished; and Sunday was the only day that the girls were given lunch as there was no breakfast. The girls were expected to take communion at Mass; then, the rest of the morning was taken up with singing hymns, and reciting the rosary in the convent chapel. At lunchtime, they would be allowed two slices of bread, spread with a smear of dripping, and for dinner, they would be given a bowl of greasy gruel.

The girls were not encouraged to socialise. Only the bare minimum of conversation was allowed between them, and that was only in the context of their work. As the pregnant girls' time grew closer, they would be transferred to the maternity section of the convent. After they had given birth they would be sent back to work in the laundry for a further twelve weeks; at which time they would be shown the front door and sent on their way. They would never see their child again.

Mary had been at the convent for six months, and was now into her eighth month of pregnancy.

She had still not been told of her mother's death. Some nights she had cried herself to sleep, wondering why her mother had not come to visit her. The insecurity of wondering about her mother was causing her undue stress, and with reluctance she had spoken to Sister Catherine.

Sister Catherine was small in stature, and kind-hearted. She always had a happy nature, unlike the other nuns, and she seemed to have an affinity with her pregnant charges. Mary had made no attempt to allow anyone at the convent to get anywhere near her emotions, but she had warmed slightly to Sister Catherine. When she had first noticed a few specks of blood on the inside of her petticoat, she had ignored it, but now Mary was feeling sick most of the time. The discharging blood was thicker, and she was getting sharp pains in her stomach, and she was scared.

Sister Catherine was leaving the laundry when Mary suddenly called out. 'Sister, Sister!' Mary doubled over as the pain tore through her stomach.

'What is it, girl?'

'I think I'm havin' me baby, sister.'

'Come with me girl, and we will have a look at you.'

'I can't walk,' Mary retorted as she held her stomach.

'Your water hasn't broken, so of course you can walk, it's probably just cramps, so get over here and lie down.' Mary lay down on the hard day bed, and Sister Catherine gave a gasp as she raised Mary's skirt.

'How long have you been bleeding for girl?'

'I dunno, I had a few specks yesterday. Why ya askin' me all these questions. Is me baby comin' or not?'

Sister Catherine examined Mary, and she came to the conclusion that the baby was still some time away. 'Now you just lie there, and don't try to get out of bed. I will go and find Sister Harriet.'

Sister Harriet was the convent midwife. Although she had no formal qualifications, she had overseen the birth of many babies. When a newborn died, she just put it down to being the will of God, and that the mother was being punished for her sinful ways.

Mary lay doubled up with pain, and it was almost an hour before Sister Harriet made an appearance. She didn't believe that there was such a thing as an emergency when it came to wayward girls giving birth. Sister Harriet was big-boned, and intimidating. She was in charge, and she had the utmost belief in her abilities when it came to delivering babies. Although never having given birth, she still prided herself on being an expert on the subject.

'Right, now let's get you out of these clothes so that we can have a good look at you. You, you girl,' and she waved her arm at the girl she had just got the attention of.

'Help me get this girl out of these clothes.' Between them, they undressed Mary before covering her in an open-fronted cotton gown. Sister Harriet asked the same questions as Sister Catherine, but included, 'How many months are you, girl? I have here,' and she looked at her notes, 'that you are not due for another four weeks. Is that correct?' She looked at Mary as she asked the question.

'I dunno, can't ya do somethin' ta make the pain go away, geez it hurts, I think I'm dyin' sister.'

'How dare you take the lord's name in vain! There is no need for blaspheming girl. I will not tolerate it, do you understand? You brought this trouble upon yourself, and you are not dying. This is all part of the process, so stop carrying on as though you are the only person who has ever had a baby!'

Mary gave a shriek, and doubled over across the bed. Sister Harriet noticed the red stain on the sheet becoming larger. She looked at Sister Catherine and whispered, 'I think that this girl is about to lose the baby, but something is not right as she is not due yet, but let's just keep an eye on her and see if things settle down.'

Sister Catherine wasn't sure that this was the correct way to deal with this situation; but as she found Sister Harriet intimidating she didn't want to disagree openly with her. If she had her way, the child would be sent straight back to the hospital. Sister Harriet brought a large cotton towel and placed it between Mary's legs. 'Now don't move around girl just lie still, and we will see if the bleeding stops.'

The pain kept coming in waves, and after an hour the towel was almost entirely red. The two nuns were perplexed with what to do. Sister Catherine suggested that a doctor should be called, citing that if the girl keeps losing blood at this rate, she will surely die.

'Yes, maybe you are right, Sister, I'll go and see if Father Aldridge is at the presbytery. Maybe he will need to give the girl the last rites because if the bleeding doesn't stop, I don't think that she will see the night out.'

Father Aldridge arrived, and after taking one look at Mary's pale face he asked Sister Harriet if she had experienced this sort of thing before. Father Aldridge was uncomfortable within this environment. He believed that all that he would be able to do would be to say a prayer for her, and if that didn't work then he could administer the last rites, but it was too soon for that, and he suggested that the girl might be better off in hospital.

'We can't just take her down to the hospital father. The girl is just a street urchin.

'We would need a doctor's referral for her to return to the hospital. No, I think that we should see if we could get the district nurse to come and have a look at her. Father, would it be possible for you to call at her house, and ask if she would be good enough to get here as a matter of urgency, and if possible bring Mrs Bishop, the midwife, with her?'

'Certainly sister, I will go straight away!' He was only too glad to have an excuse to get away.

✲✲✲

Mrs Bishop examined Mary, as district nurse Nugent took her pulse before asking, 'How long has this girl been in this state?' She was irritated that she had only been asked to attend the convent less than an hour earlier.

Sister Catherine replied, 'Only a couple of hours or so, nurse.'

'And how long has she been bleeding?'

Mrs Bishop prided herself as a midwife, and her annoyance was now clearly showing. She took her duties seriously and she knew that her patient was having severe difficulties.

'Have you treated her with anything?' Mrs Bishop asked.

'No, we don't dispense drugs to the girls here. Sister Harriet believes that the pain of childbirth is good for them, and it helps keep them on the straight and narrow after they leave us.'

Mrs Bishop had never been one to mince words, and upon hearing what the nun had said she retorted, 'What a load of codswallop. This girl is in pain, and if we are not careful we will not only lose the baby, but her as well. Now I'm going to give her some morphine and scopolamine. Hopefully, that will settle things down, but be warned sister that this girl may need to be admitted to hospital. I've seen this thing before. If it is what I think that it is, then this girl may need an emergency caesarean delivery, and it can't be done here.'

She opened her medical bag, and brought out two small vials and a syringe and injected the painkiller into Mary. She sat with her patient who was now sleeping. Over the next hour, she monitored Mary's pulse, and kept her hand on her belly until she felt the baby move.

Sister Harriet was annoyed. She prided herself on knowing how to deal with the many medical emergencies that happened within the convent. Bleeding before childbirth was never something that she had worried about. She saw herself as the instrument that did the work of her God, and it was up to him if the individual lived or died. She would never question what she perceived as God's will. If the mother and/or the baby died then that was what God had wanted, and it was not up to her to question his reasons. But now, the midwife had questioned her ability. She had done it in front of others, and she was now feeling affronted.

Mrs Bishop looked at nurse Nugent and said, 'I think that this child has a deformation of the pelvic bone, do we know if she has ever suffered from rickets?' When no one answered she said, 'Well if I'm right, I think that this baby is stuck in the birth canal, and that means that she will have to have a caesarean delivery. What do you think nurse?'

'I don't have your experience with pregnancies Mrs Bishop, but she has very low blood pressure. I can barely feel a pulse. I do know that if it gets much lower then she may die, so I would agree with you that we should try and get the baby out as soon as possible. That will mean getting her to the hospital as quickly as possible. Now it's too late for me to get a doctor's referral, but I'm sure that when I explain the situation they will find her a bed at the hospital.

'Now what I should do is get on down to the hospital and see matron, or the doctor if he is available. It will only take me about ten minutes on my bike. I will also see Father Aldridge, and see if he could be disposed of to let us use his carriage to get this girl to the hospital.'

She pedalled to the presbytery, before cajoling Father Aldridge into letting them borrow his carriage, and then she went straight to the Barracks Hospital. She had known Matron Emmitt for many years, and she had a good relationship with her. After explaining the situation, it was agreed that the patient could be put straight onto the lying-in ward.

They brought Mary to the hospital in the carriage, and then transferred her to a wheelchair. Sister Emmitt met them at the front entrance, and ushered them along to the maternity lying-in section for pregnant women. Matron gave the night nurse her instructions.

'The patient's name is Mary Bridges, and until recently her mother was a patient of ours before she died. She has been administered with morphine and scopolamine about an hour ago.

'I will need to consult with the doctor on how we should proceed from here. Mrs Bishop believes that the baby may be stuck, and if she is correct, then the girl will have an obstructed labour.

'If that is the case, then we will have to perform a caesarean, and we will probably have to do it soon as the patient's blood pressure is very low. I will go and find Doctor Conrad, so please prepare this patient for the operation.'

Doctor Benjamin Conrad was less than pleased with the news that Sister Emmitt had just delivered to him. He had finished his rounds and was about to go home, and now it looked like he would have to check on another pauper patient. That meant that he wouldn't be paid. Worse still, if what Sister Emmitt had said was correct, then he would need to carry out a caesarean section on the girl before he left.

His wife was expecting him home, as they had guests arriving for dinner. He knew that she would be less than pleased if she had to entertain his guests without him. One of his guests was a member of the hospital committee with whom he was trying to arrange a fee structure for his unpaid duties at the hospital.

He examined Mary, and agreed with matron's assessment that the baby appeared to be stuck within the pelvic girdle. He knew that if he didn't operate quickly, then both the mother and baby would certainly die.

Mary was still asleep, as the morphine had not worn off when Doctor Conrad made the first cut. The operation was carried out clumsily, but the baby survived the delivery.

An hour later, Mary woke up and started screaming. She had no idea where she was, but it was the pain from her torn abdomen that was causing her to cry. Lucy Devlin was the night nurse, and she came running into the room, which was dimly lit by two small kerosene lamps hanging from the ceiling.

She looked at Mary, and said quietly, 'Is it your belly that hurts? You have just had your baby, and you are going to be sore for a few days, do you understand what I'm saying?'

The news that she had just had her baby penetrated her drowsy mind, and for a moment it took her mind off her pain, 'Where is it, where's me baby?'

The nurse put her hand on Mary's forehead and said, 'Shush, don't speak, you had a little girl, and she's been taken to the nursery.

'The doctor had to cut you open to get your baby out, but she is fine now. I've been given instructions to give you some more morphine when you woke. Now don't you move, I'll be back shortly.'

Mary wailed, 'Where's me baby? I wanna see me baby, I hafta see me baby, nurse.'

'She's sleeping now.' She looked around to see if anyone else was present, even though Mary was the only patient on the ward at that moment. 'Look, I'm not supposed to do this, but I will go and get your baby, and you can have a little cuddle. Then she has to go back to the nursery. Do you understand? Mary gave a weak smile, and nodded.

The nurse came back carrying a small bundle. The baby had been weighed at birth and barely nudged four pounds. She was wrapped up tightly, and the nurse placed the tiny bundle in Mary's arm. She looked at her baby, and hugged it as she pondered on how small she was.

'Is she orright nurse, has she got all her toes and things?'

'Yes, she is fine. She is a little small, but when you start feeding her I'm sure that she will grow up big and healthy, now I must take her back before I get caught. Give her a kiss, and I will bring her back to you when she needs to be fed. The wet nurse has already fed her, but you can feed her in a few hours' time if you are awake!'

The nurse disappeared, and when she came back, she had the syringe in her hand. She lifted the bed sheet and jabbed the needle into Mary's thigh. 'Now you rest, and I will come and see you in a few hours.' Mary looked around at the stark room and asked, 'Where am I nurse, am I still at the convent?'

'No, you are not at the convent. You were very sick, and they bought you to the hospital. This is the Barracks Hospital, now go to sleep.' Mary was wide-awake now, and asked the nurse, 'Is me mummy still 'ere. I left her 'ere when they took me to the convent, and I ain't 'eard nothing since. Tell me that she is still 'ere, please nurse! Her name is Patricia, Patricia Bridges.'

Lucy was about to walk away, when she remembered what the matron had said about the girl's mother dying. She thought, *She doesn't know, how awful! I will have to tell matron.* 'Look I don't know your mother, and she would be downstairs if she was still here. I will ask matron as soon as I see her, now just lie back and go to sleep. You will feel a lot better when you wake up, now goodnight.'

With that, she walked back to her station feeling very uneasy about her patient not being told of her mother's death.

Noreen Emmitt was in her office, and was speaking with Brigid when the night nurse knocked on the door and entered.

'Excuse me matron, may I have a word?'

She looked at Brigid who said, 'Thank you matron, I will get back to my duties now.'

'No, stay here for a moment please nurse.' Matron looked across at Lucy and said, 'Yes, what is it?'

Lucy replied, 'Excuse me matron, but that young girl that was brought in last night.'

'Yes, what seems to be the problem?'

'Matron, she asked me about her mother. She doesn't know that her mother has died, and I was wondering if I should tell her, or would it be better if it came from you?'

Brigid listened to the conversation before asking, 'Excuse me, but are you saying that Mary Bridges is upstairs, is that who you are referring to?'

Lucy replied, 'Yes that's her name, why do you know her?'

Brigid looked across at matron, who could see the shock registering on her face. She blurted out, 'But I told the nuns months ago!' She then thought for a moment before continuing. 'Actually, I went to the convent the same evening after Mary had left, I did!

'I told the sister who came to the door. She had said that she would tell the mother superior. I asked if I could see her, and they wouldn't let me. Oh my God, they didn't tell her! She will be devastated because she sat with her mother for the whole time that she was here. I can't believe that the nuns could be so cruel as to not tell her!'

Brigid was angry and shocked. Lucy just looked at her, knowing that they now had the problem of how to inform the girl that her mother had died months earlier.

Matron looked at Lucy and said, 'Thank you for telling me, I suppose that I will have to go and break the news to her, but how is she now? I know that she had a very difficult time with the birth. I might wait a little longer, just until she is stronger.' She was talking more to herself than to the others.

Lucy replied, 'She is sleeping now, but I did get to tell her about her baby before I gave her another injection of morphine. Her bleeding had almost stopped, but it might be some time before she will be able to cope with the news of her mother, but I'm sure that she will ask for her mother as soon as she wakes. Do you want me to come and get you then matron?'

Before Noreen could reply Brigid spoke, 'I will tell her matron, if you don't mind. I feel very badly because I didn't doubt that the nuns would tell her, so I would like to tell her when she wakes up. I got along with her quite well when she was here if that's all right?'

Noreen looked at her young charge, and she thought how she had been right in taking this young girl under her wing. Noreen thought that as hard as it might be telling the girl about her mother, it would be good experience for Brigid.

'Very well Brigid, I will leave it up to you as to when and how you will tell her. In fact, what I might do is to put you up in the laying-in ward for a while. That way, you can determine when is the best time to tell her, and you can become a familiar face for her and that should help her get over the shock.'

Matron looked at Lucy before asking, 'How many patients do you have on the ward now nurse?'

'Just the one at the moment matron, but I don't expect that it will stay that way for long.'

'Very well, will you take Brigid with you? And tell whoever is there that she will be working on the ward until I say otherwise. Please explain the situation to the day nurse before you go home today, thank you nurse.

'Now Brigid, I want you to stay in that area even after you have delivered the news to the young patient. I think that it is time for you to get involved with pregnant mothers and their babies. But you can use your own judgment on how long is required to assist the girl in getting over her grief. That is all for now, but please inform me as to when you have told her, because we might have to sedate her if she takes it badly, now you had better go.'

Brigid took in her new surroundings. She had only passed through this section once since she had been working at the hospital.

Strangely, she felt a sense of excitement, as she would now learn about looking after babies and the needs of their mothers. Most pregnant women still had their babies at home, and a midwife generally delivered these. A doctor was only brought in if something went wrong during the birth. Society still frowned upon males, including doctors, being present during this intimate time for a woman.

Doctors chased patients that could afford their services, and most people who could afford the services of a doctor expected the doctor to visit them in their own homes. But the poor and the destitute women would have to contend with going to a charity hospital or a dispensary.

Those places were run by a committee of men, and it was these men who would decide on who was deserving of their charity. If the decision were made to not help the charity patient, they would be left with no alternative but to avail themselves to a local nurse.

Brigid went straight to the bed where Mary was sleeping, and then she made herself familiar with the baby nursery, although at that time there was only Mary's baby there along with the wet nurse. She checked the crib where the baby lay. The note at the foot of the crib said, *Convent baby for adoption. No name.*

She mused over how sad and cruel it was when a young mother could not afford, or be allowed by society to keep, their own child.

Mary woke several hours later, and was still in severe pain, and Brigid could see no purpose in trying to talk to her.

The wet nurse continued to feed her baby, and it was several days later before Brigid could have a conversation with her.

'Hello Mary, do you remember me?'

'Yeah, I remember you, you helped me mummy. How is she, can I see her, does she know I'm 'ere?' Brigid moved the bentwood chair closer to Mary's bedside and sat down. She took hold of her hand and said quietly, 'Mary, I'm sorry to be the one who has to tell you this, but your mummy died.'

Mary looked intently into Brigid's eyes, and as she digested what she had just heard, her eyes welled up and then she wailed, 'No, no it's not true, me mummy can't be dead, you was looking after 'er!'

Brigid clasped Mary's hand with both of hers.

'I am so sorry Mary, but your mummy died on the day that you left here to go to the convent. She was so very sick, and she never woke up again after you left.'

Mary was sobbing softly, and Brigid kept holding her hand.

'Why didn't someone tell me? I should a bin wif 'er. Where did they take 'er, where did they bury 'er miss?'

Brigid was feeling uncomfortable, as she couldn't answer the questions. She guessed that Patricia would have been buried in a pauper grave, and all that she could say to Mary was, 'I could find out where they buried your mother. Then when you are better we could go there together. Yes, that's what we will do. I will find out where she is buried, and you can say goodbye.'

Mary was still sobbing, but took some comfort from what Brigid had said, 'Will ya really find out where she is miss, an' will ya really come wif me?'

Brigid squeezed her hand and replied, 'Yes Mary, I really will, now let me check your wound.'

✳✳✳

Mrs Brown was the wet nurse. Brigid had met her a few times and knew her well enough to exchange pleasantries, but now she would be asking her to bend the hospital rules.

'Mrs Brown, may I have a word with you?'

'Yes nurse, what is it?

'Would it be possible for Mary to nurse her child for a little while? Her mother was a patient here, and she died almost six months ago, but she has only just learned of her mother's death. She has been crying on and off ever since. I thought that if she could nurse her child and bond with her then it might help take her mind off her mother. She would need to be shown how to suckle the child, but I am concerned for her. Would that be all right?' May Brown had seen this situation many times before when a young mother had delivered a child only to lose it shortly after.

She had six children of her own. She had wondered how she would cope if she were in the same situation, and was forced to hand over one of her children to the authorities.

'I was told by matron that I would wet nurse the child until the nuns had arranged a new home for her, but let's not tell anyone! We can let your patient look after her baby for a few days until she has to give it up. I know that will be hard for her, but at least she will have a few memories to keep with her.

'I will get the baby now, and I will instruct her on how to breastfeed it, but that will be our little secret, won't it? I don't want to get on matron's wrong side.'

May took the baby to Mary, and her face lit up the moment her child started to suckle. She stroked its head and tickled it under her chin, and the bond was made. May then took the baby, and changed the towelling nappy before returning it to its mother.

Brigid came to Mary's bedside and sat down. 'How are you managing Mary?'

'Oh miss, she is beautiful, but she's so tiny, and I fed 'er all on me own and ya know what miss?'

'What Mary?'

'I'm gunna call 'er Patricia, after me mum, she'd like that she would!' She beamed a big smile. Brigid thought of how happy she looked at that moment. However, she was troubled with the thought of how Mary would react when the nuns took her child, and she finally realised that she would never see her baby again.

Over the next two weeks Mary grew stronger, and the bond between her and her child grew.

Brigid had learned from the mortuary attendant the location of where Patricia was buried. She had also found out that there was a train that they could catch from Central Station directly to the cemetery. She was pleased that she would be able to fulfil her promise to Mary when the time came.

By now, there were several other patients along with several other babies in the lay-in ward. Mary would proudly place her baby in the small hospital crib after she had fed and changed her. She had also got Brigid to scrawl a small name tag at the foot of the crib, even though she could not read it.

¥¥¥

It was a month later before Sister Harriet arrived at the Barracks Hospital. A tall, stately woman accompanied her. She was dressed in a three-quarter-length brown pleated skirt. A wide-brimmed hat partially hid her face, along with the lace handkerchief that she kept close to her nose. Sister Harriet spoke down to the nurse, who had asked her how she could help.

'I am here to show Mrs Bromley the baby that is wanting for adoption, so please take us to the nursery without further delay please nurse.'

The nurse had no idea of what baby the nun was referring to, and replied, 'I am sorry sister, but it is outside of visiting hours, and I cannot leave my station without permission. I will see if I can find matron so that she can assist you.'

'Please do, and don't dilly-dally nurse, Mrs Bromley has a busy schedule, and she just needs to see if the child is suitable.'

Noreen arrived onto the ward, and was equally terse with Sister Harriet. 'Good morning sister, I believe that you wish to see Mary Bridges' baby, is that correct?'

'Good morning matron, yes that is correct. This is Mrs Bromley, and she is looking for a child to adopt. She would like a girl child providing that it has no deformities, or mental defects. I am led to believe that the Bridges child meets those requirements, so we would like to see her if you please!'

'Well, sister, I am sure that you can appreciate that we are a very busy hospital. We work to schedules and time frames, as I am certain that you do at the convent.

'That is why we have visiting hours! If anyone wishes to attend for any other reason outside of those hours, we would like an appointment to be made. However, it just so happens that I am about to do my rounds. I will take you to see the child in question, but in future please respect our rules.'

Sister Harriet's face turned bright red, as she had not expected to get a dressing-down in front of her client. She was about to reply, but then thought better of it. If the matron refused to allow them to see the child, then it would amount to a severe embarrassment for herself and her standing.

'I apologise matron, now may we see the baby?'

Mary had fed her baby, and was nursing her as she slowly walked around the ward. Deep down she knew that one day she would have to give her up, but she refused to think about that day. She also knew that she would have to return to the convent, but now that she had had the baby it would only be for another twelve weeks. After that, she had no idea of what she would do, or where she would live, but as each day passed by, she was trying to work out how she could keep her child.

Noreen arrived onto the ward, followed closely by the other two women. She saw Mary and gave her a weak smile, 'Now, here she is. Hello Mary, how is the little one?'

Mary replied, 'I just fed 'er, and she is good matron.' She looked nervously at Sister Harriet, and the tall lady standing next to her. There was no acknowledgement to her from either of them except for Sister Harriet saying to Mrs Bromley. 'This is the baby that I was referring to, she is a bit small, but is perfectly formed, and has no known defects. The child has not been named.'

Mary immediately broke into the conversation, 'Her name is Patricia, I named her after me mother, so that's 'er name.'

Sister Harriet glared at Mary before retorting, 'How dare you intrude into our conversation girl, we are trying to find a good and decent home for this child, and Mrs Bromley has kindly conceded to look at her. You should be grateful that somebody of Mrs Bromley's standing would even consider taking her. So please remain quiet unless you are spoken to, do you understand?'

Mary started to cry, and she buried her face into the blanket that her baby was wrapped in. Sister Harriet continued talking, and was determined to stress the importance of why her client should adopt this child.

'Like I was saying Mrs Bromley, the child has not yet been baptised, and nor does she have a name. In fact, she doesn't even have a birth certificate at this moment!

'If you and Mr Bromley did decide to adopt the child, I'm sure that we could arrange for you to be put down as the birth mother. You could as well give the child a name of your choice, so no one need know that you were not the birth mother.'

Mrs Bromley sniffled into her handkerchief; the hospital smells were an affront to her nostrils. She was uncomfortable in this environment, and not having any children of her own made the whole adoption process alien to her. Sister Harriet could see that the deal was far from being settled. At that moment, she was unsure if Mrs Bromley would even consider taking the child.

'Would you like to nurse the child Mrs Bromley?' Before she could answer, the nun growled at Mary, 'Hand the child to Mrs Bromley girl, don't just stand there!'

Mary passed over her small bundle, and Mrs Bromley reluctantly took it. There was no warmth or joy in the way that she held the baby, as she looked disdainfully at it.

She spoke to Sister Harriet and said, 'Of course I am only doing this because of Mr Bromley's desire to have a child. I am perfectly happy with the way that things are. I did say to Mr Bromley that I would insist on having a nanny to look after it, if in fact we did adopt a child.'

Sister Harriet nodded and said, 'Of course Mrs Bromley, and I would entirely agree with you, now what do you think? Do you think that Mr Bromley would be happy if you took the child home today?'

She thought for a moment, and then handed the baby back to Mary, who grasped it as though the child had been hurt.

'Sister, do you think that I might take the child home and see what Mr Bromley thinks? He did say that he wanted a boy child, but I insisted that if we were going to adopt, then I would settle for nothing less than a girl. Now if I take her with me, and Mr Bromley insists on a boy child then, I would need to be able to return her, would that be acceptable to you?'

Sister Harriet thought for a moment before replying, 'I suppose that what you are proposing would be acceptable, but I would insist that if you keep the child for more than twenty-four hours, then the adoption must go through. So, would you like to take the child now, or wait until you can arrange for a nanny to attend to it?'

'No sister, I will leave the child here for the moment, but I will get my houseman to bring my maid back to pick it up this evening. I have already purchased a perambulator.

'My maid can look after the child until after Mr Bromley has decided whether we will keep it or not. If we do keep it then I will employ the services of a nanny to look after it.'

'Very well, Mrs Bromley, and you will call at the convent tomorrow and let us know your answer?'

It was more of a statement than a question, but Sister Harriet would cajole and bully Mrs Bromley into accepting the child while she could. It wasn't only that they were arranging a home for the child, but the adopting couple would be expected to make a generous donation to the convent.

Brigid had come onto the ward just as Mary had handed over her baby to Mrs Bromley. She had then stood discreetly in the background while the negotiations had taken place. Brigid had overheard the conversation, and had mused over the cold and impersonal way the two women were discussing the future of the child. Neither appeared to give a thought to the feelings of its mother.

Noreen came back, and was less than pleased to see the two women still there. 'Sister, I must insist that you both leave now. The nurses have work to do, and I would like you to conclude your business elsewhere!'

'Yes, we are just leaving now matron. However, Mrs Bromley's maid will be back this evening to pick up the child. So, if you don't mind, could we retire to your office to finish off the paperwork, and sort out the birth certificate details?'

Noreen Emmitt didn't like Sister Harriet, and she didn't like the way that she traded in children at the expense of the mother. She was well aware of how society viewed unmarried mothers, and how it was almost impossible for a young woman to bring up a baby by herself.

She knew that she couldn't change society, and the contempt that most had for young unmarried mothers. Unlike the nuns, she didn't judge people on their moral values. She had also developed a soft spot for Mary, and had tried to find a solution that could change her circumstances, but any hope of Mary keeping her baby was almost gone.

When the two women left the ward, Mary had gone back to her bed, and sat on the edge. She was quietly weeping, and held her baby close to her face. Brigid came and sat with her, and put her arm around her shoulder.

'Don't cry, Mary. I know that it will be hard for you to part with her, but stop and think about it! You can't give her a home, and that rich lady can. Just think about what a wonderful life she will have with servants and maids to look after her. And think of how it will be impossible for you to get a job, even if you could find some way to keep her. I'm sorry Mary, but what will you do to support yourself after you leave the convent? You will have to get a job somewhere. Have you thought about your future? Maybe you could get a job in a boarding house as a maid, or something. That way you would at least have a room to live in.'

Mary was still sniffling, but still held her baby tightly. Usually, at this time of day, it would be tucked up in the hospital crib, but Brigid was not about to suggest that Mary put the baby down.

'I don't wanna give them me baby miss. She's all I got now that me mummy's dead!' She then lay the baby on her lap as a thought came to her, 'I know miss, I know what I'll do, I'll run away, and I'll take me baby wif me. I can go now, so when they come back we will both be gone, will ya help me miss, will ya get me clothes fer me?'

Mary was looking anxiously at Brigid, but with a glimmer of hope shining in her eyes.

Brigid was shocked at the thought of Mary trying to survive by herself with no money, and a baby to look after. She was practical, and although she could understand Mary's desperation, she could not be a party to this idea.

'No Mary, that's not a good idea. Where would you sleep, and how could you change your baby's nappies and keep her warm, and how would you feed yourself? I'm sorry Mary; I can't help you run away. I can ask matron if she could give you a job as a scullery maid in the kitchen here. At least that way, you would be able to earn a few shillings a week. That would get you a room of your own, but you still couldn't keep your baby. I'm sorry Mary, but that's just the way that it is.'

Mary held her baby tightly, and showed no recognition that she had heard, or even understood what Brigid had just said to her. Brigid stood up and said, 'I have to see matron now, and I have a few things to do, but I will be back to see you shortly, now stop crying Mary, please!'

Brigid checked on several other patients, and then she went downstairs. She had made up her mind, and she would ask matron if she could give Mary a menial position down in the kitchen.

Brigid knew that she shouldn't become so involved in her patient's life. She was of a similar age to Mary, and she had no idea of what she would do if she were in the same position as her.

She couldn't find matron, and she returned to her ward. She had been gone for less than ten minutes, but when she came back there was no sign of Mary. She thought that maybe she had gone to the nursery to change the baby and she checked there. Then she remembered the conversation that she had just had with her, and her fears grew. She thought to herself, *No, she wouldn't really run away, would she? No, she couldn't!*

She knew that Mary was only wearing a hospital gown. She ran over to the nurse's station, and with a note of panic in her voice she asked the nurse there, 'Have you seen Mary?' The nurse just gave her a blank look before replying, 'Yes, I saw her walking down the corridor, I thought that she might be going out into the garden, why is there a problem?'

'I'm not sure, maybe nothing, but I have to find her quickly. If I don't come back shortly, will you tell matron that I think that Mary might have run away with her baby and that I need to look for her? Will you tell her that please?'

'Yes, I will, but she can't have gotten far, it's only been a few minutes.'

Brigid ran out into the hospital grounds, and other than a few patients being wheeled about by nurses there was no sign of Mary. She ran through the large, ornate wrought-iron front gate and looked up and down James Street. It was a long straight road, and she looked towards Circular Quay and the water. She dismissed the idea that she would go that way because she had no money, and the road only led to the ferry terminal.

Looking in the other direction, she thought that she could see a small figure about a quarter of a mile away. The figure was too far away to be able to confirm that it was Mary, but Brigid started running in that direction just in case it was her.

After running for a few minutes, Brigid could now see that it was Mary, and she started calling to her, 'Mary, Mary, will you stop? You can't do this, please Mary just stop, we need to go back!' Brigid was panting hard, and was now only fifty yards from her.

Mary looked over her shoulder, and the surprise of seeing Brigid almost behind her showed on her face, and she started running. She held her baby close to her chest. They were now near the rail yards, and close to Central Station.

Mary now seemed intent on getting to the station, in the hope that she might be able to jump onto a train. She ran down the sloping embankment, and along the culvert that ran next to the train track.

Brigid had fallen back, but was still calling out to her. She didn't want to go down the embankment, as it only led to the railway line that went to the station. She decided to stay on the road, at the top of the embankment in the hope that she could get to the station before Mary could. Brigid glanced down, and at the same time she heard the shrill whistle of the steam engine.

Mary had also heard it coming from behind her, and it had startled her. She thought that she should cross the railway line to get to the other side, and she immediately ran across the track. The engine driver was still blowing the whistle, and was wondering what the young woman was doing as she ran in front of his train. The brakes squealed, and the steam hissed from the cylinders as he applied the brake, but it was too late. He thought that he had heard a scream above the squealing wheels, as the train came to a screeching stop.

Brigid had watched the unfolding drama, from the top of the rail cutting, and saw Mary run across the path of the locomotive. She put her hand to her mouth and screamed, 'Oh God, no!' She watched, as the driver and the fireman both climbed down and went to the front of the engine as they peered between the wheels. She saw one of the men shake his head, before walking towards the station to get help.

Brigid was in shock, as she stood and looked down on the scene. People who had been on the platform and who had seen the accident were now running down towards the stationary train, but there was nothing that they could do. Brigid sat there until someone asked her, 'Are you all right miss, did you see the accident?'

And another said, 'She was just a young girl, and she had a baby with her, how dreadful. What was she doing running along the train track?'

Brigid walked back to the hospital in a trance. She was unable to believe that less than an hour ago Mary and her baby were alive and well, and now they were both dead. Noreen was standing at the front door of the hospital as Brigid returned. She could see by the haunted look on Brigid's face that something was not right.

'What is it child, did you find her?' Brigid was shaking, as she burst into tears and narrated to Noreen what had just happened.

Noreen listened in disbelief as Brigid told the story.

Noreen knew that her young charge was in shock, as she wrapped her arm around her shoulder and said quietly, 'Come with me.' She yelled at a nearby nurse, 'Bring me a blanket nurse, quickly now.'

Noreen knew that Brigid would need to be kept warm as the shock took hold. She led her to her office, and placed the blanket around her small shoulders. 'Now you just sit there, and I will go and make you up a tonic.' She went to the kitchen, and made up a mixture of warm milk and rum, and took it back for Brigid to drink.

33.

A Letter to Tom

Tommy had been on Hannah's mind all day, and after sorting out the material that she would use to make a quilt, she sat at the table and penned her letter.

February 1916.

Dearest Tommy,

It was wonderful to receive your letter from Egypt, and I didn't know if I should laugh or cry when I read about your Christmas dinner. I was overjoyed to hear that you were all safe and still together. I know that I shouldn't say this, but I will. I hope that the generals, or whoever they are, decide to keep you all there until this dreadful war is over.

I hate the thought of anything happening of any of you, but I won't speak any more of this as it upsets me.

I have been keeping very busy, as I have been making lots of jam, mainly blackberry, as there are plenty around at the moment. We have also been making vegetable pickles and filling preserve jars with it.

I have joined the Ladies Auxiliary League, and what we do is hold street stalls on Saturday mornings to raise money. We hold raffles, and sell the things that we make, so that we can send comfort billies to as many troops as we can. Many of the ladies are getting involved in doing this, as it not only keeps us busy, but it allows us to know that in our own small way we are doing our bit for the war effort.

Some of us are also working on the nearby farms as labourers. The government asked for anyone who could help with providing labour to farmers to help with the harvest and fruit picking to enroll at our local churches. When I first heard of it, I thought that it would be a good way to learn about farm life considering that you and I will, one day, hopefully have a few acres of our own.

Last week, I was working on a fruit farm down at Camden, and we spent two whole days just picking grapes for the farmer who has both of his sons overseas.

Tommy, you would have been proud of me, and I wish that I could show you my hands. I had blisters on them as big as berries, and so did the other ladies, but none of us complained because we knew that our sunburn and our blisters were of no consequence compared to the hardships that you are all going through.

There were eight of us in total, and we all caught the train to Camden, and the farmer picked us up in his truck, and we all rode in the back as he took us to his farm. After working for more than ten hours, we were all ready for a good night's sleep, and we slept in his bunkhouse.

His wife was so lovely, and she cried when we all arrived to work, as she didn't know how they would have been able to harvest the grapes if we hadn't turned up.

Next week, we are going to another farm where we are apparently going to bale hay, so that should be interesting, but like Aunt Claire says, 'There is no substitute for experience', and I want to experience farm life Tommy as I want to be a good farmer's wife. It must be very hard for the farmers who have no one to help them with their animals and crops.

The farms that we are helping on are all relatively close by, and not hard to get to by train, so I will keep doing my bit until all of you have returned safely back to us. Oh, by the way, is Des Carney still with you in your group? The reason that I ask is that we had morning tea with Brigid Blake some months ago, in fact, it was last year now, oh my, how the time just flies by!

She is training to be a nurse at the Barracks Hospital, and she was asking after him. We told her that she should write to him as a pen pal, but I think that she holds a torch for him, and I know that it would cheer her up immensely if he would write to her.

I know that I am doing a little matchmaking here, but she always seemed to harbour a soft spot for him, and it might be good for both of them if they exchanged the occasional letter. She did mention that she was hoping to get a job on a hospital ship one day. I don't know if she did, but we haven't heard from her for some considerable time now that I come to think of it.

Please write again soon Tommy, and please stay safe. By the way, I almost forgot, your mother said that she would like a nice long letter from you. She misses you both terribly as do I.

All of my love,

Hannah.

34.

A Change of Plans

Two weeks had passed by, and Brigid was still struggling emotionally after witnessing the death of Mary and her baby. Noreen knew that Brigid was blaming herself for the death and she had kept repeating, 'I shouldn't have been chasing her, if only I hadn't chased her!'

Nothing that Noreen said would appease her.

Brigid had been put back onto the general ward, not as a punishment, but Noreen had thought that it would not be a good idea for her to be around mothers and their babies at the moment. Noreen hoped that Brigid might wish to return to the laying-in ward in the future, but she would wait and see if her young charge would recover from her trauma.

As the weeks passed, and Brigid had not improved. Noreen had decided that Brigid should return home to her mother and her brothers for a few weeks. She hoped that being with her family would help her with getting over the shock. At first, Brigid thought that she was being sent home as punishment. However, Noreen had explained that she was deserving of a holiday, and that now would be a good time for her to get away from the hospital for a while.

'Now I want you to go home, and see your mother and your brothers young lady. You need to take a few weeks away from here.

'This might sound a little harsh, but if you are going to make a career out of nursing, you will have to learn how to keep part of yourself detached from what goes on here at the hospital every day.

'Now, you take as long as you like to rest and come to grips with this dreadful affair. And when you come back we will get you to sit your nurse's exam. I know that you are more than ready, so focus on that rather than anything else, do you understand what I am saying Brigid?'

'Yes Matron, and thank you for all of your help. I'm sorry that I haven't been myself recently, but it will be nice to live at home for a while. When shall I come back?'

'Come and see me in three weeks, and then we will decide about your future young lady, now off you go I have work to do.'

***

Mr Lucas Brown was the chairman of the board at the Barracks Hospital. The only time that he attended the hospital was when he had to convene the weekly board meeting, and even then, he kept well away from the wards, which he viewed with disdain.

He showed no interest whatsoever in the day-to-day operation of the hospital. His only concern was to discuss with the other board members about who could be admitted to the hospital as charity cases.

The hospital generally only accepted patients that could pay for its services. However, they had a policy of accepting one charity case per week, providing that the charity patient had a chance of survival. If it were deemed by the board members that the patient's illness would not respond to any treatment offered, then that patient would be passed over in favour of someone who was likely to survive. If the board implemented new policies, and if Mr Brown thought that it was necessary, he communicated the changes to hospital policies through his secretary. But before this week's meeting was convened, he had dispatched his secretary to Noreen's office with a request that she attend his office as a matter of urgency.

The secretary found Matron at her desk, and she coolly relayed the summons to her, 'Good morning Matron,' and without waiting for a response she said, 'Mr Brown would like to see you without further delay if you don't mind.'

Noreen scowled at the interruption, but from past experience knew that there was no use in arguing, or even disagreeing with Gertrude Sloan. She was in her forties, a spinster, and very set in her ways. She had been Lucas Brown's secretary for more than fifteen years. Her only purpose in life, as far as she was concerned, was to accommodate and implement the instructions of her superior.

Noreen sighed in exasperation, and it didn't go unnoticed by Miss Sloan, who having delivered the message turned to make her way back to her office.

As Noreen arrived outside of the boardroom, Miss Sloan rose from behind her desk, and knocked on the door before gently opening it to announce her arrival.

'Thank you, Miss Sloan, please show her in.'

'Good morning, Mr Brown. I hope that this won't take too long as I have yet to do my rounds,' Noreen stated brusquely. She didn't like being summoned to the boardroom like a manservant, and usually when she was, it was to be told something that could have easily been communicated to her by Miss Sloan.

Lucas Brown was sat at his overly large cedar desk, and he wore a pair of pincers at the end of his hawkish nose. He now looked over the top of them, and indicated with his hand that Noreen should sit down on the chair that he had pointed at.

'Good morning Sister,' and didn't wait for a response before saying, 'Sister, I have just received a communication from the Department of Army. They have asked me if we could supply a contingent of nurses to work on a hospital ship. The ship is currently being fitted out down at Darling Harbour. It is expected to be ready to sail for the Mediterranean area sometime over the next eight to ten weeks!

'I know that it is rather short notice, Matron, but I have not given them a reply as yet, as it is out of my domain of expertise. I would like to know if we could accede to their request.

'The nurses would have to be experienced, and would all have to be volunteers. There is no saying how long they will be away from home. Those that volunteer to go must also understand that they may be transferred to work at any onshore medical facilities where our troops are being transferred.

'So, Matron, could you give me an answer by the end of the week on firstly, whether or not we can provide the army with any nurses, and if so, how many? Could you also tell me who you would recommend being in charge of the nurses' contingent? Obviously, you cannot go, as you will be required to continue managing the hospital here.'

Noreen was taken aback with the request, as it wasn't expected, but she required more information and asked, 'Mr Brown, do I have complete control on selecting the volunteers, or do you want me to provide the board with their names, so that you can decide?'

'Matron, I have complete faith in your ability to select the nurses. They will have to be able to cope with what I imagine will be difficult and trying conditions, not only on board, but also once they have reached the conflict zone. All that I require from you is an answer on if we can provide any nurses, and if so, how many, and how soon?'

'Mr Brown, did the army give you any indication of how many nurses they would require to man the hospital ship?'

'Yes matron, it was suggested that the ship would have quarters for a maximum of ninety medical staff in total, and that the ship would be able to handle up to six hundred patients at a squeeze. I believe that there would be around twenty qualified nurses, and possibly a dozen ward assistant nurses required. Around forty to fifty orderlies and possibly four or five surgeons would also be needed.'

Noreen thought for a moment before replying. 'Mr Brown, I believe that I could easily obtain that many volunteer nurses to work on the ship. I have had numerous enquiries from various grades over the past few months that I believe would sign up in an instant. However, I have been thinking about it myself for some time now, and I will put my name forward to work on the ship. I don't expect to be matron in charge, but I would volunteer to be a senior nurse.' Lucas stared intently over his glasses at Noreen before speaking.

'Matron, while I find it admirable that you would consider volunteering your services to the cause, I could not permit it! You are a valuable asset to this hospital, and we would find it difficult to replace you. No, I'm sorry, but I could not allow it!'

Noreen would, and had many times stood up to the various male board members who wanted to make decisions that she had thought were incorrect or inappropriate. She was not the type of person who thought of herself as indispensable, and if she made up her mind to do something, then she would go ahead and do it.

'Mr Brown, while I am flattered that you think that I am indispensable, I can assure you that I am not! Whilst it cannot be denied that the patients that are admitted here deserve to be attended to, I cannot help thinking of all of the young men who are suffering dreadfully overseas. If what we read in the papers can be believed, then I think that they are more deserving of our services than wealthy patients who have not sacrificed anything except some discomfort.

'The majority of patients that we have here can pay for the services that we provide to them, yet we won't accept the poor and the underprivileged.

'Now, whether you like it or not, many of those boys putting their lives on the line overseas at the moment would not be admitted into this hospital as many of them could not afford to pay for our services!

'My belief is, that the hospital, and its board members should also make a few sacrifices. If by my leaving this establishment because my conscience dictates that it is the right thing for me to do, then I think that the board members should be able to suffer the inconvenience of not having me here as the matron in charge. Now, if you cannot accept what I have just said Mr Brown, then I will hand in my resignation to you this very day!'

Lucas Brown was well aware of Noreen's strong viewpoint on patient care, and he had no desire to antagonise her further.

'Matron, there will be no need for you to take such drastic action. I would prefer that you stayed here, but if you feel that strongly about serving, then I won't mention the matter again. I will recommend to the board that we give you leave of absence from your post for the duration of the conflict, however long that may be!'

'I will also recommend that you will continue to be the senior matron on board. I would ask you, though, to provide me with the names of all of the nurses that you select to work on board as soon as possible. And could you also provide me with the name of the person who you feel should replace you here as senior matron?'

Noreen had been ready to argue her case further, but now there was no need to.

'Thank you, Mr Brown. I will call for volunteers immediately, and I will select only those who I think will be capable of working under what I imagine will be very adverse conditions. I hope that the conflict will not continue indefinitely, and I appreciate the fact that you will hold open my position until I return, whenever that may be.

'If there is nothing else Mr Brown, I shall return to my duties. When I have compiled the list, I shall give it to Miss Sloan. Good morning.'

'Yes, thank you Matron, and no, there is nothing further.'

⋆⋆⋆

Noreen made her way back to her office. She had just committed herself to an uncertain future, along with an increased workload. She would have to sort through the names of the volunteers and the person that she thought would be suitable to take over the running of the wards; along with looking after eighty nurses and orderlies and the administrative duties that went with the position.

Noreen was writing out the notices that she would place around the hospital setting out the requirements for the volunteers. Her mind was wandering as she thought about young Brigid; and how this might be the very thing that she needed to do to take her mind away from that dreadful accident. Brigid had already asked if it would be possible to obtain a position on a hospital ship well before the unfortunate incident. And Mr Brown had said that she would have complete control over whom she selected to work on the ship. It was very worrying for Noreen to know that Brigid was still blaming herself for Mary's death. She also knew that she had become very fond of the girl. Being childless had never really bothered her before, but she now mused that if she had had a daughter, she imagined that she would be someone like Brigid.

She made up her mind that if Brigid still wanted to volunteer, then she would put her through her exams over the next week, having no doubt that she would pass them with flying colours.

***

The long days over the next eight weeks just rushed by for Noreen. The volunteers had all been interviewed and selected, and Brigid had passed her exams. She was excited at the prospect of not only working on the ship, but also with the thought of travelling across the world to see places that she had only read about in the newspapers.

They set sail from Sydney, on the hospital ship 'S.S. Karoola' in mid-September 1915. On board were Noreen, Brigid and twenty volunteer nurses, along with ten surgeons and forty orderlies.

35.

France

It was a balmy, sunny day when Tom and several thousand others embarked from Southampton to sail for France.

Twelve hours later they all arrived in the old farming village of Boulogne where they set up camp on a farmer's field. From there they marched through green, peaceful farmlands that were separated by vine-covered stone walls. They were less than twenty miles outside of Paris, and it was hard for them to imagine that a deadly war had been raging not far from here for more than a year.

As the convoy rolled by, local villagers lined the sides of the road. Some just stared, while some handed soldiers small parcels of food, or a loaf of bread. Each group of villagers acted differently. Some clapped, and ran over to the soldiers to shake a hand or two muttering, 'Merci, monsieur.'

Each evening, camps were set up in fields on the edges of towns. They marched for almost two weeks covering between six and ten miles a day, and then the landscape changed.

✳✳✳

They came across deserted villages that had been all but destroyed. Nothing had been spared from the destruction. What were once stone houses and churches were now no more than piles of rubble, and what had once been a road was now no more than a crater-filled bog.

The blackened stumps of charred trees stood like sentinels next to giant craters. Cannons had created a muddy lunar landscape from what were once crop-filled fields that now looked like they had been turned over by giant moles. As the convoy marched further into the decimated countryside, the atmosphere became tense. To their left were the trenches. Some were empty, and soldiers from Canada, India and Great Britain occupied others.

The trenches stretched from the English Channel, and zigzagged their way to the Swiss border two hundred and fifty miles away. Tents lined the roadside, sometimes for a mile or more. Field ambulances were now winding their way along the road, together with an assortment of motorised vehicles including trucks towing cannons.

Ambulances were taking wounded soldiers to the casualty stations that had been set up many miles from the battle zones, while others were returning to the front. Mountains of used brass shell casings stood ten feet high and hundreds of feet long in piles alongside of the road. The road itself was chaotic.

The convoy of foot soldiers wound along the road for more than a mile, and mixed among them were the light horse cavalry brigades and dispatch riders on motorcycles. There was a sense of dread amongst the men as they marched through more burnt-out villages. Something told them that this was going to be a much different conflict to the one that they had been involved in, in Turkey.

The memories of Turkey had almost been forgotten during their rest break in England. They had played cricket and football on friendly fields, far from the bloody nightmare and noise that they had all experienced amongst the jagged hills of Turkey. But now, looking at this destruction, the horrors that they had lived with there had all come back to them. The bravado that they mostly wore as a shield was now disappearing as the sights of the destroyed villages reminded them of how precarious their hold on life really was.

The demarcation line was to their left, sometimes no more than a half a mile away from where they marched. At the end of each day they made their camp in barns and fields, but each night they could see the glow of the Very lights arcing across the sky before floating down to hiss and sputter on the ground. Some nights all would be quiet, while at other times they would hear the rumble of heavy cannon that sounded like thunder, and the distant sky would light up with what looked like flashes of lightning across a night sky. After fifteen days of marching across France, they finally arrived at where the Australian contingent was dug in.

Although the Australian battalions had seen action in Turkey, they were regarded as inexperienced. They were initially placed into the quiet trenches on the peripheral edges of where the nightly battles would take place. It was known as the nursery; where the newly arrived soldiers would spend time with those who had come before them, and who had already been christened by the explosive forces of the German guns. They stayed there for several weeks before being rotated to the front line.

Orders were being barked, and the battalion was broken up, and men were ordered to various parts of the camp. Tom and his group led the way to the sleeping tents.

'You men stow your gear, and then muster behind the field kitchen. You will be given your instructions for tonight, and then you can eat.'

The sergeant yelling out the orders was short and stocky. He had signed up at the very start of the conflict and was battle-hardened and weary. His name was Thomas Fegent, a Welshman. He had been a coal miner in Wales before he had come to Australia to try his luck at gold mining in the gold fields of Western Australia.

He had been in Australia for more than two years before the war had started, and he had been considering going back home just as the war had been declared. He had had no luck with finding gold, and the stark isolation and the harsh red earth had him longing for the heather-covered hills of Wales. He was almost penniless, and he saw joining up as a way of getting himself home. He was a good soldier, and it didn't take him long to get promoted, even though he was happy just being a foot soldier.

He had the respect of the men that he commanded as he was relaxed with discipline when the hierarchy was not around. He liked to play cards, and at times he would join in a friendly game with his men. He greeted the new arrivals as they mustered behind the camp kitchen.

'Orr right you lot, my name is Sergeant Fegent, but you can call me Sarge! My job is to train and teach you in how to use some of the new weaponry that you won't be familiar with. Now fortunately for us, the Tommies seem to be getting more attention from Fritz than what we have. That don't mean to say that they won't turn their big guns on us at any time. So, we must all be ready for when that time comes, so you will spend a lot of your time doing training and taking supplies up to the dump.'

Des piped up, 'Scuse me Sarge, what's the dump?'

'Oh, that's right, I forgot that you blokes are from the nursery. Right, the dump is at the start of the front-line trench. Now they need ammo up there, and lots of it, so every night a dozen of you will carry rifle and machine gun ammo up to the dump. Now we do this under cover of darkness, we have to really because each of you will carry an ammo box and it's easier to do it by walking along the top of the trenches instead of through them, it's also quicker that way.

'But understand this, you might think that it's an easy job just carrying ammo boxes up to the front line in the darkness. However, a lot of blokes have been shot doing it, because Fritz lights up the sky with them Very lights. They go up and down like they were dancin' on water and when them lights are up there,' and he nodded skywards, 'they light the place up like you was out the front of the Moulin Rouge in Paris. Now, before you ask me, the Moulin Rouge is one of the Frenchie cabaret places in Paris, where the sheilas all dance around on stage in their frilly knickers.'

They all looked at each other and grinned, and all thinking the same thing as the thought of dancing girls and cabarets took their minds off the reality of where they were for a few moments.

Sergeant Fegent looked at the grinning faces standing before him and said, 'Right you lot settle down. If yer lucky you might get to see the show one day, but in the meantime, I gotta teach you something. Now as I was saying, when the Very lights go up you have to drop down to the ground straight away and don't move. Cause as soon as them lights light up the place, then Fritz will have his snipers out, and most of them only need one shot at you. So, remember as soon as you hear the whoosh, and you will hear 'em, you got about twenty seconds before the whole place is like daylight.

'They don't just fire off one. They keep firin' em one after another for about fifteen minutes, so if you're out there when they go off you will just have to lie there and don't move until the lights go out. Have you got that?'

They all looked skyward as they heard the roar of an aeroplane engine. The small biplane flew directly over their heads and they instinctively ducked. The red, white and blue roundel of the British insignia was clearly visible below its wings and on its tail.

Fred was the first to speak, 'Geez, did ya see that? I never seen an aeroplane so close before, I didn't see none in Turkey.' They all spoke among themselves until the sergeant interrupted.

'Well you're gunna see a lot of them around here, and you're gunna see the balloons that Fritz puts up in the sky too.'

They were all curious now as they weren't sure what the sergeant was even talking about.

'What balloons Sarge?'

The question came from the ranks, and the sergeant replied, 'Orright, where have you blokes been? Haven't seen an aeroplane, and don't know what an aerial balloon is.

'Right, the Tommies have got em, and Fritz have got 'em. They stick a couple of blokes in the basket below the balloon. The balloon is filled up with some sort of gas so it can float, and it's tied to the ground by a long rope so it don't blow away. Now, the blokes in the basket can see right over our trenches and they draw maps of our movements. Then they stick them in a canister and drop it back to earth. That way, their brass can work out as to where they should aim their big guns.

'Now, when you see them you can't mistake ours for theirs, because theirs has a bloody great black iron cross sewn on both sides of the thing.

So, if you get near one just start shooting at it cause they will probably drop hand bombs on you! The Tommies do the same with Fritz, but it's bloody dangerous for the blokes in the basket because everyone takes pot shots at them cause they can only go up during daylight. You want to see what happens when somebody gets a lucky shot into the balloon part. We brought one down a couple of weeks ago, an it went off like a big candle. We saw the poor buggers jump out when it was about a hundred feet off the ground, doubt if they would have survived though!

'Well, you would have seen the hand bombs in Turkey that we used; well now they got these new ones. They are called Mills grenades. They are smaller than the old hand bombs, and you can toss 'em a lot further. So, it's my job to show you how to use them. I'm gunna take you all down the road a bit to an old quarry, and you're gunna learn how to throw 'em.

'Now, the other thing that we do a bit different than what we done in Turkey is that if you are in the reserve trenches and you're not on ammo duty, then you can go for a wander into the town down the road. The town's name is Locre, and if you can find somewhere to sleep in a barn or somewhere then that's up to you, but you still hav'ta be back by reveille. Some of the old sheilas in the town make up stews and soups, which aren't bad at all. They also sell coffee. They charge you a few francs but you can have seconds for nothing. Anyway, you can make up your own minds on what you do in your spare time. Right then, if there's nothing else that you want to know I'll leave you to get yourselves settled in.'

They looked at each other, and Tom commented, 'Well, he seems like a decent sort. I like the idea that we can go fer a walk if we want, so how about it?'

'I dunno if we can go now, shouldn't we wait until the Sarge says we can go?'

Tom replied, 'Yeah, I suppose ya right, anyway we need to put our stuff somewhere before it starts rainin.' The sergeant came back, and Tom asked, 'Sarge, can we go fer a walk down to the village now?'

'Well if you want, but I want you all back here in three hours, so make sure that you don't get lost because you are all going out on patrol when it gets dark, understood? Also, you need to be issued with new supplies, but we can do that tomorrow morning. So, go and relax for a while, but before you go stow your gear in the barracks tent over there,' pointing in the direction that he wanted them to go.

'Righto, Sarge we will be off now, so who's comin'?' asked Tom, and a dozen of them sauntered off.

As they walked toward the village, they noticed the marquees that were used as first aid stations, and wooden buildings that served as dining rooms and officers' quarters. Near the officers' tents were the larger tents that held up to twenty men, and served as dormitories for the men who were in the reserve area.

Further down the road was a large marquee with a red cross painted on its walls. This was the hospital, and they noticed that there was a steady stream of soldiers entering. Some were being carried on stretchers, and others were hobbling with crutches. Des commented, 'I'll do me best to keep away from that joint, bloody hospitals. I dunno how them doctors and nurses can cope with dealing with all the mangled blokes in them places.'

Tom replied, 'Think I'd rather be in there mangled up than the alternative. I got a lota time for them doctors and nurses. Must take a special type to handle the kinda stuff that they hafta deal with!'

A thirty-minute walk brought them to the small French village. It looked almost deserted, but in an old converted barn at the end of the street was a temporary store. A worn wooden plank nailed across the top of the door was painted with the words, 'YMCA Comfort Store'.

'Let's get some supplies lads, I need some tobacco.' Jack led the way into the dim interior. Ammunition boxes held up the shelves. Each shelf held an assortment of goods from tinned jam to drinking chocolate and tobacco. As the group entered the darkened interior, a young woman behind the counter looked up and greeted them.

'Hello boys, you must be the new arrivals, I haven't seen any of you in here before, now what would you like?'

Quick as a wink, Des replied, 'I'd like a ticket 'ome please miss, one way.' She smiled and replied, 'Sorry soldier, we are all sold out of them today, but hopefully you will get one soon, now what else would you like?'

They purchased their provisions of tobacco and drinking chocolate, along with some magazines and books. Other than the comfort store there were no other shops in the village, and they slowly made their way back to camp.

As night fell, the shelling started. At first, it was just a rumble in the distance, but then the noise intensified, and there was no ignoring the fact that the battle that was being fought along the demarcation line was getting closer.

For the next month, they spent their days training in how to use their gas masks and how to throw the hand bombs. Occasionally they would all go for a long route march carrying their full pack before returning back to camp. Some nights, they would patrol into no-man's-land, and at times they would become embroiled in small skirmishes, but for the most part it was as though the war was elsewhere. It was hard for them to imagine that less than twenty miles away the British and French soldiers were embroiled in a disastrous and deadly battle with the enemy, in an area known as the Somme.

⁂

The weather was warm, as it was almost summer. Red poppies and wildflowers surrounded yellow haystacks and golden trees across the fields. In their spare time, they would walk across the cornfields where the local women, many wearing black, would be harvesting their crops.

As the battle raged throughout the Somme valley over the next few weeks, the road behind the camp became a non-stop cavalcade of vehicles. Dozens of ambulances passed by, some horse-drawn while others were purpose-built trucks carrying the wounded to hospitals. Going in the other direction were convoys of trucks carrying supplies and ammunition and towing heavy cannons closer to the battleground. They all expected that it would only be a matter of time before they would become fully embroiled in the fighting that was now less than a dozen miles from their position.

It was the end of September 1916, and rumours had been circulating for days that the Australian battalions would soon be sent up the line to join the British troops. Very little information about the fighting was given out.

However, the ambulance drivers, who had been ferrying the wounded from the fields to the hospitals, had told harrowing stories of there being thousands of casualties among the British and French soldiers.

Tom, Jack and the others had just finished a four-day stint in the front-line trench. They had all made their way to the communal baths behind the rest trenches. They unpacked their spare uniforms before stripping off and climbing into the tin vats that were lined with tarpaulins and served as baths. Their dirty uniforms were steam-cleaned to blow out the ingrained mud, and to kill the lice that lived in them.

Fred had become mates with Seargeant Fegent, as they were of a similar age and the sergeant had said to him, 'Listen mate, I'm not into all this formality and officer stuff, so just call me Thomas unless the brass is around. Don't get me wrong, I'm happy to be getting a sergeant's pay, but I'm only doin' it for the money.

'I'd been digging for gold for the past two years outside of Kalgoorlie before this circus started. I was down on me luck, and feelin' homesick, so I just seen joining the army as a way of savin' a few bob and gettin' a free trip home at the same time. If I hear anything I'll let you know, but the big brass keeps everything close to their chest, but sometimes we get to hear things!'

Fred was enjoying his bath, and was looking forward to relaxing for a few hours at the Irish Club.

The Irish club was a canteen set up by the YMCA. They sold wine and beer along with tobacco. They also provided a letter-writing service for the soldiers who had trouble writing to their relatives back home. It was a popular place with soldiers who had just finished a turn of duty at the front line, as it tried to provide some normalcy in an area where life was anything but normal.

The club was full of cigarette smoke, as several hundred men laughed and joked and drank cold beer. They were all hoping that their war would not get any worse than what it was now. Thomas made his way into the smoky interior and got himself a beer. He saw Fred sitting by himself and made his way to his table.

'G'day.' Thomas gave his mate a nod before whispering to him, 'Got a bit of news mate, and it don't sound good.'

Fred drew back on his smoke, and his eyes narrowed as he looked at his mate and asked, 'What's up?'

Thomas took a long swig from his glass before saying, 'I was over at HQ earlier with the other NCOs, and we were given a briefing by Captain Wallace.

'As you know, the Tommies and the Frenchies are holding the line some miles away. Well, there was a big offensive started over a month ago between them and the Germans.

'The English Generals needed to push the Germans back across the Somme River. They thought they could make a go of it, but apparently the Germans had dug in, and they were prepared for the attack. The story is that the Tommies and the French blokes have taken a big beating, a really big beating mate! The captain said that the Tommies lost at least twenty, or even thirty thousand blokes in the last month alone. If that's true, then it might be our turn soon. The captain told us that the brass was thinking about sending our three divisions up the line as reinforcements for the Tommies.'

Thomas took another long drink from his glass before saying, 'My personal feelings are that I hope that what the captain said turns out to be wrong, I would hate to get this close to home and not make it. If there are as many casualties as the captain said then our next battle might be our biggest. I can't say that I'm looking forward to that.'

Tom and the others wandered over to where Fred was sitting, and Tom noticed the frown across Fred's brow.

'What's the matter with you? You look like you just lost a bob and found a penny.'

Fred looked at Thomas who said, 'Go ahead and tell 'em, but if anyone asks the information didn't come from me, orright?'

'You bet,' replied Fred, but before he could speak, Thomas stood up and said, 'Look I hafta go, and I hope that the information is wrong, but don't blame me if it isn't. See you later mate!'

They watched him make his way through the smoky room, as they digested the information that Fred had relayed to them.

Tom stood up and spoke to his mates, 'I think I'll go and write a letter to Hannah. I was meanin' to write to 'er for the last week or so. After what the Sarge has just said, I should do it now while I still have some time, so I will see yous later.'

He picked up some writing paper from the stack at the door, before going to his bunk to write what he hoped would not be his last letter to the woman that he loved.

Somewhere in France
September 1916

Dearest Hani,

Well here we are, somewhere in France. At the moment it is early autumn, although it still feels like summer and the weather has been pleasant. I must say though, the French summers are nothing like the Australian ones as the days are quite mild, and it still rains frequently, but at least it is not cold at the moment.

It is nothing like being in Turkey, as we regularly go on long marches, although it is an exaggeration to say that we march anywhere. It is more like a long amble. The countryside is quite beautiful, and in some areas, it is hard to imagine that there is a war being fought at all. The sides of the road are littered with wildflowers growing freely, and hedges of red fuchsias mark the boundaries of the fields. I just wanted to sit among them and forget about the madness of this war.

The fields are full of corn, and we help ourselves to the fruit that is in abundance in the farmers' fields.

But there is a war going on, and it is sad to see the French women struggling to harvest their corn with not a man in sight. We go into the little villages, and the only people that we see are old men and young women, and so many of them are wearing black mourning dresses.

Anyone old enough to carry a gun is already in the French army.

The old gang from home, along with a couple of our mates from Sydney, go into the villages of an evening. The French people take us into their homes, and they make us welcome. I think that it is their way of saying thank you to us for helping with the war effort. We have met old people who have lost their sons, and you can see the pain in their eyes as they show us photographs of them, but still they make us welcome, and they insist on sharing their meals with us.

We have been learning a bit of the French language, just so that we can hold a basic conversation with these friendly people.

I spoke with Des and suggested that he should write to Brigid. He said that he would, but you remember how shy he was around any girl, so I would not be surprised to find that he still hasn't written to her. Maybe you should get Brigid to write to him firstly, because it may make it easier for him to respond to her, as she was never backward in coming forward.

Anyway Hani, I must say that all of the comfort billies that we receive are most welcome, and you might tell the other ladies in your auxiliary group that we are very appreciative of those gifts.

I am proud of you for helping out on the local farms, and how I long for the day when we have a smallholding of our own.

I must tell you about our trip to Paris. About a month ago, we were all given a ten-day leave pass which was the first leave that we had been given since we had arrived over here. A couple of the chaps wanted to go to London, but it would have taken almost three days to get there. As we had no relatives to visit, we all agreed that we would better spend our time in Paris, which only took us a few hours to get to in the back of an army lorry.

We found some digs in a little boarding house about an hour out of Paris. On our first night out, we went to a place called the 'Follies Bergere'. The place was lit up so brightly, that I'm sure that if you were living on the moon, you could have seen it quite clearly.

I must say, that if you had told me what went on inside there I would have found it difficult to believe. But Hani, the stage was full of ladies wearing clothes that left little to the imagination as they kicked up their heels and danced about to music that was called the Can-Can.

What can I say, other than it was a very lively show, and I can only imagine the outrage from the straight-laced ladies of Sydney should the show ever be put into production there.

It was so very strange walking around the streets of Paris. It was like being in a different world. The ladies walked around the streets in their finery, and carrying parasols to keep the sun from their faces.

Everyone was going about their daily lives, and I wondered if the people even knew that there was a real war being fought no more than eighty miles from their city. The fancy dress shops were all open, along with the wonderful cake shops, and everything in between including the cabarets and theatres. I must say that after seeing Paris, I am unsure about what we are fighting over. Paris is a beautiful city, although I would much rather be at home in Sydney town with you strolling by my side.

Anyway, it seems such a long time since we were in Paris although it was only a month ago.

How is mother? Jack and I both wrote to her recently, and I do hope that Davin and Claire are both well.

How I miss those days when the only thing that I had to worry about was keeping the coals hot in the forge.

I am tired of this madness Hani, and we have no idea of how long it will endure. Can you believe that it almost eighteen months since we all enlisted, and yet there appears to be no end in sight to this conflict? I can remember the papers saying that the war would likely be over in three months, and that there would be a good chance that we would all be home for Christmas. I am not looking forward to spending winter here, as some of our chaps spent the last winter here, and they tell us that it will become bitterly cold and wet.

I am trying to be an optimist, in the hope that there will be a resolution to this conflict soon, but I fear that my optimism is nothing more than a fanciful dream. I must finish this letter off now Hani, as I want to get it in the morning mail. The word is that we will shortly be moving up the line to join the British group, so I don't know when I shall get another opportunity to write. Think of me Hani as I think of you.

Yours forever

Tommy.

The sound of the bugle penetrated their sleepy minds. Sergeant Fegent roused them fully awake. 'Everybody up, pack your kit and muster outside in fifteen minutes.'

Fred was the first out of his bunk. He said nothing, as he packed his things and then rolled a smoke. The others had also guessed that the rumours that they had been hearing about moving up the line would soon become reality.

They made their way to the field that was the parade ground, and joined several hundred others already there. A few officers and the battalion commander stood on the makeshift podium. He addressed his men through a megaphone.

'Stand at ease men,' and they all relaxed.

'We have received our orders, and we will be moving camp and joining up with the Tommies who are about twenty miles up the line. Over the past month, the allied forces of Britain and France have suffered heavy casualties in the conflict with the Germans.

'You men are now being called up to the front as reinforcements. I want you to be clear about what is ahead of you. The Germans, although they have also suffered heavy losses, are still a formidable force. Our objective is to push the Germans across the river Somme. Until we have achieved that objective there will be no further leave granted, nor will you be able to leave the camp boundaries.

'After assembly, you will proceed to the supply tents where you will be issued with ammunition, gas masks and a blanket. The Germans have been using mustard gas recently, and you have all been trained in the wearing of your masks. May I give you all a word of warning? When you are in the trenches, and you hear the gas-warning gong, make sure that you do not waste any time in putting on your masks. I want to be blunt about this. You will die an agonising death if the gas enters your lungs, and do not remove your masks until you hear the all-clear bell.

'Now, "C" company, you will stay behind and load the lorries with the ammunition and equipment. The rest of you will make formation here in one hour, and we will then march up the line until we reach the British contingent. It will take approximately two days before we reach that area. That's all men, and good luck to you all. Dismissed.'

They stood huddled together, but there wasn't much for them to say. Their thoughts went back to their miserable months spent in the cold, soggy trenches of Turkey, and they all had a sense of dread of what lay ahead.

Two days later the rain started. They had made their camp behind the rubble of houses that had recently been destroyed by heavy artillery. Little stone walls, and a spire that held the remnants of coloured glass from what was once a stained-glass window was all that was left of what had once been a small church. The remains of the other buildings, now blackened by the flames that had followed the explosions, stood starkly against the foreboding sky. The village had stood high above the valley, and it afforded views across the river, and all the way to the German lines. The trenches around it had been dug by the British soldiers, but were now partially collapsed after the shelling of the area. Then, along with the rain came the first hint of a cold winter.

They had been laying the duckboards along the base of the rebuilt trenches all day, but the water seeping through the soil was already reaching the planks.

They were also repacking sandbags at the front of the dugouts that would serve them as their sleeping quarters.

It was now almost a week since they had left the relative comfort of their previous camp. The new camp was exposed to the cold north winds that had sprung up and seemed to blow continuously. As it was autumn, they could only wonder how harsh the weather would become if they were to stay here throughout the coming winter. They had seen no action yet, but the rumble of the big guns was never far away and they all expected to get involved at any moment.

Their orders arrived from headquarters the next morning and read:

'General offensive will be at 10 am today. Platoon to create extensive diversion to the right flank of German lines. If possible engage with the enemy within their trench lines and hold for as long as possible.'

Roll call was at 8 am, and the order to stand ready was quickly passed along the trenches. Tom looked at his brother. His heart was racing, and the nervous bile was building in his throat. Jack looked at Tom and knew what he was thinking, and he whispered, 'When we go over the top spread out and find a crater and get into it as quickly as you can, and we can work out what we will do from there, orright?'

Tom nodded before saying, 'I'm a liar if I say that I ain't scared Jack, 'cause I am. I don't wanna die, but I'm shit scared, not only fer meself, but fer all of us.

'I know that when we go over the top, I won't have time to be scared. But right now, I can see all them blokes in Turkey that was blown ter bits and the bloody rats eating at them. I don't wanna end up like that. I don't want Hannah and mother to have to think of me, or you bein' blown ter bits with not enough of us left to even bury.'

Fred had been listening to the conversation and joined in, 'Now you blokes know I'm not one fer botherin' God, but just in case he exists you might ask 'im to look after ya this time. I didn't wanna talk religion, and I hafta say that with all the shit and madness that this war has brung, I hafta wonder even more if there is a God at all!

'When I was a kid, me parents made me go to church, and when bad things happened they always said that it happened because it was the will of God. Since I been here, I have often thought about that, and I must say as I got older I remember me old mam used to always say that God was good and merciful. Now I hafta wonder how that can be true because of all this.' He waved his hand around in the general direction of no-man's-land.

'I dunno what it is, but if yer time's up, then it's up, and there's nuthin' that we can do about it, but I do wonder over who decides that yer time's up!'

Des was the first to speak, and when he did he sarcastically said to Fred, 'Geez, yer a bundle of laughs today, ain't ya? It's all about luck if ya live or die and nothin' else. I bet them Germans are thinkin' the same as we are. War is stupid. If it was up to me, I'd rather go over the line and say G'day, and have a beer with 'em, rather than try ta kill 'em. But it ain't up ta me, so I'm gunna hedge me bets and hope that there is a God. I hope that he can hear me when I ask 'im to look after me, and you lot,' he added as an afterthought, 'of course, but me first.' He looked at them and smirked.

***

Their conversation was cut short, and the ground suddenly reverberated and trembled, as shells from the German Big Bertha guns exploded all round their position. As they landed, they sent geysers of dirt and rock skywards and sideways annihilating any soldier in its path. An inferno of massive explosions followed as they criss-crossed the fields. Some found their mark, and tore the life from a hundred soldiers at a time. Then as quickly as the barrage had started, it stopped.

The front-line trench was partly demolished, and they all sat dazed and shaken as they looked at the carnage the barrage had inflicted on those further along.

Stretcher-bearers made their way through the area. Soldiers scraped away the mud and dirt as they searched for survivors. Men who had their skin burned off and limbs shredded were screaming, as the first aid attendants injected them with morphia to silence their pain. Others scraped up body parts, before placing them on stretchers to be carried back to the burial ground behind the camp. As they dug away at the mud and debris with their bare hands, some would heave and vomit as the sight and smell of destroyed flesh became too great for them to handle.

NCOs were barking orders. 'Everyone out of these trenches who doesn't need to be here, now move. Make your way back to the reserve trenches. 'A' company will stay here and help with recovery operations.'

Over one hundred yards of the trench had been destroyed including almost all of those in it.

The stretcher-bearers were in recovery mode as the survivors of the barrage had already been removed to the dressing stations.

Jack and the others were still dazed, as they made their way back to the relative safety of the reserve trenches two hundred yards behind the front line. They had no sooner settled down, when a corporal came by and called out, 'Stand to men. The captain will address us shortly!'

The platoon captain emerged from his dugout, and he spoke to the soldiers through his megaphone.

'Stand easy men. Our orders are to create a diversion, so that the other groups, that is, the Tommies, French and the Canadians, can make a push through the German lines on their north flank. Command believes that until we can push the Germans back across the river, we will not be able to achieve our goals of driving them out of France altogether.

'At 10 am our artillery will attack the south flank of the German lines with heavy mortar. The entire division will stand to until the heavy artillery stops. Your job then will be to cross over no-man's-land, and attempt to get into their communication trenches and finish off any enemy still standing. Command believes that the enemy will not be expecting a frontal assault from this quarter. When the barrage stops, the hope is that our shelling will decimate them, and your job will be to finish off anyone that is still standing! You will all be ready to attack as soon as the barrage is over. That's all men and good luck.'

They all looked at each other, and they all knew that if they survived the run across no-man's-land, they would be in hand-to-hand combat with their enemy.

The wind had swung around to the north, and it brought more light rain and mist with it. The soldiers were being issued a tot of rum, and some knew that the fear that they had already tasted, along with the rum, may be their last taste of anything.

At nine o'clock, the order passed through the trenches for everyone to stand to on the fire step with bayonets fixed. The ladders were positioned against the sandbags and they stood in the rain as the time slowly ticked by. Some attempted a show of bravado with their small talk; others were quiet and deep in thought, whilst others openly prayed.

As the first explosion reverberated through the misty gloom, it was followed by the bellowing of a hundred cannons and mortars each spitting death and carnage with every round fired.

The ground shook with the force of an earthquake, and as the shells landed within seconds of each other, volcanic eruptions of dirt and rocks spewed skywards.

The fields were now pockmarked with mountainous craters. The shelling had further pulverised the blackened human remains of a thousand men, and countless animals that had littered the landscape.

They stood on the fire step, and flinched as the whistling of the shells overhead, combined with the noise of the explosions coming ever closer, terrified them all. As suddenly as the shelling started, it stopped. But before the ringing of the noise in their ears had settled, the whistles blew, and the order was shouted down the line. 'Over the top, get over those bags, now!'

Several thousand men lining the trench walls scrambled up the ladders and leaped over the top and out into no-man's-land.

The mist, mixed with the gun smoke and dust swirled eerily across the shattered ground. The dust and fumes along with the smell of burnt flesh hung heavily in the air. As they ran, they stumbled over decimated tree roots and branches. Before they had reached fifty yards, they were unsure of the direction that they should take, such was the gloom that surrounded them.

Tom had stuck closely to his brother as they went up the ladder, with Des, Doughy and Fred close behind them, but then they quickly separated as they ran through the thickening drizzle. They stumbled across the remains of the barbed-wire barriers, and they could hear the chatter of machine gun fire, but they weren't sure of where it was coming from.

Jack lay in the mud, and looked around at the ghostly silhouettes of hundreds of soldiers. Some were running, while others were standing still and fully exposed to the enemy. But the mist that shrouded them also protected them from a sniper's bullet. Men were cursing as they tripped, or stumbled as they moved towards the enemy trenches. The chatter of a nearby machine gun startled them, and they watched as the bullets hit a soldier who shuddered before doing a slow pirouette and falling to the ground.

Several soldiers fired towards where the shots had rung out, and the machine gunner returned fire confirming that they were close to the

German lines. Men began to crawl across the destroyed ground. Some gagged, as they lay among the rotting human and animal carcasses that had lain on the field since the last engagement.

Jack whispered, 'Can't see a bloody thing in this fog, but we must be close to their trenches.'

Jack looked over his shoulder, and then realised that Tom and the others were missing and that he was talking to himself. He had no time to wonder about the others as a machine gun chattering nearby had startled him. It sounded as though it was almost next to him, and he was terrified. When the racket finally stopped he heard men speaking in German. He was disoriented, and didn't know how far away they were, or from what direction their voices were coming, but he knew that they were close. As he lay in the mud and the carnage, the wind picked up. The mist suddenly cleared, and he could see the destroyed trenches, along with German soldiers standing amongst the remains of their comrades.

Before he could think clearly, and as he was contemplating his next move, he heard the shouts and voices yelling in English.

A soldier to his left stood and yelled, 'C'mon you blokes!' Several hundred soldiers rose from the mud and the rising gloom, and ran towards the German trenches. With a fear of dying, and the adrenaline coursing through them, they jumped into the German trenches and fought like men possessed.

They all struggled in the confined space; driving their bayonets deep into the bodies of their enemies. Lunge and withdraw. That's what their training with straw dummies had taught them; and as another soldier gasped his last breath they pushed past him to kill another.

Fear and hatred drove them all, as they swung their bayonets left and right. Screams of pain and anguish mingled with swearing and cursing and the occasional shot could be heard. They stumbled in the confined space, as they thrust and stabbed and tore the life from men who were just like them.

They fought for the next two hours, and when the battle was over New Zealander, Australian and German soldiers lay like brothers three deep within the trenches. Some were dead, and some were dying as their lifeblood seeped from gaping, ugly wounds to stain the ground that they were all fighting for.

✻✻✻

When the rain stopped, the clouds parted and revealed a scene from hell. The water at the bottom of the trench was stained dark red. Several hundred men lay slaughtered, grotesquely twisted and entwined with each other.

Their contorted faces were stamped with their last emotion in life, and their vacant eyes stared sightlessly as the realisation of death had flowed over them. They had been enemies in life, and were now partners in death.

The surviving, fatigued soldiers surveyed the carnage through haunted eyes. They cursed their King, and the blessed generals who had issued the orders for them to sacrifice themselves, while they had remained bunkered down in safety.

In the distance, they could hear another battle being raged, but for now in this area they had achieved their goals. The German line had been breached and was now controlled by the Australians and the New Zealanders.

They smoked cigarettes as they stood among the blood and the slaughter. It was almost six hours since they had gone over the top. Most were splattered with blood and mud and their pale, haggared faces reflected their shattered nerves.

The sound of NCOs barking orders broke through their thoughts. There was no time to celebrate their small victory. They needed to contain the area that they had just won from the enemy. That meant removing the dead from the trenches, and repairing them before the battalion could move forward.

Now that the mist and smoke had cleared, they could see their own lines behind them. They had gained no more than half a mile of ground. The stretcher-bearers arrived and checked each man for a pulse, before dragging his corpse from the trench.

The rain had come back, now heavier, and the mist swirled around as though to hide the hideous scene. Soldiers stood in the trench and lifted a body up to those at the top. They would lay two to a stretcher, before carrying them to a crater where they would lie forever with their enemies; and when the crater was full they moved to another.

As each hour passed the rain became heavier, and the mud had turned into molasses. As they walked, their legs were like lead as each step they took sent them deeper into the oozing quagmire. At times, they had to place the stretcher down, so that they could extract themselves and their boots from the mud before they could move forward, and now they were totally exhausted.

After the battle, the survivors were ordered back to camp where they rested for two days. At roll call several hundred names never answered. Tom was thinking about the nameless men that he had killed. He wanted to speak about the battle, and he wanted to know how the others were feeling because he was struggling with his emotions.

'Do yer know how many blokes ya killed Jack?' His brother looked at him before saying, 'I didn't keep count now don't worry about it. You had to do what ya had to do. It was kill or be killed! Would ya rather they had killed you?'

'But I keep seein' their faces, and it don't seem real. I never really thought that I would actually kill someone!' Doughy had been sitting quietly, and then he looked at Tom.

'Ya shoot at people don't ya?'

'Yeah, course I do.'

'Well, if ya kill someone with a bullet instead of a bayonet they are still dead, so what's yer problem?'

Tom thought for a moment before replying, 'Well, it seems different somehow. When yer shoot a bullet, you don't see where it goes, and yer don't know if it's hit somebody or not. But, when you are fightin' with a bloke, and you stick him with yer bayonet you're lookin' at his face, aren't ya? And you know that he will kill you as soon as look at you, but he might be just like us, you know, he might have a family, or a sweetheart.'

'I killed some blokes the other day, I dunno how many exactly, and I don't wanna know how many it was. But I don't feel good about it, and I keep their faces in me mind all the time.'

Fred was rolling a smoke, and without looking up he asked Tom, 'Why did ya join the army?'

Tom thought for a moment before replying, 'I dunno now, I really don't! It seemed like a good idea at the time, and the papers and the priests were all telling us that it was our duty to sign up. I dunno if any of us had any idea of what war really was. I think that I figured that it was gunna be some sort of big adventure. Oh, I dunno what I thought at the time. I don't suppose I even gave the killin' side of it any thought at all.

'All I know is, that I don't like the way I'm feelin' about killin' them Germans. I know that they coulda killed me, you, any of us, but they didn't, and we killed them. I don't feel no hatred for them because I bet half of them German fellas don't know what they are fighting for either, just like us.'

They all thought about what Tom had just said, and Des was the first to speak.

'Wada ya reckon God thinks?' He had asked the question to no one in particular, but Jack looked at his mate and said to him, 'What sort of question is that? How the hell would any of us have any idea of what God thinks about anythin' ya dumb bastard?'

They were all looking at Des now, and all thinking the same as Jack, but Des was unperturbed, and answered Jack with, 'We all believe in God, don't we?'

Before anyone answered, he went on, 'Wasn't we all brung up as Catholics? I know I was, and I know you and yer brother was.' He looked at Jack before continuing, 'And yer all went to Mass every Sunday. So, I'm not getting' all religious, but I'm just curious about God, that's all.'

Fred squinted, as the smoke from his cigarette wafted up to his eyes, and he still wanted to know what Des was alluding to.

'So, what's goin' to Mass on Sundays got to do with what God's thinkin'?'

'Well if you shut up for a minute I'll tell ya. Now, when we were kids we were all taught the Ten Commandments, right?' They all nodded. 'Well, one of the commandments says, thou shalt not kill, right? So, I suppose I'm a bit confused 'cause if there is a God, and if the commandments are one of God's laws then what do yer think he's thinkin' when he sees all of us killin' each other? That's all that I'm sayin'.'

Doughy looked at his friend and shook his head, 'What's the matter with you? Did you get hit on yer head or somethin'? There is no God. I used ter think there was too. That was before this bloody war started, but if there was a God, do yer really believe that he would let us all go around killin' each other?

'Me old mam used ter say that we were all God's children. So, if that's the case, God must be like a parent, and the Germans and us would be his kids, and yer know when the kids are squabblin' the parent always stops 'em. So, if God existed why hasn't he stopped all this killin'? That's what I wanna know!'

'Geeze Des, ya sure know how ter ask awkward questions,' said Jack. 'I know what you're tryin' ta say, and I dunno the answers mate, but we gotta do what we gotta do to survive, so if there ain't a God then it's all a matter of luck if anyone survives.'

⁂

Sergeant Fegent made his way to the group, and nodded to them along with a 'G'day, sorry to have to tell you blokes, but we will be doin' a trench rotation today, and you blokes, and all of "B" company are goin' back to the front line. I know you haven't had much of a break, but them's the orders. The brass thinks that Fritz will try and take back the ground they lost the other day.

'Intelligence says that the Germans have been movin' a couple of platoons along the river, and that means that they are gunna be on our doorstep soon. So, they want every bloke that can still carry a gun to be in the front-line trench. Maybe nothin' will happen, but who knows. All I know is that we all must be ready for another onslaught either tonight or tomorrow!'

'Oh, I forgot! They also said that the wind will be blowing in our direction by nightfall, so H.Q. thinks that we should prepare for a gas attack if the wind don't die down.'

He gave them all a grin before saying, 'Now that I've cheered you all up, I better go and let the others know what's cookin'.'

They had all been carrying their gas masks around in their kit bags. Each man had been issued with two masks, which were good for up to five hours of use. They had all been told that they must carry them at all times including when they slept. They had been warned that the gas could cover a large area very quickly when the wind was favourable. Although they had all been trained in their use, they had never yet been exposed to an attack.

The lethal black canisters containing the chlorine and mustard gases were rolled out and lay on the muddy ground in a nightly ritual. Each canister weighed around ninety pounds, and required two men to carry it along the communication trenches. Then it would be positioned above the trenches facing out onto no-man's-land.

Each canister contained enough gas to kill a hundred or more men. The toxic gas would only be released when the wind was blowing with sufficient force and in the right direction. The small hemispherical anemometer placed next to the canisters whirled slowly and then almost stopped.

The soldier, whose job it was to monitor it, was nervous, as he knew that the weather conditions were changing. The rain had stopped, and the grey clouds had parted to reveal a wispy, pale blue canopy of sky. Every few minutes he monitored the wind speed, and as dusk fell the anemometer fluctuated between zero and five knots.

His orders were to continue monitoring the wind speed, and if it picked up to ten knots or higher he was to immediately sound the gas gong alarm. The Germans would also be monitoring the wind speed, and as soon as the wind had a consistent force, the gas valves on several hundred German canisters would be opened.

The troops in the rest area had been rotated, and now they all stood anxiously on the fire step unsure of what the coming night would bring.

As the night drew down, they could hear the rumble of cannons in the distance.

The clouds scurried across the sky, and the moon came out and lay its cold silvery light across the battlefield. They were all uneasy, and a nervous tension could be felt throughout the trench line.

The quiet was suddenly shattered by the tinny sound of the gas gong banging out its warning like a child beating a saucepan with a spoon.

The wind had picked up, and was now blowing consistently at more than ten knots in their direction. Orders were being yelled out, 'Get those gas masks on now, quickly!'

It would take as little as twenty seconds for the first cloud of gas to float across no-man's-land and reach them.

As they hurriedly and clumsily tried to fit their masks they saw the sparks flying from the tail of the Very flares as they flew skywards to explode several hundred feet above the ground, before arcing across the sky.

As the flares danced across the night sky, they showered the muddy ground with a pale ghostly light. The light from the flares reflected on the insidious green gas cloud that was floating towards them across the open fields. It floated and swirled eerily a few feet above the ground, and it came towards them like a ghostly apparition. As they watched the cloud of death dancing towards them their blood ran cold. They hated the canvas gas masks as they were uncomfortable to wear, and the chemicals that were impregnated within the canvas lining gave the wearer an unbearable headache, but not wearing them was an open invitation to the lurking angel of death.

The wind was now bringing the gas towards them faster than had been anticipated. Panic made their fingers fumble as they watched the toxic tentacles of poisonous mist floating towards them.

As the gas reached the trench it was floating at head height, and because it was heavier than air, it slowly filled every trench and dugout leaving nowhere to escape its deadly tentacles. Some soldiers jumped from the fire step in panic, and they tried to get away from the toxic green cloud that was now enveloping them all.

Doughy had been smoking when the gong had gone off. But he took the time to have one long last drag on his cigarette before expelling his smoke-filled breath, and flicking the smouldering butt into the water at the bottom of the trench. He had fumbled with his mask, and had pulled it onto his head before he had realised that it was on back to front. As he pulled it from his head to position it correctly, he saw the deadly green cloud dancing in the wind, flicking its gossamer fingers of death towards them.

In a panic, he dropped the mask, and as he bent to retrieve it the gas swirled, and flowed over the edge of the trench like a river falling over a ledge of stones. It enveloped him, and as he opened his mouth to scream, he inhaled the insidious cocktail of gas.

The gas turned into hydrochloric acid as it mixed with the moisture from tear ducts and the fluid within his lungs. He put his hands around his burning throat, and his eyes bulged as they burned, and then popped in sheer terror as the gas seared the lining of his throat and lungs and suffocated him.

The others watched in horror as the gas stole the life from their friend. They saw the frothy blood spilling from his mouth and nostrils, as he convulsed uncontrollably for a few seconds before he died on the muddy floor of the trench.

They couldn't speak, but none could take their eyes from their friend. Others had also succumbed to the green veil of death as it swirled through the trench, and it was half an hour before the 'all clear' bell rang. As they gingerly removed their masks, they could still faintly smell the disappearing vapours of the gas cloud.

Des was the first to bend down and cover his childhood friend with a wet blanket. He had no sooner done that when the shells whistled overhead, and they all instinctively ducked.

The Germans had followed up the gas attack with a few rounds of heavy artillery as a distraction to allow their troops time to clamber out of their trenches. The Germans, looking like grotesque aliens, with their faces completely covered by their gas helmets, and wearing linen coloured overalls made their way across no-man's-land. There, they entered the communication trenches that had been taken from them by the Australians a day earlier, and opened fire along the trench line. Twenty men had died before the Australians had realised that the Germans were now amongst them. The Germans were running forward, jabbing and thrusting their gleaming bayonets into the surprised troops.

Fred had noticed the German troops coming their way just as he had taken off his mask. He had enough time to yell at the others, 'Look out, Fritz is comin'!' He nodded in the direction that they were coming from.

Jack had kicked his brother to get his attention. Tom and Des had been bending over Doughy, and as Tom stood, the German bullet ricocheted off a rock in the trench wall and buried itself into Tom's shoulder splintering his collarbone. Fred and Jack were too busy to notice Tom falling, and as Des was about to engage with a German, he had twisted around to look momentarily at Tom now lying in the trench. As he did, the German buried his bayonet into Des's left arm rather than his chest. The German soldier withdrew his weapon, before lunging at him again, and Des gave a scream as the bayonet sliced along his forearm with the tip of it cutting into his bicep.

Fred looked around as Des had screamed, and as the German withdrew his bayonet to strike again, Fred brought the butt of his rifle up to strike the German under his chin. He heard the bones break in the soldier's jaw and the German soldier collapsed.

Des had dropped his rifle, and grasped his arm as the blood flowed freely through his fingers. He had almost passed out with the pain and had leant back against a dugout wall with his eyes tightly shut. Through the fog of his pain, something was telling him that if he did pass out then he might never wake up, and so he fought the urge to sleep. The fighting continued around him. Men were in mortal combat standing above him, and tripping over bodies in the confined space. But, the surprise element that the Germans had started with was gone. Now, two or three soldiers were attacking a single German, and rifle butts were bashing heads, and the Germans were in retreat along the communication trench.

Tom lay in the mud unable to move. Dead and wounded men lay all around him. He knew that he had been hit with something, and he thought of Hannah. He was sure that he was going to die. He was aware that he was in pain, but somehow he seemed to be removed from it, and it wasn't bothering him like he thought that it should, but as he floated in and out of consciousness he imagined that he was talking to Hannah, 'I'm sorry Hani, but they got me, and I hate meself for lettin' you down, please forgive me.'

***

The dead and the dying lay together, and Australian and New Zealand blood mingled with German blood as the medical staff made their way along the trench. Some couldn't see, and the medics wrapped a blindfold soaked in water around their heads, and across their eyes after the residual gas had blinded them. Others were nursing wounds and moaning, but a few were screaming, as they nursed bloodied hands with severed fingers after they had grabbed a bayonet to prevent it from penetrating their body. Jack was with his brother, and Fred was standing on the firewall.

'Medic, we need a medic down here, quick man!' He waved to get their attention as several stretcher-bearers ran along, and across the trench wall.

Jack was looking with concern at his brother's shirt, and at the ever-increasing red stain that was slowly spreading across it.

Tom was now deathly pale, and barely breathing. Jack was sure that his brother was about to die, and if he did he was already wondering how he would tell his mother and Hannah.

The medical officers were hurriedly going from soldier to soldier, and doing a quick assessment of their condition.

A medic was cutting the now blood-soaked shirt from Tom, while another was wrapping a bandage around Des's torn arm.

The area where the bullet had entered Tom's shoulder had now turned purple and black, and the round bullet hole could be seen with the blood still weeping out. The medic jabbed Tom with a syringe of morphia, before he raised his arm across his chest causing Tom to moan. He then ordered one of the orderlies to bandage the arm tightly across his chest.

'He's me brother sir. How is he sir, he's not gunna die is he?'

The medic replied, 'I can't tell you yet, he will have to be assessed at the field hospital, but if the bullet hasn't hit any vital organs, and if he hasn't lost too much blood he might recover. I can tell you however that with this wound, even if your brother survives, his war will be over! Now that's all I can tell you soldier, good luck.' He then moved along the trench to his next patient.

The orderlies carried Tom and Des through the blood-soaked trench to the first aid mobile medical unit.

At the front-line casualty clearing station, they laid the stretchers on the damp ground. Field ambulance officers checked each patient as they arrived, and assessed and diagnosed the wounded in order of the most serious. Some were rushed to the temporary operating area where screams and groans were heard as limbs that could not be saved were amputated. Dozens of soldiers were arriving at the field hospital after being assessed at the casualty clearing station. The hospital was almost a mile back from the front line, and covered an area of almost four acres. Some of the buildings were converted farmers barns, but most were tents capable of holding twenty beds. The wounded kept arriving; some were standing, while some were being carried. Most of the new arrivals were bloodied and wore head bandages, or arms wrapped up in slings.

Des was taken into the tent where the emergency operations were taking place. The morphia, and the loss of blood had left him unconscious. The orderly gasped as he removed the blood-soaked bandage and inspected the wound.

The bayonet had entered his forearm at the wrist. It had penetrated almost the entire length of it, leaving the skin ripped and the muscle torn and the bone exposed to his elbow.

Captain Lacy had looked carefully at the wound and muttered, 'That's nasty, but you're a lucky man soldier because we might just be able to repair your arm. But, you would be dead if that thing had gone into your guts.' He was talking to himself, as he knew that Des was unconscious, but he always spoke to his patients as though they could hear him. He had treated so many young men just like this one. It was his way of coping with the conveyor belt of mutilated bodies that passed across his operating table almost every day.

Captain Jonathon Lacy was forty-five, and he had been working as a general surgeon at a London hospital when the war had broken out. He had signed up almost six months later when the first soldiers were being repatriated home. He had been repairing the damaged bodies that had been patched up on the hospital ships that were moored off the coast of Turkey. As he tried to repair the disfiguring wounds of young men, he had decided to enlist. He thought that if he could attend to an injury before it healed, rather than attend to it after being hastily patched up on the battlefield, he would save the soldier further months of pain and rehabilitation by not having to be operated on again. But his honourable idea had never been achievable, and from the first day that he had arrived at the battlefield hospital not far from Gallipoli, the sheer volume of the wounded had overwhelmed him.

He had been repairing torn and mutilated bodies for over three years now, and he was worn out and tired. The lines on his face, and the greying of his once black hair now reflected the price he had paid for the horror of trying to save too many young men. He was angry over the political decisions that had seen thousands of young men cut down in their prime, for an ideal that he no longer believed in.

He abhorred politics, because he believed that it was political idealism that created the tensions that led to wars. As he looked at Des, he knew that it was not young men such as this that created the barbarism of war, but bewhiskered, powerful men who roamed the corridors of power, who held a sense of self-entitlement over others that did not.

As Captain Lacy looked at Des's torn arm, he mused that in the three years that he had been operating on the battlefield, not once had he operated on a general or a politician. He despised the generals almost as much as he despised the politicians.

It was the politicians that made the decision for a country to go to war, but it was the generals who made the bad decisions that cost the lives of thousands of young men like this one laying before him.

His orderly asking, 'Will I set up the guillotine Sir?' interrupted his thoughts. The orderly had been working alongside the captain for almost as long as the hospital had been set up.

He had seen countless wounds, and he knew that this wound to Des's arm would probably necessitate it being removed, as it was swollen with the blue-black blood that had congealed under the skin that hadn't been torn. It appeared that it was only the skin that was holding the arm together.

The French surgeons had realised, during the Napoleonic wars, that they had needed an instrument to remove damaged limbs from injured soldiers. A smaller version of the executioner's guillotine had been manufactured, with the express purpose of amputating arms and legs.

The captain thought for a moment and said, 'Let's have a look at it after we clean it up. The arm might be saved if we are lucky. In the meantime, orderly, please wash the entire arm with carbolic lotion and tie a tourniquet just below the shoulder.'

'Yes, Sir.'

The tent was a hive of activity, with stretchers being brought in at almost the same time as they were being taken out and loaded into the ambulances. The wounded were then transported to the permanent hospital, some miles away in the town of Healy.

Tom had woken up, as the pain from his wound overcame the effects of the morphia that he had been injected with in the trench a few hours earlier. He was lying on a stretcher on the open ground in the midst of a few dozen others waiting outside the operating tent.

The late autumn sunshine washed over the rows of stretchers, as the orderlies walked among them and assessed the wounds. He had been lying on his back, and as the pain intensified he tried to roll over to take the pressure from his injury.

He groaned; he could hardly move as every time that he did the white flashes of pain would stab at him again. As the cool, watery sunlight shone upon his face, his blurry eyes watched the small spots of red that appeared to be dancing in the wind a few yards in front of him. His dazed mind was now curious to know what the small red objects were, and he squinted though his pain until his eyes could focus on the small red poppies that were swaying in the breeze as they hung onto the last vestiges of a summer now gone.

He stared as they danced, and as his eyes focused further, he noticed the freshly dug earth, and the small wooden crosses that stood behind the gently swaying poppies.

The realisation of what he was looking at cleared his mind for a short time. He was lying next to a small cemetery that was the final resting place for those who hadn't made it from the operating tables.

Tom didn't know where he was. He couldn't help wondering if he was dying, and if he too would be buried in this cemetery, and have a small wooden cross planted above him.

Captain Lacy was examining Des's arm, and was wondering if he could save it. It would be far easier for him to just place it under the guillotine and remove it. He had checked Des's age from his dog tags, and he didn't want to remove the arm of a twenty-one-year-old man if it could be helped. He carefully examined the savage cut, and his biggest concern was if an infection took hold. He had to make a judgment call, because whatever happened after the soldier left there, he would never know if he had done the right thing or not.

'Orderly, I'm going to try and save this boy's arm, so bring me some Bismuth Paraffin paste and some gauze.'

'Sir.' The orderly gathered up the equipment along with a scalpel, needle and some horsehair thread. The Captain opened the wound with his scalpel to fully expose the red and sinewy forearm muscle. He cut away the damaged ligaments, and plucked out the small bone fragments. Then he smeared the bloodied mess with paraffin paste in the hope that it would ward off any infection that would necessitate having the arm removed. He then stretched the skin that he had peeled back, and using a long needle he rejoined the severed tissue. Captain Lacy was speaking to his unconscious patient again as he admired his handiwork, 'Well, that's the best that I can do for you lad; the rest is up to you. If you don't get an infection in it, you should get to keep your arm. It might never be fully functional, but you should be able to pick up a knife, or a fork with it, so good luck soldier, you will be going home soon!'

He turned to his orderly and said, 'Now wash the wound with carbolic lotion, and cover it with gauze then wrap it up tightly. Do his paperwork and ship him out to the hospital. Right, who have we got next?'

They carried Tom to the operating table. He was anaesthetised with chloroform even though the last injection of morphia and the loss of blood had put him back to sleep.

Captain Lacy cleaned his wound, after removing the bullet fragments and the bone splinters from his collarbone, before binding it and fitting a metal brace over his shoulder.

'That's you done son. I know that when you wake up, that's going to hurt like hell, but as long as you don't get an infection in it, that wound should see you going home. Good luck soldier.'

The orderly scribbled down the injury, and the treatment in the record book as the stretcher-bearers carried Tom to the ambulance.

The ambulance was a horse-drawn wagon, and it could hold up to six patients. They were all still anaesthetised as the wagon jolted and swayed its way along the muddy, rutted road to the hospital six miles from the front line.

⁂

Tom and Des had been transferred to the Number 2 Australian General Hospital, which was run by the Red Cross outside of the small town of Wimereux. The hospital covered several acres of land. It was a mixture of tents and wooden buildings, and a cemetery had been established almost a quarter of a mile behind it. Each day the row of crosses grew larger, as the lack of medicine and infections took their toll.

Des was awake, and lying on a portable bed and taking in his new surroundings. A white blanket covered each bed, with a bright Red Cross emblem in the centre of it. He was still groggy from the anaesthetic, but he knew that he was in a hospital. He was starting to remember the fight in the trench, and as his mind cleared he remembered the burning pain in his arm as the bayonet entered it. He looked at his arm, and saw that it was bandaged entirely from his shoulder to his hand. He turned his head and saw that every bed in the ward had a soldier in it. He vaguely remembered seeing Tom falling over in the trench, and he wondered if he was in one of the beds here, or if he had been killed.

Tom was still asleep, having been checked out by the ward doctor and given another dose of morphine. Sergeant Fegent had made enquiries at the casualty clearing station regarding the condition of Tom and Des. He was informed that they were both alive when they had arrived there. But to be sure, he had asked a corporal whose job it was to drive the wounded to the field hospital if he could make enquiries about the welfare of his two soldiers.

Several hours later, and after taking more injured soldiers to the hospital, he had returned to his station and reported back.

'Sergeant, I have enquired about the condition of the two men that you were asking after. Private Carney has been operated on, and the surgeon was able to save his arm. However, I was informed that his arm is severely damaged, and that it will probably never function properly again. The other man, Tom Fields, has a broken collarbone and a gunshot wound to his shoulder. I was told that it would necessitate him having extensive physiotherapy before he will regain the use of his shoulder.

'I was also informed by the sister-in-charge that both men will be transferred back to England at the first opportunity. However, the sister cautioned that she didn't believe that either man would be able to return to active duty again, due to the nature of their injuries.'

'Thank you, corporal, I appreciate your diligence in obtaining this information for me.'

The Sergeant made his way back through the trenches and found Jack. He relayed the information about his brother and Des before saying, 'Well, you can stop worrying about both of them now, as it would seem that their war is over. I will be betting that they are back home before any of us here.'

Jack was grateful for the information, and felt better about writing to both Hannah and his mother. He was sure that they would both be mortified if they learnt how close Des and Tom had come to being killed. He decided that he wouldn't disclose that bit of information when the time came to write to them both.

36.

Moving to the Country

Hannah's bags were packed, and they stood on the front doorstep. Claire was busy packing a lunch basket, while Davin stood with his hands clasped behind his back, his pipe cold, but still clenched firmly between his teeth. He had his back to the two women in his life, as he stared vacantly out of the kitchen window.

Claire closed the lid on the basket and said, 'Now that should keep you going on the train, and I am sure that you will be able to get a cup of tea at one of the railway refreshment rooms along the way.'

Davin turned away from the window, and took the pipe from his mouth before saying, 'Will you stop fussin' woman. Hannah is more than capable of finding somewhere to get a cuppa tea, now look at the time, if we don't get her to the station soon she won't be goin' anywhere!'

Claire had been doing her best not to cry, and as Davin had chastised her, she pulled her handkerchief from her sleeve and sniffled into it.

Hannah was sat at the end of the table her hands clasped together, and now she stood up and moved to her aunt and embraced her, 'Don't cry, Aunt Claire, it's not like I'm going off to the war. I promise that

I will write to you every week, but you know why I have to go, and I promise that I will come home at every opportunity. Oh look, you have me crying too!' She gave her aunt a final squeeze before she dabbed at her eyes.

Claire took her shawl from the coat rack that stood in the hall. She wrapped it around her thin shoulders, before removing the small hatpin with the imitation ruby on one end of it from the side of the hat where she always kept it.

She looked at it for a moment, before she slid the pin back through her hat that was now back on her head. She smiled at her niece and said, 'Do you remember when you bought me this pin?'

Before Hannah could reply she went on, 'You were only twelve, and we went to Saint Bridget's church bazaar on the Saturday before Lent, and you asked me if you could have a penny for a lucky dip, and you reached into the bin and brought out the biggest parcel that was in there. I remember how we laughed as you kept unwrapping the newspaper. And the look on your face, as you finally found this little pin wrapped up in what seemed like an entire newspaper.'

Hannah was smiling at her aunt and said, 'I wanted so desperately to buy you a present because of how kind you had been, and for everything that you had done for me. I must say that it was worth the money, even though you paid for it.'

They both embraced again as Davin called out from the front door, 'The taxi carriage is here, it's time to go!'

The smile was now gone from her face; Hannah took one final look around at the place that had been her home and refuge for the past ten years. For a fleeting moment, she almost changed her mind about leaving. But Davin was loading the suitcases onto the tray at the back of the carriage, and she knew that she had to go.

Doris was standing on the footpath, and waiting for her future daughter-in-law to come outside. She had not wanted to intrude on Hannah's final moments with her aunt and uncle. Nevertheless, she wanted to say goodbye to the girl she now loved as her own daughter, who God willing, would one day marry her youngest son.

'Oh Lordy, I am going to miss you. I can't believe that you are leaving us. I know that you have to go, but having you around has made my life bearable while this blessed war has been going on.'

The tears were now running down Doris's face as she said, 'Now look dearie, I have something for you.' She fumbled in her apron pocket before bringing out a small gold ring. Doris placed it in Hannah's palm and closed Hannah's fingers over it.

Hannah opened her palm to look at the little band of gold, and she gasped, 'Oh Doris, this is your wedding ring, I can't take that!'

Doris took hold of Hannah's hand that held the ring, and folded her fingers back over it again.

She clasped Hannah's hand and said, 'I want you to have it. I have my memories of my Barry, and this ring would have been yours anyway. I would have given it to Tommy, and he could have given it to you, so you might as well have it now. I love you like you were my own, and with you having this ring it will bond us tightly together. Every time that I touch my hand, and the ring is no longer there I will be with you, and every time that you feel that little ring, I hope that you will think of me. Now don't argue with me, just go.' Doris was now openly crying, and as they embraced Hannah whispered, 'I will wear this around my neck on a chain Doris, until our Tommy can place it on my finger. Thank you, and Doris I love you very much.'

She climbed into the carriage, and the driver released the handbrake and loosened the reins of the horses. As they moved off, she turned her head and looked back to wave. She took one final look at Doris, who was standing forlornly on the path outside her house.

Doris stood on the pathway, and watched the carriage until it had mingled in with the other traffic to disappear from sight. She went back inside. The curtains were still drawn in the front room, and she didn't bother to open them. She sat in her darkened parlour as the house closed in around her. The silence surrounding her was deafening, and her heart ached as only a mother's could, and as the loneliness engulfed her, her tears fell.

✳✳

The carriage pulled up outside of Central Station, and her bags were unloaded and put onto a trolley. Claire looked up at the station clock, and suggested that they had time for some refreshments from the cafeteria.

They had finally run out of things to say, the lack of conversation, now cutting the ties that had held them together since Hannah was a child. Davin suggested that they find the platform where the train to Lithgow would be leaving from. They stopped at the barrier gate, and Hannah turned and said, 'You don't have to wait until the train goes. I will go and find my carriage and get settled in. I have plenty of time, and I think that I shall write to Tommy. I have my pencil, and I brought a new writing pad. If I write to him now, I can tell him all about my big adventure!'

At the gate to the platform, the red sign announced that platform tickets were a penny each, and that non-travellers needed to purchase one before they could enter the platform. Claire said to Davin, 'Go and get a couple of platform tickets from the machine.

'We might as well wait, just in case something goes wrong with the engine, or something.'

'No darlin', it's no use draggin' it out, let's just say our goodbyes now and leave!' Without waiting for a response from Claire, he held out his arms and embraced his niece. Hannah looked at her uncle's face and squeezed him tightly before saying, 'I hope that you are going to keep my room vacant for when I come home Uncle Davin. I don't want to have to share it with a lodger.'

Davin spoke into her ear as he held her and said, 'There will be no lodger young lady. It will always be there for whenever you come home. Now go, before you have me cryin' like yer aunt.' He gave her a final squeeze, and kissed her cheek before gently pushing her away. Claire put her arms around her niece and burst into tears.

'I'm sorry darling, I wasn't going to cry, now off you go, and make sure that you write to us every week, and don't forget to write to Doris too. I will go and see her when we get back, because she is going to be so lonely until her boys get back home. Now off you go. I love you darling, and don't you ever forget it!'

'I love you too, Aunty.'

Claire dabbed her eyes, and watched as Hannah gave her ticket to the station assistant standing at the barrier gate. Hannah made her way to her carriage, and after settling in she penned her letter.

September 1916.

My Dearest Tommy,

It seems so long since we have heard from you. Are you still in France? I know that you and the others have been having a tough time of things if what we read in the newspapers is true. I am writing this letter to you now as I sit on a train. I am in the process of moving away from home. I am going to be living on a farm, yes Tommy, a real farm. It is near the township of Lithgow, which is way over the other side of the Blue Mountains, and it must be about one hundred miles from Sydney.

You will recall where I told you how some of us joined the volunteer land army. We helped farmers bring in their harvests and did general farm work.

Well, I enjoyed working out in the fresh open air so much that I thought that I should learn as much about farming as I could while there was an opportunity for me to do so. I was introduced to a lovely lady, and she lived and worked on her parents' property. Her name is Harriet Murdoch, and her parents are both elderly and can no longer do as much as they once could. The property is called Megalong, and covers almost a thousand acres. Oh, Tommy, it is a glorious place, and the property shares its name with the valley that it is nestled in. It is very isolated, but there are wonderful views from the house of rolling hills within the valley, and they stretch all of the way to the rocky sandstone cliffs that rise to over a thousand feet from the valley to the top of the Blue Mountains.

I am already in love with this place, and I pray each night that you will be here with me one day. I am being a bit presumptuous in thinking that you will even want to live here once the war is over, but if you don't want to live in such an isolated location, then I won't complain as long as we are together.

Well, anyway, I met Harriet at a country women's auxiliary meeting, and we hit it off, and she invited me to visit her parents' place. I spent almost a month there. Harriet taught me how to milk a cow and how to round up the sheep, of which there are many, and the outcome was that she offered me a full-time job on the farm. They cannot afford to pay me much, but they have offered me ten shillings a week, plus free accommodation and food, which I thought was very generous of them.

They have a small farm cottage that I can live in by myself, although Harriet said that we could both live there after you come home and we are married if you wanted to.

It's such a big place, and there is so much work to do. It reminds me somewhat of my childhood home in Cork.

It was so very hard and emotional leaving home, and your mother was ever so sad. I will miss her dearly, the same as I miss you. Your mother gave me her wedding ring. She was going to give it to you when you came home, but what with me leaving she insisted that I take it.

I won't wear it until you put it on my finger, but I told your mother that I would carry it around my neck on a chain until you have returned to us.

How is everyone? Did Des ever get to write to Brigid? And talking of Brigid, did you know that she passed her nurse's exam, and she has volunteered to work on a hospital ship? It sailed from Sydney about a year ago shortly after I had spoken with her about Des. I hadn't seen her for so very long, and then one day she arrived home and told us that she had passed her exams and was going overseas as a nurse on a ship. I have received one letter from her since she left Sydney, and she said that they were anchored somewhere near some island in the Mediterranean Sea. I hope that she and Des have communicated with each other. I think that I shall do some matchmaking with those two when I get the opportunity.

I cannot believe that this dreadful war has been going on for almost three years now, and nobody seems to know how long it will continue for. The newspapers are reporting that some of the politicians wanted to bring in conscription to force other young men to the battlefields, but the government held a referendum, and everyone voted against the idea, and now the politicians are arguing again over how they could get even more young men to join up. But everyone is heartily sick of the war, and the killing of so many young men; so hopefully, the generals and the politicians will finally see common sense and end this madness.

I am sorry for talking about the war, and I won't do it any more other than to say that most people think like I am, and everyone here, although supporting you, all just want it to end.

The train journey will take over six hours, and I fear that I will be terribly exhausted by the time that I get to Lithgow. Harriet said that she would be waiting at the station for me. We are going to stay in the town at a hotel for the night, as it will be too dark to drive the buggy back to her farm, as she informs me that it will take almost another two hours to get to the farmhouse from Lithgow.

Tommy, please write to me soon, and please write to your mother too, because she will be feeling terribly lonely now that I am no longer there.

Yours Forever,
Hannah.

37.

The Hospital Ship

The medical staff had boarded the ship, and settled into their cabins the night before departure. Friends and family had gathered at the number one terminal at Circular Quay to see them off. The Salvation Army band had played Auld Lang Syne as the gangplank was raised, and a sea of smiling faces standing at the dockside waved handkerchiefs and scarves.

The sea was sparkling, and there was a sense of excitement amongst those on deck as the ship steamed out through the heads. There was still work to be done even though the wards were empty, and they had very little time to enjoy the warm balmy days that followed. Noreen oversaw the stocking of cupboards with bandages and medicines along with other medical equipment that had been stowed on board a week earlier.

After departing, it took almost a week before the civilian staff had gained their sea legs, and to get over the seasickness that most of those working in the hot, airless wards had suffered from. Training classes were held each day, so that the staff would be ready to deal with what lay ahead.

Six weeks after leaving Sydney, and one month before the Australian and New Zealand troops left Turkey for the last time, their ship dropped anchor off the coast of Gallipoli. The fifty transport ships lying at anchor were expected to carry an estimated thirty-six thousand troops that would be evacuated from the peninsula.

Meanwhile the hospital ships would take the wounded to the land-based hospital on the island of Lemnos, twelve miles off the Turkish coast. On the hills behind the beach, the battles continued between the opposing forces, and the wintery weather brought increased misery and hardship to the troops standing in frozen, waterlogged trenches.

As the transport ships waited for their orders, the landing barges kept bringing the wounded and the dying to the floating hospitals. Noreen had called a meeting of her nurses and orderlies as the ship dropped anchor.

'Ladies and gentlemen, the captain has informed me that we will be receiving our first patients soon. So, we should all prepare for a large influx of wounded soldiers. Now I just want to again warn you, that you will very likely see some severely injured men. Some will probably have wounds that none of us will have dealt with in civilian life. The chief surgeon has suggested that amputation of limbs is a real possibility with many of our patients. Irrespective of the nature of the wounds, I would suggest that we all remember to act in a thoroughly professional manner, and to treat each man with respect and compassion. That means that we must all make an effort to hide our discomfort, no matter how badly injured the patient is.

'Now, none of us has been in a war zone before. I expect that we will find that it will be entirely different to working on the wards back home. But, if anyone has a problem with dealing with their patients, or if you feel that you cannot cope, then please come and see me and I will see what I can do. That's all I have to say for now, so may I suggest that you all go to your respective stations in anticipation of the arrival of our first patients. I cannot say how long any of us will spend on the wards after today, and I am sure that you will all do your best. Thank you, staff, that will be all for now!'

After an initial bout of seasickness, Brigid had spent her days reading medical journals and playing deck games with the other nurses. She had not forgotten the recent tragedy of Mary's death, but she had now learned to live with what had happened. She vowed that once the war was over, she would devote her life to helping young pregnant women, and she would do that by studying to become a midwife.

Brigid leaned on the wooden railing, as a cold breeze blew across the water. She looked at the stark, distant hills of Gallipoli. For a moment, her mind was back in Australia and she thought of those happy days when they were all just barefooted children, running carefree and wild through the cobblestoned streets of Sydney.

Now, Des and the others were but a distant memory. Des had been on her mind for longer than she cared to admit. She had taken Hannah's advice and written to him with no expectation that he would write back, but to her surprise he had written. In his letter, he had spoken of his fear of never returning to Sydney, and how he was missing the simple days that they had lived before the war.

Brigid had the distinct impression from his letter that he really didn't believe that he would survive the war. She wondered if his talk about coming home to resume his previous life was just wishful thinking. She wondered if it was her imagination, and it was his way of saying to her that their relationship may just be a fleeting thing.

The shouting that filtered across from the starboard side of the ship interrupted her thoughts. She looked over the side, and watched, as wretched soldiers were unloaded from the barges. Doctors and nurses scurried between each man to make a preliminary decision on how soon they should be treated.

Brigid hurriedly made her way down to her station. Suddenly, the serenity of the ward was replaced with organised chaos. More orderlies had arrived below decks carrying stretchers, and laying the patients on the floor in rows, so that they could be assessed before being operated on. Each man was checked and categorised before they were carried to the operating theatre. Orders were being yelled, and hands were waving as doctors pointed to where they wanted the patient taken.

There were six operating tables in the cramped theatre, and all were being utilised at the one time. The barges kept ferrying a seemingly endless procession of dishevelled men to the ship, their once youthful faces now gaunt, aged and grey, and sometimes bloodied. Most were wearing rags, caked in mud and dried blood that were barely recognisable as being uniforms. Some could manage a weak smile to the nurses, while others wore a glazed, unfocused look with eyes haunted by the imagery of looking through the windows of hell. These were led to the wards like little children.

Feeble, flickering kerosene lamps, along with dim electric light bulbs powered by the ship's generator, lit the operating theatre.

Surgeons worked to repair the jagged wounds inflicted by the shrapnel shells, as orderlies mopped up the puddles of blood that lay beneath the operating tables.

Others carried out the dead and rotten tissue, along with the overflowing blood buckets that were positioned below the cutting slabs.

The stench of blood and the dried sweat on unwashed bodies was as overpowering as the phenol that was used as an antiseptic on the blood-soaked floors.

Brigid went about her duties with quiet efficiency. At first, she was shocked at seeing the condition of the men that had been brought on board. Those that weren't wounded, but who were trapped within a shell-shocked mind, were taken to the communal showers, before being led to a bed.

It was 1915 and early December. The hospital ship had been at anchor for more than a week. In that time, the wards had filled up, and the medical staff had dealt with over six hundred patients. The nurses were overworked and exhausted, but they all knew that the war in this part of the world was finally coming to an end. Their orders were that when the ship was at capacity, it would sail to the island of Lemnos. There, the patients would be transferred to the established hospital on shore, before returning to help evacuate the last contingent of soldiers from Gallipoli.

Brigid had grown up quickly. She had to learn new skills that a woman would never have been allowed to learn back at the Barracks Hospital. She would bathe soldiers and wash their private parts, and she had held the hands of dying men. She had written letters to their loved ones, as foul-smelling, malignant puss had wept from their infected wounds.

She had comforted men whose hearts had once harboured love, but who now questioned why God had allowed this madness to go on. She had wiped away their tears as they were told that they had lost a limb, or that they could never again father a child because of their injuries. Then, when another soldier had succumbed to his injuries, and his body had been wrapped and weighted in a funeral sheet, she had cried for him as his body was lowered over the side, to sink into the murky darkness of an unmarked, watery grave.

✲✲✲

The mood among the staff had lifted, with the realisation that within another twenty-four hours they would be transferring all of their patients to the island hospital. Then they would have time to relax as they steamed back to Gallipoli.

It took almost two days to remove all of their patients at Lemnos, and Noreen supervised the cleaning of the wards.

Hundreds of sheets and blankets were washed in the steam room, before the beds were remade.

Cupboards were restocked with medical equipment until finally, the entire medical staff could relax as the ship returned back to the coast of Turkey.

Exhausted, Brigid had slept for almost ten hours, and now with time on her hands, she took the opportunity to write to her mother and Hannah.

December 1915.

To my Dearest Hannah,

I am writing this letter to you from my ship as we sail back to Turkey. I have just written to mother, and it has been far too long I know, but our days have been taken up entirely with caring and tending to the wounded, and any spare time that I have had has been spent sleeping.

That sounds terrible, but I can't describe how weary we get with looking after all of these poor, wretched boys who are brought on board covered in filth, mud and sores. They are all covered in vermin and lice, and some of their wounds are almost indescribable. I am so very tired Hannah, and at times I feel sorry for myself until I look around and I see all the suffering and misery that surrounds me. Then I must thank God that I am well, and I tell myself that I have nothing to complain about, considering the condition of some of these chaps.

We are captive within our wards, and I see nothing other than sadness, despair and death. Is it really only four months since we sailed from Sydney? It seems like a lifetime ago.

I don't want to burden you with my problems Hannah, but I feel that if I don't speak about some of the ghastly things that I have seen, I think that I shall go mad.

At first, working on the ship was just like being back at the Barracks Hospital. That was until we arrived off the coast of Turkey. There must have been at least one hundred ships there, along with several hospital ships such as ours.

We moored about a mile from the coast, and every evening the captain would turn off all of the outside lights on the ship. They said that was so that the enemy couldn't fire their guns at us. When we first arrived here, I had no expectation of anything, but then, shortly after we had moored, the landing barges started coming alongside, and I think that we were all quite shocked. I have spoken with some of the other girls, and none of us had any idea of what dreadful condition our patients would be in.

The hospital beds are fitted with large wheels, and it makes it somewhat easier to move the boys around. We buried two chaps the other day, just after we set sail for the hospital at Lemnos Island. The hospital is only about twelve miles from the coast of Turkey, but by the time that we drew anchor, and navigated our way to the island it took us the best part of one whole day to get there. Lemnos Island is such a miserable place. It is flat and windswept, and the wind blew bitterly cold the entire time that we were there.

I must say though, that I was impressed with the way that the place has been set up. There must have been over one hundred large marquee tents set up as hospital wards. However, because of the flat terrain and the dreadful wind, it necessitated them having to be tied down very securely for fear of them being blown away.

We were going to load up some of the wounded that were on the mend, and transport them back to England, but our orders were changed, and now we are sailing back to Gallipoli to pick up more wounded. I was looking forward to going to England, but never mind, my problems are few compared to some of these poor devils.

Some of the lucky ones have just lost a leg or a hand. I shouldn't call them lucky, but God give them strength Hannah, as some of the ghastly wounds that those dreadful shrapnel bombs have inflicted upon some of these boys are just too horrible to describe.

The ward where I work holds one hundred men. There are only forty of us here, and the workload is enormous, but I shall not complain other than to say how very tired we all are. Oh, how I would love to be able to walk down a street again and see a life of normality.

I do not think that I shall ever forget the sounds of men screaming in pain, or the sounds of men wheezing and coughing and trying to find breath from their damaged lungs.

Hannah, I cannot understand this dreadful war, and I'm sure if the politicians could only see what we see, then they would surely stop this madness.

I dread doing my morning rounds, as hardly a day goes by without me finding another poor chap who has passed away during the night. It is such a sad sight to see them place the body on the slanting board, after being wrapped in a sheet and weighed down with sandbags. Then he is covered with a Union Jack. The padre then says a few words over him, as the officers stand at attention as they lower him into the water. It is so terribly sad to think that a loved one may never get the chance to stand by his graveside and place a small posy of flowers upon it.

I am so sorry Hannah, but I have spoken enough of myself; so, tell me, have you heard from Tommy and the others? I forgot to mention that I got a letter from Des and I wrote back to him, but as yet I have had no reply.

He sounded so terribly depressed, and was looking forward to the day when he could resume his apprenticeship with his father. For my part, I have no idea as to where I shall end up. There is talk that we may all end up in an Australian-run hospital in England somewhere, but I will go where I am needed, although I would be so happy if this blessed war ended quickly and we could all go home.

Write to me soon Hannah, and tell me all of the gossip as we all look forward to mail days, which are few and far between. I am weary again now, and I shall see if I can manage a couple of hours of rest before we arrive back at the peninsula.

Take care Hannah, and please do write back quickly, as I am desperate to hear of home.

Yours truly

Brigid.

38.

The Telegram

Davin and Claire caught a tram back home after dropping Hannah off at the station. They sat together, but each alone with their thoughts as they tried to come to terms with the fact that their little Hannah, whom they had loved as their own daughter, was about to make her own way in the world. They had given her a home so many years ago, and they remembered the happy times that they had shared, but now she had left them feeling empty and lonely.

As they had arrived home, Davin said, 'I think that I'll go over to the forge and see how the boys are getting on.'

He glanced at Claire as he spoke, and she nodded before saying, 'I'll go and have a cuppa with Doris. I'm sure that she will need cheering up.'

He kissed her cheek, before leaving to go the stables to get his horse.

✻

Claire found Doris washing her windows and she smiled as Claire asked, 'Is the kettle on the boil?'

'It will be shortly luvvy, now you go and get the pot warm, and I'll be in, in a minute.' She climbed down off her chair that she was standing on, and wiped the seat before entering her kitchen.

'So, she got away orright?'

'Yes, the station man said that the train would depart on time, but Davin didn't want to buy a platform ticket, and Hannah didn't want us to stay until the train left. She said that she would cry if she saw us waving goodbye, so we all had tea and cake at the refreshment rooms and left her at the barriers.' Claire stopped talking for a moment as she relived the departure.

'Oh Doris, I feel so lonely now, and I know how you felt when your boys left. I know that I'm being selfish, and that she has to live her own life, but why did she have to go and live so far away? I hadn't really thought about it, but I suppose that somewhere in my mind, I always thought that she would have stayed here, at least until after the war, and until she got married!'

Doris was pouring the water into the teapot as she replied, 'Yes luvvy, I was a bit shocked too, when she told me that she was leaving. I will miss her dearly, but we all have to go where our hearts take us. I have got used to being alone now. I sure miss my boys, doing their washing and making their dinners, but I don't expect either of them to live back here after the war. Well not for long anyway, and I've come to accept that, and I take solace from running Jack's fuel yard.

'Mind you, havin' you and Davin next door has helped me a lot. You miss your kids, you really do, but having good friends is important too.' Doris stopped pouring, and flashed Claire a smile. The tapping on the front door made them both stop talking, and look towards the sound. Doris frowned, as she was not expecting anyone. She put down the teapot, wiped her hands on her apron and opened the door.

The soldier was skinny, tall and in full uniform. He wore a small satchel across his chest. His khaki-painted pushbike was leaning against the lamp post, and as the door opened he raised his cap and said, 'Good morning madam, are you Mrs Fields?'

Doris looked at the stranger. She tried to think if she knew him or not, but then the realisation dawned on her, and her hand went to her mouth and she cried out, 'Oh no, no...' and her voice trailed off as Claire rushed to her side.

'What is it Doris?' She too, looked at the soldier and her blood ran cold. She had heard the stories of the telegrams that had been sent by the army to arrive on people's doorsteps, informing them of their son or husband's passing.

Doris's voice was quivering, and with barely a whisper she said, 'Yes, I'm Mrs Fields.' The young soldier looked sheepish, as he handed Doris the small brown envelope that he had removed from his satchel.

He tipped his hat before turning around to mount his bike.

Doris held the envelope, and with shaking hands she tore open the flap. It read,

Department of Army 18th October 1916.

Dear Mrs Fields,

It is with regret that we have to inform you that your son Thomas has been wounded in action in France. Your son was involved in a skirmish with the enemy. His injuries are no longer life-threatening, and by the time that you receive this communiqué, your son, and those injured alongside of him will have been transported away from the front line and should by now be in a repatriation hospital in London.

You may contact the army recruitment centre in York Street Sydney, regarding information on how you may contact your son.

Sincerely

Department of Army.

Doris was staring at the telegram, and her hands were still shaking. She had expected the worst, and she had to read it over again just to ensure herself that her youngest son was still alive. She could hardly speak, and she handed the telegram to Claire and muttered, 'He's alive, he's alive, thanks be to God.' She blessed herself and muttered a silent prayer. Claire placed her arm around her friend's shoulder and led her back to the kitchen. She took down the bottle of cooking sherry from the top shelf of the small dresser, and poured a good splash of it into Doris's teacup saying, 'Drink this, it will settle your nerves.'

Doris had a dozen questions that she wanted to ask about how, and where and what were her son's injuries, but there was no one to answer them, and her mind swirled with worry over the well-being of her youngest child.

39.

Repatriation

The niggling pain wormed its way into Tom's sleepy mind, and then he felt the sensation in his shoulder. It felt like something was pushing into it, and he tried to move to stop whatever it was that was burrowing into him. The anaesthetic was wearing off, and as he opened his blurry eyes, he thought that he was looking at an angel.

The vision was standing over him, and was wearing a white veil that flowed to the floor. For a moment, he thought that he was in heaven. His eyes wouldn't focus clearly, but he saw the angel bend down and come closer to him, and in his drug-induced mind he heard the angel say, 'Don't move, just lie still.' He was trying to work out why the angel was talking to him. He felt the angel's hand touch his forehead, and then the angel touched his wrist and held it for what seemed like an eternity.

His mind slowly cleared, and his mouth felt like it was lined with fur, and then he realised that his angel was a nurse, and that she was wearing a white apron and a triangular veil on her head, and he tried to smile as he whispered, 'Water, I need water.'

The nurse moved to the trolley standing at the end of his bed, and poured the water from a tin jug into an enamel mug. She then placed her arm under the back of his head, and lifted it high enough to pour the cooling liquid into his mouth.

He asked, 'Where am I?' and his angel replied, 'You are in the clearing hospital at Heilly, and soon you will be taken to Amiens.' The pain in his shoulder was intensifying, and he asked, 'What happened to me?'

'You were shot in the shoulder, and the bullet has fractured your collarbone, but luckily for you, you will recover. The bullet did some serious damage to the bone, and you are likely to be out of action for some time. I won't be surprised if they send you home, but that's not up to me to decide, now lay still. The doctor will see you as soon as he has a moment, but in the meantime, I will get you some food. I'm sure that you are hungry!'

As she was about to walk away, he asked, 'Can ya tell me, nurse, did they bring anyone else here with me?' She looked at her patient list before replying, 'There were about twelve of you, was there someone that you were looking for?'

'I'm not sure nurse, but I vaguely remember seeing me mate Des Carney goin' down, and I'm not sure about me brother Jack.'

The nurse referred back to her patient list, and scrolled through it before declaring, 'Des Carney, yes, he's here, and your brother's name is Jack. No, there is no Jack Fields here, but your other mate, Des Carney is in the ward somewhere. I'll see if I can find him for you.'

Tom lay with his thoughts, and wondered about Jack. He hoped that he had come out of the skirmish without injury. He had no idea of how long he had been in the hospital, although he was happy with the thought that his wound might see him being sent home.

He thought of Hannah and his mother, and he hoped that they wouldn't worry too much about him once they found out about his condition. He would ask the nurse if she would write them a letter.

The nurse came back carrying a tray, which she set down on the trolley at the foot of the bed. 'I've brought you some broth, soldier. You won't be able to eat much because of the morphine in your system, but it will take the edge off your hunger.

'Oh, by the way, your mate Des Carney is at the other end of the ward, so after you have eaten and I have checked your dressing, I will move your bed next to his.'

Des was awake when they wheeled Tom's bed through the ward to be positioned next to his. His face broke into a wide grin when he recognised Tom.

'Glad to see you here Tom. So, they didn't kill ya? I saw you go down, but I was a bit busy with Fritz, so I couldn't help ya. Did yer get stabbed or shot?'

'I got a lump of lead in me shoulder, and it busted me collarbone. Geez, it hurts like blazes, but bloody hell, I'm so glad to still be alive. Although, I ain't lookin' forward to the next couple of months. So, what happened to you? You're all trussed up like a Christmas turkey.'

Des glanced down at his arm before replying, 'I was tryin' to get out of the way of a German. I remember him comin' at me with his bayonet, and somehow he got the bloody thing right up inside me arm, but it was better than gettin' it in me guts. Christ! I remember how much it hurt. I nearly passed out, and the last thing I remember was that someone smashed his head in! I don't remember nuthin' after that until I ended up here.'

'I'm glad that you made it mate, so how long have we been 'ere? I only woke up a coupla hours ago!'

Des was silent for a moment before he replied, 'We been 'ere for two days. I slept for the first day meself. The doc had a word with me yesterday, and he told me that the bayonet cut right through the sinew and the muscle and that he had sewed it up as best as he could. He wanted me to know that me fightin' days are gone, and he said that they are gunna ship me out soon. I dunno where to, someone said that we were gunna go to England, but I really don't know mate!'

They lay quietly for a time, before Tom asked, 'So will ya be able ta go back to your cabinetmaking?' Des thought for a moment before replying, 'I dunno, I hope so, but the old man is gunna be upset if I can't finish me apprenticeship. He always expected me to take over his business, but I dunno what else I could do. Sometime ago I thought of going bush and doin' some shearing, but that's out now.' He gave a hollow laugh as he said, 'What do ya reckon, think I could make it as a one-armed shearer?'

Tom could hear that his mate was struggling with what had happened, and having thought about it he said. 'You don't hafta make up yer mind right now, the doc might be wrong, and yer arm might come good. Only time will tell.'

'Yeah, you're right, I'm just feelin' a bit sorry fer meself. Once I can get out of this blessed bed on me own, I'll probably feel a lot better.'

Three weeks later, they were both transferred to England for rehabilitation. The railways had been used extensively throughout Germany and France to transport heavy artillery, horse fodder and general supplies to the front lines, and now, the railways were being used to carry the wounded back to the coast.

The train took six hours to reach Boulogne, and the patients were transferred onto a ferry that took them across the English Channel to Dover.

⋆⋆⋆

The Shepherd's Bush hospital in Hammersmith had been set up as a rehabilitation centre, and the wounded soldiers were categorised by injuries. Those with physical injuries were easy to deal with, but those suffering from 'shell shock' were seen as malingerers.

If a soldier had no physical injury, but clearly showed psychological problems, then he was regarded as a weakling. When a soldier was seen crying, the authorities saw him as a failure as a man, and he was regarded as a sissy. Many of these men were sent straight back to the front lines to harden up, and to overcome their fear of death.

Tom and Des had been back in England for a month, and it was almost Christmas. Both could now walk around inside the hospital, and their days were filled with exercising, reading and sleeping. But, for the most part, they were trying to get used to the fact that there would be no more trench life, gunfire, or barbed wire for either of them.

40.

Leaving Turkey

Another day's sailing saw the hospital ship moored back in Turkish waters. The captain gathered his officers, along with the senior medical staff, for a briefing. His voice bellowed, as he relayed the information that he had received from army H.Q.

'Ladies and gentlemen, I have been informed that the withdrawal of all allied troops from the Suvla Bay area on the Gallipoli peninsula is almost completed. Now Matron,' and he looked directly at Noreen as he spoke. 'Could you inform me when the wards are full? I would like to get under way as soon as possible, and there must be a bed for each of the wounded. There is another hospital ship, the Barkarolla, and she is moored nearby. Her orders are to stay until the last troops have left the peninsula. I am told that it could possibly take several more weeks for that to happen. So, we can be under way as soon as you give the word. I am anxious to be out of these waters as early as possible. The weatherglass is falling, and I would prefer that we are not caught in the approaching storm!'

That night, during dinner in the mess hall Noreen addressed her staff. 'Thank you everyone, for your professionalism in assisting with the wounded over the past few weeks. I am pleased to announce that we will be sailing for Southampton, after we take on coal and provisions in Malta. From there, we will sail directly to our destination. The captain has informed me that it will take around ten days' sailing before we reach England.

'I am unsure if this ship will be required after then, as those wounded on the battlefields in France will probably be attended to in local hospitals there.'

Noreen looked at the weary faces of her staff before asking, 'Does anyone have any questions?' Brigid was about to speak, but another nurse posed a question to Noreen first. 'Matron, will we be transferred to another ship, or what is likely to happen to us?'

There were murmurings among the nurses and orderlies in agreement with the question being asked.

'I am not sure at this time, but I have been led to believe that there are several Australian-run hospitals in and around London. So, there is a good chance that our services may be required there. But I will be in a better position to answer your questions after we arrive in England. Now, in the meantime please carry out your duties as allocated to you. I understand that we could all do with a good rest, and I can assure you that I shall arrange for you all to receive a leave warrant once we reach London. Now if there is nothing further, please return to your stations when you have finished your meal.'

41.

Anguish

After the initial shock of receiving the news about Tom, Doris had made her way to the army headquarters in York Street. A clerk greeted her.

'May I help you, madam?' Doris was clutching the telegram that had delivered the bad news.

'I wonder if you might be able to help me, son? You see, I got this telegram.' She held it out to the clerk for his perusal.

'I would like to know where I might get some more information about me son. The telegram doesn't tell me much, so can you help me here? I just want to know how bad he's been hurt, and what's going to happen to him?'

The clerk read the telegram, and frowned. 'What battalion was he in?'

Doris snorted, 'I dunno son, but this is where he came to enlist so you should have his name on your files, Fields, Thomas Fields that's his name.'

The clerk looked uncomfortable and replied, 'I'm sorry madam, but we have over 100,000 soldiers at the front, and it would help me locate the information if I just knew what battalion he was with.'

Doris thought for a moment and said, 'Well I think that he's in the fifth battalion, it's either the third or the fifth. Silly of me, but I can't remember what section he's in, even though I write to both me sons every month!'

The clerk asked, 'You don't have the actual address that you send his letters to, do you? That would be a big help in locating him.'

'No, sonny I don't have the address with me, but who can I contact? There must be someone who keeps track of all our boys.'

The clerk thought for a moment, before deciding that he would pass the inquiry down the line. 'I will go and have a word with my superior, madam, so if you would just take a seat I will see what I can do.'

Doris sat down and looked around her. Behind the counter were a dozen or more clerks clacking at their typewriters, while doors behind their desks opened and closed as uniformed staff came and went with no particular urgency. Her mind went back to the time when her boys had come home with their recruitment papers. Her thoughts were interrupted by the uniformed officer asking,

'Are you Mrs Fields?'

'Yes, I am, do you have some news?'

'I have checked your son's file Mrs Fields, and both of your sons were stationed in an area known as the Somme in France. The details that we have are sketchy, as you would expect. However, we have been able to ascertain from recent cables that your son, along with the others who were with him, have been transferred to London. The last cablegram that has reached us, gave us the names of every soldier, including your son who has been sent to a repatriation hospital in London.

'Now, Mrs Fields I don't have an address for that hospital in London where your son was taken. However, I can assure you that your son's injuries are no longer life-threatening, and that the injury that he sustained was a broken collarbone caused by a gunshot!'

Doris was clearly relieved, but insisted on asking the young officer, 'Are you sure that he's orright? I couldn't stand it if I lost me baby, just tell me again that he's not going to die.' Doris was sat on the bench, and the officer was standing above her, but now he sat next to her and said. 'Mrs Fields, I only have the weekly communiqués,' he waved them in front of her before continuing, 'that we receive from the front, and the information sent to us is all that we have to go on, but the information that we receive is usually accurate when it is sent. It is made up of reports from the front line, and always includes casualties, transfers and the nature of the injury sustained. That information is relayed to us directly from the medical staff.

'I can assure you Mrs Fields, that right now as we speak your son is in a London hospital recuperating, and if you write to your son at his last known address then your letter will get to him. I'm sure that he will have already written back to you by now, and that you should receive a letter from him at any time now!'

'But sir, if he has a busted collarbone then he won't be able to write to me, will he?'

The officer stood up to leave, and with a parting word he said, 'Mrs Fields, there are people in the hospitals that write letters for soldiers all of the time. I'm sure that a letter will arrive at any moment, as it has been well over a month since your son was sent to London. Now forgive me, but I have to attend to other business.' Then, as an afterthought he said, 'I forgot to mention Mrs Fields, that your son's injuries will prevent him returning to active duty, so when he is released from the hospital he will, in all possibility be sent home to be discharged. Now, that is all that I can tell you at the moment. Goodbye Mrs Fields.' He then turned and walked away.

Doris made her way back home. She checked her mailbox before going next door. Claire was also waiting for news, before she made the telephone call to Hannah that she was dreading.

'How did you go Doris, was there any more news?'

'No luvvy, they couldn't give me much more information. Lord, I have to sit down and rest me bunions!' She dragged a chair out from under the table, and sat down with a sigh.

Claire had made a pot of tea, and placed the tea cosy over it before taking two cups from the dresser. 'So, who did you see, did you see the man in charge, what did he say?'

'He said that he had received a communiqué from the front where Tommy was. I suppose that's some sort of telegram, anyway he reckons that Tommy is in a hospital in London somewhere now. They said that he has a busted collarbone, and that he was recuperating and doing orright. But, I forgot the best bit! The general, or whoever it was that I saw there, says that he won't be able to go back to the war because it is going take a long time for his arm to mend properly. He said that they are probably going to send him home after he gets out of the hospital!'

Doris took a sip from her cup, and smiled before going on, 'I don't know when that's going to happen because he didn't say, but thank God he's out of danger now. I will be glad when Jack is on his way home too!'

'That's very good news Doris, and I will feel a little better when I telephone Hannah and tell her.

'Oh, my Lord, I am not looking forward to that conversation. I've put it off long enough, so I will go to the Post Office tomorrow and book the call, or do you think that I should just send her a long telegram?'

'No, I think that you should talk to her, personal like. If you just send a telegram she will panic, and probably jump on the first train and come back here. Not that we wouldn't like to see her, but she will have hardly settled in just yet, and she will be in a real flap. No luvvy, just telephone her, and make sure that you have plenty of copper coins with you. I was told that a long distant telephone call costs four pence for three minutes, and if you don't put in more money when they tell you to, the telephone girl shuts down the line. I've got a few pennies in me tin on the shelf if you want some.'

'No, I don't need any thanks Doris, as I have my little stash in the larder. Well, we can be grateful for small mercies for at least we know that he will be coming home soon.'

42.

London

The ship berthed into the port of Southampton. The wharf was lined with horse-drawn and motorised ambulances. Six hundred patients were transferred from the ship, and it was midnight when the last of them was driven away, leaving the wharf deserted.

The nurses gathered in the dining room, and the cook had provided them with a late meal. After doing a final check of the now empty wards, Noreen joined her staff and sat down as Brigid poured her a cup of tea. Although tired, they were all now in a state of anxiety. The captain had informed them that he had not received any further orders from the war office other than to prepare the ship to be handed back to its owners, the P & O line.

The ship had previously been a passenger liner that had plied its trade between Australia and England, and now it was deemed to be surplus to requirements, but the captain had told them that his orders could be changed at any time. After the meal, Noreen addressed her staff.

'Tomorrow, we will attend to packing all the equipment that needs to be transferred to shore. Hopefully by then, we will have received notification of what the war office expects of us. There is a good chance that if our ship is to sail back to Australia that we might accompany it.

'However, I am told that several Australian hospital annexes have been established in various counties throughout England. These annexes are to be, and are staffed by Australian nurses.

'Positions may be available to any of you who would rather stay here to assist with the rehabilitation of wounded soldiers. Now, this has not yet been confirmed, and if it comes to fruition rest assured that I shall inform you!

'I wish to thank you all, for your dedication and hard work over the past few months. I know that it has been a trying time for all of us. Now it's late, and you should all get some rest, so goodnight!'

Over the following two days, they cleaned equipment and scrubbed floors along with packing up medicines and equipment. An official from the British Ministry of Ships, along with two members of the British Hospital Commission, arrived at the pier on the third morning after they had docked. They came on board, and were led into the captain's stateroom. Noreen had been summoned along with the other senior medical staff and took a seat. Introductions were carried out, before Mr Jerome Lancet from the Hospital Commission addressed those gathered.

Mr Lancet wore a black suit, complemented by a white shirt. The shirt cuffs were held together with silver cufflinks showing below the sleeves of his dark topcoat. He adjusted the pincer glasses sat on the end of his thin nose, before placing the papers that his assistant had passed to him on the table in front of him.

'Ladies and gentlemen, good morning! You are all no doubt awaiting your instructions.' He raised his head, and gave them a weak smile before continuing, 'I can officially tell you, that with the last of the troops removed from the Gallipoli peninsula, our war in that part of the world is over! However, as you will all be aware the war in Europe is far from over. Mr Peters,' and he nodded in the direction of where Mr Peters was sat, 'is from the war office, and he will no doubt be able to answer your questions in that regard. For my part, I am here to explain your options.

'We are well aware that the entire medical complement on board are volunteers, and as such neither the war office, nor the Ministry of Shipping can order you to stay here, nor can we stop you from returning to Australia if you so wish! That being said, I am here to suggest to you matron, now that your turn of nursing duty aboard this ship is over, that you and your staff might consider working in one of the many temporary hospitals that have been established around the country.

'We have a variety of hospitals that specialise in different afflictions, and we at the Hospital Commission believe that it would assist the recovery of Australian troops if they were treated by familiar voices that have a commonality with their homeland.

'You and your staff would, of course, be paid for your services, and it goes without saying that your accommodation would be provided for! I have also been assured that when the war is over, should you choose to do so, you may be repatriated back home at no cost to yourselves for your passage. So, matron, if you would be good enough to talk to your staff and relay our offer to them it would be much appreciated.'

Noreen thought for a minute before replying, 'Mr Lancet, I cannot speak for my staff as yet, but I am more than willing to help out. Nursing has been my vocation for all of my adult life, and I will probably be of more use over here than back home at the moment, so my answer is yes. I am sure that once I relay your offer to my staff that most, if not all, will also stay and assist. How may I contact you to give an answer?'

'Thank you, matron, my clerk, Mr Kemp, will remain on board until after you have spoken with your staff. He will make the necessary arrangements for the postings. If any of your staff would rather work on another hospital ship, then Mr Kemp can also facilitate with them being transferred. While your ship is being taken out of commission as a hospital ship, we have other ships that will be required to repatriate wounded soldiers from hospitals in Egypt and other locations. Those transfers will take some considerable time, so if any of your staff would rather be allocated to those duties, please let me know. Thank you for your time matron, and I will bid you a good day!'

He spoke quietly to his clerk before he turned and walked from the room. Noreen stood and acknowledged the clerk with, 'I shall talk with my staff immediately Mr Kemp. Where shall I find you?'

The clerk looked up at Noreen and said, 'I shall be here, if that's acceptable to you captain?'

The captain nodded and replied, 'Yes, of course you may conclude your business here Mr Kemp. I wish to talk to Mr Peters about the submarine threat, as I have heard that we had another hospital ship attacked by the Germans recently.'

Mr Kemp thanked the captain and went back to his papers.

After speaking with her staff, Noreen had returned to the Captain's quarters and spoke with Mr Kemp.

'My staff are all willing to volunteer to work in a land-based hospital Mr Kemp, so we are all at your disposal.'

He gave a weak smile and said, 'Thank you matron. I shall make the necessary arrangements for the transfers. We can accept ten nurses at the Shepherd's Bush Hospital. That is almost in London itself. However, there is an Australian annex at the hospital at Harefield, which is in Middlesex. That hospital is about twenty miles from London however, but there is a good train service from there to London, and if you would let me know your preference at which location you would like to be stationed at, I will make the necessary arrangements.'

***

Doctor Jason Smyth-Davies was doing his rounds at the Shepherd's Bush Hospital. The hospital was stretched to its limit, along with the nursing staff that were attending to the large influx of wounded soldiers that had arrived over the past month.

The hospital board had made the decision, that the patients who could walk should be moved to other nearby hospitals. Room was urgently required for the more seriously wounded patients that would continue to arrive from France. Matron Helen Jordon accompanied the doctor on his morning rounds, and as he examined each patient, she took down the name of each man deemed fit enough to be moved.

Des could walk, although his arm was still heavily bandaged, while Tom could walk with difficulty as his shoulder was still encased in plaster, but mostly he was wheelchair-bound.

'Matron, I think that we shall transfer these Australian lads to the hospital at Harefield. How many Australians do we have here?'

'We have thirty Australian patients in total, doctor, but ten of those are still seriously ill, so we could move twenty.'

'Very well, do we have any idea how many patients are at Harefield?'

'I believe that there are approximately two hundred there at the moment, so there should be no difficulty in them accepting another twenty from us. I will make the necessary arrangements when we have completed your rounds.'

⁕⁕⁕

The first Australian Auxiliary Hospital was established in June 1915 in the small hamlet of Harefield. It was situated twenty miles from London. The hospital had previously been an eighteenth-century manor house.

An expatriate Australian, whose family had built and owned the manor for the past two hundred years, had donated it to the Australian government. It was donated on the proviso that it would be used to treat only Australian soldiers wounded in the conflict. The building was in a run-down state, and after it had been donated, the government had refurbished the rooms into wards and offices that would eventually accommodate a thousand patients. As the grounds were substantial around fifty small temporary buildings were hurriedly built as mess huts and specialist wards. Each was connected by a covered, planked walkway.

Noreen, Brigid and the rest of the staff from the hospital ship were all issued with leave warrants along with their wages, which had not been paid to them since leaving Sydney. They had all been billeted in the nurse's quarters at the Shepherd's Bush Hospital over Christmas before being transferred to Harefield in January 1916. It was the middle of winter, and other than the weather, Brigid thought that it was not all that different to being back at the Barracks Hospital in Sydney.

43.

Waiting for Mail

Doris was standing at her front door, as she did every morning. It had been a month since she had spoken with the army officer, and still no mail had arrived from France. She watched as Bert Wilson, the postman, dropped the occasional letter into a mailbox, before blowing his whistle and moving along the street. He passed by next door without stopping, and then he tipped his cap, before saying,

'Mornin' Mrs Fields, I reckon this might be what ya be after,' as he handed her two letters. Her hands trembled as she took both letters that were postmarked from France.

'Thank you, Bert, looks like both me sons have finally written to their mother. Do you want a cuppa? I got the kettle on if you would like one!'

'Thanks all the same Mrs Fields, but I got a few more letters to deliver before I'm through. Looks like the overseas mail came in, cause I gotta lot with a foreign post mark stamped on 'em.'

'Orright Bert, and thanks for bringing these two.' She waved the letters that were now clutched firmly in her grasp.

She opened the first one, and it was from Jack. In it, he gave a rundown on the skirmish that had wounded Tom. He apologised as though it was his fault that Tom had been hit, but he assured his mother that Tom was alive, and the medics had assured him that he wasn't going to die.

There was some small talk, but he didn't go into any detail about the miserable conditions that they had been enduring. He signed off with, 'I hope that we see each other sometime soon as we are all heartily sick of this war, and have a Merry Christmas mother.'

She still held Jack's letter as she poured the hot water into the teapot. She then opened the other letter that bore a stranger's handwriting.

Somewhere in France. October 1916.

Dearest Mother,

You will have noticed that I have not written this letter. I suppose that Jack will have written to you by now and told you the news? We were involved in a small skirmish with Fritz, and somehow, I managed to take a bullet in my shoulder. It hit my shoulder bone and broke it, so now I am trussed up like a Christmas turkey, and unable to do things like wash and dress myself. The doctor tells me that the wound is healing up nicely, but he is of the opinion that it will be some months before the fracture has fully healed.

We are still in France. Oh, and I forgot to say that Des Carney is here with me. He sustained a nasty gash on his arm during the same skirmish. He is well, but has been told that it will take some months for his arm to heal. It is quite amusing watching us both trying to do everyday things with each of us short of one arm that is functional. We have been told that we are likely to be transferred to England sometime soon, and if that happens, I will let you know where we will be stationed.

The weather here is freezing, and I feel for Jack and the others stuck in the mud while I am here at the hospital, clean and warm. I received a message delivered by an ambulance orderly that Jack came out of the skirmish unscathed.

I haven't been told officially yet, but the doctor has said that my fighting days are over. I am sure that the injury that Des has sustained to his arm will see him out of the war also. I haven't thought about it much, but it will be strange to be out of the army, but I can't say that I will be sorry. They are a good bunch of blokes here, and as much as I'm looking forward to coming home whenever that may be, I just wish that Jack and the others could also come home. I have written to Hannah, and in her last letter to me, she told me that she is living on a farm somewhere in the mountains. She told me that you gave her your wedding ring. I hope that she will still want me to place it upon her finger when I finally return. Since I have been lying here with nothing to do, I can't help thinking of her and how I miss her.

Not that I don't miss you mother, also Claire and Davin, but somehow, it's different, it seems so long since I have seen any of you. I can't believe that it's almost three years since we packed our kit bags and left Sydney. So much has happened, and I have seen so much that it pains me to think that I have changed. I know that I have changed; I suppose that we all have. How could we not mother? I cannot describe the things that we have seen, or the things that we have done.

It may sound silly, but the one thing that I am longing for is to once again hear the sound of silence. Mother, I cannot describe the noise of the battlefield, what with cannon and bombs, and the chattering sounds of angry guns going off all around us at all times of the day and night. The trenches are a strange place where we were subjected to weeks of sheer boredom and monotony, which were occasionally broken up by moments of sheer terror as the guns of the enemy pounded us. Well mother, there is not much more that I can tell you, as life here in the hospital is very mundane. If you see Mr Carney would you tell him that Des is all right, and that he is looking forward to going home? I will write to you again after we arrive in London.

All the best, mother,

Your son

Tom.

Doris still held Tom's letter in her hand as her mind deciphered what she had just read. She needed to talk to Claire, and show her the letters, and so she went next door.

***

Later on that morning, Claire made her way into the city and went to the General Post Office to make a telephone call. The call would go through a series of exchanges and operators and along the inland wire before the good news would be relayed to Hannah.

44.

Horace Taylor

Brigid had quickly settled into the routine at Harefield hospital. Spring had finally arrived, and the patients could now walk, or be wheeled around the grounds to enjoy the watery sunshine that had eluded them over the long, frigid English winter.

She had written to Des again, but he had not replied. Brigid was hoping that nothing had happened to him, but there was no way for her to find out. She was constantly busy, but when she did manage a quiet moment by herself, she wondered why her thoughts invariably went back to him. She didn't think that she loved him. They had been childhood friends and nothing more. She put her thoughts of him down to her just feeling lonely and homesick.

Brigid didn't like the English climate, and often thought about the hot summers back in Sydney. Her thoughts turned to home, and she made her mind up that at the first opportunity after the war she would return. It wasn't that she didn't like being in England, she did, but months of wet and cold days had left her longing for the consistent blue skies of home.

In the meantime, she would write to Hannah in the hope of gleaning any information about her friends and what had happened to the boys.

Her ward consisted of a dozen beds that three nurses presided over.

Brigid now found that she had time on her hands to catch up with reading old medical journals, along with an occasional novel from the hospital library.

All the wards had been hurriedly constructed as temporary accommodation. They were built directly behind the old manor house, and Brigid's ward held soldiers that had had limbs removed, or who suffered from minor burns.

A young soldier had been admitted a week earlier with serious wounds. His right arm had been blown off, and his face had been burned as a German mortar shell had exploded in his trench. He hadn't been expected to live long enough to leave France, but he did, and was transferred to Harefield. His name was Horace Taylor and was known to his mates as Horrie.

He was still sedated when he was brought in. The orderlies placed him down gently onto the clean starched sheets, and left him there. Brigid made him comfortable before reading his medical file. The doctor in France who had removed the remains of his arm had signed them. The file gave his service number, and his age along with his battalion. She glanced at his face, and to the side that wasn't covered in the gauze bandage. It was so pale and young-looking that she had to check his age. He had turned nineteen only three months earlier, and Brigid wondered if he would still be alive by his next birthday.

She folded back the sheet from across his chest, and flattened the pillow around his head and said quietly. 'You're safe now, Mr Horace Taylor, so you just rest, and between us we will make you well again.' As she made her way back to her station, she couldn't help wondering if Tom, Jack and Des were also lying in a ward somewhere like this.

***

It was almost two weeks after Horrie had been admitted before he was well enough to speak. Brigid had been giving him special attention. She had changed his dressings daily, under the instructions of the doctor who was concerned about the likelihood of infection. The gauze covering his face was soaked in carbolic acid, and had to be changed every two hours if infection was to be held at bay. He had been awake for some time before Brigid had reached his bedside, and he greeted her with a quiet, 'Hello nurse, where am I?'

She bent over him to look at the burn to his face. 'Hello soldier, you are at the Harefield Hospital in England, and you have been here for almost two weeks. I was wondering if you were going to wake up and join us soon.'

She spoke with a smile in her voice, that didn't reflect how she was feeling after looking at the festering wound on his face.

'How are you feeling, you must be hungry?'

'No, I'm just thirsty nurse, could I have some water?' She poured him some water and gently lifted his head as he drank greedily.

His thirst quenched, he asked, 'How did I get here?'

Brigid thought for a moment and replied, 'I suppose that they brought you here on a hospital train, that's how a lot of you boys ended up here. But you're safe now, so it's up to you to get better as soon as you can. Where are you from soldier?'

'I signed up in Sydney miss. I signed up on me eighteenth birthday. That was just over a year ago. Me old mum had to sign the papers, but she didn't want to and I just kept naggin' her until she give in. Suppose they will send me home now miss? Dunno what I'm gunna do with me wing missing,' and he turned his head towards the bandage. 'How about me eye miss, have I still got it? Cause I remember the flash as the shell went off, and I don't remember nuthin' after that!'

Brigid thought of the first time that she had changed his facial bandage. She had gasped as she looked at his wound with its loose folds of dead and dying skin, and the yellow fluid seeping from the pus-filled blisters that covered the entire left side of his face. She was concerned over his burnt eyelid, and the shrunken eye. She thought that it might eventually be replaced with a glass one, once the skin had healed.

She didn't want to lie to him, and she didn't want him getting depressed, so she replied, 'We won't be able to tell just yet if we can save it or not. Your eyelid got burnt, but that doesn't mean that you have lost the sight in that eye. We will just have to wait until the bandages can come off before we can tell for sure, now is there anything that I can get for you?'

He spoke quietly, and with some embarrassment as he asked, 'Could I have a bedpan please nurse, and could someone write a letter to me mum?'

Brigid understood his discomfort, but the war had changed a lot of things, and nurses did things now that they would not have had to do before the war.

Nurses would never bathe a naked male patient, or assist with a man's toilet needs in the days before the war, but now, with a shortage of male orderlies, the niceties of Edwardian decency were nothing more than a memory.

'I'll get a pan for you soldier, and then when I've finished with my other patients I shall come back, and you can tell me what you want to say to your mother.'

'Thank you, nurse.' She tended to her other patients, before taking a notebook back to Horrie's bedside.

'Now soldier, what would you like me to say to your mother?' Horrie thought for a moment before he replied, and Brigid was mortified with the words that he spoke.

> *September 1916. Harefield Hospital England.*
>
> *Hello mother,*
>
> *I'm sorry for not writing to you sooner. I know that it's been a long time and that I am very tardy. I am so sorry that I nagged you to sign my papers, and I don't want you to feel badly because you did, but I am afraid that by the time that you receive this letter, I shall be dead!*

Brigid froze when Horrie uttered those words and she exclaimed, 'Oh Horace, you cannot say that to your mother! You are not going to die. I won't let you; we won't let you! Look how much you have improved since you have been here. You are young, and you are going to get stronger every day. I promise you, you are, now let me reword that, please. I won't let you die, I just won't!'

She pulled out her handkerchief and surprised herself with her emotion, but then she remembered about Mary, and how she had died so violently in front of her, and those memories now came flooding back as she dabbed at her tears.

Horrie could see how upset he had made Brigid, and with his one usable hand he placed it over Brigid's and said, 'I'm sorry nurse, I didn't mean to make you cry, and if you don't wanna write me letter I understand, but I know that I'm gunna die here. Don't ask me how I know, but I know things aren't right inside me. I seen the angel in me dreams.

'Don't laugh at me miss, I just wanna let me mum know that I was thinkin' of her, that's all.

'She's gunna blame herself for what happened, and if I don't write and explain, how will she ever know that I didn't blame her. I gotta write and tell her miss.

'If she gets a letter from me, and she knows that I'm orright with dyin', then she will get over it. But, if she don't hear nuthin' until the army telegram arrives, she is gunna always blame herself. Do you understand miss? That's why you hafta write and tell her, please miss!'

His good eye gleamed at Brigid with an intensity that she couldn't ignore, but at the same time, it scared her like she had never been scared before. 'All right Horace, we shall write to your mother, but I'm going to prove you wrong. You are going to get better, I promise you!' She picked up her pencil and prepared to write again.

I have to tell you like this mother, because I know that you are going to be upset when the army telegram arrives, but you always told me to be truthful and honest. Do you remember when that horse bolted from outside the store, and he knocked over old Mrs Gilmore and she died? And I asked you why God had let it happen and you said, 'That it wasn't up to us to question God, and that God would have had a reason.'

Well, I copped it pretty bad mother, but I didn't get it so bad as the others. I at least got to write to you, so I don't know why God has let all this killing go on any more than I know why he lets some people live, and he don't let others. But I can thank him, and so should you, because he gave me the time, so that I could at least write to you!

I'm just glad that I didn't have a wife or children, and will you say sorry to my sister for me that I missed her wedding. Tell her for me that I hope that she has a dozen babies, and if she does then she might name one after me.

It is spring over here now mother, and I can just see the apple blossoms budding on the tree outside of my window. You used to get so excited when you saw the apple blossoms, because you hated the winter so bad, and you always said that winter was gone when the blossoms came out.

We don't have any blue skies just yet, and all that I ask is that when my rendezvous with God arrives, that he will let me be buried under a nice blue sky.

Goodbye mother, I love you, and when you look up at a starry night sky, I will be the one twinkling back at you.

Your son,

Horace.

Brigid's tears fell upon the pages as she finished writing. She dabbed at her eyes again before standing up and saying, 'That's a lovely letter Horace. I shall rewrite it tonight on some proper paper, and I will take it down to the village post office tomorrow, and I will post it myself. Now you just lay still, and I will bring you some food shortly.'

***

Two weeks after posting the letter, Brigid noticed a change in Horace's wounds. As she removed the bandage that covered the stump of his arm, she recoiled with the smell. The stump had now festered, and the skin was turning green and black as the gangrene set in.

She had been bathing the wound daily in salt water and iodine, and the torn skin had looked like it was improving. It was almost a month since he had been admitted to the hospital. The doctor had said that with every day that passed the risk of infection was lessened. In her mind, she had thought that the worst was now over for Horace, and how she had been hoping against hope that Horace's premonition was wrong. She needed to get the doctor to attend to him immediately. She had seen how quickly other patients had succumbed once that septicaemia had taken over.

The doctor had arrived, shortly after Brigid had sent an orderly to find him. He noted that Horace was running a fever, and as he removed the gauze that covered the burn on his face, his frown deepened. The burn was now changing colour, and the pus-filled blisters had turned black. The wound had stopped weeping as the blood poisoning took hold under the skin. Brigid wanted to ask the doctor how bad the wound now was, but she was a junior nurse, and as such, she dared not ask him anything. He finally spoke, 'Nurse, this patient is dying, I can try cutting away the gangrene in his shoulder, but the face is also severely infected, and all that I can do is make him comfortable. I will give him a vial of morphine now, and I will increase the dose every twelve hours.'

'Doctor, what should I do, will I keep bathing his wounds in iodine?'

The doctor scowled at her before answering gruffly, 'Nurse this patient will probably be dead within twenty-four hours. There is no point in wasting your time in cleaning his wounds. He has septicaemia, and keeping him sedated with morphine is all that we can do. I will increase the dosage as he deteriorates!' He then filled the syringe and forced it under the skin.

When the doctor had left, she sat at Horace's bedside and held his hand. She thought of the letter that he had dictated to her, and she wondered how he could have prophesied his death.

***

Horace died less than twelve hours later, and arrangements were made for him to be buried in the local community cemetery.

The small community of Harefield was appreciative of the Australian soldiers that had come to the assistance of England. They didn't understand why anyone would volunteer to fight in a war that didn't concern them.

Yet, the Australians had fought and died alongside of their own sons and husbands, and for that they were grateful.

Saint Mary's Church at Harefield was one mile from the hospital. It was originally built in 1086, and by 1629 they had built a turret tower that housed six large bells. A small graveyard surrounded it. Harefield had only been a small farming community, but when the manor house had been turned into a hospital, and Australian soldiers had started dying there, they had expanded the cemetery behind the original one.

They laid the coffin holding Horace's body, onto the back of a dray that was pulled by two horses. His coffin had been draped with the Union Jack, and as the dray made its way to the cemetery the soldiers that could walk followed the cart. Some wore slings, and others hobbled along on crutches, while others still, were pushed in wheelchairs. The locals, and school children lined the laneway that led to the church. As they lowered the coffin into the damp earth, those assembled could just hear the sombre strains of the church organ playing 'Abide with Me' as the apple blossoms wafted down and carpeted the ground beneath a clear blue sky.

After the funeral, Brigid's tears fell upon the paper as she wrote to Horace's mother and gave her an account of her son's funeral.

***

Brigid worked through the spring and the summer of 1916, and over those months she held the hands of many young soldiers. Some died, but some would recover, and then she would be overjoyed as they were moved to a rehabilitation hospital in another county.

Noreen now only saw Brigid occasionally, as her position as senior assistant matron kept her extremely busy. But she would keep a distant eye on her young charge. She was getting regular reports on her progress from the senior nurses who worked on the wards with her.

It had not gone unnoticed by Noreen, how Brigid had grown and matured since they had left Sydney. She had learned quickly, and Noreen was pleased with her decision to let her work on the hospital ship. She had watched as Brigid learned to deal with trauma, and that itself was a blessing.

Noreen was standing at the window, and reflecting over how quickly the past year had gone by. So much had happened, and now it was almost Christmas again, and preparations were already being put into place to celebrate it.

The dispatch from headquarters had just come through to the hospital, and they had been told to prepare for another fifty casualties that would be arriving shortly from France. She wondered how many more would arrive, carrying obscene wounds that her staff would have to deal with. She, along with everyone else, just wanted the war to end, and for the killing and the maiming to stop. The newspapers were full of gloom, and they seemed to take a perverse pleasure in publishing the growing casualty list each week as they tried to outdo each other with a different view of the war and where it was going.

The new arrivals were allocated to the wards that specialised in various wounds. Although Tom and Des could walk, they were both placed in wheelchairs and pushed by orderlies. Brigid was at her station when the door opened, and the orderlies wheeled their patients forward. At first, she didn't recognise either of them. She had given them a cursory glance, but as she read their medical records she gave a gasp, and then a small shriek. They all looked at her, and then as recognition dawned Brigid started crying as she bent down to embrace them both.

She exclaimed, 'Oh my Lord, I can't believe it! Let me have a look at you. I was only thinking of you both this morning and you, Des Carney, why didn't you write back to me. I wrote to you months ago, and I thought that you were both dead!' She wiped at her tears as Tom and Des sat grinning at her.

Des looked sheepishly at Brigid and muttered, 'I was gunna write to you again, I really was,' but before he could go on Tom said,

'He never stopped talkin' about ya, Brigid.'

Des looked sideways at his mate, embarrassed, and was about to reply, but said instead, 'What are ya doin' 'ere?'

'It's a long story, and I'll tell you sometime, but now I need to get you both settled.'

She showed them to their beds, and then she read their medical records, but didn't dwell on how close her friends had come to being killed.

It was almost Christmas, and decorations had been hung throughout the wards. The nurses did their best to bring some seasonal cheer to the patients, and although the celebrations were muted, most were happy just to be away from the fighting. Early snow had ensured that the festivities were restricted to inside activities, and the long dark days of winter dragged on.

It was early spring before the doctors had given both Des and Tom the news that their involvement in the war was over, and that they would both be shipped home at the first opportunity.

✗✗✗

Although it was intended that the wounded would be sent home, the German attacks on allied ships meant that there were no vessels available for the journey. There were a thousand soldiers recovering at Harefield by the middle of 1917. The soldiers that had recovered from their wounds, but who were not well enough to be returned to the front line, spent their days just lounging around, or strolling on the common.

On some days, an impromptu game of cricket would start, and the nurses played alongside their patients. Those that were well enough to work were sent off to surrounding factories to help out, and in some cases to learn new skills.

Tom and Des had fully recovered, but the arm injury that Des had sustained would always be a hindrance to him. Tom, on the other hand, could move his arm, but the fractured bone in his shoulder had set badly and had caused his shoulder to be stooped. He jumped at the chance to work on a nearby dairy farm, as he was determined to work the land as a farmer when he returned to Australia.

He had written to Hannah every few weeks, and she had proudly informed him that she could now milk a cow, and churn butter along with a multitude of other jobs that she had never dreamed of ever doing.

Tom was impatient to return home and start his new life as a farmer, whereas Des was happy to work in the old manor garden. It was the vegetable garden that had been used to feed the house for more than a century. It was overgrown with weeds and run-down hothouses. Des and a dozen others had torn down the old glasshouses, and dug over the rows of weed-filled garden beds. Over the next six months, the garden had sprung back to life.

While Brigid's days were filled with caring for her patients, the seeds of love were germinating between her and Des.

45.

The War is Over

It was 1919, and the war had ended six months earlier. Two thousand men, who had once been soldiers, lined the ship's railings as it sailed down Sydney Harbour.

It was early winter, but the sun still shone and sparkled on the friendly waters of home. Several dozen ferries had left Circular Quay to escort the ship on its long, slow journey down the harbour to its berth at the number two jetty at Woolloomooloo wharf. The ferries were festooned with bunting and streamers, and 'Welcome Home' banners were tied to the outside railings. They were crammed with wives and families all waving madly, and anxious to try and get a glimpse of a loved one.

Although happy to be back on their home soil, most were quiet as they stared at the city from the decks of the ship. At times, many of them had harboured doubts that they would ever see their home again. Mostly, they had left as boys almost four years earlier, but they had returned as scarred and battle-hardened men.

The less fortunate had arrived back home on a hospital ship. They were the blind, the maimed, the legless and the insane. Then there were those who would spend the rest of their lives gasping for breath through withered lungs brought about by gas attacks.

But, the government had an obligation to bring them all back, and not be selective about it, and there were thousands more waiting back in France and England to be repatriated home.

But due to a shortage of ships, it would take at least another year to get them all back.

Tom had returned without Des, as Des had surrendered his berth after he had decided that he would stay in England until Brigid returned. Des was in love with Brigid, and since being wounded, he had lost the brashness that he had worn since childhood. It seemed that he was using Brigid as a crutch, and as a replacement for the self-confidence that he had lost.

Tom looked down, and scanned the decks of the ferries in the vain hope that he would see Hannah, or his mother. He had no idea where his brother was, and he was hoping that he had been able to see out the war unscathed. They had exchanged a couple of letters during the last months of the war, but when peace had been declared he had heard nothing from Jack. He pushed the thought from his mind that anything had happened to him, and now that he was back in Sydney, he expected that his mother would know where he was.

The ferries were blasting their steam whistles, and the ship responded with noisy blasts from its foghorn sat high up on the funnel. The tugs manoeuvred the ship to its berth at the wharf, and the gangplanks were lowered. A sea of khaki-clad men carried their kitbags down the gangplank for the last time. A large corrugated building covered the wharf. Inside a hundred trestle tables had been set up as a dispersal centre to assist with the demobilisation of the soldiers disembarking. Each table was stacked high with various forms that each man would have to fill in before their discharge was completed.

They each underwent a basic medical exam, which would then form the basis for their eligibility to a pension in the future. Then they filled in multiple forms that enabled them to receive their final pay, along with a clothing allowance of five pounds. When the paperwork was completed, they were given a rail warrant that entitled them to a single train ticket back to their hometown.

After obtaining their rail warrants they said their goodbyes. Some had made plans to meet at the nearest pub, while others were desperate to return to their families and civilian life. They made their way through the final door to be greeted by a throng of smiling faces of excited wives, mothers and children waiting patiently. They were standing three deep behind the wharf barriers, and each of them scanned the face of every man that came through the door.

At times, there would be a shriek, followed by a wave as a wife or mother pushed their way through the crowd to embrace their loved one.

At first, Tom walked hesitantly towards the crowd. He was looking for a familiar face, and his frown suddenly transformed into a grin as he glimpsed the women in his life.

Doris was frantically waving her straw hat to get his attention, and next to her were Claire and Hannah. His steps quickened, and he dropped his rucksack. He kissed his mother on the cheek, and then he embraced the three of them. He didn't say a word, but just held them tightly as he savoured the moment.

He kissed his mother and Claire again before turning to Hannah. They stared at each other, and at that moment there was no one else but the two of them. Hannah was feeling shy, and she lowered her gaze. Tom took hold of both her hands. He looked at her intently before saying quietly, 'How I have longed for this moment, just to see your face and to hold you.'

He lifted her chin and kissed her gently. The tears ran down her cheeks, and he relished their salty taste as she returned his kiss.

They embraced for what seemed like an eternity, and then he heard the noise of the crowd along with his mother's voice.

'Well son, are they finished with you yet?'

'Yeah Ma, I'm a civilian again, and I won't be in no hurry to sign up again, I can tell ya!'

Doris put her arm through her son's and squeezed it. 'I'm glad son. I prayed every day for you both, and you had me worried sick until I knew that you were safe, now let's go home.'

'Ma, I hafta ask you, have ya heard from me brother?'

He was about to continue when Doris replied, 'Jack's been home for nearly three months now. He said that he would see you tonight, because he was going to buy you a beer. But he had to open up his fuel yard. He said to tell you to call in if you had enough time.

'I've been a bit worried about him. He started working down at the yard the day after he got home. He doesn't say much, and he seems healthy enough, but he won't slow down and relax. Now that you're home again he might settle down a bit, I hope so.'

Tom looked at his mother and gave her a squeeze before saying, 'It's orright, Ma. I'll have a word with him. He has seen a lot of stuff. It will probably take us all a bit of time to get used to not bein' shot at, or for that matter just not bein' in the army. I been lucky, 'cause I had time in England in the hospital to get back to normal.

'But Jack, well he had to keep fightin' on the battlefield, and he didn't get no time away from the shootin' and the noise. I gotta say Ma, you got no idea how bloody noisy war is, and I'm lookin' forward to some real peace and quiet.'

They caught the tram back home. Flags, 'Welcome Home' signs and coloured bunting was displayed everywhere from shop windows to lamp posts. The streets were far busier than normal, and there was an air of excitement as reunited families strolled along the footpaths. The Salvation Army band was playing a medley of tunes outside of Central Station. The pubs were full of rowdy ex-soldiers, as bar bums befriended them in the hope that a free beer might come their way, while out the back of the pub some were playing two-up, and gambling with their final pay.

Doris had hung streamers from the pelmet in her front room, and a small hand-painted sign read, 'Welcome Home Son.' Someone had wrapped the Union Jack flag around the gas lamp pole in front of their house. Doris was beside herself with happiness, and ushered them all inside. She stoked her stove hot, and put the kettle to the centre of the hot plate.

'I'll make us a nice cuppa, and Hannah has baked you a cake son. Now put your kitbag in your room. All that stuff in there is Hannah's, so you will just have to share with it till after the wedding. I'm sure that you won't mind.'

Tom put his arms around his mother and said, 'Stop fussin' ma. It's orright. If you saw some of the places that we hadta bed down in, it would make my room look like Buckingham Palace.'

Tom asked Claire, who was slicing up the cake, 'How's Davin?'

'He's good, he said to say hello, and that he was sorry that he couldn't come to meet you, but he is so busy at the forge, and his new bloke is lazy and not very good. He has had trouble getting staff since the war began really. Oh yes, he has had a few men that could do the job, but what with the shortage of labour, people can pick and choose where they want to work. I know he's hoping that you will go back and give him a hand, but that's something that he needs to talk to you about.'

'Well if I don't see 'im tonight, tell 'im that I will call over to the forge tomorrow.'

'Now sit down son and have your tea.' Doris was pouring and generally fussing about. Hannah was quiet, and Claire commented, 'Are you feeling tired darling? You haven't said much all morning.'

'No, I'm all right Aunt Claire, it's just that it's been a hectic few days, and now I can stop worrying about this man.'

She glanced at Tom and gave a smile, 'It's just that I have so much on my mind, and I'm not sure if I should go back to Megalong next week, or not.' She put her hand over Tom's and said, 'Oh Tommy, we have so much to talk about, and I don't know where to start.' Tom finished his cake before saying, 'We don't have to catch up with all the news today. I'm done with the army, and I got me pay, so I'm not in any hurry to do anything fer awhile. So me and you can go for a walk in the park this afternoon if you like.'

'Yes, Tommy, that would be lovely.'

Tom stood up and asked his mother, 'Do ya still have me old duds Ma? I just wanna get out of this uniform. They give us five quid to buy some new civvies, but me and Hani can go into town some other day to pick up some new clobber.'

'Yes son, I didn't get rid of any of your stuff. I took your clothes out of the boxes, and hung them up behind the curtain. I had them packed in mothballs while you were away. The smell should be gone by now as I have had them airing for awhile!'

He changed his clothes, and after saying goodbye to Claire and his mother, he and Hannah left the house. He held her hand and said nothing for a while. He wanted to hold her, but he wanted a private place to do it, and they walked in silence to the park.

It was full of couples and families, along with children running amok. They walked on further and cut across the grass, and then he stopped and stood behind a large sugar gum. They embraced and kissed, and both savoured the moment until he finally asked, 'Do you still love me, Hani?'

'Oh Tommy, you do ask some silly questions. Of course, I still love you. Not a day has passed since you left that I haven't thought of you. It's a wonder that I am not as grey as your mother is, and when Aunt Claire rang me and told me that you had been shot I was beside myself. It wasn't until I received your letter from London before I stopped worrying about you.

'Tell me about Des and Brigid. Are they really in love? I got a letter from her about two months ago, and I gather from it that she harboured more than a soft spot for him. Is it serious?'

He was leaning with his back against the tree, and he had his arms around her waist, and she rested her head on his shoulder. He smiled as she asked the question. 'Well, Des was supposed to come back on the ship that I came back on, cause the brass was arranging the berths to bring us back 'ome. There are thousands of boys still over there, and so few ships to bring them back.

'Well, Des went and seen the officer-in-charge, and he said that he wanted ta stay there, but he said no, cause if he didn't take his berth then it might be a long time before he could get another one.

'Des said he didn't care, as he wasn't goin home without Brigid. And she didn't try to talk him out of stayin', so he got some digs with an old couple in the town, and he goes back to the hospital every day. He likes workin' in the garden there. I dunno if he will finish his apprenticeship with his old man though, cause he has a lot of trouble with his arm.'

Hannah was frowning, and she asked, 'How bad is the wound?'

'He has trouble closing his left hand properly. I don't want to upset you, but when he was stabbed, the bayonet tore out most of the muscle up his arm. They sewed it up, and his arm looks orright until he turns it over, and then you can see where they stitched him up.

'He gets a bit annoyed with it at times, like when he's tryin' to close his fist, but like I told 'im, if he hadn't stopped the bayonet with his arm, then he wouldn't be here now. He knows that, but he still gets a bit down cause he don't know how he can keep doin' his woodwork. That's why he likes working in the hospital garden, 'cause he can use a pick and shovel orright, but holdin anything smaller gives him some grief.'

Hannah gave a slight shudder at the thought of how close Des must have come to being killed, and then she had to ask Tom about his wound.

'If you don't want to talk about it I'll understand Tommy, but how is your shoulder?'

He was quiet for a moment and said, 'I was luckier than Des, me shoulder gives me a twinge every now and then, and it hangs down a bit, but it couda bin worse!' He tightened his grip around her waist and grinned before saying, 'It don't stop me from squeezin' you my girl, and you don't know how many times I thought of you, and wished that I was holdin' you!

'I didn't know if I'd ever get to hold you again Hani. You got no idea how cold it was in them trenches. Up ta yer bloody ankles in frozen water and mud fer days. Oh, beg me pardon fer swearin' Hani.'

She smiled and said, 'I forgive you darling. I can't imagine what you and the others went through, and I won't talk about it again unless you want to.'

'It's orright, a lot of things happened over there, and me thinkin' of you was all that kept me goin' at times. I kept your letters in me pocket, and some nights I would read 'em over again. I could see you workin' on the farms, and I wished I was with ya.

'We had weeks and weeks of doin' nothin', but drill and cleanin' our guns, and then all of a sudden, the world exploded.

'When them Germans let loose with them big guns, all we could do was huddle in the bottom of the trench, and pray to God that we wouldn't get buried, or blown to bits.'

He stopped talking for a moment as his mind took him back, and he gave a slight shiver before saying, 'I'm sorry Hani, I don't wanna be reminded of some things. So, tell me, do ya still wanna marry me? It's been over four years since I asked you, and I got nuthin' to offer yer but meself!'

Hannah put her hand over his lips and said, 'Shush Tommy, of course I still want to marry you. I want to spend the rest of my life with you, and I want you to give me a dozen babies. I want us to live out in the country where the air is fresh, and where our children can chase rabbits and fish for yabbies.'

He gave her a squeeze before saying, 'Well, we need to work out where we are gunna live before we get married. I dunno if I can work at the forge, considerin' how me shoulder is. That's not to say that I won't go and give yer uncle a hand fer awhile if me shoulder can stand it. Now, tell me about this farm where you been workin'.'

'Oh Tommy, Megalong is such a lovely place, and Harriet is so kind. She really does want us to go and live there after we are married, but it's up to you. I know that they are struggling to maintain the place because of the shortage of labour, and they sure could use some help with the animals, and the fencing. She has a very nice little cottage where we could live. It was where I was staying, and she said that we wouldn't have to pay any rent if we worked there.

'It is very isolated, and it takes over an hour to get there by motor lorry from the train station. Harriet suggested that I telephone her if you would like to go and see the place. She thought that we might go up for a weekend. We could catch the mail train up on Friday night, and that would get us to Lithgow in the early morning, and she would meet us. What do you think Tommy?'

He thought for a moment before saying, 'It might be nice to get away for a coupla' days, but before we do I think that you should make the arrangements fer our weddin'. I want you so bad Hani I can't say no more. I'll leave the arrangin' up to you and yer aunt and me mother, of course.'

'I'll go and see Father Aldridge tomorrow. I spoke with him when I found out that you were on your way home.

'He said that once we let him know that we were going to be married, he would have to announce the Banns over three weeks from the pulpit. Once he had done that, then it would be up to us when we got married, although he did say that the longer that we left it, the longer it would take, as he suspected that there would be a lot of couples looking to be married now that everyone was coming home. You do want to be married at Saint Bridget's don't you, Tommy?'

She had expected him to say yes as a matter of course, and when he didn't she looked at him. 'Why Tommy, whatever is the matter? I thought that as we have always gone to Saint Bridget's that we would be married there, but if you would rather go somewhere else then tell me!' He looked down, and shuffled his feet as he tried to find the words to say to her.

'Hani, I'm not sure how to put this, but at this moment I'm having trouble with the whole church thing. I don't mean to offend you, or me mother. Yes, I really want to marry you, but all the years that I been going to Mass I never once doubted what the priest and the nuns told me about God.' He fidgeted some more before continuing, 'But Hani, we seen stuff over there that's got me doubtin' and wonderin' if there really is a God!'

'Remember, when we was taught the Ten Commandments, and the nuns had us sayin' them almost every day in school? Well, one of them commandments said, "Thou shalt not kill", and we were told that if yer killed somebody then that was a mortal sin, and you would go to hell forever. I'm sorry darlin', and I ain't happy admitting to this, but I killed people. I dunno how many, but it was a few, and I killed them cause they was gunna kill me. Then, there was all me mates that I seen die. Gettin' all blown to bits, and when the shootin' and shellin' was goin' on, I would be prayin' madly to God to save me and Jack, and the others.

'But when it were all over, and we hadta pick up the pieces of our mates, I would curse God, an ask him why was he lettin' all this killin' and maiming keep happenin', so I'm sorry Hani, but me faith in God has taken a bit of a batterin' lately, and I suppose that I'm a bit scared of goin' back to church to pray to a God that I doubt even exists!' Hannah had been listening intently. She was a little shocked, as she had never questioned her religious beliefs. To now hear the man that she loved casting doubt on those beliefs was a little confronting to her. She could see the pain in his eyes, and she wrapped her arms around him.

Neither spoke for a few minutes, and then Hannah said, 'I am trying to imagine what you have all been through, and for the life of me I can't, but Tommy, I won't preach at you, and only you can decide what you believe in. If you no longer want to go to Mass on Sundays, then I won't insist that you do.

'I will talk to Father Aldridge tomorrow, and I will explain to him how you feel. I'm sure that he can hold the wedding ceremony without holding a Mass. In fact, I shall insist on it, so if we get married on a Saturday, there will be no need to hold a service, other than for the wedding. Aunt Claire and your mother will be expecting a church service. I will tell them that we are just going to have a standard service, and if they ask why I will tell them that that's the way that we want it. Now, we won't talk about it anymore.'

The tension that had been building in him evaporated, and he wrapped his arms around Hannah, and they kissed.

The next few weeks rushed by. Hannah had spoken with the priest, and arranged the details of the wedding service. Over three consecutive Sundays, the Banns were called. Father Aldridge stood in his pulpit and called out the challenge. 'Anyone who has an objection to the upcoming marriage between Mr Thomas Fields and Miss Hannah Townsend should stand up, and show cause as to why the marriage should not go ahead, otherwise forever hold your peace.'

Doris had insisted on having a welcome home party for her two boys, and she was beside herself with happiness as she made the arrangements. Claire had busied herself with adjusting her mother's wedding gown to fit Hannah, and then insisted on taking Hannah to the emporium to buy some new clothes for her to wear on the honeymoon.

Tom had gone to see his brother, who was now living in the house that Mr Johnson had left him. Doris was insistent that Hannah and Tom would both stay in Jack's bedroom after the wedding until they moved away. Tom had also seen Davin, and had told him that he would work for him until the wedding. He had his mind set on moving to Megalong even though he had never seen the place.

They had all finished dinner, and most of the talk had revolved around the wedding, which was to be held in less than two weeks.

Jack asked Tom, 'Have ya made the arrangements fer yer honeymoon yet?' His mother replied, 'Of course he has.' Tom smiled, and winked at his brother. Doris had been like a clucky hen for the past few weeks, as she and Claire had ticked off the things that needed to be arranged from the lists that they had both compiled.

'So where are ya goin?'

'We are goin' up to the Blue Mountains. I got us booked into a fancy pub there. It's called the Carrington Hotel at a place called Katoomba. It's up the top of the mountains, and apparently there are lots of places to walk around and see the sights.'

Hannah interjected, 'It's not a pub Tommy Fields; you won't be taking me to some old pub for my honeymoon. I read the brochure, and it all sounds very flash. They have waiters and silver cutlery and everything.'

Jack looked at his brother and asked, 'How much is that costin' ya?' Tom replied, 'Twenty quid a week fer the two of us, but that includes all our tucker and mornin' teas, and I think we get a couple of motor tours as well.'

Jack whistled though his teeth, 'Twenty quid fer a week, and yer stayin fer two weeks? That's a lot of dough, it will wanna be pretty special for ten weeks of army pay!' Hannah broke into the conversation, as even she was slightly shocked at how much it was going to cost, and up to that moment she had no idea.

'Why Tommy, I didn't know that you had paid that much, we could always cancel and go somewhere cheaper.'

'Nup, we won't cancel it, and will ya all stop worryin' about what I paid fer our honeymoon? I picked up me last army pay. Then I got the dough that they give me for me new duds, and I had saved most of me pay when I was in England. It's all paid for now, except for the train, and I still got a bit left over for tickets, so lets talk about somethin' else, orright.'

Jack was stuffing his mouth with his mother's cake. After washing it down with a mouthful of beer, he wiped the back of his hand across his mouth. He then said, 'Orright that's settled, I been wonderin' as to what to get yer both fer yer weddin' present, so I'm gunna pay fer yer honeymoon!'

Tommy looked at Jack and replied, 'Don't be silly, I told ya, it's all bought and paid for.' Doris then broke into the conversation. 'Why, that's very generous of you son.'

Hannah smiled, and said, 'Jack, that's very kind of you, but it's far too generous. Thank you for the offer, and if you wish to give us anything at all, you could give us some pots and pans, or something practical.'

Jack took another gulp of his beer and then said, 'I'm not gunna argue about it. I'm gunna pay for it, and that's it. When old Mr Johnston died and left me his business, he also left me a big pile of money.

'I haven't spent any of it, and its just been sittin' in the bank since before the war. As ya know, Ma's been lookin' after the yard and she kept the dough comin' in, so I ain't short of a quid if that's what's botherin' yer both.' He looked over at his mother who was beaming. 'So, I'm gunna pay fer yer honeymoon, and that's the end of the matter!'

They were all silent for a moment, then Hannah went around the table and put her arms around Jack from behind before she kissed him on the top of his head. 'Thank you, Jack, that's a wonderful gesture, and I'm sure that Tommy will put the money to good use.'

Jack was embarrassed and replied, 'Well Hani, you're the closest thing to a sister that I'm ever gunna get, and what are families for if we can't give each other a present every now and then? Now stop kissin' me before ya make me brother jealous.' He smiled, and looked across the table to his brother.

Tom stood up, and walked to his brother and clasped his hand before shaking it. 'Well, if that's what ya want to do then we accept,' and he smiled as he said, 'but just cause yer payin' fer the honeymoon, don't go getting' it inta yer head that we will be thinkin' of ya while we're on it.'

The banter went on between them as Hannah and Doris stacked the dishes. Tom spoke about their plans for the future, and he said, 'We will go and spend a few days after the honeymoon up at the farm where Hani's bin workin'. I s'pose we will probably stay there fer awhile, at least until we can save enough dough to get a little place of our own.'

Jack looked startled for a moment, and broke into his brother's conversation, 'That just reminded me, I got a letter a few weeks ago from some government department. I just thought of it when you were talkin' about getting' yerself some land.' They were all looking at Jack now and Tom asked, 'What did it say?'

'I'm tryin' to think. I was gunna show it to ya last week, but then I forgot. The government has set up some department. I think it's called the War Committee department, or something like that. They sent me a certificate as well. It was called a qualification certificate. Apparently, you qualified fer one if ya had been overseas in the war, so you should get one too.'

Doris had been listening intently, 'What's it mean son?' Jack replied, 'It's somethin' called a Soldier Settlement Programme. I didn't take a lot of notice at the time cause I was busy, but I'm sure that it meant that we could all apply fer a land grant.'

'Look, I can't remember exactly what it said. I'll go and get it, come on Tom, let's go around to the yard, and ya can read it fer yerself!'

'Nah, we can get it tomorrow.'

Jack had already stood up and said, 'It's orright. I think that there is something in the letter that you need ta read. I'll be back shortly!' With that, he was gone.

Doris was the first to speak, 'He's got me all curious now, but knowing your brother, he's probably got the bull by the horns again.'

Tom replied, 'Well, somethin' certainly got him excited.'

Shortly after, Jack returned holding a bulky envelope. 'Here it is. Have a read of this.' He handed the letter to his brother. Tom read it and then frowned. Doris looked at him and asked, 'What's it say son?'

'I'm not sure what it means, but it looks like we can apply to get a parcel of land out in the bush somewhere.'

'Read it out son, you got us all curious now.' Tom said, 'It's from the government War Committee in Canberra.'

To Mr Jack Fields,
No 8 Clyde Street Redfern. N.S.W.
Ex private. Formerly of the Third Australian Infantry Division.
VX 1912745

Dear Sir,

On behalf of the Australian Government, we wish to acknowledge your war service.

In recognition of your service as a member of the Australian Infantry Forces over the past four years, we are pleased to announce a government initiative that may hold some interest to you.

In conjunction with your state government, we have set aside over half a million acres of land throughout the state of N.S.W. to be developed as farming land. The programme is called The Soldier Settlement Act 1916. You are invited to put your name forward to go into a ballot. Attached is a list of the parcels of land available to be developed, and the areas therein.

Please mark the ballot paper in the order of your preferences from the attached list of sectors.

If you are unsuccessful in your first choice, you will be notified, and then you may be granted a parcel of land from your further preferences. You may select from the following.

- Parcel 1. 100 acres of first class prime grazing land. Batlow area. Price to be determined.
- Parcel 2. 200 acres of second-class land combined grazing and bush. Western District. Lithgow/Bathurst area. Price to be determined.
- Parcel 3. 300 acres third class land consisting of bush and scrubland. Tumut District. Price to be determined.

If you are successful in obtaining a parcel of land of your choice, you will take notice and agree to the following conditions.

The land will be leasehold for a period of five years. In that time, you must live upon it and develop it to the extent that it will be self-sustaining.

Within three years the entire property must be boundary fenced, and a dwelling must have been established within the property boundary.

Depending on the property and the location, a perpetual lease may be offered.

However, if after establishing the property, and after the expiration of five years, a sale contract may be issued to purchase the freehold of the Crown land allotment.

In either case, the land will be rent and mortgage free for the first five years. If after five years you wish to enter into a mortgage arrangement with the government the terms will consist of the following.

A payment of 102 pounds per annum, including interest at 2.5 per centum is to be paid in equal instalments over a minimum fifteen-year period. The freehold title to the land will then be issued under the Crown Lands Act 1916.

If you accept this offer, the government will also make available a sustenance allowance of two pounds per week for a period of five years while the property is being developed.

If you wish to avail yourself of this offer, please sign the attached form and return it promptly to

The War Committee,

Parliament House Canberra. ACT. Your qualification certificate number is VX 1912745.

Signed

Harold Cartwright

Secretary to the Minister of Defence.

Tom was silent for a moment, as he took in the contents of the letter. Doris was the first to speak, 'That sounds like they want to give you some farmland for serving in the army, is that right, son?' Tom looked at his brother and asked him, 'What are ya thinkin' Jack? Do ya wanna have a go at farmin'?'

'Nar, it's not fer me, but it sounds like it's right up your alley. That's why I wanted to show ya the letter. Looks like everyone is gunna get one. That's a lotta land they got on offer. Where do ya think you would go?'

'I dunno, it seems like if ya go south, you get less land, and more if ya go west. Hani and me will hafta talk about it. I dunno nuthin' about farmin'. I know that we said that we wanted a bit of land. Now it sounds like a good offer, but we hafta fence the whole place, and then build a house. I needta talk to someone who knows somethin' about farmin'!'

Hannah had been thinking about the letter and said to Tom, 'We should talk with Harriet and her parents. They have been farming for years, and they could tell us what we need to know.'

Tom reread the letter and said, 'I'm glad that ya got this. It will give us a bit of time to think about what we should do before I get mine!' Hannah replied, 'Well, I think that it's all very exciting, although having to build a house, and fence the whole place will be a big job.' Tom was still thinking of what equipment they would need if they took up the government offer. He also wondered how much money they would need to buy the materials to build a house. He was also thinking of what they would grow, and what sort of animals they would need to breed to be able to make the property productive.

Tom said, 'I suppose that the first thing that we would have to work out is where our parcel of land was, and from there it would depend on whether it was flat land or hilly.'

Doris broke into his thoughts by saying, 'Well son, you will have plenty of time to think about those things while Claire and I sort out your wedding, now take your beer and let me clean up these dishes.'

46.

The Wedding

It was Saturday morning, and the arrangements for the wedding were completed. The ceremony was to be held at eleven, at Saint Bridget's. Doris had been up since before daybreak. She had rechecked the icing on the cake that she had made, along with putting the finishing touches to the food platters. The fire was lit under the copper as soon as she had risen to make sure that there was plenty of hot water available for them to have their baths. Then she had laid out their clothes after ironing them, and now there was very little to do.

Doris and Claire had hung the white and cream streamers around the front windows, and over the backyard paling fence. The frontdoor step had been given a fresh coat of white paint. Several planks were sat across fruit crates that had been set up in the back garden to accommodate the wedding cake and flowers.

Doris had insisted that the wedding reception would be held at her house, after Hannah had spoken to the priest. He had wanted three pounds for the use of the church hall and Doris was indignant over the cost. 'We will have the reception here luvvy. Three pounds to use a hall that is empty most of the time! Does he think that we are made of money?'

Claire had been up almost as early as Doris. Hannah's wedding dress was laid out on the table in the parlour.

She had double-checked that there were no pins left in the hem or the bodice where she had taken it in.

Over the preceding weeks, Claire had been thinking of her mother and of her own wedding as she had made the alterations to it. She had never asked her mother where, or how she had obtained it, and it had never crossed her mind to ask. Now it was too late, but she knew that her mother would have been pleased that her granddaughter was now wearing it.

The dress was Victorian in style, and had once been white, but now it had faded to a soft cream. It flowed freely from the waist to flare out from the hips into a modest train, and Claire had adjusted the sleeves to meet the long silk gloves that Hannah would wear.

After several fittings, Hannah stood in the gown until Claire was finally happy with her handiwork. 'Now child, let me fit your veil', and she made the final adjustment to it.

'This veil was also your grandmother's.' Then she stood back and admired her niece. 'Darling, you look like an angel. I wish that your grandmother could see you now, she would be so proud.' Claire gave a sniffle as her thoughts turned to her mother.

Hannah lifted the veil, and hugged her before saying, 'Thank you Aunt Claire. It's such a beautiful dress, and I hope that one day I may be able to pass it onto a daughter of mine.'

Claire smiled and replied, 'I hope so too darling, but Doris's genes have given her boys, so I hope that you are blessed with at least one daughter, but time will tell child.' She stopped talking for a moment as her mind thought about what she was going to say.

Hannah looked at her aunt, and saw the troubled expression upon her face and asked, 'What wrong, Aunty?'

Claire busied herself with tucking in the veil, and then said, 'I know that I have tried to talk about your wedding night before, but I am compelled to mention a few things darling.'

Hannah smiled and said, 'It's all right Aunt Claire; Doris has explained a few things to me. I'm sure that we will muddle our way through the night, in the same way that you and Doris and all the young girls that have married before me have managed to do.'

Claire stopped and looked at her niece, but before her resolve weakened she said, 'No darling, I need to say this, so just let me say it and we will speak of it no more.' She took hold of Hannah's hands and led her to the couch.

'A man has different needs to a woman, and I have heard that some men will implant their seed into their wife in a rush, and then just roll over and fall promptly to sleep.

'They may not understand the needs of the woman, and they may even not care. Other men may be gentle, and given time may try and give their wife a modicum of pleasure.

'If you are lucky my child, Tommy will be such a man. However, he may not satisfy his lust from one session, and he may insist on lying upon you more than once in a night. Your vows will ask you to love and obey him, and as such it will be your duty to accept him as he desires.

'Your wedding night will be filled with many emotions child, and you cannot be expected to understand them all in one night. If love is true, then it will take time to blossom over many nights before you both come to understand the wants and needs of each other. Now, I will speak no more of this, and I will light a penny candle and pray that you have a long and happy marriage together.

'Now, one last check. We mustn't forget tradition. *Something old, something new, something borrowed, something blue, and a lucky sixpence in your shoe.*' Claire smiled as she half sang the rhyme.

'So, let's see, something old, that would be the dress, and something new, well that will be your shoes and gloves. Something borrowed will be your wedding ring that Doris has given you, and your garter will be something blue, and I have the sixpence for your shoe darling.'

Hannah said, 'I understand everything else, but why do I have to put a sixpence in my shoe?'

'That's for wealth darling. It doesn't mean that you will be rich with money, but there are other forms of wealth like having a happy marriage and a big family. Anyway, it's just tradition and it can't hurt.'

✶✶✶

A few months earlier, Davin had bought a motor lorry for the business. Tom and Jack stood up on the tray as they made the five-minute journey to the church. Davin dropped them at the steps and yelled out, 'I'll be back after I pick up Doris.' With a crunching of gears, he disappeared back down the street in a cloud of oily smoke.

A few passers-by had stopped. Weddings always attracted a few well-wishers, and Hannah's wedding would be no different.

Father Aldridge stood at the front door of his church awaiting his clients, while Tom nervously rolled a smoke.

Doris was dressed in her finery and went next door.

Hannah was standing in the doorway, framed by the weather-beaten doorjamb. 'Oh luvvy, you look beautiful, that son of mine is a lucky man, and that dress looks like it was made just for you.'

'Thank you, Doris, yes, it's a beautiful dress, and Aunt Claire has spent hours on adjusting it to fit me. It was worn by her mother you know!'

An open carriage, pulled by two horses from Holliman's carriage service, had been ordered to take Hannah to the church. The driver was asked to wait until after the service to bring them home, before again taking them back to Central Station.

✶✶✶

Davin was as proud as any father as he led Hannah down the aisle to the strains of The Wedding March. A dozen people gathered in the first two pews, and they all stood and stared as the couple slowly made their way to the altar.

Tom only had eyes for Hannah, as Jack fumbled in his waistcoat pocket for the ring that had once belonged to his mother. As the ceremony ended the priest said to Tom, 'You may now kiss the bride.'

Arm in arm, they turned and walked from the church. A small crowd of women and dirty-faced children stood on the footpath, waiting for a glimpse of the bride and her dress.

Tom and Hannah rode home in the carriage before the guests left the church. Doris had insisted that it was customary for the bride and groom to stand at the doorway and greet the guests as they arrived for the wedding reception. The gifts had been dropped off at the house before they had left for the church, and now they were in the parlour for all to see.

Doris had taken complete control of the reception. The wedding cake had been positioned on the bench. The cake was cut and finally as the time came closer for them to leave, Davin stood up and called, 'Quiet please, everyone quiet.'

He raised his voice to be heard, and at the same time he banged a fork on the side of a beer bottle to get the guests' attention. As the noise tapered away, he cleared his throat and said, 'I would just like to say something.' He was looking at Hannah as he spoke, 'You all know that Claire and me was never able to have any children of our own. Now Hannah was left an orphan child, and we was asked by the nuns to take her and give her a home, and we done that and we never had a moment of regret with our decision. I don't suppose me and Claire,' he looked towards his wife before continuing, 'ever thought then about the joy that this,' and he then looked at Hannah, 'child would bring into our lives.

'I… we knew, a long time ago that young Tom was sweet on our girl, and we did wonder at times if he would ever get around to asking for her hand. He did that, and then the war come along and that mucked up their plans to get hitched up.

'Well, young Tom was the best apprentice I ever had, and I got to know him pretty good when he was working fer me down at me forge. I knew then that he was a hard worker, and if he survived the war, then he would marry out little Hannah, and I could notta been prouder when he come home!

'We were a bit upset about the thought of them leavin' us, but like Claire said, we ain't lost a daughter, but we gained a son, and I'm proud of yer both. Now they has to go, but before they do, I propose a toast, so if everybody could raise yer glasses.'

They looked at Hannah and Tom, as Davin raised his beer bottle and said, 'I wish you both every happiness, and if you insist on livin' out in the bush somewhere, then I hope that you're blessed with a dozen little bairns to gladden yer hearts like you have gladdened ours. Here's to Hannah and Tom everyone!'

They all raised their drinks and cheered, 'Here, here,' before gathering to embrace them both.

47.

The Wedding Night

It was almost dark as the train pulled into Katoomba Station. It had been a long journey, and the nervous tension was building within them as they wondered what the coming night would bring.

The station porter had removed their luggage from the guard's van at the rear of the train, and it was now stacked precariously on his trolley.

'Evenin' sir. Would you be wantin' a taxi carriage, and might I ask where you be headin' to?'

Tom responded with, 'G'day cobber, we will be staying at the Carrington Hotel. Could ya tell us how far away it is? And yep, we would like a carriage if ya don't mind.'

'Very well sir.' He tipped his cap before saying, 'The Carrington is just across the road sir. You could walk to it in less than ten minutes.' He pointed in the direction that he was referring to. 'It's that big building over there, on the top of the hill with all them lights on, but it's a bit of a climb sir, especially with the luggage!'

Tom looked across the train tracks, and could just make out the top floor of the hotel and said, 'Nar, we will take a carriage if yer don't mind.'

'Very well sir, if you will follow me I will arrange it.'

They walked down the station ramp that led to the crossing, and the porter waved his hand to get the attention of the coachman, sitting idle at the kerb.

'Evenin' Samuel,' the porter addressed the coachman. 'These folks be off to the Carrington. I'll just load their luggage for you.' He lifted the canvas flap at the rear of the cab, before tipping his cap once more and saying, 'Samuel will take care of you now sir. I hope that youse has a pleasant stay. Good evenin' sir, ma'am.' He tipped his cap once more before turning and making his way back to the station.

Gas lamps lined the road, and along the side of the large circular driveway that wound its way to the base of the dozen stone steps that led up to the reception area. The doorman, resplendent in his maroon uniform with gold-braided epaulettes across his shoulders, greeted them. 'Good evening, madam, sir. Would you be Mr and Mrs Fields?' And without waiting for a response said, 'We have been expecting you.'

Hannah stopped at the entrance, as it was the first time that she had been called Mrs Fields, and for a moment she was taken aback. Tom replied, 'Too right we are,' he grinned at the doorman. 'I hope we are not too late for dinner, are we? I could eat a horse!'

'No sir, the dining room is still open, and I will arrange for your luggage to be taken to your room. The reception is to your left, if you would care to sign in.' He held the door open and pointed towards the counter.

Two life-sized bronze statues, holding flaming torches that were lit by flickering electric light globes, adorned each side of the entrance. The torches imparted a soft glow on the polished wooden walls, and a long marble table sat against one wall. A large urn-shaped vase sat upon it, and was overflowing with flowers. The carpet was red and thickly piled. Hannah tucked her arm through Tom's. She was feeling nervous, and after entering the foyer she was feeling intimidated by the sumptuous surroundings.

After Tom signed the register, a uniformed bellboy appeared, and he led the way upstairs to the honeymoon suite. He opened the door, but didn't enter. 'There is a pull bell by the window sir. If you ring it, I shall be back to take your instructions, and your luggage will be here shortly.' He closed the door discreetly as he left.

They were now alone. Her heart was beating fast, and to contain her nervousness she slowly took in her new surroundings. There was a small drawing room filled with elegant furniture that led to the bedroom, and a bathroom led off from the entrance hallway.

'Oh Tommy, this is so beautiful.' Before she could speak again, Tom took hold of her and drew her to him.

'And you're so beautiful, Mrs Fields!' Then he kissed her, his desire swelling, but now unsure of himself he asked, 'Do you think that we should go and have dinner Hani?'

She replied softly, 'Yes, I think that we should, but I want to freshen up first.'

¥¥¥

The dining room was sumptuous, and neither of them had been anywhere so grand. Tom looked at the table setting, and laughed. Hannah smiled, then asked, 'What's so funny?'

He whispered, so that the other diners seated nearby couldn't hear him. 'We got two knives, and two forks. I dunno what the extra ones are fer, but I don't wanna ask the waiter bloke. He might think that I'm just a hick from the bush!' Then he smiled again.

'I dunno what them little rolled up towels are fer, neither. I didn't know that the joint was gunna be this posh. Mind you, we 'aven't tried the tucker yet. I was just thinkin' Hani, if me mates could see me now; I'd never hear the end of it. When I think of how we ate our tucker in them blessed trenches. Most of the time we just used our knives for everythin'.' He smiled again before saying, 'I'm sorry fer bringin' up the war Hani. It was just a silly thought that flashed through me mind.'

She reached over and put her hand over his, 'It's all right Tommy. I think that it's perfectly normal to think of the things that you did during the war.' She leaned closer to him, and said softly, 'If it makes you feel any better I don't know why we need two knives and forks either, but I think the little towels are for stopping food from dropping on your clothes. I have been watching that old couple over there,' and she discreetly nodded in their direction before saying, 'The lady keeps wiping her mouth with it, and then she puts it in her lap.' Hannah smiled before giving Tom a quick kiss on his cheek.

The meal was over, and the conversation between them waned. She put her arm through his as they climbed the stairs. Both of them were nervous, and each of them was lost in their own thoughts of unknown expectations of the coming night.

The hotel generated its own electricity, and it boasted that it was the first establishment in Katoomba to do so. At the top of the stairs, two small wall sconces cast a soft glow along the hallway.

Once inside the privacy of their own room, Tom stopped and brought Hannah to him. He kissed her tenderly, and his manhood swelled again. 'I love ya Hani. You got no idea how I have dreamt and longed fer this moment. Is it wrong fer me to say that I want ya?'

Hannah looked into his eyes as she said quietly, and almost defiantly, 'No darling, it's not wrong. I want you too, and I told Father Aldridge this morning that I would love you until I died, and I meant it. Aunt Claire told me to remember that I was a lady, and I couldn't tell her that I wasn't! I want you to love me Tommy. I want you to give me babies, and you have no idea of the lonely nights that I had spent thinking of you when you were away. I too have dreamt of this night, and I remembered how you said that you wanted to lie on a feather mattress with me. Do you remember when you said that to me Tommy?'

He looked down at her and replied, 'Yeah I remember, and I have re-lived that moment over and over again.'

They kissed again, more passionately than before. Hannah released herself from his grasp and said, 'I need to change my clothes, so you go and do what you have to do and I will be out shortly.'

She closed the bedroom door behind her. She let her hair down and undressed. She glanced at the naked woman staring back at her from the full-length dressing mirror. She stared at herself for a moment as her emotions took hold. She couldn't understand her feelings. Everything that she had read about the wedding night told her that what she was feeling now was wrong.

An English Vicar's wife had written the *Wedding Night Book* almost fifty years earlier. Hannah had been given the book to read by her aunt. She had remembered one paragraph which said, '*A lady must endure the dirty habits of the male because it was her duty to do so, but under no circumstances should lustful feelings be allowed to germinate within you. The sole reason for allowing a man to insert his article into a woman was for his gratification only, and to impregnate his seed for the sole purpose of procreation.*'

Hannah didn't want to believe that silly nonsense, but she was filled with self-doubt. She wondered if her lustful thoughts made her a loose woman. She wanted to make love to her husband, and she wanted to enjoy it, rather than think of it as something dirty. She was still standing naked in front of the mirror, as she brushed her hair and splashed lavender toilet water over her body. She was enjoying the sensuous feelings that had been aroused within her, and she stared defiantly at her image as she brushed her hair. She didn't care what some silly book had said.

She wouldn't allow her erotic thoughts free rein just yet, but she knew that she wanted Tommy to awaken her dormant passion.

And at that moment she didn't care about how society expected young women to behave. She wanted her husband to pleasure her, and she would do whatever he wanted her to do for that to happen.

She pulled her muslin nightdress over her head, and then slowly opened the bedroom door. The fire in the bedroom had been lit before they had gone to dinner, and now the coals glowed red within the grate. Hannah turned down the bed covers, and pulled on the light switch cord. As the light clicked off, the coals cast a soft pink glow across the walls as she lay upon the bed.

Tom's heart was racing as he came into the bedroom. There was a dressing screen in one corner, and he moved to go behind it, but then Hannah said quietly, 'Take off your clothes darling, tonight there will be no secrets between us.'

He looked at her, and although her eyes were hidden by the shadows, he could feel her watching him. He sat on the chair and pulled off his boots. He then stood and removed his shirt before throwing it over the dressing screen. With his back to the bed, he slowly removed his trousers. He was feeling sheepish, but was also aroused by the thought that his new wife was watching him. He turned around, and as he did he heard her gasp, for there was enough light from the glowing fire for her to see his arousal.

He lay beside her, and he moved his arm so that she could rest her head upon it, and they kissed. He touched her breast, and she stiffened, but almost immediately relaxed again. His hand gently moved down her body, and he slowly lifted her nightdress. His hand explored her, and she flinched as his finger pushed inside her. She slowly relaxed, as she remembered the pleasure of that arousal the first time that she had given herself to him. She buried her face into his chest, and moaned softly as she shuddered in ecstasy.

She lay panting for a moment, and she whispered, 'Oh Tommy, what exquisite delight you give to me!'

He rolled over and lay upon her, and as he slowly entered her, her eyes glistened and her toes curled. Her face was flushed, as he gave a final thrust, and he groaned with the ecstasy of his orgasm that sent a spasm of pleasure throughout his whole body.

After the passion had abated they lay in silence before falling asleep, entwined in each other's arms.

48.

Des and Brigid

Des was enjoying his life as a gardener at Harefield. His damaged arm hindered him more than he cared to admit, and sometimes it continued to give him pain. Most of the wounded soldiers had been repatriated back to Australia, and the nurses now found that they had more time for sightseeing and relaxing.

Brigid was the one who had pushed the friendship between herself and Des into the budding romance that it had become. She had received another letter from Hannah, which told of their wedding and their plans for the future as farmers. Brigid and Des spent their weekends together, and as the months passed by they had became almost inseparable.

There had been rumours around for weeks that the hospital may soon close its doors. It had gone from caring for a thousand soldiers in the last year of the war to now caring for less than fifty, and the nurses now outnumbered the patients. Noreen Emmitt was now fully in charge of the nursing staff, and had gone to London for a meeting with government officials to discuss the future of the hospital.

Upon her return, she gathered her staff together to inform them of the outcome of the meeting.

'You are all aware that I have been to London to discuss the future of this establishment. The authorities have decided that the remaining long-term patients will all be transferred to larger hospitals throughout the county.

'As you all know, this hospital was formerly a manor house, and it was only through the generosity of the owner, and through funding by the Australian and British Governments, that it was set up as a hospital at all! Now that the war is over, the Australian Government will cease funding its operation as a hospital. Talks are being held to see if the British Government would take over the funding arrangements, as there is some talk that they might be interested in using the facility as a training hospital sometime in the future. It is far too early to know if this will be the case. In the meantime, I have been instructed to inform you all that your services will no longer be required after the last patient has been transferred from here.'

There were a few groans, as the nurses came to realise that they would all have to relocate, and look for another job.

Noreen continued speaking, 'Any Australian nurse who wishes to return home will have their passage paid for and arranged by the government. If you wish to avail yourself of this offer, you must leave your name with me. I'm sorry, but you will have to make up your minds within the next seven days. Otherwise, the offer will be withdrawn, and if you wish to return home in the future you will have to pay for your own passage.'

Brigid wore a frown as she put up her hand to speak; Noreen looked at her and asked, 'Yes Brigid, you have a question?' She stood up and asked, 'Matron, what about the boys who are still here and working in the grounds? Will they be shipped home also?'

Noreen smiled before replying, 'I know who you are referring to young lady, and I can't say for sure, as his transfer is an army matter, but I can make an enquiry and I will let you know!'

When the meeting was over, Brigid found Des, and she sat on a garden bench as he finished raking up the fallen leaves that were scattered across the lawn. He smiled at her and asked, 'What brings you over here? You look like you just lost a shilling, and found a penny, what's botherin' ya, girl?'

'They are going to close the hospital and send us all home. Matron has just told us. I don't want to go back without you. I don't even know if I want to go home at all! I like it here, but if I don't go, I will have to move somewhere else to get another job. What do you think that I should do Desmond?' Brigid always called him by his full name when she was cranky with him, or when something was bothering her.

He stopped raking, and thought for a moment before saying, 'Well, you could marry me fer starters!' She looked up at him before replying, "Oh Des, stop foolin' and be serious.

'Don't you understand, I have to give Matron an answer by next week, or I will miss out on my berth and then I won't have a job, or anywhere to go.'

Des dropped the rake and looked at Brigid before saying, 'I am being serious, do ya wanna marry me?' She looked at him, and then studied his face for a moment before she stood up and asked him, 'Was that a proposal Desmond Carney, or are you just foolin' still?'

He walked over to her, and took hold of her hands and said, 'Yep, I'm proposing' to ya girl. I was gunna do it this week sometime anyway, so it might as well be now. So, wada ya say girl. Do ya want to marry me, or do ya want to risk bein' left on the shelf?' He gave her a cheeky grin.

'Desmond Carney, that's the worst proposal that I ever did hear! And what are you inferring, that if I don't marry you, then that will be my last chance? Anyway, I might not want to get married, and even if I do, what makes you think that I would want to marry you?'

She smiled at him as she feigned anger, and then he wrapped his arms around her before saying, 'Now don't you be playin' hard ta get with me, Miss Brigid Blake. Ya know that ya wanna marry me, so all ya gotta do is say yes, and then I'm all yours ta keep forever.'

She grinned, 'You're such a clown Des Carney, but I do love you and as you're the only one to ask me then I suppose that I will have to accept. After all, I would hate to end up as an old maid'.

She flung her arms around his neck, and kissed him before saying, 'But that still doesn't solve our problem. Are we going to stay here, or are we going to go back home? What do you think, and be serious Desmond?'

'Maybe we should just go home. I been thinkin' about it for some time, but I was puttin' off makin' a decision. I wanted to ask ya ta marry me, but I didn't know if you wanted ta take the risk.'

She looked at him and asked, 'What risk? What are you talking about Des Carney? Sometimes I think that you just talk in riddles.'

Des looked at her before lowering his head and saying, 'Look at me arm.' He turned it over to expose the ugly scar before quickly turning it back. 'I don't have no prospects, and all I know is woodworkin' and soldierin'. I been worried about goin' back 'ome and seein' the ol' man again. Yer know that he's been waitin' fer me to get back, so that I can take over the business!'

He was looking down at his feet, and he stopped talking for a moment as he tried to gather his thoughts. 'I know that I can't finish me apprenticeship cause me arm's buggered. Oh, sorry sweetheart, I never meant to use no coarse language around ya!'

Brigid smiled and said, 'Don't be silly. I've been around boys and men all of my life. You seem to forget that I have nine brothers, and look at all of the men I have been around here with, so don't apologise. Anyway, look at what you are doing here. The garden is beautiful. You could always get a job as a gardener, and you're good around horses. We could get a few acres somewhere, and you could breed them. I'm sure that there are plenty of things that you could do once you put your mind to it. I will talk to Matron, and tell her that we will be going home. You will have to talk with your Captain, so that he can arrange a passage for you.'

Des looked around the garden, and he thought that Brigid was right. He did like to grow things, and since he had been working in this garden it had soothed his soul, and it had helped with blotting out some of the memories of the war.

'Orright, that's settled then. We will go home. It will be nice to see the ol' man and the others again. I'll go and talk with the captain today, and see what he can do for me. Ya know that we might hafta go back on separate ships?'

***

Several weeks later, Noreen spoke with Brigid, 'We have obtained a berth for you, but the Army has not released your Desmond's transfer papers as yet, and it is now highly unlikely that he will be able to travel with you. Even if they did come through in time all of the berths have been allocated on your ship. I'm sorry Brigid.'

'That's all right Matron. I will just have to wait for him to join me, whenever that may be. Actually, it will give me a bit of time to arrange somewhere for us to live. I haven't written to Mother as yet, and she will be happy that I am coming home, although she will be surprised with the news of my wedding.' She was silent for a moment before continuing. 'I will miss you Matron. I just wish that you could be at my wedding. I will never be able to thank you for everything that you have done for me!'

Noreen stood up, and came from behind her desk and gave Brigid a hug. 'You're very welcome young lady. Yes, I would love to be at your wedding, but I haven't made any plans for myself as yet. I have been offered a position at a country hospital down south, but I have to think carefully about my own future. I miss Australia, and the blue skies and the sunshine, but I have no one waiting there for me.

'I have come to like the lifestyle over here, and I have made a few friends, and as they say, home is where the heart is.'

Noreen was staring out of the window as she spoke, and at that moment she realised that she would not be returning to Australia.

49.

The Honeymoon

Hannah had woken early, even though they had made love several more times throughout the night. She was exhausted, but deliriously happy. Hannah looked at her sleeping husband, and she thought how strange it was to now be sharing her bed with the man that she had grown up with, and had loved for years.

The smell of food wafted up from the kitchen below, and she realised how hungry she was. She got up and ran a bath. She had seen pictures of enamel baths in store catalogues, and she had heard stories of how some establishments had taps that ran hot and cold water. Her bath had always been a tin tub that had to be filled with hot water that had been heated in the copper that they washed their clothes in. But, here was one of those fancy baths that she had only seen pictures of, and she couldn't wait to use it.

Over the next two weeks, they spent idyllic days walking along scenic trails that meandered alongside of rocky ponds and streams. The gurgling streams ended at a cliff face, and then became raging waterfalls as they plunged over a thousand feet to the valleys below. They would walk along rutted paths that curved along the cliff face walls, to give spectacular views of smokey blue valleys and distant mountains. Then in the evenings, they went back to the hotel and snuggled up in front of warm fires, before they went to bed to entwine their bodies once more before falling asleep.

Katoomba to Lithgow was just over an hour's journey by train.

Hannah had rung Harriet Murdoch, who had insisted that as they were nearby they should immediately come down and stay for a few days. Tom could then decide if he would like to work on the farm. Hannah had no doubt that he would love Megalong as much as she did.

Harriet met them at the train station, and Tom smiled as he shook her hand. She was tall and tanned, and wore grey jodhpurs and riding boots below a faded brown shirt. The women embraced, and after loading the luggage Harriet drove them along the potholed dirt road that led to the farm. Hannah and Harriet sat at the front, and chatted and giggled like schoolgirls while Tom sat in the back and was happy to just take in the scenery.

It took almost two hours before they arrived at the farm, and Tom was then introduced to Harriet's father. Bill Murdoch had been a tall man once, but as his body had aged, he had developed a stoop brought on by wrestling too many sheep and calves in his younger days. His eyes were still bright, and his smile was warm and friendly. When he shook Tom's hand, it was with a firm grip that belied his seventy years.

'It's nice to meet you son. I heard a lot about you from Hannah, and I'm glad that you got home safe. Harriet tells me that you might be interested in becomin' a farmer. Is that, right?'

Tom took an immediate liking to the old man and replied; 'Yep, we been thinkin' about getting' a bit of land fer ourselves fer awhile now. Hani never stopped talkin' about yer place since I got home, and lookin' around here I'm not surprised. It's a pretty place! How long have ya been here?' Bill smiled broadly. We have been here for over twenty-five years now. I never intended to become a farmer, it just sorta happened.' Harriet interrupted, 'Now dad, let Tom and Hannah get settled in. You will have plenty of time to talk to Tom and tell him your story. I'm sure that Hannah would like to freshen up, and Tom, the washhouse is over to your left.' and she pointed towards the tin hut.

'Mother has just baked some scones, so as soon as you are settled in come up to the house and we will have a Devonshire tea, and Hannah, you will have to tell me all about the wedding.' They cleaned themselves of the brown dust that had continually swirled under the canvas hood of the car as they had driven along what was more of a goat track than a road. Hannah had unpacked the suitcases, and Tom had stripped to his trousers in the washhouse to splash himself with the cool water from the tank.

They walked towards the main house, and Tom noticed that the outside walls were made from thick, rough-sawn slab planks.

Gaps were showing between them from where the timber had shrunk. They had been painted once, but the harsh elements had taken their toll, and the once white paint had flaked and faded to almost match the greying timber.

The house itself was small, but looked much larger due to a wide verandah that enclosed the entire building. The others were already sat on the verandah as Tom and Hannah joined them. Tom was introduced to Harriet's mother. She was thinly built, and her hair was mostly white. She gave him a motherly hug before saying, 'It's so nice to meet you son. You're every bit as handsome as Hannah said you were. Welcome to Megalong farm, and our little piece of heaven.'

Tom smiled, and said, "It's nice to meet ya too, Mrs Murdoch."

'That's enough of that formality Tom. You can call me Dorothy. Now tell me, how do you like your tea?'

They sat around and finished the scones, and Tom looked at Bill and asked, 'You were gunna tell me the story of how ya came across this place Bill.'

Bill knocked the ash from the bowl of his pipe on the heel of his boot, and repacked it with fresh tobacco before he spoke.

'It was just before Federation. When was that?' He looked at his wife for confirmation before continuing. Dorothy thought for a moment before replying, '1901. I get my dates mixed up a bit too. I can't remember properly, but it was just before Queen Victoria died, or just after. Anyway, it doesn't matter, get on with the story.' She gave her husband a smile.

Bill said, 'They had discovered gold out here about twenty years earlier. They got some big nuggets from around Bathurst, and through this area all the way to Blayney. That's just down the road about twenty miles, or thereabouts. So, I come out here by meself.' He looked over at his wife before continuing. 'We were married a coupla years earlier. I had heard all them stories of blokes coming out into the bush, and pickin' up big nuggets in the creeks and streams around here. I thought to meself that I might be able to find a nugget or two, and get a coupla bob together so that we could buy a bit of dirt of our own.

'Well, I left Dorothy back in Sydney with her mother, and I told her that I wasn't comin' back until I had found some gold. I had a horse, and I bought a pick and a shovel, and a few other bits and pieces. I got a sack of flour and some salt, so I could cook a damper.

'I had me gun and I was a good shot, so I was plannin' to kill some rabbits to eat. It took me about three weeks to ride from Sydney to Blayney on me old horse, but we got there eventually.

'When I got there, the locals said that the gold was all gone and that the rush was over. Well, I come all this way, and I thought that I would at least have a go. So, I followed the river out of town. I had this feelin' that I was gunna find somethin', and I did!

'It wasn't much, but I followed the creek inta the hills fer miles, and sometimes the bush was so thick I hadta leave me horse tied up, so I could walk along the creek bank.'

Tom and Hannah were enthralled by Bill's story, and they hung onto every word as he continued telling it.

'I didn't know nuthin' about gold mining, but I met this old joker who showed me how to pan for gold along the creek edges. So, I was way out into the bush and I couldn't think that anyone else had ever been there cause the bush was so thick. But I hacked me way through the scrub for about a week before I came out into the grasslands.

'I set up me camp and let me horse graze, and I went back into the bush area each day. I found a small nugget, and that got me all excited to keep goin'!

'I spent about another three months in the bush by meself. I lived on rabbits mainly. I couldn't write to Dorothy cause I was miles from nowhere. But, the further I went along the creek, and into the bush the more gold I found. Don't get me wrong, they were all just little pieces, but I had it stashed in a sock. I never saw no one in over three months, and I had run out of flour and bullets, and I hadta go back into town.

'I never told no one about the gold that I had in me spare sock, and I rode me horse inta Bathurst. There was a place there that had a big sign up sayin' that they bought gold. I went in, and asked the bloke how much was he payin'. I dropped me sock on his counter, and he weighed it, and blow me down if I didn't have nearly 20 ounces. He wanted to know where I had been pannin', but I wouldn't tell him. Me plan was to catch the train back to Sydney, and go home for a spell, and then come back again.'

Hannah asked, 'So what happened, did you get back there?'

Bill smiled, and took another deep drag on his pipe. 'Nar, I never did. It was always my intention to go back, but after I bought the land I never found the time. I was walking back from leavin' me horse at the stables. I paid the bloke to look after him for a month, and I was headin' for the train station when I seen the sign.'

'What sign?' Hannah eagerly asked.

'They were sellin' off land, cause the government was trying to set up a farmin' industry, and they had just opened up a big parcel of land out here in the backcountry. I asked the bloke about the land, and he told me that I should go and have a look, and I did. He gives me a map of the area, and I went back to get me horse, and it took me two days ta get here.'

Bill stopped for a minute, and relit his pipe before going on. 'There were marker pegs in the ground, all painted white, and I reckon I stopped about here.' Bill pointed along his verandah.

'I looked up at them cliffs on the other side of the valley, and I knew that this was where I would build me house.'

Hannah was sat on the edge of her chair, and was impatient to hear the rest of the story and said, 'Go on Bill, what happened then?'

'I went back and seen the land bloke, and I asked him about how many acres me block was, and how much was it. He said that it was two hundred acres, and that some other bloke was lookin' at it and was probably gunna buy it, but he had to go to the bank to arrange a money transfer. The bloke said that it were five shillings an acre, and the first bloke that give him one hundred pounds could have it. I had a hundred and ten pounds in me pocket from me gold, and I pulled it out and dropped it on the desk. The bloke's jaw almost hit the ground cause a hundred quid was a lot of money then. It still is today!

'Well, he counted out all them one-pound notes, and then he counted them again, and then he got the title deed out. He filled in all the details and he give it to me. He shook me hand, and wished me well and I caught the train home.'

Dorothy was away with her thoughts, as her husband had narrated his memories and then she spoke. 'I had no idea that he was coming home, and I looked up and there he was. He was smiling like a Cheshire cat. He looked like a hobo, and I hardly recognised him. I asked him if he had found our fortune, and he just stood there with that silly grin on his face. Then he picked me up, and he gave me a twirl and said, I got us some land, and all that we have to do is build a house.'

Bill chuckled as his mind wandered back to those days. 'She never stopped talkin' and askin' me questions.' Dorothy broke into the conversation and said, 'He was always such a joker, and I wasn't sure whether to believe him or not. He eventually convinced me when he showed me the deed. He suggested that we should go back, so that he could show me our place.

Bill looked at his wife and smilingly said, 'I remember your mother not bein' happy. She was very skeptical about me findin' enough gold to buy two hundred acres, and she didn't mind tellin' me, neither!'

Hannah asked, 'So how long was it before you moved here after that?'

Dorothy answered, 'We packed some things, and I didn't know what to expect. I suppose that I was excited, and when I said goodbye to my mother I had no idea when I would see her again. Well, we caught the train to Bathurst, and then Bill borrowed a cart from the stable man, and we bought a tent and some supplies, and then we out came here. After living in the city all of my life, I couldn't get over how isolated it was. But then, we got to the top of the rise here,' she pointed forward, 'and I knew. I just knew that this was the place from how Bill had described it.'

Tom was listening intently, and hanging onto every word of the story and asked Dorothy, 'So what did you think?'

Dorothy thought for a moment as she answered. 'I remember it as though it was only yesterday. It was a beautiful morning, and I was already planning on how the house would be situated. I wanted a front verandah to face the cliffs over there,' and she pointed in their direction. Her eyes glazed over as she was transported back to that day. Other than for the buzzing of a few blowflies and the rustling of the gum tree leaves, there were no other sounds. 'I couldn't get over how quiet it was, and I loved this place from the moment that I first set eyes on it, and I still love it.' They sat engrossed within the visions of the story.

'Now, who would like another cuppa?' asked Dorothy, as she picked up the teapot. Hannah asked Bill, 'So how long did it take you to build this house?'

Dorothy was pouring the tea and answered, 'It took almost three years after we arrived.'

Tom still wanted to know what happened after they had arrived and asked Bill, 'So when you came back here, how long did you stay?'

'The first thing that we did was to erect the tent. My intention was just to show Dorothy our land, and spend a day here before going back to Bathurst. But, we walked around as much as we could. Some trees would need clearing, but there was also a good patch of open grassland.' He pointed down the hill. 'See that section down where them sheep are? Well, that was pretty open then, just as it is now. I suppose if that hadn't been the open country we wouldn't have been able to see the view to them cliffs.'

He pointed again. 'So, we walked down the gully and up the other side cause we hadta find our boundary marker. I remember that we walked around for hours before we found it in the bracken. But once we found it and the others, we was feelin' pretty happy with ourselves.'

Dorothy broke in with, 'Once we knew how big the place was, we just sort of felt like we belonged somehow.'

Then Bill continued, 'I wanted to see how many trees I would need to chop down to make us a little house. There was a big stand of trees right down at the bottom of the clearin'. I reckoned that I would need to chop down about a hundred, and haul 'em all back up here. Well, we stayed for a week and I cut down a couple of the long, skinny ones. By that time, I had a good idea as to how long it would take me to get enough to build the house.'

'We had to get the cart back to the bloke at the stables before he started thinkin' that I had run off with it. We packed our gear up, and went back to town.'

Tom asked, 'So Bill, when did ya come back here permanently?'

'Crikey, it wasn't so much time fer me, but it was nearly a year before Dorothy could get back. What happened was, I took her back to her mother's cause we didn't have much money, just a few quid. Me plan was that I would get a few tools together, like me axe and a crosscut saw and some nails and stuff. Then, I set up a proper camp for meself as I started cuttin' down the trees.

'I reckon that it musta been about a month before I had chopped down enough wood to start. I chopped down all the tall skinny ones. They was easy, and I sawed them in half before I dragged them up here. Anyway, I had the frame up, and filled in all the gaps with mud to stop the wind blowin' through, and I got the roof frame done, but I didn't have no money to buy any tin for me roof.'

Hannah asked, 'So, what did you do?'

Bill gave her a wispy smile before saying, 'I wanted to see Dorothy again and let her know what was happening, so I went back to Sydney, and I spent three months there working down at the docks unloadin' ships. In that time, I saved enough money to buy the tin for me roof with a bit left over. I got it all bundled up, and I sent it on the train to Bathurst. There was a bullocky there who delivered it to the block for a quid. So, once I had me roof on all I hadta do was buy a coupla windows to seal the place up.'

Dorothy broke in, 'And that's when I came up here to live.

'It probably took another two years before I had the house respectable because we still had no money.' She looked out over the paddocks as her mind wandered back to those early years, and for a moment she was lost in her memories.

Tom asked, 'So excuse me fer bein' nosey Bill, but I'm curious as ta how yer stocked the place. Ya see, me and Hani want a bit of land and do what you done, so I'm really interested in getting any tips on how ta get started.'

'That's orright, son, I don't mind tellin' you. Once Dorothy got the place liveable I went back into town. Down behind the railway station was the cattle yards. They would load the rail trucks up with sheep and cows, and once a week the train would cart the animals back to Sydney for slaughter. So, I got a job there. It paid me ten bob for a day's work loadin' the sheep.

'I'd been workin there for a few weeks, and after we loaded all the trucks, there was one sheep that was left in one of the yards. She was pregnant, and had found a spot to hide, but we didn't find her till after the train had left. So, I borrowed a cart and tied her legs together and I brung her out here. A couple of days later she had a lamb, and that was the first of our flock. Then I started buying a young lamb or two direct from the blokes shippin' them to Sydney. After a year we had about twenty sheep, and then I got meself a ram, and that's how we started son.'

⁎⁎⁎

They were all quiet for a moment, Bill and Dorothy remembering their early years, and Hannah and Tom dreaming of what was to come.

50.

The Discovery

The next morning, Bill saddled the horses and took Tom around the property. By mid-morning they stopped by the creek, and lit a small fire. Bill said, 'I know that it's only half an hour back to the house, but I like to boil the billy down here. I used to make a bit of damper, and have a cuppa here when I was choppin' down me trees. Now I just like sitting here, and watching the birds, and listening to the wind rustling the leaves.'

He threw a few twigs onto the small fire, and lifted the billy with a small branch to the centre of the hot ashes. He sat down and filled his pipe as he rested his back against a tree trunk. He took a long drag from his pipe and said, 'Well son, what do you think? Could we persuade you and Hannah to come and live here? We sure could use some help around the place. I'm getting on as you can see, and I got fences to mend and sheep to be shorn in the season. I couldn't pay you much, probably just a couple of quid a week. But you can live in the house where you are now for free, and we can supply all the tucker, so what do you think son? Are you interested?'

Tom was squatting down on his haunches, and was scratching at the ashes at the edge of the fire with a stick.

'Well Bill, I sure do like it out 'ere, and I learned more about farmin' in the last day or so than I learned ever. Before I say yes or no, I want ya to know that Hani and me is gunna 'ave our own place one day. I dunno when that will be, but I gotta tell yer Bill just so ya know!'

'Me brother got a letter from the government, offerin' him some land ta develop. I'm expectin' ter get one meself at any time. I dunno all the details, but it's something ter do with all us blokes comin' back from the war. The government is gunna open up some land fer farmin' across the state, and they want the soldiers to become farmers. I dunno when that is gunna happen Bill, but when it does Hani and me is gunna build us a little place of our own, just like you done. So, if we say yes, and move here ter help ya, I can't say how long we will stay!'

Bill drew back on his pipe, and as he expelled the smoke, he said, 'I understand son, but any help that you could give us would be appreciated. As much as we love it out here you can see that it's pretty isolated. Because it's off the beaten track it's hard to find any labour.

'We get the occasional traveller passin' through, but we don't usually see no one until we go into town for our supplies, or to sell the sheep.'

Bill stopped talking for a moment. 'I just thought of something! What you said about the government and the land! About a year ago we had some fellas traipsin' around out here. I figured they was lost. There was about six of 'em, and I asked them what they was up to.

'They had horses, mules and tripods, and lots of stuff like that with them. It turned out that they was government surveyors, and they was markin' out areas. Now come to think about it, they said something about it bein' for settler land. I didn't take much notice of it then cause it was no concern of mine.

'But one of the fellas, he said that they were gunna mark out some blocks at Jamison. There's nuthin' there, just bush and hills. No town, or nuthin, but it's a beautiful place. It's called the Jamison Valley, and it's about two miles from here. It's the next valley over.' He pointed in the direction.

Tom stood up and took the last gulp of his tea before saying, 'Do ya think that it's fer the soldier settlement blocks?'

'Well, I dunno what else it could be for, considerin' how far we are from town. We could ride over there, and have a look if you like?'

'Can't hurt, but if it's land fer soldiers maybe we should take Hani. She loves it out 'ere, and if it is settler land then she can make up her mind if she likes it or not. I got no preference fer where we go, but if we seen somewhere that we both like we might be able ter make an application fer it.'

'Orright son, we can go back to the house and get her. Dorothy don't do much ridin' these days, but I'll ask her if she wants to come.'

✶✶✶

The journey to the Jamison Valley took over an hour. There was no road, and the path could only be regarded as a goat track. Bill said, 'They call this road the Ration Track cause the bullock trains used to bring the rations out this way to Blackmore in the old days. They use the other road now, as this becomes impassable after it's been rainin' for a few days.'

They continually stopped to take in the views over rocky gorges and fern-filled gullies. The track wound its way down to the stony creek, before gradually climbing up to the ridge. There they dismounted, and they looked across the valley. The bushland had opened up to reveal rocky hills with pockets of natural grassland. The small stream wound its way across the valley floor, before disappearing behind a hill, only to reappear in the haze-filled distance on the other side.

They could just make out the giant sandstone cliffs, which were about twenty miles away, and they formed the backdrop to the pristine valley below them.

Hannah was the first to speak, 'Oh, what a beautiful place. What glorious views!'

Bill spoke, 'Yeah, it's been sometime since I was here. I first come over here when I bought our plot. I was out hunting for rabbits, and I stopped right about here just like we done now. I don't think nobody has ever farmed here. I dunno if there is a road on the other side, but Lithgow and Sydney is over that way somewhere.' He nodded in the direction. 'I got a feelin' that the only road in is the way past our place, and that leads to Bathurst, as you know.'

He fell silent, as they drank in the serenity of the area and Tom asked, 'So where did ya reckon they marked out the plots?'

'I dunno son. All I know is that they had a lot of white poles tied to them mules, so if we keep going down we might come across them.'

They remounted, and followed the now rough stony trail into the valley. The creek widened, and became a small stream, and they followed it for about a mile before Hannah cried out, 'Up there.' She pointed excitedly. 'See, on the side of the hill. I can see a white pole, up there!' She kept pointing until they could all see it.

'There's another one over there,' said Tom. The ground rose gently to the area where the pole was situated.

The horses picked their way through the rocks, and up the slope. They made their way around the natural fold in the hill that was almost flat. The flat area was about a quarter of a mile from the track below them.

Tom was the first to discover the dam. From the track below, it looked like a flat piece of ground jutting out from the slope above it. As Tom gave his horse a gentle prod to its flanks, he drew in his breath and whistled. He yelled over his shoulder. 'Come over 'ere, and 'ave a look at this!'

Hannah and Bill encouraged their horses up to Tom's, and they all stared.

'Oh, my goodness,' cried Hannah, and Bill said, 'Well I'll be blowed. I never would have knowed.'

They stood and looked at the dam that spanned the natural contour of the hill. It was about a hundred yards across, and appeared to be about twenty feet deep. The ground surrounding it was almost flat, before it rose again to level off at the top of the hill. A few exposed rocks and boulders jutted out from beneath the grass. On the far side of the dam stood a solitary ironbark tree. Its trunk was knotted and twisted, but it stood tall and strong, and its leafy canopy partially shaded one corner of the dam.

Tom rode his horse around the perimeter, but he could see that there was no room to build a house. The dam took up more than three-quarters of the flat land. He dismounted, and walked up the last part of the hill. His heart was beating faster, but not from the exertion of climbing, but from the thought of owning this parcel of land.

He watched as Bill and Hannah slowly made their way to him. He looked back down the valley, and in the far distance he could just make out the rusty tin roof of Bill's house. He scanned the open grassland behind him. It was slightly undulating with a scattering of rocks and boulders. It looked similar to the area where Bill grazed his sheep. He could see a patch of bushland to the south. To the north, he could just make out what he thought was smoke rising midst the blue haze that wafted through the valleys from the eucalypt trees.

He was deep in thought when Hannah sidled up to him. 'Oh Tommy, isn't this such a glorious place? Wouldn't it be a wonderful spot to build a house?'

Before he could answer, Bill had joined them, 'I had a look at them poles son. The first one we seen has got the same number on it as the one over there.' Bill nodded his head in the direction that he was looking. 'That means that the dam, and right across to here, must be one of them parcels of land that the government surveyors was markin' out.'

He looked at Tom before saying, 'Whoever gets this bit of land will be lucky. I reckon that an underground stream must fill that dam. I just had a taste of the water, and it was sweet. Not stagnant at all, and it hasn't rained out here for a while. You can see that there ain't no run-off comin' down the hill, so it would be handy havin' a constant water supply wherever it's comin' from.

'It's a real surprise about that dam, cause we know that you can't see it from the valley. It's a nice bit of sheep country here, so with the water you could grow almost anything. Yep, somebody's gunna have it made if they win the lucky dip for this bit of dirt.'

Hannah had been taking in the view, and she asked Bill, 'I can just make out some smoke on the horizon, down there.' She pointed, and they looked. Bill said, 'Yeah, there is a town over there. It's called Blackmore. It's probably at least five miles away. It's about twenty miles from Lithgow, but in the other direction to the way we come from Bathurst. I have been over there a few times. It's probably closer to go there from here, than it is to go to Bathurst.'

'How big is it?'

'It's a bit smaller than Bathurst, no that's wrong, it's a lot smaller than Bathurst, but it's got a courthouse, and a big school. I think that it's some sort of boarding school. They found gold over there about a hundred years ago. I believe that it's all petered out now. But, I gather that it was prosperous in its heyday. It's only a farmin' town now, but just goes to show how high up you are here that you can see that far.

'Mind you, it's a beautiful day today, but it gets mighty cold around these valleys and hills especially when the south wind blows. Up in the higher peaks, they get the occasional snowstorm in winter.'

Tom was still looking around and said, 'I wonder how much land there is on this parcel. How much land would a fella need, do ya think Bill, ter be able to make a decent livin'?'

Bill thought for a moment before answering, 'Well, it wouldn't handle too many cows. It's too rocky, so unless it flattens out further down the paddocks, it would only be suitable for sheep. I can grow three sheep to an acre down at my place. I usually have about a hundred ewes at any one time, and a ram. Mind you, my place isn't as rocky as this. You might get to farm two to an acre in a good season!

'It all depends son, on how many acres it is. If it's two hundred, you might be able to run up to three hundred head in a good year.

'But it would take you time to build up a big flock like that. You would have to fence it all off first, and that will take time.

'But, as beautiful as this place is, I suspect that if it were only about a hundred acres, you would struggle to make a livin' from sheep. If you could clear the place of rocks you might be able to grow some grain.'

Bill looked across the open area, and as he filled his pipe he mused, 'I know that it's a nice lookin' selection son, but if you're gunna put yer hand up for this,' and he waved his arm in the direction that he was looking at, you really need to think about what lies in front of you. Just lookin' around now, I would think that you would have at least a year's work in just clearin' the stones and them trees down there.' He pointed toward where the trees stood. 'I am not trying to talk you out of getting' this selection. I just want you to be aware of how much blood and sweat you're gunna have to invest here, in getting it to be productive to the point where you can at least make a livin".

Hannah walked over to a pole. She took a small pencil from her purse, and wrote down the numbers. 'What are you doin' Hani?' asked Tom.

'Well, I was thinking that if this is one of the settlement blocks that Jack was talking about it, then it might help if we knew the number of the block. Jack's letter said that you might have to go into a ballot, so if we are aware which block has the dam on it we might be able to bid for it.'

***

At the end of the following week, it was time for them to return to Sydney.

Tom had thought long and hard about whether they should continue to live at Megalong, but in the end it would be Hannah's decision. They had been married for almost a month. A few nights earlier Hannah had broached the subject. 'What are your thoughts, Tommy? Do you think that we should stay here, or do you want to return home?'

Tom pursed his lips, and thought for a moment before saying, 'I sure do like it out here, and Bill could certainly teach me a trick or two. God only knows that he could use some help around the place. I'm not sure of what to do. I know that we need to go back to Sydney to see if me letter has come. What me thoughts is, that I should go back to the forge, and work fer your uncle fer a while.

'I was thinkin', that when we get to wherever we go, we will need some decent tools.

'I will need a shovel, and a pick and a crowbar fer starters, and if I go back to the forge I could make them tools and save some money. The problem that I got, is that if we live out here on Bill's farm we might miss out on getting our own place!'

Hannah frowned, 'I don't understand Tommy. What do you mean?'

'There sure is a lot of work to be done around Bill's place. Don't get me wrong, I like it out 'ere, but the longer we stay, the harder it's gunna be to leave. I want me own place, and if we get one of the army blocks it's gunna take a lotta work ter build us a house, and to make a livin'. If we go back to Sydney, we can live with mother until we know where we are gunna get our land. Bill said that he could only pay us a quid or two a week between us. I can earn more than that with yer uncle. The only reason that I'm thinkin' about the money is that once we get our own block, we ain't gunna have any money comin' in! We won't have ter pay no rent at 'ome, and that means that we could save a bit before we move out to the bush permanently.'

Hannah was quiet for a moment. She had her heart set on staying at Megalong, and was now surprised to hear her husband saying that they should move back to Sydney.

'We have some money Tommy, if that's all that you are worried about.'

'I only got about forty quid saved up Hani, plus a few bob from me last army pay. I need ter save a few 'undred quid before we could move to the bush. We need a horse and trap, and a tent. We will hafta live in a tent fer a long time until I can get us a house built.'

Tom was now frowning, as the thought of exactly how much equipment they would need was starting to sink in. Hannah sidled up to him and said, 'Give me a minute. I have something for you.' She didn't wait for a response, but went back to their lodgings to return shortly after. She handed him a small bank passbook. He looked at it and asked, 'What's this?' He opened it up, and his eyes widened and he asked, 'Where did all this come from?' She smiled and said, 'Remember when you went off to the war? You sent me a pound a week from your army pay. Well, I didn't spend any of it, well not much anyway. So, Tommy, you have over one hundred and fifty pounds, and it's all your money. That should be plenty for you to buy what you need once we get our block!'

Tom looked at his wife before embracing her and saying, 'Yer full of surprises. I knew that I made the right decision when I married yer.'

He kissed her, and Hannah replied. 'We will go back home now, and stay there until we get our block and what will be, will be.'

51.

Plans for the Future

Sydney had changed after the war. The streets were bustling, and appeared to be more crowded. The pubs were always full, and one-legged men walked around on crutches. Others, who had lost arms, had the armless shirtsleeve tucked away, and motorcars were beginning to outnumber horse-drawn vehicles on the streets.

Factories were back in full swing with many now displaying vacancy signs, and although the memories of the war were still raw to many people, life was falling back into mundane routine for most.

Tom had gone back to working at the forge, and Brigid and Des were now back in Sydney. Des continued to have trouble with his arm, and he had finally convinced his father that he would never be able to finish his apprenticeship due to his injury. He had managed to secure a job as a labourer at the Botanical Gardens, while Brigid had secured employment back at the Barracks Hospital. Matron Irene Clarke had replaced Noreen. She had implemented many changes over the following years, after the board had altered their policies and allowed the poor to be admitted, irrespective of their financial circumstances.

✳✳✳

The images of treating wounded soldiers were still fresh in Brigid's mind. She wanted a change in direction, and had now begun studying midwifery in earnest.

Three months after returning to Sydney, Tom finally received the letter from the Soldier Settlement Board. After reading it several times, he carefully filled in the details that they required, including the number of the plot that they would like to obtain, before he returned the letter. A further six months elapsed before they received a response.

Hannah heard Bert blowing his whistle long before he had arrived at her door. It had been so long since they had posted the application back to the settlement board that they had almost given up on hearing from them. Bert handed her the long brown envelope. All official letters from the government arrived in brown envelopes, and had 'On His Majesty's Service' stamped upon them. Her heart was beating faster as she read the small, red printed letters on the back of the envelope. 'If not delivered return to Soldier Settlement Board. 2 York Street, Sydney.'

It was addressed to Tom, and she thought about riding over to the forge to give it to him, but then she dismissed the idea. She knew how busy they were, and there was no point in interrupting their work. They had waited this long to receive it, so another few hours would be of no consequence.

Tom had arrived home tired and dirty, and Hannah was beside herself wanting to know about the contents of the letter. He kissed her on the cheek and frowned at his wife's agitation. 'What is it Hani?' Before he could go on, she waved the envelope at him and said, 'Here it is! Open it please Tommy, I am dying to hear what it says.'

Tom took the letter and read it out loud.

Dear Mr Fields,

We are pleased to announce that you were successful in obtaining the land that you had nominated under the Soldier Settlement Act as your first choice. The parcel of land is two hundred acres, and comprises a combination of open land and light bush.

The land is in the Shire of Blackmore, in an area known as Jamison. It is situated twenty-five miles south-west of Bathurst City on what is named as The Ration Track. The nearest town is Blackmore, and is approximately three miles to the east of the Jamison property.

If you accept the following terms, the board grants to you the right of tenancy to the land as previously described for a period of five years.

You will be required to fence the property in its entirety within three years of taking possession of the land. You will also be required to have built a habitable dwelling before the expiration of five years.

It will be at your cost to have the land fenced. However, once the land is cleared and fenced you may apply either to the State Agricultural Bank, or the New South Wales Cattleman's Bank, for the financing of stock and machinery. Those loans will be at the current commercial rate at the time.

During this development period, the board will provide you with a sustenance allowance of two pounds per week. If, after the expiration of five years, and if you have complied with the above terms, the board will enter into a new arrangement with you. Whereas, you will be offered favourable terms that will allow you to purchase the property freehold at market value, less the value of the improvements that you have made.

If these terms are acceptable to you, please sign at the bottom of the acceptance form (attached) and return it to the board at your earliest convenience. You may take the signing and returning of this document as a contract between yourself and the board. As such, you may take possession of the land at your convenience.

The official documents will be posted to you in due course to your current address.

Yours sincerely,

Morris Hodges. Secretary to the board.

Neither said anything for a moment as they digested the contents of the letter. Hannah threw her arms around his neck. He put his arms around her waist before stepping back saying, 'I'm all dirty darlin'. Let me have my bath, and then we can talk about it!'

Doris had heard the excitement, and came into the hallway. She looked at their happy faces and asked, 'Did you get it? Did you get the block that you were after?'

Hannah took the letter from Tom, and waved it at Doris, 'Yes Doris, we got our block. The one with the big dam on it. Oh, thank God. I had almost given up hope!'

Doris was smiling, but her face reflected some doubt. Hannah noticed the troubled look on her face and said, 'Why Doris, what is it? Aren't you happy for us?'

Doris was holding a tea towel, and dabbed the corner of her eye, 'I am so happy for you both, I really am.' She stopped for a moment before going on, 'I knew that this moment would come some day when you would finally leave for good. I know that I'm just being silly, but you two, and Jack, of course, are my whole world.'

Her voice trailed off, and she dabbed her eyes again, 'I'm sorry; I'm just being silly. Now son, the water in the copper is boiling, so go and have your bath. Tea will be ready soon.' She turned, and went back to her kitchen.

The next few days were hectic. Tom had signed the agreement, and Hannah had posted it the following day. They now had to decide when they would move, and it had just dawned on them the enormity of the task that they now faced.

＊＊＊

Jack had come around a few nights later, and they told him their news, and how they would be leaving shortly.

Jack took a long swig of his beer before saying, 'I wouldn't mind seein' this block of yours, so how about we load me truck up with yer gear and I'll drive you there. We should be able to do at least forty miles a day, and I'll be able to give ya a hand with choppin' down a few trees before we come back. Wada ya say?' Jack didn't wait for his brother to reply, and he gulped down the contents of his bottle before saying, 'Well, that's all settled then.'

He called out to his mother, who was filling the copper with water. 'Mother, can you look after the fuel yard again fer a few weeks? Tom, and me is gunna take a load up to his new place!'

Doris came into the kitchen and asked, 'What did you say son?' Jack repeated his question.

'Of course, I will look after the yard. When are you going?'

'As soon as we can get loaded! Probably in a coupla days. We will go and pick up the canvas tomorrow, and get a couple of water barrels from the cooper. If we can get everything loaded by tomorrow night, we can head off at daybreak the next mornin'! You orright with that Tom?' Tom was suddenly excited, and the sooner that they were underway the better, as far as he was concerned.

✳✳✳

The journey took them almost three days, and as they stood at the edge of the dam, Jack took in the view and whistled through his teeth. Tom scrambled up the final few hundred yards to the peak, and Jack followed him. He immediately started gathering up fallen branches. 'We better get a fire goin' it's already getting cold. I'll do that if ya wanna start unloadin' the gear!'

The wind was picking up, and coming directly from the south. They made a camp of sorts, and they spent their first night under a cloudy sky with the canvas flapping, and it reminded them of the war.

The morning light brought cold drizzle and a swirling mist. They finished unloading, and then they set about making a weatherproof dwelling.

✳✳✳

Hannah had continued with her millinery work after arriving back in Sydney. She now had a regular clientele, and she was producing a small income from sewing cushion covers, and repurposing worn dresses and garments into children's clothing. She was generally happy, and although Tom had only been gone for a few days, she was already missing him. She was also anxious about how long it would take Tommy to build them a house. They had discussed it, and although Hannah would have accepted living rough while the house was being built, Tom wouldn't hear of it.

***

Hannah had awoken early again. This was the fourth morning in a row that she had woken up and immediately felt queasy. She made her way outside to the toilet.

The smell of raw sewage from the toilet pan only worsened the way that she felt, and the blowflies showed her no mercy as she vomited. They swarmed around her, and she tried to brush them away from her face, and be sick at the same time. When Doris saw her, she said 'You look dreadful, luvvy. What is it, was it something that you ate?'

Hannah patted her face with a towel before replying, 'I don't think so Doris, but this is the fourth morning that I have felt like this. I'm usually all right after I have some breakfast.'

Doris was quiet for a moment and said, 'Maybe you should call in and see the district nurse. It's none of me business, and tell me to mind it if you want, but have you had your cycle this month?'

The shock registered on Hannah's face, as she thought of what Doris had said.

'Oh, my goodness Doris. Do you think that I might be pregnant? I had forgotten, but…' she paused for a moment, and then said, 'Last time, just after Tommy went to the war. I did feel like this.' Her hand was at her mouth, as she remembered the first time that she had fallen pregnant.

The district nurse confirmed the pregnancy, and this time they were all ecstatic. Claire and Doris, both started making plans immediately. Claire said, 'Well, that will be a surprise waiting for Tommy when he gets back.'

Doris was equally happy, with the thought that her daughter-in-law would now have to stay, at least until her son had built them a proper house to live in.

***

When the brothers arrived home, Claire called in and said, 'Tommy, Davin asked that you and Jack come around to the forge as soon as you can, and bring the truck!'

They looked at each other, wondering what was so urgent that Davin couldn't tell them later when he arrived home.

'Orright Claire, we will go over as soon as we have a bite to eat. Ya don't know what he wants to see us about, do ya?'

Claire smiled, before saying, 'You will find out in due course.'

They looked at each other, and Jack shrugged his shoulders at his brother, who was now busy eating.

The brothers finished their meal, and they made their way over to the forge. Davin was hammering metal when they arrived. He looked up and gave a grin. He rammed the red-hot metal into the water bucket standing at his feet. The water hissed, steamed and bubbled as the hot metal was rapidly cooled. He greeted them with, 'How ya goin?' and they both nodded. Tom looked around, and he knew that he already missed the place. Davin had read his mind and said, 'You can always come back here, yer know that. There will always be a place for you here lad. Even more so now, considerin' the news.'

Tom gave him a quizzical look, 'What news, what are ya talkin' about?'

Davin, taken aback by the question said, 'Oops, sorry, none of me business,' and quickly changed the subject.

'Come out the back, I got somethin' for you.' Without waiting for an answer, he turned and walked through the forge.

He stopped, and then lifted up a sheet of green canvas. 'I made this fer you and Hannah! It's a present from Claire and me.'

Sitting on two logs was a small cast-iron fuel stove. Tom looked at Davin. 'You made this? You've done it fer us?'

Davin grinned, 'Yep, I made a couple since you been gone. Every house needs a cookin' stove, and I seen how much they was at the Emporium. I thought to meself, I could make them, and I could sell 'em cheaper than the bloke at the Emporium. Mind you, to be fair, he has to bring them in from England, cause nobody makes 'em here. I think that it came up pretty good even if I do have to say so meself.' Davin then pointed towards the rear of the foundry. 'So, as you can see, we have made a few changes.

'We finally finished building the foundry. I first had the idea after you went off to the war. But, we never had the manpower to build it, but it's done now. It's taken almost five years to get it finished. It's a lot smaller than what I first envisaged, and it cost more than I wanted to spend. But now I can build stoves, and do that fancy metal fretwork that people put around their verandahs.

'So, we made a couple a stoves to see if we could, and we sold 'em both, and then Claire suggested that I should make one fer your new house. Wada ya think?' He was looking at his son-in-law to gauge his reaction. Tom took hold of Davin's hand, and shook it vigorously. 'I can't thank ya enough, Davin. I had a look at one, and they wanted almost forty quid fer it. I thought that we would hafta do with an open fire ter cook on until I could afford ter buy one of these.'

Davin had another surprise and said, 'I got somethin' else for yer both.' And he pointed to the far wall. Sat in the corner of the shed was a bath. Slightly higher at one end, and made from galvanised tin.

'A bath!' Tom gasped, 'That's fer us too?' He shook Davin's hand and said, 'Ah Dav', yer a really good fella. Hani is gunna love havin' a proper bath to lie in, and me too. I just can't thank ya enough.'

'That's why I wanted you to bring the truck. The stove weighs nearly a quarter of a ton. I dunno how ya gunna get it off the truck, but there is enough of us here to get it on.'

It took them almost an hour to load the stove and bath, and then they made their way back home, and an excited Hannah greeted Tom.

'Tommy, I have something to tell you.' He looked at his wife, and said, 'More surprises! Look what yer uncle gave us. He pointed to the bath and stove sat on the tray of the truck. 'Now, what do yer hav'ta tell me?'

She took hold of his hand between both of hers, and said, 'I'm pregnant, Tommy. We are going to have a baby!' She was nervously waiting for his reaction, and he didn't disappoint her. 'Seriously?' He picked her up, and gave her a twirl before putting her down and kissing her. 'Are ya sure? What are we havin'? When is it due?'

'Oh, Tommy you are silly, yes I'm pregnant, and I have no idea of what it will be. I don't care, as long as it's healthy. It's due in about seven months, and that's about all that I can tell you! Are you happy Tommy?' He gave her another squeeze. His arms wrapped tightly around her. 'Of course, I'm happy, and I don't care either. Boy, or girl it don't matter, as long as it's not crook.'

As he gave her another kiss, Jack joked, 'If yer finished canoodling ya misses, I could use a hand 'ere. Oh, and by the way Hani, thanks fer makin me an uncle. Now if ya don't mind, me and Pops have got work to do.'

✶✶✶

They stayed at home for another two days before returning to Jamison. Jack was deep in thought as they made their way up the mountain road that led to Lithgow.

'What's on yer mind?'

Jack didn't speak for a few moments, but then said, 'I been thinkin' about how we are gunna move that stove. We can't just slide it off, and leave it down at the dam. So, I think that the first thing that we should do is make a road up to the top, so that we can drive the truck up there. Wada ya think?'

Tom replied, 'Tell ya the truth, I didn't give it no thought, but we could give it a go. I reckon that we can get to about two hundred yards from the top of the hill with the truck. Now, it's too steep to go straight up, so what we need to do is make a zigzag road just wide enough to get the truck over the ridge. Wada ya reckon?'

'We could do it. We hafta have a track from the dam anyway, so we might as well build a road now before we do anythin' else.'

Tom said, 'It's only a couple of months before it'll be winter. I'm guessin' that once it starts to rain up there you won't get nothin' upta the top. So yeah, let's get inta it as soon as we get there.'

Jack said, 'I think that I'll make one more trip before I hafta get back to the yard. So, how are ya gunna get yer horses up 'ere?'

'I got that figured out. I'm gunna get them sent up on a cattle train to Bathurst. I'm gunna get on the mail train first. I'll be in Bathurst fer a day or two before me horses get there.

'I should be able ta buy meself a cart while I'm waitin' fer the horses. If I can't, then I'll just go next door and ask to borrow theirs when I need to get some supplies.'

Jack was packing his pipe as they drove at a snail's pace. He struck a match, and cupped the flame in one hand as he drew back on his pipe.

He took a long drag before asking,

'So, when are ya gunna bring Hani up 'ere? It's gunna make it awkward now that she's gunna have a baby!'

Tom replied, 'I ain't bringin' her up 'ere until I built the place, and got it liveable. Besides, I reckon that it's gunna be as cold as a witch's kiss durin' the winter. No, I know that she was prepared to live a bit rough and give me a hand, but now everythin's changed. I ain't told her me thoughts yet, but I can't see her bein' here before next summer. I dunno how much I will get done. It will depend on the weather, and how much money I can spend. I thought that I would build two rooms, and get them both finished.

'I could build the kitchen inside now that I got a stove. I know that Hani would like an inside kitchen, just like them fancy houses have in them magazines that the women are always readin'. Then I will do the bedroom. Bein' it's just me, I can sleep in the kitchen while I'm buildin' the bedroom.'

Jack interrupted, 'Ain't ya forgettin' somethin'?' Before Tom could ask, Jack went on, 'What about yer dunny? You won't have a cartman out 'ere. It's orright fer us, doin' our business out in the paddocks, but yer can't expect a woman to live that rough. So, you will hafta build a bog before she arrives, and it'll have to be presentable. It will need to be close to the house, cause if it's blowin' a gale, and pissin' down ya don't wanna be walkin''alf a mile to yer dunny with a candle in the middle of the night!'

Tom was silent, as he mulled over the issues that he faced. He knew that the money that Hannah had saved would not go far, and he didn't know how long it would be before the government started paying his two pounds a week allowance.

His mother would not expect any money to provide for Hannah, but his mother was struggling to get by with her small railway pension. It was barely enough to provide for her. He knew that Hannah would also want to contribute to her keep, as she would not expect Doris to feed her. He also knew that the only money that Hannah would have was the small amount that she could earn from her millinery work. As the truck rattled on towards their destination, Tom was now seriously wondering if he had made the right decision.

Jack speaking broke into his thoughts. 'Have ya worked out what ya gunna do on the land yet?'

'I spoke to Bill about that. He mainly grows sheep. He said that he just gets by with a flock of around three hundred. I was thinkin' that I'll havta grow some crops of some sort.

'It will take me years before I got a flock like Bill's. I'm gunna grow some stuff that we can eat first. Put in an apple tree, and a few chooks. I can grow a few spuds and turnips. If we grew some veggies, I could trap a few rabbits, and if I can get me a cow and a calf, we will have some milk. If I can get the house finished with the dough that we got, then we got a chance at makin' a go of it!'

Jack was thinking, and he said, 'If ya plough up about fifty acres ya might be able to grow some wheat, or corn. I dunno; but see what the other blokes are growin' around 'ere. It will be hard work ploughin' up yer land, what with all the rocks, but once ya done it, and got some seed in, you should be set. If you could get a few bags of wheat, or corn for yer first crop, you could swap them for a few sheep, or a cow or somethin'. Yer not havin' second thoughts, are ya?'

Tom was thinking about what his brother had said, 'I s'pose that it's just dawnin' on me, about how much work it's gunna be to make a go of it.

I ain't scared about the work. I just dunno how long it's gunna take me. I can't expect Hani to live rough for years. It wouldn't be fair on her. Then, we will have the little one, and maybe one day we will have a few more.'

Jack interrupted him, 'I think that yer worryin' too much. Look at the bright side. At least you won't have the rent man chasin' you for money. The government letter said that you had three years to fence the whole place. Look at all them young saplin's you got growin' down at the back of yer land. I reckon that you could put up a post and rail fence right around yer property with them young trees. The letter don't say what sort of fence you gotta have. I would just make a couple small paddocks first and fence them off. Then, if you get a cow, or a coupla sheep, you can keep them there.

'Stop worryin' about things you got no control over. We survived the war, didn't we? I tell ya what; I'll come up and spend a week with you every now and then. So, you do the things that you can do yerself, and when you got a job that needs some extra hands, we will do them when I come back. Wada ya say?' Jack turned his head and grinned at his brother.

Tom looked at him, and gave a weak smile. 'Yeah, you're right, there's a lot of things that I can do meself. Once I got a coupla rooms done on me shack, I'll feel better!'

They drove for several more hours, before finally stopping the truck at the side of the dam. After marking out the side of the hill where the road was to be built, they used crowbars and a pick to dig out the rocks, and level it off. Then, after two days' work they could finally drive to the top of the hill. Shortly afterwards, they returned to Sydney, and Tom spent another week making the final arrangements for his move to Jamison.

Hannah woke early on the morning of Tom's departure. She had cooked his breakfast, and packed some bread and fruitcake to take on the train with him. She had intended going to Central Station with him, but Tom had insisted that she stay at home.

'I'll just catch the tram; there's no point in you coming out just to say goodbye at the station. I will be back in about six weeks, but I will go over to Bill's house, and telephone you a coupla days before just to let you know when I'm comin' home! I'm gunna go and see Bill, and Dorothy on me way to our place.

'That sounds strange, our place. Anyway, I'll call in there, and have a cuppa with them. Now, if you have to contact me in a hurry, then telephone Bill, and I will call you back. I wanna get as much work done as I can. I dunno what the weather is gunna be like over winter, but me first priority will be to get a coupla rooms built and weatherproof.'

Hannah wrapped her arms around his neck and said, 'I'm going to miss you, but at least I know that you're not going to be blown up or shot.' She kissed him on his cheek as he got up from the table.

'Well, I'd better be off, I don't wanna miss me train. He kissed his mother and said, 'Bye ma, I'll see you in a month or so. I know that you will look after Hani fer me. Say goodbye to me brother will ya? Now I'd better go!' He gave them both a hug before picking up his swag, and the brown paper bag with his food and left.

Claire and Doris took charge of advising Hannah on what she should do, and how she should do it, as they all prepared for the new arrival that was still not due for another six months.

***

After arriving in Bathurst, he made enquiries about when his two horses would arrive, and was informed that the cattle train would not be arriving for another twenty-four hours. He thought about booking into a hotel, but as the weather was fine, he decided to camp for the night by the river, and save himself the cost.

As he made his way towards the river, he couldn't help noticing the burnt-out remains of a small hotel. It had been a single-storied building, and the front area was completely destroyed except for the brick facade. The name of the hotel was scorched, but still readable. Blackened posts stood starkly upright in the burnt-out ashes holding up the remains of the roof trusses. The roof had partially collapsed, and sheets of tin lay twisted and bent among the rubble. The rear section, although scorched, was mainly intact.

To one side of the building, two men were sat on a tree stump and smoking. As Tom walked by he gave them a nod, to which one of them said, 'How you doin?'

Tom stopped walking, and replied, 'Not bad. Looks like you had a bita trouble here?'

The older one replied, 'Yeah, had a fire here last week, and just deciding on what we are gunna do. I was gunna rebuild the front bit, but the fire got inta the roof in the back bit. I reckon that it will be easier to pull it down and start again. Me mate here,' he nodded towards his offsider, 'said that we should just rebuild the front bit. But before the fire, I was gunna extend the place. It was built about fifty years ago. Cobb and company used it for a stopover for their coaches before the railway got here! Me old man bought the place after they shut the coaches down, and he turned it inta a pub. That was over thirty years ago. It's handy to the station, so we used to get a lot of travellers stoppin' overnight. But we only had four rooms, and some nights we could use a dozen.

'Lucky there was nobody stayin' the other night when the fire started. It was me own fault. I didn't check the fireplace before I locked up, and I suppose a log must have rolled out, and set the floor on fire. It's no good cryin' over spilt milk. I'll just hafta find a coupla blokes and demolish the place!'

Tom was about to go when he asked, 'So what are you gunna do with all the stuff that ain't burnt?'

The owner replied, 'It'd be easier for me if I just burn the lot, then I can just clean up the site and start building. Why do you ask?'

Tom dropped his swag, and moved towards the two men. He held out his hand and said, 'Me name's Tom Fields,' and he shook both of their hands. 'I just got here offa the train. I'm gunna make me camp down by the river cause me horses don't get here till tomorrow.'

The men shook Tom's hand, and introduced themselves. 'I'm Eric Eaton, and this is me son Gerard.'

Tom smiled as they finished the introductions. 'I just got meself a few acres outa town, and I'm gunna build me a house. I was thinkin' that I might be able to buy a few windows, and a bita tin for me roof offa ya, seein' as you're just gunna get rid of it. Would you be interested in sellin' me the stuff that you don't want?'

Before answering, Eric asked, 'Are you a farmer, where's your land?'

Tom replied, 'Nar, I ain't a farmer yet, but I wanna be. I used to be a soldier, and the government's opening up a bita land for soldier settlers. I got meself coupla hundred acres about twenty miles out, in a place called Jamison. Me and me brother been comin' up here for a while. We brought up most of me gear in his truck, and like I said, me horses will be here tomorrow. I'm gunna go and camp there, till I can build meself and the missus a shack. We got the uprights, and a coupla roof beams in, but now I gotta put some tin on the roof, and buy some planks and windows. I dunno how much it is gunna cost me, and I ain't got a lota money. I was gunna find the mill, and get them to slice me up some planks. So, what would you be askin' for the wall planks and the roof?'

Eric thought for a moment, and then replied, 'Tell you the truth Tom; I never gave it no thought to selling the scrap! All I want is to clear the plot, so that we can rebuild the place and get it up and runnin' as soon as we can.' He thought some more before saying, 'So, you was a soldier, was you?'

'Yep, me and me brother was in the third division, and then later on we was put inta the fifth. We been back almost a year now, and I put me name in the bin to get a bita land. Then me number come up, and now we got two hundred acres of rocky ground at the top of a hill.'

Eric smiled and said, 'I was gunna join up, but they said I was too old at forty-eight, so I stayed at home. Sorta glad that I didn't go now after reading all about it in the papers.

'Me boy here,' and he looked at his son, 'he tried to sign up, but he wears spectacles cause his sight isn't so good, but they wouldn't have him. I'm glad now that he didn't go. I couldn't help but notice your shoulder. Did that happen over there? Tell me to mind me own business, cause it ain't me business, but, I was just curious that's all!'

Tom smiled as he replied, 'Its orright, I don't mind tellin' you. I was lucky; I got hit in the shoulder by a lumpa lead. It put me outa the fightin', and got me banged up in a hospital in England for awhile.' His voice trailed off as his mind wandered back, but then he said, 'I dunno that I'd be in any hurry to sign up again.

'I still dunno what it was all about now. The battlefields were such a noisy place. That's why I want to live out here in the bush. I like the quiet now!'

They all fell silent for a few moments, then Eric said, 'I'll tell you what I'm prepared to do for you Tom. You want some material to build your house, and I want me building knocked down. If you're willing to help us knock the place down, I'll give you all the material that's here for free! Let's say that it's my contribution to the war, and it'll make me feel better for not going. What do you think, is it a deal?'

Tom was pleasantly surprised at the offer, and jumped at it. 'Well Eric, that's a very generous offer, and I'd be a fool to knock it back, so yep, I'll give you a hand. In fact, I'd be just as willin' to knock it all down by meself just to thank you. That way I can sort out the stuff I wanna keep!' He put out his hand, and sealed the agreement with a handshake.

Tom camped at the site for a week. Eric had supplied the tools, and Tom was up at dawn every morning. He carefully prised out the window frames before stacking up the roofing iron and the useable wall planks. They left the front brick façade standing, and would use that as the frame for rebuilding the new building.

Tom had picked up his horses, and they were grazing in the paddock next door. He spent a further two days burning off the rubble and the unsalvageable wood. Finally, there was only levelled off ash to show where the building had once stood.

Tom looked at his haul. There was far more material than he had expected to save. He knew that he would now have to buy a cart, and he anticipated that it would take him several trips before he would be able to haul it all to his land.

Eric arrived, as Tom was about to go into town. 'I was hoping to catch you. You done a good job, and I know that you're looking for a cart to buy. But you won't get all this on a cart, so I had a word with Herbert Murray. Old Herb is a bullocky. He carts wool, and other gear from the farms hereabouts! It just so happens, that he's gunna leave for Blackmore tomorrow. I told him to come, and load all this gear up and take it to your place. He knows your neighbour, Bill Murdoch. He's picked up a few bales of wool from his place.

'Herb said that he would charge you twenty quid to deliver it all to your place, but you will have to help him load it up. He doesn't have any offsider, so I took the liberty to say orright. He's gunna be here this arvo. Is that orright with you?'

'Thanks Eric, I really appreciate all the help you have given me, and for all this material.

'I'm only gunna build a little place at first, but now I've got so much stuff I'll be able to build three rooms at least. Me missus will be so surprised when she sees the place. If the bullocky can get all this stuff loaded on one trip, I won't have to spend any dough on getting a cart just yet!'

Eric smiled broadly, and said, 'You done a really good job on cleaning up me site Tom. I'm glad we met when we did. I'm gunna start building me new pub in a coupla of weeks now. Make sure that you come and have a drink when you come into town. Well, I've got to get going now, and I expect that old Herb will be around shortly.

'All the best to you fella!' They shook hands before Eric climbed onto his horse and left.

It was late in the afternoon before Tom heard the bullock train coming down the road towards him. He could see the lead animals, but the rest, along with the wagon, were almost hidden by the dust cloud that they generated as they approached.

There were six pairs of bullocks pulling the wagon. The biggest beasts were directly in front of the heavy wagon, and the younger, slimmer ones were at the front, and in the middle. Heavy wooden yokes around the necks kept them in pairs, but slightly separated. Thick heavy chains went through each yoke from the front pair of beasts to the large wooden drawbar that was attached to the wooden axles.

Old Herb wasn't that old, and Tom thought that he might have been about fifty. He walked to the side of his team, and he carried a long-handled whip that rested over his shoulder. He spoke to his beasts, which he called by name, and who were just ambling along at a snail's pace. Herb stood over six feet tall, and he wore a battered felt hat that was grey and holed, and tilted towards the back of his head.

He wore a frayed green flannelette shirt that hung loosely over his worn and stained dungarees that were held up by a knotted length of rope. The sleeves were missing from his shirt, and his arms were long and sinewy. His biceps were the size of a small man's thighs, and his face, along with his arms, were the colour of worn dark leather.

As he approached Tom, he pulled back on the long leather leads that had been draped over the wagon step, and were attached to the front pair of steers. The animals stopped, and the yokes groaned and creaked, as the chains clinked and the dust rose to hang heavy in the still air.

Herb looked at Tom. He didn't offer his hand, but said, 'G'day, you the bloke who wants yer gear delivered to yer farm?'

Tom nodded, 'Yeah, me place is out at Jamison, on the back road to Blackmore. This is all me stuff here.' He waved his arm and pointed.

Herb gave a cursory glance. He didn't seem that interested in what the load was. 'Did Eric tell ya that me fee is twenty quid, and ya hafta help me load and unload it?'

Tom replied, 'I got yer twenty quid. Do you want it now?'

'Yer pay me when I deliver yer stuff, and yer pay me before I offload yer stuff!' Herb looked towards the stacked-up materials. He pushed his hat back, and scratched his head.

'Righto, I'll get up on the wagon, and you bring yer stuff over to me. That's how the deal works. The same with the unloading.'

Tom was taken aback by Herb's gruffness. 'Well, could you bring yer wagon a bit closer, so I won't spend all day walkin' back and from?'

Herb thought for a moment about Tom's request. When he had decided that it made sense he said, 'Righto, stand back, and I'll bring 'em closer.' With that, he gave a whistle, along with a shake of the leads and the wagon edged closer.

Herb pulled out a pocket watch from his trouser pocket, glanced at it, and noted the time. 'We got less than two hours to load up. I wanna be out on the Blackmore road before it's dark, so you better get a move on!'

He didn't look at Tom as he spoke, and Tom thought that if Herb gave him a hand to carry the materials to the wagon, then they might have some show at loading it within the specified time. He wasn't going to start an argument with him as he seemed cantankerous enough, and the last thing that he wanted was for Herb to take his bullocks and go.

Tom carried the materials to the wagon, and Herb bent down and took each piece, and carefully positioned it onto the cart. It took two hours to load, and Tom wondered how Herb could have known precisely how long the loading would take. The sun was low on the horizon by the time the load was tied down.

'Righto, I'll be off! I has me spot out on the road where I makes me camp. It's about three miles out, and it takes us about an hour to get there. Where 'bouts is yer farm agin? Are ya gunna be there when I get there?'

'It's twenty miles out, and about a mile past the Murdoch place. I'll stay here overnight, and I expect that I'll catch up to you in the mornin' sometime. Don't you worry, I'll be there to unload you!'

Herb said nothing, but gave Tom a nod. With that, he raised his whip and gave it a twirl over his head. The plaited leather whirred as it first flicked backwards, and then with a flick of his wrist the twenty-foot long whip darted forward. It cracked like a gunshot, as the knotted end lightly skimmed the back of the lead bullock. The heavy wagon creaked, and the chains stretched and clinked as the animals pushed into their yokes and took up the slack. The wagon lurched forward, and the wooden wheels groaned as it started to roll. Tom watched as the bullock train made its way down the dusty road, and disappeared into the deepening gloom.

The next morning, he had risen early as he had picked up his supplies from the emporium the evening before. The sacks of flour and sugar were attached to his spare horse, and he had ridden for almost an hour before he caught sight of the bullock train.

It was lurching and wallowing from side to side, like a broken masted ship in a swell as the wheels followed the furrowed track. The road narrowed, and the bush closed in around the train. The red dirt swirled and eddied around it, as the beasts plodded on to the cracking of Herb's whip.

He sat behind for some time, as there was little room to overtake the lumbering wagon. When he did, he gave Herb a nod as he passed by. It took almost five hours before they arrived at Jamison, and a further two hours before the wagon was finally unloaded.

✷✷✷

Tom worked on his house over the next four weeks. He cut saplings, and de-barked them before positioning them as roof trusses, and it took a week before his roof was covered with his salvaged tin He nailed the weatherboard planks into position, and then after fitting the salvaged windows, he stood back to admire his work.

The house was small, and comprised of a kitchen and a small bedroom that was lit by a single window.

Tom spent another week gathering stones to make the chimney for his new stove. It was heavy, tedious work and after building the chimney, he cautiously lit a small fire in his new stove. The smoke gently wafted skywards, and he stacked small logs outside his door, which he hoped would see him through the increasingly cool nights.

The fire burning brightly in the grate cheered him up immensely; and the shadows from the fire danced across the walls as the wind whistled through the gaps in the wall planks.

He placed the billycan over the main grate, and watched how quickly the water boiled, and as he drank his tea he pondered how he could line the walls and the floor. He decided that his most pressing problem now was in obtaining and installing a windmill to pump the water from the dam up to the house. He would need to do that before he could finish building a bathroom, as it would be impossible to boil any water for a bath if he had to carry it up from the dam in a four-gallon kerosene tin.

52.

Conversations

Hannah was becoming increasingly restless. Her body was changing, as were her emotions. She had spoken with Tom only once in the past six weeks. Her telephone call had only lasted for three minutes, and had cost sixpence.

Hannah had asked Tom how long it would be before she could come and stay, and he had replied, 'The place is still very rough, and I still hafta build a washhouse and a privy. I got a small bedroom built, but I don't have a floor yet. Do you think that you could ask yer uncle if he might be able to make us a windmill?

'I couldn't pay him, but I could give him a few weeks' labour if he could make us one. I hafta be able ta pump the water up from the dam to the house. I can't keep carryn' it up from down there! If we had a windmill, I could get us a pump to use in the kitchen. I was also thinkin' that if we had water up here, we could have one of them flushin' toilets like they had at the Carrington Hotel. I still got me drawin' that I done of that fancy one there. I seen one of them inside toilets advertised in one of them emporium catalogues, and I could make it work if we had water pumpin' up here all the time!'

The beeps started, indicating that there were only thirty seconds left before more money would have to be put into the coin collector if the telephone call was to continue.

Hannah spoke quickly, 'When are you coming home Tommy? I miss you!'

'I miss you too Hani. I will ring again in two weeks and let you know. Say hello to everyone for me!'

The telephonist broke into the conversation, 'Do you want to continue the conversation? If you do, then insert sixpence into the box immediately!'

'No thank you.' And the line was disconnected.

Hannah had asked Davin about the windmill, and he agreed to make them one. They were sat around the kitchen table talking. Claire was sewing buttons onto a small coat that she had made for her grandchild that was still four months from being born. The material was from a discarded overcoat that she had brought with her from Ireland almost twenty years earlier. It was tattered and moth-eaten, but the lining was still in good condition. She had removed the coat lining, and after sewing the edges it was filled with kapok that she had taken from her mattress. Doris had been wondering what they could use as a baby crib, and she thought that as she had an old leather suitcase, she might be able to use that. Jack had removed the lid and the studs holding the hinges, and Claire had lined the inside with the bottom half of her old coat. The kapok mattress was made to fit. The rest of the garment was remade into a child's coat, although the baby would be at least two years old before it would fit.

Doris had been collecting flour and sugar sacks from her neighbours for several months. She had cut them open, and bleached them white to make nappies for her grandchild.

The sound of knocking on Doris's front door took their attention. Doris opened the door to be greeted by a stranger.

'Good morning, madam. Are you the mistress of the house?'

Doris smiled, 'I'm no mistress, but this is my house. What can I do for you?'

The stranger stood around six feet tall, and was in his mid-forties. He wore a worn brown suit, and a wide-brimmed hat, and he carried a leather suitcase. He raised his hat before saying, 'Me name's Alfred Doran, and I'm a salesman madam. I got a few bits and bobs that I would like to show you, if I may?'

Doris smiled again, she was used to door-to-door salesmen knocking at her door. She rarely bought anything, but she usually let them in to show her what they were selling.

She knew that times were becoming hard, and while the government had increased spending on infrastructure projects, non-government jobs were becoming harder to get.

'Well, you can show me what you're selling young man, if you stop callin' me madam. My names Doris Fields, and you can call me Doris, but that don't mean that I'm gunna buy anything from you. Now, wipe your feet and come in.' She turned, and went back inside followed by Alfred. He removed his hat, and nodded at the others sitting at the table and again introduced himself.

Doris asked, 'Would you like a cuppa? I just made a fresh pot.' She didn't wait for a reply before taking down the last cup from the shelf.

'Now, how do you like your tea?'

'As it comes missus. I ain't fussy. I used to be in the army. I got used to takin' what was on offer when I was in the trenches!'

Doris looked at the stranger before asking, 'Were you overseas? Both me boys was in France, and Gallipoli before that. You might know them, Jack and Tom Fields!'

She looked expectantly at Alfred who replied, 'I'm sorry missus, their names don't ring no bells, but that don't mean nuthin' as there was so many of us over there. I was in the twelfth cavalry meself. Spent most of me time in the Middle East.' His voice trailed off as his mind wandered back for a moment. 'I'm sorry missus. I would rather not talk about them days if you don't mind. Now could I show you me wares?'

'I understand Alfred, me boys don't like to talk about the war neither. So, let's have a look at what you have.'

He placed his suitcase down on the table, and opened it up. It held sewing and knitting needles, pencils, hatpins and assorted studs, along with several jars of shirt and coat buttons.

While none of them had had any intention of buying anything, they now looked at his assortment of small goods with interest. Claire took a reel of cotton, and a few buttons, and Hannah purchased a packet of nappy pins. Alfred drank his tea, and pocketed the coins.

'Well thank you ladies, I'll be on my way. I still got a lotta doors to knock on 'cause a bloke has to make a living somehow!'

He gave them a weak smile, before closing the lid on his suitcase and making his way to the door. Doris sat down again, and poured herself another cup.

'I think that it's such a shame the way the government is treating all them boys who come back from the war the way they are.'

Claire replied, 'I agree with you Doris. The government was quick enough to get them all to sign up, but now that the war is over they don't seem too keen to help them.

'I read in the newspaper just the other day about the rising unemployment. It seems like all they want to do is increase farming and little else.'

Hannah was sewing the edges of flour sacks together, and spoke to no one in particular. 'I was down in George Street the other day, and I was quite shocked at how many young men were just sitting around on the steps of the pub in the middle of the day. I wonder what is going to happen to them all?

'I must say that I am growing a distaste for the city. When I was living with Harriet at Megalong I just loved the bush. The air was clean, and the only thing that we could hear was the sound of the wind blowing through the trees and the birds singing. I feel so sorry for all of those young men who don't seem to be able to get a job!'

Claire spoke, 'I know that you want to be a farmer's wife darling, and that you want to live way out in the country, but many people will never get the opportunity of owning a selection of their own. I doubt if many will ever get a chance to even own a house of their own.

'The government just doesn't seem interested in helping working-class people. I can't believe that they allow the eviction men to just throw anyone out of their houses onto the street like they do. I was passing by

Mrs Dooley's house just the other day. She lives next door to the Chinese laundry shop, or rather she used to. Poor old Mr Dooley only passed away a month or so ago. There they were, these three big thugs just throwing her possessions onto the street. How was she supposed to pay her rent? I don't know what the place is coming to when the housing authority people can throw old ladies out of their homes and onto the street.'

Doris replied, 'She is such a gentle soul. I suppose that she will end up living down by the river like all the rest. If I had the room, I would let her live here. I know that I can't, and it makes me so angry that the government has no desire to help people like her.'

Another knock on the door interrupted their conversation. The door opened, and Brigid called out, 'It's only me, hello everyone.' She didn't wait for a response before asking, 'Is that tea fresh? I really need a cuppa!'

Doris stood up, 'Yes, it's still fresh. I'll just wash a cup. We just had a salesman drop by. I really do need to get a couple more cups, now sit-down dearie.'

Brigid bent over, and gave Hannah a peck on her cheek and asked, 'Are you all right? How are you feeling?'

Hannah smiled and said, 'I'm feeling wonderful now that I have stopped feeling sick every morning! I haven't seen you for a week, have you been busy?'

Brigid replied, 'Yes, there are lots of ladies having babies at the moment. I suppose it's because their husbands all came home from the war at the same time. Of course, the new policy has increased the number of ladies having their babies in the hospital now!'

Claire pushed the needle through the button that she was stitching onto a vest and asked, 'What new policy is that dear?'

'You know how hospitals could only take in one charity patient a week before the war?' Claire nodded. 'Well, the government has changed the hospital policy. If you are having a baby, and you don't have any money you can go to the hospital to have your baby as long as you pay for your keep.'

Doris had been quiet after pouring out the tea, 'What do you mean, paying for your keep?'

'Well, you go to the hospital about a week before the baby is due and they allocate a bed to you, but you have to help with other patients. They have to wash bed sheets, and nurses' uniforms, things like that. They don't have a baby nursery either, not like they used to do!'

Hannah frowned and asked, 'Where do they keep the new babies if not in a nursery?'

'They had to make more room for more patients after they changed the policy, and so they turned the nursery into a new ward. They keep the babies in cribs next to the beds, and they keep the mothers in for about three weeks before they send them home. The government did something good for a change when they set up the mothers' infirmary. They give every mother a voucher when they leave so that they can get free milk and feeding bottles. There is also talk that the government is going to build a hospital just for ladies. I may apply for a midwife's position there if they do, because I don't think that I shall ever go back to primary nursing!'

Brigid stopped talking for a moment as she thought about the wounded that she had attended during the war, and she knew that she no longer had the stomach to tend to mangled bodies.

She changed the subject and said, 'Have you heard from Tommy?'

'Not since we last spoke. I can't wait to see what he has built! I know that our new house is going to be small, but that doesn't matter. He can always add extra rooms if we have any more babies.'

Brigid snorted, 'What do you mean, if? You're going to be a farmer's wife. How do you think that you are going to run a farm if you don't have half a dozen sons?'

'I don't mind having six sons, but I would like a daughter or two, but we will see. What will be will be. I just want one at a time. I don't really care what it is. I just pray that it's healthy.' She patted her stomach, and then rested her hand there.

Claire was rummaging through her sewing box and said, 'Yes darling, whatever God blesses you with will be fine by me. My only regret is that we won't get to see the child growing up. I know that we will come and visit occasionally, but it's not the same as seeing the little one every day.'

They went silent for a moment before Hannah stood, and went to Claire and gave her a hug. 'I'm sorry too Aunt Claire. I'm torn with leaving, but I don't know how to get around it. I want to live in the country, and I know that Tommy does as well. I suppose that means that our babies will grow up in the country, and we will all miss each other.' Hannah took out her handkerchief, and sniffled into it before wiping her eyes.

Doris stood and gave her a hug, 'There, there, dearie, it's no good upsetting yourself. You won't be leaving tomorrow, and I think that it will be some time before Tommy has your house ready. Is Davin building the windmill?'

'I asked him to, and he said that he would get right onto it. Uncle Davin stated that he might as well build two, as it was just as easy. He said that if he could sell the other one, then that would pay for our one!'

Claire looked up and said, 'You have him twisted around your little finger. When has he ever refused you anything that you have ever asked for?'

Hannah smiled, as she knew that the love between her and her uncle knew no bounds.

53.

Getting Established

Tom had made a basic shelter for his horses to protect them from the biting south winds.

It was mid-afternoon when Bill Murdoch rode up the hill. 'G'day fella, thought I would come and see how you're goin'!' He looked around and said, 'Well, I can see that you been busy. We been waitin' for you to come down to the house and have a feed. So, I thought I better come up and see that you're still here. Well, that's wrong. It was Dot who said that I should check up on you. Oh, by the way, she sent you up some chops. I killed a sheep yesterday, so we thought that you might like a bit of fresh meat for your tea!'

He climbed off his horse, undid his saddlebag, and handed Tom a small parcel wrapped in sackcloth.

'Have you got a meat safe? You better put it out of the way of the flies. It don't take long for meat to get flyblown out here.'

'Well thank Dorothy for me. I could use a good feed, and I haven't had no proper meat for a couple of weeks except for a few rabbits. I'll cook 'em up tonight. No, I haven't got a meat safe. That's something else that I hafta get meself. I been setting the rabbit trap, I only got one, but I seem to get one every time that I set it. When I catch a rabbit, I skin and gut it, and then I stick it in me camp oven till I'm ready ta cook it. Anyway, I'll put these chops in the oven in the house. I ain't lit the kitchen stove just yet, but the flies won't get to 'em in the oven. Can I interest you in a cuppa tea?'

'I'd rather have a beer, but I expect you got none of that either, so a cuppa tea it is.' Bill walked around the house, and inspected it as Tom explained his luck in obtaining his building materials.

'I still gotta find somethin' to line the inside walls with, and make a floor yet. It's still pretty breezy inside, but once I done that, and make the bedroom weatherproof I can start buildin' an inside privy, and a room to put me bath in. When I got that done, I can bring Hani up 'ere. She's bustin' to move here, but bloody hell Bill, I can't bring her here until I got the house liveable. I'm thinkin' that she should stay in the city at least until she's had the bub.

'I'm a bit worried about how much time it's takin' me to get me house finished. I really need to get a plough, and start turnin' over some soil durin' the winter while the ground is soft!'

Bill asked, 'Have you decided yet what you're gunna grow?'

Tom replied, 'Nar, not really, but I thought that if I could grow some potatoes, I might be able to bag some up, and sell, or swap them for some seed, so I could grow some barley, or corn. Somethin' like that.'

Bill struck another match and relit his pipe, 'I got an old single furrow plough back home. I don't use it much these days, so I can let you borrow it for awhile if you want. It's hard work usin' it, but it will do the job.

'The first time that you use it will be the hardest, cause you're gunna hit a lot of buried rocks. You will need to pile them up. Mind you, if you get enough of them you could make a stone barn, or add another room to your house. Once you plough up a couple of paddocks, it don't matter what you grow cause you can grow somethin' different the next year.'

The conversation waned before Bill said, 'Well, young fella, I should head home. I don't like riding when it's dark. Too many rabbit holes, and I don't wanna break me horse's leg!' He stood up, and emptied the dregs of his tea into the ashes.

'Well, enjoy yer chops, and call in on your way back from town. Dot will be happy to see you. We don't get that many visitors. I can tell you Tom, she don't shut up about how happy she is gunna be when your missus gets here. Her and Harriet are knittin' bits for the little one. They are getting very excited about having a baby in the area! Well all the best son, and I'll see you in a couple a days I expect.' He climbed onto his horse, and gave Tom a nod before turning to head down the hill.

Tom checked his money belt. He had saved a lot by not having to buy the building materials.

However, the linoleum he would need to cover his dirt floors and the plaster powder for his walls would eat into his dwindling funds, and there were so many other things that he needed to purchase, and he wondered how he would manage.

He made up his mind that he should travel back to Sydney, and see Davin because he needed the windmill before he could realistically improve his house. The next morning, he began formulating a plan that might raise him some much-needed capital. He started counting the mature gums that were in abundance at the lower end of the property. There were more than a hundred, possibly even double that. Some were close together, and he knew that they would be the most dangerous ones to fell.

He didn't know what species of tree they were, but many of them were straight and tall. Some towered over sixty feet, and had a girth of over twenty feet. He thought that if he could harvest some of his trees, then he could have them milled. If he could sell his trees to the sawmill, he might kill two birds with one stone. They could mill him the planks that he would need for his floor, and he could sell the rest to generate some income.

He was excited at the prospect of turning his trees into useable lumber. He then made up his mind to catch the evening mail train back to Sydney and surprise Hannah.

After cleaning himself up, he realised that he would need half a day to ride to Bathurst. As it was too late to leave now, he decided that he would ride over and see Bill after he had cooked his chops. He hoped that Bill would know what sort of trees were growing on his plot. Once he knew the species, he would be able to sound like he knew what he was talking about when he negotiated with the mill owner.

It took him almost an hour to ride to Megalong, and the barking of Bill's dogs brought Dorothy and Harriet out to greet him. Harriet was the first to speak, 'Hello stranger, Dad said that you had been busy and that you might call in. The kettle's almost boiled. Of course, you are going to stay for tea, aren't you?'

Bill appeared from his shed, 'You decided to leave earlier, did you?'

Tom climbed from his horse, and raised his hat, 'Hello ladies,' and he nodded to Bill before saying, 'I wanted some advice Bill. Yeah, I'm going back to Sydney. I was gunna catch the mail train tonight, but it was too late by the time that I made up me mind. So, I'm gunna leave early in the mornin' cause I want to go to the mill. I had this idea that I wanted to run by you. By the way, I was wonderin' if I could leave me other horse 'ere while I'm gone? The old saddler charges me five bob a day fer each horse, and I don't know how long I'm gunna be away.'

Dorothy smiled, 'Of course you can leave your horse here Tom, now come inside and have some tea.' She turned, without waiting for him to answer and went inside followed by Harriet. Bill took the reins of the spare horse, and led him to the shed yard.

'Put them both here son, listen, why don't you stay here tonight? That way you can get an early start, and it will give you some time to do your business in town before the train leaves.'

'That's kind of you Bill. I bought me swag. It's always so damned cold on the night train, so I thought that this time I could wrap meself up in me swag and keep warm. I can just sleep on yer verandah. I don't want Dot makin' no fuss. I been sleepin' rough fer a while now, and it don't bother me none. Just like bein' back in the army, without the noise!'

'Well, you can have that conversation with her, son. I don't get involved with indoor stuff.' He smiled as he said, 'But, if I was you I would just sleep wherever she tells you. Forty years married teaches you it's easier to just go along with a woman and let them have their own way.'

'You said that you needed some advice son. What's the problem?' Tom took another gulp from his cup before saying, 'I wonder if you could tell me what sort of trees I got growin' on me block? You see, after you left I noticed all them big trees that are right down the bottom end of me land. Some of them are giants and would have a lot of timber planks in 'em! What I was thinkin' was if I could chop some of them down, and get old Herb the bullocky to get the logs to the mill for me, then I might be able to do a deal with the mill boss. But I don't know nuthin' about wood, and I was wonderin' if you knew what sort of trees they are?'

'We got two main gum trees growin' around here son. Them big tall ones is spotted gum, and the darker ones is Black Butt. When they dry out, they are as hard as nails. You might also have a bit of Yellow Box. If you got a few of them, they would bring in a bit of dough.'

Tom was curious now, 'How do I tell the difference, and what's so special about the Yellow Box?' Bill was again filling his pipe, and he answered, 'The railways use Yellow Box for their railway sleepers, cause they're hard as nails, and they last for years just lyin' on the ground. But if you got any Yellow Box I can't see how you will cut them down.'

'Why not?

'In me younger days I seen how they cut them big trees down. They had a gang of young blokes with muscles on their muscles.

'Two blokes stand on each side of the trunk and swing their axes. I remember thinkin' at the time that if one of them axe men misjudged with their swing they would take the head right off the other bloke. One bloke would swing his axe into the trunk, and as he pulled it back, the other bloke would bring his axe in. They would cut a big wedge out of the trunk, and there would be chunks of wood flyin' in all directions!

'When the wedge was cut halfway through the trunk, they would move to the other side and start cuttin' another wedge until the trunk was just balancin' there. Then, all of a sudden, they would hear the timber creakin' before it would give an almighty crack as it started to sway. Some of them trees was a hundred feet tall, and someone would yell, 'Timber' and down she would come!

'The axemen would have to judge which direction the thing was gunna fall, and they would watch it as it started to lean before bolting. The thing would go off like a cannon as it hit the deck. Sometimes, the trees were so big that they would take some smaller ones with them when they come down!

'To answer your question, as to why you couldn't drop a big tree by yourself, I think that it would take you a week just to chop one. Then, even if you did drop one, you gotta cut it into twenty feet lengths. That's about as long as Herb could get onta his log jinker. Just to cut one of them giant trees in half, takes two men with a long-crosscut saw about an hour. You could never do that by yourself. I'm sorry to dash your hopes son, but short of blowin' the thing up with a stick of dynamite, I couldn't see how you could manage by yourself. Mind you, that don't mean that you couldn't chop a few smaller trees down as long as they was straight. I was talkin' about the giant gums I seen them choppin' down in the Blue Mountains when they was building the main road through to Lithgow. That was about fifty years ago when I was a young bloke.'

Dorothy smiled, before saying, 'That was a long time ago, old man. We have been married for over forty years, and it was before we met.' Bill smiled as he remembered his younger years.

'I think that it's still a good idea son to talk to the mill boss anyway. You never know, he might come and chop them down for you. No harm in askin' is there?'

***

After spending the night with the Murdochs, Tom rode into Bathurst, and made his way to the sawmill, which was five miles out of town. He saw the smoke rising from the burning sawdust heaps long before he reached the mill. At the mill, men were loading freshly cut planks onto drays, while others were hoisting large logs onto the saw table with chains and pulleys. The saw blade was six feet in diameter, and was steam powered. Men were working in pairs using long crosscut saws to shorten the logs, so that they could be fed onto the sliding saw table. Others were splitting logs that would be sold as firewood for the townspeople.

Everywhere he looked he saw people working, and the mill was a hive of activity. He rode up to a group of men who were loading timber, and he asked to speak to the mill boss.

'The boss is over at the blade,' one man yelled and pointed. 'The big red-headed bloke.' He nodded at Tom, and then went back to work.

Tom tied his horse to the hitching rail, and made his way to the milling shed. The big blade was turning fast, and Tom gave a shiver as he thought of how easy it would be for a man to fall onto the sliding saw table. Two men were at the rear of the rotating blade, and they were lifting the smaller planks as they passed through the blade. Two others were feeding the logs onto the table, and positioning them to be cut to the required thickness.

The big red headed man was standing by the levers that stopped or moved the sliding table. He noticed Tom, but continued to hold the lever down until the log had completely cleared the spinning blade. He pulled down on the lever, and the long drive belt went slack. The blade slowly spun to a stop along with the whine of the machinery. He looked at Tom, before asking gruffly, 'Can I help you?'

Tom moved forward and said, 'You might be able to. Me name's Tom Fields, and I got some trees that I would like sliced up inta floor planks.' The man moved towards Tom and put out his hand, 'I'm Jerome Whishart, and I'm the mill boss! Now, where are these logs of yours?'

'I got a parcel of land out near Blackmore. I got some big trees, and some not so big. I was wonderin' if I got 'em cut down if I could sell 'em to your mill. I'm buildin' me a house, and I need some planks for me floors and walls. So, I was wonderin' if we could come to some arrangement?'

Jerome pushed back his hat to reveal a mop of scraggly red hair. He held the rim of it as he proceeded to scratch his forehead.

'So, you got any idea of what sort of wood you got?'

'I got a hundred or more spotted gum, some great big ones. Then I got a few yellow boxes, and I got quite a lot of Black Butt. I'm open to suggestions as to how I can turn them inta a bit of money.'

The saw started up again, and they moved away from the noise.

Jerome said, 'If you can get your timber here, then we could do a deal. How many, and what size planks do you need?'

Tom thought for a moment before saying, 'I dunno, I got two rooms built now, and they be about ten-foot square each. I recken that I'm gunna build at least another three rooms sometime inta the future, so let's say that they are all the same size. That'd be about five rooms and a hallway down the middle.' He looked expectantly at Jerome for an answer.

'Well, just doin' me sums, roughly mind you, I recken that you will need about forty yards of timber for each floor. If I cut you about two hundred and fifty yards of wood that should get you sorted. I assume you ain't got any money, so I'm gunna need four logs from you. They must be about twenty feet long. It will take two trees to cut up what you want, and I will want two trees the same size as payment for cuttin' your planks. Does that sound orright to you? But don't forget, you gotta get em here to the mill!'

Tom replied, 'That sounds fair to me. I'm off to Sydney on the train tonight and won't be back for a few weeks, so I'm thinkin' that I should be able to get them trees knocked down in a couple a weeks, so I expect that the bullocky will get 'em here in about eight weeks' time if that's orright?' A handshake completed the deal, and Tom made his way to the station.

✱✱✱

He arrived home before lunchtime the next day, much to Hannah's surprise, and gave her an update on everything that he had done.

Doris was pleased to see her son and asked, 'How long are you here for son?'

'I was thinkin' that I might stay about a month. I'm going over to see Davin tomorrow.' Hannah broke into his conversation, 'Oh I forgot to tell you, Uncle Davin said that he had finished building our windmill, and that he was going to get Jack to take it up to you on his truck.'

Tom smiled, 'I was hopin' that he would have it finished before I went back. I'll go and see Jack tomorrow.

'I was gunna get it loaded onta the train, but if me brother can bring it up he could give me a hand to build it!'

Hannah leaned across the table, and placed her hand on Tom's. 'Does that mean that when the windmill is installed that I can come and stay?'

Tom frowned before saying, 'I want you to stay here Hani, at least until the baby is born, and maybe a while after that.' He saw the disappointment on her face, and before she could say anything, he said, 'Hani, I miss you so much, but I still got a long way to go before the house is liveable fer you and the baby. I ain't got the bathroom anywhere near finished, and we still ain't got no floor.' He explained about the deal that he had done with the mill boss. 'I am gunna chop down some trees, and they are gunna be turned into planks fer us.

'Hani, yer got no idea how cold it's gettin' of a night up there now. Our baby will freeze to death if we was to bring it up to the shack in the middle of winter. I gotta get the floors done. Our stove works a treat, but the kitchen is real draughty, and I gotta seal the walls so that we got at least one cosy room!'

Hannah listened, and she understood, but was still upset. 'I know what you are saying is right Tommy, but I'm busting my girdle to move there. I hate us being apart. How long do you think it will be before the house is ready? It doesn't have to be perfect, and I don't care if it only has two rooms. We can make it bigger as we need to.'

Tom stood up and had a stretch, 'If I can get Jack to spend a week helpin' me, then I reckon that it will only take us a few days to get the water pumpin'. When I got the water up to the house, I can fix up the bath and the privy. Mind you, I will hafta work fer a week just to buy the privy. I suspect that it will take me another couple a weeks to get that workin', and Bill showed me how to line the inside walls. I'm thinkin' that I should have the house sealed, and liveable in about eight to ten weeks after I go back. That's about the time that our baby should be getting' here.' He patted Hannah's swelling belly, and gave her a smile.

'Do you know how long you will be in confinement?'

'Brigid said that I should go to the hospital about a week before it's due, and then I think that I have to stay there for about three weeks.'

Hannah looked at Tom with concern and asked, 'You will be here when our baby is born won't you Tommy?'

'If you telephone Harriet a few days before you think that you will be goin' in, then I will catch the train down as soon as I can.

'I will take you home as soon as the weather starts to warm up. I'm thinkin' that by the end of winter, or early spring, the house should be ready.'

Doris asked, 'So what are your plans for the next few weeks son?'

'I will go and see Jack in the mornin', and then I thought I would go and say hello to Davin. I want to give him a couple a weeks' labour fer makin' our windmill. I believe that's only fair. I got no money to pay him, so depending on what he is doing I will work for free fer a couple of weeks to help him out.'

Hannah replied, 'Uncle Davin said that we didn't have to pay him anything for the windmill, but I know you Tommy Fields you won't be happy unless you give him something in return. He won't be happy with you, you know that, don't you?'

Tom smiled, 'Yeah I know, but this way I get to spend a bit of time with you before I go back. I can't see that I will be back after this. Not before the baby is born anyway. I really want to make a start on ploughing some ground by the spring. Once I got some spuds in the field, I can make a start on puttin' up some more fences. I gotta grow something that we can eat, and something that I can sell in town. So, spuds it is!

'I want to get a few sheep, and I need to have a couple of paddocks fer them to graze in. Bill said that he was gunna help me build up a bit of a flock over the next couple a years. You got no idea Hani, as to how many stones there are on our place. It's gunna take me awhile to clear 'em up.'

Doris was smiling, 'You should hear yourself, son, you're already starting to sound like a farmer.'

'I know Ma, but its somethin' that I wanna get me teeth into.'

***

Jack was getting busy at his fuel yard as the nights were getting colder, but as he could now afford the wages for a labourer to do the deliveries, he could afford to spend some time away.

Tom spent the next three weeks working at the forge, and now it was time for him to return to Jamison. The truck was loaded with the windmill and the associated piping, and it was time for them to go. Tom held Hannah, and both were feeling the pangs of loneliness, and knowing that there was nothing that either of them could do about it.

54.

Bleak Days

After arriving back at Jamison, they had wasted no time in erecting the windmill. They spent time arguing as to where it should be placed, but Bill had arrived and offered his advice on its positioning, and they gladly accepted it.

Jack had helped Tom chop down the four trees that the mill boss had asked for. The logs were dragged from the forest, and they were carefully placed onto the open ground before Jack had returned to Sydney. Herb had been contracted to take the logs to the mill, and a month later he came back with several tons of milled planks.

The next month was spent laying the floor, and building the bathroom that he had promised Hannah that she would have.

The days were getting shorter, and were generally bleak and misty. The darkness closed in early, as it was now full winter. It was impossible for Tom to chop down any more trees, as the ground in the forest was too wet and slippery for the horses.

He had never had the time to plough any ground. Now, with the rain falling intermittently he hitched the horses to his plough, and draped the long harness around his shoulders. He held the wooden handles and gave the reins a flick.

The horses lurched forward, and he almost stumbled as the rusty plough blade bit into the virgin ground. The horses strained, and the harness stretched as their shoulder muscles bulged, and their hooves fought to grip the flat, slippery ground.

They snorted, and their warm breath expelled through their nostrils like the steam from a boiling kettle. The pointed prow of the blade cut through the wet soil and furrowed it. At other times, the blade would catch on a rock, and the horses would snort and stamp the ground impatiently as their hind legs lowered and strained as they gave their all to move it.

The misty rain fell lightly, and the air was cold and bitter. At times the sleet flew horizontally, and it stung his face like a hundred pinpricks. He fought the urge to go inside and sit at his fireside.

He ploughed the furrows towards the south, and used the dim outline of a tree on the horizon as his guide. The plough blade furrowed deeply into the wet, soggy soil until it struck another rock. Then he dug around before he could wrestle it free from the sticky mud. He hung onto the worn handles of the plough with frozen hands. Then it faltered again, as it bit through scrubby tree roots before stalling against a bigger rock, and he gave out another curse.

Some furrows took him an hour to dig, while others took longer. His legs ached, as the sticky mud built up on his boots and trousers, and his mind flashed back to the muddy fields of France. The grains of dirt inside his boots tore at his skin, and rubbed blisters on his feet. And as the darkness closed in around him, he turned to the shelter of his home.

He unharnessed his horses within the confines of the small stable. Their withers were covered in foam and mud, as he dragged out several bales of hay to feed them from where they were stored under the tarpaulin. The light was almost gone, and with a mud-laden, aching body he made his way inside his house. His frozen fingers fumbled with the matches as he lit the hurricane lamp. He cupped his hands around the glass in an effort to restore some warmth to them. The fire in the stove had burnt out hours earlier, and he quickly filled the hearth with dry kindling.

The crackling of the fire in the hearth lifted his spirits, and he lit the two kerosene lamps that hung from the ceiling before he stripped off his sodden clothes. His hands were now blistered and stinging, but he felt satisfied. He hadn't eaten since breakfast, and the hunger pangs were now gnawing at him. He had some old damper stored inside a biscuit tin, and as he chewed on it he opened a can of beans to go with it. After eating, he loaded up the fire, and placed a four-gallon kerosene tin filled with water over the firebox. An hour later he was scrubbing himself clean in his barely warm bath.

He draped his wet clothes over the back of his kitchen chair, and placed them to dry before the stove. He was asleep moments after he put his head upon the straw-filled flour sack that was his pillow.

Tom ploughed his field from sunrise to sunset over the next seven days. Then he cross-ploughed his furrows, and after ripping over around twenty acres, he decided that he would concentrate on clearing that area before he ploughed up any more. He had no idea how much land he would need to turn over. All that he was focused upon was to plough his virgin fields for the first time, and hoping that it would get easier as the rocks were removed.

⁕⁕⁕

The early light filtered through the small bedroom window. Tom had woken feeling cold, and his body ached. The air felt colder than normal, and his swag didn't prevent the cold seeping up through the floor on which he lay. He quickly dressed, and prodded the fire back to life before making his way to the bathroom to undertake his morning ablutions. He glanced at the window, but it was completely frosted over with condensation. He wiped the window with his sleeve and stared outside. The ground was covered in snow. The paddocks had disappeared into an eerie white fog, and icicles hung from the window frame. He stared through the frosted glass, and the ground was layered white for as far as he could see.

The weather had deteriorated during the night, and the snow had fallen softly to lie heavily on the ground. Bill had told him that it did occasionally snow up in the hills above Blackmore, but he hadn't expected to see much more than a little sleet. As he had ploughed his field, the pile of rocks had grown larger. He knew that he should stack them in one location, and as he looked across his snow-covered fields he decided that today would be as good as any to move them.

He didn't have a thick coat, and he knew that if he couldn't keep warm when outside, then he would probably not survive the day. He had a few hessian potato sacks, and he needed to make himself a coat of some sort, but before he did that he would make some damper, and have half for his breakfast and the rest for his dinner.

He mixed the flour and salt with a cup of water, and placed the mixture into the now hot oven. He checked his larder, as his supplies were getting low. He had two eggs and several cans of beans, along with a little flour. He knew that unless he caught a couple of rabbits, he would have to make a trip to town very soon.

While the damper was cooking, Tom made his way out to the stable. The horses gave a snort, and waited patiently as Tom dragged out several bales of hay for them. He gathered up the hessian sacks, and some baling twine and took them back inside. His boots crunched upon the frozen ground, and for a short period he was tempted to stoke his fire up and spend the day in front of it.

After eating his meagre breakfast, he set about making a coat. He joined the ends of two sacks with baling twine and left enough room to poke his head through. He had seen the canvas ponchos that the officers had worn during the war, and his potato sacks would be made similarly. He roughly sewed the third bag across the shoulders to give a little extra protection and to cover his upper arms.

He needed to gather and stack the rocks, and his mind went back to the war. He remembered how some wounded soldiers had been dragged behind a horse on a makeshift stretcher as they were transported to the field hospital. He had cut some long saplings weeks earlier to use as supports for the roof extension of his next room, and he tied several together with wire, and attached them to either side of his saddle. He would load the rocks upon his stretcher, and drag them behind his horse to where he could stack them.

The snow had stopped falling by the time that he had saddled up one of his horses and adjusted the stretcher. Little black mounds of dirt from the furrows contrasted starkly against the white snow.

He moved along the furrows, and kept moving the rocks, even when the snow started falling again and his sweat dried cold upon his skin beneath his sackcloth coat. It was early afternoon when the light began to fade, and he heard the shout from across the paddock.

Bill Murdoch was sat on his horse, and was beckoning to Tom.

Tom was exhausted, and he didn't need any prompting to return to the house. Bill had disappeared inside, and his horse was already in the stable by the time that Tom had reached it.

He trudged his way inside. Smoke was billowing from the chimney by the time that he got there as Bill had stoked up his fire.

The sack coat was saturated, as was the calico shirt that he was wearing. Bill turned Tom towards the fire in the hearth.

'You need to get out of these clothes man, before you freeze to death!' Tom's teeth had started to chatter, and his frozen fingers fumbled with the buttons on his shirt. He rummaged through his kitbag, and dragged out some dry clothes as he shivered uncontrollably.

Bill was loading firewood into the grate in an attempt to generate more heat from the stove as Tom had struggled from his wet clothes. He held his hands almost to the top of the stove in an attempt to thaw them out.

Bill looked at Tom before saying, 'Whatever were you thinking of man, working out in this weather?' He didn't wait for an answer before continuing, 'I was going to come over yesterday, but I had a problem with one of the horses. It's a good job that I come when I did, and Dot sent some tucker over for you.'

Bill placed the billycan onto the stove. 'It's full of rabbit stew. Dot thought that you could probably use a good feed. Oh, by the way, I forgot the reason for my trip. Your mother telephoned the night before last. She said that Hannah was due at any time, and that it might be a good idea if you got yourself home.'

Tom smiled, 'I was only thinking that she must be getting close to her time just the other day. I suppose that now is as good a time as any fer me to go home. I can't do no more around here until this weather fines up a bit. At least I got a few acres cleared and dug over, and all I gotta do now is plant somethin' in them!'

Bill said, 'I thought that you were gunna grow spuds. It's a bit cold at the moment, but you should have them planted by October. That gives you about six weeks to get them in the ground.'

Tom was thinking, and replied, 'I hafta buy some first. How long before they grow? I need a cash crop, and do yer have any idea as to how many spuds I will need to plant to start me crop?' Bill replied, 'Last year I got about a pound for a ton of potatoes. I'm not too sure, but I think that I had to grow about twelve bags of spuds to make a ton. That's hard work to grow a few tons of spuds, and I hardly broke even. Mind you, we didn't have no help. There was only the three of us, and we spent a few days diggin' them up before we could start bagging them up.

'I s'pose it must have taken us about a week in total to dig and bag up two tons. Then we carted them into town, and then they had to be sent by train to the Sydney market. So, two tons of spuds give me about two quid, less the five bob it cost to get them to Sydney.

'Whatever you grow son, it's gonna cost you money! Sheep is a better option, but you have to build up a flock, and that takes time.

'Even with a good flock you still have to get the shearers in, and pay them before you can sell your wool.'

Tom looked unhappy, as he stirred the stew that was now simmering on the stove. 'After today, it's just dawned on me as to how hard this farming lark is!'

Bill packed his pipe and lit it before asking, 'You havin' second thoughts? I don't think anyone said that it would be easy. If you can get over the first couple of years you should be able to make it. The problem with farming son is that it gets a hold on you. There's something about living on the land. I can't explain it. Maybe it's the satisfaction that you get when you plant something, and then you harvest it, or watching your sheep dropping lambs in the early spring.

'Farmin's not just one thing son, it's lots of things! It can bring a smile to your face, or it can make a grown man cry. Maybe it's because every day is a new day, and you never know what it will bring. Then there's the weather. It rains when you don't want it to, and when you want it to rain it generally doesn't. If farmin' has taught me one thing son, it's that you just have to take one day at a time, and accept the things that happen. If you can't do that, then you will never be a farmer!

'You been working hard son. You've achieved a lot since you been here. You built your house, and got some fencin' done. You're just tired. You need to have a good feed, and a long sleep. Go home and meet your new child, and then you will find the motivation to keep going!'

Bill looked out the window at the grey sky. 'I'd better get a move on. It will be dark in less than an hour, so I had better get going. Call in on your way to town. You can leave both the horses, and Harriet can drive you to the station. Then you can telephone us, and let us know when you are coming home. Enjoy your dinner son.'

Tom thanked him for the food and the advice, and then watched from the door as he rode away.

55.

The Arrival

Doris had gone to the Post Office, and placed the long-distance call to the Murdoch farm. She asked that the message be passed on to Tom about the imminent birth of his child.

Tom had completed the building of another room. The floor was laid with freshly milled timber, and the walls were now lined with plaster mix. The windmill was standing proudly on the brow of the hill, and the pump was bringing up water from the dam to the kitchen and bathroom.

***

Hannah was feeling more uncomfortable with each passing day. She arrived at the hospital after being advised by Brigid that she would be better off there, rather than giving birth at home. Doris and Claire accompanied her. She was feeling nervous, and her imagination had been running wild. She had heard the many stories of women dying during labour. It wasn't the thought of dying that was really bothering her, but rather of not seeing Tom, and being able to hold and kiss him before she went to the hospital.

She had asked Doris a dozen times if she was sure that Tom had received the message about her being almost at her time. Doris patiently told her again. 'Stop worrying luvvy; he will be here as soon as he can. Why he might be on his way over here as we speak.

'If he doesn't arrive today, then I'm sure that he will be here tomorrow at the latest.'

Brigid had told her that she should expect to have her baby at any time, and within a few hours Hannah felt the tightness around her protruding belly. Hannah's contractions quickly escalated, and with each new contraction she moaned louder, until finally her water broke.

After four hours, she gave a final push and a scream as Brigid took hold of the baby. The nurse cut the umbilical cord, and Brigid gently massaged the baby's tiny chest and rubbed the souls of its feet. Several long seconds passed, before there was a raspy squeak, followed by a tiny wail as the baby gasped its first breath. The nurse wiped away the grey mucus, and wrapped the tiny bundle in a soft cloth. Hannah, with her hair bedraggled, and spattered with body fluid took her baby from the nurse. 'What is it?' she asked.

Brigid smiled and said, 'It's a little boy. You have a son.'

'Is he all right?' Please tell me that he's all right Brigid, is he?'

Brigid bent down, and moved the wrap from across the baby's face. 'He is very small, but he has all of his fingers and toes, and he is breathing well. His head is normal, and I think that he is perfectly healthy. I will get the nurse to bring some warm water, and she will clean you up and we can get you into a clean nightdress. After that, I will show you how to feed your little man, and then you can get some sleep!'

✻✻

Hannah woke and saw Tom sitting beside her bed. He smiled and said, 'Hello sleepyhead. I thought that you were going to sleep all day.' He leant over the bed, and gave her a kiss on the cheek.

'Have you seen him, have you seen our son yet?' asked Hannah.

Tom looked towards the cane basket. 'Yes, I seen him. He isn't very big, and he's makin' some funny squeakin' noises, but Brigid says that's normal fer babies to sound like that.'

'Tommy, are you happy?' She looked at his face as she asked the question.

'Yes Hani, I'm thrilled. Have you decided what his name is gunna be yet?'

'I thought that we might call him Jimmy. I was thinking that we would call him Jack. He has helped us so much, and he has been so good to us.

'I thought that he might be happy knowing that we have named our baby after him. But then I thought of your little brother Jimmy.

'I know that nobody talks about him, because he died such a long time ago, but your mother mentioned Jimmy to me a while ago. She told me about how he got sick, and I thought that we could name our little one after him. If you would rather that we called him something else, then I won't mind.'

'Nar, Jimmy is good, and me brother won't mind, and Ma will be happy.'

Hannah asked, 'Have you held our son yet?'

'No, me mum was holdin' him when I arrived and you was asleep. Then Claire arrived, and they kept nursin' him between each other. I'll get to nurse him when we get home.'

'Oh Tommy, go and pick him up now, he won't bite you I promise!' Tom smiled sheepishly.

'I'm a bit nervous; I haven't ever held a baby before. I'm a bit scared that I might drop him.'

'Oh Tommy, don't be silly. You won't drop him, now just pick him up and give him a cuddle.'

56.

Clarence Homer

Clarence Homer had arrived back from the war a different man than when he had left. He was the last, and the youngest of eight brothers to leave the dirt farm where they had grown up on the outskirts of Bathurst.

His mother had borne ten children to her husband Ned over twelve years. She had all but given up hope of having a daughter, but then her last two babies were both girls.

Clarence had watched as each of his brothers had left the farm to join up and go off to the war, and one by one they had said goodbye. He was still at home when the khaki-coloured motorcar had driven up the dusty driveway and stopped outside the house for the first time.

'Are you Mrs Homer?' the young man asked through the window of his car.

'Yes,' was all that she could manage as her heart weighed heavy within her chest; she already knew what he was there to tell her.

The young corporal stepped from the car, and handed her a small brown envelope. He was young, and had trouble making eye contact with the woman who could have been his mother. He gave a weak salute, before turning around and almost running back to his car.

Clarence remembered that his mother had cried after she had opened the envelope that had informed her of which of her sons had been killed at Gallipoli.

Over the next eighteen months, the army car had called at the house and delivered another six envelopes. She didn't cry after the second envelope had been opened and read.

His mother was staunchly religious, and she had come to the conclusion that she would sacrifice all of her sons to a war that she didn't understand if that was what God had wanted. She would never understand why God would take her sons. She would say a rosary each evening before she retired, and take solace in thinking that her sons were now safe within the bosom of the Lord.

Clarence was just fifteen when Harry, his oldest brother, packed his swag and kissed his mother goodbye saying, 'Cheerio'. He was never seen again. Three years later, Clarence followed in his brother's footsteps and went off to the war.

The last thing that Clarence remembered was being up to his waist in muddy water. The shells had been exploding all around his troop of twenty men. They had all taken cover in the crater when the shrapnel bomb had exploded nearby. The chunks of screaming metal had torn the life from all of those around him, but Clarence had woken up in the field hospital with bandages covering his head and his left hand.

The war was still raging three months later when the doctors had signed his discharge papers.

They read,

'Discharged due to brain injury. Long-term prognosis is poor, and the patient will suffer from a mental impairment that will possibly see the patient institutionalised into the future.'

There was no mention of the three fingers missing from his left hand.

✻✻✻

Clarence had returned back to his parents' farm a year after he had left. His mother had aged far beyond her fifty-five years. She gave him a hug, but not a joyous one. It was as though she was scared to show her emotions, in case he too would die and leave her. She spoke softly saying, 'Welcome home son, it's been a bit quiet around here since you all left.' That's all that she had said before turning and returning inside.

Clarence felt that his mother was admonishing him, as though it were his fault that all of his brothers had been killed. His youngest sister Lucy gave him a peck on the cheek, and said, 'I never thought that you would come home, don't think Ma thought so, neither.'

Clarence smiled; they had never been a close family. They were just simple people who had always accepted their lot. As children, when they had complained about being hungry, their father would always say, 'Be grateful for what you got, cause it's a lot more than most folks have.'

Clarence asked, 'Where's Nellie?' Lucy looked at her brother with surprise, 'I thought you knew! Nellie run away with a travellin' salesman almost a year ago. We ain't heard a peep from her since she left. She broke father's heart. Mind you, she was always his favourite!' She said it with a little sarcasm.

Clarence looked at his sister, 'I never got no letters. You never writ to me. I got one letter from Ma in all the time that I was away. I never really expected ya to write. Where's the old man? I ain't seen him around.'

'Father is out boundary-ridin'. He doesn't come home much now. Ma gives him a tongue-lashing nearly every time that he comes home. She doesn't say much, but I think that she blames him for the boys.'

Her voice trailed off slightly, 'You know how they went off one by one, and she sorta blames father for that!'

Clarence was making swirls in the dirt with the toe of his boot.

'Why would she blame him? We all wanted ta go. They was all old enough ta go without him havin' ta sign our papers. I was the only one that had ta get the papers signed, and Ma signed 'em. Anyway, what's happenin' around here? Don't look like there's bin much work carried out fer awhile.' Clarence turned, and saw the fallen fence posts, and the dried weeds lining what used to be his mother's garden.

'Father doesn't do much since Timothy died. We been waitin' for the notice to vacate. I'm surprised that we haven't got it yet. He's been dead for about a year, and other than one letter from a solicitor, we ain't heard nothing from no one.' She looked at her brother before asking, 'You wasn't plannin' on staying, were ya?'

Clarence took out his tobacco pouch and rolled a smoke. He squinted as the smoke curled around his eyes. 'How about ya start at the beginning. I don't know no Timothy, and what notice is ya talkin' about?'

Lucy looked at her brother and laughed, 'Of course you know Timothy. He was always out here before the war.

'Him and father were partners when they were gold prospecting. You must remember the story about them both, you must!' She frowned at her brother. 'What's the matter with you? You haven't been gone for that long that you can't remember.'

Clarence looked at his sister, and he wasn't smiling. 'I dunno what's the matter with me. I got something wrong in me head. The doctors said that I still had a bit of steel or somethin' left inside me head. I was in the hospital in France fer a long time, and when I got out I had trouble remembering things.

'I know what day it is, most of the time, but then I can't even remember if I had me breakfast. Stuff like that. So, no, I can't remember Timothy. Do ya wanna remind me? And what's this about havin' to vacate? I always thought that Pa owned this place. I got nowhere else ta go. That's why I come home. This is me home. We bin here all our lives. I thought that I could help with the stock, and do a bit of work. Are ya sayin' that I gotta go?'

Lucy was serious now; 'I never knew that you got hurt. Nobody from the army ever come, unless it was just to tell us that one of the boys was dead. Ma isn't well. Most of the time she just sits and prays with her rosary beads. I dunno where we will go after they kick us off here. I was thinking of going to the city and getting a job somewhere. Every time that I make up me mind to pack up and go I think of Ma. I can't just leave her and father. I know that father would be happy being out in the bush, but Ma couldn't live in a tent. I know that the house ain't too flash, but it's better than living under canvas!'

Clarence asked his sister, 'Ya say that this Timothy is dead. What's he got ta do with this place?'

Lucy took her brother's hand, and led him inside like a child. 'Sit down; I will make a cup of tea. Are you hungry? I got some fresh drippin' in the icebox. I cooked up some muttonchops last night, and I made a loaf of bread. I can make you a sandwich if you want?'

'I could do with a bite of somethin'. I ain't eaten since last night. Well, not that I can remember anyway. Show me where ya keep the bread, and I'll take a slab fer meself. I haven't had drippin' since I left home, I don't think.'

Lucy gave the ashes in the stove a poke, and placed the kettle to the centre of the stove. Clarence looked around the small kitchen as though it was the first time that he had seen it. His mother was sat in a chair in the corner with her eyes closed.

Her hands were clasped on her lap, and she was holding her rosary beads. Lucy made the tea, and Clarence ate his bread and dripping.

'Are ya gunna tell me about what's-his-name?'

'Timothy, that was his name. Timothy Backhouse. Father had told us the story of when they met. Father was young, and he had gone off to the goldfields. He told Ma, that when he come back he would have his fortune, and then they would marry. Ma's parents were very strict, and our grandfather who we never met was a parson, or a priest, or somethin'.

'Well Pa and Timothy scratched around the old diggings for a few years. They found a few specks of gold, but not enough to make them rich. Father had run out of money and missed Ma. So, he came back to Hillston. That's where Ma lived in them days with her parents! According to Timothy, it wasn't long after father left that he found a vein of gold. That's when he decided to help Pa out, and he bought this property. Timothy weren't much of a farmer, but he was happy for father to run the place. They built this old house, and we were all brought up here, as ya know.

'Father said that Timothy never charged him a penny in rent in all the time that we lived here. But, Timothy bought a pub in Bathurst, and then he bought the Emporium. I dunno what else he owned. Anyway, he died. Musta been about a year ago. That's when we got the solicitor's letter tellin' us that we would hafta leave. We never got another letter from no one. We keep waitin', but nobody's come ta kick us off yet, so we just stayed here. Ma hasn't ever been herself since the boys went. She goes crook at father every time that he comes home. Ma gave up with lookin' after her little garden. She said that she didn't see no point in growin' anything cause everything dies!'

She looked at her brother, but didn't bother to lower her voice as she said, 'Ma's been slowly dying inside, ever since Harry was killed, and every one of them other army letters bein' delivered took a piece of her. She never speaks of the boys, or you! It's like she don't want to acknowledge that she had all these children, and there's only three of us left. Might as well be just two of us now, cause we won't probably never hear from Nellie again.'

Lucy gave a quick glance at her mother, who was rolling her rosary beads through her fingers and quietly praying.

Clarence thought for a few moments, and considered his words carefully before he spoke. 'I dunno what I'll do now. I always had this thing in me mind that I would just come back here and spend me days farmin'. I don't like cities; I don't even like big towns.

'I was expectin' to see a few improvements around here, but it just looks all neglected now.'

Clarence walked out into the sunlight before rolling another cigarette. He stared over the dry, weed-infested land, and he had trouble remembering what the farm had looked like. He vaguely remembered that his mother had grown vegetables and a few flowers in the front garden. He drew back deeply on his smoke and exhaled. His mind was confused, and he was now trying to come to terms with what he should do.

Lucy said, 'You can still sleep in the shed. The bunks are still there, and nobody's used them except for a couple of shearers. I can't say when father will be back, but when he comes home, he sleeps out in the bunkhouse. Are you gunna hang around for a few days?'

'Yeah, I got nowhere to go. I was looking forward to settling down here, but if ya gotta vacate then there is no point in me hanging around.'

Lucy exclaimed, 'Oh, I forgot. There is a letter here for you. It looks official. It musta come about two months ago. I just gotta remember where I put it. I was gunna send it back, cause I never thought that you would come home.' She went inside and returned shortly after.

'I stuck it on the mantle!' She handed the brown envelope to her brother and watched him intently as he read it. Clarence read slowly, and when he finished reading it he frowned.

'What's it say, what's it say?' asked Lucy, excited now by the intrigue of the contents of the letter.

'Who's it from?' she asked before Clarence had responded to her first question. He kept looking at the letter as he replied to his sister's questioning.

'It's from the Army. I don't understand it properly, but I think that they wanna give me some land of me own. Here, you read it and see if you can make any sense out of it.' He thrust the letter at his sister. She read it slowly, and then again. 'Yep, it sure sounds like you're right. You have to reply back to them though. When was it dated?'

He looked at the black franking that covered the one-penny stamp. It was dated the 22nd April 1920. 'It's orright; they only posted it three months ago. I still got time to send it back.'

✱✱✱

Clarence replied to the letter, and filled in the section that gave the land options with, 'Doesn't matter'. Then he promptly posted it.

57.

The Move

Hannah had been excited all week. She was finally moving, but along with the excitement was a sense of sadness. Doris, Claire and Davin had all put on brave faces, but as the time of their departure had grown closer, the conversations had become strained.

Jack had loaded up his truck with the things that would accompany them to Jamison, and he had departed early. It would take him a day and a half to drive there. Doris had scrounged two chairs, and a rickety table from an elderly neighbour along with several dented pots and pans. Tom had also asked the storekeeper if he could have a few ply tea chests that were stacked in abundance at the rear of his shop. The tea was packed into the chests in Ceylon, and sold by the pound in stores and emporiums across the country. When empty, they would usually be chopped up as firewood, and sold for a shilling a wheelbarrow full, or sixpence each. Stacked sideways, and laid on top of each other made them useful as storage shelves.

More cars were now appearing on the streets, and Davin had concluded that the motorcar would eventually replace the horse.

He was still shoeing horses, but that side of his business had declined as those with jobs could buy a car on the time payment scheme. Davin had purchased a car, along with lessons on how to drive and start the contraption, and he drove them all to the station to see them off.

Just before they boarded the train, Tom said to his mother, 'As soon as we can arrange it, I will get one of those telephone gadgets installed at our place. And Ma, we have arranged a little surprise for you too.' Doris wiped her eyes and looked at Tom, but before she could ask he said, 'Ma, Jack is arranging for a telephone to be installed into your house too. The Post Master General's people said that it would be installed sometime in the next three months. But when you have your telephone, and we have ours we can talk to each other whenever we like.'

Tom and Hannah looked at Doris to see her reaction, 'Oh Son, that will be wonderful. I will still write, but to be able to hear your voices will just gladden my heart.'

Davin looked at Claire and he said, 'Maybe we could arrange to get one too darlin'. What do you think?'

Claire replied, 'It would be nice if we could all talk with each other occasionally. I will miss you all terribly, but if I can hear your voices every now and then, it won't feel as though you are so far away.' They said their goodbyes amidst the tears, the steam and the smoke, and as the train pulled slowly away from the platform, they kept waving their handkerchiefs until it was out of sight.

⁂

The journey had taken longer than expected due to a breakdown along the line, and by the time that the train had arrived at Bathurst Hannah was exhausted.

Harriet was standing on the platform as the train squealed and creaked to a halt. She ran to embrace Hannah as they got off.

'Well show him to me! I have been waiting so long to see him.'

She took the baby from Hannah and smothered him with kisses. 'Mother and I are so looking forward to having you here as neighbours. Oh, hello Tom! I forgot to say welcome home, and you are home now and we couldn't be happier!'

With the luggage stowed, Harriet drove them back to the farm where they received a rousing welcome from Bill and Dorothy, which was followed by a late lunch. Tom was now anxious to get back to the farm. 'I don't suppose that you have seen me brother go by, have you?'

Bill replied, 'He hasn't called in here as yet; mind you, he may have come in from the Blackmore Road. Was he bringing your things up?'

'Yes, I thought that he might have beat us here because the train was so late. If you don't mind Bill, I think that we should get home while we still have some light. I want to show Hani what I been doin', and I will need to get the fire goin'. I'm sure that it still gets cold of a night.'

'Too right it does son. I'll take you now, it will only take half an hour!' They said their goodbyes with promises of returning soon.

***

With the sun sitting low in the sky, and with no more than an hour of daylight left, Hannah stood in front of the small house and smiled.

'Oh Tommy, it's beautiful. Our own little house!' Tom beamed as he opened the door. They stood inside the kitchen, and she looked around. The setting sun filtered through the window, and filled the room with its orange glow.

Tom looked expectantly at Hannah and asked, 'Well, what do you think? I know that it's small, but it's cosy. Here, have a look at the bedroom.' He ushered her to the doorway. 'We ain't got a door on it yet,' as he stated the obvious. Hannah looked around the tiny room and she was still smiling.

'Oh darling, you must have worked so hard. It's bigger than what we had at your mother's. I just hope that Jack turns up tonight with our bed, because it will be awfully cramped if we have to sleep together in that.' She nodded at the makeshift bed that Tom had been sleeping on. The bed consisted of two long poles tied together at the ends by two smaller ones. A rope had been crisscrossed around the frame, and several potato sacks lay across the rope.

Tom looked sheepishly at Hannah, 'I didn't put a lot of effort into makin' it, but it's fairly comfortable. I used ta drag it out in front of the fire when it was really cold, and I slept like a baby. If Jack ever gets here, I can get our bed set up, but he better be here soon.'

The baby started to cry, and Hannah said, 'He needs to be fed, and I will have to change him. Bring the suitcases in, can you Tommy? I need somewhere to sit.'

Tom dragged the cases inside, and then set about making a fire. Hannah attended to the needs of Jimmy, and then Tom exclaimed, 'I haven't shown you the bathroom. I hope that it's orright!'

It was just on dark, when they heard the crunching of the gearbox, as Jack coaxed his truck past the dam, and up the rise to stop outside the house.

'Thought that ya must have got lost,' Tom smiled at his brother.

'Well, you got that right sport. I did! I took the wrong turn at Blackmore, and I must have been three miles down the road when I realised that I was goin' the wrong way. Anyway, I'm here now, don't s'pose ya got a cold beer in there?' He nodded towards the house.

Hannah said, 'No, I'm sorry Jack, I'll make sure that we have some for you the next time that you come. Mind you, we will have to buy an icebox first. I'll make you a nice cup of tea, and then I will boil you a couple of eggs. We haven't many supplies just yet, but Dot gave us some fresh eggs, will that do?'

'Eggs will be good Hannah. I could eat a horse right now. I didn't stop in Blackmore. I was tempted to call into the pub there, but I was runnin' late, so I just kept drivin', that was until I got lost. Anyway, I need a kero light outside, so we can see what we are doin'!' They unloaded the truck by lamplight, and spent their first night together in the new house.

***

The days rushed by and became weeks, and the land was cultivated and paddocks were fenced. Then springtime blended into summer, and their first meagre crop of potatoes along with a few pumpkins was harvested.

***

They woke one morning to the distant sounds of muffled explosions. Tom stood at his door and rolled a smoke. He wasn't too sure where the sound of the explosions was coming from. Then, as he listened, he heard them again.

Hannah held Jimmy, and stood beside Tom. 'What is it?' Tom listened again before he spoke, 'It's too loud for gunfire, but someone is blowin' up somethin', and it isn't that far away. Sounds like its comin' from the south. I think I'll saddle up, and go and take a look.'

'Be careful Tommy!'

'I'll be orright; it might be the government people makin a new road, or somethin'. Anyway, I'll go over and have a look.' He gave Hannah a kiss on her cheek before climbing onto his horse. He rode down towards his gully where he had been chopping the trees. He stopped again, and listened. The explosions appeared to be further off to his left. He leant forward into his saddle, as his horse picked its way through the bracken and up the incline on the other side.

He reached the top of the rise, and he could just see the distant smoke from the chimneys at Blackmore. The barren hills stretched away from him into the hazy, grey blue distance, but about half a mile away in the valley below, he noticed the solitary figure scrambling about at the base of a gum tree.

Tom could not make out what the stranger was doing. He watched as he stood, and then started running away from where he had been a few moments earlier. Tom was about to ride down to the lowland to where the stranger was, but then he saw the puff of smoke a second before he heard the explosion. The giant tree shook, and its branches gave a shiver, and then it tottered for a moment before it leant over and crashed to the ground. The trunk hit the ground, and then bounced before settling in a cloud of dust and debris.

Tom nudged his horse's flanks with his heels, and pointed him in the direction of the valley. The stranger looked up, and saw Tom riding his way. He stopped what he was doing, and took his pipe from his waistcoat pocket. Tom rode towards him and nodded.

'G'day, how ya doin'? I heard the explosions from the other side of the hill,' He nodded towards the rise, and climbed off his horse. He threw the reins over the broken branches of the felled tree. He put his hand forward, before saying, 'How do ya do, me name's Tom Fields, and I own the land on the top of the hill and down the other side.'

The stranger came forward, and took Tom's hand before shaking it vigorously. 'Me name's Clarence, Clarence Homer. I just got this block from the government. Gunna take me six months just ta clear it, before I can start puttin' a plough through it. I never seen it before last week. I was a soldier, and the government is givin' all this land away to soldiers, well, retired soldiers like me. If I knowed that it had all these trees on it, I wouldn't 'ave taken it.

'Dunno, how they expect a fella to do all this work, and make a livin' as well! Good job I was raised on a farm, so I got some idea what ta do. Anyway, it's mine now, so I'll just hav'ta do me best. I bin camped here fer a week now. I had to wait till I could get me gelignite and fuses together. It's the quickest way I know to drop these big bastards.' He looked at the dozen trees that were already on the ground.

Tom smiled, 'I was in the army too. That's how we got our block. Mind you, it ain't as scrubby as yours is. What outfit was ya with?'

Clarence thought for a moment before saying, 'Yer know what? I ain't real sure. I think it was the 64th, but I might be wrong.'

Tom gave Clarence a puzzled look, and Clarence continued, 'I forget things. I got hit in the head with a lump of shrapnel in France.

'I know all me mates in the hole with me was killed, but I don't remember nothin' after that.' Clarence spoke matter-of-factly. Tom rolled a smoke and listened to him. 'I was in the hospital in France somewhere fer a long time. Some days, I wake up, and me head's real good. I can remember me name and stuff. But then, sometimes I dunno who I am. Ain't nuthin' I can do about it. I'm still better off than me mates though!' For a moment, Clarence was somewhere else as his mind wandered, but then Tom's voice brought him back to reality.

'Wada ya like to be called, Clarence or Clarry?'

'Ar, I don't mind, I bin called useless, and all sorts of other things, so call me Clarry if ya have a mind to.'

Tom smiled, he liked his new neighbour. He liked his down-to-earth honesty, and he liked the thought that he had another neighbour nearby.

'So, where are ya camped, Clarry?'

Clarry looked around, 'I got meself a tent set up about a half-mile down the road. I'm supposed ta build meself a house somehow. I got a letter somewhere. It told me what I gotta do. All these blessed instructions on it. The first thing I gotta do is get these bloody trees down. Then I'll burn the stumps out so ya might smell a bit of smoke fer a month or so. I'm gunna live in me tent fer a while. I grew up on the other side of Bathurst on a farm, and the old man, well he's got some machinery that I can use. He's got a harrow, an' a plough, and when I got all these stumps burnt, I'll get the bullocky to bring 'em over fer me.'

Tom looked around, and he knew that Clarence would have at least a year's work before he would be in a position to put a crop into the ground.

'Well, it's been nice to meet you Clarry. I just come over to be nosy and see what all the noise was about. Now, if yer follow the road,' Tom nodded toward the Blackmore road, 'and you turn left at your front gate, that will take you directly to our place. You will see the windmill on the top of the hill. Now, you come over and have a feed with us sometime, and if yer need a hand with anything that ya can't handle just come and get me. I'd better be getting' back. I left the missus wonderin' what was goin' on.'

Tom climbed into the saddle, gave Clarry a nod, and then rode home.

58.

Desmond

Although Des enjoyed working in the Botanical Gardens, he was still restless. His mates had gone to live in various parts of the state, and he was missing the camaraderie of his days in the army.

On the weekends when he wasn't working, and Brigid was at the hospital delivering babies, he would catch a tram and go out to Randwick. Randwick was the major horse-racing track in Sydney, and was a hive of activity every Saturday. Des wasn't a betting man, but he had always liked horses. As the horses raced around the oval track to the cheers of the punters, Des could usually be found talking to the stable hands, or the trainers. He had gotten to know many of them as he saw them regularly. Part of his gardening duties was to drive a large wagon out to the racecourse and load it with stable manure. It would take two draught horses to pull the fully loaded wagon, and when it was full he would return it to the gardens to be used as fertiliser.

Des had spent several hours loading the cart, and was returning to the gardens. Shortly after leaving the racetrack, he noticed that one of his horses had developed a limp. It was mid-morning, and the road was quiet.

Des climbed down, and lifted the front leg of the horse that had gone lame to check the hoof. He spoke quietly as he lifted up the leg.

'Now Winkles, let's have a look at what the problem is.' He poked around the hoof and kept talking. 'It looks like you have picked up a pebble or something lad!'

He always spoke to the horses as though they were human. Des opened his pocketknife to remove the offending item, and balanced the horse's hoof above his own knee.

'Now, what have you got here lad? Ah, there it is. I'll soon have that out, and you'll be as right as rain.'

He was absorbed in his work, and he didn't take any notice of the motorcar clattering and weaving its way along the wide dirt road towards them.

The other horse, that went by the name of Wally, was stamping the ground impatiently and snorting as Des worked. Des was still on the road, and he had not bothered to tether his animals as they usually stood where the wagon stopped. The horses were now restless, as the motorcar drove erratically from behind them and came closer.

The driver was almost next to the wagon, when he gave a blast from the vehicle's klaxon horn. Wally reared up in fright to the extent of his harness, and that in turn spooked Winkles, who now lurched forward and caused Des to stumble. He dropped his knife and had time to yell, 'Steady boy,' as he tried to grab the halter and let go of the horse's leg. The horses, now fully spooked by the sound of the horn, lurched forward and knocked Des to the ground. As they panicked, Des had fallen and the big hooves crushed his face, before the fully laden wagon was dragged across his prone body crushing the life from him.

A crowd gathered. The wagon had stopped, and someone had hitched the reins to a fence. Des lay dead on the gravel, and a pool of blood formed around him. The police arrived, along with the black mortuary wagon. They asked questions, and it was ascertained that the deceased worked at the Botanical Gardens.

Constable Colin Wotherspoon, of the Randwick area police station, was given the task of finding the relatives of the deceased.

He was told that the deceased's name was Desmond Carney, and that he was married with a wife who worked at the Barracks Hospital.

Brigid had just delivered another baby, and was about to take a break when Matron Fisher found her. She called out, 'Oh Mrs Carney, could I please have a word?'

Brigid looked at matron, who wore a troubled look, and to the policeman standing by her side.

'Yes matron, what is it?'

Matron Fisher spoke quietly to Brigid. 'Mrs Carney, the constable would like to have a word with you if you don't mind. You may use my office.' She then nodded in the direction and walked away.

Constable Wotherspoon looked uncomfortable, but asked, even though he knew the answer, 'Are you Mrs Carney, and are you the wife of a Desmond Carney?'

Brigid was worried now; her voice rose slightly. 'Yes, why do you ask, has something happened?'

Constable Wotherspoon had taken off his helmet, and twirled it between his hands. His eyes glanced into Brigid's before he lowered them. 'I'm sorry to have to tell you Mrs Carney, but your husband had an accident out on the Randwick Road today.' But before he could finish speaking Brigid broke in.

'Des, what's happened, is he... all right?' She was staring intently at the constable, and trying to read his facial expression.

'I'm sorry to have to tell you Mrs Carney, but your husband is dead.'

Brigid's hand flew to her mouth. Her eyes wide, and she bit down on her hand that was now folded into a fist.

'What, what happened? Are you sure that it's Des?'

'I'm sorry, Mrs Carney, but your husband was trampled by his horses, and the wagon that he was working on.' Brigid gave out a scream before covering her face with both hands.

'Not Des, I can't believe it. He was so good with horses. He loved them. I want to see him.' She spoke between her sobs, her voice quivering.

'I want to see him, where is he? I need to be with him! Tell me where you have taken him?'

Matron Fisher had been standing just outside of her office and now entered. 'Thank you, constable. I'll take care of Mrs Carney.'

Constable Wotherspoon was looking more uncomfortable as he said, 'I'm sorry, but I have to inform Mrs Carney that her husband's body is at the government mortuary in Glebe. I have been asked to tell you that you will have to make the arrangements for Mr Carney's body to be picked up and taken to your own undertaker. As Mr Carney's death was an accident, the government mortuary cannot hold bodies when an inquest is not required. It is up to the deceased's family to make the arrangements for the funeral.' He put his helmet back on and quickly turned away.

Brigid sobbed uncontrollably, and Matron held her close. 'I'm so sorry dear. You will need to go home of course. Is there someone that you can talk to? Would you like me to get the chaplain to come and talk with you? Now what about your husband, did he have any family here? Someone will need to tell them. Will you do that, or would you rather I get Father John to see them?'

Matron Fisher was talking quickly, more to herself than to Brigid. She was uncomfortable, and was trying to make sense of the accident.

Brigid stood back and sniffled into her handkerchief. 'No thank you matron. Desmond's father has a small business out in Chippendale. He works by himself. I will have to go and see him. He will be devastated. He still hoped that Des would take over his cabinetmaking shop one day. But Des couldn't use his arm properly after the war. That's why he loved working at the gardens.'

She began to tremble and cry again as she thought of telling Des's father, and everyone else, that Des was gone.

59.

Doubts 1921

Tom sat on his verandah step and nursed his son. Hannah was sitting on an old bentwood chair. It was late February, and the sun had burnt the paddocks and hills brown for as far as the eye could see. The heat within the interior of the house was almost unbearable, and the night-time temperatures hardly varied. Jimmy was now a year old, and the past few months had been as hectic as they had been frustrating.

They had both been shocked to learn of Desmond's death. By the time that they had heard of the accident Des had been buried for three months. Tom had thought of the many times that they should all have been killed during the war, but weren't, yet his mate would die at home while carrying out a simple chore.

He had built a verandah down the length of their small house. The hot, breezeless nights had forced them to move the bed and the cradle onto the verandah, and they slept with a mosquito net covering them. Hannah was looking at her husband and her son. They had been on the land for just over a year, and she wondered if their lives would improve, or if life would always be this hard.

Jimmy was sat on his father's lap dribbling and blowing bubbles, as he played with the swaying corks that adorned the brim of his father's hat.

Tom wanted to smoke, and handed the baby back to Hannah. He packed his pipe, and drew back the smoke before expelling it.

The sweet, acrid smell hung in the air as he asked, 'Are ya happy here Hani?' She looked intently at her husband before answering, 'Why Tommy, whatever makes you ask that question? I am happy, why shouldn't I be?'

'I just been wonderin' if you miss the city, that's all.'

Hannah pondered for a moment before answering, 'I miss seeing your mother, and Aunt Claire and Uncle Davin. I worry about them, as I'm sure that they worry about us. I miss Brigid, but I can't say that I miss the noise and the grime. Sometimes, I do miss being able to just walk around the footpaths and window shop. I miss our evening strolls through Redfern Park, but that's all. What about you? Do you think that we should go back? I thought that you wanted to be a farmer. Have you changed your mind?'

'Nah, I still love the bush and the quiet, but I never realised how hard it was gunna be. Other than the two quid a week that the government gives us, I ain't brung in no money fer a while. It's a good job that we get that, cause without that money I think we would starve. When I was workin' fer yer uncle, I always had a few bob in me pocket, not that I need any money out here, but it was nice to have some.

'Look at all them spuds that I planted. I thought that all I hadta do was dig a hole and drop them in it. I know that we got a few to grow but, all we ended up with was enough fer ourselves fer a coupla months. I thought that we might have got a coupla tons that we coulda sold, but instead we only got a few hundred pounds!'

He took another long drag on his pipe, and stared out across the valley. 'I dunno how we woulda survived this long if we didn't have the dam down there, and the windmill.' He nodded towards the glistening water. 'I wonder about Clarence, and the others who all came here with wantin' to make a better life. At least we are lucky enough to have plenty of water, unlike them. I gotta keep going with them fences. I done one whole side of the property so far, and we only got another two years to get the rest of the place done.' He stopped talking for a moment as Hannah lay Jimmy down.

'I just wanna make sure that you got no regrets Hani. I need to get a few lambs and another cow, but there ain't much feed out in them paddocks. I gotta plough up some more dirt come the autumn, but it's too hot and dusty at the moment.'

He went silent again as his mind wandered. There was so much to do, but with almost no money, he had reservations if he would be able to realise his dreams for the future.

Hannah pulled the net across the cradle, then went and sat on the step next to him. The afternoon heat hung heavy and oppressive in the still air. The windmill had stopped turning, as there was not even a hint of a breeze to turn the blades.

'I am a bit worn out. I got so many things to do. I wanna build another room, and I need to extend the horse yard, and I need to get some barley and wheat seed planted by the autumn.

'I can't do no more around here until I get some dough, and the only way I can get any is by felling them trees over there.' He nodded in their direction. 'I will start tomorrow, and it should only take me a coupla weeks to get 'em on the ground. It'll take me another coupla weeks to get 'em sliced up inta shorta lengths, and when I done that I'll go and see 'em at the mill.

'I don't want to harp on it, but I just wanna be sure that you want to stay here because things might get a bit harder before they get better. I read the paper, and the government bloke said that meat prices was getting lower for farmers, and we might be headin' fer a recession. I dunno what that means, but the paper bloke said it was gunna increase unemployment, and make things tougher for people on the land.

'He was also talkin' about how bad the drought was getting in some parts of the country, and that was what was sending the price of mutton down. All them blessed sheep across the country and no food for them.'

Hannah rested her arm across Tom's knee and said, 'I love living out here, it's our home. Look at what you have achieved since we have been here.' She waved her hand around. 'You have built this house for us, and we have food on the table every night, unlike some poor souls. We have lovely neighbours, and Bill gave us that milking cow. I'm sure that he must have known that the cow was pregnant when he gave her to us. So now we have a young bull calf, and in a year or two we can get another cow, and before you know it we will have our own herd. I think that you are worrying too much. You're just tired. Why don't we take the cart and spend a day in Blackmore? We haven't been there in so long. We could call and see if Brigid is home. I've been worried about her, and I would just like to know that she is coping. Besides I want to see her anyway.'

Tom looked at her with a puzzled expression. 'Why do you need to see her? There's nuthin' wrong, is there?' Hannah went silent for a moment. She looked at Tom before saying, 'I'm not sure, but I may be pregnant again. I wasn't going to say anything until I knew. I didn't want to give you any more worry.'

He took hold of her hand, and leant over to kiss her cheek. 'Well if you are, another mouth to feed won't make any difference, especially a little one. I don't mind if we have a dozen babies Hani. We will manage, so we will go and see Brigid in the next day or so if yer like.'

He looked at Hannah to gauge her reaction, but she just slid closer to him. 'Tommy, I married you for better or worse. We will just take each day as it comes. There is nothing else that we can do. We are so much luckier than many people. I read that article that said a lot of workers in the cities had to work for less money in the factories because the government was running out of money. At least we can grow our own food. If worst comes to worst, we will just grow vegetables, and what's left over we can sell to Mr Lauder at the general store. We have each other, and we'll get by.'

60.

Brigid Moves to the Country

It took Brigid many months to accept the fact that her Desmond was dead. After the funeral, she had thrown herself into studying and she worked every day at the Barracks Hospital. She attended to the needs of the many pregnant women who now threatened to swamp the new maternity section of the old hospital.

The newspapers had applauded the government initiative of building a new women-only hospital in the heart of the city. But, that would not be fully functioning for at least another two years. Brigid wrote to Hannah on a regular basis, and she often wondered if she too would have eventually moved to the country had Des lived. She thought of how many times he had spoken of his dream to live in the country and raise horses.

Brigid had no plans for her future. She purposely spent as much time as possible at work, so that she had very little time to reflect on what might have been. Her life consisted of working and sleeping, and she had moved from the small house that she and Des had shared to a small room in the nurses' quarters.

Now, as a qualified midwife, the hospital board was more than happy to provide her with free accommodation along with a small salary to have an on-call midwife at their disposal.

It had been more than six months since she had opened Hannah's letter that had motivated her to change her life. Inside was a small newspaper cutting from the *Bathurst Chronicle* that had quoted a councillor as saying:

> 'We are in need of suitably qualified medical staff to move to Bathurst, and take up various appointments within our hospital system.'

The article also suggested that a midwife was desperately needed to service the growing rural area. That night, after attending to her duties, Brigid had responded to the newspaper story, and within a month she had received a reply.

> *Dear Mrs Carney,*
>
> *The hospital board is in receipt of your letter, dated November 3, 1921. We have read your testimonials and references, and you would appear to be suitably qualified to take up the position of Rural Midwife and Area Nurse.*
>
> *The position will involve the monitoring of expectant mothers, along with assisting them at delivery. You would also spend several days per week at the clinic that has been established in the rural settlement of Blackmore.*
>
> *Blackmore is a growing township, and it is situated about twenty miles south of Bathurst. Here, as part of your duties, you will weigh and monitor the well-being of infants and their mothers, along with giving advice to expectant mothers.*
>
> *You will also dispense milk vouchers to those mothers whom you deem to need a supplementary source of calcium.*
>
> *While the board is impressed with your references, we note that you do not have the ability to drive and control a motor vehicle.*
>
> *The position will require the successful applicant to travel vast distances, and as such it will be imperative that should your application*

be successful you would need to be instructed in the operation of a motor vehicle, which will be provided by the board.

Could you please make arrangements to contact this office at your earliest convenience? You may do this by telephoning Bathurst 213, and asking to speak to me during normal business hours. Alternatively, you may correspond by the royal mail service. Please state when you could start at the practice, and if the terms of employment are acceptable to you. This includes your acceptance to be instructed in the use of a motor vehicle.

A small house will be provided for your accommodation at the rear of the clinic. The rent shall be charged at ten shillings per week. This will be deducted from your weekly salary of two pounds fifteen shillings per week.

I look forward to your earliest response.

Yours sincerely

Mr Martin Brodhurst.

Chairman, Bathurst Hospital Board Trust.

Brigid readily accepted the position, and gave her notice at the Barracks Hospital.

***

The train squealed to a stop at Blackmore. Brigid looked around at the town that would become her new home, as the train belched smoke and steam as it continued on its journey to Bathurst.

The small station was at the end of a long wide street. A variety of buildings were dotted about and faced each other. Although small, the town appeared to be well serviced. The Post Office was built from red bricks, and was overly ornate. It had been built during the gold rush days, when money was flowing quickly into the government coffers. The town hall and its clock tower were cladded with lemon-painted weatherboards, and the Union Jack hung limply in the still air from its flagpole. An ornate sign attached to the building wall announced that it was also the town library. Further along the street was a saddler, butcher shop and drapery.

Across the road was a hardware shop, sitting alongside the emporium. Both establishments were displaying their wares across the footpath at the front. Hitching posts stood next to concrete horse troughs. These were scattered along both sides of the wide gravel road that made up the main street.

It was mid afternoon, and there were very few people on the street. The train guard had placed her suitcases on the platform, along with a few parcels. The stationmaster had taken her ticket, and asked if someone was to meet her.

Brigid smiled and said, 'Yes, I was told that someone would be here to meet me. They must be running late, but never mind, I'm sure that they will be here shortly.'

The stationmaster tipped his cap and said, 'Very well madam, if you need any assistance just knock on me door.' He nodded towards the large green-painted door that held his title above it.

She watched the motorcar weave its way along the street. A cloud of dust followed its progress.

The vehicle clattered to a halt, and more dust rose around it. The woman driving it gave Brigid a smile as she stepped out. 'I'm sorry that I'm late. You must be Mrs Carney. The one day that the train is on time, I'm late. I hope that you haven't been waiting long?' She put out her hand, 'How do you do, I'm Mrs Wood, but please call me Nellie.' She gave Brigid another smile as they shook hands.

Brigid smiled back, 'No, don't apologise. I'm Brigid Carney, and please call me Brigid. I haven't been here long at all. I was just gathering my thoughts and looking at my new home.'

Nellie waved at the stationmaster, who was now picking up the suitcases and bringing them to the car.

'Good afternoon, Mr O'Leary. This is Mrs Carney. She is going to be our new nurse and midwife at the clinic.'

Maurice O'Leary again tipped his cap before saying, 'It's nice to meet you, madam. I hope that you settle in easy and that you get to like our little town. You come from Sydney, do you?'

'Thank you, Mr O'Leary. Yes, I have been working there, and I thought that it was time for a change.'

As the suitcases were loaded, Nellie said, 'All right, I'll take you to your quarters now. Everyone is excited about your arrival. It's been hard at times, not having anyone in the town with medical experience. Most people with an ailment, or pregnant ladies, have to catch the train all the way to Bathurst if they want some help with a sprain, or some such. I hope that you like us. I'm sure that we will all like you. It's a very friendly town, and I hope that you will stay.

'We had another nurse come out here some time ago, but she left as she said that it was too quiet. Goodness me, that must have been more than eighteen months ago now.'

Nellie crunched the gears and over-steered the motorcar along the dusty street. A few minutes later, they stopped outside a small shop front. It was newly painted, and above the window hung a large sign that read, *Clinic and Dispensary*.

'Well, here we are. I do hope that you will be comfortable.' The front door was unlocked, and Nellie led the way in.

'Now, this front room is what we have set up as the clinic, and your accommodation is behind here.'

She opened another door, which led into a small kitchen that led through to an even smaller bedroom. Out the back was a compact bathroom, complete with an enamel bath serviced by a woodchip water heater at one end. The toilet was outside, and stood against the back fence.

Nellie took charge and said, 'I'll make us a nice cuppa. I'm sure that you can use one after your long journey.' She didn't wait for a response from Brigid, as she moved the simmering kettle from the warming plate across to the hot plate.

'I took the liberty to light your stove before I picked you up. I hope that you don't mind, but the nights are still a little cool!' She gave Brigid a quick smile before busying herself with the teapot and cups. 'Now, you just sit yourself down. Mrs Kelly made you a lovely fruitcake to welcome you. You will meet her soon. She has been a godsend to us. She was a nurse's assistant during the war.

'She bandages up all the scrapes and cuts that the children are prone to get, and she is always the first to volunteer when someone needs a hand. She is looking forward to your arrival, but said that she would let you settle in before she came around. She lives by herself, across the road in that tiny house of hers next door to the drapery shop.' Ellie looked toward the direction that she was referring to.

'Is she married?'

Nellie poured the tea and said, 'No, she was engaged before the war, but...' and she hesitated for a moment before continuing, 'he was a lovely boy, but he was killed in the first wave of the fighting. I still find it hard to understand what it was all about. We lost over a dozen of our boys from this town alone. I knew all of them that never came back. It's been a few years now since it ended, and I can still see their faces when I run into their parents.'

Nellie stopped talking for a moment before changing the subject.

'Now, I was told that I have to teach you how to drive a motorcar!'

Nellie smiled, and gave a giggle as she thought of the trouble she had when she first learned to drive. Brigid smiled and asked, 'Is it hard? I'm afraid that I am not very mechanically minded. I would rather ride a horse, but I know that I gave the committee my word that I would learn to drive, although I must say, I am not looking forward to it.'

Ellie was grinning and said, 'I will teach you the things that I had to find out the hard way. The driving part is easy, as long as the ground is hard and not wet. It's the little things that you have to do before you start.

'I was just put into the seat, and told how to put the thing into a gear to make it go. I was shown how to use the handbrake to make it stop, and I had to work out everything else myself.

'You will probably think that I am a bit of a dill, but I never knew that you had to put petrol into the tank to make it go.' She smiled again as she thought of something else.

'The first morning that I had to drive it from Bathurst to here was so funny. It wasn't funny at the time, but I had done everything right, and it should have just started up, but as much as I kept turning that blessed crank handle, it just wouldn't start.

'Nobody mentioned to me that you have to put petrol into the thing before it would run. I turned that handle so many times that my arm was aching. Then a few men stopped to give me advice on how they thought that I should do this, or that to make it go. Well, I tried everything that was suggested, and it still wouldn't go. All the men were scratching their heads when this lady was walking by, and she suggested that the car might need some fuel. None of us had even given it a thought.'

Brigid asked, 'So what did you do?'

'I had no idea where you got petrol from, or even where it went. So, I walked over to the hardware store, and I asked the attendant if he knew where I could buy some petrol.'

'He asked me how much I wanted, and I had no idea. Well, as it turned out the hardware store sold petrol in one-gallon tins. I bought a gallon. He charged me one and sixpence. One shilling was for the tin, and sixpence was for the petrol. Imagine that, I never knew that petrol was so expensive. I eventually got my money back from the committee.'

Brigid was listening to Nellie's story and asked, 'So how much petrol does one have to put into the contraption, and how often?'

Nellie replied, 'You won't have to worry about the fuel because the committee has an account with several shops that sell petrol.

'They have a new shop in Bathurst. It's called a chemist shop. It used to be the dispensary, but it sells a bit of everything now, including petrol. Now, the motorcar takes four gallons in total. I will show you where you have to fill it up. One gallon will take you almost twenty miles. Imagine that, twenty miles in less than two hours. It takes a horse all day to walk twenty miles!'

With the tea drunk, Nellie rose and said, 'Well, it was nice to meet you Brigid. I'll go now, and you can get settled in. I will bring Mrs Kelly around in the morning and introduce her.'

61.

Worrying Times

The long dry summer had slowly edged its way into the cooler months of autumn. Hannah was overjoyed to have Brigid living only three miles away, and as Brigid had learned how to start and control her motorcar, she would now regularly visit Hannah.

Tom had cut down his trees, but he had received less money from the mill owner than he had expected. By the time that he had paid for his trees to be taken to the mill, he was left with less than ten pounds, although he had been expecting to receive around thirty.

He had ploughed another fifty acres in the first month of autumn. He had intended to sow most of them with barley seed, but having far less money available, he would now have to re-evaluate how much seed he could afford to buy. The drought had crept slowly down from Queensland. It had parched the inland waterways and dams as it spread across the rural inland of New South Wales.

Many people were feeling the effects of the economic downturn. Cattle and sheep were dying from thirst and starvation in vast numbers across the country. Wheat crops had been smaller, and workers were

441

being laid off in their thousands all along the east coast of Australia.

The days were getting shorter, and the light was now fading quickly. They had gone back to using tallow candles for light, after the price of kerosene had risen by more than five shillings for a four-gallon tin. The candles burned for almost five hours and only cost a penny each.

The railway electric company had been slowly expanding electricity to the farms, and the outlying areas around Bathurst. A power pole was placed outside of the Murdochs' boundary fence, and now their house was supplied with electricity, and a pay-as-you-go meter. The power company would not service Tom and Hannah's farm. They had deemed that it was too difficult to run the service from the road, and up the steep incline to their house.

The telegraph company had told them that they would have a telephone service connected to their house in the near future, but that was over a year earlier. Hannah had given up hope that it would ever be supplied, and she was thankful that at least they could use the Murdochs' telephone.

Hannah was expecting her baby at any time. No matter how much she moved around she continued to have the same tight, uncomfortable feeling around her belly and back. She had suggested to Tom that he should go to the Murdochs' and ring Brigid. As he rode off she sat near the window, and by the light of a candle she unpicked the stitches of the flour sacks that she would bleach and use as nappies for her baby.

Baby Billy was born in the early hours of a cool autumn morning. Their new baby had arrived in a rush, and Brigid had stayed with Hannah all night, before she had gone home with a promise that she would return later the next day.

***

Another year of struggle had passed, and it was the middle of 1923 before the heavy rains finally came. It drenched the parched earth, and the rivers and creeks flowed once again.

Tom had purchased four chaff bags of barley seed for five pounds. He had planned on only planting one, and he wasn't sure if the seed would even germinate. However, the rats and the field mice had chewed through the sacks, and they had eaten through a pound's worth of seed before he had discovered it.

He swept up the seed that was scattered over the dirt floor, and scattered it across his furrows.

As spring arrived, so did the small shoots of the germinating barley. The first crop grew sporadically, but by the time it came to harvest it, Tom had enough seed to fill several bags.

Over the next two years, the rain had fallen almost on cue, and his small successive crops had flourished. Tom had made enough money to add two more rooms to his house, and buy a second-hand truck. His boys were growing quickly, and after the harvest Hannah had told him that she was pregnant again.

∗∗∗

Their third baby had arrived into the world in the usual way on the evening of March the 12th 1925.

Hannah had been having contractions on and off, for more than 12 hours until she gave a final, primal scream and a push, and the newest member of her family had arrived with barely a whimper. The child's breathing was laboured and weak, and she was so small that she could be held in the palm of the doctor's hand.

Doctor Silas Bartholomew had been at Hannah's side for the past two hours. His weather-worn face wore a troubled look. His patient was weak from blood loss, and sleepy from the laudanum that he had administered an hour earlier. He thought that there was a good chance that Hannah may die. He was equally sure that the baby would not last out the night as it gave raspy little squeaks with every laboured breath, but Brigid had other ideas.

She had delivered Hannah's two other children, and had helped nurse them both into healthy strapping lads. She held the small bundle into the nape of her neck, and she constantly massaged it as she whispered quiet prayers. 'Dear God, please don't take this baby,' and 'Dear God, give this child the strength and the will to live.'

She paced the room for the next few hours, occasionally looking at her friend lying in the bed and checking on the baby in the crib. Hannah was deathly pale, but was now sleeping peacefully.

Tom came and went from the bedroom. He was restless and feeling uncomfortable. He had come into the room after the birth, and held Hannah's hand. He looked at his baby daughter, and he was happy to have a little girl. But, she was so small and frail that he didn't want to touch her. All that he could do was to gently run the back of his callused finger down the side of her small face.

He went back outside and lit his pipe, and Silas joined him. 'How is she doc?'

'As well as can be expected, she's lost a lot of blood, but if she doesn't lose any more she should get stronger.' He dragged back on his pipe before saying, 'Tom, I'm worried about the baby. She is too small, and she weighs less than a sparrow. It was a difficult birth, and I want you to understand that she might not last out the night!'

Tom gave a grunt as he took a long draw on his pipe, and he replied with, 'I don't want to lose either of them doc, but what will be, will be.'

They finished their smokes and went back inside, Silas to check on his patient, and Tom to sit by the bedside of the woman that he loved.

***

As Hannah woke, her eyes focused, and she saw Brigid sat at her bedside.

'Hello, sleepyhead.'

'Where's my baby, what did I have?' she quietly asked.

Brigid stood, and picked up the small bundle. She leant over the bed, and handed the baby to Hannah. 'You have a little girl. She is very small, but seems to be getting stronger. We were worried about her for a while, but please God she will keep improving.'

Hannah removed the small linen wrap that partially covered the baby's face. 'Is she all right Bridgy, are you sure that she is all right?'

Brigid sat down at her friend's side. She wore a worried look and gave a weak smile. 'You probably don't remember much, but you had a difficult time. To be honest, there were times when even the doctor was worried because you had lost so much blood, and your little girl gave us a scare too!'

Brigid held Hannah's hand, and was silent for a moment as she gathered her thoughts before she spoke. 'I'm not going to lie to you darling. Your little girl is very weak, and there is a chance that she might not survive.'

As Brigid spoke, Hannah gripped her hand tightly. 'The next few days will be critical. If she survives the next week, there should be a good chance that she will be able to grow up and play with her brothers. In the meantime, we can only pray that she will get stronger. Mrs Dickson has been kind enough to wet nurse the little one. She is a saint that one, and with five kiddies of her own as well as her newborn. Her husband has been kind enough to bring her over in the truck, and she has fed your baby while you have been asleep. Anyway, I will tell Mrs Dickson that her services are no longer needed.'

Hannah was crying softly and said, 'Will you thank her for me please? Where is Tommy?'

'Tom took the boys over to Bill and Dorothy's. Dorothy offered to look after them until you were in a fit state again.

'He should be home shortly. He said that he wasn't staying. Now, I expect that you are hungry. I have made some broth, and you need to eat it. Now you get to know your daughter, while I get you some food.'

Hannah looked at the tiny child. Its features were perfect, but ever so small. She had not expected to have a daughter. Doris had said that as she had given birth to two sons, then it was highly likely that she would deliver another one. She mused over how nice it would be to have a little girl, but all that she really wanted was to have a healthy baby.

Tom arrived home an hour later, and parked the truck behind the stables. Brigid met him at the door and told him of her conversation with Hannah. 'I have told her, Tom, that the baby might not live. I think that you should arrange for the priest to baptise her as soon as possible! Have you thought of a name for her? She will need one before she can be baptised.'

'Nar, I haven't given it a thought. I have been expecting the little one to die after what the doc had said. I never give it a thought of having her baptised. I'll go and talk to Hani now. How is she?'

'She is still in a bit of pain, but she has taken a bowl of broth, and that's a good sign. I want you to understand Tom that she is not out of the woods just yet. She has lost a lot of blood, far more than last time. What she needs now is lots of rest and quiet. Are the boys settled in?'

'Yep, Dorothy is in her element. She is going to look after them until Hani is back on her feet. I'll go over each day of course, just so they remember who I am,' he said dryly.

He went into the bedroom, and took off his hat, and then hung it on the coat hook hanging off the wall. The floorboards creaked as he tiptoed to the bedside. A sputtering candle stood on the small side table next to the bed. It cast a soft glow across Hannah's face. Her eyes were closed, but as Tom bent down to kiss her, she opened them.

'Oh Tommy, I'm so scared, Brigid has told me that out little girl might not live.'

'I know Hani, the doc told me too! We need to find her a name, and get the priest here to baptise her just in case. Have you thought of a name for her yet?'

'I thought that we might call her Peggy. I've always liked that name. What do you think Tommy?'

Tom gave a smile, 'It sounds good to me.' He looked at his sleeping daughter, and whispered a quiet prayer to a God that he had not yet forgiven.

62.

Struggling

Peggy was three, when the year had rolled over into 1928 and Hannah had given birth to another daughter.

Doris and Claire were sat around the kitchen table talking. Claire and Davin had just arrived back from Jamison after spending a few days there, and Doris was keen to hear the latest news.

Doris poured the tea, and she was bubbling with anticipation to hear about her grandchildren.

'So, tell me, how is the new baby, and how are the children? Oh lord, how I miss them.

Claire stirred her tea, 'Those children have grown. All that fresh air is making them grow like weeds. It's hard to believe that darling little Peggy is now three. She is such a delightful child. Mind you, she is still very small for her age. I do worry about her though! Hannah said that she is not all that strong. Mind you, when we were there she didn't stop running around and chasing her brothers. Those boys are so good with her. She climbs on Jimmy's back, and he piggybacks her everywhere.

'And Doris, you should see the new baby. She is beautiful, and they have called her Molly. Brigid told us that the baby is strong and healthy. She weighed over five pounds when she was born!

'I do wish that we could see them more often. The two boys go to school in Blackmore. It's so funny to watch them sitting together on the back of their pony.'

Doris looked quizzically at Claire. 'Ride a horse! Gracious me, it's three miles to Blackmore, isn't it? Aren't they too young to be riding horses?'

Claire smiled as she remembered the sight of her three grandchildren all sat astride the horse.

'Tommy taught the two boys how to ride, and they are very good. Jimmy puts the halter on, and he climbs up on the stable fence before he helps Billy get on. They ride bareback all the way to school. All the children leave their horses in the churchyard behind the school until it's time for them to ride home. Peggy is still too young to go to school, but she doubles up with the boys when they go for a ride.'

Doris refilled the cups, 'I keep hoping that they might come back to the city. I know that it's selfish of me, but I have sometimes wished that they hadn't made such a success of living out there. Does that sound awful?'

Claire took a sip from her cup before replying, 'No Doris, I have had the same thoughts at times. I don't begrudge them their life out there. They have both worked so hard, and I watched Tommy plough up those fields. He must have at least eighty acres dug over by now. He was telling me that he was hoping to plant his biggest ever crop this season.

'He knows that it's a big gamble, but he spent almost all of his money on grain seeds. He was telling Davin that if he had a good season, they would have enough money to tide them over for a whole year, as well as for paying his bills. He desperately wants to buy one of those mechanical tractors, but he can't afford to just yet.

'Hannah is worried, because she said that they are in another drought up there. It's only been a couple of years since the last one.'

Claire continued, 'Hannah asked me not to say anything to Tommy, but she knows that he is taking a big gamble on spending all of their money on that seed. She is worried, because she has six mouths to feed now. She said that if something happened to the crop before they could sell it, they would have no money at all.'

Doris was quiet for a moment before saying, 'Don't they still get that two quid a week from the government for their food allowance?'

'No, they lost that after they signed the deed agreement with the government.'

'What do you mean lost it, how could they lose it?'

Claire gave a sigh of mock exasperation as she explained again, 'Doris, when they signed up for that block they had five years to put a house on the land and get the whole property fenced.

'That's why they were paid the two pounds a week allowance. Well, they did all that, and the government man who came around to see that they had finished everything told them that the government would now give them a mortgage.'

'The government expects the settlers to be self-sufficient after five years, and that's why they stopped paying them. So now, they have to pay for the land, which the government still owns, until it's paid off. I forget how much they said that they have to pay back; I think that it was something like a pound an acre. If they don't pay all the money, then the government gets to sell the land, and all of the improvements. It doesn't matter to the government if it rains, or if they have a drought. They still have to pay for the land. I don't know how the government expects a family to live if there is no money coming in.'

'She said that they could pay the money once a year, but that's about thirteen pounds every year. That's an awful lot of money, and I have to say Doris, that I'm really worried for them!'

Doris retorted, 'You mean to tell me that they can just get thrown off their land? All of those poor boys that went overseas and fought and got injured are being treated like that. I thought that they got the land as a thank you.'

'No Doris! The government has given them fifteen years to repay the loan. If they don't make the payment every year, then they lose the place.' Doris wore a frown as she emptied out the tea leaves from the pot.

'I'll make us another cuppa. I wish that there was something that I could do to help, but I'm as poor as a church mouse. You know dearie, it's been over fifteen years since my Barry was killed. The railways still only give me ten bob a week for his wages. It don't go anywhere as far as it did then. They have never offered me a rise in all that time. I bet that they are paying more than that down at the rail yards now. I'm not complaining Claire. It's just frustrating that I can't help them. God knows that its getting harder to make ends meet now, and there doesn't seem to be a week that goes by without something going up.

'I know that Mr Dougherty at the store has to make a living, and it's not his fault that the prices are going up almost every week.

'I had to buy a sack of flour the other day. It was a shilling dearer than when I bought the last one. He's a good man, is Mr Dougherty. Why, he even offered to let me put my groceries on tick. I couldn't take up his offer, of course.

'I thanked him, but I told him that as long as I have a couple of bob in me purse then I would pay for me stuff as I needed it. Getting off that subject, did you read last week's paper?'

Claire looked quizzically at Doris before saying, 'I just glanced at it, what are you referring to?'

'I've been following the strife with the workers' unions. It seems like the wharfies and the coal miners have been goin' on strike for more money. The government has said no, because apparently the economy is not going too well. The government bloke said that all the workers might have to take a pay cut. That's got all the unions riled up, and their bloke has said that nothing will be loaded, or unloaded onto any ship until they get what they want.

'Then the government bloke said, if the union blokes wouldn't unload the ships then he would employ what he called, un-unionised labour and get the goods off the ships that way. I don't understand all this political or economic stuff except that the government bloke said that if the strikes continue then prices for everything will go up.'

Claire took another sip from her cup before replying, 'Yes, I did read about that, but I can't help wondering where it will all end.'

63.

Sowing the Seed

The summer had long gone, and it was the end of April. Tom looked across his furrowed paddocks. The land was parched and brown as far as he could see. He had ploughed over a hundred acres over the summer, and now all that was left to do was to plant his seed. The sky was still cloudless and blue although the days were now cool. The autumn rains had not arrived, and the churned-up clods of dirt were still hard and dry.

Bill had advised him that he should have his crop sown by June if he was to have a November harvest. He was nervous now. The thought that the drought might continue was a distraction, but if he didn't plant his seed, he would have no money.

They had fifty pounds left, and that would have to last them until after the harvest, which was seven months away.

If he took a gamble that the rain would come after he planted the seed and it failed, then he knew that he might have to borrow funds from the newly established Farmers' Bank. If that option didn't work out, there was the very real chance that they would have to walk away from their farm and return to the city.

He was leaning against the stable yard fence when Hannah walked over. He had gone over his options a dozen times, but he was more confused than ever. She was holding baby Molly, and Peggy was tagging along behind. She noticed the frown on her husband's face and asked, 'What's bothering you?'

He finished rolling his smoke and said, 'I'm just mullin' over planting me seed. I gotta say Hani; it's got me worried. The ground is so dry. It shoulda rained by now. I dunno much about farmin' and I know even less about planting seed. I do know that there should be some moisture in the soil before the seed goes in. Bill told me that. But, it's as dry as a sandy well, and I'm worried that if I get it wrong, then we are finished unless I can borrow some money to tide us over. I'm at a loss as to what we should do. What do you think Hani?'

She passed the baby to Tom, and said, 'Here, hold your daughter, she's getting heavy.' She squinted against the glare, as she looked across the dry paddocks and thought about what she was going to say.

'We took a gamble when we came out here. We had nothing except a pocket full of dreams. We don't have much more now, but somehow, we have survived. We have four healthy children, and we have managed to put food on the table every night.

'I don't think that you should worry about the "what ifs." What will happen will happen anyway. Look Tommy, if you plant the seed and it doesn't grow, then we will get by one way or the other. What's the worst that can happen?' she asked rhetorically.

'The government will repossess it, and we will have to go back to Sydney. You know that Uncle Davin would always give you your job back at the forge. So, my advice to you is, just to go and plant the seed and let's see what happens.'

Tom thought about what Hannah had said before replying, 'I knew that I could count on you to make up me mind fer me.' He handed the baby back before kissing Hannah on the cheek.

'I'll have to round up those boys. They can give me a hand to spread the seed before I change me mind. Have you seen them?'

'I think they might be down by the dam. Jimmy said that he was going to catch some yabbies.'

¥¥¥

It took two days for them to disperse all of the grain. When the seed was spread they walked over the hundred acres again. This time though, they tried to bury the seed as they broke up the sods with their feet. Tom wore boots, but his children walked and ran everywhere in their bare feet. That night his boys lay on their beds and were asleep within minutes.

Tom had still not made his peace with God, but as he looked at his sleeping sons lying in their beds, he mouthed a silent prayer that his seeds would germinate. Tom was fast asleep when the black of the night faded into the grey of the early dawn. The screeching sounds penetrated his sleepy mind, until the fog of confusion cleared and woke him fully. For a moment, he just lay there trying to work out what the noise was. Slowly, it dawned on him and he jumped out of bed and pulled on his trousers.

He ran to the door and swung it open. The raucous squawking of a thousand sulphur-crested cockatoos filled the air in the early morning light. He looked past the stables towards his paddocks, and what he saw filled him with rage and panic. The birds covered his paddocks in a sea of white and yellow as they greedily ate his freshly sown seed. Hannah was just getting up, and baby Molly was demanding attention.

'What is it, what's happening?' she asked, as she pulled her shawl across her shoulders.

'Blasted cockatoos. I'll get me gun,' was all that he could mutter.

He quickly dressed, and checked the magazine on his rifle. He walked as far as the stables before he fired off several shots. He was still loath to kill anything, and it would just be a futile exercise as there were so many birds. He fired over their heads, and as the shots reverberated in quick succession, the birds rose as one in a sea of flapping wings and raucous protest. The birds were now panicked, and flew in circles above the ground. A few landed quickly, and as Tom fired more shots they flew higher, and squawking loudly they turned to the south.

Tom stood there for a few minutes as his rage and consternation simmered. He was wondering how long the birds had been out there before he had woken up, and he was filled with dread. He had expected to lose some seed to field mice and rats, but not to birds. When he was sure that the birds had gone, he went back inside.

Despondently, he sat at the kitchen table as Hannah ladled out lumpy porridge into the children's bowls. As he ate his breakfast, he was wondering how he could stop the birds from coming back. Hannah could see that Tom was upset. She put her arms around him and kissed the top of his head as he sat at the table. She said, 'I have never seen so many birds. I do hope that they weren't out there for too long before we woke up.'

'I'll go and have a look when I've finished me porridge. I'll take me gun in case they decide to come back.

'One thing is for sure Hani. I'm gunna hav'ta get up before sunrise every mornin' from now on. At least until the seeds sprout!'

Jimmy was finishing the last mouthful of his porridge and sputtered, 'I'll chase the birds away, Dad.' And Billy followed with, 'We both will. We will get up before the birds do, and we will guard the paddocks. Won't we Jimmy?'

Hannah piped in, 'How many times have I told you not to speak with your mouth full? I know that you both want to help your father, but your manners come first, so no talking while you have food in your mouth. Do we both understand?'

'Yes Mummy.' And they gave each other a secret smile across the table. Peggy was still playing with her bowl, but that didn't stop her from chiming in, 'I like the birds.'

Hannah laughed, and smiled at her daughter, 'We all like the birds darling, but we can't let them just eat all of our seed because if they did that then we wouldn't have anything to eat ourselves, and that would be no good, would it?' Peggy had lost interest in the conversation as she played with her spoon and just nodded her head.

Tom finished his breakfast and made his way across the paddocks with the boys in tow. He could see that the seed was scattered randomly and he was unsure if it was because the birds had eaten it, or just because they may not have scattered it properly. They walked the entire length of the paddocks, and by the time that they got back to the stables, Tom still had no idea of how much seed he had lost.

64.

The School Teacher

Mr Adam Francis was thinly built and had a pale, sallow face on which he wore small silver-framed pincer glasses. He was forty-two years old and single. He wasn't shy, and there was no particular reason as to why he had never married. He had known a few young women who may have said yes to a marriage proposal, if he had ever had a mind to developing a friendship into something more. The truth was though that he preferred to be single. His passion was reading about history and playing the piano.

Circumstances had led him to Blackmore some years after the war had come to an end in Europe. He had tried to enlist at the beginning of the conflict, but without his glasses, he was almost blind. The army medical board had given him an exemption from going to war based upon his poor eyesight. His disappointment was tempered when the army medic had pointed out to him that if he lost or damaged his glasses while on the battlefield he would be as good as dead.

He had been working as a store clerk in Sydney as the war was being fought across Europe. Adam lived a simple life, the highlight of it being when he assisted with Sunday School for the parishioners' children at the

Methodist Church where he worshipped. He would play the piano and teach the children the words to hymns before telling the children bible stories. He liked children, and putting his own interpretation on bible stories made him popular.

He had occasionally thought that he would like to be a teacher, but the opportunity had never arisen. That was until he had taken a train trip to Bathurst over the Christmas holidays in 1928 to visit his sister and her family.

He was reading a story to his three nieces. His sister Marion had watched as her brother kept her children enthralled with his storytelling, and noticed his natural ability to communicate with them. She recalled an advertisement in the local paper a few weeks earlier. The council had listed a vacant teaching position in the township of Blackmore. The council required a teacher to take up residence and begin teaching at the start of the New Year. The position was at the new school that had been built almost a year earlier.

Marion had cajoled her brother into applying for the position. The interview had been a success. The committee was aware that he had no formal teaching qualifications, but they were having trouble finding people who were prepared to live and work in small, isolated farming communities.

The council committee gave him a six-month trial along with free accommodation. After six months, the council offered him the position on a full-time basis.

Adam looked around the small room that was now his classroom. In it were ten small desks plus his, which was positioned to one side of the large portable blackboard. On his desk was a large globe of the world, along with a coloured abacus and a wooden-handled brass bell.

Along one wall were a series of coat hooks, and a shelf holding a few dog-eared books. There was also a box of chalk sticks that the children would use to write on their slate boards. The slates were wooden-framed and were stacked on top of each other at the end of the shelf. Next to the blackboard hung a painted canvas map of Australia. He had painted a sign on a piece of board and hung it on the front fence. The sign read that enrolments were available for children aged between three and ten years old. On his first day, there were three girls and four boys who varied in ages from five to nine years old in attendance. As he was the only teacher, he was required to teach the fundamentals of reading, writing and arithmetic. But as history was his passion he would also teach that, if time permitted.

Adam stood in front of his class and looked at the grubby young faces that were staring up at him.

They all looked as though they could use a bath, and he thought that their heads were probably plagued with lice.

Most had runny noses, and Adam noticed that some had chilblains on their fingers and cold sores on their mouths. One child had an angry boil on his neck. He knew that he could not fix their ailments, but he would do his best to teach them all to read and write.

He started his first lesson with, 'Good morning children. My name is Mr Francis, and you will call me that, or sir. Now as I point at you, you will tell me your name.' The morning was spent getting to know his pupils, and by lunchtime it was obvious that none of the children had brought any food with them.

'Now children, each day we will stop for a lunch break. You will take your food and sit outside. When you have finished eating you may play for thirty minutes. When you hear the bell ring, you will come back inside and sit at your desks.' Nobody spoke, but one hand cautiously went up. Adam stared at the child and said, 'Yes David, do you wish to say something?'

The boy looked at his teacher and said, 'Sir, we don't have no food for lunch!' He stated it as though he was surprised that the teacher didn't know about their eating habits. 'Me mum feeds me and me sisters at six o'clock each night. That's when we eat. We never eat nuthin' durin' the day, unless we nick an apple from an orchard!' He gave a grin as he spoke about pinching an apple, but then looked serious again before saying, 'If I ask me mum fer something to eat at school, she will probably whack me.'

Adam looked at his young charge. He was a little shocked at the revelation, but he needed to confirm what he had just been told.

'Are you telling me truthfully David, that you only have one meal a day?' Before David could reply another hand rose, and Adam asked. 'Yes Monica, do you have something to say?'

457

Monica was six years old and replied in a tiny voice, 'We have porridge for our breakfast and bread and dripping for our tea, but we don't have no lunch neither. My mummy says that only rich people can afford to eat more than twice every day. I don't think that we are rich sir, cause sometimes we don't have no dripping to put on the bread!' Adam was becoming more concerned, as it had never occurred to him that children would be sent to school without eating something. He then asked, 'Now tell me, how many of you had breakfast today?'

The children all looked at each other, then slowly two hands went up followed by two more. Adam wanted to teach his pupils, but he also needed to know about the children he had under his care.

'Now children, you will all tell me something about yourselves. All right David, we will start with you. Where did you come from and what does your father do?' David fidgeted, and looked uncomfortable before Adam coaxed him with, 'Now David, don't be shy. We won't have any secrets here, so speak up.'

David lowered his eyes and murmured, 'Me dad took off. We dunno where he's gone!'

Adam looked at the boy, and although surprised by the revelation he prodded David for more information.

'So, tell me lad, do you have any brothers, or sisters and where do you live?' David looked more uncomfortable before answering, 'I got two sisters sir, but they are younger than me. I think me baby sister is about two, and me other one is about four, but I ain't too sure.'

Adam asked, 'Don't you know how old your sisters are David? You said that you think.' He looked at the boy for a response. David was now on the defensive and looked defiantly at his teacher.

'I dunno how old neither of them is sir. We don't have no birthdays in our house. I think it's because me mum don't have no money for presents and stuff like that. That's why me dad took off because he had no money. That's what me mum says, anyway.'

Adam was intrigued. He knew that there were plenty of people struggling to get by, but being single he had never had to struggle to make ends meet. He looked at David and asked, 'Why did your dad leave you and your mother David, and how long ago did this happen?' David, no longer embarrassed by the personal questions, was starting to enjoy being the centre of attention and replied, 'Me mum said that me dad was a soldier in the war. She said that it weren't his fault that he drunk every penny he got. She said that something bad 'appened to him in the war. The government people gave us some land, and Dad hadta put up a house after the war. He didn't have no money, so he built us a house from all sorts of stuff, but it used to leak bad when it rained and the floor was always a bit muddy.' He stopped talking as his mind went to the place that he had once called home.

Adam asked, 'Is that where you are still living David?'

'No sir, after Dad took off we had to leave cause the government men came and told us to go. We live down next to the river with the others now!'

Adam knew that there was a growing shantytown about a mile out of town. The families who had not been able to make a go of living on their settlement blocks had been moved on, and with nowhere else to go had made their camp along the riverbanks.

He looked at the innocent faces staring at him, and he couldn't remember a time when he hadn't partaken of three meals a day, yet if these children could be believed most would have been surviving on barely one meal a day. He found it concerning that parents who had mainly lived on farms, could not provide their children with enough food to give them two meals a day, let alone three.

In his mind, he resolved to do something about this problem, and after school he went to the emporium and purchased a large tin of Arrowroot and Oat biscuits. He also ordered a gallon of fresh milk to be delivered to the school each day, which he would pay for. He concluded that while his pupils may be poor, he would not teach hungry children.

***

From that day on, he made sure that the children received a glass of milk and two biscuits each at lunchtime.

65.

1929

The rain had fallen sporadically over the following months. Most mornings Tom had risen at dawn and had walked across his paddocks. The cockatoos were never far away, and he would listen to their raucous screeching as they flew overhead before landing in the nearby trees. A few landed on the ground and were eating the seed until he fired off a few rounds. After several mornings, the birds had flown away after seeing Tom guarding his crop.

Each morning, Tom looked over his dry paddocks. He would scan the sky hoping to see rain clouds. He was dreading that his crop would fail, but hoping that it wouldn't. The few early winter rains they'd received were so light that they barely damped down the brown dirt.

It was six weeks after he had spread the seed, and he was deep in thought when he noticed a few wispy green shoots appear from within the furrows. He was so taken aback that at first it didn't register that some seeds had germinated. He looked, and then with his heart pounding with excitement he stooped down and took a closer look. Some shoots were already two inches tall, and others were just breaking through the heavy soil. He was breathing hard as he walked quickly over the paddock. Everywhere that he looked he could now see the germinating seeds. He was almost running with excitement, as he moved across the field to his boundary fence.

Once there, he stopped walking and looked around. He stood still; his heart was thumping loudly as he listened. The sound of the cockatoos had disappeared. All that he could hear was the sound of the cool whispering breeze, and with a smile on his face he raised his eyes towards the cloudy sky and said out loud, 'Thank you God!'

***

That morning, Tom took his sons to school, and then stopped at the emporium to buy some tobacco.

As Tom crossed the verandah of the shop, he noticed the newspaper banner in its wire frame leaning against the wall. The headlines were in large bold type and stated, '*Major Financial Disaster in the USA. Hard Times Ahead.*' He nodded at a couple of acquaintances that were reading the paper that was spread across the counter.

'So, what's the news? What's so important about things happenin' in America that we gotta read about it here? Isn't there nothin' happenin' here at home that's more important than some money problem overseas?' Tom asked with a touch of sarcasm in his voice.

One of the readers, having perused the article just shook his head, while the other kept reading and ignored Tom's question.

Ned stood behind his wooden counter and said, 'Mornin' Tom, what's happened is that the Wall Street stock market in New York has crashed. According to the article thousands of people have gone broke overnight cause all their life savings was invested into the share market. Why, it even says that some stockbrokers have jumped out of their office windows cause they have lost all their money!'

Tom didn't understand the stock market and the vagaries of buying and selling shares in companies. He was a working-class farmer, who spent every waking moment just trying to make ends meet. He didn't have any money other than for the bare necessities, and at that moment he had no real interest in what was transpiring on money markets across the world.

He looked at Ned and said, 'I know that I'm a bit thick between the ears Ned, but what I wanna know is if any of this is gunna affect me and you. Cause if it don't, then I ain't about to start worryin' about what's goin' on over on the other side of the world.'

'I can't answer that Tom. Maybe it will have an effect on the economy over here, but I dunno enough about them kind of things. All that I know is that things are already getting tough in the city.

'As you know, I get all me supplies from Sydney, and I take the truck down there every couple of months. The last time that I was down there I seen a lot of unemployed blokes all just hanging around the wharves looking for a few days' work.

'I don't think that it has anything to do with what just happened in America though. I was told that it was because most of those blokes used to work on farms. The drought has been bad enough around here for the last couple years, as you know. But one of the bullockys told me that he went north to pick up a load of wool bales just recently. He said that the farmland west of the Darling River was nothing more than a giant dustbowl.

'So, there is no work on them outback stations cause the rivers and creeks have just dried up. I'm guessin' that's why all them poor sods are flockin' to the city in droves. Dunno how a fella is supposed to pay his rent and buy his food if he ain't earnin' any dough.

'Well Tom, what can I get you? Oh, and by the way, how's that crop of yours lookin'?'

'I'll just have some tobacco, Ned. Can't afford nothin' else until me crop comes in. I'm assumin' that I'll be able to meet me debts if I can get a half decent harvest. You better give me two packets. Dunno when I will be able to afford anymore.'

Ned looked at Tom and said, 'Tom, I told you, and I told Hannah, that you can have anything that you want. You can put in on tick and pay me when you get your crop money!'

'Yeah, I know that yer did Ned. It's very kind of you, but Hani and me we worked out our budget. We don't get no government development allowance any more. So, we hafta save our loan money payment fer the government first. Provided that me crop comes up, I can get their money together. Cause if I don't give them back me annual rental money they will take our place off us, and I got too much blood and sweat in that patch of dirt to let them government fellas take it offa me now!'

'Orright Tom, I understand. None of us knows how these money problems are gunna pan out. Better to be a bit conservative when the future is uncertain.'

'Thanks Ned, I'd better be off. I'm gunna go and see Clarence Homer. I ain't seen him fer awhile, so I'm gunna go and have a sticky at him. I'll see yer around Ned after me crop comes in. Cheerio fer now.'

✳✳✳

Clarry was patching up the walls of his house when Tom arrived. The house was barely a habitable structure, and only provided primitive accommodation. Clarry had cut a dozen tree saplings, and the ends had been dipped in creosote to stop the ants and borers attacking them after he had buried them. He had cut open potato sacks before stretching and sewing them together. Then he had tacked them onto the upright poles and poured a wet slurry of cement over all of the bags and smoothed it off with his bare hands. As the cement set, it gave the sacks some strength and provided him with little more than a windbreak.

He had thrown a large tarpaulin over the single room structure. A central pole was positioned beneath it to raise it and allow the rain to run off it. A couple of loose flour sacks formed his doorway. The floor was dirt, and he had swept it constantly, until all that was there was hard-packed earth.

Potato sacks had been roughly sewn together and filled with straw to make his mattress and pillow. The mattress lay atop of a bed made of saplings, and held together by fencing wire and nails. There was a fireplace built of stone outside the entrance of his dwelling. He nodded at Tom before wiping his hands down the sides of his worn canvas trousers.

'Haven't seen you fer awhile,' said Clarry. 'How ya been?'

Tom climbed from the cab of his truck and held out his hand to shake Clarry's. 'I been good, how about yerself? Couldn't help noticin' that you got yerself a little herd down there.' He looked in the direction of the animals.

Clarry poked the ashes of his fire, and moved the billy to the flames. 'Do ya wanna a mug? I was about ta have me smoko.'

Tom opened his tobacco pouch and rolled a cigarette. 'Yeah, thanks, I could do with a cuppa.' He offered his pouch to Clarry, who took it, and he placed the mixings in the palm of his hand before returning the pouch to Tom.

'Thanks, I been meanin' ter go inta town and get meself some supplies, but since I got me stock I been a bit busy makin' fences.'

Clarry levered open a battered tin with the edge of his pocketknife and tipped the tea leaves from it into the boiling water. He gave the billy a stir with a twig, and then placed it under the wire handle to lift it to the side of the fire. Tom was leaning on a fence railing and was staring at the cattle.

'So how long you had the beasts? If ya don't mind me sayin', they are lookin' a bit ragged! Although ya look like yer got a bit of feed fer 'em.'

'I only had 'em fer a week. I wasn't expectin' to get me loan approved, but when the bank fella came out 'ere a few weeks ago, yer could 'ave knocked me over with a feather. He brung me out a cheque fer two 'undred quid. Can ya imagine that, two 'undred quid! That's how I could afford ter buy me cows.'

'Sorry ter interrupt yer Clarry, but what loan? Who give yer a loan? I thought that you was still getting' the sustenance allowance from the government.' Clarry found a second mug, and filled it from the billy before handing it to Tom. 'I hope ya likes it black and strong. I ain't got no sugar neither!'

Tom took the mug and said, 'Nar, I been havin' it black since the war. You know how it was. We never had no milk or sugar then, so we just got used to it. Anyway, you was about ter tell me about yer loan.'

Clarry sat down on a blackened log that had been moved to the front of his house. He took a noisy slurp from his tea, before placing his mug onto the ground. 'I couldn't bite ya fer another smoke, could I?' Tom handed him the makings, and as Clarry rolled his cigarette he spoke. 'About three months ago I got a letter from the government. It wos all official lookin', and it said that the government had set up somethin' called a Commonwealth farmers' bank. The bank was ter help people like you and me, and we could apply fer a loan of up ta six hundred quid. Imagine that, six hundred quid! I never seen a 'undred quid let alone six!

'There was a form in the envelope, and all I hadta do wos fill it in and send it back. Didn't you get one? I wos under the impression that all the land settlers wos gunna get one.'

He didn't wait for Tom to respond but continued, 'Well, I filled it in. I never asked fer any amount of money. It just said that ya could get up ta six hundred quid!' He took a long drag and inhaled deeply before he continued. 'I posted the letter back.' He thought for a moment before saying, 'Geez, it musta bin over three months ago. I had forgotten about it, what with all the work that hadta be done around 'ere. Well one day, this fancy lookin' bloke drives up here, bold as brass he was. I thought he was lost, but then he asked fer me. He says he's from the bank and that he was here ter check that I met the terms of me contract. I didn't know what the hell he was talkin' about. Then he reminds me about me contract about havin' a house and the fencing all done.

'He poked his snooty nose inside, and made a note on his pad. Then he walked around and looked at me fences and writ some more. He doffed his hat and disappeared. The next thing I know is that he comes back and hands me a cheque fer two hundred quid.

'Says I hafta sign some papers, and then he says that I can spend the money on anything, as long as it was gunna improve the place. Tells me that I got five years ter pay it back in instalments. So, I takes the cheque inta the bank at Blackmore. I asked the teller bloke if it wos real, and he says it was. He tells me that it will take a coupla weeks before it has cleared and then I can spend it. Well, after it cleared I went inta the cattle sales yard in Bathurst, and that's where I bought me herd.

'The drovers had bought a big herd down from around the Darling River area. The cattle was starving, cause there was no feed, cause of the drought. Well anyway, not many bidders were at the sale, and I bought meself fifty cows and a bull. I got the whole lot fer fifty quid, and I herded them out here by meself last week. All I gotta do now is fatten em up. If I ain't mistaken, I reckon that one or two of them cows might be carryin.' He looked at Tom before saying, 'If yer look closely yer can see that a couple of them has got swollen bellies and udders. Now that might just be because they was short of feed, or it might mean that I might be able ter expand me little herd if I'm right. Anyway, time will tell.'

Tom was staring at the animals, but his mind was elsewhere. He thought that if Clarry could get a loan from the government farmers' bank, then he should qualify too. After all, his property was much more established than this one, and if he were to improve his place, then he would need to find some money from somewhere.

He turned to Clarry and asked, 'Could ya show me the original letter that yer got from the government Clarry. I ain't doubting ya fer a second, but I just wanna know what the address is and the fella's name that's givin' out the loans. I could use a few quid. Me crop is just startin' ter shoot, but I don't expect to get a big harvest. I could use havin' a few cows and some sheep. I read that the drought is spreadin', and that the price of mutton is pretty low right now. We still got a bit of feed in them bottom paddocks that I haven't ploughed. Could be an opportunity to getting a few sheep on the cheap. Mind you, a bloke would hav'ta have a bit of cash lyin' around ta do that, and I'm runnin' a bit short. So, if I can get onta this bankin' bloke, I might stand a chance.'

Clarry disappeared inside and came out carrying a small satchel. 'Me contract and all the details is inside. Take it 'ome with ya, and when ya got the details, ya can bring it back. I ain't in a hurry ter get the papers back as I got me money. All I gotta hope is that me bull will do his work and give me a few heifers, come the spring.'

66.

The Depression

The government had been continually expanding the infrastructure of the cities across Australia. Roads were being sealed, and trenches that would hold the cast-iron sewage and water pipes were dug with picks and shovels.

The Harbour Bridge was also being constructed above the slums and brothels of what was known as the Rocks area. The expansion of the electric railway system was also under construction, along with the underground tunnel system that it would run through when it was completed.

The Australian government had been borrowing heavily from the Bank of England to fund their infrastructure programmes. However, as the drought across the east coast of Australia was now into its third year, commodity prices continued to fall as crops again failed. Thousands of sheep were in such poor condition that the meat was unpalatable and they were almost worthless.

Farmers had been laying off workers across the country, and men were flocking back to the cities in the hope of picking up a job on a government-funded project. It was well known that once a person had secured a government-funded position that it was almost impossible to be sacked, or laid off.

✶✶✶

Doris was beating the dust from a rug with her broom handle. She had dragged the rug from her parlour and thrown it over the clothes line. She was struggling to keep herself busy and had resorted to cleaning things, even though she had precious little to clean. She had been feeling lonely for some time now, as Claire had been spending more time at the forge shop since Davin had finished his last contract.

Davin had been forced to lay off his workers, as the government contracts that had sustained the forge for years had suddenly dried up. He was now working alone, and had resorted to making small trivets and pokers that could be sold cheaply in the shop.

Doris, like many others, didn't understand why things had changed so dramatically. She had stopped buying the weekly newspaper in order to save a few pennies. Claire would bring around her copy for Doris to read after she had finished with it.

The electricity was supplied to her house and the others who lived in housing authority dwellings by meters. Each house had a meter placed next to the fuse box. The tenant would put a penny in the meter and turn the handle. This provided enough electricity to power several bulbs for an hour. It had cost Doris threepence a night for her power, but since the start of the depression, she could save almost two shillings a week by using candles and her kerosene lamp. Jack had gone crook at her, and demanded that she let him pay for her power, but her pride would not let her accept anything that she regarded as charity, even if it was from her son.

She was still beating the rug just as Jack called out, 'Ah, there you are. I thought that you had gone out when there was no answer.' He bent down, and gave his mother a peck on the cheek.

'Hello son, what brings you around here? Do you want a cuppa?' and she answered her own question by saying, 'Of course you do. I'll just go and stoke up the stove.'

'I just thought that I would bring around some coal mother. I didn't know if you were running short or not.'

'I am running a bit low, but that's me own fault. I lent Mrs Stubbs a scuttle full, not that I expect to get it back. Poor woman, I ran into her down at the general store. She had bought a few things, and she was so embarrassed. When she went to pay for her goods, she was four pence short. Old Mr Carlton behind the counter said that he couldn't give her any more credit until she paid what was outstanding already.

'I thought that it was a bit rude of him, cause he said it out loud, and other people in the store could hear what he said. She was trying to decide which of her things that she would have to leave behind.

'I had a few bob in me purse, and I slipped her a shilling. I could see that the poor woman was uncomfortable. She was trying to give me the money back without making a fuss. A few people were watching, and I said loudly. 'Just take the money Mrs Stubbs, you can pay me back when you get home.' I only said that for the benefit of the nosy parkers who was in the store. Anyway, she took the money and gave me a smile. I could see that she was grateful and then I got me things.

'She was waiting outside the store, and she said that she wanted to tell me that she didn't really know when she could pay me back. Well, we got talking, and I told her to come and have a cuppa with me as I could use the company.

'It's a funny old world son, I must have known Mrs Stubbs since you were a boy and she only lives around the corner. But that's the first time that I really got to talk to her other than to say hello. Once she started talking, I just let her go.

'I got the impression that she didn't have many friends. Turns out that her old man is a drunk. When he gets drunk, he belts her around, and then when he's sober he can't remember what he's done. Can you imagine that?'

Jack was pouring the tea and asked, 'Is her old man workin'?'

Doris carefully measured out a half teaspoon of sugar and replied, 'I think that he is a rigger and is working on that new harbour bridge. She told me that some weeks he would give her a quid to buy the food, but that's only if he hadn't started to drink. The rest of the time he just buys beer with it.'

'How old is her kids?'

'She's got two boys, but they must be grown up and be as old as you and your brother. She has a girl, but I think that she is a bit retarded. I know the poor child has fits. One day, I seen her having one, but she must be nearly thirty. The crosses some people have to bear!' She muttered it more to herself than to Jack, and shook her head.

'Do ya think that I should drop a bag of coal around to her?'

'That'd be a nice gesture, son, but she would be terribly embarrassed if she knew that I had spoken to you about her problems. Besides that, things are gettin' tough for a lot of people now, what with this blessed depression. If it got out that you were an easy touch, you would have half the neighbourhood wanting free coal.

'I might call around and have a chat with her in a few days. It would be easier if I just told her to bring her pram around and take home a bucket full when she needed it.'

'Orright Ma, I don't mind bringing around a bit extra. I know what yer sayin' about things gettin' tough. I musta had half a dozen blokes knockin' on me door at the yard lookin' fer work over the last week alone.

'I was down at Darlin' Harbour a few days ago, and I seen all these fellas just standing around outside the gates of the dockyards. Some had swags over their backs and most was carryin' their billies. I asked a fella what was going on, and he said that the dockyard boss would come and pick a few fellas out from the crowd when he had a ship to unload, or load up. He said that sometimes a bloke might get a day's work. But apparently, they hafta get there early, and sometimes they stand there all day in the hope that they might get picked.

'The government sacked all them union blokes who wouldn't unload the ships because they wanted more money. Now them same blokes are standin' outside them big gates begging fer a few hours' work. One fella that I got talking to said that the docks was called Poverty Road. There musta been a coupla hundred blokes all standing against the wire fences. I never seen nuthin' like it!

'I ain't never seen so many shops shut up in the city neither. Why it only seems like yesterday that the factories would have their big employment signs hangin' up on the factory walls lookin' fer labour. Now all they got is big signs sayin' no vacancy.'

Doris frowned, 'I wonder how your brother is getting along with his farm? I do hope that this downturn in the economy don't affect all them country folk. The last time that he was here he said that they was still waitin' for the government people to connect his telephone. I do wish that I could just talk to him and Hannah. I'm grateful that at least you have your own business. People need coal for their stoves whatever happens with the economy.'

Jack took the last sip from his cup and asked, 'How's Davin goin'? I ain't seen him or Claire for such a long time. Claire used to be here just about every time I come here. I was just thinkin' of them the other night after I read about the government cancellin' contracts and work orders. I know that Davin did a lot of government work and I was just curious.'

Doris stood up, and emptied the tealeaves from her cup into the sink before she removed the tea cosy from the teapot and checked its contents. 'I'll just top the pot up. Do you want another cup son?' She filled the pot again and placed the cosy back over it.

'Davin had to lay the last of his workers off, let me think. It must have been nearly six months ago now. He said that he was expecting to be able to fill his contracts.

'He was making some light brackets for the roadway that will go across that harbour bridge. Apparently, it was the biggest contract that he ever had. He even put on a coupla extra blacksmiths just so that he could fill the order on time.

'Then lo and behold, he came home one night, and he was in shock. The government bloke who he dealt with for all of his contracts had called around and told him that the government had run out of money, and as such they were cancelling all contracts. That included the one he had for the light brackets.

'Claire was in a terrible state when she came around here. Davin had all these iron brackets that he had made and then the government tells him that they can't pay for them so don't deliver them. Well, as you can imagine it left him in a fine pickle. He had to tell the new chaps that he had just hired that they were all fired!'

Doris stirred the tea in her cup before saying, 'What I don't understand is how could the government possibly run out of money. I don't understand politics, but I seen all them poor men that you was talking about too! I bet a lot of them fellas served their country just like you done son. That's no way to treat all those boys. If it were up to me, I'd give them all a job. How many came home not right in the head after all that they done? It's not right son, and I haven't read anything from the government to explain to any of us about what's going on!'

Jack wore a frown and said, 'I was deliverin' a coupla bags of coal around to the church last week, and I was speakin' to Father Davis. He's that new bloke that's been doin' the nine o'clock Mass on Sundays. We was talkin' about this very thing. At least the church is doin' more than just preachin' now!'

Doris looked at Jack and asked, 'What do you mean son?'

'Well, this Father Davis has set up a soup kitchen. He said that so many people were knockin' at his door lookin' fer a feed that he should do somethin' about it. So, he gets a few ladies to help him cook up pots of vegetables, with a bit of mutton donated from the butcher's.

'He's been givin' out a free feed to anyone who wants one every Friday night. Says he's gunna keep doin' it as long as he can get the food. He's been goin' around all the shops and puttin' the bite on them to help with donations so that he can feed the people. That's why he wanted a few extra bags of coal from me.

'He's got the presbytery stove goin' extra now, just so that the ladies helpin' him cook the tucker can get it ready in time. I told him that I would donate two bags of coal to the church every week as my contribution.

'Well anyway ma, he explained to me about why the government has been cancellin' all their contracts as well as layin' off workers. I didn't understand it neither, until he spelt it out in plain language.

'The money it uses for building things, like roads and railways, is borrowed from the Bank of England, but the English government had borrowed all its money from the Americans during the war. Now the Americans want their money back and the English government can't pay. So, because it's borrowed money, the English banks want all the money that they lent to our government back.

'After that American stock market collapsed, there wasn't much money left to go around. Well, the bank blokes in England have come out here and apparently demanded from our government that they pay all the money back, and all the interest as well. And they have told the government that they aren't giving them another penny until they get all their dough back.

'That's why it was in the paper the other day that all the people who work for the government have to take a ten per cent pay cut. That's why all them union fellas was pullin' strikes and things, cause they reckon that they can't live and pay their bills with less money comin' in!

'Father Davis reckons that it's even gunna get worse. There's talk that the only money that the government has got now is some gold that they got stashed away for a rainy day. He says that if the government has to sell all its gold, then a lot more people are gunna get laid off. That's why Davin lost his government contracts cause they wouldn't a been able to pay him.'

Doris was staring at the wall. Her mind was elsewhere. She knew that if it weren't for Jack and Claire, she would be struggling more than what she was. She was grateful that she didn't have to pay any rent as more people were facing eviction now because they had no money. She looked at Jack and said, 'We should be grateful for small mercies son. Me ten bob a week I get from the railways don't go far these days, but it's more than some poor souls are receiving right now!'

67.

Hungry Children

Within three months of the school being opened, new enrolments had expanded the class to twelve children. The government had extended the land available to soldier settlers, and now more than twenty new families were developing their allotments on the outskirts of Blackmore.

At the same time, more settlement evictions were being carried out. Those evicted invariably ended up living in the ever-expanding shanty town down by the river.

Adam could no longer afford to pay for his pupils' milk and biscuits, and he had asked the council to fund the purchase of what he now regarded as essential sustenance for the children.

At first, the council had refused. They were struggling with unemployment on an unprecedented level. The government was forced to provide the unemployed with a sustenance payment, and they tasked the councils across the country with distributing the funds.

Adam had persisted with fighting with the council to provide sustenance for his pupils. He had written a terse letter to each member of the council, and he was summoned to address the council in chambers at the next monthly meeting.

He was nervous, as he knew that the council could easily sack him and replace him with any one of the hundreds of unemployed that were searching for a job. He had confided in his sister Marion, and told her of his moral dilemma.

'Marion, you should see the state of the children. Nearly every one of them is undernourished, and more than half of them told me that they only ever have one meal a day.

'I just don't think that it is right that I should be expected to teach hungry children! I am convinced that some of the children are being sent to school just to receive the milk and the biscuits that I can no longer afford to supply!'

'I agree with you Adam. But you know how tough things are right now. You are aware that they might just get rid of you if you become too much of a thorn in their side. Go to that meeting, be respectful, and put your case forward. Have you written your speech yet?'

'No, I haven't written a speech. I will say what is on my mind. If the councillors are so narrow-minded, and they wish to remain oblivious to what is going on around them, then I don't care if they sack me. I will find another job somewhere. But, I have to stand up for what I believe in!'

***

Adam rode his bicycle to the station in time to catch the afternoon train to Bathurst. From there, he walked the half-mile to the council chambers and waited nervously for the meeting to commence. It was seven o'clock before he was ushered into the chambers. The walls of the room were panelled in dark burnished wood and the ornate Deco wall sconces imparted a soft glow upon them. Sepia-coloured photographs of former councillors hung from within dark wooden frames along the wall.

Mr Jefferson Searle was the council mayor. He was educated, opinionated and generally cantankerous to all that he met. He sat at the centre of the long table, and on the table in front of him was a copy of

Adam's letter. He acknowledged him by pointing at a vacant chair that was positioned at the end of the table.

Adam sat down. His heart was thumping loudly. Ten pairs of hostile eyes stared at him, while the mayor cast his glance down the length of the table to glare intimidatingly at him.

Mrs Janice Taylor sat behind the councillors with her note pad, and was ready to record the minutes of the meeting in shorthand. The mayor banged his gavel hard upon the table and declared, 'This special meeting of the council will come to order.

'Mr Francis, I have called this meeting tonight to give you a chance to explain to council the meaning of your extraordinary letter to each of us!' The mayor looked around at the others sat at the large table before saying, 'Sir, I must say that I feel personally affronted by your letter. So, would you be kind enough to explain the meaning of its tone to us?'

Adam stood up. He looked directly at each of the councillors before he turned his glance towards the mayor. He was silent for a moment, but then he took a deep breath and began to speak.

'Gentlemen, thank you for giving me the opportunity to talk directly to you all. Firstly, let me state that I thought it appropriate that I should write to you all individually. I wanted you all to understand fully my frustration at the situation that I am facing with my young pupils.

'If my frustration was portrayed in my correspondence as anything else, and if I in anyway have caused offence by my brusqueness in the tone of my letter, then please accept my humble apology!'

Mrs Taylor was writing quickly, and recording every word that was spoken. Each councillor was now watching Adam intently, and the room was silent. Most had expected him to show nervousness, and they were somewhat surprised at his eloquence and the air of self-confidence that he exuded.

'Gentlemen, I have been the teacher at the Blackmore school for almost a year. I fully understand that times are very hard for many people across this country. The children that I teach live in abject poverty. There is no other way of describing their plight. Most are fortunate if they have one decent meal a day. Their parents are generally as poor as church mice, yet many of their fathers served their country in the war.

'Some of my pupils don't have a father. Some men have abrogated their role as a father, and absconded from their duty of raising their children. I do not stand here and judge these men, for I have no knowledge of why they struggle to cope. Whilst I can show empathy to a woman struggling to put food on her table for her children, I believe that we cannot just turn our backs, and ignore the hungry young innocents that I am charged with teaching!

'Many of the places that these children live in could only be described as little more than basic shelter.

'Calling them houses is wrong, as most are barely hovels. I have visited some of these primitive dwellings where the floors are dirt, and the roofs are made from flattened kerosene tins.

'Only recently, I had cause to visit the accommodation where several of my charges reside. Gentlemen, I would like to describe this dwelling to you, where five children and their mother live. Cardboard boxes had been broken up and were laid atop of the dirt floor in a vain attempt to weatherproof the floor. The walls of the single room where they all lived were made from hessian sacks that were stretched between tree branches that had been inserted into the ground. The sacks had been rendered with a mixture of lime and animal fat, which I was told were boiled in salt water. This mixture, when dry, gave the hessian enough strength to remain rigid for a period of time.

However, the smell within the confines of the room resembled what one would expect to find around a decaying animal carcass that had been left to rot in the sunlight. The children sleep on potato sacks filled with dried grass gathered from the paddocks. The only cooking facilities were a wall of stones to contain the fire. They were laid in a semicircle facing the entrance of the abode.'

Adam stopped talking for a moment, in the hope that what he had just described might shock the councillors. He looked around at the gathering. Most were no longer glaring at him, but held their gaze to the table. Some twirled their pencils, and others just clasped the fists as their minds visualised the picture that he had just portrayed. Adam knew that they were feeling uncomfortable, and he took heart from this before continuing.

'Sadly, gentlemen, what I have just described to you is all too common around the settlement allotments, and the shanty town at Blackmore. The government appears to have washed its hands in helping the soldier settlers and their families. I am aware that I have not been summoned here tonight to discuss the rights or wrongs of what many of us see as a failed government policy.

'However, whether we like it or not, the failure of several government policies has a direct bearing on the situation that I am pleading with you all to rectify. These children, along with many of their parents, are malnourished. I fear that if we continue to ignore what is happening, then some of these children will surely perish. If not from starvation, then certainly from illnesses brought about by infections associated with malnutrition. Some of my pupils arrive at school wearing potato sacks that have been manufactured by their mothers into short pants and are held up by twine.

'I can say, gentlemen, with total honesty, that not one child who attends my school has a pair of shoes to wear. Shoes cost money, and money is the one commodity that these families have precious little of!

'I have met and spoken with some of the pupils' fathers. By all outward appearances, they seem normal, but most if not all of them are struggling with their inner demons. A legacy no doubt, of their involvement in the Great War.'

Adam looked at each of the councillors again. They, in turn, kept their eyes averted, but didn't interrupt.

'Gentlemen, I am not asking the council for help in changing the settlers' lives. We cannot alter the way that things are. We cannot generate jobs for these people as much as we may wish to see better times for them. However, the children are the responsibility of their parents, but we as custodians of their minds are also responsible for them. If we agree as a society that children should be educated, then it follows that we build a place of learning for them. But, do any of you honourable gentlemen,' Adam stared at each of them individually and held their collective gazes before proceeding, 'really believe that all that the council is required to do is provide these children with slate boards, chalk and a teacher? May I ask again, do you really believe that our responsibility to these children ends there?

'I would invite any, or all of you honourable gentlemen to visit my school and see first-hand how difficult it is for these children. Some are as young as four years old. They try to absorb the lessons that are being taught, while the pangs of hunger in their bellies growl louder as the day wears on!

'When I first started teaching at Blackmore, I had no idea that these children were almost starving, and that they had arrived at school with little or no food in their bellies. When I found out, I arranged to provide them with a single glass of milk and an oat and arrowroot biscuit each. I could not, in all good faith, ask them to provide me with a penny each to soothe their hunger pangs. That was my cost to provide each child with what I gave them.

'The trouble was though gentlemen, I could afford to do that when I had three or four pupils, but now I have almost a dozen, and I expect that number to increase as more of the settler children reach school age.

'Gentlemen this is why I stand before you all tonight. I am pleading to your sense of decency for help. I am asking that the council develop a policy to provide my children with at least one proper meal a day, or at least a glass of milk.

'I understand that if you vote to accept responsibility for providing some manner of sustenance to the settlement children it will no doubt become the norm for all school children within this council's boundary.

'May I give you all a reminder of how the citizens of each town in our mother country and Ireland were charged a rate to feed starving prisoners almost a hundred years ago? Prisoners were not provided with food, and if they had no one who could provide a meal for them, then they literally died of starvation in their cells. It was an act of parliament that levied a rate on every landlord and business within the community. The community administered the levy for one purpose only, and that was to provide funding to buy food for those in custody.

'Gentlemen, these children are the innocents. They did not contribute to the Depression, nor did they cause it. But, they are the victims, and if you reject my plea for help, then I have no idea as to what I shall do other than spend all of my wages on dousing the flames of their hunger to the best of my ability.'

He lowered his eyes before again looking around the chamber. He then said, 'Thank you, gentlemen, for giving me this opportunity to speak to you all.'

The councillors shuffled uncomfortably in their seats for a moment before the mayor looked directly at Adam and spoke.

'Mr Francis, the council wishes to express its thanks to you for informing it of the plight of your needy children. We will now discuss in chambers what our response should be. As you rightly pointed out, times are extremely tough, and the council is working within tight monetary guidelines. I cannot give you an undertaking that the council can, in fact, do anything to resolve your problem at this moment in time.

'Rest assured though, that the council will give every consideration to your request, and if we are able to find a financial solution that will meet your expectations without impacting on other areas, we will do our best to accommodate you!' The mayor spoke quietly to his colleagues for a few moments before returning his attention back to Adam.

'Mr Francis, in light of your concerns we will contact the district nurse, Mrs Carney.

'We will direct her to make a weekly call to your school, and she can decide what will be the best course of action to take regarding the well-being of your children.

'We will inform you in due course of what action, if any, that we will take regarding the nutritional requirements of the children. Thank you, for your attendance Mr Francis.'

The meeting was concluded as far as Jefferson Searle was concerned, and he turned from Adam in a dismissive manner.

68.

Looking for Work

It was almost springtime and the winter rains had not eventuated. The days usually dawned cloudy, and they promised rain, but by mid-morning the clouds had disappeared leaving only a cool wind and more disappointment.

Tom's crops were still growing sullenly, sustained only by the heavy dews left behind from the cold nights. He nervously walked across his paddocks every few days to check the growth. By the end of winter, the wheat was standing over two feet tall, while the barley was half that as it struggled to grow in the almost dry soil.

Hannah was also worried about their future. While she could grow a few vegetables and Tom could trap a few rabbits, they would be able to survive, but she wasn't confident that they would still be on their farm next year if they didn't get any rain soon. The few sheep that they had were far too small to kill, and they needed to keep the two cows, and the one bull that they owned in the hope that they would be able to breed from them.

Tom had told her that they had just over forty pounds left in the old molasses tin, and that had to last them at least until the crop was harvested. Hannah knew that it wouldn't go far, and she tried to put it from her mind what would happen to them should the crop fail. She had also read the weekly paper that Tom had brought home, and although she didn't understand the implications of the Depression, the tone of the articles left her with the feeling that things would probably get worse before they got better.

Tom walking into the kitchen interrupted her thoughts. He was tired, and the furrows upon his face showed it. Hannah moved the kettle to the hotplate, and it was soon boiling. He gave a weak smile to Hannah before saying, 'Well at least the chooks are still laying,' and he took four still-warm eggs from his jacket pocket. 'I suppose that we could buy a few more chooks, and we could sell the eggs,' he said dryly.

Hannah smiled and said, 'Just come and sit down. I have made a johnnycake, and I will make another for the children. Now eat, we aren't on death's door just yet!'

Tom broke off a slab of the doughy bread. He hadn't realised just how hungry he was until he took his first mouthful. He took a swig of his hot tea to wash the mixture down and said, 'I done some thinkin' Hani.

'I been thinkin that as I can't do nuthin' until the crop is grown proper, I should try and get meself a payin' job in Bathurst, or somewhere.' Tom stopped talking for a moment as he tried to put his thoughts into perspective. Hannah sat down at the table next to him. She placed her hand over his, as she knew that he wouldn't have taken this decision lightly.

'If that's what you think is best darling, but the papers are saying that jobs are getting harder to get everywhere. Where will you go, what will you do?' She was looking intently at Tom. He squeezed her hand before saying, 'I'll take a couple of quid from the tin and drive to Bathurst. I'll take the truck and me swag and sleep rough, just like I done when we first got 'ere. I might be able to do a few deliveries. I dunno Hani, but I gotta try and get somethin'. I'll go to the mill and the rail yards. There must be jobs somewhere, and I'll do me best to find one!

'If we were still getting the sustenance money, we could survive, but we aren't! I don't like leavin' you and the kids, but I'm not gunna lose this farm without a fight Hani. If it rains, then the grain will swell, and we might be lucky enough to get a few more bags, but I ain't waitin' any longer. If I could get a month's work, it might just be enough money to tide us over until the crop money comes in!'

Hannah stood, and said, 'We will be all right. The boys are big enough to manage without you for a few weeks. When will you leave?'

'There's no point in waitin', I'll go tomorrow, but before I go I gotta be sure that you got enough food to last for about a month. I might be back sooner, but if I can get some work, I will go to the post office and telephone Bill. I will ask him to get a message through to you.

'If you need anything, anything at all you better tell me in the mornin' and I will go to the store and get it before I leave. I'll leave me gun here, not that I expect you to need it, but I been seein' a few swaggies walkin' along the track over the past few weeks. They are probably just like me and lookin' fer work. Anyway, if you need any sort of help at all, just get the boys to ride over to Bill's place. I'll go and check me truck now. It will save me doin' it tomorrow!'

The door opened, and Jimmy came inside followed by his brother. Hannah looked at her boys and said, 'If you're looking for something to eat you will have to wait, I have a johnnycake in the oven and it will be ready shortly. Where's your sister?'

Billy looked at his brother before saying; 'She was having a rest outside. She said that she was tired and just lay down. I think that she was just being silly cause she wouldn't play with us.'

Hannah stopped what she was doing; a frown creased her forehead. She looked at the boys, 'What do you mean she just lay down, lay down where?' Billy shrugged his shoulders, 'I seen her over at the stables, but she does that all the time. She's just cranky because she wanted to play down at the dam and we wouldn't let her go by herself. You told us mummy, that we wasn't to let her go there by herself!'

Hannah was feeling uneasy now; it was unusual for Peggy not to follow her brothers everywhere. She wiped her hands on her apron and said with a tinge of panic in her voice, 'Come and help me find your sister boys. Show me where you last saw her.' They went straight to the stables and saw Peggy curled up on the ground. Hannah's heart was thumping, as she thought that a snake might have bitten her. She knelt down next to her daughter and breathed a sigh of relief as Peggy opened her eyes, then sat up and smiled.

'Oh darling, you gave mummy a scare,' and she gave her a cuddle. 'Were you tired my little one, or do you have a tummy ache?' Peggy looked up at her mother and said, 'My legs are tired mummy, and my arms are sore.'

Hannah placed her hand on Peggy's forehead, and it was warm. She picked her up and carried her back to the house. Tom came back inside after packing his swag and supplies onto the truck. He looked at Hannah as she lay Peggy down. 'Is she feelin' crook?' He asked casually.

Hannah wiped her daughter's face with a damp cloth. 'She has a slight temperature, so she might be getting a fever. I'll keep her in bed for a couple of days. She will be all right; now don't you worry. Have you got everything that you need?'

Tom looked at Peggy, and ran his hand through her hair. 'You will feel better soon my little angel.' Peggy gave her father a smile and snuggled down into her bed before closing her eyes. Tom stared at her for a few moments before saying, 'I think that I will call in and see Brigid tomorrow. I'll see if she can come out and give her a check-up.'

'Oh, stop your fussing, she probably has just picked up something. I will give her a dose of castor oil before she has her dinner.'

***

Tom left after breakfast and took two hours to drive to Bathurst. The bullock trains had been using the road for fifty years, and had supplied goods to the township of Blackmore. It was then that it had become known as the ration track.

He passed several men walking in the opposite direction. They all wore the same look of despair, as they carried their swags and billies as they trudged the back roads in the hope of finding work.

Tom called at the clinic and saw Brigid. 'Why Tommy Fields, what brings you here at this time of day? Is Hannah with you? It's been ages since I have seen any of you. I have been so busy here, you have no idea!'

Tom smiled, and bent down to give Brigid a peck on her cheek. 'I've missed you too. What I called to see you about, is Peggy.' Before he could continue Brigid said, 'She's not sick, is she? I worry about that child. Don't get me wrong, I worry about all of you, but little Peggy, well she's such a darling. I will never forget the day she was born, and what a scare she and Hannah gave us both. So, what's the matter with the little tomboy?'

'I don't know if there is anything wrong with her. She has been acting a little strangely of late that's all.'

'What do you mean, acting strangely?' Brigid gave all of her attention to Tom, as she wanted to know exactly what symptoms Peggy was displaying.

'I dunno, she has a bit of fever, and she said that her legs were tired. It just seemed a strange thing to say. So, if you could go out sometime and take a look at her, it would put me mind to rest.'

'Oh Tommy, you didn't have to drive all this way. You could have telephoned me from Bill Murdoch's place. You know that I would have come straight out.' Tom smiled at her, 'I know yer would, but I was coming in here anyway.

'I'm on me way to Bathurst to see if I can get me a job of some sort!' He went on to explain about his financial situation. 'Well Brigid, I'll be off. I ain't goin' home until I find meself a payin' job. Hani will be pleased to see ya.'

'Don't worry Tommy. I'm sure that it will just be a virus of some sort. Anyway, I will call out this afternoon. Now, you go and do what you have to.'

***

Tom drove out to the mill, and saw Morrie Fletcher, the leading hand. 'How ya been doin, Morrie?'

'Just takin' one day at a time Tom. What brings you out here? You got a few more trees you want slicin' up, have ya?' he asked expectantly.

'Nar, I was just wonderin' if you had a bit of work going vacant. I'm hopin' that me crop might make it through the drought. But I won't know for another two months yet. I ain't got much dough left, and I haven't got enough to spend it on the farm, so I thought that I might look fer a bit of work to tide me over. I ain't fussy about what the job is as long as it pays a few bob. I got me truck.' Tom turned and nodded towards it. 'I could do a bit of haulin' if yer wanted somethin' delivered.'

He looked expectantly at Morrie who replied, 'Sorry Tom, I'm strugglin' meself to keep the mill goin'. I got two fellas left, and I hadta cut their wages as it stands. As you know, I had a dozen men here a year ago. I said that I hadta give 'em a pay cut and they hadta work a twelve-hour day if I was to keep the mill goin', but they all packed up and went. They all said, no! Bet they wished they had stayed on now! Anyway, we lost our government contracts, and we only got one council one left. So, them two fellas that I still got will get laid off when the council contract is done. I reckon' that I got about two months work left if I'm lucky!'

Tom rolled himself a smoke and offered his pouch to Morrie.

'That's orright mate, just thought that I would ask. I didn't really expect ya to say you had some work. I seen a few blokes walking the track on me way in here. You know when things are getting tough when yer see men carryin' their swags way out 'ere!'

Morrie handed the tobacco pouch back and said, 'Where you gunna go now?'

'I dunno, last time I was here they was puttin' up streetlights and poles in town, so I might go and see if they got any work.

'But other than that, I'm gunna keep on drivin' onto the next town. I'll call in on any farms that look like they got some stock in the paddocks. I got me swag, and I can sling the canvas over the back of me truck and sleep under that.

'I ain't that worried, while I'm out drivin around I gotta chance of getting' somethin'. Better than sittin' around the plot at home waiting for me crop to grow.'

Morrie took a long drag on his smoke, and he scraped the dirt with the toe of his boot. He was thinking, and with his thoughts in place he said,

'I just remembered somethin'. This contract that we got at the moment is for the council. They are gunna build a wharf down on the Macquarie River. It must be gunna be a big one cause we hafta supply a whole pile of thirty-foot-long logs.

'We been dragging in some big ironbarks from out your way. I think that we gotta supply about forty more of them. We only delivered about half a dozen so far. Why dontcha go down to the river? You should be able to find them easy, cause they will hafta set up a big pile driver before they will be able to drop the poles inta the river.'

***

The riverbank was lined with tin shacks, and boat builders' sheds, although most were deserted. It didn't take long to see the pile-driving derrick sitting high at the water's edge. It was mounted on a low barge that was over one hundred feet long. The derrick was built over the centre of the barge while at the other end stood a smaller crane with an assortment of coiled-up ropes and assorted pulleys laying haphazardly about.

A few men stood around smoking, and Tom parked his truck behind a shack. He walked over to the group, and gave the men a nod of his head before he asked, 'One of you fellas the boss?'

'The boss is on the barge. You lookin' for work, are you?' Tom nodded before saying, 'Heard that there might be a coupla days' work goin' down 'ere.'

The others looked at Tom, and one spoke; 'They haven't started employing anyone just yet. That's what the boss fella told us this mornin'. Said he might put on a few blokes to help with the crane. That's why we are standin' here twiddlin' our thumbs. Its gunna be first in first served. That's what he told us, didn't he?' He looked at the others for confirmation of what he had just said.

Henry Brinkley was the foreman. He was tall, and heavyset with an ample belly hanging over his trousers. He wore a green flannelette shirt that did nothing to hide his bulging biceps, and his hands were the size of small legs of mutton.

His face was burnt brown by endless hours in the sun, and his whiskers contained tinges of grey. He didn't wear a hat, which was unusual in its self.

He came out of the engine room of the barge wearing a scowl. He gave a cursory glance towards the men standing on the shore, before climbing over the stored gear. He looked at Tom before asking, 'You lookin' fer work?'

'I could use a job. Don't care what it is, or how long it lasts. I just needta earn a bita dough. Have ya got any work goin? I don't wanna waste yer time, so if ya say no, I'll just say g'day and be gone.'

Henry looked at Tom before replying, 'I might have some work for the right men, but I don't want no shirkers. This job is gunna be tough. It's gunna be from sun up to sun down, and it's gunna be a six-day-a-week job until the job is finished.' He was staring at Tom through squinted eyes as if he was sizing him up.

'Well, you look fit enough, but looks can be deceivin', so I'll get you to do somethin' for me, and we will see!' Tom wasn't too sure what was required of him, but asked, 'So what do yer want me to do, and if I do it, do I get the job?'

'Well son, before we talk about whether or not you got the job let's see what yer made of. See that rope over there?' He pointed to the coils stacked upon the deck.

'Go and pick up that top coil, and carry it up the derrick. Get it all the way to the top.' He pointed skyward before continuing, 'That coil weighs seventy pounds, and it's a hundred feet long. If you get it to the top platform without droppin' it, and without fallin' off I'll give you a start!' He looked at Tom in a challenging manner before saying, 'In case you're wonderin', the top platform is sixty feet off the deck, are you up for it?'

Tom looked up at the top of the rig. There were three different levels, each with a wooden staircase rising and connecting to the next. The legs of the derrick splayed out across the deck and were bolted to the steel frame of the barge. Each leg was bolted to another crossbeam, and as the rig rose, the legs came closer as they neared the top. Where the legs joined above the top platform, another smaller ledge jutted out, and attached to that was a small wheel that hung directly over the water below. Another large rusty steel wheel with an equally rusty handle was bolted to the top platform. The top wheel itself was over six feet in diameter, and it was grooved to take the rope that would wind around it.

Tom looked at the staircases, and he wondered how hard it would be to carry a seventy-pound length of rope to the top, but if he didn't try there would be no job, so he held his hand out to Henry. 'You got a deal', and they both shook hands.

He slung the large coil over one shoulder, after putting his head through the centre. The coil was larger than what it looked on the ground, and Tom gave a grunt as the rope weighed heavily on his shoulder. By the time that he had reached the first landing, he was sweating profusely. At the second landing, he stopped, and gave his pounding heart a rest as he gasped for breath.

He hadn't noticed it before, but now that he was almost at the half way mark he was aware that the derrick was rocking gently. The movement was exaggerated by the wash of the waves lapping at the hull of the barge. He looked down at the others looking up at him. The last staircase was narrower as it rose to the top platform and the wheel, but he focused his mind on the farm and his family. They were the reason that he was taking on this challenge. With the thought of his family entrenched within his mind he slowly reached the top. Tom dropped the rope and looked down. He was bent over as he regained his breath and the sweat dripped from his brow. The top platform had decidedly more movement, and he steadied himself on the handrail. He noticed the strange looking trap door and the large lever protruding from the floor.

With his heart beating normally again, Tom slowly made his way back to ground level. Henry stared at him before saying, 'That wasn't so hard, was it? I'm a man of me word, and you got that rope to the top, so now I'll tell you about the job, and you can make up yer mind if you want it or not.' He turned and walked to the shady side of the derrick before speaking again.

'The job is to build a jetty. We are waitin' for the logs to arrive from the mill. When they do, we have to drive them into the riverbed. That derrick,' and he looked skyward, 'is the pile driver. You seen that big wheel up there and the trap door?' He looked at Tom to confirm that he had. 'Well, the rope goes over the wheel, and the rope is attached to the actual pile driver. See that lump of steel sittin' over there?' He pointed to where the steel block lay. 'We call it the monkey. That lump of steel weighs nearly half a ton, and when you drop it from way up there,' and he pointed skyward again, 'it drops onta the end of the pole, and belts it inta the river bottom.

'So, we have got to drive forty of them poles into the riverbed. Each pole is thirty foot long, and we hafta drive it twenty feet into the mud.

'When we done that, we will build the deck part. That will stand on top of the poles and should be about ten feet above the water. So, that's the job, and bein' such a strong fella, your job will be to be one of the donkeys. We work from sun up to sunset, which is about twelve hours. We work six days and don't do any work on Sundays. We aren't heathens! The job pays five bob a day and yer tucker. I need forty men, so are ya interested?'

Henry looked at Tom, with no expectation that he would turn the job offer down. Tom asked, 'So if I'm a donkey, what's me actual job?'

Henry gave Tom a hard look before saying, 'I thought I told you. I will have forty men on the rope, and you will be one of them. The rope is attached to the monkey. You blokes pull the rope until the monkey gets to the top. Then the bloke on the top locks the rope inta place with that lever that ya seen up there.'

Henry half-heartedly pointed skyward again. 'The donkeys lay the rope on the ground and move aside before the bloke at the top lets the lever go, and the monkey drops about twenty-five feet before it hits the top of the log. Each time it drops, it should knock the pole about twelve inches inta the mud.

'I told ya that it was gunna be a tough job and I don't need no sissies. It takes about ten minutes to do one drop, so that's six drops an hour. That means that we should have one pole in position about every three and a half hours, or about three or four poles a day. If I keep to that schedule, then all the poles should be set up in about three weeks. Then, it will take about another two weeks to lay the cross planks for the deck and the pole supports. So that's about five weeks' work son. If you don't want the job, then I'm sure that there will be plenty of others who do. You will be paid when the job is finished, and not before. So, do ya want to be a donkey or not?'

Tom thought for a moment. He knew that it would be hard work pulling that rope to the top every ten or fifteen minutes, but it was a job, and it would pay him thirty shillings a week. Five bob a day wasn't much money, but beggars couldn't be choosers, he thought to himself. If the job lasted for five weeks, then he would go home with seven pounds and ten shillings, and that would buy Hannah some supplies until his crop came in.

'I'll take it. When do ya want me ta start?'

'You can start now. Them other fellas over there,' and he again nodded in their direction, 'are waitin for the logs to arrive from the mill. When they get here, you can paint the pitch over them to stop 'em rotting in the water.

'Then you can axe the ends into a point to make them go inta the mud easier. The blacksmith is making the steel collars to go over the ends to stop the monkey from splitting 'em. Now go and wait with them other blokes. You ain't getting paid until the bullocky gets here and you start unloadin.'

Tom rolled a smoke, and went over to the others. 'Did you fellas hafta do that too?' One replied, 'What, carry the rope to the top? Yeah, we all got the same treatment. A few others tried, but they couldn't haul the rope to the top, so he sent them packin.'

They sat around for two hours before they heard the crack of the stock whip and the clinking of the chains. The stock whip resonated like the crack of a rifle shot, and as they looked they could see the bullock train slowly making its way towards them. The shoulder muscles of the steers rippled under their black hides as they strained against their yokes to pull the load. The chains stretched taught against the drawbar as the twenty animals slowly dragged the heavy cart ever closer to the river.

They could see six tree trunks at least thirty feet long stacked atop of each other and held together with heavy chains. The dray was fifty feet long and it creaked and groaned as it came towards them. Painted along the side running boards was the name, *The Bunyip*. Below the running boards, and under the deck of the dray was the bullocky's sleeping quarters, along with a compartment holding assorted chains and ropes.

The bullocky walked alongside of his beasts, and the long stock whip handle rested upon his shoulder. He wore a cabbage patch hat towards the back of his head, and fly corks bobbed on its rim. Hanging from the side of his mouth was an oversized nicotine-stained meerschaum pipe, which he gripped with equally stained teeth. As the wagon rolled slowly forward, he climbed up onto the seat and pulled back upon the leather traces.

With a cry of 'whoa' the wagon groaned to a stop, and the dust rose and mixed with the smell of leather and sweat.

The poles were unloaded, and two horses were then used to drag them to the water's edge. The ends were roughly axed into a point before they were painted in hot tar. It took another six days before all of the forty poles were on the ground and ready to be positioned into the water.

A crowd of men had gathered in the hope of obtaining work. A camp was set up along the water's edge along with a kitchen that would feed the workers. Henry gathered the men around and gave them their instructions.

'Now, I'm the pulley man, and I'm gunna be at the top of the derrick,' and he pointed up without looking, 'so listen to what I'm gunna tell ya. I will blow one long whistle, and you will pick up the rope and position it on your shoulder. When I blow two whistles, you will all pull the rope with all you got and walk forward. When the monkey gets to the top, I will blow three whistles! When you hear them three whistles, do not let the rope go. Any man who lets the rope go before I whistle will be sacked. I will clamp the rope with the lever, and when I done that I will blow one long whistle. When you hear that long whistle blow you will all lay the rope down and move away. If you don't move away the rope will probably take yer head off when I release the lever and the monkey drops, cause it will snake away very quickly!'

The crane on the barge had lifted up the first log and lowered it into position into the water. The whistle blew, and they picked up the rope.

When Henry blew the two whistles, there was an audible grunt as their feet dug into the dirt, and the monkey started to rise slowly. Henry was screaming at them from the top, 'Keep it movin', keep it goin', the first one is always the hardest. That's it men, don't look back just keep goin' forward!'

The monkey was now swinging from just below the top platform, and Henry pushed the lever forward. The lever clamped the rope around the grooved wheel, and then he blew three whistles. He checked that the rope was positioned properly before he blew the single, long whistle. The men laid the rope down onto the ground and moved away.

As Henry let the brake off, the wheel gave a clatter, and the rope spun around it quickly as the half-ton monkey fell twenty feet before slamming onto the top of the pole with a giant thud. The rope snaked along the ground rising up the derrick before it suddenly stopped as the monkey landed atop of the pole.

Day in and day out, they pulled the rope, and the monkey pounded the poles into the muddy riverbed. Little by little the jetty took shape, and five weeks later the job was finished. Tom lined up with the others and collected his money, desperately looking forward to returning home.

69.

The Harvest

It was dark by the time that Tom had arrived home. Hannah and the boys met him at the door. He gave his boys a hug before putting his arms around Hannah. She held him tighter than usual, and then she started to cry.

'What's all this, did you miss me that much?'

'Oh Tommy, it's Peggy, she is ill, and I'm so worried!' Tom stood back and looked at Hannah and asked, 'What is it, what is the matter with her?' There was a quiver of panic in his voice. Hannah wiped her eyes before saying, 'Brigid came out the day that you left. She was worried because Peggy was having trouble moving her legs. She thought that she may have been bitten by something, but after examining her all over, she couldn't find anything. She got doctor Silas to come out the next day. He thought that she might have a spinal injury because she was having so much trouble with her legs. Then he did some tests and came back the next day and said that our little girl has something called Polio.'

Tom walked over to his daughter's bedside and ran his hand over her forehead. He stared at her as she slept, and he didn't know what to do.

'What does it mean?'

'The doctor said that she might recover in a few months, but he warned that she might not.

'He said that a lot of children were getting sick with this disease in the cities, and that it was contagious especially with other children. He told the boys that they had to wash their hands with soap every time that they touched something that Peggy had used, or played with. They have been very good with her, and Jimmy has been giving her piggybacks whenever she wants to go somewhere. Doctor Silas said that she mustn't come into contact with other children except for her brothers, so she can't go into town with you. He said that she could get up if she felt inclined, but he warned that she might feel very sleepy most of the time!'

Tom was thinking the question, but was loath in asking it. 'Is this polio thing dangerous, like she ain't gunna die with it, is she?'

Hannah put her arms around Tom's waist, and rested her face upon his back as Tom stared down at his eldest daughter.

'Doctor Silas said that she may become paralysed, but that was a worst-case scenario. He said that in many cases the person would recover, but he warned that because Peggy was so small, it might take a very long time before she could walk again. He said that if she wasn't walking within three months he would arrange to get calipers fitted to her legs to strengthen them and keep them straight. He said that if she had to wear calipers she would need crutches to get around.

'I have been praying a lot for her Tommy. I don't know what I would do if she was taken from us. Doctor Silas said that we have to massage her legs every day. He stated that we have to keep the blood circulating, and if we do that twice a day for about half an hour she might get to walk again.'

The next morning, Tom went out to check his crops. His heart was heavy with worry over his daughter, and he was still concerned about the viability of his crops. The wheat had grown sporadically. Some was almost three feet tall, while in other places it was patchy and stunted. He walked to his barley field, and was surprised to see that the crop had changed from green to gold. However, he was unsure if it was ready to harvest. He watched as the wind blew softly across the top of the crop and the seed heads danced like waves.

He broke off a few barley stems and took them back to show Hannah. 'Hani, look at this.' He thrust the barley at her. 'Do you think that this is properly ripe and ready fer harvestin'?'

'Is that your barley crop? It looks mature, but I don't know Tommy. How much have we got?'

'I planted about twenty acres. I'm gunna go and see Bill after breakfast. He'll know if it's ripe or not.

'The wheat is still green, so I dunno how much longer that is gunna take, but I'm sure that me barley is ready.'

After breakfasting on a bowl of oats, Tom saddled up and rode across to the Murdoch place. He found the house deserted. That was unusual as Harriet and her mother were never far away. After wandering down to the shearing shed and still not finding anyone, Tom had assumed that they must have all gone into town.

Not wanting to return home without finding out if his barley crop was ready to harvest or not, Tom decided to ride across to Clarry's place. He rode through the scrubland, and then down into the hollow where he crossed the still dry creek bed.

Everywhere that he looked he could see signs of the deepening drought. The heavy brown soil was shrinking, and in some places the cracks in the ground were so wide that a man could fit his hand into them. The leaves on most of the native trees had withered and hung limply from tortured branches. The deeper water holes along the creek course that usually held water all year round were now almost dry. The paddocks lying fallow, which would usually be green and covered by native grasses at this time of year, were still burnt brown from last summer. Even though it was early spring, the wind was eddying across the bare, dusty paddocks, and was creating small dust devils that swirled in funnels almost twenty feet tall.

Tom rode through his fern gully that was shaded by the canopy of his tall ironbark trees, and made his way up to the top of the ridge. From here he could see all the way to Blackmore, and he was also afforded a view into the valley and across Clarry's farm.

He saw the smoke rising from the shack, and was surprised to see two motorcars parked behind it. Tom was hesitant to intrude if Clarry had visitors, but he could just make out Clarry waving his arms around animatedly. He watched for a few minutes, and the longer he watched the more it appeared that Clarry was upset over something. Tom made a decision to ride down and see if he could assist.

As he rode closer, he could see that one of the two figures was the local policeman. Standing nearby was another man who was dressed in a pinstriped suit. They all looked at Tom as he rode up. Tom looked at Clarry in a questioning manner, before he turned his attention to the others. He didn't dismount at first, but looked at the two men. He recognised the copper, but he didn't know the well-dressed man.

'Mornin' men,' he said with a smile. The copper's name was Percival Thomas, and he was the sergeant in charge of the three-man police station in Blackmore.

Tom had first met him when the sergeant had called at the house about six months earlier when he had been looking for an itinerant who was working in the area, but he had not spoken to the sergeant since.

Percival was tall and overweight. He wore the remnants of a handlebar moustache, and his greying hair hung over the back of his neck. He was happy with his position, as Blackmore was generally a quiet place. He would lock up the occasional drunk, and he made an appearance of being tough, although when there was the occasional brawl in a pub, he would be elsewhere and attending to other business. He scowled at Tom's intrusion, but as he had no reason to prevent him visiting a neighbour he growled, 'I recognise you, you live around here somewhere, don't you?' Tom stayed sat on his horse, and looked down at the sergeant.

'That's right, I'm Tom Fields, and I live on the property up on the ridge.' He pointed to his left. 'You called at my place about six months ago when you were lookin' fer some fella!'

Tom looked at Clarry who was looking dazed and he said, 'G'day Clarry, just called over to see how you was goin'. I ain't been around fer awhile as I bin workin' over in Bathurst, so I thought that I would come and have a cuppa with ya and chew the fat.'

As he spoke, he noticed the man in the suit looking agitated. 'Look sergeant, could we get on with this. I have to be back in Bathurst by lunchtime for an important meeting, and I want this man to face the magistrate tomorrow.'

He looked at Tom and said, 'I don't know, nor do I care who you are sir, but this is none of your business, so I would ask you to leave now. Mr Homer will not be available to chew the fat with you today, or any other day I'll warrant, so be off with yourself.'

Tom had taken an immediate dislike to this man in the flashy suit, and now looked directly at him with a steely stare.

'I dunno who you are fella, but I will leave when I'm good and ready. I came to visit me neighbour, and what I do, and who I speak to around 'ere is none of your blasted business, now if yer don't mind I'm gunna 'ave a word with me mate!'

The man in the suit went bright red and sputtered, 'Sergeant, I demand that you send this man packing, and I demand that you immediately take Mr Homer into your custody, or I will be in touch with your superiors. Is that understood?'

Tom climbed down off his horse, and ignoring the blustering of the man in the suit stood in front of Clarry.

'What's goin' on 'ere, mate? Can I help?'

Clarry was looking more confused and said quietly, 'They are gunna arrest me Tom. They said that I stole some cattle. I never done no such thing. I got all me receipts for them cows and that bull. You seen them when I got 'em cheap from the sale yards. I don't understand what they is talkin' about Tom. Crickey, me heads hurtin'.' Clarry covered his forehead with the palms of his hands and shut his eyes. 'I never stole nuthin' from no one. I can't leave here Tom. Who will look after me stock? Why won't nobody believe me? Can ya help me, Tom?'

Clarry sat down on the log that doubled as a seat in front of his shack, and he buried his head in his hands as if to hide.

'What's going on here sergeant? What's all this about, why do you want to arrest Clarry? I can vouch that he bought all these animals from the sale yards. He never stole any of them. What stolen property are you referring to?'

Tom was getting angry, and his voice was getting louder.

The sergeant looked at him and said, 'Well, Mr Fields, this really is none of your business, but Mr Homer sold two calves that didn't belong to him recently.'

Clarry shouted out, 'Them two calves was mine. The cows was pregnant when I bought 'em. I told ya Tom, you wos 'ere. Then they birthed them within days of each other. Why won't ya believe me?'

Clarry was getting more upset and Tom said, 'Sergeant, I can't see why you would think that this stock is stolen, and who is this bloke?' Tom pointed toward the man in the suit.

'This is Mr Keene. He is the representative of the government's farmers' bank. The farmers' bank owns this property and all of the stock. As Mr Homer is only the tenant, he had no right to sell those calves, or any other animal on this property. The stock belongs to the bank, and that is why I must arrest Mr Homer. He never sought permission from the bank to sell those calves, and now I have no choice but to take him into custody!'

Clarry interjected, 'That's wrong, I own this place. I got it from the government. I'm a soldier settler. I worked this place, and I took down the trees, and I bought all them cows, and I built me house.' Clarry nodded his head towards his shack. 'How can the bank say that they own them? I signed the papers with that government fella. I got copies. I can show them to ya if ya don't believe me.'

Mr Keene had been listening to Clarry and stated haughtily, 'Mr Homer, you took out a government sponsored loan from our bank a few months ago, do you remember?'

Clarry replied, 'Course I remember, I ain't an imbecile. I borrowed two hundred quid from the farmers' bank. I bin payin' it off. That's how I bought me stock. The bank lent me the dough, so I could improve me property.'

Mr Keene walked closer to Clarry before saying, 'Mr Homer, do you remember signing papers before you received your loan?'

'Of course, I do. There was pages and pages that I had ta put me name to. What's that got to do with you sayin' I don't own me place?'

'Mr Homer, did you read those documents?'

'Nar, I just looked at them, but it was a lot of mumbo jumbo. The bank fella told me that it was just bank stuff, and I didn't hafta take no notice of what was written.'

'Well, had you read those documents before you signed them Mr Homer, you would have read that once you had accepted the loan that this property and everything upon it became the property of the bank. The bank now owns this property, until the loan is repaid in full including interest. Those calves that you sold were the property of the bank, as well as all the other stock on this property. As you had purchased the stock with money that you borrowed from my bank means that the stock belonged to us, not you. You agreed to that when you accepted the loan, so it's of no use you saying that you didn't know. You were required to notify the bank, and get our permission before you sold any of those animals. By not doing so, you have sold property that did not belong to you, and that is a crime, Mr Homer!'

Clarry had gone white, as he finally came to understood what was being told to him. 'But, nobody told me that. How was I supposed ta know that, if nobody told me?'

Tom had been listening intently and asked, 'How much did ya get fer them two calves Clarry?' Clarry looked at Tom, and Tom could see the shock registering in his eyes.

'I got one quid each fer them Tom, and I bought meself some supplies with it cause I was runnin' low!'

Tom looked at Mr Keene and said, 'How about I give ya the two quid, and you can just forget all this? I'm sure that now Clarry is aware of what he hasta do that you won't have no more trouble from him.' Tom opened his tobacco pouch, and removed his wages that he had placed inside it. He unfolded two one-pound notes and handed then towards Mr Keene.

'Now here's the dough fer the calves, so let's have no more of this nonsense.' Tom held out his hand, but Mr Keene made no effort to accept the money.

'I cannot accept your offer, sir. You are missing the point. Mr Homer stole property that legally belonged to the bank. He must face the consequences of his actions. It is not for you to circumvent the law. The bank will ask the court to impose a punishment that will send a clear message to people like you and Mr Homer that stealing from an institution such as my bank will not be tolerated. No, we will ask the magistrate to impose a custodial sentence. Nothing less will suffice. Good day to you Sir.' With that, he looked at the sergeant and said, 'Sergeant, do your duty.'

Percival glanced at Tom. He would have been happy if the matter had been settled on Tom's terms. Now he would have to arrest and take into custody a simple man, who had just been ignorant of the conditions of a loan. He knew that if he didn't comply with the bank man's directive then he would have to explain his actions to his superiors. That could result in him being demoted, or even being transferred.

He took several steps towards Clarry, and as he did he removed his handcuffs from his belt saying, 'Mr Homer, I am arresting you for stealing and disposing of property that was not yours to sell. Please turn around and place your hands behind your back.'

Clarry made no effort to comply with the directive. He stood outside his shack, and they could all see the confusion reflected on his face. The sergeant repeated his order, and for a moment it seemed that Clarry was about to obey. But then, Clarry looked directly at Tom and said, 'Will ya take care of me stock fer me, Tom?' He gave him a weak smile, and then he turned around and went inside his shack. The sergeant was about to follow when they all heard the shot.

Percival moved quickly toward the entrance followed closely by Tom. Clarry lay huddled on the floor, his body convulsing for a few moments before he died with the rifle close by. His sightless eyes were looking skyward, and a small puddle of blood slowly spread across the dirt floor as it seeped from the small wound in his chest.

***

The sergeant knelt down, and although he was sure that Clarry was dead, he checked for a pulse. He stood up, his face ashen. He looked at Tom and said, 'I'm sorry, son. It should never have got this far. I was only doing my job. I hope that you understand! I'll have to make a report to the court. You may be called as a witness.' He stood and walked outside.

Tom looked down at Clarry. The blood had formed in a puddle beneath his lifeless body. As he stared at his neighbour he was reminded of other bloodied bodies that had been strewn about him over twelve years earlier on the battlefields of France. He was shocked at what had just happened, and he thought of how the incident had caused an unnecessary waste of a life.

His mind was in turmoil, and he was angry. Couldn't they see that Clarry was still suffering from his head injury that he had sustained during the war? He thought back to the days leading up to the war, and how keen the government had been in gathering up young men like Clarry to become cannon fodder for a pointless war.

He rolled himself a smoke, as his mind wandered and his rage simmered. After the war, the generals, the politicians and the newspapers had all reiterated about the sacrifices that men like Clarry had made. The stories in the papers had spoken of the guts and the glory, and how proud the citizens of the young nation of Australia should be for the sacrifice that these boys had made. But now, those in power who had taken no part in the war had conveniently forgotten about the hardships that men like Clarry had endured for them. Tom took one last look at his friend and neighbour before he walked outside.

Mr Keene, who had not entered the tent, stood near his motorcar looking agitated. He stared at Tom before saying, 'The man must have been mad. I hope that you don't think that the bank or I are in any way responsible for this. I expect that you will take care of his stock until the bank can arrange to sell it?'

Tom gave him a hard stare before saying, 'You worthless toad. Yes, I do hold you and your blasted bank responsible for that man's death. He fought for this country and was wounded in the head, and this is how maggots like you repay your debt to men like him. I'll bet that you never volunteered your services. No, it's cowards like you who stand back and watch as others make the sacrifices. And no, I will not look after your stock. You killed Clarry for his land, so you can rot in hell for all that I care, you worthless bastard!'

Mr Keene went bright red in the face before saying, 'How dare you speak to me like that, you… you hooligan. Your friend was a worthless fellow, and he arranged for his own destiny. Now get off this land, or I will have you arrested for trespassing. And, if any of those cattle disappear I will have the law onto you.'

He wore a smug look on his face as Tom walked closer to him, but the look disappeared as Tom raised his fist and belted him on his nose.

The blood spurted across his face, as he folded up and fell backwards to the ground. He lay there for a moment, and as he held his hand to his broken nose, he blustered, 'Sergeant, arrest that man,' as he pointed at Tom. 'That madman has just assaulted me, you saw what he did, now arrest him I say!'

He was trying to compose himself as he stood up. He removed his handkerchief, and put it to his face in an attempt to stem the blood that was now freely running through his fingers to fall upon his suit.

Sergeant Thomas looked at the bank man before saying, 'I'm sorry sir I didn't see any assault. You need to be more careful about where you tread when you are on unfamiliar ground. I would suggest that you go back to your office. You will have reports to fill in as do I, so good day to you, sir.' He turned his back on the bank man and quietly said to Tom. 'I served too son, and I know how you feel. You should leave now!'

Tom rode off in a trance. The shock of the morning was only beginning to sink in. He rode back home, and relayed the day's events to Hannah. He was feeling depressed over the incident and said, 'I'm glad that we are living out 'ere darlin', but I have lost faith in anything that the government does. I can remember like it was only yesterday when the government and the priests were all tellin' us that we had to go and fight and do our duty. Then we come home, and they go and pull dirty tricks on us by tellin' us that we can borrow money to improve our properties. I cannot believe that a fella can be charged with stealin' yer own stock, just cause ya borra some money from the bank. It don't make much sense ta me Hani. How's our little girl goin'?'

'She's asleep now, but she was bright as a button earlier when you were out. Jimmy was helping her draw on her chalkboard, and they were just being silly. I never realised how much I enjoyed hearing them giggle and playing.' Hannah asked, 'Did you see Bill, and how is Harriet and her mother?'

'They weren't at home, none of them. I s'pose that they mighta gone inta town. I think I'll ride over there again. I'm feelin' a bit restless, and I still wanna know if me barley is ready fer harvestin'.' He stood up, and put his hat on before saying, 'I'll be back before dark. I need ter get me head together!' He kissed her and left.

Tom took the long way across the paddocks and rode the back trail to the Murdochs' place. They were unloading their car as Tom rode up. They exchanged greetings, and Dorothy went inside to make the tea. Harriet asked, 'How is little Peggy, Tom?'

'She was sleepin' when I left, but Hani said that she was doing good today. The doc said that there is nuthin' that we can do except wait. So, that's all we can do Harriet!'

He then relayed the morning's events to them as they drank their tea. Bill was as shocked as Tom had been, 'I called over there just a few days ago, and he seemed happy enough. I was going to sell him a few sheep. So, who is gunna look after his stock now?'

'The bank fella asked me to take care of them, but after what he done I wasn't about to start helpin him out, so it's their problem. I was gunna ask the bank fer a loan meself, but if they wanna own yer whole place, then I reckon, I will just struggle on by meself.'

Tom showed Bill the barley stalks, and it was agreed that the barley was ready for harvesting. 'How's the wheat going, is that the same colour as the barley?'

'Nar, some of it is high, but most of it is still green. I been a bit nervous cause me and Hani have got a lot ridin' on this crop. I gotta get enough dough to pay the government back for a year. So, if I can get about one hundred quid to pay me rent, then we can shoot some rabbits and grow enough vegetables to get by on till next season.'

Bill took a long draw on his pipe before saying, 'I'll bring me binder over in the next couple of days. It's old but it still works, and it's a lot easier than cutting it down with a scythe. I bought it about fifteen years ago from an old fella in Bathurst. I've used it a few times, and it will do the job. By the time we cut your barley, the wheat should be ready to harvest.'

'How's it work?'

'We drag it behind a horse. It cuts the stalks, and we have a ball of bailing twine that sits on the side. As the blades go through the crop it cuts them into bundles and ties the ends. When we got a dozen or so bundles tied we will stack them up across the paddock with the seed heads upright. That keeps them all dry until we can thresh them. Old Harry Lander has got a traction engine and a good threshing machine. I can ask him to bring them over when the wheat is dry and stacked. I'm sure if you offer him a few quid he will be glad to help. It's a dirty job, and it will take a few of us, but we will soon have your crop bagged up.'

*****

Several days later they all stood and watched as the engine hissed steam and belched smoke as Harry steered his heavy traction engine, creaking and groaning up the hill and across to the wheat field.

Bill had brought over his threshing machine, and Tom had his horse harnessed to his dray.

They started working at daybreak, and Tom and the boys threw the sheaves of barley from where they were stacked onto the dray. When it was full, they took it to the threshing machine that was now attached to the traction engine by a long leather belt. Bill manipulated the levers as the machine separated the kernels from the seed as Harry kept the steam pressure up on the engine.

It was hot, dirty work as the straw and the chaff mixed with the belching black smoke and blew in all directions. The boys shovelled bag after bag of grain into the sacks, and at the end of the third day the harvesting was finished. This was Tom's first full harvest, and along with satisfaction there was a feeling of relief.

Hannah had made lunch, and they all sat around the table and discussed the price of grain and the continuing fallout from the depression.

Harry stood up and said, 'Well I had better be on me way,' then he looked expectantly at Tom. Tom's mind was elsewhere and Hannah said, 'Thanks for all your help Harry, now how much do we owe you?'

Tom came out of his daydream and was apologetic, 'Geez Harry, me mind was so busy workin' out how much I'm likely to get from me grain that I forgot about you.' He walked over to the shelf above the fireplace and took down the treacle tin. He took out a ten-pound note, and the last one that he had. He offered it to Harry. 'I hope that this is orright for ya Harry. I dunno how we woulda managed without yer engine and the binder.'

Harry looked at the note before saying, 'That's too much son, I know yer doin' it hard. We all been there, haven't we Bill?

'I worked 'ere fer three days, and I'm happy to take a quid a day fer me trouble. So, have you got three one-pound notes in that tin of yourn? If yer don't then yer can owe it to me, and pay me when ya get yer crop money.'

Tom was about to protest, because he knew that without the help of Harry and Bill he would still be out cutting down his crop by hand. Harry spoke again, 'Now, before you say anything son I said me piece, and I won't entertain no argument. I might get you ter give me a hand to chop a tree or two down sometime, so we won't say nothin' more.'

Tom put the note back into the tin and counted out three one-pound notes. 'I appreciate what ya done fer me Harry, and anytime you want a hand with anything you let Bill know and I'll be over!'

Tom loaded his truck, and then drove to the stock agent in Bathurst.

Clive Hammond, the stock and station agent, was a weedy-looking man who gave Tom a weak handshake when he introduced himself. 'How many bags of grain have you got?'

'I got two hundred to sell. Seventy bags of barley, and the rest is wheat. I can only carry eight bags at a time on me truck, so I'm gunna hafta bring them all in over the next week. So how much are ya payin'?'

The agent replied, 'If it's first-grade barley I'll pay two shillings a bushel, and if it's second grade I'll pay a shilling a bushel. As for the wheat, I'll pay two and eight pence a bushel, and two bob a bushel if it's rubbish.'

Tom was shocked at the low prices offered. 'But, you told a mate of mine last week that the price was three bob a bushel!'

The agent scowled and said, 'That was last week. This is what I'm paying today. Tomorrow it might be lower still, so you make up your mind if you want to sell or not. The government is not guaranteeing a floor price cause the government hasn't got any money. That's the price, so take it or leave it. If you want to try your luck with the wheat co-op in Sydney, then you are free to do so. So, what will it be?'

Tom was trying to work out how much his crop would be worth at these prices, and he worked out that he would receive just over one hundred and fifty pounds if he sold it all today. He knew that would be more than enough to pay his rent for another year. But it would leave him with just over forty pounds. That would be less than one pound a week for them to live on until he grew his next crop.

'Orright, I'll take it. Me crop is all first grade, so I expect ya to pay me at today's price even if it takes me all week to get it 'ere. Is that a deal or not?'

'That's what I said I'll pay, and I'll give you to next Friday to have it all here. If it's any later, you will have to take what I offer you because the price may go down even further. I need to look at the quality of what you have today, and if I'm satisfied that it's good quality then I will give you a receipt and you can unload it down at the rail yards.

'Now, as you bring in each load you are to bring it here, so that I can inspect it, and then you take it to my area at the rail yards. I have a couple of men there, and they will stamp the bags before they are loaded.'

Tom spent the rest of the week carrying his crop to the rail yards, and each sack was stencilled with the agent's name before it was unloaded.

The rail trucks were lined up against the wooden loading platform. He watched as twenty men walked along the narrow planks that zigzagged their way from the ground to the top of the stacked wheat bags.

The bags on the rail trucks stood ten rows high. Each man carried one sack that weighed almost a hundred pounds across their shoulders. As they walked along the wooden planks, they bowed and sprang under the weight, and as they reached a new level they dropped each sack upon the other. The next row was criss-crossed to give the stack stability. As each truck reached the level of the one before it, two men would throw ropes over the entire stack and make them secure. Then the planks would be placed on the next truck until that too was loaded.

Tom spoke to the man stencilling his bags, 'That looks like hard yakka. How many sacks do they hafta load?'

'As many as need loadin'. We get ten bob a day, and some days we load a hundred bags. But ya must be here early cause they don't give the same fellas a job every day. It's first in the queue in the mornin' that gets the job.

'Some blokes don't last, and some fellas can't even pick up the bags. If ya drop a bag and it busts they take the money outa your pay, so ya could work all day and get nuthin. It's no good arguing with the foreman fella cause he just tells you to bugger off, and he calls in another bloke that's standin' at the gate.

'There's always a lot of blokes waitin' at the gate each mornin' now. I'm one of the lucky ones. The stock agent pays me. Mind you, he only pays me when I got a truck to unload and to stencil his name on the bags. But ten bob a day is better than nothin'. Some of them fellas got half a dozen little mouths to feed. I only got meself to worry about. While I got this job, I can sleep in them goods trucks and that cost me nuthin.'

At the end of the week, Tom picked up his money and was grateful for what he had.

70.

Brigid and Adam

A month had passed since Adam had requested that the council help his pupils, and he had still not received a response. As he prepared his lessons for the coming day he wondered why it should take so long to make a decision.

The knocking on the door interrupted his thoughts, and before he could answer it, it opened, and Brigid walked in.

'Good morning, you must be Mr Francis. I'm Brigid Carney, the district nurse. She walked up to Adam and put out her hand to shake his.

'Yes, I'm Adam Francis. Is one of my pupils ill?'

'No, nothing like that, it's just that I have received a letter from the council, and they have suggested that I should speak with you. The letter states that you have some concerns about some of your pupils' health, is that correct?'

Adam smiled before he replied, 'I was only just thinking a moment ago as to why it was taking them so long to reply. Look Mrs Carney...'

Brigid interrupted, 'Please call me Brigid, may I call you Adam? I don't like standing on formality with names.'

'Yes, please do Brigid. We are a very small school with a dozen pupils. Many of my pupils come to school without eating. They don't bring any food with them, and I'm sure from the stories that they tell me that they don't have much for dinner, either!

'I approached the council, and asked if they could provide my pupils with at least a glass of milk on a daily basis. The way that they went on was as though I had asked them for a pound note for each of them. Well, anyway, I have been waiting for a response, so what have they decided?'

'The council has suggested that I go and see each of the children's mothers. They want me to see how each child is being looked after. If I believe that the children require additional sustenance, then I am to get the mothers to come to the clinic once a week. I will then issue them with several tins of condensed milk on a weekly basis. Also, possibly some dried fruit, dates, or the like. They only have to mix the condensed milk with water and give the child a glass each before they leave for school. It's not as nutritious as cow's milk, but it is sweet, and it will take away their hunger pangs for a short while.

'I know that it is not much Adam, but it is better than nothing. May I congratulate you on approaching the council on behalf of the children? Many wouldn't have! If this arrangement meets with your approval then I can come back later on this morning. I will bring over several cartons of tinned milk for you, so that we can begin the programme immediately.'

Brigid looked at Adam to see his reaction and Adam said, 'Thank you Brigid, and I'm sure that the children will be very appreciative.'

'Now, what I would like to do is go and visit the parents, or the mother, while the child is here at school. Do you have the addresses of your pupils?'

'Ah well, that might be a problem, you see almost every child that attends here lives on settlement blocks, or down in the shanty town by the river. I have seen a few of their residences, and many of them don't even have lavatories, let alone street numbers.

'Most are, well… how can I put this politely? Most are hovels. Even that is probably not an actual description of their homes, but that is the best word that I can use to describe their living arrangements.

'I would suggest, Brigid, that almost all of these people have no money, and very little income if any, and that most are in dire straits. Times are extremely tough for many people right now, as you will be aware!

'The police tell me that petty crime is flourishing, and I'm also told that tattered washing hanging from clothes lines is also being stolen.

'However, I would suggest that the parents, or parent of these settlement children are as destitute as anyone is ever likely to get, and they live in what could only be described as abject poverty.

'I have met some of the mothers of these children, and they are uncomfortable when I have had occasion to speak with them. They were once proud people, and are now embarrassed with their circumstances. I would be more than happy to take you to the residences of the most deserving of them.

'May I also say, that not all of the settler children are in dire straits? We have several boys whose fathers have not gone bush, and they seem to be content. Then we have a couple of young ladies whose mothers are doing their utmost to provide their daughters with a decent upbringing.

'I would think that we probably have four or five families who appear to be struggling more than the others. As I have said, I am more than happy to introduce you to some of these impoverished people. Although I must warn you, Brigid, that I would expect that my description to you of the shanty town, and its residents would be on the conservative side.'

Brigid said, 'I passed by the camp down at the river just the other day, and I felt embarrassed by the circumstances of the people that I saw there. Some were living in tents, and others were in such deplorable looking makeshift houses. I understood that the soldier settlement scheme was to get these people to become self-sufficient, on land which they could call their own.'

'That is true Brigid. The problems with the programme are only just becoming apparent. While the government intended to encourage the returned soldiers to work in agriculture, the implementation of the scheme has left a lot to be desired.

'For instance, most of the land allocated is far too small to farm economically. There were some programmes put into place to show the settlers how they should manage their land, but they never took into consideration the vagaries of the weather, or the ability of mainly city-born men to take to farm life.

'There are also the associated problems of isolation, and living off the land when you have no money.

'We have been in drought conditions here for almost four years now, and on top of that is this dreadful depression. Then we have the mental problems that some of these chaps obviously suffer from. Many are drunks, and are occasionally violent. Some of these fellows beat their wives and their children.

'I have seen the bruises on a few of the children, and they haven't been shy in telling me how they got them.

'I don't know how to put this delicately, but ah… Oh, how should I say it? Some of these settler women have been charged with prostitution! I am not being critical of them, and nor am I judging them, because they have to get money to feed their children from somewhere. But, I wonder how the government expects these people to manage when they provide no support to them? Then, the government programme forces the settlers off their allotments if they don't make a go of it after five years.

'Many of those people to whom you refer, and who are now living in that shanty town by the river, are the displaced people who the government evicted. But Brigid, where are they to go? The government evicts them, and then they wipe their hands of them. They have no money, and the chances of the men obtaining work are almost nil considering the way the economy is right now. So, they build with whatever they can find that will provide them with a modicum of shelter. Those children that I have referred to are mainly from that area. That's why they come to school hungry and dirty.'

He stopped speaking for a moment before saying, 'I'm so sorry Brigid, and I apologise if I have spoken out of turn. It's one of my flaws. I get passionate about issues that should never have been allowed to develop!'

Brigid looked at Adam, and she noticed the intensity with which he spoke. 'Please don't see a need to apologise. I admire the empathy that you feel towards these people. I will make it my duty to visit as many as

I possibly can over the coming weeks. Now I must go, I need to open the clinic. I will return with the condensed milk as soon as I have a moment, and may I inform the council that you are satisfied with their response to your request?'

Adam looked at Brigid. He was surprised and delighted with the response, and told her so. He held the classroom door open for her, and as she walked back to the clinic Adam thought that she was a handsome woman, and he wondered about her marital status.

71.

George Edie

Tom sat on his verandah nursing Peggy. He had been doing this more often since he had found out that she had contracted polio.

He didn't say much to her, as he didn't know what to say to his seven-year-old daughter. He loved her more than he could ever explain, and he was as one with her as he held her close to him. He didn't understand her disease, and all that he could do was hope. He wanted her to be one of the lucky ones that Doc Silas had said might survive the disease.

He had looked at his sleeping daughter one morning after breakfast and he had the urge to pick her up and just hold her. She murmured softly before snuggling sleepily into her father's embrace.

He was so scared that she would die, and he needed to hold her as often as he could, so he had made a practice of picking her up and sitting on the verandah with her. Some days she would chatter incessantly, and at other times she would sleep securely with her head resting on his chest while his heart ached with fear.

He was staring across the valley, but he was thinking about the future. Peggy was on his knee when the movement caught his eye. A man was walking along the ration track, and Tom noticed him stop and look up the hill in the direction of his windmill. The house, although built close to the rim of the hill, was almost invisible from the roadway. As he watched, he saw the man turn off the ration track, and make his way along the entrance road that led to the house.

He lost his view as the stranger crossed over the dry creek, and then he reappeared as he walked across the top of the hill. The stranger stopped, and he appeared surprised to see a house before he noticed Tom. He made his way toward the verandah, hesitating for a moment before he made eye contact with Tom.

'G'day boss. I never seen yer house from down the hill. I don't mean no trouble to you boss. I jess seen the windmill, and I'm a bit skint fer a drink. Do ya think I might fill me bottle?' He held it up from the string that was attached to his trousers.

Tom looked at the stranger, and he noticed the dark face looking at him from beneath the battered felt hat. He wore a well-worn suit jacket over a striped calico shirt that was opened almost to his waist due to the lack of buttons. His trousers were grey canvas, and they were tied around his waist with torn strips of material. The leg cuffs were frayed. He wore boots, but they looked strange, and Tom couldn't help noticing that baling twine was wound around them to keep them attached to the layers of worn cardboard that passed as the soles of his boots. He carried a canvas swag that was slung over his shoulder, and a burnished leather strap held it there. Attached to his swag was a blackened, battered jam tin, with a length of wire attached as a handle, and which passed as his billy. Tom looked at the stranger more intently, as he looked vaguely familiar.

The stranger said, 'Me name is George Edie, and I would be grateful if I could wet me whistle mister.'

'Go around the back of the house, and you will see the pump. Help yerself and fill yer bottle.'

The dark man nodded his head in thanks and went to the pump. Hannah came out of the house, and with a puzzled expression asked, 'Who's that?'

Tom handed Peggy to her and then said, 'Just a fella lookin' fer a drink, nuthin to be worried about. I can't help feelin' that I seen him somewhere though!' He had an afterthought and said, 'Have ya got a johnnycake inside? The fella looks like he could use a bite. I wouldn't suggest it if yer ain't got one done.'

Hannah replied, 'You bring him in for a cuppa. I have some treacle biscuits made, and we won't turn a hungry man from our door.'

George was drinking the cool water and said, 'That's sociable of you boss. Can I do somethin' in return? I could split a bit of fire wood fer yer if I could jest get a bite ta eat.' He looked hopefully at Tom, but with the expectation that he would be sent packing.

'Me name's Tom Fields,' He held his hand out to George. 'The missus has got the kettle boilin', and we can give ya a feed. I won't charge a hungry man, so you be welcome to sit at our table, and I don't expect ya to chop wood, or nuthin else, so come inside. I'll be happy to hear of yer travels.'

'That's kind of you boss. I'll jest leave me swag here.' He placed it at the door along with his battered hat.

Tom introduced George to Hannah and the children. 'It's nice ta meet ya missus, and it's kind of you to let a black fella sit at yer table.' Hannah smiled before saying, 'We are all God's children, black, white, or brindle George, and we don't judge people by the colour of their skin, but by their actions. That's how I was brought up, and that's how we bring up our children. Now, I can't offer you milk in your tea, but please help yourself to the treacle biscuits.'

George devoured the biscuit and looked hungrily at the rest. Hannah said, 'Have some more George, please just help yourself.' He took another and Tom asked, 'How long since ya had a feed?'

George replied, 'I snared a rabbit a coupla nights ago, and I helped meself to a few wild blackberries along the track yesterday. I takes me food where I get it boss.' He ate another biscuit, and gulped down a mouthful of hot tea.

Tom asked, 'Have ya come far?' George replied, 'I come through Blackmore yesterday, but the copper told me ta clear off cause he didn't want no troublemakin' blackfellas in his town. I told him that I wasn't looking fer trouble; just some work so I could get a feed. I don't like towns I like the bush, but if I could do an odd job fer a feed I'm happy ta pay me way.'

Tom kept looking at George, and he asked, 'I don't mean to pry inta yer affairs George, but you look familiar to me. I'm sure that we have met somewhere. You didn't ever live in Sydney did ya?'

'I never lived in the city when I was a kid, but I been workin' down there after the war. That was until they started layin' off everyone.

'The first time I was in Sydney, was about ten or twelve years ago. I was ona boat, and we all got kicked off there.' Before he could continue Tom said, 'I know where I seen ya. You was on the troop ship that I was on comin' home. You were a soldier, I remember you now!'

Tom grinned. 'George Edie, well I'll be blowed. You probably don't remember me, and it's all startin' ta come back now. We was havin' a tug-a-war on deck. Twenty blokes to a side, and you were standing right in front of me.

'You was slippin' and slidin' all over the place and then you went down, and I fell on top of ya. Do you remember?

'We couldn't stop laughin', and then the commander organised a boxin' match. You took on the cook, and if I remember you knocked 'im out. Some blokes lost a few quid that day, I can tell ya George. That cook was a big fella, and everyone expected the cook to knock ya block off. I knew that I recognised yer face.

'So, tell me George, what have ya been doin' with yerself since you left the army? How many years has it been now?'

'I remember that tug-a-war on the deck, and now that you reminded me I do remember that we all went head over turkey. After we disembarked I went to the pub with all the others down at Circular Quay. Here's me in me uniform standin' at the bar with me mates, and the barman tells me that he don't serve black fellas. Well me mates start tellin' the barman to pull his head in, and one thing leads to another, and then a copper turns up and drags me out of the pub. I asked the copper why was he throwin' me out of the pub while all me mates was still allowed ta stay inside. He tells me to clear off. I sez, the captain lets me 'ave a drink on the ship the same as all the other fellas, and you won't let me 'ave a drink at a bar.

'The copper then grabs me, and before I know it I'm arrested and charged with bein' drunk and disorderly. Drunk and disorderly! I'd only bin inside the pub for five minutes, and I wondered how he could say that I was drunk considerin' that I hadn't even had a drink. That was me first day back, and it ain't been much different fer the past twelve years.'

Hannah looked at George and said, 'That's dreadful. Didn't the copper know that you had just come back from the war?'

George replied, 'I don't think that any of them cared about what we were thinkin'. I never been in a pub since, and I never touched a beer from that day ta this.'

There was an uncomfortable silence until Tom asked, 'So why are you way out 'ere George?'

'Ah, it's a long story. I was workin' on a street gang fer a few years. I had a pick and shovel job makin' new roads around Sydney. But about eighteen months ago I got laid off. Not just me, but most of us. The gang boss said that they had no more money to pay us. They just gave us all a coupla quid each and told us all to clear off. I grew up out west, and I thought that I might head back there.

'Yer got no idea of the thousands of fellas in the cities who got no work. If you ain't bin to the city fer awhile now missus, you might find the place has all changed.

'There are probably thousands of fellas sleepin' rough in the parks and railway stations. There ain't any work nowhere, and fellas wos starving. I ain't kiddin' missus. The churches got soup kitchens in the halls and places. It wos only the ladies' auxiliary groups, and the church that wos providin' any tucker to anyone.

'They go down to the abattoirs and get knucklebones to boil up fer soup. Some of the queues outside the church halls of a night time musta had a couple 'undred people just waitin' in line to get a bowl of greasy soup. There wos kiddies, old people and anyone in between all just standing around in their ragged clothes waitin' their turn. Then they brought in the sustenance card. Blimey, they made it so hard fer a single bloke ta get any money!'

Hannah asked, 'What's the sustenance card George? Excuse my ignorance, but we don't get a lot of news living way out here.'

'Well, the government hadta bring in a system that gives the people some money, so they brought in the susso. That's what it's called, livin' on the susso.

'To get a card, you hafta go down to the warehouses on the wharfs at Pyrmont and a few other places. They got these big signs up with letters on 'em. You hafta go and stand in front of the one that's got yer initials on it. Like I'm E, so I stand in line with a coupla hundred other fellas. I stood there fer two days, cause if yer move ya lose yer spot. We 'ad nowhere to go, so we just slept on the ground. The church people came around and give us all a feed.

'Well, I been waitin' there along with all them other fellas, and two days later I'm standin' in front of this fella sittin' behind a desk. He asks me me name and tells me the rules. Can ya believe that? They got rules to collect the susso.

'They were tryin' to get all the single blokes to leave the city and go bush. So, what they done is, they give yer ten bob and this card. Now the fella behind the desk, he signs it and writes on it. It says the date and Pyrmont.

'Now yer can get ten bob a week at any Police station, but you only get it if yer in a different town to the last one you was in when ya had yer card stamped. The sergeant stamps the card and hands ya another ten bob. But, if yer card ain't bin stamped at a different town to the last one you wos in, you don't get no dough at all. That's why you got all these fellas on the track. Sometimes it can take you a fortnight to walk to another town. A lot of fellas jump the goods trains to get from town ta town. But then, the railway people hired these guards, and if they caught ya riding on the goods trucks they pulled you off and give yer a kickin'!

'Some towns were better than others. If the copper was a decent bloke, he would just turn a blind eye to all the fellas hidin' in the rail trucks. Then there was the coppers who waited until the goods train came inta town.

Then, as we all jumped off, they would come out with their batons and tell us to clear off. Then we had no money, even though we had our susso cards.

'After me last beatin', I jus decided that it wos easier and less painful just to walk along the back roads to get to the next town and take me tucker where I find it.

'Now I jus' tramp from place ta place looking fer a job here and there. Sometimes I get a meal fer splittin' a load of wood, or mendin' a fence. But most of the time we hafta survive on the susso. When I was livin' in the city, I could go and find a few shellfish, or mussels, but out 'ere I look fer blackfella tucker.'

The children had been sitting quietly, and listening to the conversation and now Billy asked, 'What's blackfella tucker?'

George smiled, 'There's lots a bush tucker around, you just gotta know what yer lookin' for. There are yams and berries and lots of wild fruit. You can set snares fer catching a rabbit, and if ya near a creek yer might be able ta catch a couple of yabbies.' George looked at the boys before asking, 'Have ya ever caught any yabbies?'

Billy replied, 'We used to have lots a yabbies down in the creek, but we haven't caught any since the creek dried up.'

Hannah asked, 'So where is home George? You said that you were heading west. Have you got family somewhere?'

'Us blackfellas are all family missus, but I don't 'ave no normal family. I 'ad a mother and a sister when I was little, but I don't know where they is now.'

George looked a little uncomfortable, but then Peggy who was still sat upon her father's lap asked, 'Did your mother die?'

They all looked at her, and Hannah said, 'Peggy, that's not nice. You shouldn't pry into something that doesn't concern you.'

George smiled, 'That's orright missus. It's an honest question from an innocent, and I'm happy to answer it.' He looked at Peggy and the boys before he asked the children how old they were. Thirteen, twelve, seven and five came the respective answers. George responded with, 'When I was six years old, the government people came and took me and me sister away from where we wos livin'. We wos taken to a mission centre at Wilcannia. But they separated the boys and girls, and I never seen me sister, or me mother again.'

Billy asked, 'Why did they do that, was you naughty?'

George smiled and said, 'Nar, that's just what they did with black kids. I think it wos because they didn't like children livin' out in the bush. They wanted us to be the same as white fellas. I dunno why and it don't matter, no how.'

Tom looked at George before saying, 'I remember somethin' like that happenin' in Redfern when I was a kid. I didn't understand what was goin' on, but I do remember some men comin' inta the classroom and taking away a couple a black kids at the time. I had forgotten about that, but I remember it now. So, are ya goin' back to Wilcannia now George, what's yer plans?'

'I dunno where I'm gunna go. I'll just go from town ta town until I get where I'm comfortable. That's what us blackfellas do, we go walkabout. If I get to Wilcannia, I'll probably go out to the old mission station and 'ave a look around. Maybe someone will remember me mother, or me sister. I dunno what me mother's name was, but me sister's name was Mary. I hafta move from town ta town every week, so I might as well keep headin' west. Otherwise they will cut off me susso, and I'm a bit flyblown fer money at the moment. Mind you, I might get meself a job on a station somewhere between here and there.'

George looked across the table, and for a moment there was another uncomfortable silence. Hannah looked at George and said, 'I hope that you will stay and have a meal with us George. We are simple people, and we eat simple, but what we have we are happy to share, so please say that you will eat with us before you go.'

He smiled at Hannah and replied, 'I don't wanna put ya to no trouble missus, and I don't wanna take any food that should be goin' to your little ones,' and he looked at the four children and smiled. 'I can find some bush tucker and camp down by yer creek, if that be orr right?'

Tom looked directly at George, 'If we never had no tucker we wouldn't ask ya ta share it. Like Hani said, we would be happy to share our table with ya. If ya wanna camp down by the creek then yer welcome ter do it, but the stable is warm, and I'm happy fer yer to make yer camp there if ya have a mind to.'

George grinned and replied, 'I'm happy to share a meal with you and yer family. It's bin awhile since I had a proper feed at a table and all. I gotta say though, there must be somethin' that I can help yer with around the place. Just say the word, and I'll do it.'

Tom thought for a moment before saying, 'Well, I been meanin' to rake me paddocks since we harvested the grain. If I don't gather up the stalks I won't 'ave no summer feed fer me horses.'

'I could use a hand with that, but I can't offer you a wage. It will probably take a week, or more. But, if ya ain't in no hurry to move on, I can give ya three square meals a day, and share me tobacco with ya!' He looked expectantly at George. George gave a big grin before leaning across the table with his arm extended to shake Tom's hand.

'It's a deal boss.'

'Well, there's one other thing.'

George frowned and looked at Tom and asked, 'What's that boss?'

Tom said, 'I want you to stop callin' me boss, orright? Me name's Tom, and I ain't nobody's boss. We will feed ya, and you will give us your help. It's a fair exchange, and if yer happy with that then so am I!'

They made their way to the door, followed by the boys. Peggy asked, 'Can I go too, mummy?' Hannah gave her daughter a wispy smile. 'No darling, you stay here with mummy.'

'But I want to go with them. Why can't I go?' Her voice was trembling as she asked. Before Hannah could reply Jimmy said, 'Come on Peggy, I'll carry ya, climb onta me back. I'll piggy back ya.'

He squatted down, and Peggy almost threw herself onto her brother's back as she wrapped her arms around his neck. He put his hands behind his back and under her bottom, and they walked over to the stables before making their way to the stubble left after the harvest.

As they walked across the paddocks, George turned towards the boulders and the stones where Tom and Jack had made their camp when they had first arrived. Tom and the children watched, as George stopped and stared at the large stones.

Billy whispered to his brother, 'What's he doin?'

Jimmy shrugged his shoulders and whispered back, 'I dunno.'

George touched a large boulder, and he left his hand on it for a few moments before he walked back to the group.

Jimmy asked, 'Why did ya touch the rock like ya done?'

'I was connectin' with me ancestors. This is a spiritual place, I can feel it.' The children wore puzzled looks, and George said, 'Do ya all go to church on Sundays?'

Billy replied, 'Mum likes to go, and if she goes we hafta go, but we don't go every week.'

George squatted down before he spoke. 'Now, white fellas go ta churches to talk to their God, and a blackfella's church is country. It's the land and the sky.

'We believe that our ancestors' spirits live in the stones, and when I see big stones among the small ones I know that the spirits of my people are here, and to me, that makes this place a special place.'

George turned towards the children, and he smiled before he looked at Tom. I'd be happy ter make me camp down 'ere tonight, if that's orright boss, sorry… Tom?'

'You can camp anywhere that ya feel comfortable George.'

'Can I camp here with you tonight?' Jimmy asked.

George looked at Tom and said, 'If ya father says that ya can, then I don't got a problem with that, little fella.'

'Me too,' piped in Billy followed by Peggy. Tom looked at his children before saying, 'Look, maybe George wants some peace and quiet, and he ain't gunna get none with you all chattering at him.'

Tom looked at George and gave a shrug. 'It's upta you, if ya don't want 'em with ya just say the word.' George looked at their faces, which were all wearing the same pleading look.

'Orright, you can all camp with me, but just fer tonight. We can make a campfire, and I will tell you some blackfella stories 'bout the dreamtime.'

Peggy said, 'I have dreams, what do you dream about George?'

George knelt down in front of her and said, 'It's not about my dreams little one, it's called "the dreaming", and it's the stories of my people that have been handed down by my ancestors. They tell stories of the rainbow serpent, and the things that make up the blackfellas' history. I will tell you tonight, when we gather around the fire and we make the sparks fly to the heavens.'

Peggy asked innocently, 'Will I see the rainbow serpent?'

He touched her under her chin, and he looked into her small eyes and smiled. 'If you are very lucky, you might be able to see her tomorrow, but I think that you might have already seen her and you just didn't know.'

They all looked quizzically at George, and he smiled before saying, 'You will just hafta wait until tonight before I tell you about her. Now, we should all collect some firewood cause we want to keep warm, don't we?'

After gathering the wood, they made their way back to the house to eat. Hannah knew that she could not keep Peggy from staying with her brothers at George's campsite. She instructed Tom that he was to bring her home after she had been there for an hour or so. The nights were still cool, and Hannah was worried that if Peggy caught a chill it might compound her illness.

They sat around the fire after it was dark. The canopy of stars above them sparkled and shimmered in their millions against the endless black of an infinite sky. Jimmy was the first to speak. 'Will you tell us about the dreams please George?' George was sat cross-legged in the dirt, and he was poking at the embers with a stick. The cinders were glowing red as they floated skywards and into the darkness, before fading quickly and disappearing to mesmerise those who watched. He then knelt in the dirt, before placing his hands on the rock protruding from the earth in front of him.

George sighed, and for a moment it was as though he were in a trance. He looked at the flames as the embers hissed and crackled. The shadows bounced from the rocks behind them, and the reflection from the fire glowed across his face that now looked like polished coal. He breathed in deeply, and the children could see the white of his eyes as he started to speak.

'Children, this is the story of my culture and of my ancestors. We call it the dreamtime, which was the time of the creation of country. We are the people of the land, and the land and our spirits are one. Our spirit and the spirits of our ancestors dwell in the rocks, the rivers, the trees and the stars in the sky. We have been here forever.'

⁂

George stopped speaking, and the children sat cross-legged and wide-eyed. He closed his eyes and breathed in deeply. The only sound came from the hissing and the crackling of the glowing coals as the smoke eddied skywards. His eyes opened, and they looked into the distant, dark sky, and he raised his arm, and pointed to the east before speaking quietly.

'From the darkness of the earth, where our spirit people slept, came the glow from the heavens, and from the glow came Yingarna, and she brought the light to the earth. She is our mother, because she and the spirits created the earth. When she woke she coloured the rivers silver and green, and she painted the mountains purple and rust, and my ancestors named her the Rainbow Serpent. She comes from the darkness, and she colours the sky and the heavens each morning when she awakes, and she takes the burning sky with her when she sleeps.

'This is our dreamtime, and our spirit ancestors gave us knowledge. We are all moulded of the earth, and when we die we only die in human form.

'Our spirit returns to become the breeze that whispers through the leaves of the trees, and the water that washes over the rocks in the streams. And the light from the stars is where our ancestors dwell in the heavens. This is our identity, for without identity we are nothing.

'Our spirit ancestors gave us knowledge, and they gave us our songs. We sing our songs, and we dance to connect with our ancestors. The stars tell us when the skies will cry, and the songs tell us where to fish, and where we should camp. We all tread lightly upon the earth, so that we don't disturb Ngalyod. He is our father, and he sleeps below the earth, and in the deep waterholes that swirl below the giant waterfalls. He shaped the barren flatlands, as he slid across the earth, and he created the path for our creeks and rivers to run.

'We speak in many dialects, yet we are all brothers, and we will continue to pass down our stories, as I pass them down to you.' He held a handful of dirt above his head and said, 'This is where I come from, for this is the earth of my mother, and this is where I will sleep when my mother takes me back.'

The children hadn't moved, nor had they taken their eyes from George as he spoke. Tom had been standing in the shadows and had been watching Peggy and his sons. He bent down to pick her up and in a sleepy voice she said, 'When I die daddy, I want to be a star in the sky.' Tom was taken aback by what she had said, and with a lump in his throat he squeezed her tightly.

He said goodnight, and carried Peggy back to her warm bed. He had listened to the story narrated by George, and he wondered why he had never heard it before. But he knew that he would always look differently at the morning sunrise, and the evening sunset from now on.

***

George stayed at the farm for two weeks. Each evening the children would sit cross-legged in the dirt with mouths agape as George told them a new story. During the day, they had raked the grass stubble and built it into haystacks. On Sunday, George had taught the boys how to snare a rabbit and to tell how long ago it was since a kangaroo had crossed the land.

'Well boss, it's time fer me to move on.'

Tom replied, 'Sorry that I couldn't keep ya on George. You been a big help to me these past weeks. Whats yer plans now?'

'I'll hit the track again, and tomorra I'll take me ration card inta the police station and hopefully they will give me a few bob. Maybe, I'll get another job fer a day or two, but no matter if I don't.'

George smiled before saying, 'That's the good thing about being a blackfella. We got plenty of bush tucker ta eat.'

The boys shook George's hand, and Peggy cried as he said goodbye. They all stood on the verandah, and watched him until he disappeared into the blue haze.

72.

Poverty Road

The children were playing outside in the yard, and Adam was cleaning up after giving them their daily ration of milk. He heard the yell, and several small shrieks moments before he heard the thud. He looked out and saw young Dennis Madigan lying prone at the base of the large crab apple tree that he had been climbing. The other children all stood around him and he heard another say, 'Dennis fell out of the tree, Mr Francis.'

Adam looked at the prone boy, and for a moment he thought that he was dead. As he bent down the boy gave a moan and opened his eyes. 'Don't move Dennis!' Dennis went to stretch his leg, which was folded back behind the other, and he let out a scream.

'Me leg, I can't move me leg!'

Adam said, 'All you children move away and give me some room. Dennis try and not move, now where else does it hurt?'

'Me hand, sir. I think it's busted!' The tears welled in his eyes and he tried not to cry. Adam knew that there was a good chance that the boy's leg was broken and he called to one of the girls. 'Marjorie, run down to the clinic and see Mrs Carney. Ask her if she could possibly come straight away, and tell her what has happened.'

Brigid arrived shortly after and took charge, and after checking Dennis she said to Adam, 'We need to get this boy back to my clinic. I'm sure that he has several fractures. Did he hit his head, did anyone see?' And the other children shrugged their shoulders.

'We will need something to carry him on.' She looked around before saying, 'Adam do you think that you could go next door and see Mrs. Mathews. I think that I saw a wheelbarrow in her front yard. I'm sure that she won't mind if we borrow it.'

A few minutes later Adam returned with the barrow. 'Now, if we can lift the boy into it, we can get him back so that I can splint his fractures and check him out.'

Dennis gave out a scream as he was lifted and placed into the barrow. Adam wheeled him to the clinic, and amid more screams he was laid upon the table. Brigid gave Dennis a dose of laudanum, and as that took effect she reset his broken ankle and wrist. Adam had returned to the school and sent the other children home. He knew that he would have to see Dennis's mother and explain what had happened. He closed the school and returned to the clinic and saw Brigid.

'How is he?'

'He's sleeping now, but he is going to be very sore for a few weeks. He is a strong lad, and he should be running around again soon. Now Adam, can you give me the directions to the child's home? I think that I will go and see the boy's parents and let them know that I will keep the boy in the clinic tonight. I can give him some more laudanum so that he will sleep, and tomorrow we will take him home.

'I would normally expect him to walk on crutches, but that is out of the question with that fracture in his wrist. I know that he won't be happy, but I'm afraid that it will be bed rest for this boy for at least a month!' Adam looked troubled, and Brigid asked, 'Is there something wrong?'

Adam replied, 'Dennis's father has cleared out. I think that he's on the track somewhere. He was a settler, and he left his family to manage without him. That's why they live in the shanty town by the river.'

'Does he have any siblings?'

'He has three sisters. They are all younger than him and they don't attend school as yet. I know that his mother relies on him. She is going to be upset with the news I'm afraid. Look, Brigid, I think that it is only fair that I go and give Mrs Madigan the news. I could ask her to call in and see you at the clinic in the morning if you like.'

'Thank you, Adam, but I think that it is best if I explain to Mrs Madigan the extent of her son's injuries. I would appreciate it though, if you would accompany me and show me where the family lives. I don't believe that I have met his mother, and I may be able to assist her in some way.'

She looked expectantly at Adam, who nodded his head and said, 'I would be more than happy to show you. When would you like to go?'

'There's no time like the present, the boy will sleep for some time yet, and we may as well go now if that's all right.'

They arrived at the shanty town camp, and Brigid was shocked at what she saw. There were at least two dozen assorted dwellings built with anything that was at hand. All were standing haphazardly and looked as though they would disintegrate in any strong wind.

Each dwelling was unique in its structure, and stood about twenty feet away from its neighbor. Some had walls made from flattened kerosene tins. Others had dirty grey canvas tarpaulins slung over the structures in the hope that it would give some protection from the rain and the wind.

The ground between the buildings varied between dry dirt and mud. Adam stopped outside a small square hovel. The front wall was made from flattened cardboard boxes overlapped and held together with baling twine. Standing against the wall was an assortment of sapling branches and fence palings that were tied together with wire and twine. The doorway was made from several potato sacks sewn together.

There was nothing to knock upon, and Adam partially moved the sack door and called out, 'Hello Mrs Madigan, it's Adam Francis from the school, may we come in?'

The sack was moved aside, and Mrs Madigan looked out inquiringly. She was small in stature, stooped and skinny. Her hair was prematurely grey and Adam thought that she could not have been more than thirty, although she could have passed as being nearer sixty. Her eyes were tired and red, and the lines upon her face showed the hardships that she had endured with the life that she now lived. She gave them a suspicious look before she recognised Adam.

'Oh, hello, you're the teacher, ain'tcha?'

She gave a cursory glance around before asking, 'Where's me boy, he ain't been playin' up, has he?' Before Adam could reply, Brigid introduced herself.

'Hello Mrs Madigan, my name is Brigid Carney, and I'm the district nurse. May we come in?'

'Why, what's happened to me boy? He ain't ill, is he?' She gave them both a hard stare before turning and dropping the side of the sack. They followed her into the gloom, and the smell of mould and stale air was nauseating. Two small girls were sitting cross-legged on a potato sack in one corner.

Behind them, another smaller girl lay sleeping. Brigid thought that she couldn't have been more than three. They all wore identical dirty grey flour sacks. The sacks were sewn together and still showed the supplier's name in faded letters. They hung limply across their bony shoulders. The girls looked up at the intruders, sheepishly at first, before turning their heads away to continue the game that they had been playing.

On the floor near the girls, was a half full chamber pot. Against the back wall was a small fireplace that was made from stones stacked no more than a foot high and positioned into a rough circle. A large, blackened jam tin with a length of wire for a handle was being used as a kettle. To one side of the smouldering embers was a black cast-iron saucepan which held a glutinous substance that bubbled and simmered slowly in a grey froth. The smell from the mixture was overpowering and permeated throughout the whole room.

The floor was hard-packed dirt, except where the dirty brown sacks that were being used as mattresses lay. The sacks were filled with dry grass, which protruded from the rough sewn ends, and several small salt sacks, also grass-filled, served as pillows.

One side wall consisted of a dozen potato sacks, overlapped and sewn together. Standing in front of them were several ply tea chests that served as shelves to hold the few chipped plates and the jam jars that served as cups. Another tea chest was upside down, and served as a table on which sat an oblong bread tin. From the sheets of rusty corrugated iron that served as the roof, hung a smoke-stained kerosene lamp.

Brigid was appalled. She had visited houses where the residents were also poor, but she had never seen such abject poverty as what she was seeing now. She wanted to speak in a normal manner to Mrs Madigan. She did not want to sound aloof and wanted to appear as though the poverty that surrounded her was perfectly acceptable.

'Mrs Madigan, this afternoon your Dennis was climbing a tree and he fell out. Unfortunately, he broke his ankle and his wrist. The injuries will heal over the next month or so, but I have given him some pain killing medicine. I think that I should keep him at the clinic tonight where I can keep an eye on him. I may have to keep him at the clinic tomorrow as well, but as soon as I'm sure that he is on the mend Mr Francis will assist with bringing him home.'

Mrs Madigan thought for a moment before asking, 'How long will it be before he will be able to help out again? I rely on him, ya know. He scrounges up fruit and wheat for us. Without Dennis, I dunno how we are gunna get by.'

Brigid wanted to broach the subject of how she could help.

She had learnt long ago, that even those who struggled with just getting through the day were sometimes too proud to accept any form of charity.

'Mrs Madigan, can you tell me what sort of things your son does to help out? I was thinking that while he is laid up I might be able to help you.' Brigid looked expectantly at her, and gave her a smile.

'He gets us our wheat and the fruit. If we don't have no wheat we hafta just eat the fruit.' As an afterthought she said, 'He also gets our coal. I was expectin' him to go and fill the pail up tonight.'

Brigid looked quizzically at the woman, and asked, 'Where does Dennis get the wheat from? I can pick you up a sack and bring it back if that's all that you're worrying about.'

Mrs Madigan thought for a moment before answering, 'If I tell ya, he won't get into no trouble, will he?'

'Of course, he won't get into trouble, why would you think that he would get into trouble just for helping his family?'

'He goes up to the rail yards, and scoops it up from where they spill it when they load the bags onta the rail trucks. He fills a pail every few days, and that lasts us fer about three or four days. The railway people shoo him away if they see him, but I dunno what the fuss is about. If the boys don't pick it up then the birds just eat it. The other nights he picks up the coal that falls from the engines. He ain't the only one ya know. Lotsa people hafta scrounge a bit of coal just to be able ta keep their fires goin'.'

'Mrs Madigan, is that your entire diet, fruit and wheat?' Brigid was mortified to think that the only food that these children got was picked up off the ground in a railway yard.

'Dennis goes to the store, and the fella there gives him a box of fruit every Saturday. It's the stuff that's a bit soft and he can't sell it. There's nuthin wrong with it. I boil it up and mix it with the wheat and when it sets I just cut it inta slices just like you was cutting a loaf of bread.' She said it with some pride; as though it were a personal achievement that she could turn rotten fruit and wheat into something edible.

'That's what I'm cookin' now. I'll show ya how to do it if ya like?' She didn't wait for an answer, and lifted an old wooden crate from the floor and placed it on the tea chest. They could see that the fruit that was left in the box was almost rotten and furry with mould.

She scooped it out with her bare hands, before placing it directly into the simmering pot. Then, she stirred the mixture with a flat wooden spoon and the colour of the concoction changed from grey to almost black. After stirring the mix for a few minutes, she picked up the heavy pot with both hands and proceeded to pour the mix into a battered bread tin. She smiled for the first time, and showed yellowing teeth before saying, 'That's all there is to it. It'll settle overnight, and we will eat it tomorrow.'

Brigid couldn't believe that these children could survive on this pulp mixture, and nothing else. She asked, 'Mrs Madigan do you eat anything else, meat or vegetables?' Brigid looked inquiringly at her, and Mrs

Madigan replied, 'Sometimes I go and ask the butcher for some bones. He only throws them out, ya know! When I got bones, I boil them up for a few hours, and that makes a nice broth! She then looked worried again, 'But now that me Dennis is laid up I'll have to go out meself tonight. Otherwise we won't have nuthin to eat.' It was a matter-of-fact statement, and Brigid said, 'Mrs Madigan, I don't think that you have been to our clinic, have you?' Brigid didn't wait for an answer before she continued.

'We are supplied by the council, and we have lots of things that we can give you for free. We even have a clothing store. Lots of people leave their unwanted clothes and shoes and other things at the clinic, and anyone can come and pick up a few things. There is no charge.'

Mrs Madigan was now on the defensive, 'I ain't askin' fer charity. We can manage without charity, ya know. Our problems are our problems, and one day things will get better. The priest came around the other week, and that's what he said. Didn't offer no other help though. Why didn't he tell us about your clinic? Mind you, he didn't stay here long!'

Adam had been standing quietly. He was uncomfortable, but felt that he needed to stay. 'Look, Mrs Madigan, why don't you come up to the clinic now? You can see Dennis, and then Mrs Carney can show you the clothing store. You may see something that the children could wear.'

She looked unsure, but then after thinking about the prospect of obtaining some clothing or a blanket, she said to her eldest daughter,

'Marjorie, I'm going with these people to see your brother. Now you look after your sisters, and don't let them get into anything that they shouldn't!'

73.

1936

The depression was almost over, and slowly factories came back to life. Government policy, along with their ability to again borrow money from the English banks, allowed infrastructure projects that had been put on hold to continue.

The drought had finally broken, and after the rains had fallen the swollen rivers and waterholes brought life back to the parched regions of inland Australia. Farmers across the country were again planning for the future. Slowly, the shanty towns became deserted as people finally found work again along with their dignity. The electricity had finally reached Tom and Hannah's house in 1934, almost six years after being promised, and shortly afterwards the telephone line was installed.

The following two years passed by much the same as those before. Tom had struggled through two more growing seasons, and with the passing of each season, he had ploughed more ground and managed to plant more wheat. The rain had fallen when it was required, and after his last harvest, Tom finally had money left over after paying his annual government mortgage payment. He had purchased a few cows along with a small flock of sheep and a pregnant sow.

***

Tom sat on the verandah and filled his pipe. The aromatic smell of the tobacco lay heavy in the still air. Hannah came from inside, and sat down on the sofa. 'Where are the children?' he asked.

'The boys took Peggy down to the creek, and Molly is down there as well. She wanted to catch some tadpoles. They are so good with her. I'm sure that there would be nothing that they wouldn't do for her.'

Tom drew back on his pipe and said, 'I don't know where the years have gone Hani. It seems just like yesterday when we first arrived here. The boys are almost full grown, and I should feel proud of what we done.' He went quiet again, as he thought of what he wanted to say.

Hannah reached over and touched his hand. 'Is something bothering you Tommy? You should feel proud of what you have achieved. I am proud of you! There were times when I thought that we wouldn't make it, but somehow, we always managed. We have a lot to be grateful for Tommy Fields, but I sense that you are restless, what is it?'

'It's Peggy, for three years she has been wearing those blessed calipers on her legs. I worry that she may always have to wear them. She is still so small, and she breaks my heart every time that I watch her struggling to walk.' He took another long drag on his pipe, and stared out to the horizon.

'It ain't right that a child has ta use crutches just to move around. I know that Doc said that there was nuthin' that we could do about what ails her, but I look at her and I'd rather poke me self in the eye with a stick than watch her struggle like she does. I dunno what I would do if we lost her Hani, and I worry that one day we are gunna lose her. I love all me kids, and I shouldn't play favourites, but she's the apple of me eye. I can't help it and I would swap places with her in a heartbeat.

'I haven't bothered with God since the war. I ain't been to Mass fer years, as yer know. I know that, that God botherin' priest who calls over every now and then thinks that I'm a heathen. He can think what he likes, but one part of me says that there just isn't a God, and another part of me thinks that God is punishing me cause I cursed 'im so many times. I'm sorry Hani, but I'm feelin' a bit down today. I'll finish me smoke and go and see what the kids are doin'.'

Hannah squeezed his hand and smiled. 'Do you think that we might have a proper Christmas lunch this year Tommy? We might even be able to buy the children a small present each. I thought that we might invite the Murdochs' and Brigid as well. I can roast the turkey after you kill it, and Harriet will make us one of her delightful plum puddings if I ask her.'

Hannah stopped talking for a moment and Tom asked, 'What are you thinkin' about?'

She smiled, and then she said, 'I might even ask Mr Francis if he would like to come.' And she smiled again at an amusing thought that she had. Tom looked at her before saying, 'What are you up to Hani? Why would ya want to invite the schoolteacher to our Christmas lunch? I can only guess what the children would think of that idea.'

'The children love Mr Francis. Brigid mentions his name all the time when I see her. I know that she sees him when she calls in at the school to check the children as part of her duties. I have this sneaking suspicion that she might even harbour a spark for him that's all. She is still an attractive woman, and Adam is only ten years older than her. Well anyway, it was just a thought. I think that they might be good for each other!'

'What will be will be Hani. If ya want to play matchmaker then so be it, but has it crossed ya mind that there might be a reason why the bloke has stayed single all his life? But, if it makes yer happy then ask 'im.' He stood up and put his hat on. His pipe hung from one side of his mouth as he muttered. 'I'll take a walk down to the creek and see what the kids are up ta.'

74.

Bush Christmas

It was Christmas morning, and Hannah had risen early even though she had only been in bed for a few hours. She had attended the Midnight Mass service in Blackmore after Tom had driven her to the church. He still refused to go inside, and he was content to wait in the truck until the early Christmas service was over.

Tom had dispatched the turkey the evening before, and it sat in the icebox overnight after being plucked and trimmed. Hannah lit the stove, and it was already hot by the time that Tom had risen.

'I'll put the turkey in the oven shortly. It will need a good three hours, and I expect that everyone will be here by eleven.'

Hannah had sewn four oversized calico stockings a few weeks earlier. The children had approved of the idea, but they couldn't agree on what colour they should be. They had taken a vote, and three of them had agreed that red was the appropriate colour, Molly then had asked her mother, 'How will Father Christmas know which bag is which, what if he gets them mixed up?' So then, Hannah had sewn the children's names on each stocking and then they were all happy.

They had hung them on nails that Tom had attached to the verandah posts.

Hannah and the children had gathered the branches of the fiery red shrub that had suddenly appeared amongst the greys and greens of the wattle bushes. It was known as the Christmas bush, because its sepals would turn bright pink and red for a few short weeks of the year around December. They had also cut the soft green tips from young eucalypt trees, and the wild broom was now smothered in its bright yellow plumage. Hannah had tied them all together, and now they hung from the support posts at the front fence.

The boys had long ago stopped believing in Father Christmas, but they had been ordered by their mother not to spoil the story of his late-night arrival. Peggy and Molly were both unsure as they had not celebrated Christmas for the past five years, and neither could remember when they had last received a present from Santa.

The sun had risen into another cloudless blue sky, and by the time the first guests had arrived the kitchen was like a furnace. Hannah's face was red and flushed, and her forehead was wet with perspiration with wisps of her hair stuck to it.

Tom had placed two long slabs of timber on top of several hay bales. The tin bath was filled with water and ice from the icebox to keep the beer cold.

The children had finally woken, and Hannah gave Peggy a quick cuddle before bolting the calipers to her small legs. Molly had been slower to rise and wasn't sure why this day was going to be different to the others. But as the fog of sleep lifted from her mind she became as excited as her sister.

'Did he come, did he?' Peggy asked.

'You will just have to go and see for yourself young lady. I've been too busy cooking, but I think that I might have heard someone moving about outside last night,' she said with a smile.

Molly clambered down the side of her bed. She shared the bed with her sister, and slipped around behind her as Hannah was attaching the calipers to her sister. She reached for her crutches as her brothers entered the bedroom. Jimmy said, 'Don't worry about ya crutches, just get on me back, I wanna see if he left anything too.'

He bent down, and Peggy, now well used to being carried by her brothers, climbed onto his back and put her arms around his neck.

Squeals of delight followed the finding of the now full stockings. Peggy's and Molly's each held a rag doll along with an assortment of toys, colouring-in books and lollies.

The boys had the same sweets, but at the bottom of each stocking was a pearl-handled pocketknife, along with a small wooden spinning top.

Peggy sat on the floor, and stared at her new doll before cuddling it to her chest.

It was made entirely from scraps of material carefully sewn together. The face was made from calico, and the hair was made from wool. Hannah watched her daughter's delight with the gifts. As the children proceeded to compare the differences between their toys, the boys had run off to find their father and show him their knives.

Hannah continued preparing the lunch, as the heat in the kitchen became almost unbearable. Billy was swatting the blowflies that had gathered after being attracted by the smell of the roast. Outside, the intensity of the sun grew stronger by the hour. The song of the cicadas filled the air, and the magpies warbled in the canopy of the trees as the crows flew in lazy circles. A flock of pink and grey Gallahs squabbled and squawked as they feasted on the loose grain that lay scattered over the bare paddocks from the last harvest. In the surrounding bush the sound of the exploding seedpods of the wild broom could also be heard.

The vegetables were cooked, and the turkey was almost done when Brigid and Adam arrived. The children waved their presents at Brigid, and she bent down and gave them all a hug. She asked, 'Have you all been good?' and she smiled as they all yelled out, 'Yes!' She opened the back door of her motorcar and said, 'I have something here for you,' and she proceeded to hand them each a small present. They excitedly took their gifts and proceeded to tear open the brown wrapping paper before showing each other what they had received.

Brigid smiled and said, 'Merry Christmas, Tom.' She embraced him and gave him a kiss on the cheek. Adam shook Tom's hand and they exchanged pleasantries. Brigid went inside to see Hannah, and carried a basket of fruit and preserves that she had brought with her, as Tom offered Adam a glass of beer.

'Merry Christmas darling.' Brigid placed the hamper down on the already crowded table before Hannah turned from the stove and they embraced.

'Is there something that I can help you with, have you peeled the spuds yet?'

Hannah replied, 'It's all under control. I was up early this morning. Tom and I went to the Midnight Mass, and it was about 2 before we got to bed. Tom was asleep as soon as his head hit the pillow, but I had a thousand things running through my mind. I got about three hours' sleep, which was just enough.'

She busied herself with basting the turkey with the hot juices before she took another look around to see what else she needed to do. Hannah asked with a sly grin, 'And how is your Mr Francis? I assume that he came with you?'

Brigid was taking the cutlery from the drawer as Hannah had asked the question, and she turned to look at her friend.

'Hannah Fields, whatever do you mean, *my* Mr Francis?'

'Oh nothing.' She smiled again. 'Now, can you help me with the plates? I hope that the Murdochs get here soon. The turkey is ready to carve and I don't want it to dry out.'

Brigid asked, 'Is anyone else coming?'

'No, just us. It has been so long since we could to afford to have a Christmas. I just wanted a day that we could all remember, and what better day to remember than Christmas day?' The chatter continued and as they waited for the Murdochs. Hannah had a quick wash before going outside to join the others.

The children were playing, and Tom was finishing his beer when the movement in the valley took his attention.

'Here come the Murdochs, Hani.' Then, as he watched the car from his vantage point, he noticed another.

'We expectin' anyone else Hani?'

'No, why do you ask?'

'Well, there's another car coming along the ration track.'

He pointed, and they all looked down at the cloud of dust that showed another car about a mile behind the Murdochs'. They all watched as the dust cloud surrounding the second vehicle got closer.

The Murdochs' red Dodge reappeared on the crest of the hill after disappearing as it drove around the dam before pulling up in a cloud of dust.

'Hello everyone, Merry Christmas. I'm sorry if we are late. It's my fault,' said Bill. 'I couldn't get the blessed car to start, and then I remembered that it needed fuel.' Greetings were exchanged all around and Tom asked, 'Were you expecting someone at your place Bill?' Bill looked quizzically at Tom before saying, 'No, nobody, why.'

'We noticed another car coming along the ration track behind you that's all. It was a fair way back, maybe a mile or so.' Tom looked down at the road as he spoke, and he noticed that the car was just crossing over the creek.

'Well, we'll soon know who it is, cause they are coming up the hill.' He watched until the car disappeared as it drove around the bend behind the dam. They could hear the engine and the crunching of the gears as the car drove up the final rise. It came into view at the same time as its klaxon horn came to life, and pulled to a stop next to the Murdochs' car.

The doors opened, and Doris could be heard calling, 'Where's my grandchildren?'

The children were the first to respond with, 'Nana's here, Nana's here!' Jack got out first and gave a stretch, followed by Claire and Davin.

General pandemonium followed, with everyone embracing and shaking hands, and a dozen questions being fired from each direction. 'Why didn't you let us know that you were coming?'

Claire and Hannah embraced, and the children were beside themselves with excitement.

Doris gave Tom a hug before asking, 'How have you been son? I've missed you all.' She smiled, and turned towards the children, 'My, haven't you all grown? Now tell me, did Father Christmas pay you all a visit?'

The children all nodded, and Billy was the first to speak, 'Look Nana, me and Jimmy both got a knife each.' He proudly showed the penknife to Doris.

'Well, don't go cutting yourself, will you?' Billy shook his head and replied, 'I won't.'

Tom shook his brother's hand and asked, 'How ya doin'?'

'Can't complain'

'So, what are ya doin' 'ere? Not that I ain't happy ta see ya, but blimey I never expected ta see any of yous today. What time did ya leave Sydney? It musta been early.'

Davin had joined them and he answered, 'We went to the six o'clock Mass and we left straight afterwards. Clair and Doris hatched the plan a coupla weeks ago. I was gunna give you a telephone call and tell you to expect us, but your mother really wanted to surprise you. I think that she was worried about telling you that we were coming, in case something went wrong.'

Hannah said, 'You must all want to freshen up. I'll go and boil the kettle and make us a nice cup of tea.'

Jack smiled and said, 'Never mind the tea, a cold beer wouldn't go astray.' Bill was curious, and he asked Davin, 'So what's the road from Sydney like now? It's years since I drove it, and it wasn't all that flash the last time that I was on it. I think it took about eight hours in me truck, the last time I done it!'

Davin replied, 'It took us just on five hours. Mind you, there was no traffic on the road whatsoever. I carried some spare fuel, and I had to fill up the tank twice. Claire made a hamper, and we stopped at Katoomba and had morning tea there. The road is still very twisty, but me new car,' he nodded his head towards the black Chevrolet, 'is a lot quicker than me old truck.'

'So how long have ya had that?' Tom asked, as he looked admiringly at the now dust-covered car.

'I purchased it only a few months ago. I've must say Tom, it's been a struggle these past years. We just managed to keep the forge open. When I say we, it was just Claire and me. We couldn't afford to hire anyone. It was only shoeing horses and making shovels and spades that kept us goin'. But about six months ago we got another government contract. Remember how I had the contract to make them lamppost brackets for the harbour bridge, before the Depression started? They told me then, that they didn't have no dough to pay for what I done. They said that it was something about the government having its money stopped by the English banks. That's how all this blessed trouble started apparently. Anyway, the government reckons that the country is getting' back on its feet again, or that's what they say in the papers anyway. Well, to cut a long story short I got me contracts back to finish off the lamp brackets.

'Then, I thought, what the heck. We managed to keep our heads above water all through the Depression, so I thought, why not. We have a guaranteed income for the next few months until I finish off the contract, so I bought the car. I must ask you Tom, even though I'm sure I know the answer. I don't suppose that you would be interested in coming back to the forge, would you? I'm gettin' on a bit, and other than you I got nobody to leave it to.' Davin looked directly at Tom, as he waited for him to respond.

Tom didn't reply immediately as he was thinking of what he was going to say. But then he replied, 'Davin, there have been many times over the past few years when I would have gladly gone back to working for ya. Like you, Hani and I have had plenty of ups and downs, and there have been times when we struggled just to feed the kids. But by crikey, we done a powerful lot of work around 'ere. Even if I had an inklin' to go back and live in the city, which I don't, I would never be able to get Hani to go back. Don't ask me what it is, but there's somethin' about livin' in the bush, and it gets under yer skin after a while. I can see the sky and it goes forever, and Davin you wait till tonight. Ya are stayin' fer awhile, I hope?' Without waiting for an answer, Tom continued.

'Tonight, I'll bring ya out 'ere to watch the stars. It might sound like I'm bonkers. But, the heavens are alive out 'ere, and I never get tired of looking at the night sky. I can't recall even seeing the stars when we lived in the city. So, thank ya fer the offer, but me roots are deep in me land 'ere now.

'I know there will probably be times when I'll regret making this decision, but I know meself out 'ere. I watch me kids running through the wheat fields, and last year, me crop was so tall that the kids were playin' hide and seek out there. I'd like to think that me boys would continue on 'ere after I'm gone, but that's just a dream of mine.'

Hannah had been standing behind Tom, and she walked over and put her arm through his.

'What Tommy said goes for me too Uncle Davin. We have been here for sixteen years now, and I hope that we can put in many more, God willing.' She stood on her tiptoes, and she gave Tom a peck on the cheek before announcing, 'There's plenty of food, so please find a seat at the table and let's have lunch.'

Doris proceeded to unpack the jars of fruit preserves and biscuits that she had brought with her. She sat between the children and she couldn't stop smiling.

As Tom carved the turkey, hands were waving across the table in all directions as the bush flies invited themselves to the celebration. As the food was laid out, Billy picked up his fork and was about to fill his mouth when his mother called out, 'Billy Fields, put your fork down, we haven't said grace yet!' He lowered his eyes and laid his fork down.

Hannah, clasping her hands, said grace. 'We thank you Lord, for the food that we have, and for the family and friends that share our table and our lives. Amen.'

Conversations were criss-crossing across the table, broken by the occasional laughter. When lunch was finished the women cleared the table while the men rolled cigarettes and filled their glasses with beer. Jack took a long drink and said, 'That sun has got a bite to it. I swear that it's hotter here than in Sydney. How about we go and sit down by the dam? I'm surprised that the kids aren't already in there.'

Tom yelled out to the children, 'Who wants to go swimming?'

The boys yelled back, 'We do.' Molly said, 'No, I don't want to I'll stay with Peggy.'

Tom looked at his daughters. He was surprised that neither wanted to go for a swim. Peggy was sat on the grass, her legs straight out in front of her, and he went over to see what was occupying them. 'What are you doin'?' Peggy lifted her head, and held her handiwork up to show her father, 'I'm making a daisy chain for Mummy.'

She then went back to threading the daisies while her sister said, 'It's too hot Peggy. Let's go down to the dam?'

Peggy stopped for a moment before saying, "I'm not hot, and I want to finish off this necklace.' They were all aware of how stubborn Peggy was, and if she said that she didn't want to do something, then nothing that anyone would say would make her change her mind.

Billy sat down next to Peggy and said, 'I'm gunna carve me initials inta the tree. Do you wanna carve yours? I'll let ya use me new knife!'

She stopped threading the daisies for a moment, and then looked at her brother before saying, 'Promise? But I have to give this necklace to mummy first.'

'Yeah, I promise, now get onta me back and we will find mummy.'

Hannah was sat in the shade of the verandah, along with Doris and Margaret when Billy piggybacked his sister to her.

'Me and Jimmy are goin' down fer a swim mummy. Peggy is coming with us, but she made something for you.' Billy bent down, so that Peggy could climb off his back. Jimmy had carried her crutches, and she held out her arm and said, 'I made this for you Mummy.'

'You made them all by yourself darling, just for me. You're such a clever girl they are beautiful. I shall keep them forever!' She smiled as she placed the flower necklace over her head.

'If you're going for a swim Billy, you watch your sister. We will come down shortly, now off you go.'

Jimmy carried the crutches, and Billy carried his sister and Molly walked behind. Tom, Jack, Bill and Adam were already sitting under the shade of the tree when the children arrived.

Billy opened the blade of his knife and carefully started carving. Peggy sat and watched. They took almost an hour to cut their names into the trunk, and when they were finished they stood back and admired their handiwork.

Peggy said, 'You promised that I could carve mine there too.' Jimmy told Peggy to get onto his back, and he handed the knife to his sister.

He placed his hands behind his back and clasped them together in a makeshift seat. Peggy leaned over her brother's shoulder and scratched out her name.

Billy looked at his sister's efforts and said, 'I'll carve them deeper fer you Peggy,' and after placing Peggy back onto the ground the boys dug deeply into the bark and carved 'Peggy Fields 1936' next to theirs.

**

It was dusk when the Murdochs went home, taking Claire and Davin with them after offering them a place to stay for a few days. Doris was going to sleep with the girls, and Jack would make do with the verandah.

They all stayed together until New Year's Day, and amid the heat, the flies and the tears they said their goodbyes.

75.

Heavy Hearts

Peggy had been feeling unwell since Christmas. At first, she was just sniffling, and Hannah thought that she had caught a cold. By the end of the week, when her condition had not improved, Hannah telephoned Brigid to express her fears.

'She is having trouble breathing Bridgy, and she is very listless. I'm sure that she is in pain, and she says that her bones hurt. She can't hold a cup properly either, and I have noticed that she is very wobbly on her crutches. Oh Bridgy, I'm really worried. Tommy sat with her all night last night, and he is beside himself.'

'Hannah, I'm going to telephone Silas and ask him to come and see you. I don't know what ails her, but she might just have caught a virus, or she may have been bitten by something. I'll telephone Silas now, and then I'll come over right away.'

Silas arrived at the house an hour after Brigid had. The children were all with Peggy and Silas asked, 'Would everybody leave the room please? Not you, nurse. I want to give the child a full check-up.'

After the examination, and as he was putting his stethoscope away Brigid noticed the frown upon his face.

'What do you think doctor, is it a bite? Brigid was hoping that her worst fears wouldn't be confirmed. She had read the latest medical journals on the treatment and symptoms of polio in children, and Peggy appeared to have all of the fatalistic symptoms of the disease.

'She has a slight temperature, but it's the lack of strength in her arms that has me concerned. How long has she had the polio now?'

'About five years, doctor.'

Silas's frown deepened. 'She should have recovered by now. I am aware that there are different strains of the poliovirus and that some can be fatal. I am very concerned that she is having breathing difficulties. Polio can sometimes affect the lungs, because after all, polio is a muscle-wasting disease.'

Brigid was now having real concerns, and her heart was beating faster.

'What is your prognosis doctor? You know that I love these people as I do my own family. I don't want to give them false hope. Is Peggy going to die doctor? If she is, then I need to give them all the help and support that I can.'

Silas looked at Peggy, who was now sleeping. Her small face was red. Her breathing was shallow and raspy, and her chest was heaving as she struggled for breath. He turned his gaze to Brigid, and she knew what his answer was going to be by the pained look in his old watery eyes.

'This child should be in hospital nurse. Her lungs are failing, and I think that it will only be a matter of time before her heart stops. At best, she might last for a few more days. I need to make her as comfortable as I can. As her lungs weaken she will continue to struggle for breath, and shortly she will possibly lose what muscle function she has. It will be quite painful for her unless I medicate her with morphine. I think that her family should have the opportunity to say their goodbyes when she wakes up. Once I start with the morphine she will sleep until she succumbs. I would suggest that we take her to hospital.'

The tears welled in Brigid's eyes, and she was dreading the next few minutes. Deep down in her soul she had always had the feeling that this moment would come, and now her worst fears were being realised. She bent over the bed and straightened the bedclothes. She then gave Peggy a kiss before running her hands through her blond locks. She stood up, wiped her tears, and then asked Silas, 'Do you want me to talk to Hannah and Tom?'

Silas responded with, 'I will talk to them, thank you nurse. Will you ask them to come in?'

They were all gathered in the kitchen when Brigid found them. Hannah noticed the look on Brigid's face, and her clenched fist went to her mouth to suppress a sob.

'Silas would like to speak to you both.'

She looked at the children and said, 'I'll stay here with them, now you go and see the doctor.'

Tom and Hannah walked to the bedroom, and the children watched them go. Billy was the first to speak and he asked Brigid, 'Is Peggy gunna die?' It was a direct question, and Brigid shouldn't have been taken aback with it, but she was. She stooped down in front of them and put her arms out to embrace them. Molly was already crying as she laid her head on Brigid's shoulder.

'Your sister is very sick and she is in a lot of pain, that is why the doctor is here.' Molly was sobbing, and between the tears she asked, 'Can't he make her better? You told us that doctors made people better, why can't he make her better? I don't want Peggy to die Aunty Brigid!'

Brigid hugged them all, and their tears flowed before she said, 'When mummy talks to the doctor we can all go and see your sister. Now I want you all to understand that the doctor has given your sister some medicine and it might make her sleepy. So, I want you all to be quiet and you can give her a kiss and a hug.'

Silas looked at Tom and Hannah, and he explained what was happening. Hannah was kneeling against the bed, and she placed her arm across Peggy and wept silently. Tom was trying to be strong, and he asked, 'Are ya sure doc, that there is nuthin that we can do. What if ya just keep her on the morphine, won't that do any good?'

'I'm sorry son, if there was anything that I could do to prolong this little child's life, then I would have done it. If I don't administer the morphine she will become very distressed, and it will only exacerbate her condition. Now I can keep her comfortable, and I will stay here for however long it takes. I can take her to the hospital if you like, but that will be your decision.' He looked at their distressed faces and Tom was the first to speak.

'Tell me doc, if you take her to the hospital, will that change the outcome for her?'

Silas didn't have to think before he answered, 'I have to be honest with you both. The treatment that would be administered to your child at the hospital would be no different to what I am doing here. We can only make her comfortable, and the rest is in the hands of the Lord.'

Tom replied, 'Thanks fer being honest with us doc. If that's the case then I would rather she stay here with us? If you thought that there was any glimmer of hope then we would get her to the hospital.'

Hannah stood and wiped her tears. 'I'll go and get the children.'

They all stood in the doorway, and looked unsure of what to do. Tom smiled at them and said, 'You can go and sit on her bed. If you talk she might be able to hear you.' Molly was the first to move. She climbed onto the bed like she did every night. She then lay alongside of her sister, and put her arm across her as her tears fell. Jimmy and Billy sat on either side of the bed. They were trying to be brave, but then they also cried. Silas stood by, and after a few minutes he said to Tom, 'I need to administer the morphine now. Do you want the children to stay?'

'Yes doc, they can stay. Do what you have to do. We will all stay with her for as long as need be.'

Silas searched through his satchel and found the vial of morphine. While he was administering the drug Hannah said, 'I know what we will do. I will read a story just like we normally do. Now what story should we read first?'

Billy said, 'Read Peggy's favorite one, *Jack and the Beanstalk*,' and they all agreed.

The children sat on and across the bed with their sister. Hannah sat on a chair next to the bed, and Tom stood next to Brigid at the doorway. Silas checked Peggy's pulse before leaving the room.

Brigid had dried her eyes and went back into the bedroom. Six hours later the boys and Molly were asleep on the bed. Tom sat on another chair, and he had dozed off when Silas gently shook him. Hannah was nursing Peggy as she took her last breath. Tom stared, and his mind quickly cleared. He looked at Peggy, and then bent to take her limp body from Hannah. He held her tightly, and buried his face into her neck. His sobs wracked his body, and Hannah embraced them both. Brigid was also sobbing, her pain as much for her friends as for her goddaughter. Silas stood by quietly. He was tired, and this child's death had drained him emotionally. It seemed like only yesterday when he had helped deliver her. For over fifty years he had been a doctor, and suddenly it had occurred to him that maybe it was time for a younger man to take over the administering of the sick and the dying.

The children were all still sleeping peacefully, and Hannah tried to compose herself. She looked at Silas and asked quietly, 'What happens now?'

Silas replied, 'I will write out a death certificate, and then I will telephone the undertaker to come and collect the child.

'He will want to know what sort of service you will require, and then he will make the funeral arrangements for her burial.'

Tom wiped his eyes with his sleeve, and said in a voice that was louder than what he meant, 'We will bury her here doc. This is her home. This is where she lived and played, and this is where she is stayin'! Now you do what ya hafta do Doc, but tomorra I'm gunna dig a hole down near the dam where she loved to sit and draw. Then, we are gunna put her where we can be with her whenever we want.'

Tom's eyes welled up again, and he again buried his face into his daughter's neck.

Silas wasn't going to argue with Tom. If he wanted to bury his child on his farm then he was entitled to do so. He would just need to notify the authorities. Brigid went to her car and retrieved a blanket. She placed it over the small body that Tom was still holding.

'C'mon Tommy, let's put her on your bed, and we will all say goodbye tomorrow.'

Brigid had taken charge, as she needed to do something to hold herself together. 'We will leave the children to sleep, and in the morning, they can cry before we all say goodbye.'

Silas had contacted Father Dooley in Blackmore, and he arrived shortly after Tom had finished digging the grave. Tom and his boys had spent the morning down by the dam. The ground was compacted and hard as concrete. Tom swung the pick, and the small shards of dry clay flew like bullets as the pointed steel end bit into the hard earth, but slowly, inch by inch, the hole got deeper. Occasionally, his eyes would again well up, and he would swing the pick even harder. He was angry, and he wanted someone to blame for the death of his daughter, even though he knew that it was nobody's fault and that there was no one to blame, so in the end he blamed God.

The Murdochs had arrived, and were equally devastated. The undertaker had arrived, and although it was unusual to prepare a body outside of his establishment he did what was necessary, and Peggy was placed into the small coffin.

⁂

The funeral was a simple affair. Father Dooley pondered to his audience as to why a child who had a loving family should die at such a tender age. In the end he said, 'It is not up to us to question the motives of Our Lord'. He then finished by saying, 'God works in mysterious ways, and one might take solace by thinking that he needed a small angel to sit by his side.'

Bill helped Tom push the dirt back into the hole, and when it was full the children laid their posies of wildflowers that they had gathered earlier across the small mound.

The sounds of their sobbing were interspersed with the crows flying lazily overhead singing their raucous songs of woe.

***

The following days were filled with moments of tears, anger and frustration. But the days grew into weeks, and soon the weeks flowed into months. The seasons demanded that the paddocks be ploughed and the animals managed. The children learned to laugh again as they sat and played on the bench that Tom had built near Peggy's grave.

Hannah had kept the daisy chain that Peggy had made her at Christmas, and she pressed it between the pages of her diary. The flowers had faded, but the memory of the day that her daughter gave it to her would never die.

***

It had been more than four months since Peggy had died, and Hannah had not been feeling well. Brigid had called over, as was her habit on a regular basis, and Hannah had made a pot of tea. The children were at school and Tom was out mending fences. Hannah smiled at her friend as she poured the tea and said, 'I think that I'm pregnant again, Bridgy.'

'Oh Hannah, that's wonderful.' Brigid rose and embraced her friend. 'Does Tommy know?'

'No, I haven't told him yet. I just wanted to be sure. I don't want to give him any false hope. He misses Peggy so much, not that I don't, but she was the apple of his eye, and barely a week goes by without him sitting down at her graveside. He just lights up his pipe, and I know that he talks to her. Nothing would give me greater pleasure than to present him with another daughter, but a boy would be just as welcome. Whatever it is, I just want it to be healthy. I wanted to talk to you before I said anything to him.'

Brigid asked Hannah questions and when she was sure that her friend was pregnant she said, 'You do know that there are risks involved with having a late baby? You're forty years old.'

'Yes Bridgy, I know how old I am, and it scares me a little, but what is the alternative? I would never contemplate getting rid of it.

'If I am meant to have another baby, then I will have it. But Bridgy, we need this baby, Tommy needs it.

'It will never replace the memory of Peggy, but a baby will bring joy and happiness with it, and I will do anything to make Tommy and the children laugh and smile again.' Brigid smiled, and said, 'I will be with you every moment darling.

'I want you to telephone me day or night if you are unsure of anything, anything at all. You will, won't you? Now promise me that you will!' She stared into her friend's eyes with a burning intensity. Brigid placed her hand over Hannah's, and Hannah put her hand over Bridget's and gave it a gentle squeeze. 'I promise Bridgy.'

✳✳✳

The children had arrived home, and Tom had come back to the house for a late lunch. Hannah watched Tom eat a slab of fresh bread before she said, 'Let's go for a walk darling.' He looked at her quizzically, and stood up. 'Where do you wanna walk to?'

She smiled, and put her arm through his and said, 'Let's go down to the dam. I want to tell you something.'

He took his battered hat from the coat hook and dropped it onto the back of his head. Hannah leant on him and locked her arm through his as they walked down the track that led to the dam. They stopped at the bench, but didn't sit down. Tom gave a cursory glance at the grave before taking his pipe from his pocket and filling it.

He looked at Hannah and asked, 'So what's the big secret that ya couldn't tell me up at the house?'

She looked directly at him and said, 'Tommy, I'm pregnant.'

Tom was about to light his pipe and stopped, 'What did ya say, Hani?'

'I'm pregnant, Tommy.'

He stared at her before asking, 'Are ya sure Hani, are ya really sure?'

Hannah smiled before saying, 'Yes Tommy, I'm really sure, now tell me that you're happy.' He threw his hat into the air, before he opened his arms and embraced her. He held her tightly, his face against hers, and for a few moments he was speechless. As they embraced, his eyes fell to the small mound in the ground, and his eyes welled up as he buried his face into Hannah's shoulder, and he choked back a sob.

'Oh God, I miss her so much Hani, are you really pregnant?'

Hannah took his face between both of her hands, and she was smiling as she too started crying. He then kissed her and said, 'I love ya Hani. I have always loved ya. Have ya told the children?'

'No, I wanted to tell you first.'

Tom looked at Peggy's grave, and smiled as he wiped away his tears with the back of his hand. 'Let's go and tell the children darlin'.'

They held hands as they slowly walked back up the hill to the house.